Deadly Dominoes

By

Linda Pirtle

Copyright © 2017 Linda Pirtle
Venture Galleries LLC
1220 Chateau Lane
Hideaway, Texas 75771

ISBN: 13:978-1544012995
ISBN: 10:1544012993

All rights reserved. No part of this book may be reproduced, stored in a retrieval program, or transmitted by any form or by any means, electronic or mechanical, including photocopying, recording, or otherwise except as may be expressly permitted by the applicable copyright statutes or in writing by the author and publisher.

Book Cover Design: Laura Gordon
www.thebookcovermachine.com

Deadly Dominoes is a work of fiction. Names, characters, places, and incidents are either the product of the author's imagination or are used fictitiously. The only exception is the name Caddo Lake, a natural lake situated on the border between Texas and Louisiana. Any resemblance to actual persons, living or dead, or events is entirely incidental.

In escaping their gated community, the Prestridges may have thought to be finding rest and relaxation at Caddo Lake, but the rattling of bones (nickname for dominoes) and presence of curses lead to a very different experience. Linda Pirtle's style and character building is continued in this spine chilling fast paced story. I can see this as the early beginnings of a fine, well received series of books.

David L Atkinson, author of *Grace and Favor*

I couldn't stop reading. The twists and turns were non-stop to the end. The setting of Caddo Lake is the perfect place to hide bodies and secrets. That is until Lillian Prestridge shows up and will stop at nothing to solve the crimes. It's more than a cozy mystery. Entertainment at its best.

N. E. Brown, author of the Galveston, 1900, Indignities five- book series, and *Carson Chance, P. I., Over the Edge*

Another exciting cozy mystery featuring the inquisitive Mah Jongg player Lillian Prestridge who wanted a relaxing vacation. What she got was murders and an explosion. Linda Pirtle delivers everything a cozy mystery should have: great characters, crisp dialog, murders without too much gore. Start reading early – it's hard to put it down.

James R. Callan, Award Winning author of *A Silver Medallion*

Be prepared for unforgettable storytelling, an irresistible returning character, and unexpected murders on the shores of Caddo Lake in East Texas. In true Agatha Christie form, amateur sleuth Lillian Prestridge returns, unable to resist the pull of mystery solving while on an RV vacation despite the warnings from the locals. Author Linda Pirtle gives us what we want as she did in her previous book, The Mah Jongg Murders!

> **Patty Wiseman**, Author of
> *An Unlikely Deception*

No one does mystery, murder, and mayhem better than Linda Pirtle.

> **Dana Wayne**, Award-winning author of
> *Secrets of the Heart.*

Deadly Dominoes

By

Linda Pirtle

Acknowledgments

To be successful, an author needs a critique group in order to perfect the art of writing. I am fortunate because I know a talented group of successful authors who met with me twice a month to rip to shreds the sentences that made no sense and brought to my attention the omissions which needed to be included to avoid gaps in the flow of the story. I owe them my gratitude for their honest critiques of my book. They are Brinda Carey, Rev. Richard Hollingsworth, Stephen Woodfin, Esquire, and K Sellers, founder of the East Texas Writers Guild. I am especially thankful for the best critic of all, Caleb Pirtle, my husband. I also would like to thank my beta readers: N. E. Brown, author, and Glenn Hyde, a former educator and long-time colleague and Vivian Freeman, my editor.

A big thanks to Y & R public relations for their help with the launch of the ebook of Deadly Dominoes.

*Dedicated to my beloved sister Joy
who loved to RV with her husband Pat.
and
To my husband Caleb and
our son Josh,
My love always.*

Chapter One

"YOU'D BETTER be careful."

Lillian, lost in her own world, mentally checked off the items she had just purchased and hoped she had not forgotten anything. She barely heard the advice of the young man who was busy placing into the back of her Jeep the burgeoning sacks of groceries she and Bill, her husband of fifty years, would need while camping at Caddo Lake along with their white Standard Poodle, Eli.

For the first time, Lillian paid attention to the six-foot tall, muscular, dark haired young man who stood before her waiting for a response. "I beg your pardon – uh -- " She glanced at the name tag pinned to his shirt. "Brandon, what's that you say?"

"I said 'you'd better be careful' ."

"Why would you say that?"

"Crazy things been happening out at that RV park at Caddo Lake."

"What kinds of crazy things?"

"People have gone fishing, thought they didn't need a guide to take them around the lake."

"That's not crazy. My husband and I never hire a guide when we're fishing. We love to explore and have been lost several times, but we always find our way home."

"You don't understand. I'm saying lost souls at Caddo are never found by the park ranger. They're gone for good."

"What could possible happen to them?"

"Don't know, but be forewarned. Be careful if you go off on your own."

"I will." Lillian smiled and changed the subject. She decided to give him a pop quiz, "Okay, Brandon, all warnings aside, just how did you know I'm RVing and, to be more precise, RVing at Caddo?"

"Well, ma'am, there's that sticker on the front windshield of your Jeep...and," he paused, "if I hadn't seen it, I could guess you're RVing by what I just packed in these sacks. Most folks who go there stock up on mosquito spray, suntan lotion, quick and easy snacks, milk, eggs, bread, corn meal to coat the fish they plan to fry, and cooking oil. And since you've bought dog treats, I assume. . ."

"Okay, okay, I get it. You don't have to recite my grocery list. I'll have to say that you are an astute young man. I envision you as a detective someday."

Brandon laughed with Lillian. "Perhaps, you're the detective, ma'am. I'm enrolled at Sam Houston State University. My major is criminal justice."

"I should have known. You remind me of my son, Jake, and my adopted son, Grant. Both attended Sam Houston where they received their degrees in criminal justice. Maybe you'll have the opportunity to meet them while my husband and I are at Caddo. That is, if I can coax them to drive up for the day."

"That would be nice. I'd like to talk to someone other than a school counselor who could give me some advice, someone in the real world."

"Oh, they'd be glad to do that. Well, I've got to go. Bill's waiting." Lillian prepared to leave, but for some unknown reason, felt drawn to the young man. "I'm sure I've forgotten something. Since this is the closest store to the lake, we'll be seeing more of each other. Next time we meet, do me a favor."

"Sure, ma'am, anything. Just let me know what you need."

"ABispense with the ma'am and call me Lillian."

"You got it."

Lillian started to get in the vehicle, stopped, turned around, and extended her hand to the ambitious young man. Slipping him a twenty-dollar bill, she said, "Brandon, I wish you well, and I thank you." She put the key in the ignition, started the motor, and proceeded to pull out of the parking lot.

Before heading back to the lake, however, she glanced in her rearview mirror in time to see Brandon walk back into the store. Bill would not be happy with their choice of a campsite if she told him about Brandon's warning.

Lillian debated whether or not to go back and quiz the young man a little more. She was intrigued by his warning, and because he avoided making eye contact when he mentioned lost souls, she suspected he had not related all he knew about the missing persons. No, she decided to keep her promise to Bill. They would have a real vacation. She would mind her own business. But, unable to control her curiosity, she thought about lost souls all the way back to their RV.

* * * * *

Tall, slim, gray-haired Lillian, a retired educator, parked beside the new brown and white Forester Class C motor home Bill had given her for their fiftieth wedding anniversary. The motor home had all the conveniences of home, albeit on a much smaller scale. With a separate bedroom, a full bath, a small kitchen and sitting area, it was just right for the two of them and Eli.

Deep in thought and curious about Brandon's cautionary statement to her, Lillian had not seen Bill and her Standard Poodle Eli walking away from the Pavilion situated by the entrance to the park. She glanced in her rearview mirror and saw both man and dog hurrying to catch up with her.

As soon as she stepped out of the Jeep, Bill grabbed her in an embrace. "Hi, Sweetie, what took you so long?"

Lillian handed Bill a couple of sacks.

He laughed. "Okay, I get the hint. I'll help you unload the groceries."

Lillian reached down and gave Eli a love pat on his topknot and smiled at her husband. "You know, you still look quite handsome, even distinguished with that salt and pepper hair."

She laughed when Bill, a former investigative journalist, looked at her, and then to no one in particular. "Ah, yes, she evades the question. What has she been up to?" He reached into the back of the SUV and grabbed another sack. He carried them into the motor home and sat them on the small kitchen table.

Eli bounded up the steps and nosed around each of the bags, sniffing. Bill looked down and patted him on the head. "I bet she bought you some treats, ole boy."

Bill rummaged through one of the bags and pulled out a bag of chew bones and held one up. "Sit."

Eli plopped down. "Shake hands." Eli lifted his right paw and eagerly, but gingerly, took his reward from Bill's left hand. "Good boy."

Lillian followed her husband into the RV and placed the non-perishables in the small pantry below the refrigerator and the cold items in the fridge. "Bill, you should have been with me. I met the nicest young man at the store."

"Oh?"

"Yes, and he said the strangest thing."

"Now, Lillian, you know what you promised."

"Yes, I remember what I said, but…

"No buts. Anyway, we've been invited to a game of dominoes this evening."

"Dominoes? We've never played dominoes. I don't even know how. Who invited us and, more importantly, I can't imagine why in the world you would even accept such an invitation."

"The Gruenes asked us to come."

"I see. While I've been grocery shopping, you and Eli have been socializing. By the way, who are the Gruenes?"

"They are the couple in the white mobile home across and down the street from us."

"What time do they want us? Did you ask what we could bring?"

"We will meet them and a few others at the Pavilion. It seems that is quite the gathering place here. And we need take only what we want to drink. The Gruenes plan to grill hot dogs for everyone."

"Sounds like fun. I guess this is what RVing is all about. Relaxing, meeting new people, playing games. What do you think about that, Eli?"

Upon hearing his name, the poodle looked up, too busy chewing on his treat to answer her question.

Chapter Two

RELAXED FOR the first time in weeks, Lillian held onto Eli's leash as she walked with Bill on the way to the Pavilion. She gazed across the lake and wrapped herself in the sounds and smells that surrounded them. It was the time of day when the glow of the sun turned a muted orange in the western sky. The reflection of the trees on the water mirrored the glow of the Indian Summer sundown, and the Spanish moss dripping from their limbs gave the impression of oddly shaped golden tentacles on the water's surface. The waves on Caddo Lake had calmed to a slow ripple. Even so, the waves remained strong enough to gently rock the boats moored to the T-shaped public pier which stretched twenty feet across the surface of the water. The gentle slap, slap of the water against the boats blended with the distant sounds of laughter. The gravel crunching beneath their feet gave rhythm to the peaceful, harmonious cantata of water and distant voices.

"Bill, do you realize that for the first time in many months, we have nothing to do and plenty of time to do it?"

"Yes, and I'm glad to see you happy for a change," Bill responded.

As they entered the Pavilion, Lillian hesitated. She felt Bill protectively place his arm around her shoulders.

Eli began a low growl, a sound she had become to know as a sign of danger. Lillian stiffened.

Standing before her was an elderly man with short gray hair, rather unkempt, unshaven. The open collar of his worn, faded, khaki shirt revealed a silver cross attached to a black woven band of elephant hair.

Lillian could remember seeing a similar cross but could not recall where it was. Bill dropped his arm and placed his hand in the small of her back to nudge her forward. She ignored his efforts and walked over to the man. But before she could say anything, he looked her in the eye, nodded his head ever so slightly, turned, and walked away.

Try as she might, Lillian could not place the man, but his dark, piercing eyes reminded her of someone whom she had not thought about in a long, long time.

"Lillian, come on," said Bill, "I want to introduce you to the camp director."

Hesitating still, Lillian allowed Bill to lead her to a man who was positioned on the far side of the Pavilion where he had just fired up the grill. As they approached, Albert looked up, stopped what he was doing, and smiling, walked over to greet them.

"Welcome, Bill, I'm glad you could come." The two men shook hands.

"Thanks, Albert. I'd like to introduce you to my wife, Lillian."

Albert reached out to shake hands with Lillian but dropped his hand when Eli jumped between them. His growl told Albert to back away, and the man followed the dog's advice.

"Nice guard dog you have, Lillian. I hope he won't pose a problem for the other guests here at the park."

"He won't hurt anyone. Sit, Eli. Stay." The dog followed her command and sat close beside her and continued his warning in a little softer tone. "See, Eli is well behaved. Say hello to Albert, Eli." The poodle stopped his low growl and looked up but did not speak with his usual friendly bark. Instead, he gave a loud snort and turned his head. It was obvious to Lillian that Albert took note of the snub. He gave the animal one last, disgusting glare.

Recovering quickly, he looked at Bill and said, "I hope you two will enjoy your stay here at Caddo." Then, he exchanged his frown for a superficial smile and spoke to the dog. "You, too, Eli."

"Oh, I'm sure we'll have fun, Mr. Gruene. We always love an adventure," said Lillian who had to gently tug on Eli's leash to make sure he stayed put.

"Now, wait up a minute, you two. There's to be no 'Mr. Gruene' around here. People who know me would think I'm putting on airs. Call me Al," he said jovially.

Lillian responded, "You've got it, Al," and laughed along with him.

Lillian saw a woman approaching the table with a stack of wieners and buns. She placed her tray of food on the table and joined Al. "Hi, I'm Milly. You must be Bill and Lillian."

Milly and Al could have passed for brother and sister, five-feet, eight-inches tall, auburn hair, freckles. Both were probably somewhere in their forties.

By a quick glance at their waistlines, Lillian knew right away they enjoyed eating. Both faces were filled with laugh lines, happy wrinkles all. The two ladies, along with Eli, moved away from the men.

"Milly, do you need any help setting up for tonight?" asked Lillian.

"Oh, no thanks, we keep everything simple. Al and I usually provide hot dogs or burgers. Everything else is just pot luck. First timers are guests and aren't expected to bring anything."

"That's good because Bill didn't say anything about food. He just mentioned dominoes."

"Al likes to play straight dominoes each Friday night with any of the RVers who show up here at the Pavilion. Some of the guests prefer forty-two, but usually, we play regular dominoes."

"Well, you will have to teach me. I've never played dominoes in my entire life."

"You're kidding," said Milly. She laughed and then asked, "or rather, is this the big hustle?"

"No, I'm not kidding. My Leisure Lake friends and I play Mah Jongg...." Lillian said wistfully, remembering the loss of one of her Mah Jongg friends who had been murdered a few weeks ago by another of her Mah Jongg companions.

She took a deep breath and exhaled to erase the sadness enveloping her.

"But I'm ready to learn a new game."

"Good."

Lillian turned to find Bill still talking with Al. She smiled and spoke to some of the other guests who had arrived, some in pairs. All of them greeted the friendly dog accompanying her. Those who had brought food to share placed containers filled with deviled eggs, chips, salsa, baked beans, potato salad, cookies, and cakes on the table and began to mingle. She joined the men and hooked her arm around Bill's.

Al said, "Come on. I'll introduce you to some of the other campers tonight. I see you've already met Simon, our handyman."

"Well, I wouldn't say we met since he made tracks when Lillian walked over to him," said Bill.

"Oh, just forget about him," said Milly.

"I agree," said Bill. "We are here to enjoy ourselves, so let's get to it."

Al took a head count and walked to the center of the Pavilion and in a loud voice gained the attention of those present. "Okay, folks, I think we have enough people here to get started with the games. Everything you'll need is on your table."

Milly joined Al. "I'd like to introduce all of you to our two newbies, Lillian and Bill. Eli barked. "Oh, yes, I almost forgot you. Everyone, this is Eli. I won't ask you to tell them who you are right now, but before the evening is over, perhaps you can come by and say hello to them. They'll be at our table tonight."

A man with a New Jersey accent yelled, "Okay, Milly dear, we will. Right now, let's play."

The chatter in the open Pavilion became a low hum as everyone took their seats. Well, here goes, thought Lillian. The people knew each other by the way they chose partners and tables. Almost simultaneously, the dominoes tumbling from their containers clacked onto the tables and slid into the slow rhythms of their shufflers.

"Lillian, pick seven dominoes. Bill, I'm assuming you've played before," said Al.

"Yeah, I have. As a kid, I played with my grandfather." Bill smiled. "He was quite a shark. By the time everyone had played twice, he knew what each player had in his hand."

Al started the game. He played the double five. "Ten," he said and turned to Lillian who was still considering what she had drawn and trying to line up her dominoes in some kind of order.

"Lillian, if you have a five, just play it. If not, you'll have to pass." He looked surprised when Lillian picked up one of her dominoes.

"Ten," Lillian announced as she plopped down the blank five. "We're even, Al."

"Yep, for now, but don't expect it to stay that way, little lady," he responded.

Milly looked at Al's red face.

"I think Al's just been hustled. Are you sure you've never played before?"

Lillian shrugged her shoulders and laughed along with the other three. She noticed that Al laughed the loudest. Too loud. She didn't trust Al for one minute. By the dog's low growl, neither did Eli. She smiled and ignored his 'little lady' comment.

For the next hour, she concentrated on the strange and somewhat confusing game. All that could be heard in the Pavilion was the clack of the dominoes being slammed on the tables followed by either laughter or a groan, dependent upon the win or loss by the different teams.

Finally, after Milly had finished tallying their scores, Al stood up and yelled, "Okay, folks, when you finish the round you're playing right now, stop. Let's take a break and eat. There's a feast on the table."

"Whew, I thought you'd forgotten us," said one of the men. "I'm starving."

"I'll have these dogs ready in a minute," said Al.

"Let's mingle," said Bill.

"Yes, let's," agreed Lillian. She stood and hooked Eli's leash to the leg of her chair.

"Eli, you stay here by the table. I'll sneak an extra hotdog for you." He licked his lips in anticipation of the treat to come.

The two made their way around the room shaking hands and introducing themselves to the other players.

Suddenly, a loud explosion replaced the laughter and camaraderie of the Friday night domino competitors. Its force caused the Pavilion's foundation to shift, rattling the chairs and tables while dominoes skated off the tables.

Chapter Three

THE PAVILION shivered once more and then settled back down.

Silence.

The only sound came from Eli who yowled and used his paws to rub his ears. Lillian saw the dog, still attached to the chair. She went back to him and set him free. He ran down the steps, barking.

Stunned, everyone looked at each other for a moment. Some of the more timid players held onto the edge of their tables for support.

Not Lillian.

She followed Eli. With Bill close behind, she rushed down the steps of the Pavilion and ran to the pier. Lillian scanned the sky to see if she could determine where the explosion occurred.

"Bill, do you see that bright glow over there?"

"Where?"

She pointed above the Cypress treetops.

"There, left of that old house on the curve across the open area of the lake." She bent and picked up Eli's lead. The dog ceased barking, and he, too, looked in the direction of Lillian's outstretched hand.

"I do, but I can't tell how far away it is. Pretty dark out here. Let's go back to the Pavilion before pandemonium sets in." Bill turned to leave. "Uh oh, too late," he said.

Others had followed Lillian and Bill. They turned in circles, scanning the sky for some sign of the disturbance that brought an end to their evening. Stymied, they milled around talking among themselves. When Lillian and Bill walked up to them, the once carefree domino players fired questions.

"Good grief, what was that?"

"Could you guys see anything?"

"Of course, they couldn't, Jim. It's pitch black out here."

"I sure hope no one was hurt by that, whatever it was."

"So do I," responded Lillian to the last statement.

"I'm going to my RV," announced one of the men, his voice shaking, "Strike that. I changed my mind. Maybe, Al can learn what happened."

Heads bobbed in agreement.

"Good idea," Jim said. "We'll feel safer if we stay together."

Al stood on the top step of the Pavilion. He spoke to the crowd. "Come on back in. I'll see if I can find out what made that noise, get to the bottom of this."

"How do you propose to do that?" asked Lillian. Holding Eli's leash, she and the dog were the first ones up the steps.

"I'll call the sheriff's office. See if I can find out anything." Al stepped off the lower steps of the Pavilion and stopped. "Bill, could you – ?"

"Don't worry. I'll stay here with everyone until you return," offered Bill calmly.

"I'll help you with that," Lillian said to her husband.

She scanned the crowd, and saw Milly sitting at her table. Unlike the other frightened campers, she looked too cool, calm, and collected in Lillian's opinion. She joined Milly and asked, "Aren't we supposed to have hotdogs tonight?"

"You bet." Milly stood, turned to the other confused campers, and with feigned enthusiasm announced, "Don't any of you dare leave here until Al comes back." She walked to the grill and fired it up.

"Don't worry about that, Milly," volunteered a tall blonde with hazel eyes. "I don't care to be alone in my RV until I know what happened."

Lillian took note of her and thought it odd that a middle-aged woman would want to go camping all alone.

"Yeah, I think we need to hang around awhile," agreed one of the men who, in Lillian's opinion, did not fit in with the other campers. By the new-looking clothes he wore, she decided he was new to camping and as green as she and Bill about RVing.

"Right on, Russell. I'm not going anywhere right now," said another.

"Does anyone besides me smell smoke?" a panicky female voice asked.

"No, I don't," said Guy Steiner, the camper with the loud New Jersey accent, "and you don't either."

Lillian sidled up to Bill.

"I smell it as well. Don't you?" She glanced down at the dog standing beside her. "Look. Eli's nose is working overtime. He smells it, too."

"We don't want everyone to panic. If they think there's a forest fire coming this way, they'll pack up and leave, and God only knows what they'll get into," Bill whispered.

"You're right. We don't know which direction the sound came from," said Guy, close enough to overhear Lillian and Bill talking to each other.

"It came from the north," Lillian said.

"How do you know?" Guy asked.

"Caught a glimpse of the blaze above the tree tops."

Lillian and Bill climbed the steps by the Pavilion and rejoined the domino players. Eli made one last growl and tipped his canine nose in the air as he walked beside his owner.

Guy stepped back into the Pavilion and in his loud, nasal voice, spoke to all of the campers still standing around.

"Since Milly's cooked enough hot dogs to feed an army, what say we eat dinner while Al is tracking down some information for us?" Guy suggested.

"Grab a plate, everyone," said Milly. "Al and I can't possibly eat all of them."

Lillian and Bill stood aside and watched Milly serve the hot dogs. As Milly passed by them, she stopped. "Here, puppy, you can have one."

"Yes, he thinks he needs one," Lillian said. Eli gently grabbed the wiener from her hand and gulped it down. Lillian and Bill laughed at the dog's greediness.

Milly offered a second one, but Eli looked at Lillian for permission this time. "She said you may have it." Milly gave him a second helping.

"Hungry, are you?" Bill asked and then added, "Me, too." He lifted a hotdog off the platter and took a bite.

Lillian waited until Milly returned to the grill before speaking. "I think we ought to go over to Al's office and help him," Lillian said to Bill, quietly enough this time so no one else could hear. And in a whisper, she added, "He might not remember everything he hears. He might even withhold some of the facts."

"Now, Lillian, don't start judging Al. If he doesn't tell us everything, I'm sure he may just be trying to keep everyone calmed down. Why do you distrust him?"

Lillian nodded, "Okay, but I'm not convinced about his sincerity. I noticed that he didn't volunteer anything until someone pushed him for information. That's why I'm suspicious of him. If you were the camp director, no one would have to suggest you investigate an explosion."

Bill ignored her last comment, took her by the elbow, and led her toward the grill. "I could use a second helping," he said.

When Bill and Lillian walked up to be served, Milly said, "Why don't you join me and Al in our RV for a glass of wine. We had planned to invite you before all of this happened."

"Sounds good," said Bill.

"I'll help you clear things away here," Lillian offered, "while Al makes his report to everyone."

"Oh, no," said Milly. "Simon will do that for us."

Al returned to the Pavilion. Everyone looked at him expectantly.

Lillian was the first to speak. "What did you learn?"

"Nothing now. Too soon for an official report about it on TV, and the sheriff's dispatcher was tightlipped and would only say the sheriff was at the scene of the accident. Hopefully, by morning, I'll know more about the explosion."

Guy spoke in a loud voice. "I don't know about the rest of you, but I'm going back to my RV and turn on my television. If we continue to stand here gawking at each other, we'll miss out on the ten o'clock news."

The crowd began to disperse. Watching them, Al said, "Bill, did Milly invite you and Lillian over for a drink?"

"Yes, she did, but if this is not a good time --"

"We'd love to," interrupted Lillian.

"Good. You two go on with Milly. I'm going back to my office, call the park ranger. See if he knows anything. Bet he's probably already heard about it. I'll catch up with you later."

* * * * *

All conversation ceased when Al entered the RV. Eli had been dozing on the floor next to Lillian's chair. He raised his head and growled a soft warning to Al.

"Shh, Eli," Lillian said as she reached down to pet his head. "Stay." The dog laid his head on his front paws. His big black eyes followed Al's movements.

"Well?" said Bill.

"The park ranger, Jeff Richards, answered his cell phone. Fire department's on the scene, trying to contain the fire. Said he would contact me if he felt we were in any kind of danger," said Al.

Milly stood and walked over to her husband, hugged him, and said, "Well, dear, don't worry about it. None of our campers were hurt. So far, so good." She retrieved a wine glass from the small cabinet over the sink and poured from the bottle on the counter. "Here, have a glass of Merlot."

"Thanks, darling," Al said as he returned her hug.

Lillian looked at Bill and then at her host, "Al, when we first arrived, you mentioned that Simon is the handyman."

Al nodded. "He's a good employee. Always keeps the grass mowed and the Pavilion and pool clean. On Fridays, he works extra duty setting up the tables for the domino party. When he finishes his chores, he vanishes."

"Really."

"Simon's kind of quiet, keeps pretty much to himself," Milly offered.

"Oh, well, I guess I'll be running into him while we're here. I may need his help."

"What Lillian is really saying is that tonight is our first night ever in our RV. I'm not even sure we have the RV's power sources or septic services attached properly."

"Al, not Simon, will help you with all of that," cautioned Milly.

"That's right, and I suggest you stay away from Simon," said Al.

"Okay, we will, but is there a reason why we should?" asked Lillian.

"Simon doesn't have the best people skills," Al explained. "He likes to do his work and not be bothered by anyone. Even he and I don't talk much. I tell him what to do. He usually just nods and goes about completing the task."

Milly confirmed Al's evaluation of Simon, saying, "I see him every day, and he has not said more than two words to me. I think he's a little too creepy. Know what I mean?"

Lillian shook her head but didn't respond.

"How long have you been here?" asked Bill.

"I guess it's been at least two years," Al responded. "Felt lucky to get this job with the economy being what it is."

"When did Simon come to work here, before or after you?" Lillian wanted to know.

Al and Milly exchanged glances. "He was here before us," Al said. His wife nodded in agreement.

Lillian shivered as a warning prickle danced up and down her spine. Simon reminded her of someone. And, it interested her that the Gruenes were too quick to warn the Prestridges to stay away from him.

Chapter Four

BILL GLANCED at his watch. "Al, it's been a long day. I think Lillian and I are ready to turn in. I'd like for you to double check our connections before we call it a night. That is, if you don't mind."

"Sure. It has not been a typical Friday night. We're all tired. Let's go on over to your RV right now."

Eli walked between Lillian and Al. He did not growl but walked so closely to Lillian that she could feel his fluffy fur brush against her legs with each step she took. He never took his eyes off of Al.

"Lillian, do you have a notebook handy?" asked Al as he waved his flashlight back and forth so that the three of them could find their way to the Prestridge RV. The trio stopped in front of the steps leading into the brand-new Forrester. Eli jumped onto the top step and stood guard, still eyeing Al.

"I do. As a matter of fact, I always carry one in my purse. Why would you ask? Do I need one?"

Al chuckled, "Well, I would have bet a week's salary that you keep a notebook in your purse."

Lillian raised one eyebrow. "I hope I'm not that transparent."

"You remind me of my high school English teacher. Never seen one yet that didn't come prepared to take notes."

"You got me on that one." Lillian smiled.

Al cleared his throat, straightened his shoulders. "Besides, the instructions I'm about to give you and Bill are somewhat difficult, so I thought you might want to jot them down."

Lillian rummaged around in her handbag and pulled out a black notebook bound with a hot pink spine. The front cover was splattered with white polka dots. "I'm ready. Fire away."

"Okay, here goes. First, there are pink jobs and blue jobs."

"Let me guess," interjected Bill. "Mine are the blue ones."

"You catch on fast, don't you?" He laughed and looked at Lillian. "Now, little lady, listen carefully. The pink ones are for you. Don't want you to get hurt or nothing."

Lillian shook her head and glanced at her husband who shrugged his shoulders before directing his attention back to the task at hand.

Al bent over to examine the connectors that attached the RV to the utilities. "First thing you always do when your RV is stationary is to make sure you have it in park."

"Surely, you jest." Lillian spoke up. "That's pretty obvious if you know how to drive at all"

"You'd be surprised at the number of people who forget that step. Funny watching them 'catch' their RV to put it in park. I see you're already connected to water and electricity."

"Check that off our list of things to do, Lillian," instructed Bill.

"You've connected the sewage hookup like a professional camper. These are all of the blue jobs you really need to know."

"Thanks. I wasn't sure I remembered all of the instructions the salesman gave me when I bought the RV."

"Remembering details is important. Be alert when you disconnect the sewer service. Water's okay if it spews on you, but…"

"I get it. I understand that water might slosh on me, but I'll pass when it comes to raw sewage," said Bill. "Are you sure those are all of the blue jobs?"

"Yep," Al said as he turned to Lillian.

"Okay, now as for you, little lady, here are the pink jobs"

"Like I said, I'm ready." Lillian had her pen poised to write.

"Your list might be a little longer."

"How so?"

"Well, your job is to do everything else that needs to be done like cooking, cleaning up the kitchen, making the bed, sweeping, setting up the patio table and chairs, going to the nearby laundry."

The loud laughter he uttered following his proclamation caused Lillian to step back. She pressed her lips into a tight, straight line, tilted her chin up at least two inches, and scrunched her eyebrows together. She slammed her notebook shut.

Al winced.

"Oops. You're not one of those women libbers, are you?"

"That, sir, is a position most male chauvinists don't understand."

Eli rushed off the front steps and ran around the RV. He came to an abrupt stop and stood beside Lillian. He showed his teeth to Al and growled. Lillian grabbed his collar to hold back the poodle.

"I'm thinking I've done worn out my welcome. Sorry if I caused you two any grief. See you in the morning."

Lillian saw Al wink at Bill, who smiled. She scowled even more severely, and took a deep breath, struggling to control her temper and to restrain Eli. Before she could tell Al that she agreed with his last proclamation, he turned and jogged back down the trail. Lillian watched the beam from his flashlight dance back and forth along the path as Al made his way back to his camper.

Bill's smile disappeared when he turned around to face his wife.

"You'd think he never heard of the ERA," she said.

"Now, Lillian, don't get your dander up about Al's attitude. He was just teasing. You know I'll help you with the household chores just like always."

"I know you will, but when Al criticizes or demeans womanhood, I'd better not catch you smiling. After all these years, I know you understand how much I despise male chauvinism. Anyway, I decided it was time to give him my 'ole principal's face' so he would go away."

"Glad you did. What do you think about our new friends on the road?"

"Well, it's a little early and I don't want to prejudge anyone, but..." She paused. Bill raised his eyebrows.

"Don't you think Milly and Al are too worried about our meeting up with Simon. I will make a point to talk to the handyman before we leave Caddo."

"Uh, uh, we are not going there. I don't think it's wise for you to try to second guess what they meant when they cautioned us about him. You don't need to start pestering Simon."

"Let's turn on our television, see what the explosion was all about." Lillian walked over to the small TV attached to the header located between the sitting area and the cab of the RV. She reached up to turn on the unit. Nothing. "I forgot. We haven't hooked up to the cable."

Bill gently turned her around. He put his arms around her and pulled her toward him. "Instead, let's try out that new bed of ours."

"Yes, let's." She put her arms around his waist and kissed him.

Eli's ears perked up. Lillian, always in sync with her dog, asked, "What's the matter, my good boy. What do you see?" She stopped and looked into the darkness but could see nothing moving. "Come on, Eli. It's bedtime."

Bill opened the door for her, but Eli ran inside before Lillian had time to respond to Bill's chivalry. The dog leaped up the steps, sailing over all three in one fell swoop. He scurried through the tiny rooms of the RV and jumped onto the bed, found a spot, and lay down.

Lillian laughed. "Eli heard you say we need to try out our new bed."

"Oh no you don't, big boy. There's not enough room for all three of us." Bill patted the dog on his head. "Go on. Get off the bed, you big ole baby."

Eli gave a loud snort, jumped down, and walked into the living area where he jumped up onto the back of the sofa.

Lillian laughed.

"That's better, Eli. From there, you can look out the window and observe everything that occurs in the campground during the night. I'll expect a report in the morning."

The dog put his nose in the air and looked out the window.

* * * * *

Snuggling deeper under the covers after plumping up her pillows, Lillian looked over at Bill who was absorbed in Stephen Woodfin's new best seller, *The Compost Pile*. "This is just like that commercial on TV, Bill."

"Which one?"

"I don't know what they're advertising, but I remember a couple about our age is in it. They are in the west somewhere, and a bad thunderstorm chased them inside their camper trailer."

"Yeah, I know that one," said Bill, yawning. "The difference between them and us is that we don't have a storm raging outside."

Lillian responded, "But have you heard the crickets and the locusts? And just listen to those bullfrogs. Sounds like a storm of wildlife to me."

Upon receiving no response from Bill to her last statement, Lillian waited in silence. Soon, she heard Bill's snores, soft at first. She removed his book, marked his spot, placed it on the nightstand, and turned off the light. She eased out of bed and tip-toed into the small kitchen.

Eli looked up, but when she whispered, "Stay," he complied. He closed his eyes and dozed back to sleep.

Lillian donned the black sweatpants and T-shirt she had folded and left on the arm of the sofa. She eased the small refrigerator's door open, grabbed a bottled water, and closed it.

She glanced out the window over the sink. Darkness surrounded every campsite in the area. However, there was one glow from the window of the camp director's office. Al was in a hurry to leave after he checked the hookups. Did he withhold information about the explosion? Lillian decided to investigate. She sneaked past Eli and gently opened the door. Before stepping through the portal, she reached back to the upper cabinet adjacent the door, retrieved a flashlight, and eased out into the black night. The soft click of the RV door sounded like a canon to Lillian. She paused and waited. Eli made a soft whimper. "Shh, Eli. Stay," she whispered a stern command. All was quiet.

She stood outside the door of her RV until her eyes adjusted to the darkness gathering around her. She let the glow coming from the open window of Al's office guide her steps.

Standing outside his window, Lillian heard a different kind of storm, not the peaceful sound of nighttime wildlife. The distant careening sirens of fire trucks and emergency vehicles blended with the night songs of locusts and crickets. She risked a quick peek through the window.

She heard Eli's sharp bark in the distance and winced. Lillian wished she had brought him with her so he wouldn't wake Bill.

Chapter Five

WHEN THE door of the RV closed softly, Eli followed Lillian's command. A moment later, he barked once and then ran into the bedroom. He jumped onto the bed and gave Bill several dog kisses. Bill stirred, opened one eye, and asked, "Don't tell me you want to take a walk at this time of night."

Eli bounced up and down, shaking the bed. The dog continued making small yips as he nudged Bill under the chin.

Awake, but wanting to resume his sleep, Bill pushed Eli away, turned over, and reached over to wrap his arm around Lillian.

Gone.

"Okay, boy, now I know what you were trying to tell me."

Wide awake, he rose, put on a T-shirt, and pulled on a pair of faded jeans. Padding barefoot through the RV, Bill realized that Lillian had taken the flashlight and had indeed slipped out of the RV.

He knew the explosion was too much excitement for her and regretted not having paid for the cable hookup. Bill made a note to arrange for a connection first thing tomorrow.

He reached under the sink for the mosquito repellant and quickly sprayed some on his arms and legs. Worrying that Lillian would not, could not, ignore any kind of intrigue and fearing that she might have an accident wandering around in the middle of the night, he slipped on his sneakers, and walked outside. Where could she have gone at this time of night?

"There's nothing to do but find her. Eli, wait here. I need to get your leash." Bill stepped back into the RV.

The dog sat down and sniffed the night air. He stood, growled, and raced away.

Bill heard Eli's growl. "What do you see, ole boy? Do you see her?" he asked as he stepped outside once more. With empty leash in hand, he hoped the dog knew where she had gone. He couldn't see anything. She'll either return or . . . Bill shook his head. He didn't want to think about the alternative. He listened for Eli's bark.

Silence.

Not knowing which way either of them had gone, Bill took off in search of his inquisitive wife.

* * * * *

Lillian stood outside Al's window. For a few seconds, she heard the tail end of a news announcement then silence.

"Shoot," she muttered to herself, wishing she had heard the whole report. So much for being away from civilization. Cable service would be her first priority come morning. Then the room was filled with static.

Al's voice floated out the window. "Acer calling Shadow. Come in Shadow."

A Ham radio. Odd. Lillian didn't know anyone communicated with those anymore. Antiques, but effective and secure. She would have to remember to ask Al if he served in the military during the Vietnam War.

Al repeated his call.

"Acer calling Shadow."

"Shadow here," responded a female voice with a distinct accent.

"We heard an explosion."

"A truck exploded from the Morningside Fertilizer Plant."

"We felt the aftershock all the way out here. Where did the explosion occur?"

"Just off Highway 49."

"What went wrong? I thought we had a good plan."

"You tell me," Shadow demanded. "If your guys can't do any better than that, we may not need your services in the future."

"Now wait a minute, Shadow."

Al's stern response indicated to Lillian that he was not willing to accept the blame for a scheme gone awry. "Look, you can't hold me or my men responsible. I told you we needed to wait. You're the one who couldn't wait. You put everything into play too early."

"Don't get testy."

"Well, just don't point a finger at me," Al said. "How much damage was there?"

"One fatality, so far."

"Oh my God," Al moaned. "That's going to complicate everything."

"Ten-Four on that. But, it might work out for us after all."

"How?"

Lillian heard a tap, tap. She sneaked a glance through the window and saw Al, pen between his fingers, flicking it back and forth against the top of his desk.

"Well, all the residents in the surrounding rural areas are being evacuated to nearby Jefferson until the fires can be extinguished."

"Including everyone in Atlanta?"

"Yes. And both Texas and Louisiana state troopers have the highway blocked to through traffic."

"I assume we are behind the blockade?"

"Ten-Four. We'll be able to move -- "

Al's telephone rang.

"Over and out. Gotta go," Al said.

Lillian remained beneath the window, trying to absorb what she had heard on the news. Now, she knew what had rocked the Pavilion and ended an otherwise pleasant Friday night of dominoes. What's so important that Al received a phone call this time of night?

She heard panting and looked down to see Eli. He, too, had sneaked to Al's window.

"Shh, Eli. Don't bark." She reached down to pet her loyal companion. "We don't want him to hear us." The dog sat, his nose sniffing the night air.

She heard, "Yeah?" Pause. "The first one made it? Good. Anyone else hurt?" Pause. "Well, at least half the mission is accomplished." He ended the call.

Mission? What in the world? Lillian knew by the screech of Al's chair and the sound of his footsteps that she and Eli needed to leave in a hurry. Before the office door opened, she quickly scooted out of sight taking Eli with her. "Shh." She and the dog froze as Al walked out onto the small deck, bowed his head and stood silently for a moment before turning and stepping back inside. He looked as though he were praying. Lillian had heard enough for one night. She whispered to Eli, "We're going back to bed before Bill wakes and realizes he's alone."

Lillian with Eli beside her walked back down the trail to her RV. Before she could take two steps, Eli whimpered and with tail wagging took off into the woods. She stopped and softly called "Eli, come back."

She heard a whispered "Good boy," and then a man's voice beckoned. "Lillian, over here."

Lillian scanned the darkness trying to identify the owner of the soft voice. If whoever called her name were dangerous, Eli would have growled a warning.

Besides, she reasoned, that dog doesn't take up with people if he senses danger.

"Who are you? What do you want? How do you know my name? You'd better speak up quick, buddy, before I scream and wake up everyone in this campsite," she bravely whispered back.

Eli and a tall figure stepped out of the trees. "It's Brandon. We need to talk. Come with me."

"Brandon, from the grocery store?"

"Yes, and don't talk so loudly, please," he whispered. "Just come with me."

"Why? Why should I follow you anywhere? I really don't know you. I just saw you briefly earlier today," responded Lillian, trying to keep her voice down.

"I know. I know. But just trust me. Your dog does. Walk with me," he motioned with his hand. She followed him away from the campsite back through the thick shrub-like foliage along the edge of a path.

"Okay, but I must be nuts to let you talk me into this," said Lillian. "Eli, you stay with me just in case." She gripped her flashlight, prepared to use it as a weapon.

Brandon chuckled. "No ma'am, you're as sane as Eli. If you recall, I tagged you as a detective when we met earlier. I'm either right, or you just like to eavesdrop outside windows. Which is it?"

"Well, to be honest, I am curious about several events that have happened tonight. As for you, you do have some explaining to do. Namely, what are you doing lurking around in the dark at our campsite?"

"And you? Let's see, you always stroll around at night when you go camping?" he said.

"Okay, *touché*," Lillian conceded.

"Truce?" asked Brandon as he extended his hand.

"Truce," she said and shook hands with him.

The moon beams bouncing off the rippling waters of the lake provided enough light for Lillian and Brandon to see each other clearly. They had reached a picnic table in a wide grassy open area. Brandon motioned for Lillian to sit on the bench attached to the table. He parked himself across from her. Eli hopped up onto the table and lay down between them.

"Okay, Brandon, do you remember when we stood in the parking lot at the grocery and you warned me about strange events occurring at Caddo Lake?"

"Shh. Don't talk so loud," he cautioned. "Someone might here you." He added, "And, don't you think an explosion is strange enough, especially in an isolated area like Caddo Lake?"

Lillian ignored his question. "You mentioned lost souls. I need to know more, so enlighten me about them. Who were they?"

"Lillian, all I know is that over the past three years, four people went fishing and never returned. These were men who regularly fished and camped at Caddo. They knew their way around the lake. All four times, one went missing, the park ranger organized a volunteer search party of fisherman knowledgeable about all of the lake's bayous, but they didn't find any trace of the men. No boat. Nothing. Sounds crazy, I know, but please trust me. Be careful."

"Crazy? Who's crazy? You or I? We were both slinking around in the middle of the night. Look at us. Sitting here at a picnic table with a dog on top of it. Jolly time for a picnic, if you ask me."

"Well, I have a question for you, you peeping Tom, you." Brandon chuckled.

"Don't laugh at me. What in the world were you doing watching me while I was sleuthing, not peeping, mind you." Eli raised his head at the sound of her voice.

"It's okay, my friend." Brandon stroked the dog's back. He settled back down.

"To answer your question: I sometimes ride my Harley out to the lake late at night when I've finished my shift. Everything's more peaceful here at night. No motor boats, paddle wheels, or loud laughter. I like to hear the frogs croaking, the night owls hooting. It relaxes me after a hard day on the job."

"Oh, sure. I really believe that story," Lillian said. "You may disagree with me, but I hear that it's a little hard to sneak up on someone if you're riding a Harley. I certainly didn't hear you riding in tonight. Now, Brandon, it's time for the truth. Detective to detective. Tell me."

"I didn't expect you to believe that, but had to try anyway. To be honest, I rode out tonight to make sure everything is okay.

After the explosion, I called the park ranger, Jeff Richards. He's a friend of mine. He and the sheriff are, as you would expect, more than a little busy right now. I told him I would check on the campers."

"If you are here officially, then why sneak in?"

Brandon nodded. "I can understand your suspicions. I came to check on something else." He lowered his voice and asked, "Did you hear anything of importance while you were standing outside of Al's window?"

Lillian shivered and looked around the area. She couldn't see but knew they were not alone. She saw Brandon do the same. "I didn't hear anything that made any sense right now. Besides, why should I share any information with you when you've not told me the truth?"

"I promise. In time, I'll tell you everything. But, right now, the less you know, the better. Trust me," he said.

"Blind trust is not in my vocabulary, and patience is not one of my virtues. But okay, just so you understand one thing: When my curiosity is piqued, I usually dig until I get all the facts. I will, however, give you the benefit of a doubt only because it is late at night, I'm suddenly quite tired, and I don't want Bill to awake and find me gone. If he even gets a hint that I'm on a case, he will crank up that RV, tie me up, throw me in it, and drive someplace else."

"Seriously, Lillian, I've got to check one other thing before I expound any of my theories about this particular campsite. Call the store tomorrow if you need anything delivered. I have been known to make deliveries, tangible and intangible."

"Got it loud and clear. I'm sure I forgot something today when I shopped," said Lillian. "I will expect some concrete information though."

"What can I expect?"

"Some of my famous pimento cheese sandwiches and chocolate cookies."

"Deal. I'll walk you back to the campsite."

"No need for that."

"Don't want you to fall in the dark, and I certainly don't want anyone catching sight of the glow of your flashlight."

Eli jerked. Growled and then barked. "No. I can find the way by myself."

Lillian stood quietly watching Brandon disappear through the darkness. He pushed his Harley all the way back to the entrance gate, far away from the campsite. Lillian could barely hear the sound of his engine as he sped away into the night.

Lillian folded her arms across her chest. The breeze skimming across the lake had a foreboding chill. Swiftly moving clouds filled the sky and obliterated the dim rays of moonlight. Darkness dropped like a shroud and snuffed out all sounds of insects and nocturnal animals. Lillian did not want to turn on her flashlight, nor did she want to fall, so she walked slowly and tested where she placed each foot as she made her way back through the thicket of trees.

She stopped. Did I hear a limb crack? She quickened her pace. She reached the path that turned into the open lane. Was that the crunch of a footstep? Again, she stopped to listen. No, couldn't be. I'm imagining things. She crept on a few more steps and paused. No, there it is again. Someone is following me. Picking up speed, Lillian turned on her flashlight and hurried toward the safety.

* * * * *

Not knowing which way Lillian had gone made it difficult for Bill to conduct a search for her. Nonetheless, he raced back and forth along the pathways between all of the RVs. Surely, Eli would be barking if he found her. Bill shivered. She can't have gone far. He went down to the marina and looked out over the lake. Bill's eyes had slowly adjusted to the low light produced by the moon. Its beams danced on top of the lake's gentle waves. He heard the deep resonating voice of a bullfrog's serenade to an unseen audience. The frog croaked one last note. Total silence followed.

He heard a familiar bark and rapid footsteps. He strained his ears to determine the direction they were headed. Then he saw the dancing flashlight guiding Lillian toward the RV. She was running, Eli beside her. He ran to meet dog and master.

He wrapped his arms around Lillian.

"Lillian, are you all right?"

"Hurry, Bill, let's get inside our RV."

Chapter Six

SIMON HAD followed Lillian as she made her way back to her RV. He stayed well out of sight behind the thick foliage that lined the trail leading from the picnic area to the campground. He kept guard long enough to make sure no one else followed her. He saw Bill rush to her and witnessed their embrace. Simon was glad he was downwind from the white Standard Poodle who looked right at the group of low bushes shielding him. Simon bent down lower and backed up. The dog growled but didn't advance toward him. Eli turned toward the RV and followed his owners inside. Satisfied that Lillian was safely ensconced in her motor home, Simon walked down the trail past the Pavilion to the public boat ramp where he had left his small fishing boat. He rowed until he was well out of earshot before he turned on the Jon Boat Trolling Motor.

He trolled the boat across the lake, steered it around a bend, and entered one of the many bayous that fed in and out of Caddo Lake. Hundred-years-old oaks and cypress trees dressed in their finest Spanish moss provided a canopy through which Simon slowly guided his boat. He chugged deeper and deeper into the bayou. Its entrance was hidden by an outcropping of vegetation and known only to him. The song of the tree frogs grew louder and louder.

When he approached another smaller inlet, lily pads parted giving him safe passage, and as soon as he exited their delicate gate and made a left turn, they slowly closed. He shook his head as he remembered that in the past, several intruders had ignored his offer to serve as their guide. Simon thought about the park ranger's search for them, all for naught.

The trees were thick on each side of the waterway. Even though the cloud cover destroyed the moon's rays, Simon knew the bayous of Caddo Lake as well as the history of the Indians who once resided among the cypress knees. The white man's government had removed the Great Raft, a natural dam of fallen trees, to open up the Caddo to steamboats. After the engineers finished their desecration of the dam known as the Great Raft, the lily pads had slowly returned to guard the secret of Simon's world.

A white owl screeched and swooped across the bow of Simon's boat and soared up into an oak where it perched on a low branch.

Simon looked up. "Hello, Charlie," he said as he passed under the ancient tree. He pulled up to a dock situated directly below a gray, weather-beaten house. Its roof had patches on top of patches. A long screened-in porch stretched across the front where two black, ladder-back rocking chairs shared a small handmade table. Perched high between two giant cypress trees and shaded by their mourning branches, the house gave the appearance of being supported more by the trees than by the stilts on which it was built.

Simon slowly climbed the back stairs that led into the small, well-equipped galley kitchen. He opened the door of an elaborately carved oak cabinet and retrieved a bottle of Ménage à Trois, removed the cork, and filled a wineglass to the rim. Carrying the glass and the opened bottle with him, he passed through a hallway lined with overflowing bookshelves, walked through the living room, and stopped. Before stepping outside to the screen porch, he turned on the Bose radio/CD player perched on the table just to the right of the front door. He sat down in one of the rockers. The song "As Time Goes By" followed him out of the room. He hummed along with the orchestra. On the wall behind him, Simon had nailed a sign that contained the words:

Speak softly in shade,
smell cool dew against your feet,
hear nothing but light...

Simon glanced over at the empty rocking chair moving back and forth in sync with the rhythm of the music.

He nodded. He smiled and raised his glass in a reverent toast as he looked toward the other side of the lake.

"Here's to you, Lillian," Simon said.

Chapter Seven

LILLIAN LAY in bed savoring nature's music. The songs of the morning sparrow and the mourning doves blended with the last lines of the cricket solos. She loved that moment of the day, not quite dark and not quite daylight. She could hear Bill tiptoeing around in the RV's tiny kitchen in an effort to make coffee without waking her. She chuckled, knowing the harder he tried to be quiet, the noisier he would become. Within minutes, she could smell the dark rich aroma of Folgers brewing and the English muffins toasting.

She rolled over on her left side and saw Eli asleep in Bill's spot. She hugged the dog and whispered.

"What'd you do? Push him out of the bed?" The dog opened one eye, closed it, sneezed, and went back to sleep. "You must have stayed up late last night, you good boy." The dog raised his head, yawned, and settled back down.

Stretching, she arose, sneaked up behind Bill, and wrapped her arms around his waist. He turned, put his arms around her, and kissed her. They did their usual morning dance together. Happiness. Peace.

Click. Muffins popped up out of the toaster.

Beep. Coffee ready.

"Let's eat our breakfast outside," suggested Lillian. "I'll throw on a pair of Bermudas and a T-shirt. Won't take but a minute."

"Sounds good. I'll set up the table and chairs while you get dressed," offered Bill. He stepped outside of the camper, turned, and stuck his head back in the door, "Lillian, you might need a sweater. It's pretty chilly out here this morning."

"Okay." Lillian donned her favorite pink cardigan. From the window, she watched Bill retrieve the folding table and two chairs from the storage bin beneath the camper.

"It's ready," said Bill. He opened the door to the RV for her.

Lillian stepped out of the RV, carrying a tray laden with two cups of coffee and the English muffins. "Don't close the door completely. Eli may want out soon."

Bill gently closed the door making sure the latch didn't catch.

Lillian set the tray on the table and picked up her cup, which she held with both hands to absorb its warmth. Still standing, she sipped her coffee.

"Bill, look at that sunrise. Who can see the gray and blue of the sky and the purples and shades of yellow and gold it creates and not believe in God?"

"I know what you mean. Man can't paint that landscape and do it justice," responded Bill. "Come on over and sit down. Let's eat while the muffins are hot."

"Oh dear," said Lillian. "I forgot the sugar free orange marmalade you like. I remember the young man I met at the store mentioned we could call the grocer and place an order. He said he makes deliveries out here all the time."

"Are you serious? I didn't think anyone still did that these days," said Bill.

"I know. I think I'll call him later and ask him to bring the marmalade today after his shift ends. What do you think about my inviting him to stay for dinner?"

"Well, Lillian, I wondered how long it would take you to find someone you could adopt. You do tend to mother anyone who will let you."

Lillian smiled. "You do a good job of fathering, if you ask me."

"I didn't, but sure, go ahead. His being here will give us an excuse to forego any potential domino games tonight. "

"Amen to that. Didn't enjoy it one bit, especially with the explosion and all. I still don't understand Al's reaction to the explosion, nor do I understand why he and Milly want us to avoid the maintenance man. What was his name? Do you remember?"

"Simon. I think that's what Al said. For the record, it doesn't matter. We're going to take their advice."

"Speak for yourself, mister. I intend to talk to him."

"Lillian, I'm warning you -- "

"Wait just a minute, Bill, before you start in. I'm not going to get into any trouble. I promise. But my gut tells me there's something about Al and Milly that doesn't ring true. I'm going to ask around about Simon. He really reminds me of someone. I can't put my finger on it, though."

"Lillian, don't. If you start asking around, others might become just as suspicious as you are. Remember, James 1:19: '. . . let every man be swift to hear, slow to speak.'"

"You're right, of course. I won't cause any trouble for anyone. I'll keep my eyes and ears tuned in and will share my thoughts with only you."

"Good."

"By the way, Bill, did you hear anything unusual outside our RV after we went to bed last night?"

"No, I slept like a -- " Bill stopped mid-sentence.

A woman's anguished scream echoed throughout the campsite, a sound that ricocheted up Lillian's spine and kept her shivering long after the scream had died away.

Chapter Eight

ELI LEAPED out of the bed, bounded through the RV door, and raced past his owners. Lillian jumped up immediately and followed the poodle. Eli stopped in the middle of the road, stood motionless, one front paw raised, nose twitching, and stared at a tall, shapely middle-aged jogger. Her blonde pony tail swished back and forth as she staggered out of breath toward the campsite. Eli broke his point and slowly crept to the distressed woman who had stopped in the road bent over, hands on her knees, gasping for air. Both Lillian and Bill hurried to her. She had ceased her screams. Having filled her lungs with oxygen, the woman sobbed. Her salty tears accentuated the essence of her terror as they followed lines of anguish etched on her face.

"What's wrong?" Lillian said reaching out to the woman whose sobs grew louder and more uncontrollable. "Here, let me help you." Then Lillian noticed the blood on the woman's hands. "Oh no, something terrible has happened to you." Lillian put her arms around the woman's shoulders and guided her toward Bill.

Other campers had also heard the screams, and curious, had abandoned their morning activities. The crowd gathered as Lillian tried to comfort the woman. Eli paced around the two women, pushing back the onlookers, growling when necessary. People backed up as the dog kept enlarging the circle.

"Bill, hurry. Get her a chair," ordered Lillian. He retrieved the chair where he had been sitting only moments earlier.

"Here, ma'am. Sit down," and then to his wife, he said, "Lillian, stay with her. Try to calm her down. I'm going to dial 9-1-1. Be back ASAP." He looked at one of the women bystanders, "Could you bring her some water, please?"

Lillian lip-synced a silent thank you.

She patted the woman on the shoulder. "Miss, could you tell me your name?" Lillian thought that if she asked simple questions she could get the woman to calm down long enough to tell her what happened.

The distraught woman could not speak. She rocked back and forth in the chair.

Lillian looked around the crowd. "Does anyone know this lady?" she asked.

"Yes, I do," said a tall, muscular man decked out in black and green jogging clothes. "Move out of the way, folks." He pushed through the crowd using his elbows to shove campers aside. He sweated profusely. "She is Leigh Ann Heavener. She and I jog the same trail each day."

Leigh Ann's breath was coming in short gulps, but she glanced up and nodded an acknowledgement when she heard the man utter her name. "And you are?" asked Lillian who remembered seeing him at the Pavilion playing dominoes.

He straightened his back ramrod stiff and squared his shoulders. "My name's Russell Stokes. I'm a private investigator."

"Thanks, Russell." Lillian turned back to Leigh Ann. "Can you tell me what's wrong? What happened to you?"

Russell interrupted Lillian. "Ma'am, move aside. She knows me. Let me talk to her. I've had experience in these kinds of traumatic situations." He put his hand on Lillian's shoulder to move her out of his way. "I can – "

Before he could complete his sentence, Eli sprang in front of him, planted his front paws, lowered his body, laid back his ears, showed his teeth, and snarled, ready to spring at the stranger.

Stokes backed away from Lillian. "That dog – you'd better get him under control before I – "

Once again he was interrupted.

"You touch that dog, you'll regret you ever saw him," Lillian said. She then commanded, "No. Stay, Eli."

The dog quit growling but did not move nor did he take his eyes off the man.

Neither did Lillian. "You are not going to interrogate her. She doesn't need that." She turned her back to the man.

"It's awful, just awful. Never seen anything like it." Leigh Ann shuddered and began to sob again.

"What's awful? Can you tell me?" persisted Lillian.

"The man, he was lying face down beside the jogging trail. I thought he had tripped," Leigh Ann sputtered between sobs. "I tried to help him up. I couldn't."

"How badly is he hurt?" asked Lillian.

"He's dead," wailed Leigh Ann.

Russell Stokes spoke again but kept his distance from the women and the poodle whose growls were softer but just as menacing. "I was jogging behind her. All of a sudden I heard her scream and then she took off like a streak of lightening."

"Mr. Stokes, did you see the body on the trail?" Lillian asked.

"No, I didn't. Guess I was more concerned about her." He looked down at the sobbing woman.

Leigh Ann repeated over and over, "There's blood, blood everywhere."

First an explosion and now a body. And a pompous ass who thinks he's Sam Spade. What next?

Sirens blared. Good. Bill called them. Lillian put her arms around Leigh Ann's shoulders and squeezed.

"Okay, Leigh Ann, help is on the way. You just sit tight."

Lillian saw Bill running toward them and the onlookers who stood in a circle around her and Leigh Ann. She turned to ask Russell Stokes if he could retrace his steps back to the location where Leigh Ann had screamed, but he had disappeared. It was then she realized Eli had stopped growling.

Chapter Nine

LILLIAN STOOD beside Leigh Ann's chair and kept one hand on the woman's shoulder and one hand on Eli's head for moral support as well as to steady her own nerves. Eli barked. "Good boy," said Lillian.

"Are you okay?" asked Bill as he walked over and took his wife's hand. He gave it a squeeze. She acknowledged his support with a nod. The other campers stood, patiently waiting, watching to see what would transpire next. They, too, are in shock she noted. She heard the shrill sound of help weave its way down the county highway but couldn't discern whether it was an ambulance or a police cruiser.

The sheriff wheeled into the camp with sirens blaring. Eli howled at the intrusion. Within seconds, the siren took its last wail and settled into silence as the cruiser skidded to a stop less than fifty feet from Lillian and the group of onlookers. Eli sat down and rubbed his ears with his right front paw.

The park ranger, Jeff Richards, opened the passenger door and stepped out. He walked around to the front of the vehicle.

From the driver's side, Sheriff Jay Tomas unfolded his long legs and the gravel of the drive crunched under his cowboy boots as he stepped out of his car. He stood for a moment. His steel-gray eyes surveyed the scene. Six feet, three inches tall, Tomas overshadowed Jeff Richards who had short, blond, curly hair. Tomas hosted a face with chiseled cheekbones. As if trying to escape imprisonment, his thick, curly, salt and pepper hair sneaked out of his uniformed cap. Tomas pursed his thin lips even tighter.

Al joined the group.

Lillian tiptoed to whisper to her husband. "It's about time he showed up. I need to speak to you privately. I want to tell you about the man who —"

Before she finished her sentence, the sheriff said, "The 9-1-1 caller reported an emergency. Who made that call?"

"I did," Bill said. "This lady came running into the camp screaming and said she had found a dead man. That's when I called you."

Seeing the blood on Leigh Ann, he spoke into the two-way radio clipped to the lapel of his uniform. "Need an ambulance and the medical examiner at Caddo RV Park."

"Ten-Four."

"Al, would it be possible for you to take this lady to your office so I can get her story?" Tomas asked.

"Sure, Sheriff," he responded.

His voice tugged Lillian's memory. She wondered where she had seen him before. Tomas took control right away. She hoped he was as efficient as her first impression of him had been.

Lillian confronted the sheriff. "Sir, this lady is Leigh Ann Heavener, and my name is Lillian Prestridge. It was my husband, Bill, who alerted Al and you about this situation."

"Prestridge?"

"Yes, sir." Lillian wondered why he repeated her last name as though he had heard it before but decided not to pester him with a question about it."

"Pleased to meet you, ma'am. Now, if you will excuse me, I'll escort the lady to Al's office, and we'll find out what's happened out here."

When Eli stepped between him and Lillian and growled, he asked, "This your dog?"

"Yes, sir."

"I don't have time to deal with a hostile animal."

"He's only hostile to rudeness." Lillian met the sheriff's gaze with an icy glare.

"Keep him quiet, please."

"Okay." Lillian looked down at Eli. "Quiet, boy. Sit." Immediately, the dog obeyed.

"Impressive." The sheriff then directed his gaze to Al. "I know the way to your office. I don't need you with me. You go with Jeff. I want you two to take these people over to the Pavilion. Get their names and contact information."

Tomas turned to the crowd. "Folks, I'll need to talk to you, so don't think about packing up and leaving this campground until I give you permission. Is that understood?"

A few of the onlookers nodded.

"All of you come with me," Jeff instructed.

Lillian didn't move. She patiently waited for the sheriff to acknowledge her presence.

He looked at her for a moment. "Ma'am, do you have something else you want to say?"

"Yes, I do, as a matter of fact." She ignored Bill's tug at her elbow as he attempted to steer her away.

"Well, let's hear it," said Sheriff Tomas gruffly.

"Don't you want someone to go take a look at the body?"

"Ma'am, we'll get to that as soon as we know where to look. This lady can help us find it." He leaned down to help Leigh Ann stand. He spoke sternly. "I want you to go to the Pavilion with the other campers. Leave your contact information so I can get in touch with you later."

Lillian stood her ground and held onto Leigh Ann's arm. "This woman has been through a traumatic ordeal, and I think it's important for her to have a female present when you question her."

"Yes, please, let her come with us," pleaded Leigh Ann, her eyes tearing up.

"Okay, fine. Let's go on over to Al's office. I'd like to know exactly what happened to you and where you were when it happened," said the sheriff. Tomas reached out and gently took her arm. He held onto her while they walked the short distance to Al's office.

Inside, Lillian took note of the room's stark furnishings. Besides the desk chair, there were only two ladder back chairs and a telephone on the desk. There was no Ham radio in sight.

Sheriff Tomas moved one chair to the back of the room and placed it against the wall. He motioned for Lillian to sit down.

"Keep that dog quiet." He pulled out the desk chair for Leigh Ann to sit down. He leaned against the desk.

Bill had followed the group and now stood, his back against the inside doorframe.

Tomas glared at Bill. "And you are?"

"Bill Prestridge. I'm the one who called you. I'm with Lillian." He walked over to stand beside his wife's designated spot. "I'll try to keep her from interfering."

Lillian narrowed her eyes and frowned at Bill. Eli reached up and licked Bill's hand. Lillian smiled at her dog.

After a quick nod to Bill and a glare at the dog, the sheriff turned to Leigh Ann, and in a voice more gentle than Lillian could have imagined, he said, "Now, miss, it is Leigh Ann, right?" He pulled from his shirt pocket a ringed three-by-five-inch notebook, clicked his ballpoint pen and jotted down the date and time. "Leigh Ann – one word or two? Spelled Lee?"

"Yes, sir, it is."

"Which one? L-e-e or L-e-i-g-h?"

"It's L-e-i-g-h, two words," said Leigh Ann.

"Okay. Good. Now, can you tell me where you were when you got all of that blood on you?"

"Yes, sir." She took a deep, ragged breath.

"Take your time." The sheriff reached over and patted her hand, which she had placed on the desk.

"I was on the trail that circles the campsite. I try to stay in shape, so I jog every day. I've run each day I've been here at Caddo."

The sheriff nodded. "How long have you been at Caddo?"

"Let's see, I don't remember the exact day, but I know I've been here at least two weeks."

Tomas jotted a note in his book, looked up and asked, "Can you tell me what happened today while you were jogging?"

She sniffled, cleared her throat, and said, "I saw him."

"Who?"

"I don't know who he is."

"Well, can you remember exactly where you saw him?"

"I think I can. I had jogged about half way around the trail, passed the curve that leads back toward the marina."

"What was he doing?"

"Nothing. Are you crazy?" Leigh Ann waved her hand, palm down, left to right. "He was just lying there. Blood everywhere. So much blood."

She began to sob loudly. "I tried, I tried -- "

"Okay, Miss, you're safe now. Take a deep breath." The sheriff motioned for Lillian to come closer. "Your friend is here. We'll take a break. Can I get you something to drink, some water, perhaps?"

"No thank you, but I really need to wash this blood off of me."

"You'll have time to do that real soon, ma'am."

Lillian looked at the sheriff and asked, "May I talk to her?" He nodded.

"Leigh Ann, can you repeat what you told me when you first came back from your run?"

"Yes, I can."

"Good. Like the sheriff said, take your time. Look at me and tell me again what happened," said Lillian as she rubbed Leigh Ann's arm to soothe her.

"Well, I was jogging along the trail and saw him. He was lying face down, not moving. I thought he might have tripped and hit his head on a rock or something. So I tried to turn him over to help him. I couldn't. He was too heavy, but then I saw the blood." Leigh Ann's voice raised a decimal as she continued, "I got it all over my clothes, my hands and my arms." She looked down at her hands. "I've got to get it off."

"Okay, ma'am," said the sheriff who had been writing as she talked. "If I ask you to lead me down the trail, could you show me exactly where you found the body, er, man?"

"Yes, I think I so. Can Lillian come, too?"

"I suppose it'll be okay for her to come." He turned to Bill. "Sir, do you mind coming as well. May need some help with these." He motioned toward the women with his head.

"Of course. Glad to help," said Bill.

The sheriff looked at Lillian. "I suggest you put your dog in a place where it can't get in the way."

"Why can't he come?"

"Evidence," the sheriff mouthed the word and nodded toward Leigh Ann.

Lillian nodded. "I see. Give me a couple of minutes, Leigh Ann, and I'll return. We'll all go together."

"Okay, but hurry. I'm scared."

Lillian left with Eli beside her. She took him to their RV and left him with instructions.

"Be on guard, Eli. Don't let anyone come into our RV." He parked himself inside the door and barked as if to say, "I've got everything under control."

* * * * *

The group walked down the trail in a single file behind Leigh Ann. Lillian made mental notes about the path. The jogging trail, barely wide enough for two runners to pass each other, cut along the edge of the main road leading into the campsite. Past the last RV lot, it angled off into the woods.

A thicket of tall oaks, pines, cypress, and sweet gums provided ample shade for joggers as they ran. The pine bark and wood chips on the trail provided a soft cushion for knees and ankles. They also muffled the sounds of pounding footsteps. A person could run past the RVs and never be heard.

As the group continued its trek, Lillian eased her way up the line until she was right behind Leigh Ann. About a mile into the forest, Leigh Ann slowed her pace.

"This looks like the spot where I saw his feet sticking out of the brush, but I don't see them now."

She sounded panicky to Lillian.

"Are you sure?" asked Sheriff Tomas.

"Yes, I'm pretty sure. No, wait. Maybe I saw it around that curve," she said, pointing in the direction of a right turn in the path.

As they rounded the curve. Lillian noticed a dark figure quietly ease back into the thick foliage and disappear.

"Did you see -- ?" Lillian wanted to know if the sheriff had seen the shadow, too.

"Yeah, I see," said the sheriff as he caught sight of the dead man's feet protruding out onto the trail. "Stay here."

The sheriff walked over and pushed aside some of the undergrowth. He hunched down beside the body and felt the carotid artery. "No pulse." Just as Leigh Ann had described the scene to him, blood had pooled around the body. The sheriff motioned for Bill to help him.

They turned over the corpse whose shirt fell open. Carved into his chest was a snake, its eyes spilling bloody tears, coiled and ready to strike.

Bill straightened up and frowned. "Lillian, you and Leigh Ann go back to the camp's office."

"But -- I saw -- "

"No buts. I said go. Now. Be quick about it."

Lillian knew not to argue with Bill when he spoke that sharply. She also knew he would discuss the situation with her when they were alone. "Come on, Leigh Ann. Let's go to my RV. I'll make you a cup of tea. Tea will make both of us feel better."

Leigh Ann turned to retreat from the scene, stumbled, and would have fallen had Lillian not responded quickly to take her by the arm. As they walked back to camp, Lillian said nothing, but she glanced at her companion frequently to make sure that she wasn't going into shock after seeing the body again.

As they approached her RV, Leigh Ann finally spoke. "Thanks, Lillian, but I need to clean up. Think I'd feel better if I had a shower."

"I understand. We can stop by your place long enough for you to do that if you'd like."

She nodded her agreement.

The two women walked past Al's office, the Pavilion, and the Prestridge RV on their way to Leigh Ann's Air Stream camper. It sat on the lot farthest from the lake. It looked peaceful nestled against the thick forest of pines where azaleas had been planted beneath their thick umbrella shade.

While Leigh Ann showered, Lillian sat on the small sofa deep in thought. She had wanted to tell Bill what happened when he left to call 9-1-1. Also, she had seen the carving on that man's body. The two dots on his forehead enticed her.

Brandon was right. Strange events, indeed. Two serious incidents in two days? Coincidence? Perhaps. But the big question is why did Stokes disappear when the sheriff appeared? And where was Al? He didn't show up until the sheriff and the park ranger arrived.

Chapter Ten

LILLIAN SAT on the tiny sofa in Leigh Ann's RV and waited for her to complete her ablution. The sound of water running in the small bathroom of the Air Stream seemed to go on and on. Finally, Lillian heard the squeak of the faucet. The flow of water ceased. Wrapped in a fluffy white bathrobe, Leigh Ann, skin pink from excessive scrubbing, stepped through the small sliding door leading to the sitting area of the camper.

"I still feel dirty," she said as she sat on the chair opposite Lillian. "I just can't get over what I saw. All that blood."

"Why don't you put on some clean clothes and let's mosey on over to my RV. I don't think you need to be alone right now."

"Thanks, Lillian. I'll do that."

She opened the small closet and chose a gray T-Shirt and a clean pair of jeans. Dressed, she joined Lillian. "I'll lock up here before I go. Right now, I don't feel this is a very safe place. I just hope – " She paused.

"Hope what?"

"Oh, nothing. I'm sure I'm just imagining things. Let's go. Okay?"

"Sure. I bet Bill has some cookies squirreled away somewhere in the cupboard. He never goes very far without his sweets." Lillian smiled.

"Sounds good. As you can tell, I haven't turned down very many offers of dessert lately," said Leigh Ann trying to match the cheerfulness that Lillian exhibited.

The two ladies walked the short distance between their campsites. Eli barked a welcome to his owner. He backed away from the door so that Lillian could open it for Leigh Ann to enter. Eli gently rubbed his body beside Leigh Ann who reached down to pat him.

"Thank you. I needed your soft touch." Eli licked her hand and turned away. He jumped onto the back of the sofa and looked out the window.

A dreaded *déjà vu* sensation crept up her back and caused Lillian to shudder. Before stepping through the door, Lillian stopped briefly and scanned the area, then tossed aside the idea of being watched and walked inside behind her friend.

* * * * *

Simon followed at a distance. He had been careful to stay out of sight by moving beneath the shaded canopy provided by the low moss-covered branches of oaks standing guard alongside the lane.

He saw Lillian stop and look around the campground. She wore that puzzled expression he remembered so well. He smiled and in a low voice acknowledged her intuitiveness.

"Okay, Lillian. I see you scanning the area." Simon barely whispered to himself. "I can tell you sensed my following you. I'll have to be more careful from now on. I had forgotten just how perceptive you are. Thank goodness, you didn't recognize me when you and I stood face to face in the Pavilion. I've got to keep my cover as a maintenance worker intact. Need to clean up this campground. Keep it family friendly."

A lone figure stood on the opposite side of the lane. Simon had taken note of the person stalking the two women. He saw the man standing between two of the RVs parked on the north side of the road. Simon didn't know if the other person had seen him sneaking along behind the women, but Simon did not hesitate to let the watcher know he had been spotted.

Simon stepped out into the light and crossed the lane. He walked straight to the trash bin situated across the lane from Lillian and Bill's RV. As he approached the bin, Russell Stokes stepped out, turned away from Simon, and headed back down the lane toward his own RV.

*****

From his perch on the sofa, Eli began his menacing growl, a warning Lillian had heard too often lately. She walked over to him, bent down and looked out the window to determine what he had seen. "There's nothing moving out there, big boy. Go lie down, Eli," she said.

She turned around. Leigh Ann sat listlessly at the small dinette table. The sadness in Leigh Ann's big, blue eyes reflected the gloom of the thunderclouds gathering above.

"Let's see, I did promise you a cup of tea." Lillian smiled and reached for the tea kettle on the back of the range, filled it with water, and set it on a burner.

Leigh Ann looked up and returned Lillian's smile. "Tea is always good. I drink a cup every night before bedtime. It helps me calm down."

The tea kettle whistled, and Lillian filled their cups with the hot, steaming water. On the table there was a box with a variety of tea bags. "Here, you choose which flavor you want."

Leigh Ann chose a TAZO caffeine-free calming tea. Lillian chose Lipton black tea loaded with caffeine. The two women sat on opposite sides of the small dinette silently sipping their tea. Anxious for conversation, Lillian reached over, handed Leigh Ann a fresh tea bag, and poured Leigh Ann another cup of hot water.

Leigh Ann looked up and smiled. "Thanks. I guess I was in my own little world. How long have I sat here ignoring you?"

"Oh, not long. We both had a lot to think about. I've been sitting here trying to decide how to ask you about yourself without sounding too nosey."

"Let me guess. You want to know why I'm camping by myself, don't you?"

"I admit I do. But first, just for fun, let me guess what you do professionally."

Leigh Ann laughed. "You like games, I see."

"Puzzles are my forte." Lillian held up her hand. "Let me guess, I bet you are, or were, a teacher. Am I correct?"

"I taught Texas history in another lifetime."

"Well, Miss Texas history teacher, you are in good company. I, too, was a teacher."

"Now, it's my turn to guess." Leigh Ann studied Lillian's face. "From your speech pattern, I'd bet you taught English. That would be my first idea."

"I taught English in the Dallas-Fort Worth Metroplex area for thirty years. You mentioned 'another lifetime' and I suppose that means you are retired?"

"Yes, but 'retired' may not be totally accurate."

"Now, you've sparked my curiosity."

Both ladies laughed.

"Tell me more about your teaching career," Lillian said.

"I taught for fifteen years right out of college," Leigh Ann explained. "Then, a colleague of mine set up a blind date for me. Her fiancé had a friend who was new in town. When I met him, it was love at first sight."

"Wow, I thought love at first sight happened only in romance novels." Lillian turned serious.

"What happened?"

"I fell for a smooth talking attorney and married him six months later."

"Oh? How did that go? I guess your friend felt quite good about herself, playing matchmaker and all."

"Well, unfortunately, no, she didn't."

"Why?"

"The smooth talker was my friend's date. She refused to be my maid of honor."

"Well, bless her heart," Lillian said.

"No. You should say 'bless Leigh Ann's heart.'"

"Did you and your friend ever reconcile?"

Leigh Ann nodded. "Only after she married a wonderful guy did she speak to me again. I think she enjoyed my misery."

"In that case, she was never a true friend."

"If I had known then what I know now."

Leigh Ann sighed and shook her head. "Guess I won't go there if you don't mind."

"Does your husband plan on joining you here? Forgive me if I've gone too far."

The look on her face puzzled Lillian. Was it disappointment, anger or fear?

Which one?

"Oh, no. You see, we're separated. Camping is one decision I made, didn't ask for his permission this time."

"I'm so sorry. I didn't mean to pry."

"It's quite all right. I can actually talk about him now without feeling any semblance of heartache. I should have suspected how our marriage would be."

"Why do you say that?" Lillian doubted the woman spoke the truth about not having a broken heart. Leigh Ann's expression said otherwise. Lillian knew by experience that heart breaks preceded other emotions, both good and bad.

"We returned from our honeymoon, and the next day he insisted that I leave my job and devote myself only to him. He said it didn't look good for an attorney's wife to be a lowly school teacher."

Lillian shook her head. "How sad. Teaching is an honorable profession."

"You're right, but I was so much in love, I let him have his way. I quit my job. I've always regretted giving up my professional life."

"Perhaps, he was taught by his father that the husband should provide for a stay-at-home wife. It's old school by today's standards, but I know couples who have that kind of marriage. They are happy." Lillian said, trying to keep the conversation going.

She wanted to know more about a woman brave enough to camp alone yet helpless and hysterical in a tragic situation. "But in the twenty-first century that relationship is not for everyone."

Leigh Ann nodded in agreement and continued. "Three months later, he demanded we start our family. I told him I wasn't ready. He threw a fit, said he didn't care whether or not I was ready. He was and that's all that mattered. I knew then he would control my life."

"Still, a marriage breakup isn't ever easy, especially when children are involved. You haven't mentioned any, so am I to assume you two didn't last that long?"

"That's the only good part of my thirty-five year marriage. Somehow, we hid our disdain for each other and raised a good son. He's a graduate from Baylor Law School. His dad has offered him a position in his firm, one I hope he declines."

"Well, I wish him the best. I understand mothers and sons. I have two myself."

"I need to return to my camper now." She stood to leave.

"Well," said Lillian, "if you need anything at all — day or night — you call us." She reached for a notepad on the counter and wrote her cell phone number on it. "Here, take this. I'm serious. Call if you need us."

Leigh Ann hugged Lillian. "Yes, I will. I can't thank you enough for today."

"Think nothing of it. I was glad to help and hope to visit with you again soon."

Lillian gently closed the door and sat back down at the table. She gazed out the window and watched Leigh Ann walk down the lane and pass by the trash bin.

Eli had moved from the sofa to the king-sized bed at the back of the RV. He jumped off the bed when Leigh Ann opened the door to leave. He jumped back up on the sofa and settled in his favorite spot, the back. He looked at Lillian.

"She's a puzzle, Eli. We've got to watch out for her. You'll have to help me." The dog gave a snort at Lillian's proclamation. "Think what you will, ole boy, but we've got work to do. She didn't tell the whole truth." Lillian made up her mind to unravel the mystery of Leigh Ann's lies.

* * * * *

Lillian's cell phone vibrated and squirmed its way across the small dinette table. The caller I.D. on the screen told her that Jake, her biological son, wanted to touch base with her. She swiped her finger across the green telephone and answered.

"Hello, son. How are you and the family?"

"We're fine, but I've heard about the explosion that occurred near Caddo Lake last night."

"The shock waves caused the ground to sway where we stood. Your dad and I were at the Pavilion meeting other campers and playing dominoes."

"Bet that shook up everyone."

"It did, but that's not all of the excitement we've had."

"What do you mean?"

"There's been a murder."

No response from Jake. Lillian waited, giving him time to say something. When he didn't, she asked, "Can you hear me?"

Silence.

"Are you still there?"

Finally, she heard him.

"I'm thinking."

"What?"

"Dad took you camping to get you away from all of the murders around Leisure Lake."

"Yep, and the second night we're right in the middle of a murder investigation."

"Mom, listen to me. Stay out of it."

"Don't worry about me. I'll be very careful. By the way, have you heard anything from Grant?"

"I know what you're doing: Changing the subject, but I'll answer your question anyway." Jake paused.

Lillian could hear him turning the pages of his desk calendar. Just like him, she thought. He has to check the date of their conversation. She smiled when Jake continued.

"Grant called me last Thursday to give me his new cell phone number."

Lillian opened her notebook. "Great. I've got a pen. Read it off to me."

"I suggest you wait and let him call you. He still needs time to heal."

"Is he okay?"

"Of course."

"That's good to know. Did he tell you where he is?"

"No, ma'am. He's still reeling."

"Poor thing. I know I hurt him when I exposed Margaret for the murderer she turned out to be."

"Mom, I know my brother. He doesn't blame you. He's just disappointed."

"Disappointment is an understatement. Margaret is the second woman he's loved and lost, but he will get over it."

"He will. He's strong." Jake agreed with Lillian. "But if he calls again, I will tell him where you are."

"Tell him to call me, please. Let him know I miss him."

"Will do." Jake's phone rang. "Hold on a minute. Let me answer this call."

Lillian heard her son put the other call on hold. He came back on the line.

"Remember, Mom. Stay clear of any and all murder mysteries. I want you and Dad to enjoy your camping."

"Love you, darling." Lillian said and then pushed the red phone symbol on her cell.

* * * * *

Jake punched the blinking line on his office phone. "Hello, Grant."

"Jake, have you heard about the explosion and the murder at Caddo?"

"Yes. But how do you know about the murder? I just learned about it from Mom about two minutes ago."

"Oh no, don't tell me she's at Caddo Lake."

"Where else would she be, especially if there's any kind of mystery involved?"

"And I know her," Grant said.

"Don't know where you are, but I suggest you head toward East Texas, maybe even Caddo."

"Well, surprise, big brother. I'm already close to Mom and Dad. They just don't know it yet."

"How so? Explain."

"Do you remember Professor Tomas?"

"Best instructor we had at Sam Houston, and, as I recall, he retired from teaching and is a county sheriff now. His county is next door to Caddo."

"I've talked to him, and he asked if I could work with him on a temporary basis, help him out with the situation at the lake."

"Good ole Tomas. Tell him hello for me."

"Ten-four, and don't worry about Mom. I'll take care of her."

"You always do. Gotta go. Stay in touch."

Jake ended their talk.

Chapter Eleven

LILLIAN POURED herself another cup of tea, munched one cookie after another, and mentally replayed the events of the past two hours. Satisfied that she remembered all of the details, she picked up her laptop case and pulled out a composition notebook with white and bright pink hearts on its black cover. She listed in chronological order all of the events she could remember since she and Bill had arrived at the Caddo Lake campsite.

1. *Bill and I parked our RV in the reserved spot.*
2. *Met nice young man at grocery store. Name = Brandon*
3. *Bill checked in with the camp director.*
4. *Bill announced we had been invited to play dominoes.*
5. *Met camp's maintenance man. Simon something. Looks familiar. Don't know why.*
6. *Met Al and Millie Gruene. Don't trust them.*
7. *Loud explosion.*
8. *Found out a truck had exploded.*
9. *Next morning, Bill and I were having our breakfast and were enjoying the beautiful blue and purple sky at sunrise.*
10. *Asked and received Bill's okay to invite Brandon to dinner tonight.*

11. Heard a scream. Saw a woman running toward us. Tall Blonde. Athletic.

12. Woman hysterical. Reported a body on jogging trail.

13. Asked her name. Didn't answer me. She could not speak.

14. Russell Stokes stepped up and identified the woman. Said he was a jogger. Said he was a private investigator.

15. Woman's name is Leigh Ann Heavener.

16. Crowd gathered. Other campers? Did someone not Rving show up in crowd? Don't know.

17. Bill notified Al and authorities. Sheriff Jay Tomas and Jeff Richards, park ranger arrived.

18. Russell Stokes. He seemed assertive until he heard the sheriff's siren blowing into the campground. Why did he disappear so quickly? Does he have anything to hide? Did he know the dead man's identity? Sheriff questioned Leigh Ann.

19. Leigh Ann led us (sheriff, Bill, and me) to the body.

20. Leigh Ann and I returned to her RV and then to mine.

21. Someone followed us. Why? Who?

22. Leigh Ann – former teacher – married attorney – divorced.

23. Leigh Ann did not want to talk about ex-husband. Why?

24. One son – in law school – Dad wants him to work in his law firm – she doesn't want him working with his father.

25. Did she tell the sheriff everything she knows about the dead man? If she didn't know him, why was she so upset? What, if any, is her connection to the dead man? Why did she lie to me?

26. *Just how well does Stokes know Leigh Ann?*

27. *I need to level with Bill. Let him know about my suspicions. Would he be upset about my getting involved? Yes, I know he will be. Will he help me? Yes, I know he will. He loves Me.*

Lillian read over her notes. She reached for another cookie and realized she had finished off the packet. She picked up the phone and called Edgemon's Gas & Grocery store. The phone rang five times. A man finally answered on the fifth ring. "Edgemon's. This is Kyle speaking."

"Hello. Lillian Prestridge speaking. I'd like to place an order to be delivered today by Brandon."

"Sure. What do you need?"

"I would like to order two packages of chocolate chip cookies and two jars of sugar-free orange marmalade."

"That's all?"

"Yes, sir. Thanks."

"Whoa, hold up. I need your address."

"Oh, yes, I'm sorry. I'm at the Caddo RV Park. In the brown and white Forester RV. We are parked in the fourth lot on the main road leading into the campgrounds. You can't miss us. We're the only brown and black Forester here."

"Got it."

"Great. Again, thanks. Oh, one more thing. Could you have Brandon call me before he leaves the store just in case I think of something else I need?"

"Sure will, ma'am."

Lillian hung up the phone. She couldn't believe she had forgotten to give Kyle her location. Her mind was definitely elsewhere.

She looked at Eli.

"I'll be glad to see Bill walk through the door. He's my sounding board even though he never wants me to get involved in these types of escapades."

The dog tilted his head in understanding.

"But in the end, he always supports my decisions."

Eli laid his head on his front paws and yawned.

"Okay, I won't bore you, but just know that I am one blessed woman and you are one blessed dog."

At the sound of dog, Eli jerked his head up.

"Good. You're listening. I'm glad I thought to ask him to have Brandon call me. I have quite a few questions for that young man. Perhaps Brandon saw something on his way out of the camp last night."

* * * * *

A couple of hours later, Lillian was sitting at her laptop when Bill returned. She quickly logged out of the program and shut down her computer. She stood and walked over and gave him a hug and kiss. Lillian felt comforted and protected as Bill held her close.

She kissed him again before stepping back. Still holding on to him, she said, "Bill, you did the right thing by telling me to take Leigh Ann away from that grisly scene. She was really shook up."

"I know. You would have been, too, had you stayed," he responded. "I hope I didn't hurt your feelings by speaking so sharply, but I wanted you to understand the urgency of getting Leigh Ann away from the scene. Plus, I didn't want you to blurt out what you had seen."

"Don't worry. My feelings are intact. I knew what you were doing."

"Good. I'm glad we're on the same page here. I saw you eyeball the carving on his chest."

"A coiled snake, if I'm not mistaken."

"You're right. It was a snake. Did you see what looked like two dots on his forehead?"

"Yes, but I couldn't tell how they were made."

"The two dots were in a rectangle divided in the middle to resemble a domino, the one referred to as 'snake eyes.'"

"Strange, isn't it?"

"Strange is right," said Bill.

"A puzzle, if you ask me. And this is the second time I've heard the word 'strange' used to described this place."

"Who else has used that word? On second thought, never mind. Don't tell me. I came on back here as soon as I could because I knew your mind would be in a whirl."

"You know me well, my love."

"Yes I do, and I don't want you getting involved and maybe hurt. Let's you and I leave this situation to the medical examiner and a forensic team. They are on their way here as we speak. The sheriff and the park ranger were waiting for them to arrive when I left. They can't remove the body until the M.E. and forensic finishes with it. Sheriff Tomas was frustrated because it was taking them forever."

"Why is that?" Lillian asked.

"They're working another site right now. There's another body."

"Oh, no. Things are no longer 'strange' around here. They're dangerous."

"Remember the explosion?"

"How could I forget?"

"Well, it was a truck filled with ammonium nitrate. The driver died as a result of the explosion. He was thrown quite a distance from the vehicle. Burned to a crisp."

Lillian listened intently. She did not let Bill know that she already knew the cause of the explosion. The death of the driver was not a surprise. "What a coincidence," she said.

"Coincidence?"

Bill looked doubtful. "Coming from a lady who does not believe in such. Explain what you mean, Lillian. I've been married to you for fifty years, and I've never heard you use that term before."

"Let me ask you a question first. What do you think the chances are of two deaths occurring on the same night only a few miles apart from each other out in this secluded part of East Texas?"

"Don't know. Don't want to go there. In fact, if the sheriff would let us, I'd crank up this RV and leave right now," he said.

"I know you would prefer to do that, but don't you think we ought to welcome the fact that the sheriff has the benefit of your expertise? After all, your whole career centered around investigative reporting. You've worked hand in hand with detectives in the Metroplex area. Your eye for detail always gave them insights they would never have considered."

"Lillian, don't patronize me. I know you're not referring to my expertise. And I'm telling you now. Leave this situation alone. Two people are dead. I don't want you meddling. You might be the next victim if you antagonize the wrong person. Control your curiosity. I mean it."

"But you've got to admit something's just not kosher around here."

"Let's just enjoy the night. How about a glass of wine?"

"No thanks. Do you remember my telling you about the grocery store making deliveries?" No response from Bill.

"Well, Brandon is making a delivery to us tonight. I want you to meet him and hear the questions I ask him. I've made a list of facts that have occurred and plan to incorporate into it last night's events."

"Lillian, I'm warning you. This is a dangerous affair. Please stay out of it."

She heard him but ignored his advice. "FYI, Brandon is also bringing more chocolate chip cookies. Leigh Ann and I finished off the last of the package."

Bill nodded and sat down at the table, looked at the computer, and stated, "I didn't know you brought your laptop with you. I'm glad you did, though. I might need it."

"Sure. You're welcome to use it," said Lillian who smiled sweetly to the man she adored. "I thought you said you were going to bring your computer."

"I did, but we left in a hurry, and -- " The screen popped up on Lillian's computer and caught his attention.

She turned her back to him with the thought that her trustworthy husband had just told her a lie. And because of his blatant falsehood, she did not feel guilty about her secret. She would reveal it when she decided it was time for Bill to know.

Chapter Twelve

LILLIAN HUMMED "On Eagles' Wings," her favorite hymn, as she assembled a tray of assorted sandwiches she planned to serve with her homemade tomato bisque soup for dinner. At the end of each verse, she paused, just long enough to keep tabs on Bill. He sat at the computer, and each time she glanced his way, she noticed he was reading the headlines of different East Texas newspapers. She placed the last chicken salad sandwich on the tray and walked over to stand behind Bill.

"Have you found anything online about the explosion?" she asked.

"Yes, a brief mention about the evacuees going to Marshall. I thought there might be an update on it, but so far, there's only a mention of those displaced being allowed to return home. Other than that, I haven't found anything enlightening. Guess I'll have to talk to Al about hooking up our television to the camp's cable service. There ought to be some coverage on the major channels, I'd think."

"Surely, there will be something either in the on-line newspapers or on the television about it."

A distracted "Hmm" was Bill's only response.

She leaned over and kissed the top of his head. "Search on, darling. If anyone can find information, you can." She chuckled softly and whispered to no one in particular, "He just can't help it. Once an investigative reporter, always a. . ."

He had already tuned her out, so Lillian returned to the small kitchen to resume dinner preparations.

There was a loud knock on the RV door.

Eli raced to the door and growled. There was a ridge of fur protruding from the top of his head and the middle of his back.

"Shh, Eli. I'm sure it's Brandon."

"I'll get it," she said and opened the door. She was surprised to see Al standing on the bottom step.

"Hi, Lillian, may I come in?"

"Sure." Lillian grabbed Eli's collar to hold him back and moved aside to give Al room to enter the RV. "Everything okay?"

"So far as I know." Al stepped inside.

She looked at Bill. He exhibited a fleeting scowl which he quickly replaced with a half smile, almost a smirk. She knew all of his moods, however subtle they may be. It was obvious only to her that he was not happy to see the camp director.

* * * * *

"Bill, do you have a moment?"

"I do."

Bill closed the laptop and motioned for Al to have a seat opposite him at the small dining table. "As my sweet wife just asked, 'everything all right'?"

Al raised his eyebrows, rolled his eyes toward Lillian, and looked back at Bill as if to say "may I talk in front of her?"

Bill understood the gesture and nodded, "It's okay. Lillian and I don't keep secrets from each other." Bill said a silent prayer asking God to forgive him for telling a big, fat lie.

"Well, I just want to ask you what your take is on the body found on the jogging trail."

"To answer your question, I haven't any kind of opinion. Do you?"

"Well, I don't mind telling you many of the campers want to leave and are upset with the sheriff right now."

And that's the second question you've ignored thought Bill. "Yeah, I know, and I can understand their wanting to pack up and leave. If the sheriff would give us permission, I wouldn't hesitate to follow their lead."

He looked at Lillian as he made this last statement and inwardly breathed a sigh of relief that she followed his non-verbal request: don't say anything. "

I hope he can find the culprit soon; otherwise, he may have a mutiny on his hands."

"You got that right," Al said. "Some of the folks here have used up all of their vacation leave and need to get back to their jobs."

"Glad Lillian and I are retired."

"Yeah, that's a good thing. Well, I just wanted to pick your brain since you were there when forensics and the M.E. arrived."

"Actually, I wasn't there when they arrived. The sheriff didn't need me, and I felt I needed to come back to the camp and check on Lillian and the lady – can't remember her name -- who found the body."

"Leigh Ann's her name," said Al interrupting Bill.

"Ah. But as I was about to say, go ahead. Ask me what you had on your mind."

"I've been thinking about the carving and the things the sheriff found in the man's pants pocket."

"Wait a minute." Lillian's interest peaked. "What things?" She looked at Bill and frowned.

"I guess Bill hasn't mentioned any of that. I'm sorry, Bill, if I spoke out of turn," said Al.

"No apology needed. I just got home a few minutes ago. You know more about the man than I. Besides, Lillian and I haven't had time to talk about it."

Al spoke to Lillian. "Well, little lady, I'm referring to the carvings and the domino and note found in the man's pocket." He then asked Bill, "What's your take on that?"

"Why do you ask Bill for his opinion?" Lillian said.

"I know he's a smart man. I've read his investigative articles in the paper for years. He's usually a step or two ahead of everyone else regarding a murder."

"I have to agree with you. My husband is the best."

Bill smiled at Lillian's response to Al's compliment. "I didn't see anything of the sort," Bill lied. "I have to ask, though, how did you hear about the scene?"

"I guess I was wrong. I thought you were with him when he found the body. But, I'm curious. Why would someone want to mutilate a dead body like that?"

"Don't know for sure, but maybe someone's mad enough to seek vengeance for a wrong committed, perhaps an injustice in the past," offered Bill. "That's the only reason for it I can think of."

Bill made a mental note that Al had failed to answer a third question.

"Yep, that's kinda what I thought, too," agreed Al. "But what?"

"I guess we'll have to wait and let Sheriff Tomas answer our questions," said Bill.

"I just hope he's up to the task," said Al. "I hope Tomas will include Jeff in the investigation or at least keep him updated."

"You and Jeff work closely, I take it?" Bill knew the sheriff. If he's worth the salary he earns, he wouldn't have shared any information about the scene. It was the park ranger who had confided in Al.

"For the past year we have – ever since Milly and I took over this camp. I'd hate to know all of us here and the park ranger himself are sitting ducks for some kinda nut on the loose."

"Jeff will just have to make sure that doesn't happen," said Bill.

"Yeah, you're right. Well, I guess I better go. That's all I came to find out." Al opened the door and took one step outside. He suddenly turned back and said, "Oh, yeah, this murder plumb made me forget. Too much happening at once."

"Let me guess. The explosion?" asked Bill.

"While I was helping Jeff get information from all the campers—mostly their cell phone numbers, I already had their home addresses—we got word that it was a truck that exploded."

"The sheriff also got that news while we were on our way to the murder scene," said Bill. "Was told it carried ammonium nitrate."

"Ammonium nitrate? You don't say? Strange," said Al. "Well, anyway, I guess I'd better go. Milly will come looking for me if I don't get home pretty soon." Al left, letting the door slam behind him.

Bill did not acknowledge Al's last remark, but muttered to himself, "Strange, indeed."

* * * * *

Lillian, who had listened to the conversation between the two men, stood at the sink and pretended to be busy. She peered through the window and watched Al as he walked down the path toward the camp's office. She turned to Bill. "Bet money, he's going to make a telephone call."

Bill raised his eyebrows.

Lillian smiled, knowing he didn't understand what she meant. She skipped an explanation about her telephone call comment and continued on a different track, one she knew he would understand.

"Bill, I got the impression that Al was surprised you had heard anything at all about the explosion. Did you notice he didn't mention anything about the dead driver? Or that he didn't answer your questions?"

"I did. However, if he had mentioned the driver, I would have been suspicious."

"Why?"

"The sheriff said that information had not been released just yet. No identification of the person has been made. They are treating it as a suspicious death."

"Most interesting," said Lillian. "As I said, before: 'what a coincidence.' And, as you so aptly reminded me, I don't believe in coincidences."

"I know, but until the sheriff has more data, I don't think the two deaths can be connected."

"But what if they had some kind of link? What would those two people have in common?"

"I suggest we wait and see. Let the sheriff do his job."

Lillian wasn't ready to let the conversation end. She had more questions.

"In the meantime, let's talk about the murder here at the lake. I noticed you didn't say anything definitive to Al when he asked you about it."

"And there's a good reason for that. Other than the sheriff and me, no one else should know about that little piece of evidence."

"So, how did he know about it?"

"Not sure. I need to remember to ask Sheriff Tomas if he mentioned anything to Jeff about the note or the contents of the man's pocket. If so, Jeff may have mentioned it to Al."

Sitting in the chair Al had just vacated, she reached over and took Bill's hand. "You told me about the carving. Will you share the details of the note with me?"

"On one condition," said Bill. "You can't, and I repeat, you cannot mention it to anyone."

"I promise." She let go of his hand and retrieved her notebook.

"Okay. Write this down in your notebook."

"Wait just a second. Let me find my place." Lillian entered number *28* and wrote Bill's words as he dictated them: *In the man's pants pocket, sheriff found a domino. He called it snake eyes. It had one dot on each end.*

She looked up.

"Number one. Oh, dear, I hope there's not a number two. And the note? What did it say?"

"It was typed and in all caps. It said HE WHO BETRAYS A FRIEND MUST SUFFER THE STRIKE OF THE FANGS, and was signed The Snake."

Lillian entered number *29* and again wrote Bill's dictation. "It does sound like a curse," she said. "Guess we ought not to discuss this in front of Brandon. What do you think?"

"I agree. Before Brandon arrives, do you mind if I use your laptop again?"

"No, of course not. Go ahead. Look for anything online about the explosion or about the body found on the jogging trail."

Lillian poured some half and half and fresh basil into the tomato soup, stirred the concoction, and tasted it. Satisfied that it would pass anyone's taste test, she lowered the temperature of the small crock pot to warm. Her work completed, Lillian sat down opposite Bill.

"Would you like a glass of wine while you search the Internet?"

"Yes, please."

She opened the small wine cooler and retrieved a bottle of Pino Grigio. "Have you found anything at all?" she asked as she placed his drink in front of him. "I'd think there would be something about the explosion, at least."

"Yes, I have. There's an article about a truck filled with ammonium nitrate exploding." Bill scanned the article and paraphrased it. "It goes on to state that traffic on Highway 49 near the Texas/Louisiana state line is being re-routed. It also says that state troopers have the highway blocked to through traffic and that only residents living nearby were evacuated. But authorities have given them permission to return to their homes. I guess we're far enough away they think we're safe."

"Does the article say anything about who owns the truck?"

Bill scanned further down the page. "It says that the truck may have come from the Morningside Fertilizer Plant in Carthage and that the ATF and Homeland Security will be working with the company to determine what could have caused it to explode."

"Does the article mention anything about the driver of the truck?"

"No, it doesn't. And the fact that it doesn't supports the sheriff's decision to withhold that information. Don't you find it odd that Al—as nosey as he was about everything else—failed to mention anything about a possible driver?"

"Actually I do, especially in light of the fact he asked about the carving and the domino and note on the body found today. You said no one else knew about it."

"That's right."

"But Al did know there was at least one fatality. Need to remember to add another thought to my list." Lillian smiled and stood. "Stand up, Bill."

He did as she ordered and was surprised when she grabbed him and gave him a gentle bear hug. Bill laughed and hugged back and planted a kiss on her forehead.

"And just what have I done to deserve this?"

Lillian laughed. "I don't care what you say. You're just like me."

"How's that?"

"Once a snoop, always a snoop." Before he could object to being called a snoop, she turned around and poured herself a glass of Merlot. "I hope Brandon arrives soon. I'm hungry."

Chapter Thirteen

BRANDON DROVE Edgemon's Gas & Grocery's new white delivery van through the gates of Caddo RV Park. Brandon was glad he had met Lillian. It gave him a reason to be seen at the campground. He parked in a spot designated for guests. He reached over the console to the passenger seat and picked up the sack containing Lillian's order of chocolate chip cookies and orange marmalade.

Brandon whistled the theme song from The Andy Griffith Show, his favorite television series when he was a child. The tune became a mere whisper when he noticed a tall, blonde woman walking toward him.

He watched her for a moment. She was headed toward the Pavilion. "It can't be," he muttered. "What in the world is she doing here?"

Brandon walked past the Pavilion, knocked on Al's door and, without waiting for an invitation, opened it and walked in. Al was seated at his desk, telephone in hand. He motioned for Brandon to sit down. When he hung up the receiver, he asked, "Making a delivery, are you? Who's ordered something from the Edgemon's Gas & Grocery today?"

"Lillian Prestridge. Can you direct me to her RV?" He tried to sound as innocent as possible, not wanting Al to know he and Lillian had already met.

"Let's see," said Al. "Her RV is straight down the main drive, past the marina, fourth space on the right."

"Thanks, Al." Brandon glanced at the Pavilion on his way out the door and saw no sign of the mystery woman. He began to whistle again.

Then stopped. There she was. She was sitting on the pier, gazing out at the lake. All he could see was her back. Brandon decided to get a closer look at her.

Just as he approached the pier, she turned. He stopped.

"Oh my God, what are you doing here?" she asked.

"I'm making a delivery."

"Delivery?"

"I work at Edgemon's Gas & Grocery. More and more, these days, I make deliveries to RVers here at Caddo. Today, though, I also have a dinner invitation. What are you doing at Caddo Lake?"

"It's a long story," Leigh Ann responded. "But right now, you need to ignore me. Don't let anyone know who I am, please."

"I guess you're hiding again."

"Yes."

"What happened this time?"

"Like I said, it's a long story and we don't have time right now to discuss it."

"Which RV is yours? I'll come by later."

"I'm the last one on the left, the Casita with the yellow door."

"Promise you won't up and leave before I can talk with you," said Brandon. "I'm worried about you."

"I promise. I can't leave anyway with the murder and all."

"Murder?"

"I'll tell you later. Okay?"

Brandon nodded and leaned down to hug her. She held up her hand and waved it in a dismissive gesture.

"Don't," she said. "Remember, you don't know me."

* * * * *

Lillian saw Brandon as he left the pier and walked toward her RV. She opened the door before he knocked. "You look a little pale -- like you just saw a ghost," said Lillian, the consummate mother.

"Really? Well, I've had a hard and busy day. Besides waiting on customers, I had to restock the shelves and didn't stop to eat lunch."

"That will do it. I've got chicken salad and pimento cheese sandwiches, and I've made some tomato basil soup to go with them. How does that sound?"

"Great."

The color returned to Brandon's face.

"Great," came a voice from the bedroom.

"Sounds like an echo, doesn't it? Bill, come on to dinner. Brandon's here."

Bill came through the bedroom door, walked over and kissed Lillian on the cheek and then shook hands with Brandon. "Lillian has really looked forward to your visit. She misses our sons, Jake and Grant. Better watch out. She'll be mothering you before too long."

Lillian noticed Brandon's face blanched a little when Bill mentioned the mothering word.

"Yes, I do miss them," said Lillian agreeing with Bill. "I hope you'll have the opportunity to meet them someday."

"I hope I have that honor. When we first met at Edgemon's, you mentioned one of them is in security and the other is a county sheriff, didn't you?"

Lillian smiled.

"You have a good memory, young man. Yes, Grant is Chief of Security for Leisure Lake, and Jake is the County Sheriff. Have a seat. You guys get acquainted while I heat up the soup. Bill, why don't you get our guest a drink while I finish up here?"

"Sure thing. We have cola, tea, water, beer, wine. What'll it be?"

"I'll have a glass of tea. Thanks."

While Bill filled the glasses with ice and poured the tea, Lillian placed the sandwiches on the table, poured tomato soup into bowls, and set them beside each plate. "Bill, do you mind saying grace?" she asked as she joined them at the table.

After the blessing, Lillian waited a few minutes to let Brandon eat one of the sandwiches. Then she decided it was time to quiz him.

"Brandon, you and I have some unfinished business."

"What are you talking about, Lillian?" asked Bill.

"Do you remember my telling you about Brandon right after we arrived here? You were hooking up all of the utilities to the RV while I drove to the store for supplies. I mentioned meeting a nice, young man there."

"I remember that."

"Well, do you recall I told you what he said."

"No." Bill looked from Lillian to Brandon. "What don't I know, my dear?"

"Let me answer that question," offered Brandon. Lillian gave him a nod, and he continued. "I told Lillian to be careful while you were here. Strange events have been happening in this campground."

"Tell me about it," said Bill. "There's not been a dull moment since we arrived."

Brandon's posture grew serious. He stopped eating, placed his elbows on the table, leaned forward and looked directly at Bill. "How so?"

"First, there was an explosion. We now know an ammonium nitrate-filled truck exploded. And now, there's been a death."

"No, Bill, speak the truth. We've had a murder," said Lillian.

"Yeah, I heard," said Brandon.

"So, the word is out in town already?" asked Bill.

"No, I met a. . . a lady who told me about it," said Brandon.

"Yeah, I guess everyone is talking about it," said Lillian. "Tell me, Brandon, can you describe the lady who told you about it?"

"Why do you ask?"

"Oh, I'm just a snoop, remember?" Lillian smiled.

"I do remember calling you that." Brandon laughed.

"Wait a minute. I think you two are holding out on me," said Bill.

"Yes, dear, we are. I haven't been entirely truthful to you, and for that I sincerely apologize," said Lillian.

"Okay, but neither have I," admitted Bill.

"Nor I," confessed Brandon.

"Hold on," said Bill. "Before we have true confessions, let's finish our meal."

"Yes, let's. I'm still hungry," Brandon said as he devoured a chicken salad sandwich and reached for another one. "Do you have some more of that soup?"

"Coming right up."

Lillian passed the soup tureen around and waited until Brandon finished ladling some into his bowl.

She repeated, "Describe the woman who told you about the murder."

"Well, let me see. She was young, had short, brown hair streaked with gray. She was sitting in the Pavilion, looked lonely, so I spoke to her. She was worried and told me what had happened." He grinned, satisfied with his lie.

Lillian smiled at him and made a mental note.

He lied, but why?

*****

Lillian looked from one to the other. "Okay, boys, it's time we three tell all. Which one of you wants to go first?" Both men looked dead serious. She stood up, turned around, reached into the cabinet, and pulled out a bottle of wine.

"I will," said Bill.

"Shoot," said Lillian as she poured three glasses of Merlot.

"Night before last when you decided to take off somewhere -- Lord only knows where – Eli woke me."

Lillian looked at Eli. He dropped his head on the floor and hid his eyes with his front paws. The three humans laughed at his pitiable antic.

"It's all right, Eli. I forgive you." The dog perked up, and with his tongue hanging out of his mouth, smiled as if to say, "I missed you." Lillian looked at Bill. "Okay, go on."

"I was worried about you, so I got up and dressed. Eli and I started to search for you. I couldn't yell your name. Afraid I'd wake up the whole campsite. Then Eli ran off. I couldn't keep up with him and lost sight of him after he ran off the path. When I saw you coming down the path, I was one happy guy."

"Thank you," said Lillian, as she squared her shoulders and prepared to tell her story. "I appreciate your concern and your efforts, but I was perfectly safe. In fact, Eli and I were with Brandon. He and I. . ."

"Hold on a minute. My turn to talk," interrupted Brandon. "Yes, we had a conversation, but not until after I caught her snooping around Al's office. She was standing outside his window. By the way," he turned to Lillian, "you never told me what you were doing there."

"Just what were you doing, my dear?" asked Bill. He emphasized 'my dear' and gave raised both eyebrows.

"Well, as I've told you before," she frowned and continued, "I don't trust him. There's something about him that doesn't bode well with me."

"You made that clear the first time we saw him," reminded Bill, "and the more I see of him, the more I'm inclined to agree. But, I digress. Go on, explain."

"Yes, we're listening," agreed Brandon.

"Okay. That was the night we were invited to play dominoes at the Pavilion. I think they must play every Friday night. Anyway, while we were there, we heard a loud explosion. After all the confusion died down and everyone returned to their RVs, Al and Milly invited me and Bill over to their RV for a drink. I thought Al, as the camp's director, was too evasive or perhaps more *blasé* than he should be about everything, especially the safety of the campers here."

"And I know you, my dear. I bet you couldn't turn off your thoughts."

"You're correct. I tried to be so quiet. After you went to sleep, I got up for a glass of water and looked out the window."

"What did you see?" Brandon asked.

"I saw a light on in his office, so I sneaked out and walked over to see what he was up to."

"Did you learn anything important?" asked Brandon.

"Yes, I did."

"What?" asked Bill.

"I heard him talking to someone. It sounded like he received a report about the explosion."

"What exactly did he mention?" asked Brandon.

Lillian hesitated.

"I'm sorry, but I don't know how much of it I should discuss with you. Can I trust you?"

"Yes, Lillian, you can."

"How can you assure me you're trustworthy?" asked Lillian. She looked at Bill. "What do you think? You've always been a good judge of people."

Bill took a sip from his wine glass. He nodded. "Lillian, let's hear what Brandon has to say about himself before you divulge any more information."

"Sounds fair," responded Brandon. "First of all, Lillian, I lied to you at the store when I told you I was enrolled at Sam Houston State. I'm not a student there."

"I suspected that you're already a college graduate," said Lillian.

"I am."

"From Sam Houston?"

"An undergraduate, but I also have a J.D. from Baylor Law School."

"Okay, but what are you doing in this area? I would think you'd be an attorney in a law firm if you've passed the bar exam."

"I passed the bar. But I'm here because a little over a year ago, my grandparents were killed in an accident, a suspicious one at that. I am their only grandchild, so I inherited the proceeds of their investments as well as the house and everything in it. I like Jefferson, so I moved into their antebellum home. I'm considering turning it into a bed and breakfast in the future. But right now, I'm trying to find out what caused their accident. I have my suspicions but no proof."

"Oh, dear, do you think someone deliberately killed them?"

"I do."

"Who?"

"I have some opinions, but no evidence. Not yet anyway."

Lillian did not hear all of Brandon's last statement because once again a blood curdling scream overshadowed the sanctity of Caddo Lake.

"I've heard more screams from people at this campsite than from any horror movie I've ever seen."

Lillian jumped to her feet.

All three confessors scrambled out the door of the Prestridge RV. Eli led the way. Lillian followed her dog, dreading another murder.

Chapter Fourteen

ONCE AGAIN, Caddo RV Park was in turmoil. The crowd grew as people exited their RVs and began to mill around on the main road. Huddled together in wads, wives held onto their husbands, friends held onto each other looking up and down the lane trying to discern the origin of the scream.

"Did you hear that?"

"Could you tell where it came from?"

"Was it human?"

"Was it a man?"

"Didn't that sound like a woman to you?"

"Man oh man, I want to leave this place."

"I'll be glad when I can see Caddo in my rearview mirror."

Such statements were repeated over and over.

Beneath the murmurs of the campers' questions, Lillian could hear the echo of the scream ricocheting over the gentle waves of Lake Caddo. Instinctively, she looked at the water and was surprised to see on the far side of the lake the glow of a light which competed with the moon for its own reflection on the water.

But unlike the other campers who were frozen in place looking for the source of the commotion, Lillian scanned the area for something or someone who might be out of place. To see a crowd gather on the lane was the norm, especially with all of the recent strange events. What was not the ordinary had taken a command post at the end of the narrow graveled drive. Russell Stokes stood in the center of the road. He was pointing toward the forest with one hand and gesturing with the other. Whether he was truly gesturing for her or for someone else made little difference to Lillian. She and Eli began to run, followed closely by Bill and Brandon.

"He ran that way," Stokes shouted.

"Who?" Lillian asked.

"Don't know. He's wearing a plaid shirt and a baseball cap. Hurry."

"I'll catch him," Brandon yelled. He lunged over the azaleas and crossed the jogging trail on his way into the woods.

Lillian ran after him, but was stopped by Bill. "Stay here. Let Brandon get him."

The sounds of the men thrashing through the foliage could be heard over the muttered questions by the crowds. Lillian listened to Brandon's yells to 'stop' for a moment or two before ordering "Go help him." Only Eli followed her instructions. Everyone stood and listened. "Dear Lord, don't let Brandon or Eli get hurt." She reached out for Bill's hand for assurance and was comforted when he gripped her hand and gave it a gentle squeeze.

"Amen," said Bill who had also been silently praying.

* * * * *

Ten minutes elapsed. Lillian grew impatient. "I'm worried about Brandon and Eli. I'm going to see if he's okay."

"Look. Here they come."

Brandon had a strong grasp on the front of a man's shirt, half dragging, half supporting him. Growling, Eli held a mouthful of the man's pants leg. "That'll teach you to run from me, you sorry SOB," Brandon said. He shoved the man down on the ground. "Stay there," he ordered.

Eli pounced on the man and stood on the culprit's chest, fangs showing. Once again, Eli had blood on his whiskers.

The man's plaid shirt was torn. His baseball cap was missing. "Get this mutt off of me," he growled in his New Jersey accent.

Lillian didn't give Eli any commands. She asked, "Who are you?"

"Hey, what's going on here? Why'd you throw Guy on the ground? Get that dog off of him."

Lillian turned around and saw Al enter the lane, not from the direction of his RV but from the direction of the lake. She was quick to answer Al's question. "We heard a scream, and Stokes over there saw someone running into the woods. Brandon went after him and brought him back. Obviously, he didn't want to come. Eli has him contained."

Bill let go of Lillian's hand and addressed Al. "You called this man Guy?"

Al did not have time to respond.

"Yes, he did. I'm Guy Steiner," said Eli's captive, from where he lay on the ground, "and I'm camping here. Can't say I'm enjoying it, though. Never been treated like this in my life. Don't appreciate it one bit."

Guy attempted to sit up, but Eli snapped at him.

"Eli, stand down," Lillian ordered.

Brandon pushed the man back down. "Why did you run when I yelled for you to stop?"

"Hell, I don't know you. For all I know, you may have been the one to scare Vickie to death. Please get this dog off my chest."

Brandon looked at Lillian.

"Eli, stand down. Come here." The dog jumped off of Guy and stood by his owner. "Vickie? Who's Vickie?" asked Lillian, quick to respond to a new name.

"She's the lady in the RV across from me. She and I are -- tell them, Al. They'll believe you more than me."

Like a politician addressing the minions, Al squared his shoulders and cleared his throat. He surveyed the crowd briefly before acquiescing to Guy's request. "All of you listen up. This here's Guy Steiner. He's a regular here at the camp. Well, at least, I'd call him a regular. Since I've been camp director, he's been here every couple of weekends for the past year."

"Keep talking. Who's this Vickie person?" asked Lillian who was determined not to let Al get away without answering another question.

Guy tried to stand up but fell backwards. Al reached out his hand and helped him to his feet.

"And he's talking about Miss Vickie Parsons. She's a regular here, too. Lives in Jefferson most of the time, I think." Al paused, looked around. "Speaking of Vickie, I don't see her. Where is she?"

"I'm right over here," responded a melodious voice, dripping with an East Texas accent. With the flourish of a beauty pageant contestant, a thirtyish something brunette, her hair streaked with gray, glided gracefully off the spacious deck attached to her RV. "I owe all of you an apology for my hysteria."

"Why did you scream, ma'am?" asked Brandon.

"I drove in after work. It was dark. I walked into my RV and turned on the light so I could see, and a mouse scurried across my foot."

"Thank goodness, that's all that happened to you," Guy said.

She ducked her head, then laughed and addressed the crowd. "I'm really embarrassed, but I'm deathly afraid of mice. I jumped up on the kitchen counter. It took me this long to garner enough nerve to get off of it."

Relieved that the campground had been spared another murder, Lillian laughed along with everyone when Vickie finished her story. She did notice the woman matched the description Brandon had given earlier. Interesting.

"Do you have a mouse trap?" Al asked. "If you don't, I've got one. I'll be glad to set it up for you."

"That would be so kind of you. I may have some cheese to use for bait."

"I'll go get it right now. Be back in a jiff." He headed to his office.

Quite content that all was well, the campers, now calm but amused, began to disperse. Lillian paid no attention to their chatter as they returned to their RVs. Taking one last gaze around the campground, she noticed several things she would write in her notebook before she retired for the evening.

"I'm sorry I was so rough on you," said Brandon, offering to shake hands with the man whose clothes showed evidence of a struggle. They were in a state of much-needed repair.

Guy scowled, hands at his side, but then smiled. He held out his hand to Brandon. "Guess I would have done the same thing if I'd seen someone run off like I did. No hard feelings on my part, I guess."

"Sorry I called you a name. Don't usually lose my temper like that."

"No problem. I've been called worse."

Lillian walked over. "I hate to interrupt. But just have to ask if you saw anything out of the ordinary?"

"All I saw was that guy at the end of the lane pointing toward me. That's when I decided to run into the woods. Now that I think about it, why did he do that?" asked Guy.

Not receiving an answer, he shook his head and walked back to his RV.

"Good question," Brandon said, and Lillian nodded in agreement. Both looked in the direction of Stokes's RV. He was nowhere to be seen.

"I don't know about you, but I think we need to call it a day." Lillian walked with Brandon toward the Edgemon's Gas & Grocery van.

"Suits me. That sprint in the woods took it out of me after a day already too long."

"Let's get together again soon. Maybe, Bill and I can drive into town, and we can all meet for dinner one night next week."

"Sounds good. Thanks, Lillian, for a most entertaining evening. You do know how to give someone an interesting time." They laughed at Brandon's attempt to make light of the events of the night. He opened the door of the van, climbed in, and put the key in the ignition.

Lillian saw Brandon place his hand on something taped to his steering wheel. "One more thing before you go."

Brandon, his right hand clutching the wheel, paused and turned in his seat to face Lillian. "Yes?"

"Have you ever seen either Guy or Miss Parsons in the Edgemon's Gas & Grocery?"

Brandon thought for a moment. Fastening his seat belt with his left hand, he responded, "No, never." He started the engine. "And that's rather odd, I think, in light of Al's claiming they are regulars here."

"I wonder where they buy their supplies."

"Beats me. Maybe they bring ample weekend supplies from their homes."

"You're right, I'm sure. Anyway, I guess we don't need to know everything."

"See you, Lillian. I've got to go now."

Lillian watched him back out and drive away.

"Be careful," she said to the taillights of the van as it drove out of sight.

* * * * *

"You certainly disappeared quickly tonight," Lillian said to Bill as she entered their RV. "Wasn't there enough excitement for you?"

"Naw, no murder, no use in hanging around," he joked. "I listened long enough to hear about the mouse and decided all of the hoopla was over, so I came on back to do something constructive." He finished loading dirty dishes into the compact dishwasher.

"Thanks for cleaning up the kitchen. You're a lifesaver."

"Don't know about you, but I think a romantic walk by the lake is in order, my dear. How about it?" he asked.

"Wonderful. Just let me get my sweater. It'll be cooler down by the water."

"Good idea. I'll take the flashlight just in case." He picked it up and put it in the pocket of his jeans.

He donned a windbreaker and, bowing with a grand flourish, opened the door for Lillian. "Let's depart, milady."

And with that, the two lifelong friends and devoted lovers walked away from the lights of the RV camp to the glow of the moonlight bouncing off the mysteriously caressing waves of Caddo Lake.

Lillian looked far into the darkened shoreline but could no longer see the glimmer of light flickering on the other side.

* * * * *

Unbeknownst to Lillian and Bill, a lone watcher across the lake had his binoculars focused on their every move. Simon was glad he had turned off his light when he did. He hoped Lillian would not remember seeing it when she woke up tomorrow morning.

Simon poured another glass of Merlot and raised it in a toast. "Goodnight, Lillian."

* * * * *

"Goodnight, my dear," Bill said as he rolled away from Lillian. She immediately sat up in bed and turned on the bedside lamp. "What are you doing? I thought you'd be ready for sleep after our passionate lovemaking. I could be offended, you know," said Bill as he yawned.

Lillian looked at him and smiled. "You were, as always, wonderful, darling, but I've got to jot down some notes about tonight's events before I forget them."

Bill sat up at that. "Let me see what you write. I might want to add something."

"Okay. Great." Lillian began to write.

30. Don't believe Vickie Parsons' story about the mouse. Might if one actually turns up in the trap Al set.
31. Russell Stokes. . .always around when mayhem begins. Then disappears.
32. If mouse story is true, what was Stokes doing in the lane to begin with and why did he point out Guy?
33. Does Brandon know Vickie? If not, why did he describe her to deceive me?
34. All of the campers came outside. All except one. Leigh Ann. Why didn't she come?

"That makes me think," said Bill. "If the mouse story is true, why indeed would Stokes have been in the lane?"

"Yeah, thanks for reminding me." Lillian held up her notebook. "Did you notice Al come from the marina and not from his office or RV?"

Bill nodded and Lillian made another note in her book.

35. Al came from lake side and not from RV or office. Stokes' RV isn't close to the lake.
36. Could Al and Stokes have been together before all of the confusion?

"Good question," said Bill. He continued watching her write her observations.

37. Brandon said he didn't know Parsons or Steiner. Truth?

38. Brandon – law degree – Baylor School of Law. Truth?

39. Leigh Ann's son – law degree – Baylor School of Law. Truth?

40. Coincidence? – Don't believe in them.

41. Saw light on other side of lake? Source? House? Houseboat? Check it out.

"Check it out? Not without me," said Bill. He yawned again. "There's something else, but right now I can't think of it. Maybe, it will come to me in the morning." One minute later, Lillian heard his usual snore.

"Maybe," she said and turned off the lamp.

She waited until Bill's breathing moved into a deep-sleep rhythm, and then she slipped out of bed and took her notebook to the kitchen table. She turned to the last page and wrote: Note to self. Why did Brandon not want me to see what was taped to his steering wheel?

Chapter Fifteen

BRANDON EASED into the parking lot beside the Edgemon's Gas & Grocery and parked the van in its designated spot beneath the floodlight that lit up the entire corner of the street. He sat in the vehicle and opened up the envelope he had hidden from Lillian. He had discovered it taped to the steering wheel and was afraid she would see it. He read and reread the words written in the neat script he remembered so well:

Brandon, please do me a favor. When you make deliveries to me—and I will call tomorrow and place an order--be sure and ask for the RV belonging to Leigh Ann Heavener. Do not let them know that you have ever met me. I fear your dad knows my whereabouts. I have my suspicions of at least two people here in the camp he may have sent to find me. Love,

Brandon crumpled the unsigned note and put it in his jeans pocket. He climbed out of the van and walked over to the storage shed behind the store, unlocked it, and pulled out his motorcycle. He replaced the padlock on the door and swung his right leg over the cycle. He turned the key in its ignition. The powerful engine roared to life. Machine and man sped toward Jefferson and home.

He noticed a black Lincoln Town Car parked across the street at Pott's Bait and Tackle but paid no attention to it, that is, until he glanced in the bike's side mirror and saw the car ease out in the street to follow him. He made several unnecessary turns and finally decided to challenge whoever was behind the wheel. He pulled to the side of the road two blocks from his house, stepped off of the cycle, and faced the vehicle with his hands on his hips. He had to jump aside as the car picked up speed, practically running over him and his motorcycle as it sped away into the night. Brandon tried but could not get the license tag number in the dark. The last thing he saw fading out of sight were two malevolent red taillights.

He climbed back on his bike and, as quietly as he could, started its engine and rode home. Brandon asked himself why anyone would follow him. He answered his own question out loud. "Unless he thinks I will lead him to her. Must get out there tomorrow and warn her. She must leave no matter what the sheriff says."

Brandon parked his motorcycle in the detached garage at the back of his house.

He went straight to the library, walked to the bookshelf, which lined the back wall. He pulled *The Complete Works of William Shakespeare* from the third shelf to reveal a sliding pocket door. He took a key from his pocket, inserted it in the lock mechanism. The door and the bookcase silently slid to the right. Brandon stepped into a room hidden behind the wall. As he did so, an overhead light automatically illumined not only several computers and wall-mounted monitors but also a Ham radio.

Brandon booted up the first computer and typed an email.

Attention: Top Secret

Blonde-haired lady named Leigh Ann Heavener at Caddo Lake Campsite may be in danger. Please keep an eye on her. Let me know if you overhear someone who may be planning an attempt to kidnap her.

Satisfied with his message, he hit the send button and waited.

Three minutes passed. Then the computer's screen lit up with a reply.

Ten-Four.

Brandon logged out of the computer and left the safe room. The light cut off as he stepped back into the library. The door automatically closed and locked when he pushed the Shakespeare volume back in its place.

Chapter Sixteen

"**MORNING. THANK** goodness," were the first words that popped into Lillian's brain as she jolted awake. Three bodies were in the bed. She felt a furry lump about half-way down under the covers snuggled so close to her that if she rolled the wrong way she would land on the floor. She turned her head on her pillow and watched Bill sleep a while. He opened his eyes and smiled.

"Good morning." He propped himself on one elbow, leaned over Eli, and kissed Lillian. The lump began to move. It wiggled up and out of the covers and propped its head on Lillian's pillow. "Good morning to you, too, Eli." Bill scratched the topknot on the dog's head.

Eli stood and stretched both his front and back legs. He walked to the foot of the bed, looked through the window, and then sat back down.

"Good morning back at you. I hope you slept better than I did last night. I think I woke up every hour on the hour."

"Too much excitement for you?"

"You know it. How about some coffee?"

Bill nodded.

"I'll make it today." Lillian jumped out of bed and threw on her gray sweat pants, a maroon and white Texas A&M T-shirt, and her favorite pink sweater. Eli watched her dress and followed her out of the room. He went to the door and pawed it. "Okay, big boy, but you come right back," Lillian said as she opened the door for him. From the kitchen, she suggested, "Hey you, sleepy head, let's sit outside this morning. Maybe, nothing extraordinary will happen today to interrupt our peace and quiet."

"Sounds good, and while you brew the coffee, I'll get everything set up for our morning devotional." Dressed in a pair of khaki walking shorts and a bright green long-sleeved Izod golf shirt, Bill entered the kitchen. He stood behind Lillian and kissed her on the neck.

She turned around and hugged him and smiled. "Great idea. We've been too preoccupied since we've been here to keep up with our Bible reading."

"Yeah, but I think the good Lord will understand."

Lillian prepared a quick breakfast, a carafe of strong coffee and bagels with strawberry cream cheese. She placed breakfast, two mugs and saucers, and napkins on her favorite blue/white tiled tray and headed outside.

"I've got the table and chairs ready." Bill opened the door and took the tray from Lillian and set it on the small folding table. He held out a chair for her. "Just look at that beautiful sunrise."

The sun, in the middle of its morning ritual, made its daily debut. It peeked around an orange cloud. Beyond the cloud, a purple haze stretched languidly until its tentacles faded into a robin's egg blue. "Magnificent, indeed," she said.

Lillian sat down and reached for her cup of coffee, took a sip, and loaded her bagel with cream cheese. She took a big bite and chewed blissfully. "Yummy. You know, we ought to enjoy these crisp mornings and warm afternoons. The Farmer's Almanac predicts a cold winter." Bill didn't respond to her comment. She watched him turn the pages of his Bible. "Which verses are we reading today?"

"A verse that might keep us -- more specifically you — in check."

"What does that mean?"

"It means you, my dear, should make sure that your reactions to people and events are appropriate."

"And just what do you mean by that remark, may I ask?"

"You may ask. I'll use an event from the past as an analogy."

"I can't wait." She rolled her eyes. "Proceed. I have a feeling you will whether I want you to or not."

"Remember when you thought old Mr. Turner was dead and you organized the ladies in the church to take dinner to his family?"

"How could I know there were two Andrew Turners in our town?"

"You might have slowed down long enough to call his wife to express condolences and to ask her permission to organize a dinner."

"Okay. Okay. Go on. Read."

Not wanting to be reminded of how embarrassed she was when Mr. Turner opened the door in response to her knock, she took another bite of her bagel. "You might want to drink some of your coffee before it gets too cold."

"I still laugh when I think of you and the other ladies standing there holding trays of food." Bill began to scan the Bible looking for the verses he wanted to read.

"We all had a big laugh, relieved that our friend was alive and well. As I recall, we all enjoyed the impromptu party, also." She noticed that Bill had tuned her out.

"Ah, here's just the thing." He began to read from Ecclesiastes 3:1,5,7: "There is a time for everything, a season for every activity under heaven. . .a time to embrace and a time to refrain. . .a time to be silent and a time to speak." He looked at Lillian. She stared back.

"You know, Bill darling, those verses were the last ones we studied just before we left Leisure Lake to begin this adventure."

"I had forgotten that," he admitted.

"Well, they do have special meaning for us." She looked at the sky. The sun had gone behind dark clouds. She pulled her sweater tighter around her body to seal out the chill creeping into her bones. Eli, who had returned from his walk, sat on her feet, propped his chin on her knee.

"I agree."

"Sadly, we left a part of us there. I had so many good times playing Mah Jongg with my friends until the murders occurred at Leisure Lake. But unlike the lost souls of Caddo who are gone forever, we will return to our home. Poor Stella, so new to the lake and had to die such a brutal death."

At the mention of his former owner's name, Eli whimpered. She looked at him, touched the top of his head. "I know, you pretty boy, you still miss her, don't you?"

"Being shot and then stabbed isn't a desirable way to die, I'll agree."

"And, my poor Rachel. She was always so kind to everyone. I'll never wrap my head around the fact she was so cruelly murdered by Grant's fiancée. I will always miss them both."

Lillian remembered the happy smile of her Mah Jongg partner with whom she had played for years.

"But, my dear, remember the Good Book says

There is a time for everything, a season

for every activity under heaven. . .

and this is our time. When we leave Caddo, this season in our lives, too, will have ended. Before we go home to Leisure Lake, we'll see new places, meet new friends, experience new adventures. And, God willing, no more murders or mysterious goings on wherever we may go."

"Amen to that."

"Now let's talk about the last part."

"I know you have a lot to say about that." Lillian poured another cup of coffee for both of them.

"Not really. I have to say, so far, I'm really proud of you."

"Are you serious? I'm almost afraid to ask what I've done to deserve such a compliment."

"I'm proud you've kept your list of important questions to yourself and have shared them only with me. I'm proud you're trying to get a handle on your impulsive nature. I'm proud you are analyzing all of the facts so you can solve all of the strange events we witnessed."

She nodded. "Thank you, my sweetie." Comfortable with the silence, Lillian was deep in thought. Finally, she asked, "Did I tell you that Brandon warned me the first time I saw him at Edgemon's Gas & Grocery?"

"You did," Bill said. "You thought it was strange."

"Give me your opinion of him."

"He's a smart young man, I think. But I also think there's more to him than meets the eye. He's too interested in what happens out here. That's just my opinion for what it's worth."

"I agree. We were interrupted last night before we finished our confessions. I have more to tell you."

"Shoot."

"Think back to the night of the explosion. You know I left the RV, and you know Brandon saw me outside Al's office."

"I do. There's more, I'm guessing."

"You're correct. While I crouched beneath the open window, I learned that Al is a Ham radio operator. He had a conversation with someone called Shadow. Al's handle is Acer."

"Go on."

"During the conversation, Al said 'mission accomplished.' Now what in the world could he have meant?"

"Interesting. Do you think he had anything to do with the explosion?"

"I don't know," Lillian stated. "But I intend to find out."

"Whoa. Wait a minute. What did we just discuss about being silent?"

"I know, Bill. I promise I'll be careful and share what I learn with you." She thought for a moment. "Do you remember his saying anything about what he knew when he returned to his RV to report back to us and Milly?"

"No, I don't. Why should he have mentioned it?"

"He knew that we, along with all of the rest of the campers, were curious about what could have happened. As camp director, he should have wanted to allay any fears about our safety we might have had. He had a golden opportunity then to reveal information to us but instead said he had contacted the park ranger about it."

"As he should have done. I'm sure that is the appropriate protocol for him to follow. I won't fault him at all. As I recall, he had merely invited us to have a drink with him and Milly. That's what he did, and when we asked for his help with how we had set up our RV, he checked the hookups."

"And, later when he questioned you, he didn't mention anything about having a Ham radio, did he?"

"No."

"But he was full of questions trying to glean information from you."

"Again, don't you remember our earlier conversation, the one about responding appropriately to people and events?"

"All I'm saying, Bill, is that I don't know why he was so secretive, especially since you asked. It would have been easy for him to enlighten us. He already knew the cause of the explosion and about the road blocks, all of it."

"I see. So, Miss Curiosity, why do you think he kept that information to himself but wanted to quiz me about the corpse found on the jogging trail?"

"I don't know, but I think he is guilty of something. I just can't figure it out right now," Lillian said.

"Well, time will reveal what he's up to. Remember Ecclesiastes – keep silent until we know more."

"You keep saying *we*. Does that mean you will help me?"

"I'll always have your back."

"That's comforting to know. Let's pray now." She led them in their morning prayer for the day, ending with "Dear Lord, thank you for placing us in such a lovely part of Your creation. And Lord, give us wisdom to help our fellow visitors to Caddo. Amen."

Lillian picked up the last half of her bagel and took a bite of it. She looked at Bill relishing his breakfast. She smiled. The Good Lord knew the meaning of her prayer even though its intent had flown over Bill's head.

"You're right. I'm glad we had this talk. For the first time since we arrived at Caddo Lake, I feel that no matter what happened last night, no matter that a man we don't know anything about has been murdered, no matter what may happen today, we should continue with our plans: take a Graceful Ghost Tour of the lake, go fishing, relax in the sun, and read the novels we brought with us."

"Now that's what I call a vacation." Bill set his coffee cup on the table and entered the RV.

Chapter Seventeen

"*VOILA.*" **BILL** set a stack of paperbacks on the table. He sorted them by genre: mystery/thriller, sci-fi/fantasy, romance, historical fiction. "Boy, you really bought a variety for our reading pleasure."

Lillian ignored his comment and looked up at her husband. "You know, darling, can you think of any reason why — no matter where we are — unusual events seem to occur?"

"I guess we're just lucky," Bill said. He handed Lillian two novels: Richard Hollingsworth's *Dark Corners Cemetery* and N. E. Brown's *Galveston 1900 Indignities: The Arrival,* both historical fictions. He read the blurbs on the back covers. "Which one do you want to read first?" He paused, sat down, and said, "Choose one. I'll take the other one."

Lillian, deep in thought and gazing at the gentle waves on the lake, picked up neither book but snapped to attention when she heard Bill's next statement.

"However, the events here at Caddo are mysterious, aren't they?"

"Too many coincidences for me."

"And as you've reminded me so many times, you don't believe in them."

"I have a request." She took a sip of coffee.

"Okay. What?" Bill said.

"Would you retrieve my notebook and read over my list. It might help to have another look at the facts that have occurred. See if something jumps off the page as being inconsistent with what we do know."

"Sure." Bill put the novel aside and stepped up into the RV and returned. While he read over the items Lillian had jotted down, she scanned the other side of the lake.

"Here's something else I need to tell you."

"What?"

"I saw a light on the other side of the lake during the mayhem on this side."

"I wouldn't think that's unusual. People live around the lake, you know."

"Yes, they do, but I surely felt as though you and I were being watched."

"Watched? By whom?"

"Let's take the ghost tour today. Perhaps we can spot the source –"

"Lillian," Bill interrupted her, "put that suggestion on hold."

"Why?"

"When I opened your laptop yesterday, there was a notification in the top right hand corner of the screen. I think that's more important than a random light on the lake."

"Well, what did the message say?"

Lillian gripped her coffee cup, her knuckles turning white, dreading his next remark.

"Let me think. What was his name? Oh yes, Professor Milton – can't remember his first name – not important. But I want to know why he or any other professor would be writing to you?"

Lillian looked at her coffee cup, smiled, and handed it to Bill. "Would you mind?"

Bill smiled but did not take the cup. Instead, he pushed the carafe of coffee toward her and watched as she refilled both their cups. He grinned and looked at Lillian. "Good try. Now, are you going to answer my question, or should I call you 'Miss Al' since you so obviously tried to use one of his tactics?"

Lillian glared at him, took a big gulp of coffee, and cleared her throat. "Miss Curiosity works better."

"While I'm waiting," Bill said, "I'll continue. As I recall, Professor Milton was one of Jake's instructors at Sam Houston. And, the last time we met him at Jake's graduation, he asked if you would consider editing his memoirs since you have such a strong background in grammar?"

Lillian didn't respond.

Bill said, "Am I right?"

"You may be correct about that."

"I am. You know I am. So, Miss Curiosity, don't keep me in suspense. Why would he be emailing you? Obviously, I didn't read your mail, or I wouldn't ask."

Lillian sat very still for a good ten seconds. She continued her surveillance of the waves rippling across Caddo. Several boats cruised downstream, fishermen on their way to the best spot to catch the "big one." She could see Bill in her peripheral vision, waiting.

"Bill, darling, I guess I have one more confession to make to you."

"I'm still waiting." Bill sat his coffee cup on the small table between them. He crossed his arms. Lillian knew that he was losing his patience with her.

"It's difficult for me. You see, we've never kept secrets from each other. Not serious secrets anyway."

"You're right. Like I said, I'm waiting. Whatever it is, you can confide in me."

"I know I can, but I also know you won't like what I have to say."

"Try me." Bill leaned forward in his chair. He reached over and took her hand.

"You're looking at me so trustingly." Lillian looked down, unable to meet his gaze. "And I've been so deceiving. I feel so guilty."

He reached over and gently said, "Lillian, are you going to tell me that you're having one of those on-line affairs?"

"Oh, no, nothing like that."

"Then, out with it. I'm tired of all this skirting around the issue." He dropped her hand like a hot branding iron, catching her off guard so much so that she jerked and slammed her elbow against the arm of the chair.

She ignored the pain.

"Okay. Here it is. I've been enrolled in online courses through Sam Houston."

"That's great. We've talked about keeping our brains busy." Bill wrinkled his forehead. "Should I ask what kind of course?"

"I've just completed all of the courses necessary to earn a degree in criminal justice. I thought the degree would be beneficial for my new career."

"And, can I ask, just what is your 'new career'?" His eyes hardened and his words dripped with sarcasm.

"You may ask." Lillian smiled. She knew that her correcting his grammar irritated him. This time, though, he ignored her emphasis on the word may and did not take the bait. But she didn't care because she knew the direction this conversation would go. And she was ready for his next question.

"So, how do you plan to use your new degree?"

"Private investigator," she replied.

"You're what? Oh no, I forbid it," his voice grew three decimals louder, and no longer sarcastic. It was demanding. The vein in his neck bulged. He was angry at her.

Lillian glared at him.

"Don't you dare yell at me. And, furthermore, don't even begin to think you have the right to tell me what I can and cannot do."

"I will raise my voice, and yes, as your husband of fifty years, I do dare. Listen to me. You and I, we are retired. Retired. Do you know what that means?"

"I do. But it's you who doesn't know the meaning of that word."

He made a guttural sound. "And just what do you mean by that?"

Lillian feigned innocence by rolling her eyes upward. "Oh, I don't know. Maybe, I'm confused. Except for the days you play golf or sit at the club house playing poker and drinking with your friends, you sit at your computer and write. There's just something about waking up at four o'clock in the morning, writing for two to three hours before you begin your leisure activities and then coming home and sitting back down in front of your machine and writing for another three to four hours. That doesn't seem 'retired' to me."

Lillian knew by Bill's red face and the way he pressed his lips into a thin line that she had hit a nerve.

"You're being a bitchy female. You know that, don't you?"

"No, I'm not. I'm being realistic. And if you ever call me that again, I'll kick you from here to kingdom come. I don't like your attitude."

"Nothing wrong with my attitude."

"And don't be misled. You are not going to make me feel guilty about my plans."

"Guilty? Exactly. You should feel guilty for being so sneaky."

"Sneaky? Sneaky you say?" For the first time, Lillian raised her voice. "Just who do you think you are? The poster child for honesty?"

"Well, I haven't out and out deceived you about anything." Bill yelled. He tossed out the cold coffee that remained in his cup and stood to leave.

"Oh no, you don't. You just sit back down."

He sat. When Lillian used her school teacher voice, it was hard not to follow her instructions. She stomped into the RV. He waited. Within a minute or so, Lillian returned with Bill's laptop, the one he had kept hidden beneath the driver's seat. She threw it at him. He barely caught it before it crashed onto the ground. "Guess this falls in the 'oops, I forgot it was there, I'm innocent category'."

Bill's face went even more red.

Lillian couldn't tell whether he was embarrassed or infuriated because she had caught him in a lie. "Well, I should have known the snoop would find it," he growled. "Can't have any privacy with you around."

"If you can't defend your action, accuse someone else. Just so you'll know, I found it the second day of our trip. I was vacuuming under the seats and hit something. That's when I discovered the laptop. At least, I kept quiet. I wasn't going to take you to task about it. But now, you don't deserve my consideration. You invade my privacy, it's only fair that you lose yours. What were you going to do with it anyway?"

Bill responded with a much softer voice. "Thought I'd take notes for future blogs so we could write off this trip on our tax return."

Lillian relaxed her shoulders but was still offended.

"What a brilliant idea. Guess what? I can write off the cost of my courses."

"Good. We both win." Bill held up the carafe. "More?" he asked.

"No thanks. And no, you are not off the hook. I'm still angry at you for hiding your laptop and wanting to use mine. I think you were just trying to catch me doing something wrong."

"You don't understand. I thought you were using yours to play games and to journal about our trip. I use mine for business. My situation is different from yours."

"So your retirement means you can continue doing what you love, but I'm expected to play Mah Jongg either on or off line, attend tea parties, and participate in any other mundane activity that calls for no brains. You're crazy if you think – "

Lillian did not finish her sentence because Bill stood and stalked away. In their fifty years of marriage which had included debates worse than this one, she could not remember a single time when he had left her standing. They had always been able to work through their differences without losing control of their emotions. She watched Bill head for the marina. He walked out to the end of the dock and sat down, his back to her. She sat for a few more minutes, and then she slowly stood and put away the remains of their breakfast, rinsed the dirty dishes, and placed them in the dishwasher. She slammed its door closed, set the start button, and yelled to no one in particular.

"Damn that professor and damn that computer and damn my lack of computer savvy. I should have figured out how to program the stupid thing so it wouldn't give email alerts. I'm no more guilty than he is. We've both been deceptive. But he won't hear an apology from my lips. Not until I hear one from him. No worries. I know him. By tonight, he'll be over his anger, but my fuse burns a long, long time. Meanwhile, I have things to do."

Eli growled in agreement.

She grabbed a bottled water and left the RV. She saw that Bill had left the marina but had no idea where he had gone.

Chapter Eighteen

LILLIAN DECIDED to take a walk through the campsite. "You stay here, Eli. I need to be alone." The dog tried to push past her, but when she held him back and closed the door, he ran to the sofa and peered out the window. She counted the number of RVs at the campsite and made mental notes about each one, wishing she had paid more attention to the campers who rushed out when Leigh Ann screamed.

She stopped and looked around. She had that creepy feeling again but didn't see anyone following her. She reached Leigh Ann's RV and knocked on the door.

Leigh Ann did not smile when she saw who was standing on her stoop.

"Hi, Lillian."

"Thought I would come by, make sure you're okay today."

"Thanks. Come in." She held the door open for her visitor.

The RV was so compact that Lillian could stand in one spot and see the complete layout of its interior: living/dining/tiny kitchen on the right; bedroom and bath to the left. She noticed an open suitcase situated on the single bed.

"Going somewhere?" she asked.

"I don't feel safe here anymore."

Lillian could tell by the tremor in her voice that the woman was scared.

Leigh Ann continued. "Besides, it's too depressing now."

"Has something else happened to you?"

"No, but a dead body is hard to forget. Never thought I'd witness a murder."

"Witness? I thought you said you stumbled upon the body after the fact."

"Yes, yes. That's what I meant to say." Leigh Ann brushed away an imaginary tear.

"There, there, now. Everything will be okay. You're probably safer here than anywhere else," Lillian said soothingly and gently patted Leigh Ann on the shoulder.

She couldn't tell Leigh Ann why she wanted her to stay or that she doubted her honesty or that she had promised herself to discover the secrets the woman was hiding. She stood since Leigh Ann had not invited her to sit or stay and visit. "I'll be going. Remember, time heals many hurts. Stay a few more days. See how you feel then."

"Thank you. Guess I'll have to stay. The sheriff hasn't given anyone the okay to leave."

"You're right. I need to finish my walk." Lillian turned to go but stopped and looked back at Leigh Ann. "If you don't feel safe tonight, I'm sure Bill would let you come stay with me. He could exchange places with you. Call us if you need us."

"I'll remember that offer." Leigh Ann hugged Lillian. "Be careful on your walk."

* * * * *

Lillian wandered out of the campground, turned left, and followed a gravel road leading away from the Caddo RV Park.

"Might as well enjoy the day, see some of the area. After all, that's why Bill and I came here." She was glad no one was close by and had heard her talking to herself.

The road was narrow, just room for one car to travel. Several times, Lillian had to step off the gravel to allow a vehicle to pass. Lillian hummed one of her favorite hymns. From the melodious sounds drifting down from the trees, it seemed to her that the birds, too, sang with her as they flitted from one branch to another.

She stopped and sniffed. Food.

Around a curve in the road, Lillian saw brightly-colored tents of various sizes and shapes perched along each side of the road. At some of the campsites, families gathered around picnic tables, and at one, she saw a lady standing in front of a Coleman burner, frying bacon in a cast iron skillet. Lillian waved and the woman returned her greeting with a raised spatula.

Lillian continued past the campground. A small sign pointed the way to "Canoe Rentals." She found the park ranger's station where canoes were kept for visitors to explore the lake.

She walked down the wooden ramp leading to the front of the small building.

Unfortunately, a sign posted on the door indicated that the park ranger was out and would not be returning until two o'clock in the afternoon. She glanced at her watch and then ambled around to the side of the building where there was a bulletin board with several notifications. Lillian carefully read the notice that included safety rules about canoeing as well as the cost of rentals.

Safety Rules

Never paddle alone.

File a float plan – tell someone where you are going and when you will return.

Check weather forecasts.

Carry a map.

Wear coast guard approved Type III-V jacket.

Carry drinking water, sunscreen, and insect repellant.

Rental Prices

1 hour $10

3 hours $20

6 hours . . .

Lillian quit reading the sign. And then to anyone who might be listening: "Two o'clock. Okay. I'll come back then." No one heard her.

She walked back up the ramp and out onto the road. Lillian had gone fifty yards when she saw another sign. It pointed to a trail one-half mile in length to a scenic overlook of the lake. Without hesitating, she began the climb. It was an easy walk. Reaching the crest, Lillian sat down on a large rock and gazed out over the lake.

She cupped her hands above her forehead to shield her eyes from the glare of the sun as it skipped over the waves rippling downstream.

At two o'clock, Lillian walked back down to the ranger station to rent a canoe. There was no one in the building. A Bic pen was attached to the bulletin board by a short length of twine. She tore off the end of one of the notices on the board and scribbled the following:

Took a canoe to paddle Hell's Half Acre – Return in three hours. Lillian Prestridge.

Chapter Nineteen

BILL LEFT the dock and walked to the Pavilion. For two hours, he mentally reviewed the list of events Lillian had written in her notebook. He chuckled to himself, knowing he had gotten under her skin, but he had needed time to think. Besides, she was so mad, she didn't notice his taking her notebook. Bill had developed a theory he wanted to go over with her, so he wandered back to the RV.

Like Lillian, he spoke to the wind. "May as well get it over with. We were both in the wrong. Knowing Lillian, I'll have to be the first to apologize. Always am. Damn it. She is one stubborn woman."

As he entered the RV, he noticed that the green light glowed on the dishwasher door, indicating that she had run it. He walked into their small bedroom. "Can't believe she left you behind."

Eli lay on the bed and snorted at him.

"Guess you're mad at me, too."

The dog stood and stretched first his front legs and then his back legs. He jumped down off the bed and followed Bill back through the kitchen. Lillian's computer sat on the table.

Bill crawled into the cab and checked under the driver's seat. His computer had been stowed.

Eli sat in front of the door and looked through the lower glass. He howled.

"Don't worry, Eli. I bet she's gone for a walk. That's her usual routine when she's angry and needs to cool down. I'll read a while, and when she returns, we'll go over her notebook and the conclusions I've come up with."

He picked up *Wayfaring Stranger,* the new James Lee Burke novel he had brought to read on their trip. He grabbed a soft drink and settled down on the sofa to read.

Eli left the bed and snuggled next to Bill.

Bill lost track of time. At six o'clock, Eli began to pace the floor. He barked at Bill, who marked his page, stood, and stretched. Bill rummaged around in the small freezer, found a Marinara Chicken steamer, and put it in the microwave. As he ate, he suddenly felt a chill which caused him to glance out the window. He had been so absorbed in Burke's novel that he had not looked outside.

The sky had changed. The sun had disappeared. A loud rumble filled the sky.

"Lillian, where are you? You need to come on back. A storm is headed our way."

* * * * *

Lillian, too, had lost track of time. During the past four hours, she had gone in and out of several bayous. She waved at all the fishermen she saw and slowly drifted by their boats careful not to make any noise. They returned her silent salutation with a brief wave or nod. It was obvious to her that they were intent on catching as many keepers as they could hook. She happily continued her personal, self-guided tour of the lake.

It had been years since she had done anything as strenuous as paddling a canoe. Even though she remembered to hold a good body position by sitting in the center of the canoe and maintaining a smooth rhythm with the paddle, she began to tire.

"This was a mistake," she muttered. "I'm out of shape. Where's that cool breeze I felt earlier?"

She decided to let the canoe drift so she could rest. The canoe moved farther and farther from the shore. Lillian paid no attention to it. Instead, she reflected on the argument she had with Bill and came to the conclusion he didn't truly appreciate all of her abilities. But more than resenting his attempts to protect her, she appreciated the fact he did so because of his love. She finally decided she would complete the process of obtaining her license but would not practice unless he worked with her. A new career did not warrant a ruined marriage. After all, the vows she made more than fifty years ago were still good.

The hoot of an owl pulled her back to reality.

She glanced up and saw it swoop close, too close to her canoe. The owl flew back into the pine trees just as a slow, distant rumble began to echo over the lake. She saluted the bird as a silent thank you.

Within minutes, the thunder grew louder and sounded closer. She turned the canoe around and began to paddle toward the station. The storm arrived and brought a steady downpour of rain. Her cell phone rang. She stopped paddling and dug the phone out of her pocket. She looked at the caller ID. She propped the phone on her shoulder and tilted her head to hold it in place. "Hello?"

"Lillian, this is Brandon. I need to talk to you."

"Okay. I'll call you when I get home."

"When will you be there?"

The wind and waves grew, and it became difficult for Lillian to keep the canoe balanced and talk on the phone. Lillian couldn't hear him.

"Brandon? Are you still there?" No answer. The sky grew dark. Lillian knew she had to get off the lake.

"Why in heaven's name did I think I could still handle a canoe?" Lillian asked the rhetorical question out loud. The only response she heard was more thunder, closer every time it rattled the dark night-black sky.

A jagged streak of lightning danced across the lake in front of her. Startled, Lillian dropped her phone in the water and swamped the canoe. Over she went hanging on for dear life. She clung to the side of the canoe but let go as the strong current began to take it down stream.

Lillian tried to decide which way to swim. She had become disoriented, and the rain had become so heavy she could not see the shore. She treaded water, turning around and around, trying to get her bearings in her dim surroundings. She heard the gentle purr of a small outboard motor coming her way.

Lillian began to yell, "Help me. I'm over here. Hurry. Help me, please."

The captain of the small skiff killed the engine and floated close to Lillian. He threw a lifeline to her. "Grab that. Hold on. I'll pull you into my boat."

Strong arms reached out and gathered Lillian into the boat. Relieved but out of breath, Lillian gasped, "I can't thank you enough. So glad you happened by."

"I didn't just happen by, Lillian."

At the sound of her name, Lillian pushed back the hair that had fallen over her face and looked up.

"Richard?"

"No. I'm Simon."

* * * * *

Brandon looked at the face of his cell phone. Battery dead. He ran down the central hall of his antebellum home and into his library. He grabbed the phonebook from a desk drawer and looked up the number for the Caddo RV Park. Someone picked up the receiver.

Not waiting to hear a "hello" Brandon said, "Can you get Bill Prestridge on the phone? I need to talk to him right away."

"It's raining cats and dogs. I'm not going out in this weather."

"Millie, is that you?"

"Yes. Who are you?"

"I'm Brandon, the delivery man from the Edgemon's Gas & Grocery. Please, can you at least give me his number? It's imperative I talk to him."

"Why, what's so urgent?"

"I made a delivery to him earlier. A mistake. Please give me his number."

"Okay, but I don't see why you're so bent out of shape over a wrong delivery. Hold on just a minute. I'll pull his information." She found the registration form for the Prestridges and recited Bill's cell phone number.

"Thanks." He hung up and dialed Bill's number, and when Bill answered, he said, "This is Brandon."

"What's wrong? You sound like you're in a panic."

"I don't want to scare you, but I tried to call Lillian. We lost connection. But not before I heard a loud clap of thunder."

"Oh, no. If she's hurt, I'll never -- Brandon, hold on a minute. I have another call coming in." He answered the second call.

* * * * *

Bill took a deep breath and released it when he heard, "Bill, darling, don't worry about me. I'm okay. I'm at --"

His phone buzzed.

"Thank God. Hold on will you? Brandon's on the other line. I'll get back to you right away." He put Lillian on hold.

"Brandon, the other caller is Lillian. She's okay. I'll talk to you tomorrow."

He went back to Lillian's call.

"Okay, Miss Curiosity, you have some explaining to do. Big time. Where have you been all day?"

The line was dead.

* * * * *

Bill called the RV office and asked Al if he could help search the campground for Lillian.

"Sure, Bill, but if she did get caught when the storm began, I bet she's with one of the other campers. I'll have her call you if I see her."

"Thanks, Al. You're probably right. In fact, she's called me, said she was okay, but we lost our connection."

"The storms we have out here do affect cell service. I bet she comes home as soon as the storm subsides."

Al's reassurances had done nothing to alleviate the fear gripping Bill. He then called the Park Ranger's office.

"Jeff, Lillian left this afternoon to go for a walk and hasn't returned. I'm worried. She may be caught out in the storm. Can you help me?" Bill talked so fast he didn't slow down long enough to take a breath.

"Have you checked with the camp director?"

"He thinks she may be holed up in another camper's RV until the storm subsides."

"He's probably right. If she doesn't return after the storm, I'll come by and help you find her. Try to relax."

"That's easier said than done." Bill muttered, knowing he would have a sleepless night until she returned. The storm raged. High winds, thunder, and lightning rocked the RV. He and Eli sat on the sofa while dime-sized hail sounded like bullets as they hit and bounced off the RV's roof. But the weather outside could not compare to the turmoil raging within Bill. He spoke to Eli.

"As soon as the hail lets up, we're going to look for her."

Eli ran to the door and pawed it. "Don't worry, Eli. We'll leave in a few minutes."

The dog left the door and sat in front of Bill who continued, "I should not have walked away and left her alone. Let her follow her dreams. Back her up. Hasn't she always been there for me? Why in the world did I ask if she had been unfaithful? Never has she ever given me cause to doubt her love for me. I could kick myself for hiding my computer. Don't care what anyone says. I will find the love of my life. I'll make things right between us. I'll even help her open her private investigator's office."

The hailstorm passed over. The cloudburst continued its downpour. Bill grabbed a flashlight and put on his slicker and Wellingtons.

"Come on, Eli. We'll find her if it takes all night."

Bending forward to push his way through the deluge, Bill began knocking on doors of the campers. Each time, he hoped to see Lillian safe and sound inside.

No one had seen Lillian.

"Let's check the Pavilion," he yelled to Eli.

She wasn't there.

Eli ran toward the jogging trail.

Bill followed, "Good idea. I bet she walked that way."

The two searchers experienced some shelter from the rain as they moved along the tree-canopied path. Intermittent lightening revealed the trail, now covered with fallen pine branches. Bill's flashlight provided further illumination. They passed a sign that advertised canoe rentals. Surely, she didn't rent a canoe. They continued their search and reached a hill that provided a view of the lake. Bill, followed by Eli, climbed the slippery slope.

When they reached the crest, it was as though the rain gods turned off the faucet. For several minutes as the storm paused, Bill strained to see the lake. The wind kicked in moving the clouds. For a brief moment, he saw a dim light across the lake.

Darkness returned as more clouds assembled to empty their reservoirs. Bill sighed. "Come on, Eli. Let's keep searching."

They retraced their steps and stopped when they reached the ranger station. Trying to decide where to look next, Bill stood beneath the protection of the covered ramp. He pushed aside the recurring thought that wormed its way into his brain. Canoe? No, she wouldn't dare take one out by herself.

Eli's howl spurred Bill back to action. He raked the palm of his hands over his face to wipe the water dripping from his eyelids and once again said, "Come on, Eli. We have more places to look."

The desperate husband ran to the marina. He shined his flashlight toward the lake but saw nothing but the white caps of the waves being sprinkled with more raindrops. He turned and walked up the hill to the camp director's mobile home. He saw a light in the front window and knocked on the door.

Al opened the door immediately. "You and that dog look like drowned rats. Come in."

Bill and Eli entered. "I need your help. Eli and I have searched the whole campground. I've knocked on the door of every RV and can't find Lillian."

"I should have known you wouldn't wait to hear from her again before you forged out in one of the worst storms we seen in a long time. Did you call Jeff?"

"Yes, but would you call him again for me? Maybe, you can convince him to start a search tonight."

Al nodded, picked up his cell phone, and punched the speed dial for the ranger. The call went to voice mail.

He shook his head. "I'm sorry, Bill. Like I said, cell phone service is bad out here when there's a storm."

"Thanks for trying." Bill took a deep breath and opened the door.

"Wait a minute," Al said. "I still say she's safe. I bet she's at one of the homes that line the far side of Caddo."

"I hope you're right, but I still have to try to find her." Bill pulled the hood of his slicker over his head. "Let's go," he said to his dog.

As he walked away, Bill prayed. "Dear Lord, let her be safe. Keep her warm until I can find her."

Chapter Twenty

AFTER PULLING her out of the water, Simon took Lillian to his house, gave her a pair of his warm ups and an old sweater, and pointed her toward the bathroom. While she showered, he popped two TV dinners in the microwave, took two wine glasses out of the cupboard, filled both with Clois du Bois Pinot Grigio.

Lillian entered the small kitchen. She saw the two glasses he had placed on the counter. "You remembered my favorite white wine. Thank you, Richard, for bringing me here." She picked up a glass and looked for a place to sit down. He pulled out a chair for her.

Simon walked around to face her. "Lillian, look at me when I say this: You cannot call me by that name. While you are here at Caddo, I'm Simon. Please try to remember that, will you?"

"Yes, I'll try but why an alias?"

"Can't answer that question right now. I've tried to avoid you since that first night you walked into the Pavilion to play dominoes. I was afraid you recognized me."

"I knew you looked familiar, but I must say you've changed. Where is the ivy leagued young man I knew once upon a time?"

"He's here inside, but right now no one must know my true identity. Trust me when I say you will be safer if you act as though you don't know me when you see me around the campsite. Can you do that?"

"If you say it's important I ignore you, I will."

She took a sip from her glass and looked him in the eyes, those beautiful steel-blue eyes she once loved. "Simon, there have been a couple of times I felt I was being watched. Can you explain that?"

Simon smiled and reached out his hand but withdrew it before he touched her.

"I knew you sensed something when I saw you stop and look around, searching for something or someone. I'm afraid I'm guilty. I've been keeping an eye on you. Don't want you to come to any harm."

"Why would I be in danger?"

"Things are going on at Caddo that you don't need to know about."

"You do know how to pique my curiosity, don't you? But then, again, you were always good at that – among other things."

Simon smiled but made no response.

Lillian took another sip of wine and looked around the kitchen. She saw the row of bookcases in the short hallway. Taking her glass with her, she walked over and read the spines of the books.

"You always did enjoy a good book, Simon. You've quite a collection of classics here. Is that what you do when you're not doing your job?"

"Don't try to change the subject. Remember, I've been watching you, and I know you are getting too involved in the lives of some people at Caddo."

"If you've been watching me, then you know I've not gone looking for trouble."

"I guess your eavesdropping outside Al's office wouldn't fall into that category?"

"Guess you were the one who followed me that night. If you were close enough to me, then you probably heard his side of the conversation."

Simon narrowed his eyes but did not acknowledge her statement. She remembered that expression of his and understood how stubborn he could be.

Lillian decided to distract him by introducing a bit of nostalgia to their conversation.

"Do you remember when we first met?"

Her question caught him unawares. He smiled and in a soft voice, said, "Always. I fell in love with you the first moment I saw you scamper into the student center, scoot right in front of me, and try to convince me you would be late for class if I made you go to the back of the line."

Lillian laughed. "You were so gallant that day, not to mention handsome."

"Despite the grumbling from those waiting in line behind me, I would have picked you up and carried you if you had asked me."

"You should have carried my tray."

Simon chuckled.

"I'll never forget how you looked when you tripped on the mat beside the salad bar."

"Don't remind me," Lillian shook her head. "I was so embarrassed."

"Well, I thought you were beautiful, spaghetti and all."

"I never did get that stain out of my blouse."

Lillian grew serious.

"Richard – I mean Simon – we had some good times back in the day, but we're older now and have lived full lives. At least, I have. What about you? Has life been good to you?"

"For the most part."

"Can you talk about it?"

"Of course. After graduation from the University of Texas, I joined the military, served in Vietnam came home and entered law school."

"Did you practice law until you retired and moved to Caddo?"

"No."

"Why not?"

"Uncle Sam beckoned again."

"You were called back into the army?" She paused. "No, I bet Uncle Sam wanted you for another reason. Right?"

"Could be." Simon smiled. "I think the line goes like this: If I told you what I did, I've have to kill you." The smile vanished. "Let's don't go there."

Undaunted by his warning, Lillian persisted. "CIA? FBI? Which one?"

"Forget I said that." Simon paused. "On a lighter note, I am a partner in a law firm in Dallas."

"Which one?"

"Ford and Townsend."

Silence.

Simon reached across the table and took Lillian's hand in his. "I have only one regret from our college days."

"What's that?"

"I introduced you to Bill."

Lillian snatched her hand back. "Let's come back to the present. You said you saw me outside of Al's window."

Simon nodded.

"I don't trust that man. He's up to something. I just can't figure it out."

"Stay away from him, Lillian. In the past, your curiosity has gotten you in some pickles."

"Did you see anything or hear anything else out of the ordinary that night?" Lillian wanted to know if Simon had overheard her conversation with Brandon.

"I saw you with the young man who works at Edgemon's. What was that about?"

Lillian gave Simon a coy smile. "If I told you, I'd have to kill you."

"*Touché*, but enough of our sparring."

"That was always our forte."

Simon breathed deeply. "Right now, I know Bill must be worried about you. That brief message you left him did not, I'm sure, alleviate his concern about you."

"That wasn't a message. He answered the phone and then put me on hold. How dare he? So, if I'm not more important to him than that." She paused. "I hung up. Let him wonder."

"And, as I recall, you did have a temper. I see you haven't changed in that regard. I remember that chin in the air." He laughed and shook his head as she lowered her chin and raised one eyebrow.

"Well, actually, I've mellowed some. To tell the truth, I will be glad to get back to camp. I really don't want him out in this weather looking for me."

"I'll get you back tomorrow. Storm's too bad right now. I suggest you use my bedroom and get some sleep."

"I hate to do that. Where will you sleep?"

"I'll bed down on the sofa. I want to watch the storm. Make sure all's well before I go to sleep. May read a while."

Lillian stood and walked over to Simon. She stood in front of him, then tiptoed so that she could kiss him on the cheek.

"Good night, my old friend. Thanks for saving my life."

"Good night, Lillian."

He watched her walk away. *Good night, my love.*

Simon sat down on the worn sofa in his living room and waited until he heard her even breathing and a slight snore. Then he left the house and walked to the small anteroom behind the kitchen. He booted up his computer and entered:

> Woman named Lillian Prestridge stranded
>
> She's safe. With me. Asleep.
>
> Will arrange pick up when she wakes.
>
> Meet me in usual place at 2300.

Chapter Twenty-One

BRANDON HAD been relieved to hear Bill say Lillian was "on the other line," so he took a quick shower and donned his pajamas. Worried about the chasm between his parents -- especially about his mother -- he lay in bed and listened to the wind's whistle as it swept by the corner of the house. Sometime after midnight, when the eye of the storm passed, the gentle pelting of the rain on the metal window awning outside his bedroom lulled Brandon into a peaceful sleep.

A loud clap of thunder woke him. He looked at his alarm clock. Morning. Five o'clock. Rain pinged on the awning, telling him the day would be another gloomy one. He crawled out of bed with the knowledge Lillian was okay and hoped he could soon feel the same about his mother. He decided he would visit with her later in the day. It was a good thing that his work schedule didn't begin until seven o'clock. He was certain one or more campers would call the market and request a delivery. He would be able to fake a delivery to his mother. Brandon wanted to know what she was doing all alone at the Caddo Lake campsite.

Regardless of the weather or his schedule, Brandon always awoke two hours early. First thing on his agenda was a run through the historic streets of Jefferson. As usual, he dressed in his blue sweat pants, put on his Nikes, and grabbed the door keys. He added one more layer to his clothing: a bright yellow rain poncho. Before exiting the antebellum home he had shared with his grandparents, he walked through the parlor and paused by the large window on the front of the house. He pulled aside the lace panels and peered past the spacious front porch to check out the street. He looked as far as he could down each side. There was no sign of the black Town Car.

Stepping outside, he began his run. His spirits soared. Brandon enjoyed jogging through the historic district, particularly this leg of his run. He always admired the stately turn-of-the-century homes. Some had been converted into bed and breakfasts. As he passed the Captain's Castle, The Carriage House, The Old Mulberry Inn, The White Oak Manor, House of the Seasons, and the Steamboat Inn, he thought about the name he would give his B&B when it opened. How would the name reflect its history?

He admired the continuous blooming Encore azaleas that graced the lawns of the Victorian cottages along the street. He could hear the crunch of autumn leaves under his feet as he leisurely jogged along East Clay. Looking ahead, Brandon saw that the light was green at the intersection of Clay and Highway 49, so he picked up speed and sprinted across the road before the light changed.

He left Clay for the final lap home and saw the black sedan parked at the corner, two blocks from his house.

Its tinted windows made it impossible to identify the driver. Not to be intimidated by the unknown, Brandon stopped, walked toward the sedan. But before he reached it, the driver revved the engine and wheeled around the corner. Brandon made a mental note of the license plate number and watched the car until it turned right on Highway 49.

"I know my father sent those thugs to keep tabs on me. He either thinks Mom might be in Jefferson, or this is his way of convincing me to work for the firm."

He spoke to a father miles away. "Well, Dad, you can send them all you want, but the answer is still the same: No. I didn't get a law degree so I can keep your sorry ass out of jail."

He paused, imagining his dad's response and then answered, "And, I'm not going to lead you to Mom."

He ran up the sidewalk and entered the house. Brandon closed the front door and walked down the hall to the library. From the pencil holder on his desk, he grabbed a pen and jotted down the tag number of the sedan on a Post-it note. He folded the paper and put it in his wallet behind his driver's license.

Half an hour later, dressed for work, he pulled back the curtain and double checked the street for any sign of the sedan. It was nowhere in sight. He walked swiftly to the garage, started the Harley's engine, and arrived at Edgemon's, happy to be at work.

Brandon worked at a steady pace until nine o'clock, sacking groceries and loading customers' automobiles with their purchases. Between customers, he remarked to Kyle, his boss, "Guess everyone is stocking up in case the rain doesn't stop."

"I watched the news this morning and heard that the water is rising out at Caddo, and more thunderstorms are on their way," Kyle said. "As soon as you can, why don't you make these deliveries out there before the next wave hits."

Brandon had not forgotten about the chance meeting with his mother. At ten-thirty, he grabbed a sack, packed it with two T-Bones, a head of lettuce, and two potatoes. He filled another sack with chocolate chip cookies, a loaf of bread, and a jar of peanut butter. In another sack, he loaded three cans of Wolf Brand chili, shredded cheese, and a box of saltine crackers. He scribbled a different name on each sack and loaded them into the store's van. He drove to Caddo Lake.

Al was locking his office door when Brandon stopped the van and waved to make the camp director aware of his entering the campground. "Who are you delivering to today in this kind of weather?" Al asked.

"I've got three different deliveries. One to a person I don't know."

Brandon reached in his shirt pocket and produced a sales slip. "Leigh Ann Heavener. Can you tell me which RV is hers?"

"It's the last one on the left." Al pointed down the lane. "You sure are making more and more deliveries out this way."

"I've spoiled Lillian Prestridge for sure. She called again today for something. I'm making a delivery to a couple named

Patterson, a Joy and Pat. They called just before I left the store and gave me directions to their RV. They're next door to the Prestridges. Guess everyone out here has such a good time they hate to leave even to drive into town to buy groceries."

"Normally, I'd agree with you, but lately, this rain has everyone feeling trapped." Al paused and looked up into a bleak sky. "Looks like we're in for another storm."

Brandon nodded in agreement.

"I know what you mean. But, you see, I don't mind deliveries, rain or shine. I earn some good tips. And I can always use the extra money."

Al laughed. "Every little bit helps, don't it?"

"Sure does, especially for a student like me. Thanks, Al."

"Since you're here, why don't you join us for dominoes tonight?"

"Dominoes?"

"Yeah. Most all of the campers meet on Fridays to play dominoes. Because of this weather, I'm sure they want to have some reason to leave those cramped RVs. They'll be looking for a diversion tonight, so I'm going over to the Pavilion now to get everything set up."

"Thanks, I just might take you up on that."

Brandon drove away but glanced in his side mirror. He could see Al watching him. He eased slowly through the campsite and did not relax until he saw Al turn and walk toward the Pavilion.

Brandon drove past Leigh Ann's RV and turned the van around before stopping. He hoped that because he had parked at the end of the street and not beside her RV, anyone who noticed his van would not pay particular attention to it. He opened the back and looked at a slip of paper. He checked his list and then scoped out the campsite as if he were trying to locate the various RVs where he would be making his next delivery.

He walked first to the Prestridge RV and knocked on the door. No one came to the door. He knocked again. Silence. Brandon shrugged and decided to try again after making the rest of his deliveries.

He walked next door to the Patterson's RV. He tapped on the door and was greeted by a beautiful, tall brunette whose smile was contagious. He could not help but smile back at her. "Ms. Patterson, I'm from Edgemon's Gas and Grocery. I have your order." He paused and looked at the itemized slip. "Two T-bones, two potatoes, and a head of lettuce."

She invited him in while she looked at the ticket and counted out the correct change. "I'm really glad you make deliveries, young man. I don't think I got your name."

"It's Brandon, ma'am, and anytime you need something from the store, you just call. Ask for me. I'm glad to be of help to you."

"Thank you."

She gave him a five-dollar tip and another smile. "I will." Brandon left with a big grin on his face and silently thanked Ms.

Patterson. Because of her tip, he could justify the fact that he had not told Al a lie.

Brandon went back to his van, checked his list again, grabbed the last sack, and walked over to Leigh Ann's RV. He tapped on the door. When she opened it, he hurried inside. As soon as the door closed behind him, he grabbed his mother and gave her a big bear hug.

"Mom, what in the world are you doing here?"

"Sit down, son. I have a lot to tell you."

"I'm anxious to hear what you have to say about your camping all alone."

Leigh Ann shook her head as if to dismiss Brandon's comment. She spoke louder than necessary, emphasizing each word. "First, do you think you were followed?"

The blunt, sharp edge in his mother's usual soft voice caught Brandon off guard and made him wonder whether or not he knew the woman who stood before him. He had never heard her sound so stern, nor had he ever witnessed such a cold, piercing, stoic expression on his mother's face.

Brandon squared his shoulders and answered in an even, controlled voice, hoping that a calm response would help Leigh Ann relax. Perhaps, she would admit why she was concerned that he would expose her whereabouts. He wanted to know why she was hiding from his father.

"I don't think I was followed this morning on my way here. And, even if I were, I've made another delivery and visited with someone else -- just in case – plus, I have one more delivery after I leave you."

"I'm glad you were careful, but you're not good at hiding the truth from me. You lost all color in your face when I asked if you had been followed. Has anyone given you any trouble lately?"

Why would she think someone would have caused a problem for him?

Brandon decided to follow her lead, despite the feeling that he should change the subject. "As a matter of fact, someone has."

Leigh Ann stood and took a step away from her son. Then she whirled around to face him. "When?"

"Last night and earlier this morning."

"Tell me exactly what happened."

Brandon looked into Leigh Ann's eyes and saw a dark, red glowing ember. He felt a shiver dance up his spin and pounce into the frontal lobe of his brain. It warned him to stop talking, but he continued. "I was followed last night by someone in a black Town Car. I spotted it and parked my Harley to confront him or them. Was nearly run over."

Leigh Ann Leigh Ann asked between clenched teeth. "What happened today?"

"Same sedan. Whoever is driving it tailed me as I jogged."

"That does it. I'm leaving. If I stay, you will be in great danger. I'm afraid he'll use you to get to me. He knows I won't stay away from you for very long."

"I guessed it was Dad who's having me tailed. He wants to keep up with me. Keeps asking me to join the firm."

"Whatever you do, don't do that. You have no idea what his practice involves."

"Don't worry. I won't. But tell me, why are you hiding from him now? I thought you and he decided to go separate ways. Why would he use me to find you? What's he done this time? Why are you afraid of him?"

"It's not what he's done, but more like what I've done. I am really afraid I'm in serious danger now, more than ever."

Leigh Ann sighed and patted Brandon's back and softly said, "I love you."

"I love you, too."

"You know I wouldn't do anything to cause you harm."

"Tell me, what have you done?"

"Can't tell you. Trust me. The less you know, the better off you are. Suffice it to say, I hurt him where it hurts the most."

"That would be money. How much did you take?"

"Enough. He's gone too far this time."

"Why do you say that?"

"Because of the men who keep coming to our house."

"What about them?"

"I'm not sure, but I think they're connected to the government."

"You know, Dad has always done business with unsavory characters. Maybe, the FBI is investigating some of his clients."

"Maybe the FBI is investigating him?"

"Are you afraid the feds are investigating you because of him?"

Leigh Ann shook her head. "The feds have no reason to look into my affairs, but I've seen a man who resembles one of his so-called business associates here at the lake."

"Is that why you wrote the note to me?"

She nodded

"Then you have to leave, go to another location ASAP."

Leigh Ann took a deep breath, and continued. "I hate to say it, but before I ran away, I overheard him talking on the phone. I think he may have orchestrated the explosion we heard last Friday night."

"I don't believe that and neither do you. Don't let your imagination take control of you. You're not making sense. Dad wouldn't be involved in anything like that." As if nature agreed with him, thunder rumbled across the sky and shook the RV.

Leigh Ann hugged Brandon.

"It's supposed to rain all day and storm again tonight. I want you to leave now before it gets any worse. Call me tomorrow. She passed him a phone number. "This is for a burner phone and can't be traced." She reached below the bench on which she sat and opened a drawer. It contained a stack of unused phones. She handed one to Brandon. "I suggest you use this one so our calls cannot be monitored. And don't call from inside the house, please. It's probably bugged."

"Don't you think you're being more than a little paranoid?"

"Please do as I say."

Brandon nodded, but his gut told him that his mother had omitted telling him everything. Brandon knew his father would not give up what he wanted or what he felt he owned. He also knew his mother understood her husband.

"I hate to leave you alone. You're scared. Come home with me. We'll leave East Texas. Go somewhere else. Together, we might be safer."

"That's impossible. I'll leave, but I don't want to worry about you. Please call me, though."

"I'll do so only if you promise to keep me updated about your destination and your safety."

Leigh Ann hugged her son again. "I promise. Go now. I worry about you."

With a heavy heart, Brandon gave her one last hug and left the RV, headed back to the van. He saw Bill and Eli walking in the middle of the road. The man and dog were completely drenched. Bill shuffled along, and Eli looked so tired that, when he walked, his whole body swayed from side to side. Brandon stopped the van in the middle of the lane, climbed out, and ran to them. Bill looked confused.

"Come on, my man. Let me get you inside." Brandon escorted Bill inside the Prestridge RV and seated him at the table and cranked up the Keurig. He handed Bill a mug of coffee. "You need to warm up."

Bill's hands shook. Brandon kept his hands on the mug and watched Bill take a couple of sips. "Where have you two been?"

"Looking for Lillian. She didn't make it home."

"I thought she called you while we were talking."

"She did. But when I put her on hold to answer your call, we lost our connection. She assured me she was okay and told me not to worry about her."

"You report her missing?"

"Yes. I called Al and Jeff. Both of them said she was probably with another camper waiting out the storm."

"Did you ask the other campers if they had seen her?"

"Yes. I knocked on every door. Talked to all of the campers except one."

"Had anyone seen her?"

"No, but I'm going back to ask the person who wasn't home last night."

"Who was it?

"The Heavener lady. She didn't answer her door."

Brandon was taken aback. From his conversation with his mother, he assumed she would stay close to the campground if she were afraid to be seen by anyone employed by his dad.

"I just made a delivery to her. Lillian wasn't there."

Bill's shoulders slumped. "I'll call the ranger again. Maybe, he'll come and help before another wave hits the area."

"You do that. He's a friend of mine, so I'll make sure he listens to you. In the meantime, take a warm shower and put some food in your stomach before Jeff arrives. You're going to need your strength."

Bill nodded.

Brandon sat down on the sofa and watched Bill shuffle into the bedroom. As soon as he heard the shower, Brandon hit speed dial on his cell. When Jeff picked up, Brandon said, "Bill Prestridge called you last night?"

"He did. Said something about his wife not coming home. I told him she probably found shelter with another camper if the storm caught her unawares. Why are you calling me about her?"

"I just talked to Bill. He's going to call you again. I'm asking you to help him get on the lake and search for her."

"I hope we can find her. Didn't have much success with the last four people who lost their way."

"I know. Their disappearance bothers me, too." Pause. "Hey, listen. I have a suggestion."

"Let's hear it."

"You know the maintenance man at Caddo Lake?"

"Simon?"

"Check with him. He's an odd character for sure, but he may have seen her."

"I'll do that."

"Call me if I can be of any help."

"Ten-four."

Brandon ended the call. He heard the door to the bedroom open.

"You look better now, but promise me you will eat something."

"I heard you talking. What did Jeff say?"

"He's going to contact the maintenance guy. Perhaps, Simon can help locate her. Jeff said he would get in touch with you."

Satisfied that he had done all he could for the moment, Brandon said, "I've gotta go now. I'll check back later."

He shook hands with Bill and left, closing the door behind him. He walked to his vehicle, climbed in, turned the ignition, and drove down the lane. As he neared the exit to the campground, he saw Al leaving the Pavilion. Al motioned for him, and Brandon stopped.

"Hate to cancel an invitation, but no one's going to play dominoes tonight. I heard on the news that we're in for a big blow. Expect some high winds and hail. In fact, the weather man predicted rain for the next three days."

"Will that affect the campers?"

"It could. Jeff called a few minutes ago and said the sheriff will release them if the rain causes any flooding."

"That's good. I heard the water's rising."

Al nodded. "Be careful now."

Brandon slowly drove away. He glanced in his side mirror. There it was, as black as any evil demon could be. The Town Car followed him to the store and parked on the street. It stood guard as he put the van in the garage and returned to the store. It was raining so hard that Brandon could barely see across the street.

At three o'clock, Brandon's boss told him to take the rest of the afternoon off. Because of the intensity of the storm, he doubted there would be any customers.

Once again Brandon put on his yellow slicker and exited through the back of the store to retrieve his Harley. He eased the bike around the building and stopped to look right, then left before he pulled out of the parking lot onto the road. Halfway home, the hair on the back of his neck sent a warning message that crawled up and down his spine.

He felt eyes on him. Brandon glanced in his side mirror. Even though the rain fall had somewhat slowed, and the image was distorted by the raindrops running down the mirror, the reflection of two headlights announced an unwelcome visitor behind him. Like a sinister cat stalks its prey, the black Town Car crept along behind him all the way home and watched him park his Harley and lock the garage. When Brandon reached the front porch and looked toward the street, the car was gone.

"Now what?"

Chapter Twenty-Two

BRANDON'S CELL phone rang. He clicked it on. It was Bill. "I'm assuming Jeff has already contacted you?"

"Right. Jeff is on his way over as we speak, and we're leaving in a few minutes to go look for her. He advised me to let him take me out on the lake. Said I might get lost if I went alone and then he'd have two people to find."

"He's right. People get lost on the lake all the time. He's the guy to help you search. He's found other people wandering around, no sense of direction. He knows all the tributaries of Caddo. If she's out there, he'll find her. Let me know if you want me to help." Brandon didn't tell Bill that, as a child, he had spent every summer with his grandparents who taught him the ins and outs of the lake.

"Thanks. I will."

"Well, at least the rain seems to be letting up a little bit. Hopefully, the next wave will hold off while you search. Don't worry. Jeff will find her."

"Got to go. I see Jeff at the marina." Bill ended the call.

Knowing Lillian would be okay, Brandon smiled. He retrieved several pieces of mail from the mailbox beside his front door and went inside. He entered the library, sat down at his desk, and shuffled through the envelopes filled with junk mail. Tossing all of them in the wastebasket, he stood and walked over to the wall of bookshelves on the opposite wall.

He removed the copy of *The Complete Works of William Shakespeare* and inserted a key in the pocket door hidden behind the frame of the bookshelves. The door slid into the wall crevice behind the shelving. Brandon sat down at the first computer hidden in the small room.

There was a message on his computer.

Brandon leaned back in his chair and smiled.

* * * * *

Brandon made another call, one he had sworn to himself he would never make. But he was worried about his mother. He decided to swallow his pride and telephone his dad. He knew there was no love between his parents, could not imagine what his father had done to cause his mother to flee. He had to find out what was going on between them.

Brandon did not want to talk to his father, but more than anything, he wanted to know why his mother was so afraid of her husband. He scanned the contact list in his cell and chose the number for his dad. He heard the phone ring twice.

"Well, my prodigal son finally saw fit to call his father," said Franklin Ford. "It's good to hear from you, Brandon. After our last conversation two months ago, I didn't think you'd be calling so soon."

"This isn't a social call."

"Good. Business, it is. I hope you've reconsidered my offer. There's an empty office in my firm with your name on the door."

"I've given you my answer regarding your offer."

"Just know it'll be here when you're ready. I understand you want to make it on your own, and I know you can. It's just that I'd always planned on adding '& Son' to the plaque outside my office."

Throughout his childhood, the verbal abuse Brandon received from his father had taught the son how to use flattery to soften his dad's attitude.

"I know, and believe me, I have always appreciated your being there for me. But today, I'm calling for another reason altogether."

"If you're still not willing to join the firm, why did you bother to contact me? Do you need a loan? If so, I'm afraid that's impossible right now. Thanks to your mother, I'm a little short on funds."

"No, sir, I don't need your money. Actually, I have a question to ask you."

"Out with it."

"Have you talked to Mom lately?"

"Hell no."

He paused.

Brandon could hear him grind his teeth. "Furthermore, if I ever see her again, it'll be in court." Franklin spoke in the courtroom voice he used to question hostile witnesses. "Why do you ask?"

"I'd like to see her, but she's never at the house when I call."

"I'm surprised she hasn't contacted you since you two are so close."

"I'm worried about her. She always returns my calls. Do you have any idea where she could be?" Brandon wanted to know if his dad had anything to do with the men in the black sedan.

"No, I don't. Wish I did. Shortly after she cleaned me out, she disappeared."

"What do you mean 'cleaned you out'?"

"She withdrew every dime we had in our joint account as well as the firm's business account."

"How could she do that?"

"Unfortunately, like a fool, I had her signature on file for both accounts."

"Why would Mom do a thing like that?"

Franklin answered Brandon's question with one of his own. "Well, if you do see her, will you do a favor for me?"

"And what might that be?"

"Tell her she'd better fork over the three and half million she stole from me and my investors. They don't take too kindly to a thief. Those who double cross them have learned that lesson the hard way. Tell her she's in danger and not from me."

"My God. What do you mean?"

"Just tell her they're coming for her. She'd better come back to me and face the music. I'm the only one who can help her now, but I can't protect her if I can't find her."

"Do you think they may try to find her by following me?" Brandon held his breath waiting for an answer. He wanted to know if the men in the Town Car worked for his dad or for his dad's investors."

"I wouldn't put anything past them. These guys don't deal kindly to anyone, man or woman, dumb enough to steal from them. Why do you ask about them?"

"Someone's been following me, nearly ran over me the other night."

Franklin growled. "Can you describe them?"

"No, I've not seen the driver or a passenger. The windows are tinted black, but I can describe the car."

"Tell me."

"It's like the fleet of cars you own – a black Town Car."

"Be careful. You and I have our differences but know I wouldn't cause or order any of my employees to harm you or your mother in any way. Let me know if it continues."

"I hoped that would be your answer."

"One more thing: Were you able to get a tag number?"

"I was."

"Email it to me. I'll get one of my men to investigate, find out who's stalking you."

"Thanks, Dad."

"And, if your mother returns your call, warn her. Tell her she's in danger. Tell her to let me know where she is. Better yet, tell her to come home."

"I'll do that, and if you see her, tell her to call me."

Franklin made no such promise to his son. "Got to go. My next client just walked in. Take care, you hear?" With that, Franklin ended the call.

Brandon sat down at his desk. So, that's what Mom didn't want me to know. How in the world did the bank let her get away with that much money? And why am I better off not knowing about it? Dad may not be her biggest problem, or was he lying? Investors? What is Dad up to? More to the point, what is Mom up to? Why would she steal from Dad? He's always been as generous to her with his money as he has with his sharp criticism of everything she bought with it.

Chapter Twenty-Three

LULLED BY the gentle rain pelting the roof of Simon's cottage, Lillian slept all night and until one o'clock the next afternoon. She awoke to the aroma of coffee and the sound of bacon sizzling. She threw back the covers, jumped up, and headed for the bathroom. She turned on the vanity's faucet and splashed cool water in her face. With her eyes closed, she reached out and fumbled around until she felt a towel. Face dried, she caught a glance of herself in the mirror. She frowned at her reflection and ran her fingers through her long hair to straighten it as much as she could before heading for the kitchen.

Simon looked up and smiled. "Good morning, or should I say good afternoon? Thought the smell of coffee and bacon would do the job."

"I think I slept better last night than any night since parking our RV."

"I'm glad. I know you were tired after your ordeal. Don't know how much you swim these days, but you did a good job treading water until I could get to you."

"No long distance swimming these days. Just water aerobics at the health club. Richard, I mean, Simon, I don't know how I will ever thank you."

He interrupted her. "No thanks necessary. Actually, you've done me a great favor."

"How so?"

"Now I don't have to hide from you. It will make my job so much easier if I don't have to dodge you all day long. But, I promise, I will still keep an eye on you for safety's sake."

"I wish you could tell me what it is you're investigating. That is what you are doing—investigating, right?"

Simon smiled but ignored the question. "You assume too much, Lillian."

"If you will share with me, perhaps I could listen and observe and help. I have to tell you I've helped my sons solve a couple of murders."

"When?"

"Just before Bill and I arrived at Caddo."

"Who was murdered?"

"A newcomer to Leisure Lake as well as one of my best friends. Broke my heart."

Lillian took a deep breath. "That's why Bill bought me the RV, to get me away for a while."

"So, he brought you here and first thing, a murder."

"Did you know the man who was found on the jogging trail?"

"No, I'd not seen him before. Don't know what he was doing here. I saw you take the woman who found the body to your RV. Leigh Ann, I believe, was her name. Correct?"

Lillian nodded.

Simon continued. "Funny, I didn't hear her scream until after she reached the road leading into the campsite."

Suspicious by nature, Lillian wondered why Simon would mention her screams.

"Why is that funny?"

"Sound carries on the water, and I was in my boat near the edge of the trail. If she had screamed when she first saw the body, I would have heard her."

"Her screams disrupted the peace and quiet we were all enjoying. That's for sure. From what she told me, she has a sad story. But before we say another word, I need some coffee."

"There's a cupboard right behind you. Reach up there and get two cups."

Lillian found two mismatched coffee mugs and set them on the table. Simon filled them with the strong, black, caffeinated, heart-jumping brew. "Tell me about Leigh Ann. I've wondered why she came to Caddo."

"Why? Have you been watching her, too?"

"Watch everyone. But with regard to her, I've thought it odd that a woman alone goes camping but never participates in any of the camp's activities. She jogs. It's like she's running, always running. Does she like to run for exercise, or is she running from something or someone?"

"From what she told me, from someone, her ex-husband. He's been abusive to her and to their son. Sad situation, I think."

"Where's her son? Why isn't he with her?"

"He's grown, attending law school or maybe he just graduated. I'd have to think about our conversation to answer that question correctly."

Lillian wondered why Simon was so interested in Leigh Ann and her son.

"No more about Leigh Ann and her problems," Simon said. "Sit down. I'll scramble some eggs. We'll eat and then I'll get you back to the marina."

* * * * *

"It's beginning to rain," Bill said. Try as he could to stay calm and not panic, Bill's patience was depleted in proportion to his increased worry and concern. Time was running out. Another storm threatened their search, making it difficult to find Lillian. But he knew he wouldn't quit until he held her in his arms. In fact, he might never let her out of his sight again.

"Look, Jeff, we've been in and out of every nook and cranny, one after another. We've stopped at every house beside the lake. No one has seen her." Bill waved his arms. "How big is Caddo Lake anyway? I'm telling you: We've got to hurry."

"I know, but don't worry. Keep calling her name."

"Don't worry, you say? Look up, Jeff. Look at the sky. Those clouds are ominous. Another cloud burst is on its way. She can't survive another night with the sky pouring down a deluge of rain and the water level of the lake rising." Bill slammed his right fist on the edge of the boat's open window. "Do you understand that?"

"I understand. Try to hold on a little longer, Bill," Jeff said. "We're headed for our last stop. If we don't find her at Simon's house, I'll call for a recovery team."

Bill grabbed the bullhorn and stalked out of the pilot's cabin. He braced himself against the railing of the boat's bow and yelled Lillian's name again and again, hoping she could somehow hear him and answer his call. She just had to be alive.

He prayed she was warm and dry in someone's kitchen. Right now, he didn't care whose house. He needed to see her, to touch her, to hold her, to tell her how much he loved her.

* * * * *

"Thanks. Thanks for everything, Simon. You were right last night. I know Bill is beside himself with worry."

"I bet he's looking for you now." Simon tilted his head, listening. "Hear that?"

She heard a voice in the distance calling her name.

"That's Bill. He's out there on the lake. Sounds like he's talking on a megaphone."

"Go out on the porch." Simon handed her a bright, red dish towel. "Yell back to him and wave this. When he gets here, tell him to tie up and come on in. There's enough coffee for all us."

"Like old times." Lillian grabbed the towel, hugged him, and ran outside. She heard the small engine coming closer to Simon's cabin.

Bill continued to call out her name. "Lillian. Where are you?"

When he got close enough, she called to him and waved the flag. She could not see him and feared he wasn't able to see her. Simon's cabin was well hidden.

Simon stood beside Lillian and yelled, "Jeff, can you hear me?"

Lillian heard one short blast of the horn on the patrol boat. "He heard you," Lillian said. The deep rumble of the park ranger's boat drew closer.

"Idle your engine. I'll come out to you." Simon climbed down to his boat and started the small engine. He slowly eased away from his dock. He disappeared into the steady gray mist.

Lillian stood on the porch and scanned the lake, straining to see any movement. The rain muffled the sounds of the engines, but one sounded as if it were moving farther away from the cottage. Another one with a deep roar grew closer.

It finally came into sight.

The patrol boat had two occupants—Bill and the park ranger. Ignoring the rain, she left the cover of the porch and raced down the steps to greet them.

Jeff secured the boat. Bill jumped out, grabbed her, lifted her up, and swung her around. "I thought I'd lost you."

He blinked back tears. "I searched all night for you. Never been so worried."

"You shouldn't have worried – " She didn't get to finish her sentence. Bill's lips stopped whatever protest she had intended. When he released her, she looked up and said, "I'll never leave you, you know that."

"I do." Bill turned to Jeff. "Can't thank you enough for all of your help today."

Jeff, standing in the gently swaying boat, had looked away as the couple embraced, but turned around, and cleared his throat.

"No thanks needed. Just doing my job. Glad things worked out for the good." He grinned. "You two lovebirds ready to go?" He handed a rain poncho to Lillian.

"You bet," Lillian said.

Jeff extended a hand to the couple. After they were seated in the dry cabin, he untied the ropes and pointed the boat toward the marina.

Bill and Lillian cuddled together on a straight-back bench behind Jeff. She leaned over and whispered. "We have much to discuss."

He nodded.

Lillian pushed back the hood of the poncho when she heard the short-wave radio crackle. She listened to the conversation between Jeff and the caller who didn't give Jeff time to say hello.

"Jeff, this is Al. A few minutes ago, I found your missing canoe."

"Great. Where?"

"It's moored in the last boat slot at the marina."

"That's good. Thanks for letting me know."

"So, have you found the missing little lady? She okay?"

"Yes sir. She was at Simon's cabin. I'm headed your way right now. I have the Prestridges with me. See you in less than five minutes."

"Come by my office when you get here."

"Ten-four."

The radio went silent, but Lillian's brain went into overdrive. She leaned over and whispered, "I wonder who found and returned the canoe I rented?"

Bill shrugged and shook his head. "I'm more interested in learning why in the world would you think you could handle a canoe all by yourself. Would you like to clue me in?"

"Once upon a time, my arms were stronger. In fact, I was rowing quite well today – that is, until lightening struck too close for comfort to my canoe. I lost my phone and was treading water when Simon happened by."

"Coincidence?"

"You know I don't believe in them. I'll explain more later." Lillian made a writing motion with her hand.

Bill smiled and responded in a low voice. "Yes, ma'am, we have much to write in your notebook. We'll wait until we get home to talk."

Lillian nodded.

At the marina, Jeff slipped the patrol boat up to the dock.

Bill hopped out and tied the ropes to secure the boat, then walked back and helped Lillian climb out. Husband and wife ran to their RV holding the hoods of the ponchos tightly to their faces.

Jeff followed them.

"Come in out of this weather," Lillian said, turning her head so she could see him

"Thanks, but I need to see Al before the weather gets worse," Jeff said.

Chapter Twenty-Four

LILLIAN, ANXIOUS to get inside and out of the rain, beat Bill to the door. She stepped into the RV where she was met by Eli whose yelps and happy whimpers indicated he was just as glad to see her as she was to be home. He stood on his back legs and placed his front paws on her shoulders, then covered her face and ears with wet, sloppy, dog kisses.

Lillian put her arms around the dog.

"I'm glad to see you, too, you beautiful big boy." She lifted his paws off her shoulders and patted him on the head. He danced in circles, wagging his tail. He jumped onto the sofa and leaped off again. His excitement was contagious.

Lillian laughed at his antics. "Okay, Eli, I can tell you're glad to see me. Time to calm down."

For once, Eli did not obey his master. He continued prancing around her until she turned and put her arms around Bill's waist.

Bill pulled Lillian into his arms, put his hand under her chin, and lifted her face. Her teal colored eyes met his gaze.

"Both of us missed you. I was so afraid something bad had happened to you. Promise me you won't ever take off in a canoe by yourself again."

"That's an easy promise to make. When I swamped the canoe, I was afraid I'd never see you again. I'd kiss you, but right now my face is a little slurpy." She laughed.

"Eli's kisses do that to a person." Bill smiled. "Go take a warm shower, get out of those wet clothes. I'll make some hot tea for us."

"Sounds wonderful. Won't take me long."

Twenty minutes later, Lillian sat on the sofa with Eli squeezed between her and Bill. They sipped their green tea and munched on chocolate chip cookies.

"Brandon delivered these to replace those he ate when he visited with us." Bill reached for a third cookie. "Lillian, I have an apology to make."

"So do I." She sat her empty cup on the end table and turned to Bill. "I'm sorry I lost my temper. I'm also sorry you had to worry about me. It was foolish of me to think I could handle a canoe after all these years."

Bill reached over Eli and took Lillian's hand. He raised it to his lips. "Forgiven. Now, it's my turn. I over-reacted to your wanting a new career. I should have encouraged you. I thought about it all night and came to a conclusion."

"What might that be?" she asked.

"If you'll have me, I'd like to be your partner."

"You're already my partner. We've been married forever."

"That's not what I mean."

"I'm listening. Explain things to me."

"If you want to be a P.I., I'll get my license, and we will work together. What do you think about that idea?"

Lillian jerked her hand out of his. "Other than you're being my wedded partner, what makes you think you'd be a good P.I. partner to me?" Lillian kept a stern face.

"So, you want to hear my qualifications?"

"Most people have to submit a resumé and wait to be contacted by the employer for an interview." She still had not bestowed a smile on her beloved.

He nodded. "I understand." He stood and walked over to the dinette table and sat down in front of the laptop.

Lillian opened a new bottle of merlot and filled two wine glasses. Bill covered the computer screen as she placed one beside the laptop. She chuckled at his being so secretive, but honored his attempt to hide what he was typing. She heard a low rumble outside and walked to the door.

"It's getting dark early today. Guess another storm is on its way. Let's be sure to watch the evening news, get an update on the weather."

Bill nodded once, kept typing.

Lillian moved back to the sofa and sat by Eli, who flipped onto his back and offered his tummy for a rub. His master complied.

Ten minutes later, Bill handed a single sheet of paper to Lillian. "Please overlook any typos. I prepared this resumé for an emergency interview."

In a stern business-like voice, Lillian read.

Name: William (my wife calls me Bill) Prestridge

Address: Wherever my wife resides. Currently: RV Park, Caddo Lake.

Position Applicant is Seeking: Private Investigator

Qualifications for Position: Thirty years as an investigative reporter for the *Fort Worth Star Telegram*. Helped FWPD solve crimes. Descriptions available upon request.

Computer Skills: Proficient with Microsoft Office

Other Skills: Good kisser.

Lillian looked up, then laughed. She leaned over Eli and pulled Bill toward her. The dog grunted and tried to sit upright, but he was trapped on his back. "Come here, you kisser you."

Bill obliged. After their embrace, he said, "I assume applications are closed."

"Your qualifications meet all expectations for a working partnership."

"Then let's get to work," Bill said. "I have one more confession to make."

"I'm listening."

"When I walked away from you, I took your notes and read over the items you made about the events here at the camp."

"Did you come to any conclusions?"

"I did."

Bill stood and walked over to the dinette. He picked up the notebook, opened it, and showed Lillian some of his notations in the margins.

She ran her finger down the list and stopped at one with Bill's comment: Al and Russell Stokes – suspicious of their actions. Al tells lies, and Stokes is always near when trouble arises. Al is late to events. Need to check their backgrounds.

Lillian continued scanning down the page. Beside her note about Leigh Ann, Bill had written: Why is Leigh Ann always afraid? Is she in hiding? From whom?

She stopped reading.

"I'm glad you agree with me about Al and Russell Stokes."

"What about Leigh Ann? Do you think she is as helpless as she wants us to believe?"

Lillian considered his question.

"I have my doubts about her, nothing definitive."

A loud rumble rocked the RV. Bill reached over the back of the sofa and closed the window blind. "That sounded close." He stood and walked to the kitchen, closed the blind to the small window over the sink, looked outside, and said, "Storm's here."

Lillian and Eli moved to the open door. The gray day had succumbed to total darkness.

A jagged streak of lightning lit up the sky. Lillian jumped back and pulled Eli with her.

"Quick, Bill, close the door. That lightning's too close for comfort."

"Let's unplug all of our appliances," he said. "Hate for lightning to strike anything." He took care of the coffee pot and the television.

"What about our laptops?" Lillian bent down and unplugged her computer. "By the way, where is yours? I'll take care of it, too."

"It's okay. I left it under the driver's seat. Battery's probably dead by now."

The lights in the camper flickered once, came back on, flickered again. Darkness. Lillian felt her way across the living area and down the short hallway to their closet. She opened the door, reached up and grabbed the battery-powered lantern she had ordered online just before their trip. She turned it on high. Its low-wattage was enough to light the entire camper. She joined Bill at the kitchen table. He sat with his hand under his chin propped up by his elbow.

"Glad I remembered to bring this with us." She sat the lantern in the middle of the table.

"Always prepared. That's another reason I love you." He had her notebook in front of him. "I've been thinking, he said, "and I agree with you about the maintenance man. We need to talk to him. He may be able to tell us more about some of the strange events Brandon mentioned."

"Hand me that pen over there, please." Lillian pointed to the pencil holder she had placed on the end table.

Bill stood to retrieve the pen but stopped at the beep of a car's horn.

"What in the world?" Lillian said. "Sounds like it's right outside. Open our door. Check it out."

When the door opened, she saw a Mercedes SUV parked a foot away from the bottom step. Leigh Ann jumped out and hurried into the camper, carrying an overnight bag in her hand.

"Come in," Bill closed the door and turned around. "Let me take your raincoat."

"Thank you." Leigh Ann slipped off the wet garment, handed it to him, and looked for Lillian. "There you are," she said.

Bill spread the black and white checked slicker over the back of the RV's passenger seat to dry.

Lillian, puzzled by Leigh Ann's abrupt entry, saw her new P. I. partner standing behind the woman.

He raised both eyebrows and mouthed, "What's with her?"

Lillian responded with an almost unnoticeable shrug of one shoulder. "What are you doing out on such a stormy night?" Lillian motioned to a chair opposite her. "Have a seat. I'll pour you a cup of tea. I think the water is still hot." She looked at Bill. "Would you care for another cup, dear?"

"Please." He pulled out a chair for Leigh Ann and then sat across from her. Lillian poured three cups of tea and sat beside Bill.

Leigh Ann spoke in a quavering voice. "I hate to bother you, but you did say I could spend the night with you if I ever felt threatened."

"Yes, I did," Lillian said, "but tell us, what scared you tonight. The storm?"

"Heavens, no, I'm not afraid of storms. But I am scared of some people."

"Has someone bothered you?" Bill wanted to know.

"Not yet, but I'm afraid he will."

"Tell us who scared you," Lillian said gently. "Perhaps, we can help."

"I don't know."

"Then why do you think you're in danger?" Lillian closed her notebook and put it aside with the hope that their guest had not seen any of its notes. She waited for Leigh Ann to answer her question.

"Someone's been lurking around my RV for the past several nights."

"Did you see the perp?"

"No, but I've heard him. Tonight, he walked up onto my step and rattled my door. I guess the lightning scared him. So, I waited, and when I thought I could get in my car safely, I drove here."

"You're welcome to stay," Bill reassured her. "In fact, you and I will switch places. I'll stay in your RV tonight. See if I can catch the culprit if he returns."

Lillian shivered. "Bill, there's no need for that. I'll make out the sofa for Leigh Ann. You don't need to leave." The memory of almost dying on the lake frightened her, and Lillian dreaded being away from him tonight. For some reason, his not being close enough to touch did not bode well with her.

"I'll be fine," Bill said. "I'll take my cell phone. Call me if you feel uneasy."

"Remember," Lillian said, "I lost my cell. I can't call you."

"Okay, if Leigh Ann doesn't mind, use her phone."

"Sure, she's welcome to call from mine."

Bill left them and went into the bedroom. A few minutes later, he returned with his gym bag in tow. He carried his flashlight in his left hand when he entered the living room again. "Do you mind if I take your laptop?"

"Take it. You're always researching something." Without moving her head, Lillian turned her eyes in the direction of their guest.

Bill laughed. "You know me well."

Lillian walked him the short distance to the door. She put her arms around his waist and stood on tip-toe to kiss him goodbye. "Love you. Be careful, darling."

Bill turned and darted out into the black chasm of the night. Lillian watched the bounce of his flashlight until he was half-way to Leigh Ann's RV. After that, her view was blocked by automobiles parked along the drive. She silently prayed, "Dear Lord, keep him safe."

Chapter Twenty-Five

WITH BILL out of sight, Lillian watched Leigh Ann who sat with arms bent, elbows on the table, holding her head in her hands. She looked tired and worn out. Determined to learn more about Leigh Ann, Lillian pulled out a chair and sat across from her but said nothing. She waited for the other woman to speak.

Finally, Leigh Ann looked up. "You must think I'm either a paranoid wreck or just plain crazy," she said.

"No," Lillian said louder than she intended, but then with a kind and gentle expression, she added, "But I'd like for you to tell me the truth about yourself."

Leigh Ann straightened her back and defensively folded her arms across her chest. "I've already told you. I taught school and married an attorney. Had a son who graduated from Baylor. What else do you want to know?"

"I want to know why you are estranged from your husband."

"That's personal and I don't care to discuss it."

Lillian nodded and continued. "I also want you to tell me why you're camping all alone. You have to admit that's not the norm."

Leigh Ann took a deep breath and exhaled. "Of course, you think it's odd. But that's my business."

"Since you barged in on us and since my husband gallantly left our warm RV to allow you a safe, good night's sleep, I don't think it's asking too much of you to answer my questions." Lillian's tone made it clear that she expected Leigh Ann to be honest.

"Since you put it like that, I guess you have a right to know more about me."

"Thank you."

Lillian waited for the other lady to continue.

"First of all, my husband was and is an abusive man. I was so glad when our son Blake left for college."

"Did he beat your son, too?"

Leigh Ann's eyes filled with tears. "There's more than one way to abuse someone, you know."

Lillian handed her a tissue.

"I do understand. I've taught students who were emotionally abused. That's the hardest kind to prove. Sometimes it's only evident after a tragedy occurs."

Lillian paused and then asked, "So, am I correct to assume he meted out one demeaning comment after another."

"Exactly, but with Blake away at school, I could take his criticism. I had become numb to his condescending attitude."

"You've filed for a divorce?"

"No, not yet."

"I'm confused. You just said you had died out to his verbal abuse. So, tell me, why did you leave him?"

"I knew he was breaking the law. After all, he was an attorney and should have known better."

"How did he break the law?"

"I don't know. I left after learning he had become involved with a foreign investment syndicate. That's what he called it."

"Does his so-called syndicate have a corporate name?" Lillian asked.

"That's the problem. He said it was a group of rich oilmen who had invested in one of his projects. I asked Franklin to tell me about the project. He wouldn't discuss it. One night, I heard him talking on the phone to someone. More than once, he assured the person he had everything worked out. I knew by the tone of his voice that he was being threatened.

"He ended the conversation with a warning to stay away from his family. I was scared, so I packed my suitcase after he went to sleep and left."

"And came here?" Lillian wanted to know more about Franklin, whose name Leigh Ann had mentioned for the first time.

"Not at first."

"Where did you go before you came to Caddo?"

"I spent that first night in a hotel outside of Dallas. The next day, I went to the bank and cleaned out all of our accounts."

"Personal accounts?"

"And business accounts," Leigh Ann said.

"Why in the world would you do that?" Lillian wanted to know.

"Because money is his first love, not me, not our son. I knew I had to have something to hold over his head if I wanted a clean divorce."

"You do plan on filing for a divorce?"

"Yes, but not yet."

"Why not?"

"I want to make him assure me that Blake will be safe. Then, I'll take action."

"So, you and he have talked, I hope."

"No, but I've talked to my son. I think he's hiding from his father, too."

"What makes you think that?"

"He told me he was being followed."

"Do you think your husband knows where you are?"

"If he did, he would have contacted me. I think I'm being followed by one of the syndicate men."

"Why would they follow you?"

"I'm sure Franklin told them I took their money."

"How could you take money from your husband's business account?"

"I'm his business partner. I had access to the firm's account."

Lillian thought for a moment. "Let me get this straight. You made all of the firm's deposits, too?"

Leigh Ann nodded. "Lately, though, the money kept growing, money I didn't deposit – even in our joint account."

"Your personal account?"

Leigh Ann nodded again. "That's what I just said."

"What made you think the money in your account belongs to them?"

"I know my husband doesn't make that kind of money practicing family law."

"How much are you talking about?" Lillian held her breath, knowing it must be a large sum for someone to terrorize the woman.

"Over three million dollars," Leigh Ann whispered confidentially.

Lillian said the first thing that popped into her mind. "Holy Mother of God, help us all." Then she remembered Bill was in Leigh Ann's RV.

"Hand me your phone, damn it." Lillian was angry. "How could you let my husband spend the night in your RV knowing he might be in danger?" Eli had been snoozing in his usual place on the back of the sofa but jumped down and ran across the room. He growled and barked and repeatedly jumped up to the handle in an effort to open the door.

"I didn't think they would bother him." Leigh Ann rummaged around in her purse searching for her phone. "I know I put it in the side pocket. It's got to be here."

Lillian understood Eli's ability to sense danger and grew impatient with Leigh Ann. She snatched the purse and dumped all of its contents on the table, grabbed Leigh Ann's cell, and dialed Bill's number. It went straight to voice mail. Frustrated, she threw down the useless object and ordered, "Stay here. Don't open the door for anyone but me."

Leigh Ann nodded. Lillian didn't wait to hear the click of the lock. She and Eli ran out into the storm.

The power failure had left the campsite in the dark. Rain and thunder carried on a battle overhead, but for once, Lillian was thankful for the lightning. It lit the way for her and Eli as they ran to Leigh Ann's RV. There was a dim glow, to Lillian a sign of hope, from one of the windows. "Hurry, Eli. Run. Alert Bill for me. I'm too slow."

The dog had been keeping pace with his owner, but at her command, he raced ahead and bounded up the steps to the Casita, barking loudly and pawing the bottom of the door.

Bill opened the door. "What's wrong, boy?"

Eli grabbed him by his pants leg and began to pull him outside.

Lillian saw the jagged dagger dancing toward the tall pine tree behind Leigh Ann's RV and yelled, "Bill, run, run to me. Hurry."

When he and the dog reached her, she grabbed him. "Come on. You're not safe. Run." Eli heard her command and raced ahead of the couple.

She stopped when she heard a loud pop as lightning exploded in the forest followed by the scent of burning wood.

Bill grabbed her hand. "Hurry," he said. "Lightning struck a tree."

A loud crack followed the creaking and groaning of the tree. Then the sound of wood hitting metal resonated throughout the campsite as a pine crushed Leigh Ann's RV. Lillian glanced back over her shoulder.

She stopped.

"Oh, no. You could have been in there. Thank God you're okay."

"Yes, thank the Lord, you and Eli reached me before that tree fell."

The Casita burst into flames.

"And Leigh Ann's safe in our RV." Lillian added, "We have been blessed tonight."

"Damn. Your laptop is still in there." Bill dropped Lillian's hand and turned to go back to the camper.

Lillian grabbed his arm and jerked him back. "Forget it," Lillian said. "Computers can be replaced. You can't."

Across the lane, two campers -- Pat and Joy Patterson -- flashlights in hand, ran toward Lillian and Bill.

"Man, that was too close," Pat said.

"Yes, sir. It was."

"I pray the lady who owns the RV is safe."

"Luckily, she's in our RV," Bill responded.

"What about her son?"

"Her son?" Lillian asked. "Have you seen him with her?"

"Yes, ma'am. He was here recently," Ms. Patterson said.

"Did she introduce you to him?"

"No, but I could tell by the way she looked at him. I recognize a mother's love when I see it."

Lillian nodded.

"Yes, ma'am, I know what you mean." She remembered Leigh Ann's mention of her son and the fact that he, too, could be hiding from Franklin.

"Did any of the limbs hit your camper?" Bill asked.

"No. We're okay," Joy said.

"And we will be better in the next thirty minutes." Pat was adamant. "I'm hooking up my car, and we're leaving tonight. This place isn't safe. Come on, Joy."

"We can't leave." His wife reminded him. "The sheriff has everyone quarantined because of the murder."

"I don't care what he said. The sheriff knows where he can find us."

"Don't blame you one bit," Lillian said. "Drive safely."

"You can count on it," Pat yelled back over a clap of thunder. "Take care."

Bill looked down at Lillian. "How in the world did you know I was in danger?"

"I didn't, but Eli did."

Bill bent over and hugged the wet dog. He laughed when he stood. "Look at us standing out here in a thunderstorm, dripping wet. Glad we have indoor/outdoor carpet."

Lillian looked back the RV. "Guess there's no need to call the fire department."

Bill laughed at her dry comment. "I think the rain will do their job tonight."

"Come on, you two. We need to break the news to Leigh Ann." Lillian dreaded telling the woman the troubling news. "Don't know how much more she can stand."

The threesome hurried back to their RV. Before Bill could open the door, it flew open. Leigh Ann stepped outside.

"Oh my God. My RV's on fire." Tears competed with the rain that pelted her face.

"Thank goodness Eli warned us." Lillian put her arm around Leigh Ann's shoulders. "I don't have enough words to tell you how sorry I am."

She stepped away from Lillian. "I've got to go." Wild-eyed, Leigh Ann stared at the flames as though she didn't hear Lillian.

"You're too distraught." Lillian knew how trauma could cause a person to go into shock. She took Leigh Ann's hand. "Let's go inside. We're soaking wet. A cup of hot tea will be good for all of us."

Lillian led Leigh Ann into the Prestridge RV.

"That sounds wonderful to me," Bill said. He closed the door. "I'll get us some towels." He walked the short distance to the linen closet and grabbed three big, fluffy white bath towels. "We still want you to spend the night with us."

Leigh Ann ignored his invitation. She turned in a circle, spotted her raincoat where Bill had placed it, grabbed it, and put it on. "I've got to find it," she announced and ran outside.

Before they could stop her, Leigh Ann rushed outside.

Lillian motioned to Bill, and they, too, stepped into the black abyss surrounding Caddo Lake. Only an intermittent flash of light from the sky and the wet, sizzling, glow of the remaining embers of fire dancing across the remains of Leigh Ann's RV provided any kind of light for the campground.

Lillian watched as Leigh Ann used a broken tree branch to stir the ashes. Lillian heard her mumble over and over, "It's got to be here. They'll kill me if I don't find it."

"You won't be able to find anything tonight," Bill said. "It's too dark. Besides, everything in your camper is burned. If your belongings survived the fire, they're too wet to retrieve anyway."

Leigh Ann continued to shuffle around the remains of her RV, mumbling about a lost object. She sounded desperate.

Lillian got as close as she dared to the frantic woman who had stopped sifting through the ashes and was now waving the stick in the air.

"If you'll tell me what's so important, I'll try to help you," Lillian said.

"I can't stay here. Got to go." She ran to her car.

"Where could she have gone?" Bill stood with a puzzled look on his face and watched Leigh Ann speed out of the campground.

"More importantly, I would love to know what she tried to locate and who will kill her if she can't find it."

"Right now, I don't care." Bill said. "Let's get inside."

Chapter Twenty-Six

RAYS OF sunlight slipped through the blinds on the bedroom window of the Prestridge RV. Lillian opened her eyes and blinked at the brightness. She rolled over on her side with the expectation of seeing her husband beside her. Instead, two big, black eyes surrounded by white curly hair stared back at her. She stretched her arms around her adored pet and kissed the top of his head.

"I can never repay you for saving Bill." She looked lovingly at the dog's happy face. "Anyone who believes dogs can't smile has never seen you, Eli."

She smelled coffee brewing. "Yea, electricity is back."

Both Eli and his owner crawled out of bed. One on tip-toes and one with a cat-like stealth sneaked into the kitchen where Bill sat at the dinette. Lillian put her arms around his shoulders and kissed the back of his neck.

Eli put his front paw on Bill's knee. He scooted back his chair and stood to greet both of them.

"Hey, you two sleepy heads, good morning. Guess last night's events wore you down." He hugged and kissed Lillian, then opened the door for Eli. "There you go, big boy. Don't stay out too long. You might get run over."

"I hadn't paid any attention until now, but I hear traffic, lots of noise in the campground. What's going on?"

"People are leaving. After the tree destroyed Leigh Ann's RV last night, no one wants to stay. And, like Mr. Patterson said, the sheriff has everyone's cell number and home address."

"Let's hope Al gave everything to him."

Lillian heard a car's horn and went to the door. Eli stood in the middle of the road blocking a white Subaru Outback with a white fifth wheel attached to it. She stepped outside and smiled when she saw her dog on guard. She knew by his stance that Eli was protecting her. The driver's window of the Outback slid down.

"Get that mutt out of my way before I drive over him," Guy Steiner yelled.

"Come here, Eli," Lillian ordered. "Let him pass."

With the dog out of his way, Guy gunned the car's engine, and with tires spinning, sprayed loose gravel. Behind him, his RV swayed from the sudden start. The unknown driver of the car following Guy shook his head and waved as he passed the Prestridges.

"Smart, isn't he, Eli?" The dog gave a loud snort.

"My sentiments exactly," Bill said from the top step of the RV. "Come on in here, you two, before I have to fight one of these men for being so rude."

"Don't worry about that. Most of the RVers are friendly and much more courteous than that idiot."

Eli barked his agreement.

"Let's have coffee outside, wave, and wish them well as they leave."

"I'll set up the chairs if you'll bring the carafe and our cups," Bill said.

Several of the drivers of the trucks and RVs slowed down and waved at them. Vickie Parsons, the last one to leave, did not have her camper attached to her SUV. When Lillian waved, Vickie stopped and lowered her window.

"Looks like everyone else has left. Are you two staying?"

"Yes, ma'am. We want to explore this area before we head out for our next stop," Bill said. "You're not pulling your camper. Do you plan to return?"

"I'm back almost every Friday. I envy you. I'll be glad when I can spend more than a couple of days in my POD. You'll want to see Jefferson. It's an interesting turn-of-the-century town. Has a great history. If you come that way, look me up. I'll treat you to a burger or at least a cup of coffee."

"We may take you up on such a kind offer. I'm ready for a day trip," Lillian said. She placed her hand on Eli's head to stop his low growl which sounded more like a purr.

"I'll look for you. My law firm is right in the middle of town, just down from the Excelsior House and across the street from the Jay Gould Railcar." Vickie laughed. "You can't miss it. The sign over the door has my name on it." She waved and drove out of the campground.

Only four RVs remained: the charred ruins of Leigh Ann's Casita; the RV which belonged to Russell Stokes; the RV owned by Vickie and permanently parked in its slot; and, of course, the brown and white Forrester belonging to the Prestridges. The Gruene's mobile home was parked as always inside the gate.

An empty, death-like silence engulfed the campground. Neither Bill nor Lillian spoke to each other for the next three minutes. Bill picked up the carafe, poured the last drop of coffee into his cup.

Lillian looked at him. "I don't even hear any of the birds singing, do you?"

"I wonder why they're silent?"

"It's too quiet for me. Guess they'll wander out as soon as they realize everything has calmed down after the storm. Looks like it's going to be a beautiful day."

She squinted her eyes from the glare of the sun. "The water is really calm today."

"How about you and I walk down to the marina and do some fishing off the pier?"

"That sounds like a lovely idea." Lillian smiled. "I'll fill the cooler with some drinks if you'll go down to the office and buy some bait."

"I'll need to show Al our fishing licenses. I'm sure he or the park ranger will want to see them sometime today. By the way, can I ask a rhetorical question?"

"You may," Lillian emphasized the word may.

"Did you remember to bring your license?"

"It's in my tackle box."

"Should have known. You're always prepared."

Bill gave her a thumbs up and walked in the direction of the camp's office.

* * * * *

The two long-time friends and lovers sat on the pier, feet dangling over the edge. Lillian cast her rod and reel once and ignored the gentle pull of the waves on her lure which hung naked in the water. She could care less about fishing but enjoyed spending a leisurely morning with her beloved husband and dog.

The birds had returned with their cheerful singing. Lillian listened to their songs and gazed across the lake. Though she couldn't see it, she remembered the house high above the water supported by giant cypress trees. Lillian wondered if her guardian was indeed watching or whether he was busy cleaning up the campground.

Orange and red leaves of the deciduous oaks and elms had fallen prior to the storm of the previous night. Its fury had left a plethora of debris in its wake. Branches from the oak trees, needles from the pine and cypress cluttered the main path leading into the campground. What was left of the tree destroyed by lightening would need to the removed, not to mention the skeletal remains of Leigh Ann's camper.

Eli dozed in the mid-day sun and lay on his side, his back pressed against Lillian. He raised his head and yawned when Bill took a fish off of his lure. The Poodle always snorted at the helpless fish flopping its way into Bill's cooler. Eli would lick Lillian's elbow before he resumed his nap.

Deep in thought long after she cast her lure, Lillian watched the line spin from the reel into the water and thought about the sudden departure of the frightened woman during the peak of the storm. Questions ran through her brain as swiftly as the waves of Caddo Lake scooted by the dock where she and Bill sat. Someone had indeed scared her.

But who? Another camper?

What did she try to find in the ashes?

And who would kill her if she didn't find it?

The sounds of Bill's lure hitting the water and the spin of the reel each time he snapped his rod to re-cast his line, always in the same spot, provided peaceful background noise to Lillian's mental ramblings.

"I hear a motor." Bill pointed toward a mid-sized white boat with black trim approaching the pier.

"Isn't that the patrol boat?" Lillian asked.

"It sure is." Bill reeled in his line, stood, and waited for the boat to sidle up next to the pier.

Jeff Richards idled the twin motors and threw a rope to Bill who secured the boat. Jeff killed the engines and removed the key from the ignition.

"Caught anything?" Jeff asked as he stepped out of the boat. He reached down and patted Eli who had welcomed him with a wagging tail.

"A few," Bill said. "I have enough for dinner."

"Bill's caught more than a few," Lillian laughed. "We can't possibly eat all of them. Want to join us for dinner?" Lillian liked the young man.

"No can do. I'm on duty for the next twenty-four hours, at least."

"I guess you're always busy after a storm like the one we experienced last night."

Jeff inhaled and placed his hands on his hips. He exhaled and straightened his back.

"Yes, ma'am, but today, the storm's damage isn't my biggest concern." His knitted eyebrows chased the smile from his face.

"Oh? Then what is it?"

Lillian heard the worry in his voice.

Above the lake, a cloud scooted across the sky to hover in front of the sun. To Lillian, the gloom that followed was a sign that Mother Nature, too, dreaded to hear Jeff answer her question. She moved closer to Bill and waited.

"There's been an accident on Caddo Lake. The sheriff and the medical examiner are on their way here."

"You're waitng to take them by boat?" Bill interrupted.

"Yes, sir. A boat ran into a cypress tree, tore it up pretty bad."

"Medical examiner?" said Lillian. "That sounds serious." Could something have happened to Simon? Could someone else know about his mysterious reason to be posing as a maintenance man?

"Yes, ma'am. It is. At first, I thought it was only an accident." Jeff paused.

"But the driver didn't make it. He managed to stay in the boat, though."

"How do you know he didn't make it if you're just now going out to the wreck?"

"From the person who called it in, said he's draped over the steering wheel. I've already checked. The scene is exactly as reported. The man is dead."

"Who reported the accident?" Lillian hoped that Simon had been the person who called the ranger's office. She also wanted to know more of the details.

Jeff did not answer her question but continued on his way. He stopped and turned to face her when he heard her next question.

"Would it be possible for us to accompany you?"

"No, ma'am. I don't think it's a good idea for a lady to see the damage. Even though I hope it was an accident, from what I saw, there may be another cause for the wreck. It may be too much for you. Dead body and all."

"I've seen dead bodies – even some who've been savagely murdered."

Jeff's puzzled expression let her know she needed to explain.

"You see, we – my husband and I – could help you determine whether it is a homicide. And we might be able to help find the murderer."

"And why do you think you're qualified to help? Death is not fun and games."

"I understand that. I've completed my coursework to be a private investigator. Also, my husband worked as an investigative journalist for more than thirty years. Both of us are very observant, and I promise we won't get in your way."

"That's right." Bill took Lillian's hand in his and gave it a gentle squeeze to acknowledge her reference to their being a team. "Besides, we've helped our son who is a sheriff in another county solve more than one death."

"I guess it'll depend on Sheriff Tomas. I never know what to expect from him. He's the moodiest law officer I know."

"If that's the case, I'm sure he'll say a big, fat no. The last time I talked to him, Sheriff Tomas made it clear that he doesn't care about a woman getting in his business," Lillian snapped.

"When was that?" Jeff asked.

"When a camper found a dead body on the jogging trail. Remember?"

Jeff stood perfectly still. It was obvious to Lillian that he remembered her encounter with the sheriff when he laughed and said, "I remember he tried to dismiss you when he asked me to herd all of the campers into the Pavilion."

"That's right," Lillian smiled.

"You're the first person I've seen who didn't back down from the bully. I admired your spunk."

"Will you ask him if we can ride with you?" Bill asked.

"Come to think of it, I'm the Park Ranger, and the accident happened in a state park, so I can determine who's in or out of my patrol boat."

"So?" Lillian said.

"You can come," Jeff said.

Chapter Twenty-Seven

IT TOOK all of Lillian's self-control to keep calm. She wanted to grab Jeff and give him a hug. Instead, she shook his hand.

"Wait here. I'm going to talk with Al, let him know about the accident," Jeff said.

Lillian watched the ranger walk to the camp's office. "Bill, we'd better hurry if we want to be ready by the time he returns. It won't take Jeff long to alert Al."

"You're right." He dumped the fish swimming around in his Styrofoam cooler into the lake. "We'll meet again, boys," he promised. "Until then, swim your little hearts out."

They grabbed their gear and with Eli hurried to their RV. Lillian packed a quick snack for everyone, and Bill added bottled water to the small, insulated bag. They grabbed raincoats, hats, and sunglasses, ready for any kind of weather. Lillian left the RV before Bill.

"Let's wait here for Jeff and Al. I see them walking this way."

Lillian heard tires crunching on gravel. "That must be Sheriff Tomas and the medical examiner."

"There's more than just the two men," Bill said. "But they're too far away for me to tell whether the third man is with the sheriff or the M.E."

Al and Jeff stopped and waited for the men to catch up. The medical examiner motioned to the younger man, who walked behind the van and retrieved a bag.

"Must be the medical examiner's assistant," Bill said.

"No. Look again. Don't you recognize that walk?"

Eli abandoned them and ran to greet the young man. Barking and yelping, he jumped up and tried to hug the officer who removed the dog's paws from the front of his shirt, then squatted and ruffled the fur on the dog's back.

"It can't be."

"But it is," Lillian dropped the insulated bag holding their snacks and ran to greet the tall, athletically-built man with salt and pepper hair who wore a deputy's uniform. He saw her running toward him and handed the bag to Patrick Lawrence, the M.E.

When they reached each other, he grabbed Lillian and swung her around in a circle. "Man-oh-man, am I happy to see you," he said.

"Not as thrilled as I am to have you here," Lillian kissed him on the cheek. "I've been worried about you, Son, especially after all you went through at Leisure Lake."

Al stood off to the side of the group. "That woman can't help but interfere," he mumbled. "And she called him 'son'?"

Lillian heard him and gave him a stern look. Al turned away.

"What a coincidence," Bill joined the group and hugged Grant after Lillian turned him loose.

"No such thing," Grant winked at Lillian. "You know she'll correct you if I don't."

Bill laughed. "You're so right. No such thing. So, you're working with Sheriff Tomas? You've been this close and didn't let us know?"

"I came out of hiding exactly three days ago and applied for the deputy position that had just opened. Besides, when you left Leisure Lake, you didn't let me know your first stop would be Caddo."

"*Touché.*" Bill laughed.

"And with all that's been happening out this way, I'm sure glad he came on the force. His homicide experience outranks mine." Sheriff Tomas looked from one to the other with a puzzled expression. "Tell me something – how do you folks know each other?"

"It's a story for later, sir," Grant said.

"Yeah, we need to get moving. The day's not getting any longer," Jeff said.

The group turned and walked out to the pier where the patrol boat waited. Al followed behind. Again, Lillian heard him mutter, "Didn't know this was gonna be a damned family reunion."

She couldn't resist Al's grumbling.

"Family? You are so right. That may be the smartest thing I've heard you say."

* * * * *

Jeff drove the patrol boat. As park ranger, he knew the location of cypress stumps that dotted the underbelly of Caddo Lake and deftly guided the boat through one lily-pad bayou and out the next maze of bayous. At first, Lillian tried to memorize the route Jeff took, but soon, she became completely disoriented, so she left the cabin and took one of the open-air passenger seats. She sat beside Bill and listened to their conversation.

The boat eased past a group of water lilies. Lillian recognized the passage to Richard's cottage. It was well protected, almost out of sight. She smiled, remembering their encounter. She mentally corrected herself. Simon. She still had questions for the man with whom she felt an ill-defined, common destiny.

"That's unusual," Bill said.

"What?" Lillian perked up, looked across the lake, and saw only the sun glinting off the waves.

"See?" Bill pointed to a white owl flying away from them and into the thick foliage along the side of the lake.

Without thinking, Lillian responded, "That's just ole Charlie, my dear." She pressed her lips into a straight line, knowing Bill would want to know why she called the bird by name.

Bill opened his mouth to speak, but Jeff saved Lillian when he slowed the boat and pointed. "There it is," he said loudly enough for everyone to hear. Near an abandoned, dilapidated dock, the blue and white Bayliner pleasure boat lay straddled across a cypress stump, its bottom ripped open.

Only the bald top of the stump speared through the fiberglass kept it above the water. The gap caused by the collision began behind the driver's seat and stopped just short of the boat's motor. Jeff cut back the patrol boat's engines and circled around the end of the half-submerged boat. He stayed far enough away from the cypress stump to protect his boat and glided close to the other side of the crumbling dock.

"Sheriff, grab that rope and see if the dock is sturdy enough to tie up."

The sheriff nodded.

"We need to keep everything as still as possible so we can climb over the side and retrieve the body." Jeff tried to steady the boat.

"I understand."

The sheriff reached as far as he could. "Can you get a little closer? If I lean any further, I'll go overboard."

Jeff maneuvered closer. "How's that?"

"Better." The sheriff tied the boat to the dock. "Got it," he said.

"Good. Al, stand by these controls. If the wood crumbles, and I expect it will, move the boat away from the dock." Jeff climbed out of the boat and tentatively tested the dock. It held his weight.

"Don't worry," Al said.

Grant stood. "Wait, Jeff. Let me. You're the captain. Stay put on your boat."

"Yeah, Grant's right." Lillian felt the sting of Al's glare but ignored it.

Jeff nodded and said, "Thanks, anyway, Al. Be ready to take over when I help Grant move the body."

Al moved aside for Jeff.

Grant removed his gun, badge, and shoes and walked to the edge of the boat. He had one leg over the edge and stopped. "Patrick, I'll take pictures for you."

"Good. I'll put the camera in a plastic zip bag to keep it dry." He opened his black bag and pulled out a large, gallon-sized bag, secured the digital camera in it, and handed the bag to Grant.

"Be careful, son" Lillian said. "Don't fall between the dock and the boat."

"Don't worry," Grant responded.

He held the edge of the bag with his front teeth and gingerly stepped out of the patrol boat. He crossed the dock in two steps and tested the stability of the wreck. When Grant put his weight on the boat, it held securely to the stump that curved toward the bow of the wreck. He surveyed the scene. He opened the bag, removed the camera, stuffed the empty bag in his shirt pocket, and focused the camera.

Lillian heard the camera click several times.

"Can you get on the other side of the bow and take a couple of photos from that angle?" Dr. Lawrence asked.

"Sure." Grant scooted around the bow. The boat groaned and shifted from his weight, so Grant raised up on his knees and waited for the boat to settle. From that angle, he could see the man's throat.

"This was no accident," he said.

"What makes you think that?" Sheriff Tomas asked.

"There's a wire around the victim's neck." He snapped several shots and crawled toward the body. "I'll get some shots of the inside of the boat, and then I think we ought to figure out how to remove this guy. Can someone toss me a knife?"

"What's the problem?" Sheriff Tomas asked and then reached in his pocket. He tossed his Swiss Army knife to Grant.

"His hands. Someone fastened them to the steering with zip ties. I bet this boat was going full speed when it hit the stump."

"Here, Al, take over, will you?" Jeff climbed over the side of the boat to check out the scene for himself.

"Be careful, Grant," Lillian said. "Don't slip."

Bill put his arm around her shoulder and patted it. "Always the helicopter mom. He's a big boy, my dear. He'll be okay." He leaned over and kissed the top of her head.

"Look at Eli. He's not worried."

Eli was on guard. Lillian whispered to Bill, "He's definitely not worried about Grant, but notice at whom he's staring."

Bill whispered back. "I tend to agree with him and you."

Lillian nodded toward Grant. "He may need your help."

Bill inclined his head toward Al.

Lillian understood the gesture. "Don't worry, I'll watch him."

Bill leaned out of the boat, took the camera from Grant, and handed it to Patrick who put it in his black bag.

"Grant, how difficult do you think it will be to move the body?" Sheriff Tomas asked.

"He's a big man. It might take all of us."

Patrick cautioned, "Don't try to lift him. I have a fold-up stretcher in my bag. It'll take only a second to pop it open."

Lillian stepped to Patrick and took one end of the contraption and held it while he snapped the handles on it. "Hurry," she instructed.

Sheriff Tomas patted Patrick on the back, and said in a low voice. "Better you than me. I've been there."

"You don't know anything," Bill chuckled. "I live with her."

"When you guys quit chastising my mom, I'd appreciate your help," Grant said. "I'm beginning to feel more than a little soggy." Grant had moved behind the body.

The boat was breaking apart and slowly sinking deeper in its shallow grave.

Concerned about Grant, Lillian forgot all about Al and watched the rescue efforts.

Grant gripped the man beneath his shoulders and pulled. Jeff grabbed the man's ankles. The two men moved slowly and carefully to the edge of the wrecked boat. Jeff and Grant, in sync with each other, lifted the body onto the stretcher. Holding onto the ends of the stretcher, they inched their way across the dock and lined up to lower the corpse to Tomas and Bill. The wood holding the patrol boat to the dock snapped, and the boat drifted away from the dock.

Absorbed in the rescue, Lillian ignored Eli's warning bark.

"Damn it, Al. Keep that boat steady," yelled Sheriff Tomas.

Lillian turned around to yell at Al, but he was nowhere in sight. She ran to the boat's controls and steered it closer to the dock and the men with the corpse.

"That's far enough, Lillian," Grant yelled. "Hold it there."

Five minutes later, the rescuers were back on board. Grant, who had stood in the water, grabbed a towel to dry his legs, then removed the blood-sucking leeches from his ankles.

The medical examiner opened the cover he had placed over the body.

Lillian gasped.

Bill stood beside her. He, too, looked at the corpse. "Oh my God."

"Do you know him?" Sheriff Tomas asked.

"That's Russell Stokes from the camp," Lillian said.

Chapter Twenty-Eight

JEFF STARTED the engine and eased away from the abandoned, rotting dock and skewered Bayliner. "I'll get some help and come back out tomorrow morning to remove the wreckage."

"We'll need to impound it until the investigation is over." Sheriff Tomas scanned the area, lowered his voice, and directed it to the park ranger. "That's not all we'll need to impound tomorrow."

Jeff gave a brief nod. "Got it. Call me. I'll go with you."

Lillian stood at the side of the boat and scanned the water for Al.

"Wait," yelled Lillian. "We need to find Al."

Both Jeff and Tomas ignored her and continued talking.

Lillian strained to hear the conversation between the two authorities who stood elbow to elbow in the cabin. The volume of the boat's twin engines drowned out their voices.

She joined Bill and Grant on the wide bench at the back of the boat.

The sheriff followed her and sat down beside Lillian.

Lillian looked at him and said, "Can you explain why we're not looking for Al?"

"Ma'am, he knows this lake like the back of his hand. He'll be okay. I guarantee it."

"Why in the world would he run away? And where could he possibly go to find shelter?"

"Beats me. Don't worry about him," Sheriff Tomas looked out over the water.

Grant sat by Bill. He leaned forward, propped his elbows on his knees. "If you don't mind, Sheriff, let me talk to my parents."

Tomas raised both brows. His black eyes widened. "Your parents? Is this the 'Lillian' you talked so much about when you took my class at Sam Houston?"

Lillian saw the twinkle in his eyes.

"The lady who liked to meddle into police business?"

"Yes, remember I told you she and her husband took me in when my parents were killed in an accident."

The sheriff nodded. "That explains it."

"The way you two are talking about me, I guess you've forgotten I'm right here. I can hear you." Lillian looked from one to the other. "'Explains it, you say?" She smiled at the sheriff for the first time.

The sheriff returned a lop-sided grin. "That feeling of *déjà vu* every time I'm around you."

"I wondered when it would hit you," she said. "I didn't remember you right away when you first appeared after Leigh

Ann found the body on the trail, but after thinking about it, I recalled Grant talked about a Professor Tomas."

They shook hands.

"Still, I'm worried about Al. We need to do something."

The sheriff's voice had left its edge.

"Like I said, ma'am, don't worry about him. Did you happen to see the abandoned cabin up on the hill. I'm sure that's where Al ran off to."

"But what if he doesn't come back to the campground today?"

"Then, I'll personally look for him first thing tomorrow."

"Okay, but let me know if you find him."

The sheriff did not acknowledge her request.

Lillian shrugged and scooted to the edge of the bench and leaned out so she could make eye contact with Grant. "We watched everyone leave this morning, and after the self-imposed evacuation, we noticed Stovall's RV was still parked at the end of the lane. I wondered about him. Now we know why it's still there."

"I'm sorry you've lost another friend," Grant said.

"Friend? Heavens no, he was a --" Lillian looked sadly at the cover protecting the corpse. "I hate to speak ill of the dead, especially when they are within hearing distance."

An alligator slid off the bank into the lake. His splash left a small ripple of waves as he glided through the water. Inspired by the reptile's wake, Lillian ducked her head and brushed away a crocodile tear.

"But I'm sure he will be missed."

The sheriff cleared his throat. "Ma'am, we'd appreciate any information you can give us. It may help." He patted her hand. She did not jerk it away.

"I'll do everything I can to help, but right now, I need time to think. May I talk to you tomorrow?"

"Yes ma'am, I understand." He motioned with a tilt of his head. "Situation like this. Stressful, to say the least."

"Thank you, sir." She batted her eyes like a damsel in distress.

Grant and the sheriff exchanged looks.

Shock. Grief.

Exactly what Lillian wanted them to think. Bill stared straight ahead.

The medical examiner interrupted her smug thoughts. "I don't seem to be able to find my camera." He dug through his large bag.

"What's that?" Grant frowned. "I know I handed it to you."

"Yes, you did. I've put it somewhere with all this gear. I'm sure I'll find it."

Lillian doubted it, sure that it went overboard along with Al. As much as she distrusted the man, Lillian hoped Al made it to solid ground.

"Maybe I put it with the body." Dr. Lawrence pulled back the cover hiding the body of Russell Stokes. He felt the man's shirt pocket. "There's something here, Deputy." He handed the objects to Grant.

Grant motioned for the sheriff to join him. "Patrick found something strange in the man's shirt pocket."

"Same M.O," said the sheriff.

From her seat, Lillian overheard their conversation, stood, and joined the two officers. "Let me guess," she said, "a note and a domino."

Grant squinted his eyes. "You're good, but not that good. That information is confidential. We'll talk later."

Sheriff Tomas turned to Bill and pointed to Lillian and then to Bill. "Keep her with you – if you can." He stepped over the body and walked to the boat's cockpit.

Bill stood, took her by the arm, and led her back to the bench. "Hit a nerve, didn't you?" He gave her a thumb's up.

She smiled and tilted her chin. "Keep them guessing is my motto."

Jeff increased the boat's speed. "Let's get home."

"What about Al?" Patrick asked.

Lillian appreciated Patrick's appeal on behalf of Al, but not Jeff's response.

"What about him?" Jeff sneered and turned the boat in the direction of the open lake and the marina.

"Shouldn't we look for him?"

Jeff made no response.

Sheriff Tomas said, "He'll show up soon enough."

Grant shook his head and sat down. "Strange."

"In more ways than one," Lillian said.

"It's as though they know where he went and don't care to find him." Grant's voice had a hard edge to it. "Doesn't make any sense. Why would he run?"

"Good question," Lillian said, "and a challenge for you and me."

Grant frowned.

Before he could caution her, Lillian added, "I have more puzzles for you. Dinner tonight around six o'clock at the lodge?"

Grant barely moved his lips. "Ten-four."

Chapter Twenty-Nine

FIVE O'CLOCK Sunday afternoon. Refreshed and energized by a hot shower, attired in a long-sleeve turquoise tunic over purple slacks, Lillian walked out of the bedroom of their RV. The lilac headband she wore failed miserably in its attempt to corral her long, unruly, wet hair. The silver bracelets on her wrist jangled as she removed the headband and pulled her hair back and fastened it in place with a large silver and turquoise beret. She opened the refrigerator and half-filled her glass with crushed ice. She added one jigger of Scotch and doused it with water.

"You look beautiful," Bill said as he passed her on his way to clean up before their rendezvous with Grant at the lake's prestigious lodge, renowned for its fried catfish dinners and fresh, crisp salad bar.

While her new crime-solving partner did his ablution, Lillian picked up her black notebook covered with pink and white polka dots. She turned the pages slowly and scanned her notes. Her last two entries involved the two men at the center of her thoughts: Russell Stokes and Al Gruene. One was a homicide, and the other more than likely dead.

She had read newspaper reports about the mysterious disappearances of more than one person who braved the haunted bayous of Caddo Lake. The image of the alligator gliding through the water flashed through her mind. Lillian shivered. What if Simon had not seen her desperate attempt to swim? She sipped her drink.

Lillian heard Bill turn the water faucets off and the click of the door indicating he was out of the shower. She poured a bourbon and water over ice for him and placed it on the dinette table.

"You smell clean," she said as he entered the kitchen and sat across from her.

"Yeah, felt good to get rid of the stench of swamp water. Thanks for the drink." He picked up the glass, took a sip, and announced. "Perfect."

"I've been reading my notes."

"May I?" Bill asked.

Lillian turned the notebook around and pushed it across the table. "Pay particular attention to the last two items."

He read them and looked up. "Interesting, especially the one about the possibility of Al and Russell being together just before Vickie Parsons disrupted everyone's evening."

"I didn't believe her story about the mouse, did you?"

He chuckled. "It's so corny, it might be true."

"Be that as it may, both of us need new cell phones. Let's drive into Jefferson tomorrow for replacements."

"Good idea. We can sightsee while we're there." He glanced at his watch. "Time to go."

Lillian grabbed her shoulder bag and slipped her notebook in its side pocket.

* * * * * *

Grant, too, had showered and changed out of his soggy uniform. He wore a plain, navy T-shirt, tight enough to show off his six-pack abs. A black leather belt sporting a large silver medallion buckle cinched his jeans. Custom-made, black ostrich skin Justin cowboy boots and a white Stetson completed the romantic stereotype of a handsome, rugged Texan. He parked his Ford F150 in front of the lodge and scanned the parking lot for Bill's SUV.

Ignoring the stares of the drooling waitresses as he entered the lodge, Grant swaggered to the circular booth in the far corner of the restaurant. From where he sat, back against the wall, he faced the front of the building and could see the door and other diners seated around rustic tables.

Grant watched the young girls standing behind the counter flip a coin to determine who would win the honor of waiting his table. He chuckled to himself.

The bell over the door jingled signaling new arrivals. Lillian and Bill waved at him and weaved their way past the tables to the booth. He stood and allowed Lillian to slide into the booth, then hugged her to him and planted a kiss on the side of her head just above her ear. He reached across the table and shook hands with Bill.

"What a day," he said.

"Yep, you can say that again," Bill said, "but I'm more interested in how you ended up in Marion County. I expected you to be in Colorado by now."

"I won't be here long. Sheriff Tomas hired me on a temporary basis to help him. The recent events have completely stymied him."

"I don't care how you got here, I'm glad to see you, my dear boy," Lillian patted him on the arm. "I think I can say the same for Eli."

Grant laughed. "He nearly knocked me down when he saw me."

"That, my son, is unconditional love – much like your mother's." Bill reached over and touched Lillian's hand. "I have to admit she will enjoy our trip more being with you."

"I hope your broken heart has healed," Lillian said. Her eyes emphasized her love for the young man she had raised.

Grant changed the subject.

"Have you talked to Jake lately?" Grant asked about Lillian's biological son, a county sheriff. He and Grant were more than friends. They considered themselves brothers and had worked closely together solving the murders at Leisure Lake, the deep East Texas gated community Lillian and Bill called home.

"As a matter of fact, we haven't," Bill said. "With all of the --" Bill paused. The winner of the coin toss stood at his elbow, ready to take their orders.

"Do you need more time to look at the menus?" She directed the question and her gaze at Grant.

"We've heard fried catfish is your specialty," Lillian said, "so I'll take the small catch with coleslaw and green beans." She was amused at the young waitress who nodded, still gazing at Grant. "Oh, I almost forgot. May I order extra hush puppies?"

"What would you like to drink?" The waitress asked Grant.

He smiled at her and pointed to Lillian.

"Oh, yes ma'am, you want a small catch platter with green beans and coleslaw."

"Thank you" Lillian kept a straight face. "And iced tea, please."

The young girl looked at Bill. "And you, sir?"

"Same thing she's having," he said.

"Me, too. We'll make it easy on you," Grant said. He watched the teenage waitress turn away from the table. She wore a typical restaurant uniform, khaki walking shorts and a golf shirt sporting the name of the Lodge. She exaggerated the sway of her hips on her way to the kitchen to place their order.

"I think you have a new admirer, Son," Bill said.

"More like a predatory black spider, if you ask me. Be careful. I've seen teenage girls ruin a man's career."

"Don't worry, Mom. I'm not in the market right now."

"You will be some day, believe me," Lillian bumped shoulders with him, "but right now, we need to discuss the events at Caddo Lake."

"I agree."

She reached into the side pocket of her handbag and pulled out her notebook. "Here. I want you to read my notes before we talk."

The waitress arrived with their drinks and a basket filled with butter and hush puppies. Grant held the book out of sight beneath the table and waited for her to leave before he opened it. He puffed out his cheeks while he perused Lillian's observations. He closed the book, looked up, and whistled softly.

"Things have been happening so fast, I've not had time to make new entries."

"There's more?"

Lillian didn't respond.

The waitress arrived with their food and placed their orders on the table. "Will there be anything else?"

"No, thank you. We're good," Bill turned his attention to the plate before him. "Let's eat and then reconvene at our RV to talk."

"Yes, we can't have much privacy with Grant's peanut gallery watching every move he makes." Lillian laughed.

"The reviews are right, my dear. This is the best catfish I've ever tasted."

Grant swallowed his first bite. "Yep, they are. I suggest I come by tomorrow. We'll have more time to discuss the situation. Does it matter what time I come?"

"Anytime is fine." Lillian put her notebook back into her purse and continued eating.

Chapter Thirty

DARKNESS. NIGHT sky sans stars or moon. Heavy, dense clouds hovered over Caddo Lake. The beams of light from the SUV's halogen headlamps revealed tendrils of Spanish moss dangling from tree limbs. Like calypso dancers, they swayed to the beat of a silent tune as the gentle night breeze waltzed over and through the limbs of the ancient oaks, guardians of each side of the road. No light emanated from the sign over the entrance to the RV park. To Lillian, it resembled an ominous, dark orifice ready to devour all who entered. She felt Bill tense. He eased the SUV through the gate. Lillian reached down and retrieved her revolver from beneath the passenger seat.

"Don't forget your gun, Bill. We might need our weapons before this night ends." For the first time on their trip, Lillian felt isolated. No cell phone. She made a mental note to get new cells and new laptops when they visited Jefferson the next day.

"Ain't that the truth," Bill said light-heartedly, but Lillian detected the tension in his voice. He retrieved his nine millimeter from the side panel of the SUV's door.

He drove slowly by the camp director's office – dark – and by the mobile home where Al and Milly resided – dark – and into the campground – no security lights, no light from RV windows.

Silence. Then Lillian heard an eerie howl followed by Eli's angry barks. "Hurry, Bill, let's get inside. I hear Eli. He needs company."

Bill accelerated and honked the vehicle's horn.

"Why are you honking?"

"Scare away the bad guys." Bill said lightheartedly. "Beats whistling every time."

Lillian laughed at him. "Thanks. You do know how to calm a girl's nerves."

Bill slammed on his brakes.

Lillian peered through the windshield and saw two golden eyes gleaming, staring at them. "What is that?" The creature turned, ran into the woods.

"Beats me," Bill said and drove the next few feet to their camper and parked close to the front door. He hopped out and hurried to the passenger door. "Allow me." He offered his hand to Lillian.

"Thank you, kind sir." She took his hand and climbed out of the car. She reached the door of the RV and paused. Eli continued to bark and claw at the door.

"What's wrong?" Bill took her elbow.

"A creepy feeling just crawled all over me. Someone's watching us. Hurry. Get inside." Lillian opened the door and entered. She grabbed Eli to keep him from darting out the door. "Quick. Lock it, Bill."

* * * * * *

Typical East Texas weather, Lillian thought as she blinked. Once more Mother Nature provided a beautiful sunrise. A red Cardinal perched on the green cover that protected the cable and electricity hookups. His happy chirps promised a new day. Fresh coffee, the sizzle of bacon, and the happy tune her husband whistled filled Lillian with hope. She said a silent prayer of thanks for all of God's creation before she started her day.

The morning air was cool, so she chose her tight, black yoga pants, white and maroon Texas A & M long-sleeve T-shirt. Dressed, she joined her husband.

Bill stopped mid-note and kissed his wife. "Sleep well?"

"I did. Better than I thought I would."

"Me, too. I have to admit yesterday was full of surprises. I was exhausted."

"Some of those I could have done without." Lillian poured a cup of coffee. The opened door of the RV allowed the crisp autumn air to filter through the RV.

Lillian looked at the lake. "It's foggy. Looks like steam rising from the Lake."

"That's a sure sign of cooler weather," Bill said. "Here. Take this." He handed her a plate with three strips of bacon and a blueberry bagel.

"Looks delicious. Thanks." She sat down at the table. "Where's Eli? He usually wakes me up."

"He wanted to go outside an hour ago and hasn't returned. He'll wander back home when he's ready."

As if on cue, Eli barked. He bounded up the steps and into the opened door, and then just as quickly, he turned and ran outside. Lillian heard the low rumble of a vehicle's motor and the crunch of gravel as an automobile neared their RV. Grant stepped out of his Ford F150. "Hey, boy. How's it going?" Footsteps approached.

Grant knocked gently on the door's frame. "May I join you?"

"Of course. You're just in time for breakfast," Bill aid.

"Just coffee, please. You folks might have the luxury of sleeping in, but some of us have been on the job for the past two hours." He bent over and kissed the top of Lillian's head and then pulled back a chair sat across from her. "Been trying to call you this morning. Your cell battery must be down."

"Could be. Hard to keep cell phones charged when one rests at the bottom of the lake and the other is about as crisp as this." Bill put his plate and a platter of crisp bacon on the table and sat down to eat.

"How in the world?" Grant stopped. He grinned. "I'm sure you'll tell me all about it, so I won't ask. I know it's going to be an interesting story."

"More like a saga," Lillian said.

"I'm sure it is."

"You're out and about mighty early," Lillian said.

"Sheriff Tomas gave me permission to drive out here this morning to go over your notes. Do you have time now, or should

I come back later?" Grant reached over and took a slice of bacon from the platter in front of him.

"Hoped you would drop by early so we could get your input." Lillian handed Grant her notebook. "Think we can get something done without your admirers?" Lillian teased.

As Grant read, he underlined some items on the list and looked up when he finished. "Pretty thorough as always. After seeing this, I have more questions than input."

"That's okay. We can go over your questions, but first I want information about the note in Russell's shirt pocket. "Here's a pen. If you write it down, you won't have to tell Sheriff Tomas a lie. I know he doesn't want you to talk about it."

Grant took the pen and opened the book. Lillian watched him add the next number on her list and write:

#42. Double blank = nothing. Nothing = a nobody.

A nobody = A failure. Failure = death.

Beneath those lines, Grant drew a rectangle with a line dividing it in half. He said, "You were right about the domino, Lillian. There was a double blank in the man's pocket."

Grant turned the book around so Lillian and Bill could see his note. "Does this mean anything to you?"

"Not really, except that it seems to follow the theme of the first murder," Lillian said. "Did Sheriff Tomas fill you in on that one?"

Grant took another strip of bacon and big bite before he answered Lillian. "He showed me the first note. He's completely baffled, especially after this last murder with almost an identical M.O."

"Did he say anything about the truck explosion and the driver's body?"

"No, but everyone knows about it by now. It's been on all the television news stations. Besides, it's out of his hands. The Feds have taken it over."

Grant reached across the space between the dinette and the kitchen counter for the coffee pot. He poured himself another cup. He glanced back down at the notebook and with his index finger pointed to number five on the page. "You made note of it on your list."

"Yes, I did." She held her empty cup in the air. Grant replenished it.

"What do you think? Could all these deaths somehow be connected?" Bill looked at the notebook and then at Grant. "Personally, I don't see how they could."

"I trust Lillian's intuition. If her gut tells her there's a connection, I believe it, too." Grant continued. "Tell me your opinion about a connection, Ms. Private Detective."

"Whoa," Bill interrupted, "You knew about her plans?"

Grant laughed. "Mom and I share all our secrets, don't we?"

"Most of them," Lillian patted Bill's shoulder. "Don't get riled again, partner."

Bill looked at the ceiling, sighed, shook his head. "Continue, my dear. Explain."

The low hum of a second vehicle's engine entering the campsite diverted Lillian's attention. She stood and walked to the door. A green Ford pickup parked in front of the camp director's mobile home. "I wonder where she's been?" Lillian said.

Grant's cell vibrated. "Hello?" He listened to the caller and squeezed past Lillian.

"Gotta go." He ran to his truck.

"Trouble?" Lillian yelled to his back.

"Problem at a grocery store." He jumped into his truck, made a U-turn, and drove toward the exit.

Lillian grabbed her purse.

"Where do you think you're going?" Bill asked.

"Edgemon's. Make sure Brandon is okay."

"No, you're not. Brandon doesn't need you to help him make a routine call."

"But –"

"We'll stop by there on our way back home, but we need to take care of our business first."

"You're right."

Chapter Thirty-One

LILLIAN STOOD at the door for a few minutes and watched Grant's truck travel through the park's gated archway and turn right. She let Eli outside. "Don't go too far, Eli. We're taking a daytrip, first Jefferson and then Edgemon's Gas & Grocery." She turned to face Bill. He was staring at a page in Lillian's notebook.

"I don't see any connection between murder and dominoes," he said.

Lillian looked over his shoulder and studied Grant's scribbling. "Hatred, greed, resentment, jealousy. Maybe, the perpetrator is making a statement about his victims."

"Well, of course, he is. Both men camped here. Did they know each other before they came to Caddo? And if so, how?"

"Guess we'll find out soon enough with Grant on the case," Lillian said. She thought she knew the answer to his question but kept her thoughts to herself. She wanted to do a little more investigating before she divulged her theory about the dominoes. "I think our killer likes to play, the more dangerous the game, the more gratification he feels."

Bill made no response, so she continued. "Let's take Eli and drive into Jefferson. I don't want to spend another night without a cell phone. I need to powder my nose and brush my teeth before we leave." She went to the bedroom to add those final touches to her appearance.

She returned to the living room.

Her notebook was closed and Bill was not in the RV. Then she heard voices coming from outside. She joined Bill and Milly outside.

Milly was explaining her absence to Bill. "My mother fell and broke her hip. I have one sister. She and I have alternated weeks staying with her. We'd hate for her to be alone, afraid she might have another fall. I've been with her all week, left the day after that horrible explosion."

"Sorry to hear about your mother," Bill said.

"If there's anything we can do to help, please let us know," Lillian said.

"You are so kind," Milly said. "Thank you."

"What's your mother's name?" Lillian asked. "I'll send her a card. It helps to know people care."

Milly wiped away a tear. "Yes, it does. Her last name is Horton. But there's something else you can do to help me."

"You name it," Bill said.

"It's Al," Milly blinked back another tear. "Have you seen him?"

"Not since yesterday afternoon," Lillian said and felt for Bill's hand. He took it and gave it a gentle squeeze.

Milly clasped her hands together, fingers crisscrossed, released them, and let her arms hang at her side. "It's not like him to leave without letting me know his whereabouts." She waved one arm toward the campsite. "Where are all the RVs? I know it's rained, but the weather has never caused the camp to be this empty."

"Didn't Al tell you about the murder or the lightning striking a tree?" Bill asked.

Milly paled. "Heavens, no. Was anyone hurt?"

Lillian thought about saying "yeah, murder tends to hurt a body" but decided not to be sarcastic. She waited a few seconds to give the woman time to assimilate what Bill said.

"Only the Heavener lady's Casita." Lillian asked. "She wasn't in it at the time."

"Thank goodness for that."

Lillian let the more serious topic slide. She gave Milly another thirty-second wait time to comprehend Bill's earlier statement. She wanted to see if Milly would respond to his use of the word murder.

Nothing.

Milly was focused on her husband.

"You see, Al loves my mother and has called first thing every morning to check on Mom's condition."

"When was the last time you talked to him?" Lillian asked.

"Last night. He said he missed me and hoped I could come home soon. My sister arrived later last night and offered to stay with Mom all next week. I tried to call Al before I went to bed to let him know I'd see him early today. I knew he'd be happy to hear my good news," she paused, "but he didn't answer." Milly wrung her hands. "He left his cell phone on the kitchen table. He always has it with him." She paused again. "If you see him anywhere around the lake, would you tell him to contact me?"

"Doubt we'll see him today since we're going into Jefferson to sightsee," Bill said.

"Oh, I'm sure he'll surface sooner or later," Lillian reassured Milly.

"You're probably right. You folks go on and enjoy your vacation." With that last remark, Milly turned and walked to the office.

Bill opened the passenger door for Lillian. Eli hopped in first, climbed over the console, and took his usual place in the backseat right behind Lillian. He waited for her to fasten her seatbelt, then placed his head on her shoulder. Bill slid into the driver's seat and looked at his wife before starting the engine.

"You ought to be ashamed of yourself."

She stared straight ahead, chin slightly titled.

Eli walked across the back seat, put his black nose next to Bill's ear, and snorted.

"There," Lillian said. She looked back and gave her beloved Poodle a thumb's up. "Glad you've got my back, Eli."

Silence.

Bill looked in his rearview mirror and glared at the dog, then started the engine, drove under the gate's arch, and turned onto the highway.

* * * * * *

Simon moored his Jon Boat to the end of the pier. The camp director's office was his destination, but he stopped at the Prestridge RV. "Knew you wouldn't let storms or murder drive you away." He opened the door and entered. He picked up the last piece of bacon and half a bagel and walked through the RV.

"Interesting," he said as he left Lillian's RV and walked down the lane to the camp director's office.

Simon was still munching the bagel when he opened the camp director's door. Milly looked up and then continued her search, rummaging through Al's desk drawers.

"Found his list of recruits yet?" he asked.

"Nothing. It's like he cleaned everything out before he gallivanted off."

"He didn't get far." Simon leveled his gaze.

Milly gazed back at him and then muttered, "Good riddance."

Simon nodded. "My sentiments exactly."

"We'll keep looking. It's got to be here somewhere." Milly opened a file drawer and continued her search.

Simon returned to his boat and pushed away from the marina. He smiled when he rounded a bend and saw his talisman perched on the limb of a cypress tree.

"Hello, Charlie," and then more seriously, he muttered, "Guess I'll troll down to the Lodge. Promised to meet him for lunch. He's going to be disappointed if I don't show up."

Chapter Thirty-Two

BILL DROVE past the city limit sign for Karnack, Texas, a small historic town between the lake and Marshall. Lillian broke the silence. "You took a wrong turn. We're headed south. Jefferson is north."

"No, I wanted to come this way. We need a day away from Caddo. Let's see what we can find in the surrounding area."

"Fine with me. Isn't Karnack the childhood home of Lady Bird Johnson?"

"Think so," Bill said, "And right after Pearl Harbor, Lady Bird's husband, a young senator at the time, convinced Congress to approve the establishment of the Longhorn Ammunition Plant."

"Why do you suppose he wanted it so close to his wife's hometown?"

"Look around. What do you see?"

"A rural, isolated, remote little community. Perfect spot for the plant, I guess."

"You want to drive through it?" Bill asked. "I've been told Karnack is also home to several bed and breakfasts."

"Let's wait and do that another day. I'm anxious to get a cell phone. If we can't find a good buy on a laptop, I guess we can share yours."

"Sure, I'll share my computer, but I need my own phone. Like, you, I depend on my cell. Besides, it's less than twenty miles or so to Jefferson. We should have plenty of time on our way home if we decide to veer off the main highway."

Bill pulled into a driveway and backed up to turn around. He slammed on his brakes to avoid hitting an Army jeep as it sped down the road.

Lillian got a quick glance at the driver and wondered why he would be in such a hurry. As Bill pulled back onto the road, she peered through the side mirror on her side of the SUV. The jeep entered the ammunition plant's parking lot.

* * * * *

Two hours later, they walked out of the Jefferson Walmart with two new iPhones, fully charged and a new laptop for Lillian. Bill asked, "Do you know how to load Microsoft Office or should we find a computer geek to do it for you?"

Lillian looked askance at him. "What a silly question. Of course, I do. Don't you?"

Bill pointed in the direction of their SUV. "That goofy dog of yours." He laughed. "I never know what to expect from him."

"He's just playing dog." Lillian laughed when she saw Eli. He had jumped over the back of the driver's seat and stood with his back paws on the bottom of the steering wheel. His upper torso rose above the opened sunroof of their SUV. For balance, he had propped his front legs on the top of the vehicle and was barking in time with the car's alarm system.

Bill reached into his pocket and retrieved his key to end the incessant beeping.

"No telling how long he's serenaded the parking lot. Just listen to him," Bill said. "He'll do anything to get attention."

"Yes, he has managed to attract a crowd of rubberneckers with his loud barking. He must have been bored." The dog saw her coming and jumped down and into the back seat. She opened her door and climbed into the auto. "I see that innocent look, but I know you're guilty." He lowered his head at the sternness of Lillian's voice. She did not let him see the twinkle in his eye.

"Where to now?" her chauffeur aka husband wanted to know.

"Let's find a park, someplace where we can let Eli have a walk. He's been cooped up too long."

Bill slowly pulled out of the parking lot. "When we came into town and drove around, I saw a sign indicating a Lions Club Park. That might be a good place for Eli to romp around for awhile."

"That sounds great," said Lillian.

Bill turned on Polk and drove through town. He followed the signs to Lions Park and to the visitor parking area. He opened the back door for Eli, "Don't run off, ole boy. I might just leave you." The dog, eager to get out of the car, took off lickety-split. "Look at him go. He meets every adventure with enthusiasm, doesn't he?"

"That's why I love him so." Lillian walked around the car. "We might as well follow and try to keep him in sight."

"That's easy," said Bill pointing to the dog. Eli had flopped onto his back and rolled from one side to the other in the cool St. Augustine grass, all four legs waving in tandem with his body. "Real class right there." He smiled. "He is fun, though."

"Yep, what a sight. You could write a blog about that." Lillian suggested. She whistled for Eli. He ran to her and stayed in step with her as she and Bill strolled up the hill to enjoy a leisurely walk.

Thirty minutes later, Bill asked, "Are you hungry?"

"Yes. Let's get back in the car and find a good restaurant. Eli's had enough time stretching his legs. He'll be glad to rest while we search."

They passed the playground where a daddy pushed his red-haired daughter in a swing. He waved a greeting. Eli ran to the father and the little girl and ignored Bill's command to stop. The child squealed when she saw the dog racing to her. "Stop, Daddy. Let me pet the puppy."

The father complied but did not remove her from the swing. He stood in front of her.

Lillian whistled and called the dog. He made a U-turn before he reached the father and child and raced back to his master.

"Guess he thinks you're the only one he has to obey," Bill grumbled. "I think I'll walk over and apologize for that dog of yours and ask the man to recommend a good restaurant."

"No, leave them alone." She turned to Eli. "That man was afraid of you."

Eli looked at her with an innocent expression.

Lillian laughed.

"Come on. You had your fun. Let's go eat."

* * * * *

Bill drove through a neighborhood, past historic homes, many of which wore signs that designated them a bed and breakfast.

"Isn't the architecture unique on these homes? I wish I knew which one belonged to Brandon."

"Why?"

"He plans to convert it into a B&B someday."

"I see," Bill said as he turned left and entered the downtown area. "Let's park here." He stopped in the only remaining slot on the shady side of Polk Street, the main street dividing the town in half.

"Don't leave the sunroof open," Lillian laughed.

"Why?"

"I shudder to think what kind of entertainment shoppers might have from our dog."

"You mean from our Ham, don't you?"

Bill reached back and looked at Eli who was poised, ready for another adventure. "Okay, ole boy, you may walk with us."

They crossed the street and saw a mural on one side of an old brick building. "That looks good. Let's go there," suggested Lillian.

"Auntie Skinner's Riverboat Club," said Bill. "I read an article about it in one of the brochures I picked up at the lodge when we met Grant. It has a reputation for good food."

Farther down the sidewalk, several feet from the door, Lillian saw a low iron hook protruding from the brick. Above it a sign asked patrons to leave their dogs outside. The establishment provided a bowl filled with water for thirsty pets. The shadow of the building offered plenty of shade. Lillian attached Eli's leash. "Stay here. Wait."

The dog sat on his haunches and sniffed the air. After his behavior in the park, Lillian added, "Eli, leave people alone. Don't bark or try to intimidate them." He looked up with his big, black innocent eyes, lay down, snorted, and put his head on his front paws.

The interior of the restaurant was divided. One side sported a dark, carved mahogany bar with stools. A large mirror, reminiscent of a by-gone era, surrounded by shelves containing various bottles of whiskey, leered at the patrons perched on bar stools. Rustic tables and rough floors added to the ambiance and provided opportunity for visitors to enjoy a step back in time. Loud music came from the other side of the building, so Lillian did not attempt to carry on a conversation with Bill. Instead, she walked to the front window, peered out to check on Eli watching tourists pass by. On her return to the table, she picked up a tabloid that advertised historic sites in Jefferson.

"When we finish eating," she yelled at Bill, "let's walk around the block and visit the Excelsior House. It's supposed to have ghosts in the Diamond Bessie room. And there's a historic railcar across the street from it."

The moment Bill yelled his response, "I worked with a friend who used to play in the Jay Gould car," the music stopped.

His crimson face amused Lillian. "Huh? I didn't hear you," she turned her head to the side and winked at the couple seated at the next table. The waitress delivered their orders. Lillian forgot Bill's embarrassment, and they ate in silence.

Chapter Thirty-Three

LILLIAN AND Bill walked a block to the Excelsior House, Jefferson's most luxurious hotel. "Let's go inside and look at the guest register, Lillian."

"Is that the hotel where Jay Gould stayed when he visited here?"

"Yes, his signature is followed by his curse on the city."

"Curse. I think I've read enough of those lately," Lillian said. She grinned and then sarcastically commented, "He didn't leave a domino with it, I hope."

Bill shook his head. "Come on and be nice," he said and opened the door for her and Eli.

Lillian sighed and looked around the elegantly decorated lobby. "I think we ought to come here for a weekend, maybe our next anniversary."

"We'll do that before our next anniversary," Bill said. "How would you like to see a re-enactment of the Diamond Bessie Trial?"

"I'd love it. Let's stay in the room named after her."

"I'll see if we can get reservations for next April," Bill said and walked to the front desk.

While he made reservations for them, Lillian stood by the glass case containing the old registry. She looked at Jay Gould's signature followed by the words The End of Jefferson. The epitaph reminded her of the notes connected with the recent murders. She had read that the railroad magnate wanted to run his Erie Railroad line through the town. Had its citizens been willing to give up the steamboat trade, they and the town would not have suffered an economic decline.

While she could understand Gould's prediction, it was a puzzle to her why someone would leave a curse note, along with a domino, on the body of his victim. There had to be a connection, and she was determined to find it.

Bill walked up to her. "Sorry, my dear. They are booked the three nights in April and May when the play happens."

"Don't worry about it. We can stay in our RV." She walked out the front door, holding Eli's leash.

Bill followed. "You betcha," he said. "Let's go back down Polk to our car and then home."

"I'm ready. After all, we've done all we came to do," said Lillian. "Let's walk down the other side of the street so we can enjoy the architecture of the buildings across from us." She didn't wait for Bill to agree. Lillian, with Eli leading the way, proceeded.

Bill shrugged his shoulders. "Good idea," he said to her back, "but I'm not rushing. I want to take pictures." He retrieved the small digital camera he had put in his shirt pocket and stopped periodically to snap pictures of the buildings."

"Take your time," Lillian said over her shoulder. "Eli and I are in no hurry."

She and the dog passed the volunteer fire department and stopped in front of a coffee shop. When Bill caught up with them, she said, "You might want to take a picture of the fire department. Looks much different from those of today, don't you think?"

"Sure does. Modern buildings are strictly utilitarian. This one has character," Bill said. "Say, while I take some snapshots, why don't you go inside and get us a coffee to go?"

Lillian gave him Eli's leash. "Hold on to him. I'll be right back."

She entered the coffee shop, but before she could place an order, she heard a commotion outside – Eli, barking, growling loudly and Bill yelling angrily. She rushed back outside.

Struggling with the dog, Bill had dropped his camera. He held the leash in one hand to restrain Eli and stretched with his other arm to retrieve the camera.

"What in the world?" Lillian said as she took the leash from Bill. "Eli, settle down. What's wrong with you?"

The dog tugged on the leash in an effort to cross the street. Lillian jerked him back. "You'll get yourself run over." She scanned the sidewalk lining both sides of Polk. "There's nothing there to upset you."

Eli sat down and looked up.

Lillian followed his gaze.

Across the street stood a red-bricked building with a New Orleans style façade. French doors on the second floor opened to a balcony wrapped in black, ornate wrought iron. On both ends of the balcony, Boston ferns grew in blue/white ceramic pots. Two women and one man sat beneath a red and white striped umbrella at a patio table situated in the center of the balcony. The two women sat opposite each other.

The gentleman had his back to the street. One of the women had long, blonde hair which draped over her shoulders. The other was a brunette. Both women were focused on the gentleman who sat opposite them.

As he talked, he made dramatic hand gestures. Lillian thought she recognized him. She knew the women.

"Sit, Eli," Lillian said louder than she normally spoke to the dog. He obeyed her command.

"Hey, Lillian, come on up and join us." Vickie leaned over the balcony and waved to Bill and Lillian. "Bring your dog with you."

Lillian waved back. "How do we get there?"

"Go into my office. I'll call down and tell my secretary to send you up on the elevator."

* * * * *

Lillian, Bill, and Eli stepped out of the elevator into a sitting room. Its floors looked original to the structure. An Oriental rug covered wide oak planks. Turn-of-the-century, brocade-covered sofas flanked a fireplace on one side of the room, and a baby-grand stood on the other side.

Eli raced to the table. He suddenly stopped and waited for Lillian and Bill to catch up. Lillian approached the trio.

"Thanks for the invitation, Vickie. We don't want to intrude," Lillian said. She addressed the blonde. "Leigh Ann?"

"None other," said the blonde as she stood to hug Lillian and Bill.

"We're surprised," said Bill. "Couldn't figure out where you'd gone."

"When lightning struck that tree and it fell on my Casita, I decided I'd had enough of Caddo Lake. I called Vickie."

"She was sure-enough scared, so I emailed my friend here, and he made reservations for her." Vickie explained. "Oh, excuse me. Let me introduce my colleague. Franklin Ford, meet Lillian and Bill Prestridge."

Ford shook hands with both newcomers. "Glad to meet you." He offered his chair to Lillian and moved two more chairs from another table for Bill and himself.

"Thanks," Bill said. "Sure we aren't interrupting?"

"No," said Leigh Ann. "I was just telling Franklin and Vickie about how kind you were to me when I needed a friend at Caddo."

"Yes," said Franklin, "on our client's behalf, we want to thank you."

"No problem," Lillian said. "We're always glad to help our neighbors." She looked at Vickie. "We really did intend to drop by your office for that cup of coffee you promised."

"I'm glad I saw you when I did," said Vickie. "It's been a sunny day to visit Jefferson."

"Yes, we've had a good day. Bought new cell phones and a new laptop for Lillian," Bill said.

"The day's complete now. We know Leigh Ann is okay," Lillian said.

"She is that," said Franklin. "I'm glad I was here when she called Vickie."

His quick glance to Leigh Ann did not get past Lillian.

"Do you practice here in Jefferson, too?" Lillian smiled sweetly. She felt Bill's shoe tap her left foot but ignored his non-verbal warning.

"Oh, no," said Vickie.

Lillian noticed she was quick to explain. "Franklin lives in Dallas. He and I went to law school together. He's of counsel with my firm."

Franklin nodded in agreement but did not look at Lillian. He gazed at Leigh Ann.

"I guess I'm ignorant, but tell me, Franklin, exactly what does 'of counsel' mean?" Lillian asked to get him involved in the conversation.

He laughed. "It means I do everything that Vickie doesn't think a lady of her standing in the community ought to do."

"I bet you do it well," said Lillian.

"Yes, he does." Vickie laughed.

Franklin cleared his throat and reached for his glass, took a sip, looked down at the street, and then back at Lillian.

Leigh Ann patted the dog who had laid his head on her knee. Vickie, too, reached for her coffee cup. An awkward silence ensued. It was obvious to the older woman that she and Bill had indeed interrupted a confidential conversation.

"Bill, don't you think we need to get Eli home? I'm sure he'll enjoy a long walk around the lake before it gets dark."

"Yes, ma'am. He's been cooped up in our car far too long today." He stood and pulled back her chair. "Thanks for the brief rest." He laughed. "I needed it before I take that mutt for a walk."

To Lillian, the relief shown on the faces of the three was palpable. When she and Bill were back out on the street and out of earshot, she said, "And what kind of conspiracy are they hatching?"

"Conspiracy? Don't make quick judgments, my dear," Bill said and then added,
"Perhaps, you should ask yourself why does Leigh Ann need an attorney?" Bill said.

Lillian knew the answer to his question but said, "We'll find out sooner or later."

"That's the second time today, you've used that sooner or later phrase."

Lillian smiled, but once again, stared straight ahead. Then she said, "Yes, my dear, sooner than later you'll know why I used that phrase. And sooner or later, I'll know Brandon's relationship to Franklin. They look too much alike."

Bill opened the passenger door for his wife. When she and Eli were in, he closed the door and walked around to the driver's side. "Now that you mention it, they do resemble." He started the engine, waited for a car to pass, and pulled out into the street.

"But," Lillian muttered, "the real questions are: Why did Franklin look at Leigh Ann so adoringly? Why would Vickie call in another attorney, particularly the estranged husband, to help Leigh Ann file for divorce – if that's what she's doing? What exactly is Franklin's role in the conspiracy?"

"What's that?" asked Bill.

"Nothing. Just thinking out loud," said Lillian.

Bill laughed. "That's dangerous. I guess you have more notes to make?"

"How'd you guess?"

"I know you, my dear."

Bill reached for the volume control on the radio. "Let's groove on down the highway."

Chapter Thirty-Four

BILL AND Lillian were singing along to an old Peter, Paul and Mary folk song, "If I Had a Hammer." As they neared Caddo Lake, Lillian stopped singing and said, "Let's remember to stop at Edgemon's so I can pick up a few things."

"You mean check on Brandon." Bill slowed down and parked. There were only two gas pumps available. "I'll fill up while you go inside."

Yellow crime tape surrounded four of the gas pumps. "Why would a constable park his car and block the pumps?"

Lillian got out of the SUV and walked toward the store. In the middle of the crime tape lay a mangled, black Harley. She hurried to the scene, lifted a section of the tape, and bent over to pass under it. Lillian wanted to get a closer look at the bike.

"You can't do that," said a constable. He moved in front of her to block her entry.

She peeked around him and asked, "Is that a Harley?"

"It's hard to tell from its condition, but, yes, it was one."

"What happened?"

"I suggest you wait for an official statement from Sheriff Tomas."

"But I know a young man who works here. He rides a black Harley just like that one."

"I can't give you any information, ma'am." His voice softened.

Lillian knew he was sympathetic to her concern.

"Please, I've got to know what happened."

"It was a hit and run. That's all I can say."

Lillian looked back at the pump where Bill was parked and saw him talking to a man who held a sack of groceries. The last time she had seen the man, he acted like a jerk and threatened to run over Eli. Lillian was certain he was the culprit Brandon had tackled and dragged back to camp one evening. She would know him any day because of his shiny, black hair, prominent ears, and rude manners. She left the constable and rushed back to their SUV.

"Aren't you Guy Steiner?" she asked.

"Yes. Where's that mutt of yours?" He spoke with a New Jersey accent, but it was obvious to Lillian that it was fake because the last time they met, he had a Texas drawl.

As if to respond to his questionable pedigree status, Eli poked his head out of the SUV's window and growled. His owner decided to ignore Steiner's insult to her dog. "I thought you'd be long gone by now."

"I drove up to Jefferson to another RV camp, better than the last one. Nicer people, too," he said.

"Do you know anything about the situation here?"

"The store manager was so upset they had to take him by ambulance to ETMC in Marshall. He has a bad heart, you know."

Lillian silently counted to three and reminded herself to be patient.

"No, I don't know the manager. What about the bike? Can you tell me anything about the wreck?" Lillian held her breath waiting for an answer.

"The lady who checked me out said a young man who worked here was run down when he pulled up in front of the gas pump. All I know is that they had to care flight him into Marshall. He was hurt pretty bad."

Lillian gasped, "Brandon."

"Yeah, that's the one." Guy had to raise his voice to be heard.

Lillian was already in the SUV and had the motor running. Bill hopped into the passenger seat, and his wife roared out of the parking lot without checking traffic either right or left.

"Slow down, my dear," Bill warned. "We don't want to cause a wreck."

"Hush. I'm going to Marshall, find Brandon. He needs me."

"You don't even know where the hospital is located," Bill said.

"Put that new cell phone of yours to good use. Call Grant. He'll know."

"How do you know he would?"

"Remember? He had to leave us this morning because he received a call about a problem at a store."

"Oh, yeah, I forgot about that," Bill said.

"You're going to have to start concentrating more." Lillian shook her head. "Never mind, just tell him to meet us there."

Bill followed her instructions and scanned his contact list. "I don't have Grant's number."

"For crying out loud," she said disgustedly. "Grab my purse and find my phone."

"Calm down, my dear." He rummaged around in her purse. "Always on the bottom," he mumbled. He scanned the directory and chose Grant's number. He pressed the speaker button and laid the phone on the console between them.

"Hi, Lillian. You sound as though you're traveling," Grant said.

Lillian responded. "We're on our way to the hospital."

"What's wrong?" Grant's voice revealed his concern. "Is one of you hurt? Which hospital? I'll meet you at the ER."

"The hospital in Marshall. Need the address. That's why I'm calling you," Lillian said.

"I repeat. What's your emergency?"

"It's Brandon," Lillian said.

"Brandon Ford?"

"Yes. He's the young man who was hurt in an accident at Edgemon's."

"How do you know him?" Grant asked.

"I'll explain that later," Lillian said. "Do you know the quickest route to the hospital?"

"Yes. ETMC. I'll text the information to you and meet you there." Grant said and then asked, "Bill, are you driving?"

"No."

"Lillian, drive safe. I don't want you two hurt."

Lillian ended the call without responding. "Ford? Did he say Ford?"

* * * * *

Lillian wheeled into the hospital's parking garage, grabbed the ticket from the meter, drove beneath the raised arm, and stopped. She handed the ticket to Bill.

"You park this thing. I don't have time." With those orders, Lillian grabbed her purse and jumped out of the SUV. She saw Grant waiting outside the emergency entrance.

When she reached him, Grant hugged her. "I'm so glad you're okay."

"How is he?"

"Don't know for sure. It's too soon, but I was here when they brought him out of surgery."

Lillian searched Grant's eyes. She knew him. He always tried to protect her.

"Grant, be honest. Don't try to shield me from bad news. I saw the Harley. If it's indicative of his injuries, I know he's in serious condition."

He looked past her. "Here comes Bill. Let's go up together."

"He can't join us. He has Eli with him. He can walk him and wait for us."

* * * * *

Grant dreaded the impact Brandon's condition would have on Lillian, but he knew his mother would never forgive him if he kept her away from the young man who had somehow become important to Lillian and who lay in a coma struggling for his life. Grant understood Lillian's propensity to adopt loved ones. And if Brandon didn't survive, he knew Lillian would not take his death well. She would want revenge. He had no idea how he and Bill would handle her. A call to Jake may become a necessity. Grant thought she might listen to him. He looked at her out of the corner of his eyes and recognized the tilt of her chin as they walked down the hallway to ICU. Without realizing it, he finished his thought out loud, "sooner than later, I think."

"What?" Lillian asked.

"Did I say something?"

Lillian didn't answer him. When they reached the ICU wing of ETMC, Grant took her elbow and stopped. The cold, sparkling-clean, double, stainless steel doors reflected the concern on Lillian's face. He peeked through the small rectangle of glass and saw Brandon's cubicle. Two nurses were tending to him. He prayed they were working miracles on Brandon so Lillian could have hope and peace of mind.

Before he pushed the button to automatically open the doors and announce their entry, Grant turned his back to ICU, took Lillian's hands, and gazed into his mother's eyes. "Lillian, I know you think you are prepared to see Brandon, but brace yourself before we enter ICU. It's not a pretty scene. Don't let the sounds of the machines scare you."

She whispered an okay and squared her shoulders.

Grant could feel her tense. He put his arm around her, knowing the sight of Brandon lying in his sterile environment and hooked to every life support possible would break her heart. She watched the nurses care for him. When she blew out her breath, Grant waited for her anger to boil to the surface. She took deep breaths.

Oh, yeah, Grant thought, Jake will need to visit our mom and soon. She is furious and has revenge in her eyes. The poor bastard who tried to kill Brandon will need some sympathy.

For the second time in his life, Grant witnessed her internal battle to avoid crying. Lillian blinked away the tears that threatened to spill.

"I'm going to find the person who did this to him, Grant, and neither you nor Bill nor anyone else will stop me."

"Don't worry. You and I will do this one together. And if I find him first, I will remove my badge and beat the holy --"

"Thank you, my dear." She turned to leave. "There's nothing we can do for him now but stay out of the way of the medical personnel."

"You're right. Let's go downstairs, get Bill, and drive out to Caddo."

"Plan on staying with us."

"No, ma'am. I have my own RV."

"You do?"

"It's at Caddo, next to yours." Grant smiled at Lillian's shocked expression. "Close your mouth. It's not ladylike." He took her by the arm and led her to the elevator.

"I'm speechless," Lillian admitted.

Grant laughed. "That's a first."

"But I'm so glad you will be near us."

Bill and Eli were walking down the sidewalk when Lillian and Grant stepped outside. "How is he?" Bill asked.

"Not good," Grant said. "We're reconvening at Caddo. I'll give both of you the information the surgeon shared with me."

"Good," Bill nodded. "You won't have to repeat yourself."

"See you in about thirty minutes," Lillian said. "I'll have the coffee brewed by the time you arrive."

Grant kissed her on the cheek. "Hope you have some cookies to go with it."

Lillian patted him on his shoulder. "Always."

"I'll drive this time," Bill said. "Besides, as I recall, you left the keys in the ignition. Follow me. I'll lead you and Eli to the car."

"That's fine with me. I have some thinking to do on the way home."

"Plenty of notes, I know."

Neither of them spoke again. Bill paid the parking fee and pulled out onto the street. A green Range Rover entered as they exited. Lillian saw the driver of the other car. Lillian wondered why he would be at the hospital.

Chapter Thirty-Five

GRANT'S NEW, silver and gray Winnebago Instinct nestled next to the Forrester belonging to the Prestridges. The slot next to Vickie Parsons's RV across the street held a new white and navy blue Sportscoach Cross Country motor home. Its size shouted affluence, and compared to the other RVs at the lake, it looked out of place. Lillian couldn't wait to meet its owners.

"We have new neighbors," Bill said. "Guess we'll have to make a point to welcome them to Caddo."

"Looks like it, but I suspect you already know one of them," Lillian said and smiled at Bill's puzzled expression. "Just wait. You'll see."

Bill shrugged, parked, and stepped out of their SUV. He opened the back passenger door. Eli hopped down and ran to the Winnebago and sat on the top step.

Lillian laughed. "Even Eli knows whose RV sits next to ours." She climbed the steps to their RV and walked to the bedroom and grabbed a pair of black Capri leggings and a white turtleneck tunic.

By the time Bill and Eli entered, she was pouring water into the coffee pot. She added three scoops of a Kona blend and pushed the start button before she searched through the pantry.

She found the canned chicken she needed. Eli leapt to the back of the sofa, his favorite spot to conduct his guard duty.

"Would you like some chicken salad sandwiches for dinner?"

Bill who had disappeared into the bedroom to change into his gray, everyday sweats and green T-shirt did not answer, so Eli barked a reply to her question. Lillian laughed. "At least, you're listening to me."

Bill sneaked up behind her, put both arms around her waist, and hugged her.

"I heard you, but I was deep in thought."

"And just what were you thinking?" Lillian said.

"We ought to start planning where we want to go next. Aren't you ready to leave Caddo?"

Lillian, still in Bill's embrace, turned around to face her husband. "Surely, you jest. To answer your question: No, I'll not leave Grant all alone here to solve these murders all by himself."

"Now, my dear, you know --"

"You're correct. I know I'm going to get to the bottom of what's happened out here. And don't you forget about that young man in ICU. Grant and I will ferret out who did that to Brandon. If you had seen him, you would understand how seriously he was injured." She kissed Bill and moved out of his embrace. "You are welcome to join us, or you may choose not to help."

Lillian turned back to the counter and began to chop pecans, grapes, and celery to add to the chicken. "Either way, I intend to make the culprit pay."

"Have you forgotten we agreed to be partners? Of course, I'll help you and Grant. I just want you to be careful. Don't want either of you hurt."

"On that, we are definitely in agreement." She stopped chopping, smiled at the man who was the love of her life, put her arms around his neck. "Have I told you how much I love you today?" Bill hugged her to him. His kiss told her the feeling was mutual.

Lillian heard an engine.

She looked out the window over the sink. "Here's Grant. Guess we'd better save this conversation for later. Need to finish these sandwiches for him. He's always hungry."

"I'll put them together. You'd better find some cookies for him." Bill nudged her out of the way and dumped all the ingredients into the chicken salad. He added a generous dollop of mayo and stirred.

Lillian reached into the pantry. She had two packages, Oreos in one hand and jalapeno potato chips in the other, when Grant stepped inside.

Eli jumped off the sofa and ran to Grant who squatted down and wrapped his arms around the Poodle's neck. The dog gave him a slobbery kiss.

"Good boy," Grant said.

He stood and went to Lillian and leaned down to kiss her on the cheek. "Hmm, that looks good. You know I love your chicken salad."

Lillian added ice to some glasses and poured each of them some iced tea.

"Let's eat, and then we'll plot our strategy to solve the deadly domino mysteries and the attack on Brandon." Grant's raised eyebrows and the silent exchange between him and Bill did not go unnoticed. "Grant, don't think I'm going to let you work alone on these cases. Bill and I will help."

Grant nodded and took a bite of his sandwich.

Lillian and Bill also followed his lead and ate in silence.

* * * * *

Sandwiches consumed, Grant decided it was time for a discussion of the day's events. He pushed his chair away from the table and studied Lillian as she bustled around tidying up the small kitchen. She poured coffee for each of them and set a plate of Oreo cookies on the dinette.

"Lillian, are you ready to hear about Brandon's condition?"

"Yes, and don't leave out anything. Be honest with me. What did the doctor say?"

"Doctors would be more accurate. He had three: an internist, a neurologist, and an orthopedic surgeon."

"Let's discuss the prognosis of each," Lillian said, "and begin with the orthopedist. Bones may heal faster than other types of injuries."

Grant nodded in agreement.

"Brandon has a broken arm and two broken ribs. One rib punctured his lung. The doctor had to do some repairs there to help with Brandon's breathing."

"That explains the ventilator," Lillian said.

"Go on," Bill said. "Did he have other internal injuries?"

"Yes, he did. The force of the car's impact damaged his spleen. It had to be removed."

Grant reached for a cookie, took a bite. He chewed slowly, swallowed the Oreo, and blew on his coffee. While he waited for it to cool, he watched the other two people absorb what he had said. Lillian covered both eyes with her palms. Bill stared into his coffee cup, said nothing. Lillian removed her hands from her face. Grant saw the glint in her eyes and understood she was on the hunt. Having listed Brandon's injuries, he no longer pitied the prey who could not escape his mother's wrath.

"Are those the most serious?" She nodded for him to continue.

"Yes, ma'am."

"No concussion?" Bill asked.

"No, but I think the doctor said something about keeping him sedated overnight." Grant closed his eyes and added, "Doc said they would stay ahead of Brandon's pain and not let it get too intense for the next few days."

"We will keep both Brandon and the medical team in our prayers," Bill said. "Have they notified his family?"

"Sheriff Tomas is on that. We found a business card in his wallet and gave the information off of it to the doctor."

"What kind of business card?" Lillian asked.

"An attorney from Dallas," Grant said. "The card listed the firm beneath the lawyer's name.

"Do you remember the name of the firm?"

"Ford, Dodson, and Town – something or other." Grant closed his eyes to visualize the card. "Oh, yeah. Now I remember. It was Townsend, a Richard Townsend."

He saw Lillian's surprised reaction to the name. She nudged Bill's arm with her elbow. "Tell him, Bill."

"My college roommate was named Richard Townsend. He planned to go to law school after graduation, but Uncle Sam interfered."

"Did you two keep up with each other?" Grant wanted to know.

"All I know is that instead of becoming a lawyer, Richard became a soldier. We lost touch after both of us were drafted. He went into the navy, and I went into the army. He may have studied law after he was discharged."

Lillian asked, "Will the doctors let you know if the attorney leads them to Brandon's family?"

"I'm sure they will," said Grant. He stood. "Thanks, you two, for the dinner and dessert. I'm going home right now."

"No you're not." Lillian said. "You said you had eye witness reports. What about them?"

"I'm pretty tired right now. It's been a long day. How about early tomorrow morning?

Lillian stood and hugged him. "Of course. Did you tell Bill where home is for you right now?"

Grant smiled. "I take it you didn't?"

She nodded.

Bill asked, "Okay, you two. Why do I have the feeling that once more I'm the last one to learn something? What do you know that I don't?"

Grant laughed and said, "If you look out your bedroom window, you can see my new home right next to yours."

"You're kidding," Bill said. "Next door?"

Grant nodded.

"Great."

"If you come over tomorrow," Grant said, "I'll give you the Grand Tour."

"Breakfast, first," Lillian said.

"Seven o'clock too early?"

"It'll be waiting for you," she said.

Grant smiled. "Now, you know the real reason I moved next door." With that, he left and walked to his new Winnebago.

"Ah, it's nice to be home." He sat in his black leather recliner and removed his boots. He reached for the remote control to the TV. Grant leaned back and fell asleep listening to the weather report.

Chapter Thirty-Six

LILLIAN RAISED her head. Round, black eyes stared lovingly into her clear, blue-greens. Eli laid his head next to hers giving Lillian doggie kisses. She gave him a pat on the head, looked at the clock on her bedside table, and smiled. "Six-twenty. It's early," she whispered, easing out of bed without disturbing Bill.

"Let's go for a walk."

She tiptoed into the living area carrying a pair of jeans, a white T-shirt, and her favorite pink cardigan. Dressed, she stopped by the coffee pot and filled her travel mug. She and her four-legged companion quietly left the RV. As soon as Eli bounded down the steps, he ran across the lane and sniffed around the large RV. He stopped at the camper's door and growled.

"Come here, Eli, be quiet," Lillian ordered. "You'll disturb our new neighbors."

For the first time that Lillian could remember, her obedient dog did not respond to her command. Instead, he circled the RV once more, continuing his inspection of the area. Again, he sat in front of the steps to the entry. This time he barked. Lillian knew her dog and his warning signals. They always signaled danger, but right now the campsite was the picture of calm.

Besides, most of the campers were still ensconced in their RVs, and she didn't want to disturb them, so she lowered her voice a couple of decibels. "Come here, I said, or you'll go back to the sofa."

Eli snorted but complied and raced down to the marina. Lillian trailed along behind him and stopped frequently to take sips of her coffee. She inhaled the crisp, autumn morning. Like the woman who ambled along the path to the dock, the sun was in no hurry to pop up above the tree line. The lake and the residents who lived around it would have to wait for its warm rays.

Lillian, deep in thought, felt the early morning chill and pulled her cardigan tighter to lock in her body heat. She and Bill had been camping at Caddo Lake since late summer and into the fall. Lillian knew Bill was antsy to move on to another town. She did not want to leave unfinished business and wouldn't enjoy their next stop if she did so.

She sat down on the dock beside Eli. He scooted close, pressing his body against the side of her leg. Lillian wrapped one arm around him. She sipped the cooling coffee from her mug and gazed at the water.

The lake was smooth with ever so gentle ripples. The sky gradually grew lighter as the sun made its debut. In the center of the lake, a bass boat drifted slowly, quietly. The fisherman used a Stand-to-Fish seat. By the way he cast, Lillian decided he must be a good fisherman, perhaps a professional.

She tensed when the rod he held jerked and hoped he had caught a big one. The man knew what he was doing. He calmly pulled in the line with his left hand while keeping the line taut. She saw the fish flopping and fighting to free itself from the hook.

The fisherman took it off of the lure and placed the fish in a cooler. Then he lowered the circular standing seat to a sitting position, looked around, saw Lillian, and waved. The roar of the boat's motor interrupted the peaceful moment.

Lillian glanced at the face of her watch. "Come on, Eli. Let's go prepare breakfast for two hungry men."

* * * * *

Silver, insulated coffee cup in hand, Grant stood outside his Winnebago. Like his adopted mom, Grant greeted early mornings and their promise of a new day, each one a fresh beginning. He recognized the silhouette of the woman and her Poodle backlit by the rising sun. Grant had awakened before daylight and intended to walk down the lane to the marina, but he hesitated at the sight of Lillian cuddled next to Eli on the pier.

Grant thought about joining his mom and the dog, but he heard the sound of a door open and close. He stopped and scanned the campsite.

A tall brunette stepped outside of a small Sport Airstream. She wore a green windbreaker, jeans, and brown hiking boots.

"Good morning," he said to her as she walked past him.

She neither spoke nor looked at him but nodded in response to his greeting.

Grant tried not to stare. Without turning his head in her direction, he watched her enter the walking/jogging trail at the far end of the lane. The woman was quickly out of sight. That's good. He didn't need another woman in his life right now. He waited on the one chasing the Poodle up the hill.

*****

Lillian saw Grant waiting for her and walked briskly up the path to meet him. Eli trotted ahead of her, tongue hanging out, tail wagging.

"It's going to be a beautiful day," she said with a big grin on her face. "I'm so glad you are here. Sometime today, you're going to have to show off the interior of your new home."

"Come on in. I'll pour you another cup while you inspect my new digs."

"Sounds wonderful. I bet you have our favorite flavor," she said.

"I bought some hazelnut at Edgemon's with you in mind."

She lifted her cheek to him for a kiss, and being the dutiful son, he obliged, then opened the door for her. Eli was the first to enter. He took a cursory tour of the camper, sniffing his way around each room. Finished with his inspection, the dog hopped on the bed, and after yawning, he lay down for a nap.

Grant laughed at the dog. "Looks like Eli partied too late last night."

"He woke me early this morning." Lillian, too, inspected the Winnebago. "How lovely," she said. "It looks like you. I like the brown and sage green accents." By the way he exhaled and grinned, she knew he had held his breath waiting for her approval.

Grant opened a cabinet door, "Take your pick of flavors just in case you want to experiment." He motioned to the different types of coffees and demonstrated how to operate his new Keurig.

Lillian chose the hazelnut. While it brewed, she said, "Let's talk about Brandon. You mentioned statements from witnesses."

Grant nodded. "I did, but let's eat breakfast first. I can make scrambled eggs and fry up some bacon."

"Sounds good to me," came a male voice from the open door. Bill walked in. "I guess I'm a sleepy head this morning."

"Too much excitement for you, my dear?" Lillian teased using Bill's own words he had employed many times to describe her response to a difficult situation, namely murder.

"Coffee, please." Bill yawned. "Thought I'd need plenty of rest before we discuss yesterday's events and Brandon's condition." He sat down at the table, reached for the coffee cup Lillian placed before him.

"Speaking of Brandon – I wonder how he's fairing this morning," Lillian said.

"He's good. I called the nurse on duty first thing. She said he woke up and refused to take any pain medication. He's talking about leaving the hospital today and wasn't a happy camper when she told him he'd have to receive an okay from the doctor." Grant checked the bacon, turned it over to brown on the other side. "She said he's demanding she call the doctor and get a verbal release."

Bill laughed. "If he's fussing, he's well on his way to recovery."

"We'll see about that," Lillian said. "Grant, do you need any help?"

He handed her plates, napkins, and utensils. "You can set the table." Then Grant put a platter on the table. "Help yourselves."

Lillian buttered a slice of toast and then layered it with two slices of bacon and a scoop of eggs. She took a bite. "You're a good short-order cook."

"Taught by the best." He sat down beside her and said, "Bill, would you say grace?"

"Be glad to."

As soon as she finished eating, Lillian got down to business.

"I think we've prolonged our discussion long enough. While you two clean the kitchen, I'm going next door to get my notebook."

The two men saluted and proceeded to follow her instructions.

* * * * *

"Ten minutes? I wonder what's keeping her so long."

Grant noticed the worried frown on Bill's face. "Let's go check on her, make sure she's okay."

Bill glanced out the window.

Before he and Grant could exit the Winnebago, Lillian walked in.

Bill rushed to her. "What's wrong? You're pale."

"Someone's been in our RV."

Grant grabbed his gun and holster from his gun safe. "Keep her here. I'll go check it out." He put on his gear as he ran through the door.

The Prestridge RV was in a shambles: drawers opened, some emptied onto the floor; sofa cushions tossed; pantry and refrigerator doors gaped open.

Grant whirled around and pointed his nine millimeter in the direction of the sound he heard behind him.

"Who are you?"

Chapter Thirty-Seven

GRANT FACED a short, plump, red-haired, freckle-faced lady who stood just inside the door. She raised her hand to her throat and gasped at the sight of the gun.

Grant scowled at her. "Don't you know how to knock?"

"I did knock, but I guess you didn't hear me." The woman squared her shoulders. "Do you mind?" she asked as she looked down at the barrel of the 9mm. She extended her hand. "Allow me to introduce myself."

Grant put his gun in its holster and shook hands with her. "Grant Perryman."

"I'm Milly Gruene. The camp director is my husband."

"How long have you been standing behind me?"

"I just now came inside. I stopped when I saw you."

"Do you need to speak to my mom?"

Milly did not answer his question. She saw the badge attached to his belt. "Mrs. Prestridge didn't tell me her son is a policeman."

Grant nodded. He noticed the fear in her eyes as they darted back and forth, scanning the room as if she were looking for something, as if he were no longer standing before her.

"What can I do for you?" Grant said sternly to get her attention.

"I'll come back later when it's more convenient." Milly made a quick exit.

From the open door, Grant watched her stop at the edge of the street, look both ways, and then walk to the camp director's mobile home. Before stepping inside, she glanced back and waved at Grant. He answered her wave with a scowl.

Grant kept his eyes on her until she closed her door. His investigative instincts kicked in. He knew she was guilty of something. He decided he needed to run a background check on her.

He closed up the RV and walked next door to his own.

Bill stood spread-eagled, with his arms and legs stretched from one side of the door to the other. He grinned at Grant. "Only way I could keep her contained until your return." Bill dropped his arms and moved aside.

Grant entered and after one look at Lillian, he said, "Let me guess. Her temper overcame her shock."

Lillian moved toward the door. "Let's go back and pick up the place. Get my notebook so I can make note of the witness statements you have. This is *déjà vu* all over again."

"How so?" Grant asked.

"Remember our last case?" Lillian said. "Someone broke into our house and searched for the documents I took from Sheila's house after she was murdered."

"But what could someone think you have here?" Grant wanted to know.

"Beats me," Lillian said and led the way back to the Prestridge RV.

Bill picked up sofa cushions and placed them back where they belonged. "Let's clean up and maybe we'll discover if anything is missing." He walked to the kitchen, picked up cabinet drawers, and replaced their spilled utensils.

"I'll help you straighten up the bedroom," Grant said. They replaced the mattress and remade the bed. "Someone did a thorough job here."

"Yes – oh my goodness – my notes."

Lillian went back into the kitchen. The notebook was no longer on the dinette table. She and the two men searched the whole RV.

"Well, now we know what the hoodlum wanted," Grant said.

Lillian, shoulders sagging, plopped down at the table. "If he found my notebook on the dinette, why tear up the other rooms?" She straightened her back, pressed her lips together, tilted her chin, and answered her own question. "He wanted us to think it was a burglary."

Grant waited. He knew what was coming next.

"I'm mad as hell. I'll tell you right now. I will nail the culprit who did this."

"We'll be right there with you," Bill said and patted her on the shoulder.

Grant didn't want to add fuel to the flame but felt he needed to inform Lillian that Milly had been in the RV.

"Lillian, when I was here earlier, a woman came inside and stood right behind me. Said her name was Milly."

"She was married to the camp director."

"Was? She didn't use the past tense when she identified herself as his wife."

"I guess she doesn't know," Lillian said.

"Know what?" Grant asked.

"Tell him what you saw, my dear," Bill suggested.

"Remember when we found the wrecked boat and Al jumped overboard?"

"Yes." Grant cocked his head sideways. "So?"

"Right after we turned back toward the campground, I saw an alligator slip into the water."

"You think he's dead?"

Lillian nodded.

"Until we have a body, we can't come to that conclusion." Grant said.

They sat silent for a few minutes. Lillian, convinced that a cup of tea could boost their spirits, poured water into the tea kettle. When it whistled, she sat a tin of teabags on the table and poured water into three cups.

"Wouldn't surprise me if she were the one who rummaged through my things," Lillian said. "I thought she and her husband were untrustworthy when I first met them."

"I'm sure you have your reasons," Grant said.

"It's as if they tried too hard to be friendly," Bill said. "And Lillian didn't like the way Al talked down to her."

Grant shook his head and asked, "Who besides the three of us knew about the existence of your notebook?"

"I can't think of anyone right now," Lillian said and added, "but it's okay. I have a backup list on my new computer."

Grant grinned. "Well, Madame, boot up that laptop. I have some information for you to add."

It took a few minutes for the computer to come alive. Lillian attached it to her printer and made a copy of her notes for each of the men.

"I've just had a thought," Lillian said as she handed a printout to Bill. "Eli didn't growl. That's a first for him. He always warns me if danger is near."

"You're right. What does that tell us?" Bill asked.

"He knew the intruder," Grant said. "Make a note of that."

Lillian entered the information at the end of her notes. Grant and Bill penciled it on their paper copies.

"Are you ready for more notes?" Grant asked.

"Fire away." Lillian placed her fingers on the computer's keys. She listened to Grant and then typed.

43. Eli didn't growl when RV was trashed.

44. Store manager saw the car hit Brandon

45. By the time he reached Brandon, the car was gone.

46. The young checker saw the car as it entered the gas station.

47. She said the driver revved the car's engine before it hit Brandon.
48. Customer at checkout counter thinks the car hit him and backed over him before speeding away.
49. Happened so fast, everyone shocked, no one saw tag # on license plate.
50. It was a black Town Car.

Eli growled and jumped from the back of the sofa. He ran to the door and looked through the glass.

Grant walked to the dog. "What's wrong, Eli?" His eyes followed the dog's gaze. "Well, well," he said.

"What is it?" Lillian wanted to know.

"A black Town Car just left the campground," Grant said, "and it didn't take the front entrance." He reached in his pocket and wrote down the tag number, then patted the dog on the head. "Good job."

"Coincidence?" Bill asked.

"Don't believe in them," Lillian said.

"Nor do I. However, I've paperwork to complete, so I need to leave. I'll track down background information on Milly and Al as well as the identity of the car's owner."

"Let me know what you find out," Lillian said.

Grant nodded and walked to his truck.

* * * * *

Lillian watched him drive away and then sat back down at her computer and added one more notation.

51. Black Town Car seen leaving campground.

Not front entrance.

She filled the sink with hot soapy water and washed the dirty teacups. Finished, she remained at the sink and glanced out the window. Lillian saw Milly walk from her mobile home to the camp director's office. A minute later, Milly left the office and climbed into her truck. She left the camp, using the Town Car's route. Lillian walked back to her computer and entered another note.

52. Did Milly follow the black car?

From her vantage spot, Lillian saw Simon tie up his boat at the marina. She watched as he opened the storage unit to the campground. He pulled out the riding lawnmower and cut the grass around the Pavilion.

She felt Bill's arms encircle her waist.

"What's so interesting outside?" he whispered in her ear.

"When you and Jeff came for me after I swamped my canoe in the storm, did you know the cabin where I spent the night belonged to Simon?"

"Yes, Jeff had decided we would look for you in one more bayou before giving up and calling in a recovery team. He mentioned to me that the maintenance man might have found you."

"Did you get a good look at him?"

"No. By the time Jeff moored the boat, Simon was gone. Why?"

Lillian took Bill's hands away from her waist and turned to face him. "I have a confession to make," she said.

Bill raised his eyebrows. "I can't imagine that you have anything to confess, but whatever it is, I forgive you," he said.

"Simon is one of our old friends."

Bill smiled. "My dear, all of our friends are old."

"When I tell you who he is, you will be as shocked as I was."

"Surprise me."

"Simon is Richard Townsend."

"You can't be serious. I think I would recognize my college roommate."

"No, you wouldn't. Not now."

"Something bad must have happened to him. Why would he take a job as a maintenance man? He was too smart to end up with a menial job."

"If you had seen the inside of his cabin, the books, the furnishings, you would suspect that his manual labor job is a ruse. Plus, even though we can't see it from here, the location of his cabin provides a direct view of the campground. I tell you he's more than just a guy who mows grass and cleans up."

"Did you ask him about his job here?"

"I did, but he wouldn't tell me, but I intend to find out what he's up to." She turned around looked outside.

"Have you been watching him from the window?"

Lillian nodded and glanced outside again. "He's finished mowing. Now, he's eating his lunch under the Pavilion."

Bill peered over her shoulder to see Simon. "Can't see his face," Bill said. "He has his back toward us."

"I want you to see him up close."

"I'll walk over and pretend to accidentally see him, then begin a conversation."

"No, Bill. If he sees you, he'll leave. Let's follow him when he finishes his jobs. Go rent a boat. I'll get our fishing gear together and throw some sandwiches in the cooler."

"Be sure to pack the binoculars." Bill left.

Lillian packed their lunch, stepped out of the RV, and set the cooler on the portable table.

Eli whimpered and pawed the bottom of the door.

"No, Eli, it's too dangerous for you to be in a boat. You might fall overboard."

She retrieved their fly rods and tackle boxes. Lillian smiled as the thought occurred to her that she planned to reel in more than a big bass.

Chapter Thirty-Eight

BILL TIED the rented boat to the end of the dock at the marina and joined his wife. They sat with their backs toward Simon.

"Listen for the sound of his motor so we won't have to turn around to see him leave."

"Don't you think he'll speak to us?" Bill asked.

"No, he doesn't want to meet up with you."

"How do you know that? Did he say so when you two had your *tête à tête* all nighter?"

Lillian didn't like the direction Bill wanted to take their conversation, so she ignored the implication he tried to make about her night with Simon.

"Didn't have to. If he wanted to talk to you, he would have waited for you and Jeff to dock at his house."

"You have a point."

Bill cast his fly rod toward the bank. The quick response of a hungry fish shocked him. "Didn't know I was such a good fisherman. Look at the size of this thing." He took it off the hook and put it in a bucket of water.

"Looks like dinner to me," said Lillian. "Shh. Here he comes."

Simon untied the rope and threw it into his Jon boat. Lillian and Bill concentrated on their fishing. Simon rounded the end of the dock and eased out into the middle of the lake.

"Did you get a peek at him?" Lillian asked.

"All I saw was his back. He always was the smart one, head of our class."

"Sneaky, too, as I recall."

Bill raised both eyebrows.

"Don't ask," Lillian said, "I'll explain when I have a few more facts."

"Let's try out this boat." Bill pointed to the rental.

"Yes, let's do. I think we can safely follow Simon."

Bill climbed down into the boat. "Hand me our gear." He reached up and took their rods, tackle boxes, cooler from his wife. "Now, my dear, throw the rope in here and take my hand. I'll help you down."

Lillian stepped down.

"Where are the life jackets?"

Bill pointed. "Raise the seat on that bench."

Lillian put one on and handed the other life jacket to him. She mimicked the gravelly voice of a pirate, said, "Okay, Matey, let's catch that two-legged angler."

"Aye, aye, Cap'n Curiosity." Bill's voice lacked its usual upbeat tone. He turned serious and said, "I'm sorry I brought up your night with Simon. I'm just glad he found you." He started the engine, and they eased out into the lake.

"No apology needed," Lillian said over her shoulder. She faced the bow of their rental and kept Simon's boat in sight. She swiveled around and looked at Bill. "There's one more thing you ought to know."

"What?"

"I gave him my word that I wouldn't reveal his name to anyone, but I thought if you recognized him, I wouldn't be guilty of breaking my promise."

"Did he ask for your silence?" Bill wanted to know.

"Yes, I think he's on a mission of some kind, maybe undercover."

"That why you called him sneaky?"

Lillian nodded and cocked her head to one side, listening.

"Slow down. I hear another boat. Sounds like it's coming our way."

Bill cut the engine and reached for their rods. "Here, take this. We're just a happy couple enjoying a day of fishing on the lake."

They barely had time to cast before the park ranger's patrol boat came around one of Caddo's bayous. There were two men aboard. Jeff slowed and sounded the horn to get their attention.

He called to them. "Caught anything?"

"Yeah," Bill yelled back, "a bass back by the RV Park."

Jeff waved, gave two short beeps of his horn, and drove the boat around the next bend of the lake. Lily pads parted, and Jeff's boat floated out of sight.

Lillian reeled in her line and placed the rod in the boat's hull. "Let's move on down, opposite the bend where Jeff turned."

Bill placed his rod and reel next to hers. "I wonder if they're looking for Al's body."

"Could be, but I doubt Jeff's interested in Al."

"Who was with him? Could you see?"

"Not enough to make an accurate I.D." Lillian lied. "Well, well, to quote Grant, what do we have here?" she mumbled.

"Missed that. What did you say?"

"Nothing. Just talking to myself," she responded.

The pretenders continued casting for another fish. Soon they heard the engine of the patrol boat. Jeff saw them and waved as he maneuvered out of the bayou.

Lillian felt a pull on her line. "Help me, Bill. I've never caught a fish this big."

He dropped his rod into the bottom of the boat and took her rod. The line broke, and husband and wife fell backwards. The boat rocked back and forth from the force of their fall but stayed afloat.

"That was close, my dear," Bill said.

She took a deep breath. "Too close for comfort if --"

Lillian stopped mid-sentence. "Listen. That engine sounds familiar."

"Turn around. Don't look," Lillian ordered. "Let's keep fishing until he passes by, then we're going down that bayou. Find what they were searching for."

"No, we're not," said Bill. "We're going back to the campground. We've done enough snooping for today."

Lillian frowned but didn't argue. She knew tomorrow Simon would leave his cabin to work at the campground. She was determined to search the cabin, learn more about Simon's work. Next time, she would leave Bill behind.

"Okay, let's follow Simon. He may be going to the RV Park."

Bill kept a discreet distance from the handyman.

* * * * *

A couple of worn-out fishermen sat in front of their RV. In a grassy area adjacent to the Pavilion, Grant tossed a Frisbee to Eli. Lillian was amused at the dog's agility. The poodle would catch the toy and race to the lake, dip it into the water, run back to his playmate, hand off the disk, and wait for another toss. Finally bored with the game, the dog brought the Frisbee back and dropped it behind Lillian's chair. Grant plopped down on the grass in front of his mom.

"That was good fish you fried," he said to Bill.

"Thanks, but I'm so full right now, I can barely move." Bill rubbed his belly. "I think there's something about gluttony being bad for one's body."

"I'm going to call it a day." Grant stood and left.

"Me, too," said Bill. "The thought of stretching out on the bed is pulling me inside."

"You go on. I want to watch the sunset."

Bill bent down and kissed her on the top of her head. He climbed the three steps to their RV and turned back. "Lillian, I think –"

Lillian heard a gasp, then a thump. Glancing over her shoulder, she realized Bill had fallen face down.

"Bill?" Silence.

She raced to him and knelt beside him. She saw blood spreading across the back of his shirt.

"On, no."

Then she screamed.

Chapter Thirty-Nine

GRANT LEANED back in his recliner and turned on the evening news. Over the sound of the weatherman, he thought he heard a high-pitched wail. He opened the door and heard Lillian calling his name. She sounded desperate. Grant took the steps to his Winnebago in one leap and ran to his mother.

The brunette Grant had admired came running from the dock, fishing gear in hand. She secured her gear in her RV and rushed across the lane. "I heard screams. What happened?"

As a former Dallas policeman, Grant had witnessed far too many times this type of scene, one in which a loved one bent over a spouse, a child, a friend and wept. He never considered the fact that this kind of tragedy would involve the two people he loved more than anyone else in the world. One look at the blood on Bill's shirt gave Grant an instant assessment of the situation. He reached down and gripped Lillian's shoulders.

"Get back. Let me check him." He gently turned Bill over. Blood covered the front of his shirt.

"I'll call an ambulance," the brunette offered.

"No time to wait," Grant said. "He's losing too much blood."

"What can I do to help?" the woman wanted to know.

"I'm going to pull my truck around. You can help me lift him into the back seat." Grant turned to his mother. "I'll drive Bill to the hospital. It'll be faster." She nodded.

Grant knew that people responded differently to traumatic events. Lillian's breathing was too rapid.

She was looking around and appeared to be confused like a person on the verge of shock. Thinking quickly, Grant said, "Go get a blanket to cover him. We want him to stay warm." Lillian needed movement and purpose.

She nodded and went into the RV.

He left the two women, the older one with a mission, the younger one stayed with Bill and somehow produced a compress and was holding it on the exit wound.

Grant parked his truck as close as he could to the victim. "Get in first, Lillian, and support his head. Keep it elevated. Can you do that?"

Without answering, Lillian handed Grant the blanket, hopped into the backseat and held out her arms to receive her beloved.

Grant tossed the blanket in the front passenger seat. With the help of the brunette, he lifted Bill into the truck. Grant reached over the back of the passenger for the blanket. "Here, let me spread this over him." Grant spoke softly but firmly to Lillian. "Can you keep that compress on his wound?"

"I'm not helpless. Quit worrying about me and haul it out of here."

Eli had jumped into the truck and stood between the front and back seats, whimpering. Grant closed the truck's door and ran around to the driver's side and hopped in. The brunette was already in the passenger seat.

"Thanks for your help, but I can take it from here." Grant waited for her to exit.

"You can, but I'm going with you. Lillian said 'haul it' and I think it would be a good time to do that right about now, don't you think?"

Grant gunned the engine, sped out of the campground, and headed for Marshall. Grant looked in his rearview mirror and made eye contact with Lillian.

"Where are you taking him?" she asked.

"ETMC Marshall."

"Hurry."

Grant placed his emergency red blinking light on the roof of the truck and pressed down on the accelerator.

"By the way, I'm Vickie Parsons."

"Thanks again for your help. How do you know my name?"

"It's elementary." Vickie smiled. "I heard Lillian calling, and you came running, so I put two and two together."

Grant couldn't help himself. He grinned. "Smart, too."

"I assume you have a last name?"

"It's Perryman."

"If you don't mind my asking, what's your connection with the Prestridges?"

"They're my adopted parents."

Vickie nodded and was silent during the rest of the drive to the hospital.

"Hurry, Grant. He's losing too much blood."

"Marshall's closer," Vickie reminded him.

Grant used his police radio and called Sheriff Tomas. "En route to ETMC, Marshall. Alert ER. Gunshot victim being transported. ETA in twenty minutes. I'll give you details on arrival."

"Ten-four."

* * * * *

Emergency staff met Grant as he pulled in and parked outside of the ER entrance. Two medics gently removed Lillian's grip on the still unconscious Bill, put him on a gurney.

Eli jumped out of the truck, pushed past them, and ran to the entrance. The automatic door opened.

Grant ran and grabbed Eli's collar. "Come here. You'll have to wait inside the truck."

Eli growled and tried to free himself from Grant's hold.

"Don't growl at him," Lillian ordered.

After he had forced Eli back into the truck, Grant helped Lillian out of the truck and, supporting her with his hand on her elbow, escorted her to the ER entrance. Vickie was waiting for them at the door and put an arm around Lillian's shoulder.

"Would you go inside with her while I find a parking spot."

"Sure. I'll take care of her."

Grant climbed inside his vehicle, and holding on with both hands, leaned over and rested his forehead on the steering wheel. "Dear Lord, please let Bill come through this."

Grant sat frozen, unable to move. He closed his eyes and replayed the incident in his mind, trying to remember whether or not anyone other than Vickie had been around at the time of the shooting. He kept drawing a blank, so he started the engine and drove to the visitor parking lot.

* * * * *

Sheriff Tomas opened the passenger door and slid into Grant's F150. The sheriff watched the young man wrestle with his emotions. Grant sat up straight and leaned back. Eli licked his ear.

"I think he sympathizes with you," the sheriff reached over and gave Eli a firm pat on his neck. "Good boy. You're folks are going to be okay." He looked at Grant. "We need to talk."

"Yes, sir."

"Where were you when Bill was shot? I assume it happened at the lake."

"It was at the campground. The three of us had just finished our dinner, and I left to go to my RV. Hadn't been home more than five minutes when it happened."

"Did you hear anything?"

"You mean the gunshot, don't you?"

"Yes."

"No, my TV was on. I wanted to hear the evening news."

"So, let me get this straight. You had dinner and then promptly left. You didn't visit with them for awhile after you guys ate?"

"I didn't leave right away. Eli and I went down by the Pavilion, playing with a Frisbee. All of a sudden, he ran back toward the RV and lay down. I just thought he was bored with the game, but now, I wonder."

"Did you see anyone at the Pavilion, someone you might not have seen before?"

"There have been a couple of new RVs at the park. I'll have to think about that question and get back with you."

Eli licked the side of the sheriff's face and made a guttural sound.

"If I didn't know better, I'd think this dog is trying to tell me something."

"His owner thinks he can talk." Grant patted Eli.

Sheriff Tomas opened his door. "Come by the office tomorrow, fill out a report. Maybe by then something else will come to mind." The senior officer traded Grant's F150 for his cruiser, started it, and drove away.

* * * * *

"Ten-four," Grant said to the retreating red taillights. He looked back at the Poodle. "Stay here. I'll go check on our loved ones." Grant half-lowered all four windows in the cab. "That ought to be plenty of ventilation. Temperatures are dropping." Eli lay down on the back seat to wait.

He found Lillian and Vickie in the surgery waiting room.

"Thanks for being there when we needed you," he said to Vickie who stood when he entered.

"My pleasure," she said, "but now that I know Lillian is okay and Bill is getting medical attention, I need to get back to the camp."

"I'll drive you," Grant offered.

"That's not necessary. I have a ride. I called a good friend who's probably outside as we speak."

Always the gentleman, Grant walked her to the door. "I'll wait with you."

"I appreciate your offer, but Lillian needs your company right now."

Grant nodded. "Again, thanks."

Vickie left them.

Before the automatic doors closed, Grant heard her greet her ride.

Chapter Forty

GRANT TURNED around and nearly ran into Lillian. "Did you see the driver?"

"Too dark."

"What did she say?"

"One word – 'Hello' -- to her ride," Grant responded.

"That's not what I mean. Did you hear her say a name?"

"Didn't pay any attention if she did."

"I would swear I heard her say a name, but it wasn't clear. I wasn't close enough."

"You're still reeling from the shock of seeing your husband shot."

"Maybe, but I've been trying to reconstruct in my mind everything that happened."

"That's a relief."

"Why?"

"That tells me you're okay."

"I'll be okay as soon as I hear the doctor say Bill is all right."

"While we wait, do you feel like filling me in on your thoughts?"

"Yes. I need to keep my mind busy. What do you want to know first?"

"Somebody tried to kill Bill, but I didn't hear the sound of a gunshot. Did you?"

"No, and don't you think that strange?"

Grant nodded and continued. "Did you see anyone out and about, someone you haven't seen around the campground before tonight?"

"Not a soul, but I was too engrossed with the beautiful sunset and thinking about the murders."

"Don't guess you've talked to Jake?"

Lillian shook her head. "I don't want him out on the highway tonight. Let's wait until we get the doctor's report, then bring him up-to-date."

Grant smiled and hugged her to him. "My helicopter mom. Always trying to protect her sons."

Lillian smiled. "Look who's coming."

* * * * *

Sheriff Tomas left Grant in the parking lot, but after driving halfway down the block, he remembered the second reason he had come to ETMC. He had been on his way to Marshall when Grant called. He wanted to check on Brandon's progress, so he made a U-turn stopping next to the curb.

A black Town Car slowed down and stopped outside the ER entrance. The young woman who helped Grant with Bill walked through the automatic doors and waved at the driver of the car. She opened the passenger door and sat down. The car drove away.

Tomas jotted down the tag number and parked his cruiser in a different space. He entered the main entrance to the hospital down the hall from the surgical waiting room. Passing by a connecting hallway, the sheriff glanced to his right and saw Brandon making his way slowly down the hall. He stepped out of sight and waited.

* * * * *

Grant looked in the direction Lillian indicated. He recognized the young man slowly coming toward them. She stood and rushed to Brandon, giving him a gentle hug.

"Should you be out of bed?" Lillian asked.

"I'm working on my strength," Brandon said. "I can't stand a hospital."

"You need to give yourself time to recoup," Grant suggested.

"I don't have any time to waste."

"Brandon, do you remember my telling you about my sons the first time we met at Edgemon's?"

"Yes, ma'am, I do."

Lillian reached out for Grant.

"I want you to meet Grant Perryman, one of my sons." The two men shook hands.

Grant smiled at his helicopter mom leading the young man to a comfortable chair. She held on to his good arm while he sat. She pushed an empty chair along side of his and took his hand.

"I'm so glad you can get up and around."

"Doctors said I'm healing faster than they thought at first."

"That's what youth can do for you," Lillian said.

"Do they predict when you'll be released?" Grant asked.

"If my ribs are okay, they say I can go home in a week."

"Whew, that is fast," Grant said, "but nowadays, doctors want you out as soon as possible."

Brandon nodded. "Insurance dictates recovery, I guess."

"I'm just so thankful you survived the accident," Lillian said.

"I'm surprised to see you two here. Where's Bill?"

"In surgery," Grant said and then walked across the room where another easy chair was placed. Grant could see down the hall and also keep up with Lillian and Brandon.

"What kind of surgery?" Brandon wanted to know.

"A gunshot. Someone shot him as he stood to go inside our RV, and," she added almost in a whisper, "I'm worried about him."

Grant felt so sorry for her but knew she would resent any excess solicitous alms from him; therefore, he simply observed the woman and the young man from across the room as they quietly conversed.

Brandon looked directly at him and motioned for Grant to sit beside him.

"Do you think that, perhaps, Lillian was the target?"

"Why would you make that statement?" Lillian demanded.

"Right now, we don't have enough information to make that assumption," Grant said. "But it is certainly something to consider."

"Do you know more than I about the shenanigans going on at the lake?" Lillian asked.

Brandon shook his head.

Lillian then asked, "Who are you really, Brandon?"

Brandon laughed. "Madame, what you see is what I am."

Grant could read body language as well his mom, so Brandon's response to Lillian's question interested him but did not surprise him.

Brandon pushed himself up, using his good arm. "I need to return to my room before they send out a BOLO. Besides, it's time for my meds. I don't want to miss my evening cocktail." He laughed at his own joke and then wobbled as he stood.

Grant caught him before he fell.

Brandon held onto Grant's arm. "Help me to the door, will you?"

"Sure," Grant felt that Brandon's near fall was only for show.

As they neared the entrance to the hallway, Brandon whispered, "Will you promise me something?"

"Depends. What is it?" Grant kept his voice low.

"Don't let that good woman out of your sight. Take care of her."

"Consider it done."

"That's an easy promise to make, I'd guess." Brandon hobbled away.

When Grant turned back, Lillian stood right behind him.

"What did he say to you?"

"Asked me to protect you," Grant said. "Made me promise."

"Strange, don't you think?"

"I'm glad you asked for his true identity. Did you notice his reaction?"

"Yes, sir, I did," Lillian said.

"You need to be careful around him," Grant warned. "He's involved in whatever is going on at Caddo but has adopted you."

A nurse entered the waiting area. "Your husband is out of surgery. The doctor would like to give you an update. Come with me, please."

As they passed a connecting hallway, Grant's peripheral vision provided the quick glance of a sleeve, one he knew well.

The nurse led them to a small conference room.

"Have a seat. Dr. Williams will be with you in a few minutes."

Neither sat down. Grant moved around Lillian and stood behind her.

Dr. Williams entered and approached Lillian. The surgeon's kind eyes twinkled even though his face held the staid, professional façade doctors use when they confront the family to give a report, good or bad.

Lillian's voice cracked.

"Is Bill going to be okay?"

"Yes, ma'am. He's in recovery now. When he rouses, and we know he's cognizant of his surroundings, we'll move him to ICU so we can keep a close eye on him. If he progresses the way I think he will, we'll move him to his own room tomorrow."

"Can you tell us the severity of his injury?" Grant asked.

"Please do," Lillian said.

"The bullet went completely through the fleshy part of his right shoulder without hitting any vital organs, including bone matter."

"Thank God." Lillian wiped away a tear. "And thank you, Dr. Williams."

"Don't thank me, Mrs. Prestridge. Thank your son. It's a good thing he got him here so fast. Your husband lost a lot of blood."

"Does he need a blood transfusion? I could donate some for him," Grant said.

"The transfusion we're giving him now should be adequate."

"May I see him?"

"Five minutes, no longer. I'll have one of my staff take you to him." Dr. Williams turned and entered the surgical area.

Lillian sat down. "Grant, I'm so glad Bill's going to live. With him safe in the hospital, I can concentrate on solving the murders at Caddo." Grant raised his hand, a signal to stop.

"Don't say anything about your plans. Too many ears in this place." He glanced behind her and saw Sheriff Tomas watching and listening from the end of the connecting hallway.

Tomas made a pretend telephone with his hand.

Grant nodded.

A nurse arrived. "Mrs. Prestridge, the doctor asked me to give you five minutes with your husband. Please, follow me."

Lillian stood and waited for Grant.

"No, Lillian. You go. I'll be in the waiting area."

Grant looked back down the hallway. It was empty.

In the waiting area, he saw a notepad and wrote a message to Lillian, telling her that he needed to make a phone call and asking her to wait for him. He folded the piece of paper and wrote her name on the outside, then gave it to the volunteer manning the phone.

"I'll make sure Mrs. Prestridge receives it," the man assured him.

Grant ambled down the hallway.

Chapter Forty-One

MIDNIGHT. SLEEP tempted Brandon. Every time he almost fell asleep, the scene at Edgemon's flashed through his brain. Over and over, he replayed the nightmare that put him in the hospital, and once again, he hoped his father was not behind the attempt on his life. Abruptly, his mind would do a bungee jump to the murders at Caddo. Down into the chasm of confusion he fell. The sensation was so real that Brandon had to grip the rails on the sides of his bed to maintain his equilibrium.

A light tap on his door startled Brandon who, at such a hour, did not expect anyone to drop by to see him. Visiting hours ended three hours ago.

"Come in," he said. He knew the silhouette of the woman standing in the open doorway. "What are you doing here?"

"I heard about your accident and had to risk driving into town to see how you're doing." She walked to the side of his bed and brushed back his hair and kissed him on his forehead. "I wish you had called me. I would have come sooner." She blinked back the tears that threatened to flow.

"I'm doing all right. In fact, Doc said I may be dismissed next week if I continue to heal at the rate I am."

"That's the news I hoped to hear, but when you are discharged, call me. I'll pick you up. Take you to my house. It's secluded. No one knows about it. You'll be safe."

"What you really mean is that Dad doesn't know about it."

"You know I'll do anything to protect you."

"You're my mother, and I appreciate your concern, but I don't want you seen with me. It wouldn't be as safe as you think. By the way, how did you find out about the incident?"

"Everybody's talking about it."

"By now, I'm sure the story has become more dramatic with each retelling."

"Be honest with me. Are you healing, or do you say that to keep me away?"

Brandon reached up and took her hand. "I told you. I'm doing fine. Don't worry about me." She bent over and gave him a light hug.

The embrace gave him a clear line of sight over her shoulder. Brandon recognized his next visitor who stopped, made a U-turn, and quickly moved away from the door. In a voice, the volume of which was meant to be heard by anyone in the hallway, Brandon said, "Thank you so much for coming by. Tell everyone at Edgemon's I'm recuperating nicely." Then, in a whisper. "We're being watched. Go home. Now."

Leigh Ann followed his lead.

"Well, young man, if there's anything I can bring you, call Edgemon's." She opened her purse and handed him a card. "In case the line is busy, call me on my cell. As you know, we make deliveries."

The lady put on dark sunglasses and the large black, broad-brimmed hat she had held during their talk. When she reached the door, she turned and blew a kiss, and disappeared from sight.

* * * *

As soon as Leigh Ann turned the corner at the end of the hallway, Sheriff Tomas stepped out of the utility closet and moved to Brandon's room. He closed the door.

"What's up?" Brandon said.

"Someone close to us both asked me to check on you. Said he was busy and can't be seen with you but wants a report."

"Is it safe?"

Tomas nodded. "Hallway's empty except for hospital personnel, but I suggest you wait until morning to contact him. Keep your voice down. Ears are everywhere."

"Ten-four," Brandon said to an empty room.

* * * * * *

Brandon was wide awake. Why had the sheriff lied to him? He had to send a message right away. He rang for a nurse, but he was disappointed when his least favorite one entered his room.

Her nasally, high-pitched voice reminded him of a hawk's screech just before it swooped down and snatched an innocent, little critter.

"Are you in pain?" the nurse asked.

"No."

"Dr. Williams said I could give you an injection if you needed it." She held a hypodermic in her hand.

"I don't want an injection."

"You look as though you are in pain." She stepped closer to his bed. "This will help you sleep." The nurse tore open an alcohol packet and swabbed his arm.

Without thinking, Brandon slapped her had away.

"Why you," she reached out for him again.

Brandon raised his voice. "I will ask for that poison when I want it."

"Why are you yelling at me?" she asked.

"I'm not yelling," Brandon protested.

"Yes, you are." She spoke sternly. "You are getting too worked up. If you don't cooperate, I'll call an orderly to help me administer this injection."

Brandon took a deep breath and spoke slowly. "Would you just listen? Let me tell you what I want?"

"I'm listening, but make it quick."

"I need to borrow a cell phone. Do you have one handy?"

She pointed to the phone on the stand beside his bed. "Use that one."

"I need a more private line. It's a matter of life and death."

"Sorry, but it's against hospital procedure to let a patient use our personal items."

Brandon sighed. All of his life, he assumed nurses cared about their patients. She used the word sorry but sounded about as sympathetic as a rattlesnake just before it struck someone. As if she read his thoughts, the nurse rammed the needle into his arm and squeezed the soothing venom into Brandon. Struggling against the effects of the tranquilizer, Brandon heard the buzzer sound at the nurse's station. He waited, giving her time to slither down the hall to her next victim. He slipped out of bed and staggered down to the hospital's main lobby. The information desk was not manned after ten o'clock, so he sat down and dialed a familiar number.

"Hello," said a sleepy voice.

"Cover blown. I repeat. Cover blown."

"Ten-four."

The line went dead. Brandon hung up the phone and hoped he had made the call in time.

* * * * *

Lillian read the note from Grant. Once more, she sat in the surgical waiting room. She was alone. Hearing footsteps approach, she stood, then froze and listened. The short, choppy steps did not belong to Grant but to someone else.

A woman, wearing a black hat and dark sunglasses after midnight, exited the automatic doors.

Lillian sat back down. Where was Grant? Why did he need to talk to someone on the phone at this time of night?

Footsteps again, heavier this time, sounded like a man's long gait. Ready to leave, Lillian stood. A man in an official uniform left the hospital. "And just why is Sheriff Tomas still here?" Lillian muttered to herself.

"My mama told me it's not nice to stare," came a soft whisper in her ear.

"I remember saying that to both my sons," Lillian said. "Let's go to Caddo."

"Sounds like a plan to me." Grant escorted her out into the cool, autumn night.

Eli raised his head and yawned as the two climbed into Grant's truck. He promptly dropped back asleep.

"You said you needed to make a phone call?"

"Yes, I had to return a call."

"Who talked so long?"

"No one. Got only a voice mail."

"Strange."

"You think?" Grant asked.

She yawned. "Wake me when we get there." She closed her eyes and wondered why Grant had lied to her.

* * * * *

At three-forty-five in the morning, both Lillian and Eli awoke when Grant parked the truck in front of the Prestridge RV. "Here we are."

Grant slid out of the vehicle and walked around the hood of his truck to open the passenger door for Lillian. "Sit here while I do a walk-through."

"That's not necessary. Go on home. I'll see you in the morning."

"No, ma'am. After my inspection, I'll go to my RV for my pajamas and toothbrush. I'm spending the night with you."

"Go through my RV if you must, but that's all you're going to do tonight. You've already done enough, my dear. I don't need a keeper."

"But --"

"Don't argue with me, Grant. I'm worn out. Besides, I need some time to myself."

He didn't respond but opened the door of her RV.

Lillian watched the light come on in one room after the other as Grant made his way through the camper.

Finished, he returned to her. "It's safe." Grant extended his hand and helped her climb out of the truck. Eli jumped out and ran to the door, waiting. "Call me if you hear anything outside."

Lillian nodded, stepped inside, and closed the door. There was a knock. She smiled when she heard, "Lock your door." She locked the deadbolt.

Grant's footsteps told her he was on his way to his RV.

"Move over, Eli," Lillian said as she crawled into the bed without bothering to put on her pajamas.

* * * * *

Grant walked into his RV without turning on a light. He peered through the mini-blinds of the small window over the kitchen sink. There was enough moonlight to reveal a lone figure sitting in the car parked between Vickie's RV and the newest, biggest motor home across the lane. Grant stood still and waited five minutes, ten minutes. Nothing. No movement. Grant opened his door and with his 9mm in hand walked toward the street. Suddenly, the car's headlights blinded him. The driver revved the engine and sped out of the campsite.

Vickie flung open her door and ran out, holding a shotgun. She saw Grant standing in the middle of the lane. "What in the world?" She asked.

"Beats me. Do you know anyone who drives a black Town Car?"

"No. Why?"

"There was one parked between your RV and your next door neighbor. The person staking out the campground didn't much want to talk to me."

"I don't blame him. Middle of the night isn't prime time for getting acquainted with strangers."

"You didn't hear a car's engine drive that close to your RV?"

"I don't pay any attention to traffic in the campground. As you should know, RVers come and go at all hours, night or day."

"But most of them don't park by an RV other than their own. Are you sure you didn't hear anything out of the ordinary?"

"Not until I heard it peel away. Threw gravel against my camper."

"Vickie," Grant said, "be sure and lock your door. Caddo doesn't need another --"

Before he finished his sentence, Vickie saluted him and stepped back into her RV. "Goodnight," she said without looking back at him.

Wondering why she had run out of her RV, shotgun in hand if she hadn't heard anything, Grant waited until he heard the click of the lock on her door, then ambled across the street and stepped inside his Winnebago. As soon as he closed his door, his cell rang.

"Hello."

"What was that all about? Did I hear you talking to Vickie?"

"Go back to sleep, Lillian. We'll talk about it tomorrow."

"Noon is early enough for me." She hung up.

Chapter Forty-Two

TRAFFIC IN the campground. A cool autumn breeze blew the bottom of the curtain covering the open window in Lillian's bedroom. The waving cloth allowed a frisky strip of bright sunlight permission to hopscotch across the tiny space and alight on the weary eyelids of the sleeping woman. She rolled over and looked at the clock/radio.

Nine-thirty. Lillian shot out of bed and groaned as her feet touched the floor.

She stood, stretched, and glanced around. Alone. Even her dog had left her. Needing caffeine to chase away the cobwebs in her brain, Lillian staggered through the camper to the kitchen. Eli, on guard as usual, lay stretched along the back of the sofa.

"Okay, go ahead. Call me a sleepy head." Eli raised his head and yawned. The red stains on the dog's neck and chest – Bill's blood – a sad reminder of the previous night chased away the dregs of Lillian's exhausted sleep. All too well, the blood brought back memories of the day she and Eli had become inseparable, the morning he came to her wearing the blood of his previous owner.

Lillian choked back tears. "Can't believe I didn't see these last night." She retrieved a washcloth from the small bath and, after holding it under the sink's faucet, she then perched on the armrest of the couch, cleaning the dark, red reminders from Eli's fur. "We make a pair, don't we?" she asked in a soothing voice.

As only his owner would claim, the dog grinned at her as if to say, "Yeah, you know it."

She grinned back and pulled him close. "You brighten my day, you sweet mutt. And it will be an even happier day after I see Bill this morning, especially if he had a good night's sleep. I pray he felt no pain."

Lillian threw the cloth in the trash and set the coffee pot to brew. "I'll be right back, Eli. I need to get dressed."

Lillian opened her bedroom closet and took out her favorite pair of black sweatpants, her Texas A&M T-shirt, and her favorite pink cardigan. Dressed for the day, Lillian returned and filled her insulated cup.

Her cell phone rang. She recognized the masculine voice she loved on the other end.

"Hi, darling. I was about to phone the hospital to see how you're doing. Eli and I will drive in this morning, but I wanted to give you plenty of time to sleep-in. I can't believe you're awake this early."

"Didn't sleep much last night," Bill said.

"Were you in pain?"

"A little pain, but overall, I'm fine."

"The doctor told me he intended to keep you sedated through the night and most of today. Did the meds not take effect?"

"They would have if I'd swallowed every pill the nurse gave me."

"What did you do, Bill?"

"I faked it."

"Why?"

"I was worried about you. Afraid to call you. Thought you might try to drive back into town to make sure I slept."

"No need to worry about me. You know I can take care of myself."

"Hold on a minute."

Lillian could hear muffled voices, then silence. The line went dead. Lillian immediately dialed Bill's cell.

"Hello, Lillian."

"Grant?"

"I'm with Bill. Came in early to check on him, and it's a good thing I did."

"Thank you for seeing about him this morning." Lillian could hear Bill's complaining and Grant's stern response. "No, Bill, you can't have it back. I'm talking to her now."

"He sounds angry."

Grant laughed. "He is."

"Why?"

"I took his phone away from him."

"Thank you again. Tell me, Grant, do you think he's all right?"

"He's fine."

"He told me he didn't sleep well last night. I know the doctor wants him to rest."

"Dr. Williams made his rounds right after I walked into the room this morning. He wants to keep him here for a couple of days, fill him with antibiotics to make sure no infection occurs. And, the doc assured me Bill will sleep like a baby today."

"That's good. You and I have work to do."

"Correction: I have work to do. I want you to stay inside today. You need to rest."

"Wrong, my dear son. I'm not hibernating while you do all the snooping."

"I agree with what Brandon said last night."

"Refresh my memory. I was a little upset last night, so I don't remember everything accurately."

Even though she knew Eli could not tattle on her, Lillian crossed her fingers for lying to Grant. She clearly remembered Brandon's second warning about the need for caution at Caddo Lake.

"Brandon speculated that you, not Bill, might not have been the target."

"I'll keep that in mind and promise I will be careful."

"Be careful and stay put. I'll check in with you off and on today."

"I'll see you tonight, son." Lillian ended the call.

Lillian filled her thermos with coffee and said to Eli, "It's no wonder you slept on the sofa. You, too, must have sensed we were being watched. Come on. Let's go for a walk. Both of us need exercise."

Eli barked an answer and jumped down. When she opened the door, he raced across the lane and once again sniffed around the luxurious camper across the street.

"Come on, you silly boy. You've already checked out our new neighbors."

She and her dog walked past the camp director's mobile home. Eli raced ahead of his owner and then circled back, barking at every leaf falling from the old oak trees.

Lillian heard a door open and stopped to look back over her shoulder. She made eye contact with Milly and noticed the woman's hesitation before walking out onto her deck to greet Lillian.

"How's Bill this morning?" Milly asked.

"Better, thank you."

"Does the sheriff know who shot him?"

"Not yet. Who told you about the shooting?"

"Everybody's talking about it."

Lillian wondered how everybody could have talked to Milly since only Vickie had shown concern for Bill. Lillian tried to remember if Milly had been at home the previous evening. She didn't remember seeing her. Perhaps, Grant could tell her if anyone else had exhibited any curiosity about hearing a gunshot in the campground. But for now, Lillian continued on her way and followed Eli to the end of the pier.

"After visiting Bill this afternoon, I think we need to pick up a few things at Edgemon's, don't you, Eli? Where was Milly last night? That store is where most of the locals spread the news about Caddo, but since Edgemon's closes at eight in the evening, that tidbit of gossip won't reach the owner or the store's patrons until this morning. If she didn't hear about the incident at the store, then someone else informed her. But who?"

The dog answered with a low, warning growl and stood. A strip of ridged fur down the center of his back indicated Eli's attack mode. Lillian quickly stood and grabbed his collar to restrain him.

"What's wrong with your dog this morning?" A tall, muscular man approached them. He wore army fatigues and carried an elongated, black duffle bag.

"Nothing's wrong with him. He doesn't like strangers. That's all."

The man smiled and held his hand down so Eli could sniff it. The dog growled louder and lunged toward the man.

"Sit," Lillian commanded in a loud, stern voice. "Stay." Eli obeyed.

The man quickly withdrew his hand. "I'll leave you two alone." He held the bag between him and the Poodle, moved to the far side of the pier, and warily walked backwards to the end of the marina. Eli stared at the man and gave him a toothy, canine sneer. The sound of a small engine floated over the gently splashing waves of the lake.

The man in fatigues waved, and when the Jon boat reached the end of the marina and stopped, two hands reached up to receive the black bag. Then the stranger in camo stepped down.

Lillian watched the Jon boat glide to the middle of the lake. She looked down at her four-legged guardian. "I didn't like him either. I wonder what he and Simon are planning."

Eli snorted and shook his head.

"Let's go. I need to feed you before I leave to visit Bill."

Lillian heard another boat approaching the marina. She stopped to look. Only one other boat, the park ranger's patrol boat, had an engine as loud as the one she now heard. The force of the wind rushing across the bow, blew red hair away from the face of its captain.

"Milly?" Lillian muttered. "Where are you going?"

"Looks like she's on a mission."

Lillian turned to see Franklin Ford, coffee cup in hand, standing behind her.

"Mr. Ford? Where did you come from?"

"Sorry, Mrs. Prestridge, I didn't mean to startle you."

"Just surprised, that's all. Of all people, I didn't expect to see you at Caddo."

He laughed.

"It's a small world."

"Indeed. And the older I grow, the more it shrinks."

Eli, tail wagging, took a couple of steps toward Franklin and sniffed the man's pants leg, then sat down beside him.

"I think he remembers me from Jefferson," Franklin said and patted Eli's head.

"He's a smart dog and a good judge of character," Lillian said and smiled. She extended her hand. "What brings you to Caddo?"

Franklin shook hands and said, "Vickie's been telling me I would love to RV, so I took her advice and decided to rent an RV. If I enjoy it, I might buy this one." He pointed back to the campground to the large, ostentatious motor home Eli had sniffed.

"She leaves hers parked here all the time, I think," said Lillian.

"Vickie loves camping and fishing. She spends every free moment away from her practice here at Caddo."

"Speaking of law practice, how long have you and Vickie had a relationship?"

Franklin looked puzzled, so Lillian quickly added, "Forgive me. That was a nosey question." She laughed and pretended to be embarrassed. "I hope I didn't offend you. I should have said law partners."

"No offense taken." He paused and nodded as if he had decided how to answer Lillian's inquiry. "Vickie and I have known each other longer than she would want me to reveal. She guards her age well."

"Don't we all?" Lillian said sweetly.

Franklin smiled. "How well do you know her?" he asked.

Lillian felt that Franklin and she were alike. Each of them could give a vague answer to any question.

"I'll tell you one thing: She came through for me and my husband last night. She helped take him to the hospital."

"I'm sorry he was shot. Vickie told me what happened. How is he?"

"He'll be okay. It will take some time for him to heal and get back on his feet."

"Well, that is good news. If there's anything I can do for you, let me know. I'll be here for a few more days." He reached out his hand to shake.

"Thank you. That's very kind of you."

When Franklin shook her hand, he slipped into it a piece of paper. Without looking at the item, she placed it in the pocket of her sweats. "Well, I need to feed my dog. Hope you enjoy your stay."

She tugged gently on Eli's collar. "Come on, big boy. Let's go home."

She did not look over her shoulder as she walked away, but her intuition screamed, "He's watching you," as she climbed the slight incline on her way back to the campground.

Chapter Forty-Three

AFTER SHE stepped inside her RV, Lillian read the man's business card. "I forgot to ask Franklin if he has a son. His answer might help me solve one of the mysteries at the lake."

She fed Eli and sat down at her computer and typed a note to herself, separate from the list she shared with Grant and Bill.

Eli finished his meal and trotted to the bedroom, leaving Lillian at the dinette table staring at her computer screen, deep in thought. When someone touched her shoulder, she jumped and jerked her head around to see the culprit who dared to sneak up behind her.

"Don't do that to me," she commanded, using her schoolmarm voice, but the grin on her face belied the fact that she was happy to see him.

"I thought I told you to keep your door locked," Grant growled.

"You did, and it was locked all night," Lillian said.

"That's good," Grant said and poured himself a cup of hazelnut coffee. He turned to face Lillian and leaned against the small kitchen counter.

"You're quite pensive. What's on your mind?"

"I have a message from Bill," Grant said.

"What is it?" she asked.

"Just before he conked out from the strong sedative the doc ordered, he said to tell you to stay put, don't drive into town. Those were his exact words."

"What would make him say that?"

"He said he needed to rest, not worry about you."

"Okay. To please him, I'll check on him via telephone and hang around here."

"Thank you. By the way, where is that funny dog of yours? He usually greets me, nearly knocks me down."

"He's tired. We walked down to the marina this morning." From Grant's expression, she knew another lecture was on its way, so she decided to head it off. "And before you fuss, let me tell you what happened."

"I'm listening."

Grant topped off his cup, replenished hers, and sat across the dinette table from her.

"First of all, do you remember when Bill and I drove into Jefferson to buy new cell phones and replace my computer?"

Grant nodded. "That was the day of Brandon's accident, wasn't it?"

"Yes. Did we tell you whom we saw while we were there?"

"I'm not sure we talked much about it. Enlighten me."

"We were walking down the main street of town when Eli started barking, growling, and trying to cross the street. He jerked the leash so hard that he made Bill drop his camera."

"That's not unusual. Your canine buddy is good at that – creating chaos, I mean." Grant laughed as Eli, on cue, ran from the bedroom and placed his paw on Grant's knee. "See what I mean? He has to be in the middle of everything, including our conversation." Grant patted the dog on his head. "You like attention, don't you, boy?"

"Speaking of attention. If you could let me have yours, I'll finish my story."

"Continue, ma'am."

"Second, do you remember Vickie Parsons?"

"Sure do. Every time she steps out of that RV of hers, she's hard to forget. She's a beautiful lady. Besides that, I appreciate the way she helped us with Bill."

"You're correct on both counts, but be careful around her."

"Why do you say that?" Grant asked.

"I'm not sure she's all she claims to be."

"You don't have to worry, Lillian. I'm not in the market." Grant said in a low voice.

"Let's go back to my story about Jefferson."

"What does that have to do with Vickie?"

"Vickie is an attorney and has her practice in the middle of town."

"And that's significant because?"

"We visited with her that day."

"Okay." Grant took a gulp of his coffee and waited. "So? I know there's more."

"Guess who was with her?"

"Won't even try."

"Leigh Ann Heavener."

"Isn't she the lady who found the body on the jogging trail?"

"And guess who else was with Vickie?"

"You tell me."

"Franklin – Leigh Ann's soon-to-be ex – if she's told the truth."

"That's interesting," Grant said. "Perhaps, they were discussing how they were going to divide their property."

"Franklin's gaze at Leigh Ann indicated an interest in more than property."

Lillian knew she had piqued Grant's curiosity, so she leaned back in her chair, tilted her chin in triumph, and decided to put the icing on the cake, so to speak. "Guess what else?"

Grant raised his eyebrows. They posed a question.

"Franklin's last name is Ford. Does that ring a bell?"

"It sure does."

"And I've talked to him since Jefferson."

"After Jefferson? When?"

"Guess who owns the big RV across from us."

"Damn," was Grant's only reply.

"I think you need to visit with the sheriff and find out if Franklin is legit."

"I'll do that." Grant stood and left Lillian sitting in front of her computer.

She laid the attorney's business card on the table and booted up the laptop and chuckled out loud to Eli.

"That will keep him busy and out of my hair while I put two and two together."

* * * * *

Sheriff Tomas sat at his desk proofreading his written report of the events surrounding the attempt on Bill Prestridge's life. He looked up as Grant knocked on his office door.

"I got your message to call, but your phone went to voice mail," Grant said.

"After contacting you, I decided I needed to write up a report before we discussed the shooting." He handed the report to Grant. "Let me know if you think I've left out anything pertinent to the incident."

The deputy scanned the report and handed the document back to his superior officer.

"Looks good, very thorough."

"I've been thinking," said the sheriff, "and have come to the conclusion that Lillian may have been the target, not Bill."

"What makes you think that?"

"Ever since I received that first call about the dead man found on the jogging trail, she's been right in the middle of everything that's happened. I get the feeling she doesn't miss much."

"That's my mom." Grant smiled. "Remember. I've told you about her uncanny way of getting to the bottom of things."

"I know you respect her judgment."

"Always. But sometimes, she takes too many serious risks which cause me to work hard protecting her while I perform my paying job."

Sheriff Tomas swiveled his desk chair to face the window, ran his fingers through his wiry salt and pepper hair, and then turned back to make eye contact with Grant.

"Here's what I want you to do: Go talk to her. Get any information she has or thinks she has about everything that's happened while she and Bill have camped at Caddo." He paused and then said, "Tell me, is she honest with you?"

"Most of the time."

"Most of the time?" Sheriff Tomas said.

"Yes, sir, but I can tell you up front that she will divulge only what she wants me to know."

Sheriff Tomas shook his head.

"Well, do the best you can. Then report back to me."

"I will." Grant stood and left.

The sheriff walked to his window, watched Grant get in his truck, and wondered whether or not he could trust his new, temporary officer. Was Grant more loyal to his adopted mother than he was to the oath of office he had taken?

Tomas closed the window blinds shutting out the sight of storm clouds gathering outside his office. He was tired of rain. A slow rumble escaped the one that hovered over the building. He returned to his desk and slumped down into the black leather, swivel chair given to him by fellow professors when he retired from Sam Houston.

He sighed and thought perhaps he had made a mistake trusting the person he had commissioned to oversee the most important project of his life. He picked up his cell phone and dialed the number he had on speed dial.

"Hello, sheriff. How's it going today?"

"Where is that report you promised I would have on my desk this morning?"

"There's nothing to report. Only four or five have checked in."

"I don't believe that crap." Sheriff Tomas slammed his fist against the arm of his expensive chair.

"Well, sir, why don't you drive out to Caddo and count the damned RVs for yourself?"

"You better hope I don't do just that."

"Is that a threat?"

"No. It's a promise. You better watch your back." Tomas violently punched the "end" button.

A light tap on his door interrupted his curse and announced the arrival of his worst nightmare. A lady wearing black leggings and a burgundy silk tunic stepped inside his office. She closed and locked the door behind her. Perched on the corner of his desk, she kicked off her red, spiked heels. She wiggled her toes in the spot she knew he couldn't resist. "Hello, darling. Why look so sad?" she said with a smirk.

"Lillian Prestridge. She's the problem."

"Don't worry. The plan is working. Besides, I gave you her notebook. You know what she thinks she knows."

"Yeah, but if what I've heard about her, that woman's brain never sleeps."

"Forget about her." The woman said as she slipped off the desk and onto the sheriff's lap. "She isn't Agatha Christie."

The sheriff thought about his dwindling bank account, sighed, and put his arms around his nemesis.

Chapter Forty-Four

LILLIAN HAD both laptops perched on the dinette table and moved from one to the other as she searched databases. The HP printer spewed page after page of information she gleaned from the Internet. Above the drone of the inkjet buzzing across its lines of print, she heard a knock at her door. She stopped the printer and closed the screen of the computer, which faced the open living area of the RV.

"One moment, please," she said as she scooped up the stack of printed pages and turned them over to obscure their information. Then she walked to the door.

"May I talk to you?" asked Milly.

"Of course, come in." Lillian waved her hand toward the sofa. "Have a seat."

The woman stood in the middle of the room, hands together, fingers laced so tightly that Lillian asked, "What's wrong, Milly? Do you need help?"

"I don't know."

Lillian took Milly's arm, led her to Bill's recliner, and helped her sit down. In a soft, soothing voice, she asked, "Why don't I make us a cup of tea? We can talk then."

Milly nodded. "Yes, that sounds good."

Lillian put teabags in two mugs, filled them with water, and placed one in the microwave. When she heard the timer ding, she removed the cup and handed it to Milly.

"I'm worried," said Milly.

"About Al?" Lillian put the second cup into the microwave. She turned and faced Milly in time to see her swipe away a stray tear.

"Al's dead, you know."

Lillian heard harsh undertones seeping through Milly's declaration.

"No, I don't know. Why do you think he's dead?"

"I've not heard from him in over a week. That's not like him."

"Have you reported him missing?"

"After I returned from my sister's house, I asked Jeff Richards – he's the park ranger, you know – to keep an eye out for him, and I filed a report with the sheriff's office."

"Do you think Al could have lost his way back to camp if he went out on the lake alone?" Lillian asked.

"No way could Al be lost on Caddo. He knows every inch of that lake."

Lillian patted the woman's arm. "I'm sure the authorities are doing all they can."

Milly shook her head. "I doubt they know anything since I haven't heard from them. I'm not even sure they took me serious when I talked to them."

"Don't give up hope. I know from talking to my sons that family members of the missing person don't understand the time it takes to find their loved one. Sometimes, they discover that the person doesn't want to be found. Al wouldn't willingly disappear. He's too much of a homebody. Thanks for listening to me." Milly stood and motioned toward Lillian's computer and the stack of papers on the dinette. "Sorry the camp's internet is down. Cable company hasn't been able to come. That last storm --" Milly's voice gave way.

Because of Bill's situation, Lillian discovered she empathized with the woman. "Don't worry about that. I'm just glad we have electricity."

"Me, too. Hope your husband is doing okay."

"You take care, okay?" Lillian watched the woman walk back to the camp director's office.

"Well, Eli, I wonder what that was all about? She didn't tell me anything new. Maybe she did just need to talk."

The Poodle raised his head, sneezed, and went back to sleep in his favorite spot on the back of the sofa.

Lillian put Milly's empty cup in the sink and made another cup of tea before she resumed her research. She sorted the printed pages into stacks, lined them up on her desk, and read through the information, highlighting the facts she deemed important and writing her observations in the margins. When she heard an automobile ease to a stop, she left her notes to stand in front of the kitchen sink and look out the window.

A black Lincoln Town Car stopped across the lane, and Vickie Parsons climbed into the passenger seat. The driver turned the car around and drove back through the entrance to the campground.

Movement alongside the tree line drew Lillian's attention away from the receding car. Franklin Ford, too, watched the car drive away. He held a cell phone to his ear.

"Darn, Eli. I wish he would look this way so I could read his lips," Lillian said.

And, as if Franklin heard her, he turned and walked in her direction.

"Thank you, Mr. Ford," Lillian said as he ended the call and placed the cell in his shirt pocket. "I will need to share this information with Grant." She sat down at the table and wrote a quick note on the back of one of the printed pages.

Lillian dialed Bill's cell phone. After three rings, a male voice said, "I still have Bill's phone, Lillian."

"I'm glad. Have you checked on him this afternoon?"

"He's sleeping like a baby."

"Good. When you have time, I have a request."

"Tell me."

"Could you, in your official role as a deputy, unofficially run a background check on some people?"

"There's no such thing as unofficially official. Why should I go undercover?"

"It's important to keep Tomas in the dark."

"I don't like going behind my superior's back to do any kind of investigation. It's not fair. I know. Been there."

"If you don't mind being blindsided again, go ahead and ignore me. So much for our being a team."

"Now, Lillian, don't try to put a guilt trip on me."

"That's okay. I'll call Jake. He'll do it for his mother." Lillian knew sibling rivalry well. She had used it to her advantage with the boys on more than one occasion.

"Hold on," said Grant. "I'm on my way to Caddo. Let's discuss this further."

"I'll wait for you. I have some important information to share with you. Why don't you plan on eating dinner with me tonight? I'm going to Edgemon's to buy the ingredients I need to make your favorite enchilada casserole." She smiled, knowing that Grant couldn't resist.

"What time?"

"Be here around six o'clock if you can."

Lillian shut down both computers and packed them in a briefcase along with all of her printed pages. She placed them in the cooler she always carried in the back of her SUV when grocery shopping. She slammed the tailgate shut and called her dog. "Come on, Eli. We have some shopping to do. Grant's coming for dinner, so I need to pick up some ice cream." She opened the passenger door, and her loyal companion jumped in, ready for adventure. Lillian climbed behind the wheel and started the engine, driving slowly away.

"In case of a break-in, the culprit won't find my notes this time," she said to Eli as she glanced in her rearview mirror. As expected, she saw someone step out of hiding. She drove slowly out the entrance. Once she made the turn onto the highway, she slowed down more, giving herself plenty of time to make a positive identification.

*****

At Edgemon's where gossip was the norm, Lillian methodically strolled down one aisle and up another, speaking to other customers. Satisfied that she had everything in her overloaded grocery cart for Bill's home-coming celebration, she took her place at the end of the queue at the checkout station.

She read the headlines of the tabloids beside the aisle and accidentally bumped her cart into the lady standing in front of her.

"Oh, excuse me," she said. "I got sidetracked by these." Lillian pointed.

The lady smiled. "No problem. I do the same thing, read all the news about who's getting a divorce. Don't believe a word of it, though."

"Yep, as if the problems of the rich and famous make a difference to me, but the stories are too good to resist."

The lady nodded agreement. "You must be camping at Caddo."

Lillian laughed and waved her hand over the cart. "How can you tell?"

"I did the same thing every time my family joined my brother who had a lake house on Caddo. Bought too much. You'd think we were leaving civilization to be gone a year and feared starving."

"I think we all do it, but when my husband is released from the hospital, I am having a domino party to celebrate."

"They still play dominoes out there?"

"Until recently, every Friday night. I never played the game before RVing at Caddo."

"My brother always enjoyed the games. I can't bring myself to go camping anymore since his death."

"I'm so sorry for your loss," said Lillian.

"Thank you." The woman paused. "I guess I ought to restate that. I don't know if he died or not."

"If you don't mind my asking, what happened?"

"Three years ago, he went fishing with two of his friends on Caddo Lake. They disappeared. Couldn't be found."

"How sad," Lillian said.

"More than you can imagine. I can at least talk about him now." Then the woman moved on up to the counter, paid for her groceries, and waved goodbye to Lillian as she left the store.

Lillian unloaded her items from the cart and placed them on the counter's moving conveyor belt. The chatty young checker smiled and greeted Lillian.

"Planning a party?"

"Yes, ma'am, a domino party as a matter of fact."

The checker's cheerful face turned serious. "Be careful. Strange things have been going on at Caddo."

"Do you know Brandon Ford?"

"Yes, ma'am. He worked here, but was in an accident and is in the hospital now."

"I asked about Brandon because he warned me about strange events at Caddo the first time I shopped here."

"I hate to gossip, but the lady in front of you – well, she won't leave the area. Keeps hoping her brother will turn up. At the time, there was a big write up about it in the newspaper."

The checker completed scanning and sacking Lillian's purchases and gave her the amount due.

Lillian handed the girl her credit card. After swiping it on her computer, she returned it. "Thank you, Ms. Prestridge," and added, "Be safe."

Lillian pushed her cart to her SUV and loaded everything into the back. She started the engine but sat for a moment deep in thought. Lillian decided she would ask Grant if he had heard about two fishermen disappearing about three years ago.

* * * * *

Lillian parked her vehicle in front of the camp director's office. "Stay here, Eli. Guard the car." She opened the sunroof so he could have plenty of fresh air and left him. She knocked on the office door and stepped inside.

Milly looked up, but before she could say anything, Lillian said, "I want to run something by you."

"Okay. What do you have on your mind?"

"Dominoes," said Lillian.

"You're kidding. I don't remember you having any fun the last time you played."

"Be that as it may, I'm planning a welcome-home party for Bill, and I'd like for you to come."

Milly smiled.

"Lovely. I'll be there, but dominoes and welcome-home party. Just how do those equate since you don't like to play that game?"

Lillian plastered a sly grin on her face. "I like to surprise my guests with fun activities. I'll let you know the date and time as soon as I can get things organized," she said and left the office.

Outside, Lillian stopped and scanned the area. Eli, on guard, stood on his back legs, head protruding out of the sunroof and growling.

A familiar figure walked away from her car.

The dog settled down in the passenger seat when she climbed into the car. "Good job, big boy. I don't blame you for fussing at him."

* * * * *

Groceries unloaded and put away, Lillian retrieved the ice chest from the SUV. She decided to leave the computers in the cooler until after dinner. Then, she would discuss her suspicions with Grant and inform him of her plans for Friday night. She set the table and mixed ingredients for the enchilada casserole. While it baked, she prepared a salad.

Lillian turned on the television to catch up on the world news. The next thing she knew, she heard Grant calling her name and knocking on her door. She rushed to the door and then to the oven. She placed the casserole on top of the range.

"Thank goodness, it didn't burn."

"I thought you'd never let me in. It's beginning to rain."

"Sorry. Guess I drifted off listening to the drone of the television."

"If FOX News can lull you to sleep, then it's a good day. Dull news sounds wonderful to me." He inhaled. "Do you want me to drool, or do you plan on letting me eat? This smells heavenly."

Lillian laughed.

"All of a sudden, I'm hungry, too. Let's eat." She handed him a plate.

Chapter Forty-Five

LILLIAN ATE silently and watched Grant devour every morsel of food on his plate. Finished, he took his empty plate to the sink and rinsed it off before placing it in the dishwasher, then returned to the dinette table and sat opposite Lillian.

"Thanks," he said, "I had forgotten how much I love your Mexican casserole. During my sabbatical from Leisure Lake, I mostly ate fast food or TV dinners."

"I'm glad you enjoyed your meal. Would you like something to drink while we work?" Lillian asked.

Grant's expression changed from a satisfied smile to an irritated frown. "I hate to fuss at you after such a delightful meal, but did you forget our earlier conversation, the one about my working and you staying put?"

Lillian's eyebrows shot up and she feigned innocence. "Are you sure we had that discussion? I certainly can't remember agreeing to those terms."

Grant laughed. "I should have known you wouldn't listen to me earlier today. So, out with it: tell me about your snooping."

"You'll change your tune in a minute, young man. I have some information you will want to know. It might help us find the deadly domino murderer."

Lillian stood and picked up the red and white cooler. She placed it on the table. "Open this and set up the computers while I make us some coffee. We're going to need to be alert tonight, and caffeine will help."

Grant set the cooler on the floor after removing the computers. He placed a laptop on each side of the table and booted both of them.

Finished with the coffee maker, Lillian reached into the cooler and retrieved the stack of papers she had printed.

Lillian sighed and said, "Grant, I'm going to ask you to read these. But before you ask me where I got this information, I want you to remember this: If a person knows how to listen to others, how to research, and how to surf the web, she can find out anything about anyone."

She handed the printed sheets of information to Grant and instructed, "Read, son. Read every word. And when you've finished, speak softly. Don't raise your voice."

After making sure that Grant followed her instructions, Lillian walked through the RV and closed all of the window blinds. She didn't want any peeping tom to see them or hear their discussion.

Lillian, elbows propped on the table, held her coffee mug with both hands and waited for Grant to finish reading the printed pages as well as her summary of the facts. He looked up when he had turned the last page. His face, creased with disappointment and sadness, broke Lillian's heart.

"Who would have thought it?" Grant spoke slightly above a whisper.

Lillian realized the moment Grant completely absorbed the facts when he growled, "Makes me ashamed of being in law enforcement after reading the trash you obtained on Tomas and Jeff."

"I know you always held your old professor in high regard."

Lillian stood and walked around the table. "This feels like *déjà vu* all over again." She put her hand on Grant's shoulder. "I'm so sorry, but I wanted you to be the first person to learn about your old mentor."

"Don't apologize. He lied to me when he said he retired from teaching."

Grant surprised Lillian when he suddenly stood and began pacing back and forth. Halfway across the room, he stopped, balled one hand into a fist and slammed it into the open palm of his other hand.

"I wish I could prove your theory right this minute. I'd figure out a way to arrest him tonight."

"Shh. Calm down, son. Anger isn't a solution. Plus, I might have misjudged him."

Grant's nostrils flared, but he lowered his voice. "No, ma'am, your impression of another person is correct ninety-nine point ninety-nine percent of the time."

Grant took two steps and stopped again. "And to think he had the gall today to ask me to spy on you."

"I know you're more than disappointed, but listen to me, son," Lillian said in the soothing voice she had employed throughout the years to diffuse an occasional argument between her boys.

"I have to believe something bad happened to the man to cause his morphing into such a radical, or the university would not have dismissed him."

Grant nodded and took his empty coffee mug to the counter and re-filled it. Turning to face Lillian, he held up his cup and with a lop-sided, insincere grin, asked, "Do you have any whiskey?"

"Yes, but you can't have any tonight. I want you clear-headed. We need to figure out what we're going to do next without causing any harm to innocent bystanders."

"Right. How to investigate the sheriff isn't going to be easy."

"And that, my darling boy, is where you come in the pic --" Lillian stopped.

Eli leapt from his perch on the back of the sofa and ran to the RV's door. The soft tone of his menacing low growl matched the hushed voices of Lillian and Grant, but all the same, it signaled danger lurking outside.

* * * * *

Grant immediately switched off the overhead light. He motioned for Lillian to hold onto Eli's collar. Then ever so softly, he tiptoed across the room and peered out the small window over the sink. He did not recognize the person he saw standing outside of Vickie Parson's RV. He tiptoed back to stand beside Lillian and whispered in her ear. "Someone's spying on Vickie."

Lillian nodded. "Keep Eli quiet. Be careful, son."

Grant pulled his gun and silently opened the door. Before stepping outside, he whispered, "Lillian, stay put." Then he disappeared into the darkness.

* * * * *

Lillian held Eli's collar, and she pulled him alongside of her as she, like Grant, tiptoed to peer out the kitchen window. She smiled when the man's hands shot up in the air and turned away from Vickie's RV and walked in front of Grant.

"Be nice, Eli," Lillian said before she opened the door to admit the stranger and Grant. She closed the door behind them and switched on the light.

"Franklin?"

"Yes, ma'am. It's me," he said.

"Put away your gun, Grant. I know this man." She gave Franklin a stern once over.

"But what I don't know is why he was lurking around Vickie's RV."

Grant snarled, "Sit down."

Franklin sat down in the chair Grant pulled away from the dinette. "I can explain," he said.

"You'd better start explaining. I could arrest you, and I bet Ms. Parsons would press stalking charges against you."

Franklin appealed to Lillian. "Would you please tell him who I am?"

"Yeah, Mom, just how do you know this pervert?"

"His name is Franklin Ford, and he's attorney of counsel with a young, female attorney, namely, Ms. Vickie Parsons. Your dad and I met him a week ago when we visited Vickie at her office in Jefferson, Texas."

Grant put his gun back in his holster but maintained eye contact with Franklin.

Lillian continued.

"And, I'm pretty sure he's the father of a mutual acquaintance of ours who is in the hospital suffering from injuries sustained as a result of a hit and run."

"My God, are you talking about my son?" His voice quivered. "Surely not."

"If your son is Brandon Ford, she is," said Grant.

"Where is he? I want to see him," Franklin sounded frantic.

"First, I want to hear from you. Explain what you were doing outside Vickie's RV this time of night," Grant said.

Lillian interceded on Franklin's behalf. "Wait, son, think about it. Your dad would want to see you if he knew you had been in an accident. Besides, I'd like to check on your dad before this night is over. Let's take him to the hospital."

Grant took a deep breath and nodded. "I guess you're right. The county jail's not too far away from the hospital. He can tell us what we want to know on the drive into town," Grant took Franklin's elbow, "or he can explain his actions at headquarters. His choice."

Lillian gathered the loose sheets of paper scattered on the table and unplugged the laptops. She packed the red cooler, hooked Eli to his leash, and announced, "Let's go," and led the way.

Grant opened the passenger door for her, but Lillian opened the backseat passenger door. Eli jumped in and she climbed in behind him, placing the cooler on the seat between them. With a wave of his hand, Grant instructed Franklin to climb inside the truck.

* * * * *

Three slots were available on the ground level parking at the ETMC garage. Grant drove past them to the second level and chose a spot closest to the elevator so the three of them could ride the lift and use the crosswalk connecting the garage to the main building.

"Guard the truck, Eli. Don't let anyone near this," ordered Lillian. She patted the cooler and set it between the seats. She then climbed out of the truck. Eli placed both of his front paws on top of the cooler.

Lillian waited to hear the click of the automatic lock before she joined Grant and Franklin who waited by the elevator for her.

The elevator stopped on the fourth floor where Brandon's room was located.

As they stepped into the hallway, Lillian caught a peripheral glimpse of a woman, dressed in black tights and a burgundy tunic, enter the next elevator. Unfortunately, the woman's face and hair were concealed by a large-brimmed hat and sunglasses, but she was almost positive the woman was the same one who had been at the hospital the night Bill was shot.

Grant stopped in front of Brandon's door.

"Lillian, you go in first. Let Brandon know Mr. Ford and I would like to talk to him."

Lillian nodded and pushed the door so she could peek around it. She smiled at Brandon who beckoned her inside and turned down a corner on the page of the book he held in his hands.

"Hi, it's good to see you," he said and held out a hand for her to shake.

"I'm glad you feel like reading."

"Yeah, a friend of mine brought this book to me. It's pretty good. First book I've read by this author." He held up the book so Lillian could read the title.

"I've read that one. In fact, N. E. Brown is a friend of mine. We met at the East Texas Book Fair last year right after she published *Carson Chance, P.I.*"

"Wow," Brandon said, "I've never met an author in real life."

Lillian laughed. "I'll introduce you to her sometime. She lives in Tyler, but right now, there's someone else waiting outside your door. Is it all right if ask them to come in?"

"Let's see," he began, "this is the day of Caddo Lake visitors."

"What do you mean by that?"

"First thing this morning, the maintenance man, Simon, came to visit, and just a few minutes before you arrived, Ms. Heavener dropped by. And now you, but I bet you're visiting Bill also."

"Yes, I plan on seeing him, too."

"Well, don't just stand there. Invite my visitors in." Brandon said. Lillian walked to the door and opened it.

Brandon's smile eased into a grimace when his father followed by Grant walked into the room. Son and father stared at each other.

Finally, Franklin spoke, "Hi, son." He stood by Brandon's bed.

"So, Dad, you just had to come see the handiwork of your henchmen."

The sneer Brandon gave his father as he ground his teeth was too much for Lillian. She pushed her way between Franklin and the side of the bed.

"Listen to me, young man," she scolded and pointed her finger in his face. "If you weren't in that bed, I'd turn you wrong side out. Teach you a lesson about civility. How dare you blame your father. For your information, Brandon, he didn't know anything about your accident; it was I who told your father about you."

Bug-eyed and mouth agape, Brandon didn't move, didn't breathe.

"And close your mouth," Lillian ended her tirade.

Brandon exhaled and said to Lillian, "I'm sorry I upset you."

"Forgiven," she snapped and in a softer tone added, "Shake hands with your father. We don't have time for regrets and much to discuss."

Lillian stepped aside so that father and son could make contact.

Holding his son's hand, Franklin bent over the bed and kissed Brandon on the top of his head. "She speaks the truth, son. I wouldn't hurt you or order anyone to harm you. Ever. Please believe me." Franklin raised his right hand and swiped it across his face and turned quickly away from the young man lying in the bed.

Brandon reached out and grabbed his father's arm. "I'm sorry, Dad. I do believe you, but I also believe someone tried to kill me."

Chapter Forty-Six

GRANT OBSERVED the interaction between the two men. Amused by Lillian's school-marm lecture when she stepped between them and berated the son for his rudeness, Grant waited to witness the result. After father and son reconciled, he cleared his throat. He knew he had their attention.

"Brandon, do you remember me? I talked to you the next day after the accident."

"Yes, sir. You were the first officer to arrive before I blacked out."

Lillian spoke up. "Also, do you remember the first time you and I met at Edgemon's?"

"Yes, ma'am."

"I'm pretty sure I bragged about my sons."

"You said you hoped I would have an opportunity to meet them."

Lillian motioned to Grant to come closer to the bed.

"Here's one of them. Grant is now working with Sheriff Tomas to solve some of those 'strange things' you mentioned while loading groceries into my car."

"Congratulations, or should I say condolences? I would guess working with the sheriff isn't an easy job." Brandon extended his arm and shook hands with Grant.

"Have you had any run-ins with him?" Lillian asked.

Brandon ignored her question and smiled at Grant. "Your mom said you graduated from Sam Houston State."

"That's right."

"I'm an old Bearkat myself." Brandon threw back his head and yelped a catcall.

Grant laughed at Brandon's youthful antic, then paused, and pressed his lips together. He gazed at Brandon for a moment and said, "I'd like to talk to you about the accident if you don't mind."

"Sure."

"Do you always ride your Harley to work?"

"Yes, sir. My boss lets me park it in the garage behind the store. More secure behind locked doors."

"But you were in front of the store on the day of the accident. Had you stopped to gas up your motorbike?"

"No, sir. I stopped there so people could see me. I knew I was being followed."

Grant ignored Franklin's growl and the sound of grinding teeth, but a sideways glance told him that the father was ready to do harm to the person who ran over his son.

He continued. "What made you think the car was following you?"

"Happened before."

"What are you saying? When did it happen before?"

"A black Town Car has followed me home more than once. Late one night, I stood in the road to stop them, and the car sped up. I had to jump out of the way. So, this time, I decided to confront the goons in a public place." Brandon looked at his dad. "Sorry for thinking you had anything to do with them."

Franklin shook his head. "They'll rue the day. When I find the slime --" Franklin balled his hands into fists, opened them, and repeated the action.

Lillian touched his arm. "Mr. Ford, I advise you to take care of your son and let my son do his job. He will find the so-called 'slime' who tried to kill Brandon."

Grant appreciated his mom's ability to calm the man. "Listen to her, Mr. Ford. Too many people have died." He paused and spoke slowly, enunciating each word, "Just be smart and stay safe. Whoever did this to your boy is dangerous."

In a less menacing voice, Grant added, "Besides, Brandon will need you when the doc releases him. I suggest you stay with him. Guard him until we resolve the situation."

"Consider that done. He's going to be at Caddo with me."

Grant spoke to Brandon. "Son, can you think of anyone who'd want to hurt you?"

Brandon sighed. "Maybe, but I don't have enough information to make an accusation." He looked at Lillian. "I think the shooter goofed up. In my opinion, you were the target."

"Grant told me what you said the night Bill was admitted."

Brandon fidgeted with the edge of the sheet. Lillian understood his hesitation. "I tend to agree with Brandon," Lillian said.

"Then I'll let you fill him in about our conversations," Brandon said.

Grant looked at Lillian. "I won't ask. You and I will talk later."

"We will, but isn't there something else we need to discuss with Mr. Ford before we leave?" Lillian said.

"Ten-four, but I'll ask the questions," Grant said and waited for her to agree. Their standoff lasted thirty seconds. Finally, Lillian nodded.

"Proceed."

"Thank you." He knew her acquiescence would be short-lived. He directed his next comment to the gentleman standing beside him. "Mr. Ford, tell me why you were lurking outside of Ms. Parsons's RV."

"I wasn't lurking. I wanted to talk to her about an important matter. After all, I do serve as of counsel to her."

"That being the case, why discuss work in the middle of the night? Can't you do that in the office?" Grant asked.

"Ms. Parsons has a busy schedule, in and out of the office."

"Care to elaborate about her 'out of the office' work?"

"She's belongs to a group of people called," Franklin paused.

Grant could tell he was searching his mind for the precise word.

Franklin continued. "As I recall, Ms. Parsons refers to them as Preppers. She's into that stuff and has urged me to join."

"I see," Grant said.

"No, you don't," Franklin responded.

He turned to Lillian. "You saw me and my wife talking with Vickie in Jefferson, right?"

Lillian nodded.

"Before I joined them on the balcony, I stood across the street and watched them talk to a young man. He wore some kind of uniform. But I digress. After I saw him leave and get into his vehicle, I joined them on the balcony. I had already come to the conclusion that since Ms. Parsons and I work together, a conflict of interest existed with regard to --"

Ford tilted his head sideways and looked at his son. "Hate for you to learn about us like this."

"It's okay, Dad. Mom told me she moved out and planned to divorce you."

Franklin didn't respond soon enough to his son, so Lillian interceded. "Is that what you two were discussing with Vickie when Bill and I saw you in Jefferson?"

"Partly. We talked about other things as well."

"Like what?" Lillian smiled sweetly and asked. "The "preppers" or could you have discussed money?

"Divorces always entail a discussion of money." The lawyer's demeanor changed from concerned father to a formal business-like tone.

Lillian's tone matched his when she persisted. "I should think your discussion of a little more than three million dollars would have been a little heated, but perhaps Bill and I interrupted you before that topic arose."

"How did you?" Brandon

"Wait a minute," Grant sputtered, amazed at his mother's question. "What's this about three million bucks?"

Brandon threw off his covers, lowered the rail on his bed, and dangled his feet over the edge. He stood up too quickly, and as his feet hit the floor, he swayed. Both Franklin and Grant reached out to steady him.

"Lillian, how do you know about the money?" Brandon's voice was barely above a whisper.

Franklin let go of Brandon and whirled around to face Lillian. "I'd like to hear the answer to that question, too, Ms. Prestridge."

Grant, holding onto Brandon, helped him hobble to the only chair in the room. After making sure Brandon was settled into the high-backed, faux leather recliner, he turned to his mother. "Me, too. Just what have you been up to, Mom?"

Lillian never ceased to amaze her son. Grant admired her observation skills as well as her ability to analyze people and convince them to tell the truth.

*****

The former high school administrator knew the value of maintaining eye contact if she wanted to keep a student talking and if she wanted to get a true rendition about an incident on campus.

She utilized that technique now with Brandon before leveling her gaze on his father and in a non-accusatory, compassionate tone directed her next comment to both of them.

"Mr. Ford, Brandon, I think it's time for all of us to be honest with each other, don't you?"

Brandon took a deep breath and exhaled. "Yes, ma'am, but first, I'd like for you to tell us how you know about the three million dollars."

Lillian smiled at the young man. "Your mother mentioned it to me when she confided in me that your father is an abusive husband."

Franklin Ford muttered incoherently and stalked around the end of the hospital bed. He stared out the window for a long moment, then faced Lillian.

"I don't know what Leigh Ann told you about me, but I swear I've never laid a hand on her."

"She didn't accuse you of physical abuse. Said it was verbal."

"I gave her everything." He sighed and let his shoulders droop. Then he straightened his back, squatted in front of his son, and directed his next comment to Brandon. "Do you think I've verbally abused you?"

"No, sir. You've always worked hard to support us. I don't know how you treated Mom behind closed doors, but in my presence, I never heard you demean her. But I know you weren't happy with her during our telephone conversation. Can't say that I blame you. She took a boatload of money from your business." Brandon put a comforting hand on his dad's shoulder.

Lillian watched Franklin exhale. He stood and asked Lillian, "Is that enough to negate her allegation about my abusing her?"

"Yes, sir, it does."

Grant spoke up and said, "I need to know more about the money. Most attorneys I know don't make three million dollars handling wills and divorces."

For the first time since Lillian met him, Franklin laughed out loud. "I wish I did, but unfortunately, all but a hundred thousand dollars in my business account, belonged to investors in a project I've been trying to close for a client of mine."

"What kind of project are you talking about, Dad?"

"A top secret venture between my clients and the government. That's all I can tell you until the feds say so."

"Does it have anything to do with ammonium nitrate?" Lillian asked and moved across the room to stand in front of Grant before he could open his mouth to say something. Lillian discreetly reached behind her back and waved her hand back and forth as a signal for Grant to not interfere.

Franklin's puzzled expression told Lillian that the project had nothing to do with explosives, so she turned around to face Grant.

"Why don't we let these two visit for awhile? We need to check on Bill."

Lillian led him out into the hallway.

"What was that all about?" Grant asked.

"Something else you and I need to discuss privately."

"Yeah, you never know who's hiding behind one of these and listening." Grant pointed to a closed door as they walked by. "Too many ears in this place."

"Some are indeed hiding," she said, "and in the darnedest places, too." She laughed at Grant's frown.

* * * * *

Brandon placed his hands on the arms of the chair and pushed himself into a standing position. He walked slowly back to his bed and climbed in. He lay there for a few seconds and watched his father who stood and looked out the window.

"Dad, I didn't tell Mom to contact you."

Franklin left the window and sat in the empty chair. "That's interesting, so did you talk to her after our conversation?"

Brandon nodded. "I faked a delivery to her at Caddo and tried to talk her into leaving with me. Told her I thought she would be safer someplace else."

"And, of course, she left without telling you where she was going,"

"But she did leave a disposable cell phone with me so we could communicate with each other."

"Disposable phone? You're kidding."

"No, sir. She had a whole drawer full of them. Strange, don't you think?"

"Indeed."

"Dad, do your investors know that you've met with her?"

Franklin raked his hand across his chin.

"To be honest, yes, they do. They know my plan to negotiate a return of their money."

"Do you think they tried to harm me in order to smoke her out of hiding?"

"That's exactly what I think. It's a good thing she doesn't know about your accident. She'd set herself up – and you, too – if she did."

"Hate to burst your bubble, Dad. I don't know how she knows, but she does. In fact, she came to see me. Thought she was disguised."

"Well, she didn't see fit to mention it to me during our meeting with Parsons." He paused. "I hope they find her. She deserves what she gets."

* * * * *

Dressed in gray warm-up pants and hospital gown for a shirt, legs crossed, hospital bed raised in a thirty degree position, antibiotic drip seeping its miracle cure into his left arm, and totally engrossed in the FOX News presidential debate, Bill did not hear Lillian and Grant enter his room. He jumped when his wife touched his arm and kissed his cheek. Then he smiled at the two of them.

"How are you feeling?" Lillian asked.

"Great. I'm ready to leave this place."

"Don't get in a hurry, Bill," Grant said. "The doc will tell you when you're ready."

"He hinted this morning that I might be ready in two more days if my blood tests are as good as he thinks they will be."

"That's good news," Lillian said. "I'm ready to have you home so we can plan our next destination."

"I don't care which direction you two travel, but try to find a murder-free zone, will you?"

Bill laughed at the dead-serious expression on Grant's face. He grabbed his shoulder.

"Don't make me laugh. It hurts," and then added, "I hope it's far, far away from Caddo Lake," Bill said. "I prefer another state, maybe Louisiana for a change."

A nurse came into the room. "Mr. Prestridge, I'm going to change the IV, and it's time for your breakfast."

Lillian patted his shoulder. "Grant, we'd better go and let him get back to the TV."

The nurse added, "And sleep. He's not doing much of that on his own."

*****

Out in the hallway, Lillian said, "Guess we need to go back to Brandon's room for his dad."

"Yep, we're his ride. Besides, maybe he'll open up to us and tell us more about that boatload of money his wife took."

"Maybe, but don't count on it. Also, don't let me go off and leave my purse in his room. I forgot it when we left to visit Bill."

When Lillian poked her head in the door, she saw only Brandon asleep in his bed.

Franklin Ford was gone.

She tiptoed across the room and retrieved her purse from the bedside table where she had left it.

"Franklin wasn't in the room."

"Maybe, he went down to the cafeteria. Do you think we should wait for him to return?"

"No." Lillian pressed her lips into a thin line. "He's a big boy. He can find his own ride back to Caddo."

Chapter Forty-Seven

LILLIAN PUNCHED Grant's arm when she saw Brandon's father sitting in the waiting room. She slowed her pace and thought that he looked like a man who bore the weight of the world on his shoulders. He sat bent over with his elbows on his knees and head down. She hoped that he and Brandon had enjoyed the few minutes alone after she and Grant left the room. At least, she hoped they had carried on a father-son conversation.

He stood when Grant and Lillian walked into the room. "Brandon went to sleep, so I thought I would wait for you guys here. I'm ready for you to take me to the police station now, Mr. Perryman."

Grant replied. "That won't be necessary, Mr. Ford. I think we can discuss your reason for standing outside Ms. Parsons's RV last night on our way home." Grant opened the door of the backseat driver's side of his vehicle for Lillian.

"I have a better idea," Franklin said. "I saw an I-Hop on the way into town. If you will stop there, I'll buy breakfast for all of us."

"Thanks, but I need to get you two back to Caddo," said Grant. "I need to report to duty in about thirty minutes."

Lillian, relieved that Grant declined, said, "I appreciate your offer, but since Grant can't take time to eat, I'll counter your offer with breakfast at Caddo. My treat."

Franklin turned halfway in his seat and smiled at Lillian. "Yes, ma'am, that's fine with me. From the aromas I've smelled coming from the direction of your RV, I'd say you are a good cook."

Lillian glanced at the rearview mirror and could see Grant's expression. His stare said it all: Watch your step, Mom. Her gaze matched his as she smiled and nodded an understanding of his non-verbal warning.

* * * * *

Seated at the table, Franklin dived into the scrambled eggs, bacon, hash browns, and toast Lillian had prepared for him. Lillian waited for him to clean his plate.

"Would you like more coffee," she asked.

"Yes, ma'am." Franklin swallowed the last bite of food and held up his cup for a refill. "Thanks for breakfast. Best meal I've had since I don't know when."

"Franklin, I'm determined to get to the bottom of who tried to kill Brandon."

"Do you have any theories?"

"Some, but I need some information from you before I proceed. Do you mind if I ask you a question?"

"If it will help find Brandon's attacker, by all means," he said.

"Let me know if I get too personal," Lillian warned.

"Fire away. Ask me anything. I won't mind."

Lillian nodded. "You mentioned Leigh Ann's taking money from the men who had invested in one of your projects."

"That's right," he said.

"I won't ask about the nature of the project or what our government has asked you to do, but I am interested in the investors."

"All I can say about them is that they expect a large return on their money, and they don't take too kindly to someone who steals it. I've had a hard time holding them off by promising I would find my wife and recoup their funds. She's in danger, too."

Lillian thought for a moment. "You lied to your son, didn't you? I think you did have him followed. Can you tell me why?"

Franklin nodded. "I explained everything to him after you and Grant left us alone. But since you asked, I'll tell you."

"I'd appreciate it."

"I had Brandon followed to protect him from his mother. She has always tried to keep Brandon away from me, even lied to him about how I treated her, so I knew she would eventually contact him."

"Did she?" Lillian wanted to test his honesty.

"Yes. The investigator I hired reported to me that she was camped at Caddo and that he had seen Brandon enter her RV."

"Do you mind telling me his name?"

"Russell Stokes. He works for a security firm I use from time to time. He's good. Has helped me with several of my criminal cases?"

"Did he say anything about stumbling onto something illegal going on at Caddo?"

"No. Don't know if he learned any more than what he reported about Brandon. Never heard from him again, and that's the main reason I rented the RV and drove down here. He's always been diligent about his work. I didn't decide to go camping because Vickie coaxed me into it."

"Do you trust Vickie?"

"Not anymore."

Lillian looked at Franklin and suggested, "Go home. You and I both need sleep, but promise me something."

"You name it."

"Don't do anything rash. I'd hate for Brandon to lose both his parents." She smiled at Franklin's puzzled expression.

He nodded and said, "Don't worry about me." He stood to leave. "Thanks again for breakfast."

"Take care," Lillian warned.

*****

Lillian glanced down at Eli who lay beside her feet. "Well, ole boy, what did you think about him? Is he a good guy or a bad guy ?" The dog made no response but leapt onto his favorite spot where he could watch the coming and going of the campground's inhabitants. "Let's see if I can distinguish the good people from the bad."

She laughed at Eli's snort which sounded like a human's harrumph. "Why so cynical?" she asked him.

Lillian booted up her computer, and after reviewing people she had written in her notebook, she began to Google their names. Lillian had already learned all she could about Franklin Ford and Vickie Parsons. She personally knew Richard aka Simon Townsend and previously discovered information about Jeff Richards and Sheriff Tomas. She decided to learn all she could about Al and Milly Gruene, Russell Stokes, and Guy Steiner whose names appeared in her notes more than once.

Russell Stokes had been an investigator, working for a private security firm in Dallas. One on-line source had a photo of Stokes holding up a golf trophy after he and his partner placed first in a tournament benefiting the Boys and Girls Club. Franklin had confirmed Stokes was the man he hired to guard his son. Based upon Franklin's statement and her own opinion of the investigator, Lillian concluded the nosey P.I. could have stumbled onto more than his assignment and, unfortunately, did not live long enough to report it to Ford or to any other person of authority.

Or, had he done so? Did Franklin tell the truth when he stated Stokes contacted him only once?

On-line articles portrayed Leigh Ann Ford as the typical socialite wife, a member of the Junior League of Dallas. She had volunteered for many charitable organizations, primarily the Salvation Army, and had served as a member and officer of the board of directors for the local Audubon organization. Then, two years ago, nothing, no news article mentioned her name. It was as though the lady had gone underground. Lillian rationalized that could have been when the Ford marriage began to crumble. With Brandon away at college, they no longer had to pretend to be happy. Did Leigh Ann become bored with her husband and decide to live an extravagant lifestyle after leaving him? Did she steal three million dollars, wishing to punish him for ruining her own career as she claimed he had done? Or?

Lillian couldn't think of another possibility, so she decided to Google the other names on her list. She could find no article, Facebook account, or twitter account for Al, Milly, or Guy Steiner.

Lillian stood and replenished her empty coffee cup and paced back and forth, thinking about the murder victims. Could any of their deaths be connected?

If so, how?

Lillian stopped in front of the kitchen window and watched Vickie load her fishing gear into her SUV. Something was wrong with the scene playing out across the lane. Vickie carried a bag, too short for a fishing rod, and by the slope of Vickie's shoulder, Lillian knew it was heavier than a bag of lures and hooks.

Vickie wore a white, tight-fitting T-Shirt, fatigue pants and jacket, and heavy hiking boots. The boots made Lillian think about her conversation with Franklin.

He had said he didn't trust Vickie. So, as Vickie climbed into her vehicle and drove out of the campground, Lillian reasoned, she should follow her.

"Come on, Eli. We're going fishing." Always eager for a car ride, Eli bounded out the door and waited for Lillian. She grabbed her shoulder bag, checked to make sure her thirty-eight was in it just in case, and saw Bill's camera in her bag. "Good," she muttered and ran for the SUV. Eli bounded into the passenger seat, and the two sleuths took off.

"She can't be too far ahead of us," Lillian said to the dog. Then spotting Vickie's SUV, she followed at a safe distance.

"Strange. Why is Vickie driving this direction if she's planning on fishing?"

The SUV slowed down and turned into a secluded gate. "What could she be doing at the ammunition plant?"

Three men dressed in army fatigues approached Vickie's vehicle. "Who are those men?" The SUV's hatch opened, and the men placed their gear in the cargo area and joined Vickie.

Lillian patted Eli as she spoke.

"Their bags are identical to Vickie's. Be quiet, Eli. We're going to see where she takes those men. You'll need to be a good dog and don't growl or bark when we get close."

The Poodle blinked his big, black eyes. "Good boy."

Lillian put her SUV in reverse and backed around the sharp turn in the road, staying out of sight. "If she comes back this way, she'll spot us."

Vickie eased out of the gate and turned in the opposite direction. "Whew," Lillian said as she, too, slowly proceeded south on the two-lane road.

She and Eli followed Vickie to an isolated farm several miles south of Karnack. When Vickie turned into the farm's entrance, Lillian pulled off the road and hoped the sound of her wheels crossing the cattle guard did not reach the people gathering at the farmhouse. She parked in an empty hay meadow behind a thick grove of trees. "Perfect, Eli. From here, we can see but not be seen." She killed the engine and reached in her purse for Bill's camera.

Lillian snapped several pictures of Vickie and her passengers as they retrieved their bags. They placed them on the ground. Instead of fishing rods, they removed another type of gear.

"Oh, Vickie, what are you involved in? Eli, if I'm not mistaken, those are military assault weapons."

Growling softly, Eli put his paws on the car's dash and peered through the windshield. "Shh. Sound carries. We don't want them to catch us." The dog grew silent but stayed vigilantly on guard. He turned his head toward the road. Lillian followed his gaze. "And who's coming to join the militia?" Lillian whispered.

A black Town Car parked beside Vickie's SUV. "We know him," Lillian said as she snapped a picture of the soldier who climbed out of the driver's seat and opened the back door for two passengers.

"You and I know the driver, Eli. Good heavens," she added, "I would never have guessed he would be involved in a paramilitary group."

A major whose uniform sported a row of medals stepped out of the car and saluted the driver. He turned back to the opened door and assisted a second person. Her uniform shouted high rank by the glint of metal pinned to her ample bosom.

"Of course, he'd want to be in charge, but her?"

She snapped pictures of the scene until a distant flash of light, stole Lillian's attention. "Well, would you look at that, Eli. There's another person watching this group's maneuvers. He's lying down on that hill."

Lillian pushed the zoom on the camera, focused the figure peering through a pair of binoculars. When he lowered them from his eyes, Lillian had to control her laughter to avoid shaking the camera. The click of its lenses forever froze his image, which supported Lillian's suspicions.

"Well, well, now I know."

Lillian started the engine and slowly drove out onto the highway. She dialed Grant's cell. No response.

Chapter Forty-Eight

THE RING of her car phone startled Lillian who was deep in thought about the activity she had witnessed while on a self-imposed stake-out at the isolated farm where she saw Vickie join more than seventy-five men dressed in their militia garb. She touched the telephone icon on the steering wheel.

"Hello."

"Hi, Lillian."

Bill's voice sounded strong and clear.

"Guess what."

"You can come home?"

"Yep. Doc says you can pick me up."

Without waiting for her to respond, he asked, "I'm ready to go if you can drive into town and get me."

"I can do that, but it might be faster if I ask Grant to drop by on his way out of town. That is, if it's okay with you."

She could hear the pride in his voice.

"You, my dear, are always on the ball. I'll call him right now. If he can't drive me home, I'll call you back."

"Good deal."

She pushed the phone icon again and disconnected their call. "Man-oh-man, Eli. We have to hurry. I want to download the pictures and go over them before those two arrive." She pressed the accelerator and sped toward Caddo.

* * * * *

Lillian studied the slide show of pictures she had snapped as she watched the militia group perform its maneuvers. She then turned her attention to the photos Bill had taken during their trip to Jefferson. Two of the random street scenes portrayed three of the people she saw at the isolated farm south of Karnack.

"That settles it, Eli. Now, all I have to do, is figure when I'm going to reveal their dirty, little secrets."

* * * * *

Simon, sat at Al's desk, reviewing the registrations Milly had entered in the campground's computer. He saw Vickie leave through the entrance gate. Within minutes, he saw Lillian zoom by and guessed why.

He shut down the computer and climbed on a motorcycle he kept hidden in the camp's storage unit and followed the two vehicles.

He felt confident that neither woman would recognize him in his bike helmet, especially since they had not seen him on the motorcycle. He passed Lillian's SUV and followed Vickie until she turned into the farm.

He continued riding until he found a slight rise in the highway and pulled behind a grove of trees along a neighbor's fence line.

He opened the bike's saddlebag and retrieved his binoculars. Simon found a vantage point where he could lie down on his stomach and observe the men below him. He saw the glint of a vehicle beyond the tree line on the other side of the farm.

He wished he hadn't taken Lillian's notebook so soon. He knew she always carried one in that purse of hers, but this time he didn't have to go through her bag. Lady luck was on his side. There it lay on the table. All he had to do was pick it up and hope she didn't miss it right away so he could make a copy of it. He chuckled, remembering the time he stole her notebook back in their college days. Without it, he would never have passed world literature. From her scintillating notes, Simon had developed an appreciation for the great classics and had built an extensive library.

He chided himself for thinking about the past. He needed to stay alert, forget about Lillian for a moment. But he couldn't forget her. For over two years, he had been looking for this group. They had a way of hiding in the deep recesses of East Texas forests. Not once had he considered Vickie being a part of this outlaw group.

Lillian.

Thanks to her, he could move forward with his investigation. Then, he saw the Black Town Car. "You son-ofa-bitch," he said. Again, he fussed at himself. "Why didn't you bring your camera, Simon?" Simon had to control his temper, not only at the two stepping away from the car but also at himself for being hasty and forgetful.

Returning to his bike, he decided to confide in Lillian.

* * * * *

Once more, Lillian's cell rang. She pressed the phone icon. She didn't have time to say hello. She stiffened when she heard a familiar voice. "Meet me at the lodge."

"That won't happen tonight. My husband will be coming home, and I plan on spending the evening with him."

"We have to talk."

"Not tonight. I'll let you know when I'm ready to clear up this mess."

"I don't think you can."

"Watch me."

* * * * * *

Lillian had tomato bisque soup and chicken salad sandwiches made by the time Grant parked his truck in front of her RV. She saw him walk around the hood to open the door for Bill. She ran down the steps to assist her husband as he climbed down.

Bill waved her away. "I can get out by myself." He stood by the opened door of the truck and pulled his wife into his arms. "See? I'm good."

"So glad you're home, my dear." Lillian felt his arm around her waist tighten when they reached the RV. She stepped aside and allowed him to climb the steps.

Grant followed them inside.

"Smells like you're going to have your favorite soup and sandwich for dinner, Bill."

"I'm ready. That hospital food may be nutritious, but it's too bland for me."

Lillian placed soup bowls brimming with the bisque in front of Bill. "Grant, please sit and join us."

"Thanks, I will." He laid his Stetson on the arm rest of the sofa and pulled out a chair. "Lillian, I tried to return your call earlier to let you know I had picked up Bill."

"Sorry I missed you. I ran a few errands." She had her back to the men. And when she turned back to face them, she ignored Grant's raised, questioning eyebrows.

"Did you see Brandon before you left ETMC?" she asked.

"Yes. He said he would be dismissed tomorrow."

"Great," said Lillian. "I'm planning a welcome home party to celebrate his and Bill's recovery."

"You don't need to do that," Bill protested with a big grin on his face which told his wife otherwise. "But," he continued, "it's time we had some fun at this campground."

"Then, it's settled. I'll make sure to invite guests tomorrow. We'll set it up for Friday night at the Pavilion if that's convenient with you, Grant."

"Sure. Barring an emergency, I'll plan on it. Can I do anything to help you prepare?"

"Yes. Be sure to have your handcuffs." Lillian joked. "Perhaps, more than one set," she said.

Grant shook his head. "Is that all?"

"No. Bring your dominoes, too. We're going to play deadly dominoes."

"I've never heard of that version of the game."

"No one has. I've just made up the rules. I promise you'll enjoy it."

"I'll hold you to that, but it's getting late, and Bill needs his rest." He stood to leave. "Thanks, Mom, for dinner."

Lillian hugged him and whispered in his ear, "Be careful tomorrow. I think you may be in danger. I'm serious about the handcuffs."

Grant nodded. "Lock this door after me."

Lillian tucked Bill in for the night. "I'll be along in a few minutes. Sleep tight."

Before she, too, went to sleep, Lillian scanned the phone's call log, selected the last call she had received the previous day, and sent a text message: I'm ready to talk. Come and get me, please. Be at the dock by six-thirty tomorrow morning.

Seconds later came the reply: Ten-four.

* * * * *

Thursday morning. Lillian arose early and tiptoed out of the bedroom. Eli jumped down from his lookout post to greet her. "Shh, big boy, we are on a mission today. I'll leave a note for Bill so he won't worry."

She grabbed a pad and pencil and jotted the words, *Gone to invite guests to party. Be back soon. Love, L.*

She taped the note to the front of the coffeemaker, knowing caffeine would be first thing on Bill's mind when he awoke. Removing her cell phone from its charger, she whispered, "Come on, Eli. We're taking a boat ride." She and Eli walked down the hill to the marina and waited.

Five minutes later, she heard the motor of the Jon boat and watched as Simon slowed down and sidled up to the dock. He raised his hand and helped her step down. Eli jumped down and sat between Lillian and Simon.

"Do you take your dog everywhere you go?"

"Yes, especially when it's a 'come to Jesus meeting' with an old friend who hasn't been completely honest with me."

Simon chuckled. "So, that's what you call my day of reckoning?"

"Yes."

"What made you suspicious of me?"

"First, I know you better than anyone, so I knew who stole my notebook."

Simon laughed so loudly that Lillian feared he would wake up the campground.

"But, my dear old friend, why did you make such a mess of the RV?"

"Mess? It was as neat when I left as it was when I entered."

"Are you telling me the truth?"

"Yes, of course, but that begs the question: Who else knew about your notes?"

"Indeed." Lillian continued, not answering his inquiry.

"Second, Simon, I ran into your sister at Edgemon's."

Simon gazed into the distance and then made eye contact with Lillian.

"I'm truly sorry for hurting her, but I had no choice."

"I know, but when the government finishes with you, I think you should --"

"No. She can never know. It wouldn't be safe for her to be seen with me."

"You have some explaining before you show up at the party I'm planning for Brandon and Bill."

"Party?"

"Dominoes."

"That's a deadly game, Lillian."

"Such are the games we play."

She smiled at Simon's puzzled expression.

"When we reach your cabin, I'll explain."

* * * * *

Simon pulled close enough to the shore to help Lillian return unseen to the campground. "You might want to remove your shoes, keep them dry."

"Good idea." She removed her Sperrys and stepped into the murky water. "What about Eli? If he's drenched, Bill may not believe my story."

"Don't worry." Simon stepped into the water and picked up the dog and slogged his way to the shore. He gently released the dog. "Eli, you take good care of her," Simon said. "She's pretty special, but you already know that, don't you?"

Simon returned to his boat and waited until Lillian put on her shoes. He watched her and Eli walk back toward the campground.

"Lillian, my love," he whispered.

* * * * *

Lillian saw Franklin's car beside his motor home. She was glad to see him open the passenger door and help Brandon step out of the vehicle. She quickened her pace and caught up with them before they reached the steps to enter the door.

Brandon hugged her. "Thanks for scolding me. You were right. Dad and I needed to make peace with each other."

"Ditto," said Franklin.

"No thanks necessary," Lillian said. "I stopped by to invite both of you to my domino party to celebrate yours and Bill's homecoming."

"Wow," said Brandon. "When?"

"Tomorrow afternoon at five o'clock, at the Pavilion. And, before you ask, you don't need to bring anything. I have all the fixings for burgers and homemade strawberry ice cream."

"We'll be there," Franklin smiled.

"Good."

* * * * *

Lillian waited beside the road when she heard the engine on Grant's truck come to life. He stopped even with her and lowered the passenger side window.

"Going or coming?" he asked.

"Good question," she responded. "Do me a favor?"

"Sure."

"Will you mention the party to Sheriff Tomas and invite him to come?

Grant grinned. "I think I know what are you're really planning, Mom. Do I need to bring backup?"

"No," she said, "that won't be necessary. I've arranged for that already. Federal agents will be there. I'll give you their names before the game begins. You just make sure you get Tomas here before the sparks begin to fly."

"Ten-four."

Grant left her standing by the road and, through his side mirror, watched her walk to Vickie's RV and knock on the door.

He whistled softly and said out loud, "That's Lillian, my mom, the world's greatest sleuth. Can't wait. I'll have to be prepared to protect her."

Chapter Forty-Nine

LILLIAN STOOD on the steps to the Pavilion and greeted each person. She handed them a folded piece of paper with the instruction: "Don't look at it until I tell you."

There had to be sixteen people so Lillian's plan would work. She looked around the Pavilion. Only fifteen had arrived. Then, she saw the last guest.

Leigh Ann stepped over the threshold. Lillian's greeting included the last folded slip of paper. Each slip contained one letter of the alphabet.

Also in attendance were five, muscular men celebrating their tenth college class reunion. They laughed and made jokes about their arrival in the dead of night, how they tried to be quiet setting up their tents, only to have them fall down and wake up all of the other campers.

Lillian signaled Milly to sound the cowboy's dinner triangle. Hearing the clang of metal against metal, the cluster of people standing around the tables ceased their chatter and turned to their hostess.

"I'm so glad each of you could join us tonight," she said. "I want to say thank you for coming out to Caddo Lake to help me welcome Bill and Brandon back home. As you know, these two guys have had a rough go of it lately and are lucky to be alive."

She waited for the cheerful well wishes and the round of applause to stop.

"I'd also like to thank Milly and Simon for all of their help setting up the tables and cooking the food. We'll eat first and then play dominoes. Right now, I'm going to ask Bill to say grace."

Bill stood. "Let us pray."

All heads, except five, bowed in prayer. Lillian watched the group of people, and as soon as she heard Bill's 'Amen,' she announced, "Milly's cooked enough burgers to feed an entire militia, so come on up and let her and Simon serve you."

Lillian noted the glances of some of her guests when she used the word militia.

She gave the group thirty minutes to complete their meal. "Folks, let me have your attention, please," she said. "As soon as everyone at your table is finished, let Simon know. He will roll the trash can around so you can toss your paper plates. If you want a bowl of homemade ice cream, come over this way, and I'll scoop some for you."

A loud, obnoxious voice yelled. "What flavors do you have?"

"Strawberry."

"Sorry, I'm allergic," Guy Steiner retorted.

"Good," yelled one of the newcomers. "That means more for me." He laughed and acknowledged Simon when he rolled the trash can by his table. "Thank you, sir."

Guy stood and waved toward the table where Lillian stood, scoop in hand. "Be my guest," he said. "When do the games begin?" he asked.

"After dessert," Lillian smiled, trying not to tilt her chin in defiance to Steiner.

She finished serving the ice cream and set the container aside. Lillian and Milly placed a box of dominoes on each table.

"Okay, folks, each table has a set of dominoes. Open the slip of paper I gave you when you first arrived." She watched them open the slip of paper and look confused. "You will notice that the paper has one of the following letters: A, B, C, or D."

"What does it mean?" Leigh Ann asked.

"Everybody stand, please," Lillian said. She walked to the closest table. "If you're holding the letter A, come sit at this table." Then she walked to the next table. "All of the Bs here." She indicated to the others where they should sit.

"Now, let the game begin," she announced.

She walked around to make sure people were at their assigned tables.

At Table D, situated behind all the other tables: Simon, Milly, Franklin and one of the newcomers who introduced himself as Larry; Table C: Jeff, Vickie, Brandon, and one of the newcomers who introduced himself as Curtis; Table B: Grant, Tomas, and two newcomers who introduced themselves as Mort and Ernie; Table A: Bill, Leigh Ann, Guy Steiner, and one of the newcomers named Bert.

Struggling to control her laughter, Lillian shook her head and turned away when she heard the newcomers introduce themselves to the other players. She was amazed that the others didn't pick up on the sarcasm of their names: Curley, Larry, Mo, Bert and Ernie.

This was going to be easier than she thought. She handed a slip of paper to Grant. On it, she had written the names of the agents and the table at which they sat.

Grant glanced at it and nodded. Then, he folded it and put it in his pocket.

Slam. Slam. Slam. Slam. Dominoes spilled out of the boxes. Shuffling noises filled the Pavilion as a player at each table swirled around the tiles. Then muffled sounds as the players placed their tile in the line of dominoes and announced their score or moaned when they couldn't make any points.

Lillian waited until she recognized signs that a break was in order. The click of dominoes hitting the table slowed. Some of the players went back for more ice cream or for a refill of a drink.

She decided it was time for the final game. Once again, she signaled Milly. Once again, the cowboy dinner triangle clanged, and everyone stopped what they were doing.

"Please, we are going to play a new game, and I'll walk you through it. I will give you step-by-step instructions, so don't get ahead of me."

"Is this going to be complicated?" Leigh Ann asked.

"No," Lillian said. "Will one person at each table shuffle the dominoes."

The sound of dominoes scraping across the four tables stopped. "Each player should have seven dominoes before we play the last game for tonight."

After the players had chosen their dominoes, Lillian smiled. "Don't look at your hand until I say so. I want everyone to be patient with me." Lillian saw a few heads nod. "Thanks."

She motioned for Grant to join her and waited until he stood beside her to continue. "As all of you know, we have experienced some rather strange happenings at Caddo Lake, some resulting in the deaths of campers and an attempt on the life of my husband. Those committing these crimes extended their heinous acts outside the gates of this campground in an attempt to murder an employee of Edgemon's Grocery Store."

"What's that got to do with playing dominoes?" asked Vickie.

"Good question. Listen, and as our game progresses, you'll know."

"I've asked my son, Grant, to come forward to give you some information that until now has not been made public by law enforcement."

Sheriff Tomas stood. "Grant, you don't have my permission to speak on the evidence we have."

"He doesn't need it," Simon said.

"Be quiet, Simon. It's not your turn to speak," Lillian ordered.

She nodded to those seated at Table B, and Ernie stood and stretched his back. He moved to stand behind the sheriff's chair, ready to block any movement from Tomas.

"First, Grant, could you tell everyone about the evidence found on each of the murdered victims?"

Grant nodded. "Although one was disguised as an accident, there have been three murders at Caddo Lake within the past month. I'm here working under Sheriff Tomas." Grant walked over to stand in front of Table B and spoke directly to his old mentor. "Sir, I applied for the vacancy in your department not because I needed a job but because the FBI for whom I work asked that I do so."

"Why?"

"I, too, asked that question. The Feds gave a reason, which made no sense to me. You see, I have always admired you. In my opinion, you were the epitome of an excellent law officer, and I valued the advice you gave me."

Tomas squinted his simmering coal-black eyes and glared at Grant.

"And blinded by my regard for you, I didn't understand the importance of my assignment, but my mother explained it to me. You didn't retire from the university. You were asked to leave. Is that correct?"

"That is none of your damned business," Tomas growled and tried to stand. Ernie pushed him back into the chair.

Lillian walked over to stand beside Grant.

"You'll not use that tone of voice when speaking to my son, your superior in every way." She patted Grant on the shoulder. "Continue."

Grant walked back to face all of the tables. "At each murder scene, we found a domino and a note on the corpse." He stopped when Lillian put her hand on his shoulder.

"I'll take it from here."

She instructed the players, "For this game, I want you to allow those at your table to see your hand. Turn up your dominoes."

Guy Steiner was the only one who grumbled.

"This is crazy. You don't ever let your opponent know what you're holding. I'm done with this nonsense." He scooted back his chair. Bert prevented Guy's departure from Table A.

"That's correct, Guy, but remember, this is my game."

She smiled. "I want everyone to look at the dominoes on your table. Who has a double ace?"

Four hands, one at each table, slowly rose. Lillian walked around the room, saw which person had a double ace, and stopped at Table B.

She faced the players.

"Milly, do you remember the Friday night when we heard a loud explosion?" Heads nodded.

"That was scary," Milly said.

"Yes it was, especially for your husband Al," Lillian said, "because he was in big trouble after losing a truckload of ammonium nitrate."

"That's a lie." Milly yelled and frowned at Lillian.

"You and Bill were with me when Al came back to our mobile home and told us about the accident. He had talked to the park ranger and the sheriff's office."

"Yes, ma'am, you had invited us over for a drink. You see, I didn't trust either you or Al the moment I met you."

"Why?" Milly asked.

"You tried too hard to keep her away from the maintenance man," Bill said.

Lillian heard Simon clearing his throat.

"Then, after the campground quieted down that night," Lillian explained, "I took a walk and stood outside the camp director's office. I overheard Al talking with someone who wasn't happy about the explosion. The person's handle was Shadow."

"You," Milly shouted, pointed at Table C, and tried to jump up. Larry who sat beside her placed his hand on her shoulder and restrained her.

"Let's don't continue this game," Jeff Richards suggested. "You're upsetting too many people and all for nothing."

"I agree," growled Tomas.

Grinning like a Cheshire cat, Simon drawled, "Oh let's do."

Lillian went back to Table A.

"Guy, it took me awhile to decide that you were Shadow."

"You don't know what you're saying. I don't know anything about a shadow man."

"You used a foreign accent when you threatened Al, but your cadence and mispronunciations gave you away. You see, I speak French, Spanish, and German, and I recognize speech patterns, especially those which prevent a person from hiding his original dialect. You're from Georgia, aren't you?"

"You're nuts, lady."

"When I heard you speak on the night Vickie had a mouse in her RV, you spoke with a New Jersey accent. Then at Edgemon's you had a typical East Texas drawl. You, as Shadow, were so angry with Al that you decided to give him a warning."

Lillian picked up the double ace and placed it in front of Steiner. "You were the one who killed the man on the jogging trail and left the double ace and a note in his pocket. He was your inside man at the fertilizer plant setting up the ammonium nitrate thefts. You thought he had double-crossed you and caused the truck explosion, but it really was just an accident."

"What do you mean?" Steiner asked.

"There was a witness no one knew about. He said the driver dodged a deer and crashed into a ditch. But you had no way of knowing that since Sheriff Tomas decided to keep that bit of information to himself."

Steiner glared at Lillian. "I did not kill anyone, and you can't prove it."

"Yes, I can. Remember when Brandon dragged you back into the campsite?"

"I should have filed an assault charge against him."

"Too late, buddy," said Brandon.

"He did give you a bloody nose. My dog – excuse me – I believed you called him a mutt. I refer to Eli as a detective with a long nose. Well, that so-called mutt aka detective managed to get some of your blood on him while he held you down."

"And I had it analyzed. Amazing thing," said Grant, "what modern forensics can discover."

"I didn't okay a DNA test on any of the murder victims." Tomas slapped the top of the table, sending dominoes skating to the floor.

"But I did," Grant responded.

"Finish what you were saying." Lillian urged Grant.

"The DNA on Eli's fur matched the DNA the murderer left on the first victim." Grant looked at the newcomer sitting beside Steiner. Grant looked at Bert, the agent sitting beside Guy. "Please arrest Mr. Steiner and read him his rights."

Bert looked at Simon who said, "Do what he says."

Bert nodded, cuffed Steiner, and led him to a black SUV parked beside the Pavilion.

Vickie stood.

"Where do you think you're going?" asked Simon.

"I'm going to talk to Guy Steiner. He needs a good attorney."

"No, ma'am, you're not," said Lillian. "You may have a conflict of interest."

Agent Curtis stood and blocked her exit.

"You've got a lot of nerve," Vickie said.

"Indeed, and so do you," Lillian agreed. "When you learned that Franklin had sent a private investigator to watch his wife – to make sure she was safe from his investors, you were the only camper who knew the P.I.'s identity. You knew Stokes jogged everyday at the same time Leigh Ann ran."

"I never saw Russell Stokes before the night he accused Guy of breaking into my RV. Besides, I was in Jefferson practicing law when he was killed."

Franklin joined the conversation. "Vickie, I distinctly remember introducing Stokes to you when he met with me at our offices in Jefferson. I'll swear to that in a court of law."

Lillian smiled.

"Thank you, Franklin, for clarifying my theory. Only she who plotted the act and the actual murderer knew why Stokes was in the campground."

Lillian turned back to Vickie and continued her explanation. "So, you decided he had to die. You were afraid Stokes not only had seen Guy murder the jogging trail victim and put the double ace and curse in his pocket but also would report Leigh Ann's involvement with the militia."

"Prove it." Vickie crossed her arms and sneered.

Simon laughed. "She doesn't have to prove it. I had your phone tapped. The FBI has the recording of your instructions to Guy. You told him to follow Stokes the next time Stokes took his boat out on the lake and kill him. You said you didn't care how he did it."

"How could you?" Franklin asked. "You represented both me and Leigh Ann in our divorce proceedings. I had a gut feeling that you were up to no good."

"You talk too much, Franklin." Vickie smirked. "And when you introduced me to Stokes and gave me the name of his agency if I ever needed an investigator, I knew I could help Leigh Ann destroy you once and for all. Frankly, Franklin, I'm tired of your arrogance." She cackled at her play on words.

Agent Curtis stood, handcuffs ready, and looked at Grant. "Sir?"

"Not yet," Grant said.

"Furthermore," Lillian continued, "When a sharpshooter missed me and hit Bill by mistake, I was completely devastated. Then, Brandon's warning made me realize I was, indeed, the target."

Vickie's smile was the most evil grin Lillian thought she had ever seen.

"I knew right away you'd be trouble. Had to get rid of you. I'm just sorry you moved at the last minute." She turned to Bill. "I'm sorry. You're a nice man."

"That's the first truth we've heard from you," Lillian said. "Guess you needed more time at the shooting range."

Grant nodded to Agent Curtis. "Now," he said. "Go on, Mom. Let's finish this charade."

"Yes, let's do," said Simon. There was no smile on his face. "Get it over with."

"Don't boss my wife around, Richard." Bill glared at his old college friend. "I suspect you're surprised that I know who you are."

Lillian sighed. "Behave, you two. I'm ready for the *coup d'état* myself. Tomas, Leigh Ann. Vickie. Jeff," Lillian paused between each name and then turned to face them. "You folks have built up quite an anti-government militia."

"You don't know what you're saying," Tomas said.

"If she says it, she knows it for a fact," Bill said.

Tomas mirrored Vickie when he challenged Lillian. "Prove it."

"I have photos of the four of you, along with about seventy or so militiamen. Those photos are now in the hands of the FBI and Homeland Security."

Tomas yelled. "People fed up with the government practice survival skills all over these United States. Being in a militia is not against the law." He looked at Grant for confirmation, but received only a glare from his deputy.

"Correct, but stealing ammonium nitrate and storing it in vacant government buildings at an ammunition plant for the purpose of making bombs to prevent a pipeline through East Texas is against the law, not to mention the death of the landowners – or should I say as it was reported in the papers, the disappearance of the landowners – who sold their acreage to the oil company Franklin represents." She paused and then added, "Since the name of the undercover person who's a member of the group must stay anonymous, I won't tell you who snitched your plan to Grant who, in turn, gave me the information. I passed it on to Simon who made sure we had FBI agents at this little party of mine."

Tomas snorted and addressed Simon. "So, you're with the FBI?"

Simon smiled but said nothing.

Lillian answered for Simon.

"You really don't want to know the answer to that question." Then, she looked at Simon and shook her head. "I knew you had stolen my notebook, but I couldn't understand why you messed up the RV to make it look like a burglary. When I confronted you about it, you lied and asked me if anyone else could have known about it."

Simon didn't respond.

"Milly had seen my notebook, so she approached you to find out what I knew about her. You told her about me and my suspicious nature. And after my conversation with your sister, I knew you were up to no good. I had to ask myself: Why would Richard fake his death?"

"For the sake of curiosity, what did you conclude?" he asked.

"You had gone dark. You were either in the CIA or FBI – neither of which Grant could discern – or you were involved in something illegal."

Simon smiled.

"By now you should understand that I'm always legal."

"Correct. Otherwise, you could not have called in five FBI agents for backup."

Lillian directed her next comment to Leigh Ann. "Who indoctrinated you – Vickie or Sheriff Tomas? And what did they promise you in exchange for funding the militia's activities with the millions you stole from your husband?"

Leigh Ann didn't answer the question. Instead, she looked at her son. "I'm so sorry. I didn't mean for you to get hurt."

She turned to Tomas. "You ordered your men to kill him. I hate you."

Tomas responded. "They never fired a shot at him."

"No, but they ran him down with your Black Town Car."

She looked at Franklin who wiped tears from his eyes. "And ditto to you. I hate you and your overbearing, controlling, arrogant personality. But, no matter how much I loathe you two men, I love my son."

She walked to Brandon and kissed him on the cheek. "To answer your question, Lillian, it was Tomas. He was in charge of this whole scheme. Too late, I decided he was a radical idiot." She looked at the agent called Bert and held out her hands. "Are you going to put handcuffs on me?"

He shook his head. "I don't think they're necessary."

Tomas spoke.

"No, Leigh Ann. I wasn't in charge. I had my orders to seduce you. Our leader with the code name Shadow is none other than Guy Steiner. As Vickie's lover, he knew your husband had millions from investors." Agent Mort tapped him on the shoulder. He stood and put his hands behind him.

To Lillian, the click of the cuffs represented the sad end of man's law enforcement career. Once revered, now he would live the rest of his life in disgrace.

Lillian turned to Simon and smiled. "Now," she said.

He turned to the remaining players seated at the tables. "Stay where you are." He walked to Table D and grabbed Milly. "Let's go."

Grant asked, "Why are you taking her?"

"She knows too much."

Simon saluted Lillian and said, "Good work, my dear. I knew you'd solve the mysteries at Caddo Lake."

Grant and the four agents assigned to the case waited for Simon and Milly to leave before herding the last of the guilty culprits into the waiting SUVs.

Grant kissed Lillian. "See you later." He motioned for Brandon. "You coming?"

"I wouldn't miss this for the world." Brandon stopped and called out to Grant. "Wait a minute. I have a question for your mother." He turned to Lillian. "What about Milly? Did she know what her husband was doing?"

"Of course she did. Their marriage was one of convenience."

"I don't understand. What do you mean?" Franklin asked.

"She married Al only at Simon's instructions. She works for him. After her husband's disappearance, she found Al's list of recruits and gave it to Simon. Those who joined the militia will be investigated."

"I didn't know Al disappeared."

"You'll have to ask my son about Al's whereabouts. Grant was there when Al jumped overboard. Right now, though, I don't think Al likes his new home. It's kind of cramped."

Lillian winked at Brandon who laughed at Lillian's joke. Then he said, "Grant told me his mom could see through people."

He turned and joined Grant.

The two men climbed into the F150 and left the campground.

Lillian walked over to Table C and sat down beside Jeff who had not moved from his chair. Franklin and Bill joined them.

"What a day," Jeff said. "I'm glad you didn't suspect me."

"Oh, but I did. It was Simon who told me you had joined the militia to spy for him."

Jeff nodded and shuffled the remaining dominoes resting on the table. "Anybody want to play?"

"Not me," said Franklin. "Those things are deadly.

The Games We Play Series

Book One: *The Mah Jongg Murders*

Book Two: *Deadly Dominoes*

Book Three: *Tarot Terrors* (to be released in 2018)

In *Tarot Terrors,* Lillian faces the most difficult challenges of her life. She discovers the body of her beloved husband Bill while they are camping in Sedona, Arizona, and then she has the difficult task of delivering the sad news to their sons. Though she grieves his death, she refuses to plan a memorial service and insists that neither Grant nor Jake need to fly out to be by her side. Instead, she places the carved, rosewood box containing his ashes on her bedside table. Each night before she retires, she rubs the top of the box and talks to Bill.

"I know what you would say, my darling, if you could. "Vengeance is mine, says the Lord." She smiles, remembering the sound of his voice. "But in this case," she continues, "I think the Good Lord needs my help." She promises Bill she will not rest until she finds his murderer and sees the culprit or culprits prosecuted.

Lillian begins her quest to solve Bill's murder.

Sammie Nightingale, a young Navajo woman and professional photographer, has also begun a vision quest which traditionally is taken by a young male. But Sammie is a liberated woman of the Twenty-first Century. Like Lillian, she is independent and believes in justice.

These two women – one, older and wiser; one, younger and in touch with nature and the supernatural – join forces and begin a quest of their own. Along the way, they discover an ancient cult with demonic, dangerous practices. The cult wants them dead.

Note from the author: If you have enjoyed reading Book One and Two of The Games We Play Series, you will enjoy *Tarot Terrors*. All of my books are available on Amazon, Barnes & Noble in paperback and ebooks as well as iTunes. Feel free to contact me at lsgp@suddenlink.net I value you as a reader, and your comments are always welcome.

Made in the USA
San Bernardino, CA
26 July 2017

LAROUSSE

Le journal du 20ᵉ Siècle

LAROUSSE

© Larousse-Bordas 1998
pour l'édition en langue française
© Chronik Verlag chez Bertelsmann
Lexikon Verlag GmbH,
Gütersloh/Munich, 1998.
Ouvrage réalisé par Marshall
Editions Ltd en 1998.

Conseiller de l'édition française :
Anne-Marie Lelorrain, agrégée d'histoire
Responsabilité éditoriale :
Véronique Herbold
Adaptation française et réalisation :
Copyright avec la collaboration
de Carole Hardoüin et de Cécile Edrei
Lecture-révision : Annick Valade
assistée de Laurette Heitz
Couverture : Véronique Laporte
et Sarbacane Design
Fabrication : Annie Botrel
L'éditeur remercie de leur collaboration
les personnes suivantes :
R.G. Grant, R. Boulanger, R. Stewart,
C. Phillips, N. Grant, M. Mulvihill,
D. Gould, T. Morris et M. Barratt.

Toute reproduction ou représentation
intégrale ou partielle, par quelque
procédé que ce soit, du texte contenu
dans le présent ouvrage, et qui
est la propriété de l'éditeur,
est strictement interdite.

Distributeur exclusif au Canada :
Messageries ADP, 1751 Richardson,
Montréal (Québec).

ISBN 2-03-565010-0
Dépôt légal : août 1999
Imprimé en Allemagne

Présentation 5 • Mode d'emploi 6

SOMMAIRE

Les années 1900   8
Dossier : La conquête du ciel 20

Les années 1910   40
Dossiers : La course aux pôles 44
Les civils en guerre 56

Les années 1920   68
Dossiers : La radio 78 • Les années folles 94
Football et baseball 104

Les années 1930   106
Dossiers : Des villes tentaculaires 112 • Le fascisme 120
La bande dessinée 124 • Le cinéma 140

Les années 1940   142
Dossiers : Du côté des civils 146 • Le génocide 154
La bombe atomique 162 • L'art de la mode 174

Les années 1950   178
Dossiers : L'automobile 182 • La décolonisation 194
L'ère de la consommation 208 • Les adolescents 216

Les années 1960   218
Dossiers : Agents secrets et espions 230
La pop music 246 • L'âge de la télévision 254

Les années 1970   256
Dossiers : Conquête spatiale 260 • L'environnement 268
La nouvelle génération 280 • Le terrorisme 286

Les années 1980   288
Dossiers : Les effets spéciaux 298
Les ordinateurs 314

Les années 1990   318
Dossiers : La fin du communisme 322
La génétique 330 • Les jeux Olympiques 340

Tableaux chronologiques 350 • Index 352

PRÉSENTATION

Au début du XXᵉ siècle, des rois ou des reines étaient à la tête de presque tous les pays d'Europe et la France républicaine leur semblait un peu dangereuse... Dans le port de New York, la statue de la Liberté accueillait des millions d'immigrants venus d'Europe en bateau à vapeur. Les ouvriers travaillaient 11 heures par jour, six jours par semaine sans avoir jamais de vacances. C'était le temps des bourgeois en haut-de-forme, des ouvriers en casquette et des premiers métros. Le cinéma avait cinq ans, la télévision n'existait pas ; on se retournait au passage des rares automobiles et seuls quelques « fous » croyaient en l'aviation.

Deux guerres mondiales et des milliers d'inventions plus tard, tout est différent. Au cours des cent dernières années, la vie des hommes a plus changé que durant les 1 000 ans précédents. *Le Journal du XXᵉ siècle* dit pourquoi et comment.

Jour après jour, année par année, page après page, ce livre fait revivre l'actualité passionnante de notre siècle dans le monde entier : grandes catastrophes et petits malheurs, découvertes scientifiques et inventions, événements musicaux et records sportifs.

À la une du journal, les gros titres, les événements dont tout le monde parle partout : des guerres et des révolutions, des naufrages et des exploits, des films aux records sportifs, racontés en direct dans des articles courts et illustrés par plus de 1500 photos. Des pages-magazines, thématiques, font le point sur les grandes questions de notre époque : problèmes politiques, transformations de la société, vie quotidienne...

Du naufrage du Titanic dans la nuit du 14 au 15 avril 1912 à la Libération de Paris le 25 août 1944, du premier homme sur la Lune le 21 juillet 1969 à la mort d'Éric Tabarly en juin 1998 et à la guerre au Kosovo en 1999... *Le Journal du XXᵉ siècle* retrace en direct 100 ans de l'histoire du monde pour tous les curieux de notre temps.

Anne-Marie Lelorrain
agrégée d'histoire

1950

1951

Le *Journal du 20e siècle* fait revivre jour après jour, année par année tous les événements et les personnages qui ont marqué les 100 dernières années.

Avec 1 500 photographies en couleurs, il offre un étonnant reportage sur le siècle pour les jeunes curieux de leur temps.

L'approche chronologique permet aux lecteurs d'utiliser facilement le livre et de retenir les informations proposées. Chaque année est traitée sur une double page très claire au modèle de celle qui est montrée ci-dessous.

1950 – 1959

◀ L'année figure dans un cartouche de couleur en haut de page.

▶ La décennie est toujours mentionnée dans une bande verticale de couleur.

1956

▲ Une couleur particulière signale chaque décennie.

1956

▲ La vignette-photo de l'année traitée est agrandie.

1956

Boycott des bus en Alabama
▶ 1er mars 1956

En décembre dernier, Rosa Parks, une femme noire qui ne trouvait pas de place, s'est assise à l'avant du bus, réservé aux Blancs. Son arrestation et son emprisonnement ont provoqué la colère, et le boycott des bus a été organisé. Le meneur de l'opération s'appelle Martin Luther King, un pasteur noir de la ville. L'Alabama est en effervescence avec les manifestations des Noirs contre les lois ségrégationnistes du sud des États-Unis. À Montgomery, la capitale, les Noirs ont arrêté de prendre les bus, ce qui met les sociétés de transport en difficulté financière.

Hier, la Cour fédérale a ordonné la réintégration à l'université d'Alabama d'Autherine Lucy, une étudiante noire. Trois semaines auparavant, alors qu'elle devait commencer les cours, des étudiants blancs s'étaient révoltés, et l'université avait suspendu son inscription – pour sa propre sécurité, selon l'administration. Mais la décision de la cour impose une protection. En 1954, la Cour suprême des États-Unis avait ordonné l'ouverture des écoles publiques aux Noirs, une décision qui n'a jamais été respectée dans les universités des États du Sud.

▼ Rosa Parks, assise à l'avant du bus.

En 1956 aussi...

2 janvier • Victoire du Front républicain (centre gauche), mené par Guy Mollet, aux élections législatives, en France, sur un programme de paix en Algérie.

29 juin • Marilyn Monroe épouse le dramaturge Arthur Miller.

6 novembre • « Ike » Eisenhower est élu pour un second mandat de président des États-Unis.

Indépendances en Afrique
▶ 20 mars 1956

Les Français perdent une partie de leur empire colonial. Deux pays du Maghreb obtiennent ainsi leur indépendance : la Tunisie, qui, à partir d'aujourd'hui, est gouvernée par Habib Bourguiba, et le Maroc – français et espagnol – qui est devenu le royaume du sultan Mohammed V. Le 1er janvier, le Soudan, sous domination égypto-britannique, obtenait lui aussi son indépendance. Mais, dans un des plus grands territoires français, l'Algérie, en lutte pour l'indépendance, la France intensifie la guerre avec l'envoi de soldats du contingent, c'est-à-dire ceux qui font leur service militaire.

◀ Cette année, le Soudan, le Maroc et la Tunisie sont devenus indépendants.

La crise de Suez
▶ 3 novembre 1956

Sous la pression de l'Union soviétique et des États-Unis, les Britanniques et les Français ont accepté de retirer leurs troupes de la zone du canal de Suez. La crise de Suez a commencé le 26 juillet, lorsque le dirigeant égyptien Gamal Abdel Nasser a nationalisé le canal, qui appartenait à une colonie franco-anglaise. À la suite de ces événements, les troupes israéliennes envahissent le Sinaï, en Égypte, selon un plan secret établi avec la France et la Grande-Bretagne, qui, à leur tour, envoient une armée dans la zone du canal. Mais l'URSS et les États-Unis interviennent. Ils ne veulent plus de l'influence européenne au Moyen-Orient. L'URSS menace d'utiliser la bombe atomique, et les États-Unis font pression sur la livre et le franc.

◀ Le président Nasser, entouré de la foule en liesse, à Port-Saïd.

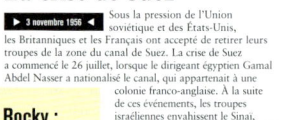

Rocky : 43 K-O et aucune défaite

Le boxeur Rocco Francis Marchegiano dit Rocky Marciano, prend sa retraite, à l'âge de 33 ans. Quoique se situant juste au-dessous des 2 mètres et pesant moins de 84 kilos, il a gagné ses 49 combats professionnels, dont 43 par K-O. Il a obtenu le titre de champion du monde des poids lourds en 1952 et l'a défendu six fois avec succès.

Inauguration royale d'une centrale nucléaire
▶ 17 octobre 1956

La reine Élisabeth II d'Angleterre a inauguré la centrale nucléaire de Calder Hall, sur la côte anglaise, qui fait partie d'un grand complexe comprenant notamment le centre de recherche atomique de Windscale. Le réacteur, refroidi au gaz, a une capacité d'environ 200 mégawatts. C'est une des premières centrales de ce type, conçue pour produire de l'électricité.

▶ La centrale nucléaire de Calder Hall, dans le nord-ouest de la Grande-Bretagne.

L'Autrichien Toni Sailer gagne trois médailles d'or
▶ 6 février 1956

Les jeux Olympiques d'hiver de Cortina d'Ampezzo, en Italie, sont terminés. Sans conteste, la star de ces jeux a été Toni Sailer, qui a remporté trois médailles d'or en ski : slalom spécial, slalom géant et descente. Il a dominé de bout en bout le slalom géant, creusant un écart de plus de six secondes avec le médaillé d'argent.

◀ Toni Sailer, nouveau roi autrichien des pistes.

De nouvelles lignes de téléphone

On peut maintenant communiquer par téléphone avec l'Amérique aussi facilement qu'avec un ami de la ville voisine. La pose du premier câble de téléphone transocéanique entre Terre-Neuve et l'Écosse, est achevée. Contrairement aux anciens câbles télégraphiques, les nouveaux sont doublés – un pour chaque sens.

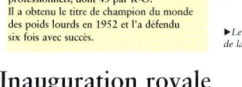

▲ Inauguration des nouvelles lignes de téléphone.

La ségrégation

Malgré l'arrêté de la Cour suprême des États-Unis déclarant, dès 1954, la ségrégation anticonstitutionnelle (illégale), les autorités blanches d'Alabama n'accepteront pas de Noirs dans les écoles avant 1963.

•

Martin Luther King veut intégrer ses frères de couleur dans tous les rouages de la société américaine. Il a fondé la SCLC (ligue des chrétiens du Sud), qui refuse la violence. Il veut faire connaître ses revendications par des moyens pacifiques.

◀ Quelques autres événements importants de l'année en cours sont cités dans cette rubrique.

▶ Des illustrations en couleur servent de toile de fond et donnent des informations en plus des grands articles.

▼ L'année traitée apparaît sur chaque double page, en gros caractères, sous le texte.

MODE D'EMPLOI

▼ *Dans les encadrés jaunes, sont relatés les principaux événements populaires ou culturels de l'année.*

Rocky : 43 K-O et aucune défaite

Le boxeur Rocco Francis Marchegiano dit Rocky Marciano, prend sa retraite, à l'âge de 33 ans. Quoique se situant juste au-dessous des 2 mètres et pesant dans les 84 kilos, il a gagné ses 49 combats professionnels, dont 43 par K-O. Il a obtenu le titre de champion du monde des poids lourds en 1952 et l'a défendu six fois avec succès.

Les dossiers du livre

Au fil de la chronologie, le *Journal du XXe siècle* présente aussi 30 dossiers qui abordent, chacun sur deux pages, un grand thème de notre époque, ou une idée majeure.

Les sujets sont très divers et se situent aussi bien sur le plan culturel que politique, social que sportif... mais ont pour point commun d'avoir marqué l'histoire du XXe siècle.

Pendant les 100 dernières années, une incroyable avancée dans tous les domaines de la connaissance s'est produite. Les pages dossiers du livre servent de repères pour le prouver et l'expliquer clairement au lecteur.

Le XXe siècle c'est tant la conquête du ciel que les villes géantes, tant la bande dessinée que la protection de l'environnement, tant la pop-music que les ordinateurs, c'est aussi les deux Guerres mondiales, la montée du fascisme, la décolonisation, les découvertes génétiques...

Ce livre est un témoin unique sur l'histoire du siècle qui, à présent, s'achève.

De nouvelles lignes de téléphone

On peut maintenant communiquer par téléphone avec l'Amérique aussi facilement qu'avec un ami de la ville voisine. La pose du premier câble de téléphone transocéanique entre Terre-Neuve et l'Écosse, est achevée.

▶ *Des doubles pages-dossiers informent sur des thèmes importants et intéressants.*

◀ *Dans les colonnes en marge sont décrites les inventions de l'année ou les innovations dans tous domaines.*

De 1900 à 1909

1900

À l'aube du XXᵉ siècle, les États-Unis et l'Europe ont confiance en l'avenir. Ils dominent le monde grâce à leur économie et à leur culture.

Dans les dix premières années de ce siècle, au moment où l'automobile, le téléphone et l'électricité entrent petit à petit dans la vie de tous les jours, le progrès technologique semble illimité. Tandis que l'Empire britannique poursuit son expansion, les États-Unis sont sur le point de devenir une puissance mondiale.

▲ *En juillet 1900, la première ligne du métropolitain est en service à Paris.*

La folie du cake-walk

Le cake-walk est la dernière danse à la mode. Elle est d'origine noire américaine. Les couples évoluent sur la piste en formant un carré. Le rythme est syncopé, et les pas, assez compliqués et fantaisistes. Un jury attribue des notes pour la créativité des danseurs, l'élégance des hommes et la grâce des femmes. Le couple vainqueur gagne un gros gâteau décoré.

L'Exposition universelle

- Elle s'étend sur 6 000 hectares dans Paris.
- La grande roue est un manège géant qui mesure 106 m de diamètre, compte 80 nacelles pouvant contenir chacune 20 personnes.
- Quelque 76 000 exposants sont présents, dont 36 000 Français.

L'Exposition universelle à Paris

▶ 14 avril 1900 ◀

L'Exposition universelle ouvre ses portes à Paris. Cette manifestation, destinée à célébrer le nouveau siècle, est la plus grande jamais vue en Europe. En l'inaugurant, le président de la République, Émile Loubet, a lancé un appel en faveur de la paix dans le monde.

De nombreux pavillons ont été édifiés pour présenter les produits et réalisations de chaque grande nation.

Deux Expositions universelles s'étaient déjà tenues quelques années auparavant, en 1878 et en 1889, dans la capitale. C'est à l'occasion de l'exposition de 1889 que la tour Eiffel fut construite.

▼ *Paris vu du ciel, avec, au premier plan, quelques pavillons de l'Exposition universelle.*

1900 – 1909

Paris a son métro

▶ **19 juillet 1900** ◀ Le métro est inauguré à Paris. La première ligne mise en service est Porte Maillot-Porte de Vincennes. De nombreuses stations sont décorées avec des motifs végétaux dans le style Art nouveau. Certains trains, équipés de pneus en caoutchouc, permettent un voyage confortable. Le métro devrait rouler sur 192 km dans Paris.

Un nouvel appareil photo

La compagnie américaine Eastman Kodak lance un nouvel appareil photo, le Brownie. Celui-ci ne coûte qu'un dollar, et l'innovation est révolutionnaire : pour faire développer les photos, on extrait la pellicule du boîtier et on l'envoie chez Kodak. Jusqu'alors, il fallait renvoyer l'appareil avec la pellicule…

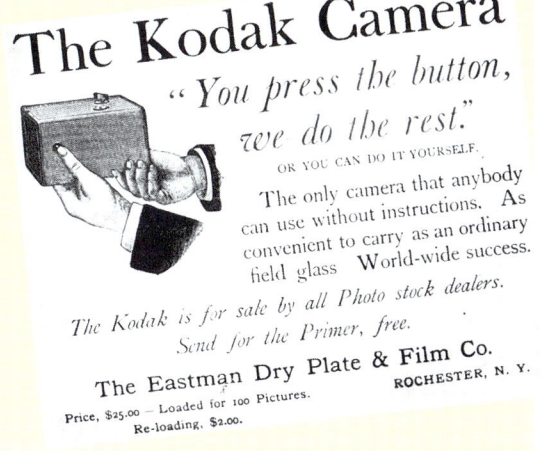

▲ *Scène de guerre en Afrique du Sud.*

Fin de la guerre des Boers ?

▶ **30 septembre 1900** ◀ En Afrique du Sud, lord Roberts, commandant en chef des forces britanniques, a annoncé la fin imminente du conflit qui oppose les colons hollandais – les Boers – et les colons britanniques. En décembre 1899, les Boers s'étaient révélés d'excellents combattants, et les Britanniques avaient subi trois sévères défaites. Mais l'envoi de renforts permit à la Grande-Bretagne de remporter une victoire à Mafeking en mai 1900. Toutefois, les Boers ne s'étaient pas rendus : la guerre n'était peut-être pas finie.

Des fouilles à Cnossos

▶ **19 mars 1900** ◀ L'archéologue anglais sir Arthur Evans découvre en Crète un palais qui serait le labyrinthe de la légende ; les rois y ont sûrement vécu. Le palais de Cnossos date de 2 000 ans av. J.-C. Ses fresques représentent, entre autres, des taureaux, évoquant le Minotaure, monstre mi-homme mi-taureau de la mythologie grecque.

▼ *Fresques ornant l'ancien palais de Cnossos, en Crète.*

Pékin délivré des Boxers

▶ **14 août 1900** ◀ Les forces internationales ont délivré le quartier des ambassades de Pékin, assiégé depuis cinquante-cinq jours. Elles ont ainsi mis fin à la révolte des Boxers. Ces Chinois, qui refusent la domination étrangère, ont tué à Pékin des missionnaires européens et des chrétiens chinois, et occupé des ambassades. Les forces internationales, composées de 10 000 soldats, anglais, français, américains et allemands, se sont heurtées à la résistance des Boxers, avant d'entrer dans Pékin.

◀ *Un Boxer en armes.*

1900

Premier vol d'un zeppelin

▶ **2 juillet 1900** ◀ Le comte allemand Ferdinand von Zeppelin a essayé en Allemagne son premier dirigeable rigide, le *LZ-1*. L'appareil est constitué d'une armature en aluminium, de 128 m de long, comportant seize arceaux, et d'une enveloppe extérieure en coton. À l'intérieur sont disposés dix-sept réservoirs d'hydrogène, gaz plus léger que l'air. Deux moteurs de 15 chevaux permettent au ballon d'atteindre la vitesse de 29 km/h. Deux grands gouvernails, situés à l'arrière, servent à le diriger.

Le Meccano

▶ **30 novembre 1900** ◀ L'Anglais Frank Hornby a mis au point un nouveau jeu de construction en métal pour les enfants.

Ce comptable, habitué à fabriquer pour son fils des accessoires en métal pour son train miniature, trouvait qu'il n'y avait pas assez d'éléments interchangeables. Il eut alors l'idée de percer des pièces en cuivre et de les fixer avec des vis et des écrous minuscules. Sa première boîte de Meccano permet de construire une grue articulée miniature.

Le docteur Freud interprète les rêves

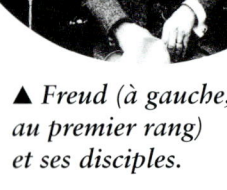

▲ *Freud (à gauche, au premier rang) et ses disciples.*

▶ **14 octobre 1900** ◀ La publication du livre de l'Autrichien Sigmund Freud, *l'Interprétation des rêves*, jette les bases d'une nouvelle science : la psychanalyse.

Le docteur Freud pense que, si certaines personnes souffrant de troubles nerveux lui racontent leurs rêves, il pourra les soigner. En effet, selon lui, les rêves sont remplis de symboles révélant des souvenirs ou des désirs refoulés. Ils expriment les frustrations des individus. L'analyse du docteur Freud a suscité un très vif intérêt dans le monde.

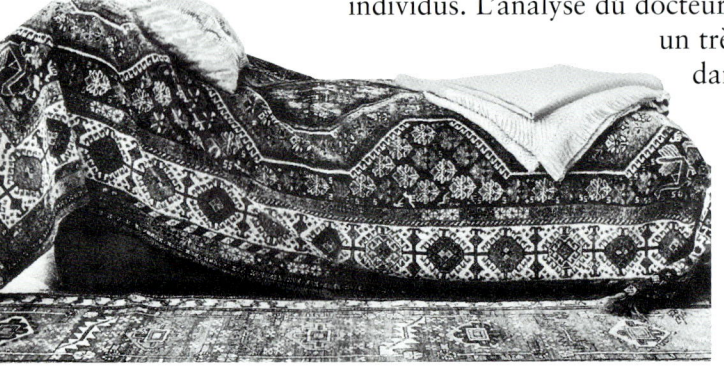

◀ *Divan sur lequel s'allongent les patients de Freud au cours des séances de psychanalyse.*

Les États-Unis remportent la première Coupe Davis

Les tennismen américains ont battu les Britanniques A. W. Gore et Roper Barrat, au Longwood Cricket Club, à Boston, par cinq matches à zéro. Ils remportent la première Coupe Davis. Le trophée, une coupe en argent massif appelée le « saladier d'argent », a été offert par Dwight Filley Davis, le fondateur de la compétition.

1900 – 1909

Les Russes en Mandchourie

▶ **3 septembre 1900** ◀ Les Russes contrôlent une partie de la Mandchourie, région du nord-est de la Chine actuelle. Le 13 août, les cosaques russes avaient mis en déroute les troupes chinoises. Depuis, plusieurs villes situées sur les rives du fleuve Amour ont été occupées, et leurs habitants, expulsés. Le but, selon le gouverneur russe, est d'inciter la Mandchourie à respecter le pouvoir russe ; il est en réalité de donner à la Russie un port libre de glace dans le Pacifique, Port-Arthur.

▲ *Soldats russes surveillant la plaine du Liao, en Mandchourie, région du nord-est de la Chine.*

◀ *Les premiers dirigeables avaient une forme de fuseau et une hélice mue par un moteur à vapeur.*

En 1900 aussi …

2 janvier • Mise en circulation du premier bus électrique à New York.

14 mai • Ouverture des jeux Olympiques à Paris.

22 mai • L'âge minimal requis pour travailler dans les mines en Grande-Bretagne passe de 12 à 13 ans.

30 septembre • Loi Millerand-Colliard « limitant » à 60 heures la durée hebdomadaire du travail, qui ne l'était pas jusque-là pour les hommes.

La théorie des quanta

▶ **14 décembre 1900** ◀ À Berlin, le physicien allemand Max Planck explique sa nouvelle théorie sur la nature de l'énergie et bouleverse le monde de la physique. Jusqu'à présent, on pensait que l'énergie était émise de façon continue. Selon Planck, l'énergie ne peut exister que sous forme de particules – les quanta – et son émission se fait de façon discontinue. Cette théorie ouvre une ère nouvelle aux scientifiques et leur permet de mesurer avec précision les unités d'énergie comme la chaleur, la lumière et les ondes radio.

▶ *Max Planck.*

Le premier hamburger

Les clients d'un restaurant de New Haven, aux États-Unis, ont dégusté le premier hamburger. Il s'agit d'une sorte de sandwich garni de bœuf haché assaisonné d'oignons. Cette spécialité serait inspirée de la cuisine des immigrés allemands de Hambourg.

▼ *Un paquebot transatlantique de luxe, le Deutschland.*

Record sur l'Atlantique

▶ **13 août 1900** ◀ Vingt-quatre heures après le transatlantique *Kaiser Wilhelm der Grosse*, c'est le *Deutschland* qui bat le record de vitesse de la traversée de l'Atlantique. Le *Kaiser Wilhelm* avait relié l'Amérique à l'Europe en 5 j 19 h 45 min. Le *Deutschland* a amélioré ce score de huit heures. Le Ruban bleu, qui récompense ce genre d'exploits, lui a été décerné.

1901

Mort de la reine d'Angleterre

▶ **22 janvier 1901** ◀

La reine Victoria s'est éteinte à Osborne, dans l'île de Wight, à l'âge de 82 ans. Elle a régné 64 ans ; c'est le plus long règne de l'histoire de la monarchie britannique. Elle est couronnée à 18 ans, en 1837. On la juge d'abord frivole – elle est gaie, elle aime la danse. Elle devient populaire au moment où elle tombe amoureuse de son cousin, le prince Albert, qu'elle épouse en 1840. Ils ont neuf enfants, dont plusieurs se marièrent avec des membres des grandes familles royales européennes. Parmi leurs petits-enfants figure l'épouse du tsar de Russie Nicolas II.

Victoria a été si affectée par la mort de son mari, en 1861, qu'elle s'éloigne de la vie publique. Pour célébrer ses cinquante puis soixante années de règne, on organisa de grandes fêtes, au cours desquelles elle réapparut devant ses sujets. En 1900, des problèmes de santé l'obligent à se retirer dans son château d'Osborne, sur l'île de Wight.

Un nouveau rasoir : le rasoir Gillette

Un nouveau type de rasoir devrait être lancé l'année prochaine sur le marché américain. Il a été imaginé par l'homme d'affaires King Camp Gillette. Bien que le brevet ait été déposé dès 1895, il a fallu plusieurs années pour mettre au point la double lame de ce rasoir. Le principe est simple : une fois usée, on jette la lame pour la remplacer par une neuve.

▶ *Le rasoir Gillette, présenté dans une jolie boîte.*

◀ *Le cortège funèbre de la reine Victoria devant le château royal de Windsor.*

Première Mercedes

▶ 31 mars 1901 ◀ Le constructeur automobile Daimler a lancé une voiture révolutionnaire, s'inspirant d'un modèle qu'il avait expérimenté en 1899. Elle a été fabriquée pour Émile Jellinek, consul général de l'Empire austro-hongrois à Nice, qui n'a pas hésité à lui donner le nom de sa fille : Mercedes.

La voiture est dotée d'un moteur de 5,9 l à quatre cylindres, combustion interne et refroidissement à eau. Elle ressemble à une voiture à cheval et peut atteindre la vitesse de pointe de 85 km/h.

De nouveaux disques

Les premiers disques pour Gramophone sont mis en vente par la firme La Voix de son maître. Le disque, gravé sur une face, a été enregistré par le grand ténor italien Enrico Caruso. Il interprète un air de *Paillasse (I Pagliacci)*, un opéra de Ruggero Leoncavallo.

1900 – 1909

Premiers Nobel

▶ 10 décembre 1901 ◀ Les premiers prix Nobel sont décernés par la fondation créée par Alfred Nobel, un riche industriel et chimiste suédois. Ils récompensent des travaux dans cinq domaines (physique, chimie, paix, littérature et médecine). Parmi les lauréats : pour la paix, l'économiste français Frédéric Passy avec le Suisse Henri Dunant, fondateur de la Croix-Rouge ; pour la physique, l'Allemand Wilhelm Röntgen, père des rayons X.

▼ *Alfred Nobel, l'inventeur de la dynamite.*

En 1901 aussi ...

25 janvier • Ouverture du Salon de l'automobile, du cycle et des sports au Grand Palais, à Paris.

18 mai • Une éclipse totale du Soleil s'est produite à l'île Maurice.

24 juin • Première exposition du peintre espagnol Pablo Picasso à Paris.

9 septembre • Mort du peintre français Henri de Toulouse-Lautrec, à l'âge de 37 ans.

Les Juifs russes fuient vers la Palestine

▶ 1901 ◀ De nombreux Juifs russes s'exilent en Palestine, pour s'installer dans des colonies agricoles financées par le baron de Rothschild. Ces hommes et ces femmes sont les victimes des pogroms, mouvements de violence populaire soutenus par le gouvernement russe. Ce dernier pratique l'antisémitisme (racisme envers la communauté juive) et rend les Juifs responsables des grèves et du terrorisme révolutionnaire.

▼ *Les Juifs russes s'installent en Palestine, sous des tentes.*

Le Concours Lépine

▶ 30 septembre 1901 ◀ Louis Lépine, préfet de Paris, lance un nouveau concours. Destiné aux fabricants de jouets français, il récompensera les créations les plus originales et les plus ingénieuses, à condition qu'elles soient bon marché. Louis Lépine s'engage à aider les inventeurs à vendre leurs produits.

1901

Le président McKinley est assassiné

▶ **14 septembre 1901** ◀ Le président américain, William McKinley, meurt huit jours après l'attentat commis sur sa personne par l'anarchiste polonais Léon Czolgosz. Il avait 68 ans. Il est le troisième président à avoir été assassiné, après Abraham Lincoln en 1865 et James A. Garfield en 1881.
Le vice-président, Theodore Roosevelt, qui se trouvait dans le Vermont, a aussitôt pris un train spécial pour se rendre au chevet du président. Malheureusement, il n'arrivera que douze heures plus tard. À 43 ans, ce dernier devient le plus jeune président du pays.

◀ *Ce tableau évoque l'assassinat du président McKinley par l'anarchiste Czolgosz.*

Le cinéma bon marché

Aux États-Unis, le public afflue dans les *nickelodeons*. Ce sont des salles de cinéma où, moyennant un *nickel* (5 cents), les spectateurs peuvent assister à la projection de plusieurs petits films pendant une heure. Ces pionniers doivent cependant faire preuve de patience, car des incidents techniques, comme la défaillance d'un projecteur, interrompent souvent la séance.

Création du Commonwealth d'Australie

▶ **1er janvier 1901** ◀ À Melbourne, environ 50 000 personnes célèbrent la naissance du Commonwealth d'Australie. Le but de cette fédération est de réunir dans une même nation les différentes colonies australiennes. Le Premier ministre, Edmund Barton, a annoncé la formation du premier gouvernement fédéral. Il occupera le poste de ministre des Affaires étrangères. La constitution de cette fédération devrait améliorer la défense du pays, permettre de mieux contrôler l'immigration asiatique, et garantir la liberté de commerce entre les colonies australiennes.

1900 – 1909

Un Noir à la Maison-Blanche

▶ **16 octobre 1901** ◀ Quarante ans après l'abolition de l'esclavage des Noirs, les États du sud des États-Unis, esclavagistes jusqu'en 1865, sont sous le choc : le président Theodore Roosevelt a invité l'éducateur noir Booker T. Washington à un dîner à la Maison-Blanche. Né esclave, ce dernier est convaincu que seule l'éducation peut aboutir à l'unité entre Blancs et Noirs. En 1881, il était directeur d'un collège formant des professeurs noirs. Depuis, il est le leader incontesté des Noirs américains.

▶ *Roosevelt reçoit B.T. Washington.*

Premier train suspendu

▶ **1er mars 1901** ◀ En Allemagne, dans la région de la Ruhr, le premier train suspendu du monde a été inauguré. Conçu par l'ingénieur allemand Eugen Langen, il ne nécessite qu'un seul rail. Il traverse l'étroite vallée de la Wupper pour relier Vohwinkell à Barmen, villes distantes de 13 km.

Halte à la poussière

Un ingénieur anglais, Hubert Cecil Booth, a déposé un brevet qui va révolutionner la vie domestique. Il s'est inspiré d'un engin de voirie américain soufflant la poussière dans un conteneur. En inversant le procédé, il a créé une pompe électrique munie d'un tuyau pour aspirer l'air et d'un filtre en tissu pour retenir les poussières qu'il contient. C'est le premier aspirateur.

Empreintes digitales

À Londres, pour empêcher la fraude, la police relève les empreintes digitales des prisonniers. Les traces laissées par les doigts étant propres à chaque individu, cette méthode est infaillible pour identifier quelqu'un. L'administration anglaise l'avait déjà adoptée en Inde pour éviter que des personnes ne réclament indûment une pension.

La vogue du style Art nouveau

▶ **1901** ◀ Le style ornemental appelé Art nouveau connaît un vif succès. Apparu dans les années 1890, il se caractérise par des lignes sinueuses et des formes empruntées au règne végétal. L'Exposition universelle de 1900 à Paris et le succès des lampes et vases en pâte de verre colorée du décorateur américain Louis Comfort Tiffany témoignent de cet enthousiasme. Le terme « Art nouveau » a été inventé par une galerie parisienne qui en expose beaucoup.

◀ *Cette affiche représentant Sarah Bernhardt illustre le style Art nouveau.*

1902

Inauguration du Transsibérien

▼ *Train circulant sur le Transsibérien.*

▶ 1902 ◀ La ligne de chemin de fer, le Transsibérien, est ouverte à la circulation. Longue de 9 297 km, elle relie Moscou à Vladivostok, en Sibérie, sur la mer du Japon. Le premier coup de pioche avait été donné, en 1891, par le futur tsar Nicolas II. La fin des travaux est prévue pour 1904. Les ouvriers qui ont construit la ligne ont dû bâtir des ponts pour franchir des fleuves tumultueux comme l'Ob ou l'Amour, combler de profonds marécages et lutter contre le gel. Il a été impossible de contourner le lac Baïkal, à cause du relief accidenté. Les trains le traversent donc sur des bateaux à vapeur pour gagner la Mandchourie à Port-Arthur, devenu russe en 1900, où ils empruntent le chemin de fer chinois. Le voyage complet dure plus de dix jours, avec des arrêts dans plus de 1 000 gares.

Un gratte-ciel étonnant

▶ 1902 ◀ Aux États-Unis, l'achèvement de la construction du « Fer à repasser » (Flatiron Building), à New York, annonce une nouvelle ère architecturale. C'est l'œuvre de l'architecte Daniel H. Burnham. Celui-ci avait déjà transformé l'aspect de Chicago dans les années 1880. Il fut le premier à concevoir des édifices dotés d'une ossature métallique. Cela permettait, grâce à l'utilisation d'ascenseurs puissants, de dépasser les seize étages des bâtiments traditionnels en brique. En 1885, William Le Baron Jenney avait déjà construit à Chicago un gratte-ciel à cage d'acier revêtu de béton : le Home Insurance Building. Le besoin croissant de bureaux dans les villes risque de modifier le paysage urbain en profondeur ces prochaines années.

▶ *Le « Fer à repasser » à New York doit son nom à sa forme triangulaire effilée.*

Pierre le Lapin enchante les enfants

Dans les librairies, on s'arrache l'*Histoire de Pierre le Lapin (The Tale of Peter Rabbit)*, publiée par Beatrix Potter, d'origine anglaise. Dans cet ouvrage, elle raconte les aventures d'un lapin, Peter Rabbit, et de ses amis, d'autres animaux. L'auteur a également illustré ses textes avec de jolies aquarelles.

96 mineurs tués

▶ 31 juillet 1902 ◀ Une explosion dans la mine australienne du mont Kembla, dans l'État de Nouvelle-Galles-du-Sud, tue quatre-vingt-seize mineurs. Cent cinquante-quatre sont encore bloqués au fond. C'est la première catastrophe minière d'une telle envergure dans le pays. Cette mine avait la réputation d'être si sûre que la flamme des lampes des mineurs n'était même pas protégée. Pourtant, le grisou – gaz combustible – s'est enflammé.

1900 – 1909

Le barrage d'Assouan est achevé

▶ **10 décembre 1902** ◀ En Égypte, un premier barrage à Assouan sur le Nil, à 950 km au sud du Caire, est inauguré. Sa construction par les Anglais a duré quatre ans, et 11 000 personnes environ ont permis de la mener à bien. Il mesure plus de 2 km de long. Ce barrage doit retenir les crues annuelles du fleuve et relâcher l'eau progressivement pendant la saison sèche.

▲ *Le barrage d'Assouan, haut de 40 m.*

En 1902 aussi …

9 février • À Paris, le docteur Eugène Louis Doyen sépare les célèbres sœurs siamoises du cirque Barnum.

28 mai • Thomas Edison invente la première batterie automobile.

9 août • Couronnement du roi Édouard VII à l'abbaye de Westminster, à Londres.

29 septembre • Mort, à Paris, de l'écrivain Émile Zola, à l'âge de 62 ans. Il est l'auteur, entre autres, de *Germinal*.

Le volcan tue à la Martinique

▶ **8 mai 1902** ◀ Environ 40 000 personnes auraient péri dans une éruption de la montagne Pelée, volcan du nord de la Martinique. Le seul survivant serait un prisonnier … protégé par les murs de son cachot. Saint-Pierre, chef-lieu de canton de l'île, est complètement détruit.

Voyage sur la Lune

Le dernier film du réalisateur français Georges Méliès est une aventure de science-fiction évoquant de façon fantasmagorique la vie sur les autres planètes. *Le Voyage dans la Lune* est le récit d'un voyage en fusée dans l'espace. Ses « effets spéciaux » sont très appréciés par les nombreux spectateurs. Méliès a réalisé plus d'une centaine de petits films dans les studios de tournage qu'il a créés à Montreuil. Ses ingénieux trucages passionnent le public.

▼ *Le parcours du câble sous le Pacifique.*

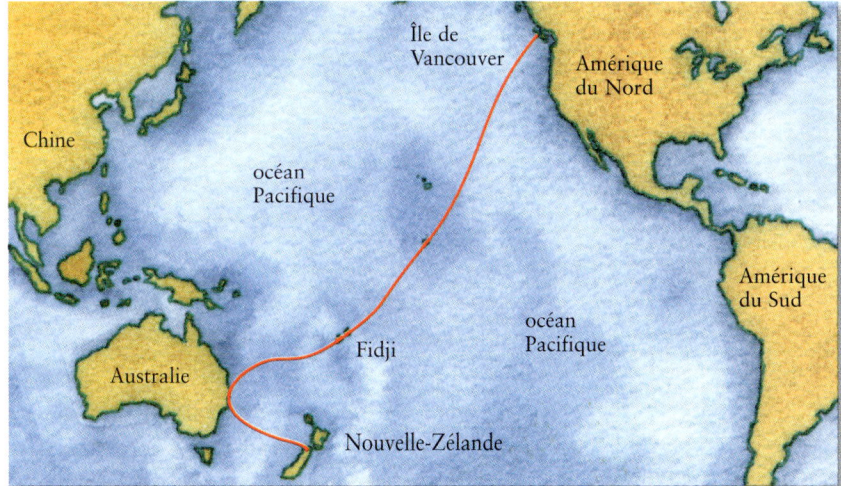

Sous le Pacifique … un câble

▶ **31 octobre 1902** ◀ La pose d'un nouveau câble télégraphique sous-marin est achevée. Il traverse le Pacifique de l'île de Vancouver, sur la côte ouest du Canada, jusqu'à l'Australie et la Nouvelle-Zélande, via les îles Fidji. Il comporte un seul fil conducteur, gainé par une enveloppe en résine naturelle – la gutta-percha – et protégé par des fils de fer galvanisés. Ce câble transatlantique, comme les précédents, sert uniquement pour les communications télégraphiques et transmet un seul signal à la fois. Il faudra attendre encore un peu pour pouvoir téléphoner à l'autre bout du monde…

1903

◀ Les frères Wright entrent dans l'Histoire. À Kitty Hawk, ils réussissent à voler à 3 m du sol pendant 12 secondes.

Décollage réussi

▶ **17 décembre 1903** ◀ Un peu après 10 h 30, ce matin, à Kitty Hawk, en Caroline du Nord aux États-Unis, Orville et Wilbur Wright effectuent un vol de 36 m dans le biplan à moteur qu'ils ont conçu, *Flyer 1*. Il n'a duré que douze secondes, mais c'est le premier vol mécanique d'un tel engin. Les frères Wright, qui ont un magasin de cycles à Dayton, dans l'Ohio, s'entraînaient à voler depuis 1896. Ils ont construit leur premier biplan planeur en 1900 et l'ont testé à Kitty Hawk. En 1901, après avoir volé sur 118 m avec un planeur plus grand, ils décident de fabriquer un moteur à essence à quatre cylindres. Celui-ci, fixé au planeur, entraîne deux hélices grâce à un système de chaînes et d'engrenages. *Flyer 1* est né. Il n'a pas de roues : il est lancé par un chariot roulant sur un rail en bois. Pour le vol de ce matin, les Wright s'étaient entraînés dans un tunnel doté d'une soufflerie qu'ils ont construit près de chez eux.

Le tour du monde en six heures

Le 11 juillet, à 11 h 55, le journal *le Temps* a envoyé un télégramme ; il lui est revenu à 17 h 55, après avoir fait le tour du monde. Jamais aucun message n'avait parcouru autant de kilomètres en si peu de temps. Le succès de cette expérience prouve la qualité des moyens de communication modernes.

Premier film de gangsters

Le public américain peut assister à la projection d'un film d'un genre nouveau. Il dure douze minutes. *The Great Train Robbery*, réalisé par Edwin Porter, est bâti autour d'une véritable intrigue : l'attaque d'un train par des bandits. Ceux-ci sont poursuivis par les hommes du shérif, qui finissent par les rattraper. La scène finale surprend par son originalité : le chef des hors-la-loi braque son revolver vers les spectateurs et tire.

L'aspirine est en vente en Allemagne

▶ **10 octobre 1903** ◀ Un nouveau médicament, l'aspirine, a été commercialisé en Allemagne par la firme Bayer. Cet antidouleur soulage notamment les maux de tête, et il aurait aussi une action efficace contre la fièvre. C'est un dérivé de l'acide salicylique – provenant de l'écorce du saule – obtenu par le chimiste français Charles Gerhardt en 1853, et redécouvert par un chercheur de chez Bayer en 1893.

◀ Attaque du train dans une scène de *The Great Train Robbery*.

1900 – 1909

Ours en peluche

Une usine est créée, aux États-Unis, pour fabriquer des ours en peluche. Le président Theodore Roosevelt, qui refusa de tuer un ourson lors d'une chasse, est à l'origine de ce succès. Émus par son geste, le commerçant Morris Michton et sa femme confectionnèrent un petit ours en peluche – le Teddy Bear, Teddy étant le diminutif de Theodore. Michton vendit l'ours exposé dans son magasin en cinq minutes. Le soir, on lui en avait commandé une douzaine...

Championnat de base-ball

▶ **13 octobre 1903** ◀ Aux États-Unis, les Red Sox de Boston – American League – ont battu les Pirates de Pittsburgh – National League – par cinq matches à trois, dans les premières World Series de base-ball. Cette compétition opposait les vainqueurs de chacune des deux ligues. Fondée en 1876, la National League a longtemps refusé la création d'une ligue rivale. Elle a dû céder en 1901, lorsque la Western League est devenue l'American League.

▲ *Première rencontre entre les deux ligues rivales américaines de base-ball.*

Garin gagne le premier Tour de France

▶ **19 juillet 1903** ◀ Le premier Tour de France a été remporté par le Français Maurice Garin. Cette course de dix-neuf jours, créée par Henri Desgrange, comporte 6 étapes de Paris à Paris, via Lyon, Marseille, Toulouse et Bordeaux, soit un total de 2 428 km. Sur les 60 engagés, seuls 21 coureurs ont terminé le périple. Après avoir gagné 4 des 6 étapes, Garin a remporté la course avec près de trois heures d'avance sur son compatriote Pottier.

◀ *Maurice Garin (à gauche), vainqueur du premier Tour de France.*

En 1903 aussi…

Juin • Henry Ford fonde la Ford Motor Compagny.

11 juin • Alexandre Ier Obrénovitch, roi de Serbie, est assassiné, avec son épouse, à la suite d'un complot militaire.

10 octobre • En Angleterre, Emmeline Pankhurst fonde l'Union féminine, sociale et politique, afin d'obtenir le droit de vote pour les femmes.

Prix Nobel pour les Curie

▶ **10 décembre 1903** ◀ La Française Marie Curie a reçu le prix Nobel de physique pour ses travaux sur la radioactivité : c'est la première fois que ce prix est attribué à une femme. Elle a découvert que des éléments comme le thorium, le polonium et le radium sont radioactifs. Elle partage cette récompense avec son mari, Pierre, et Henri Becquerel.

LA CONQUÊTE DU CIEL

L'homme a toujours cherché à voler, et les inventeurs ont créé des machines volantes depuis des siècles. Déjà, au XVIᵉ siècle, Léonard de Vinci étudia ainsi l'aérodynamisme et inventa des engins volants. Le Français Clément Ader, en 1890, a été le premier à voler avec un appareil plus lourd que l'air, qu'il appelle « avion ». Les frères Wright effectuent, en 1903, un vol de 36 m en douze secondes au-dessus d'une plage de Caroline du Nord. En France, les frères Voisin construisent des avions en série dès 1904. En Allemagne, Zeppelin fabrique des aéronefs, moins lourds que l'air. Ces dirigeables font des vols réguliers, avec des passagers, à partir de 1910. La guerre de 1914-1918 accélère les progrès de l'aviation, pour les besoins des armées.

▶ *Louis Blériot, aux commandes de l'un de ses appareils.*

L'exploit de Blériot

L'ingénieur français Louis Blériot est le premier homme à voler au-dessus de la mer. Il fonda une entreprise d'accessoires automobiles, puis se consacra à l'aviation et fit des essais, avec deux planeurs tirés par des canots, sur la Seine. Il utilisa ensuite les moteurs légers de motocyclette sur ses prototypes, des monoplans à hélice.

Blériot veut remporter le formidable prix de 1 000 livres offert par le journal londonien *Daily Mail* au pionnier qui traversera la Manche en avion. Il essuie d'abord des échecs : ses avions décollent mais s'écrasent vite. En 1908, il améliore le monoplan et emprunte le gauchissement des ailes aux frères Wright, ce qui lui permet de tourner en vol. Le 25 juillet 1909, il décolle des environs de Calais, sur le *Blériot XI*, équipé d'un moteur Anzani de 25 chevaux. Il atterrit trente-sept minutes plus tard près de Douvres, sur les côtes anglaises, après un vol de 41 km. Son succès est tel, que de nombreuses commandes affluent, et il doit créer une usine pour fabriquer le *Blériot XI*.

◀ *Louis Blériot dans son* Blériot XI.

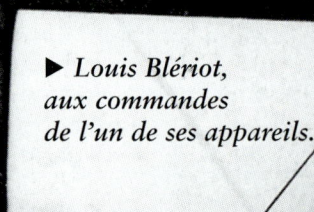

L'homme-oiseau

L'Allemand Otto Lilienthal, pionnier de l'aviation de la fin du XIXᵉ siècle, pense qu'il faut maîtriser la technique du planeur avant de s'intéresser aux avions, encore propulsés par des moteurs lourds et inefficaces. Son engin ressemble aux deltaplanes actuels. Le pilote effectue de longs vols, tournant, montant ou descendant dans le ciel en modifiant ses appuis. En 1896, surpris par une rafale de vent, il s'écrase et se tue.

L'essor de l'aviation

L'avion constitue un nouveau moyen de transport, entre les deux guerres. Les premiers vols réguliers Paris-Londres débutent en 1919, les liaisons transatlantiques, en 1939. Les hydravions, qui se posent sur l'eau, sont très utilisés à cette époque, car ils ne nécessitent pas d'aéroport, mais c'est le Douglas C-3 (DC-3), ou « Dakota », dont certains sont encore en service, qui connaît le plus grand succès. Les progrès s'accélèrent à partir de la Seconde Guerre mondiale. Les engins gagnent en sécurité et en vitesse. Les hélicoptères (premier vol en 1907) et les avions à réaction (premier vol en 1939) se diversifient. À partir de 1950, les avions remplacent les bateaux sur les longs trajets et concurrencent le train. Depuis 1976, le supersonique Concorde est en service. C'est un avion franco-anglais.

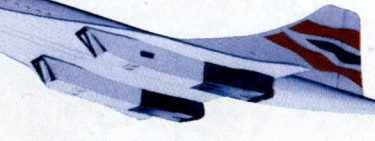

▲ *Le Concorde baisse son nez au décollage et à l'atterrissage pour élargir le champ de vision du pilote.*

L'aviation
France : premier voyage en ballon des frères Montgolfier en 1783.
•
Brésil : Alberto Santos-Dumont construit le premier U.L.M. – ultra léger motorisé – en 1906.
•
Allemagne : le Heinkel He 178 de 1939 est le premier avion à réaction.

▶ *Le chantier du Concorde. Rapide et beau, l'avion est bruyant. Sa fabrication a été arrêtée en 1979.*

▼ *En quelques décennies, les « coucous » fragiles et bizarres se sont transformés en appareils de haute technologie, aussi performants pour le transport de voyageurs que pour l'action militaire.*

▲ *LVG CV1, 1917*

▲ *De Havilland Comet, 1949*

▲ *Panavia Tornado GR1A, 1986*

◀ *Boeing 747 Jumbo-jet, 1969*

▶ *DC-3, ou « Dakota », 1934*

1904

Un prix Nobel pour Pavlov

▶ **10 décembre 1904** ◀ Le biologiste russe Ivan Pavlov reçoit le prix Nobel de médecine. Il a découvert que les messages envoyés par le cerveau jouaient un rôle important dans le processus de la digestion. Ses expériences sur un chien montrent que, si le repas de l'animal est interrompu, son estomac continue à sécréter des sucs digestifs ; mais que, en neutralisant ses nerfs, la sécrétion cesse, même avec l'apport de nourriture jusqu'à l'estomac. Pavlov fit également sonner une cloche plusieurs jours d'affilée, juste avant de nourrir l'animal. Il nota que le chien salivait au seul son de la cloche, sans qu'on lui donnât d'aliments. C'est ce qu'il a appelé un réflexe conditionné. Le chien associa le signal extérieur, la cloche, à la nourriture.

Le Japon déclare la guerre à la Russie

▶ **10 février 1904** ◀ La flotte japonaise a coulé 7 navires russes ancrés dans la rade de Port-Arthur, port de Mandchourie occupé par la Russie. Environ 8 000 soldats japonais ont également débarqué en Corée et marchent vers Séoul, la capitale. L'empereur du Japon vient ainsi de déclarer officiellement la guerre à la Russie : il lui reproche ses ambitions en Corée et en Mandchourie. Le tsar est alors à l'Opéra de Saint-Pétersbourg. Ses officiers attendront la fin du spectacle pour l'en informer.

Caruso triomphe à New York

À 30 ans, le grand ténor italien Enrico Caruso a le monde à ses pieds. Il triomphe au Metropolitan Opera de New York dans *Élixir d'amour,* de Gaetano Donizetti. Pour chaque représentation, il reçoit 1 000 dollars. Il a également enregistré son premier disque aux États-Unis : un extrait de l'opéra de Verdi *Rigoletto*.

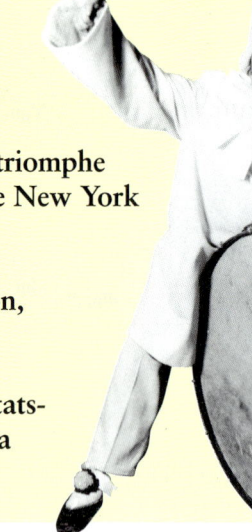

▲ *L'artillerie japonaise en action.*

Peter Pan à Londres

▶ **28 décembre 1904** ◀ L'événement théâtral de la saison sera sans doute la nouvelle pièce de l'Écossais James Barrie, *Peter Pan ou le Petit Garçon qui ne voulait pas grandir*. La première représentation, donnée hier soir au Duke of York's Theatre, à Londres, a révélé que le public adore les contes de fées. L'auteur, qui n'a pas d'enfants, est le tuteur des cinq fils d'une amie. C'est pour eux qu'il a inventé les aventures de Peter Pan et du capitaine Crochet.

1900 – 1909

Inauguration du métro à New York

▶ 27 octobre 1904 ◀

La première ligne de métro est mise en service à New York, après quatre ans de travaux. Elle relie Broadway à la 4ᵉ Avenue. Pour sa construction, les ingénieurs se sont inspirés du chemin de fer existant dans la ville et du métro de Londres. Son originalité est d'avoir plusieurs voies. Ainsi, des métros express qui ne s'arrêtent pas à toutes les stations circulent.

◀ *Vue du nouveau métro souterrain de New York.*

L'Entente cordiale

▶ 8 avril 1904 ◀

L'Angleterre et la France ont signé ce matin un accord historique, l'Entente cordiale. Cet accord règle plusieurs différends, dont les rivalités coloniales. Il définit notamment les droits territoriaux et les droits de pêche de la France et de l'Angleterre à travers le monde.

L'exploit d'Helen Keller

▶ 1ᵉʳ septembre 1904 ◀

Helen Keller, une Américaine de 24 ans, a soutenu sa thèse de doctorat au Radcliffe College de Cambridge, dans le Massachusetts. C'est une réussite exceptionnelle, puisque la jeune femme est aveugle, sourde et muette depuis l'âge de 19 mois… Quand elle eut 7 ans, un professeur malvoyant, Ann Sullivan, commença à lui apprendre le braille, système d'écriture où les lettres sont dessinées en relief, qui allait lui permettre de faire ses études. En 1902, Helen Keller a raconté son combat dans un livre poignant, *Histoire de ma vie*.

En 1904 aussi …

8 janvier • Le pape Pie X condamne le port des robes du soir décolletées.

18 avril • Parution en France du premier numéro du journal l'Humanité, fondé par Jean Jaurès.

9 mai • L'explorateur britannique Henry Stanley meurt à l'âge de 63 ans.

Premières glaces en cornet

L'invention d'un Italien, Italo Marcioni, a fait fureur à la foire internationale de Saint Louis, aux États-Unis. Le cornet à glace, fabriqué simplement avec de la farine, du lait et du sucre, permet en effet de déguster une glace en se promenant. C'est un vrai plaisir pour les gourmands … et les gourmandes !

◀ *Helen Keller, aveugle, sourde et muette, réussit son examen.*

1905

Dimanche rouge à Saint-Pétersbourg

▶ 22 janvier 1905 ◀

À Saint-Pétersbourg, les troupes du tsar ont tiré sur la foule des manifestants et de leurs familles, venus présenter une pétition au tsar Nicolas II : ils manifestent contre les impôts et le manque de nourriture. Beaucoup ont été tués et blessés au cours de ce qu'on appelle déjà le « Dimanche rouge ». Cette marche, conduite par le pope (prêtre de l'Église orthodoxe russe) Gueorgui Gapone, a commencé vers midi. Les participants brandissaient des icônes (images religieuses), des bannières et des portraits du tsar. Devant le palais d'Hiver, ils se sont trouvés face aux soldats. Ces derniers avaient reçu l'ordre de disperser les manifestants. Mais ils ont fait feu sur les hommes, les femmes et les enfants. Le pope a réussi à s'échapper, mais des meneurs ont été arrêtés. Ce massacre détruit l'image de protecteur des pauvres que le peuple a du tsar et marque la rupture entre le peuple et le tsar.

▼ *La Garde impériale refoulant les manifestants devant le palais d'Hiver, à Saint-Pétersbourg.*

▲ *Dans cette scène du* Cuirassé Potemkine *(1925), film du Russe S. M. Eisenstein, les mutins sont rassemblés sur le pont du cuirassé.*

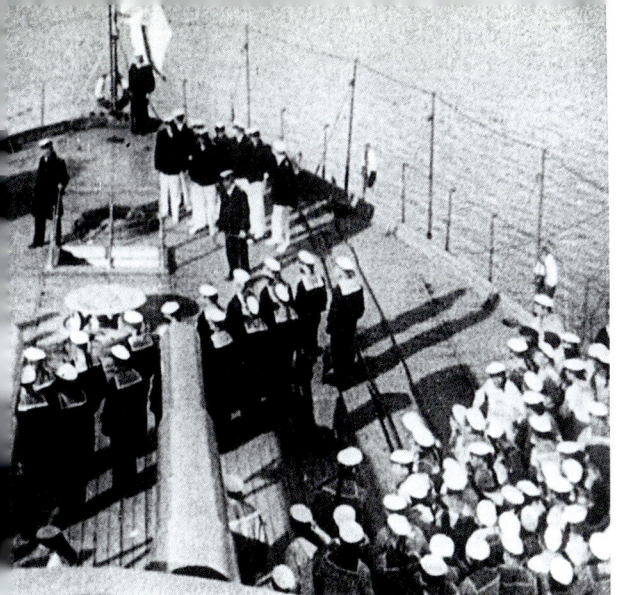

Mutinerie sur le *Potemkine*

▶ **27 juin 1905** ◀ Les marins du plus puissant cuirassé de la flotte russe, le *Potemkine*, ont déclenché une mutinerie à Odessa, port de la mer Noire. Un marin, qui s'était plaint de la mauvaise nourriture, a été tué par un officier. L'équipage, révolté, rejoint par huit officiers, a jeté par-dessus bord le commandant et des officiers. Deux autres bateaux ont rejoint la révolte. Huit membres d'équipage seront condamnés à mort.

Des ampoules plus lumineuses

Les nouvelles ampoules électriques éclairent mieux et durent plus longtemps. Les anciens filaments, en fibres végétales, ont été remplacés par des filaments en carbone, ce qui augmente nettement la luminosité des ampoules ainsi que leur durée de vie.

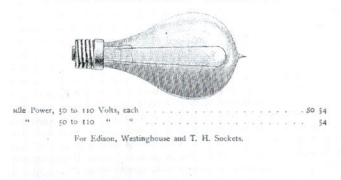

▲ *Lampe à incandescence.*

La folie des cartes postales

La dernière mode, pour prendre des nouvelles de quelqu'un ou lui en donner, est d'envoyer une carte postale. Même les amoureux n'ont pas trouvé de meilleur support pour déclarer leur flamme. Depuis sa création, en 1861, à Philadelphie aux États-Unis, et sa commercialisation en France, en 1872, jamais la carte postale, noir et blanc, sépia, ou délicatement colorée, n'avait connu un tel succès en Europe.

▶ *Carte postale sépia envoyée par le président Roosevelt à sa mère.*

◀ *Le roi Haakon VII de Norvège, en compagnie de la reine Maud et du prince Olaf.*

L'indépendance de la Norvège

▶ **7 juin 1905** ◀ Le Parlement norvégien – le Storting – proclame l'indépendance de la Norvège. Cet État avait vu son destin lié à celui de la Suède par l'Acte d'union d'août 1815, consécutif à l'invasion de la Norvège par les troupes suédoises. Le souverain suédois Oscar II régnait sur les deux États. Les Norvégiens ont voté le rétablissement de leur propre monarchie et ont porté sur le trône le prince Charles de Danemark. Il régnera sous le nom de Haakon VII de Norvège.

Les fauves scandalisent Paris

▶ **1er octobre 1905** ◀ Plusieurs peintres qui exposent au Nouveau Salon d'automne, à Paris, utilisent les teintes primaires pures et affirment que la couleur est en soi un moyen d'expression. Devant leurs toiles, un critique s'écrie « [...] mais ce sont des fauves » : ce nom leur restera. Le chef de file des fauves, Henri Matisse, a réalisé un portrait de sa femme qui a scandalisé le public.

▶ *Nature morte de Matisse, 1907.*

1905

▲ *Albert Einstein établit la théorie de la relativité.*

La relativité restreinte d'Albert Einstein

▶ **1er juillet 1905** ◀ Un savant allemand, Albert Einstein, vient de publier ses travaux sur la relativité restreinte, lesquels contredisent totalement la théorie d'Isaac Newton. Selon Einstein, il n'existe ni temps ni mouvement absolus ; tout dépend de l'observateur. Supposons qu'une fusée survole la Terre. Depuis la Terre, la fusée semble devenir de plus en plus petite, et le temps, s'y écouler lentement. Pour le pilote de la fusée, en revanche, le temps semble s'écouler normalement à bord, et plus lentement sur la Terre. Einstein en conclut qu'il y a un rapport d'équivalence entre la masse et l'énergie, et qu'une petite quantité de masse correspond à une grande quantité d'énergie. D'où l'équation $E = mc^2$, où E est l'énergie, m la masse et c la vitesse de la lumière. Selon Einstein, la seule valeur absolue est la vitesse de la lumière.

New York découvre la pizza

▶ **1905** ◀ Célèbre plat italien, la pizza est désormais servie à New York. Cette pâte à pain aplatie, garnie de tomates, de mozzarella et d'huile d'olive, cuite au four et servie chaude, est une invention napolitaine. C'est aux nombreux immigrés italiens de New York que la pizza doit son succès.

Naissance de *Little Nemo*

Une nouvelle bande dessinée comique vient de paraître dans le *New York Herald*. *Little Nemo à Slumberland* a été créé par Winsor McCay. Little Nemo se rend chaque soir à Slumberland et rencontre des personnages farfelus. Ce monde imaginaire est décrit avec beaucoup d'humour et de gentillesse, ce qui devrait assurer un franc succès à cette nouvelle publication.

▲ *Quatre dessins extraits de* Little Nemo à Slumberland.

Le Nobel pour Bertha von Suttner

▶ **10 décembre 1905** ◀ La femme de lettres autrichienne Bertha von Suttner obtient le prix Nobel de la paix. En 1876, elle entre au service d'Alfred Nobel, à Paris, comme gouvernante et secrétaire. Au bout d'une semaine, elle repart pour Vienne et épouse secrètement le baron Arthur von Suttner. Elle ne revoit Nobel que deux fois, mais ils s'écrivent jusqu'à ce qu'il meure, en 1896. Leur dernière rencontre, à l'issue d'un congrès pour la paix, à Berne, remonte à août 1892. C'est sans doute cette femme pacifiste qui a décidé l'inventeur de la dynamite à créer un prix de la paix. Son roman *Bas les armes !* (*Die Waffen nieder !*) a eu beaucoup d'influence.

1900 – 1909

En 1905 aussi …

2 janvier • Victoire du Japon sur la Russie. La garnison russe se rend à Port-Arthur.

24 mars • Mort de l'écrivain français Jules Verne, à l'âge de 77 ans..

4 avril • Un tremblement de terre fait plus de 10 000 victimes à Lahore, en Inde.

5 octobre • Les frères Wright effectuent un vol de trente-huit minutes.

Une étoile est née

▶ **1905** ◀ Une jeune ballerine russe, Anna Pavlova, a obtenu un triomphe pour son interprétation talentueuse d'un magnifique solo du *Lac des cygnes*, ballet du compositeur russe Tchaïkovski. Âgée de 23 ans seulement, elle a rejoint le ballet de l'Imperial Theatre il y a déjà six ans. Michel Fokine a réalisé la chorégraphie de ce ballet. Cette danseuse est douée d'un charme et d'une grâce extraordinaires.

Les artistes de Dresde

▶ **7 juin 1905** ◀ Quatre étudiants en architecture ont fondé, à Dresde, en Allemagne, une nouvelle association artistique, Die Brücke (« Le Pont »). Karl Schmidt-Rottluff, Fritz Bleyl, Erich Heckel et Ernst Ludwig Kirchner veulent rallier tous les artistes révolutionnaires. Les peintures des artistes de cette association se caractérisent par des coloris violents et des lignes d'une grande simplicité.

Succès du blues aux États-Unis

Le blues, chanté à l'origine par les esclaves noirs américains dans les plantations de coton, gagne les villes. Cette musique mélancolique est accessible à tous les interprètes. W.C. Handy, compositeur et trompettiste, souhaite créer une société d'édition de partitions de blues.

Photo-Secession

▶ **Novembre 1905** ◀ Alfred Stieglitz, célèbre photographe américain, a ouvert une galerie à New York. Il y expose des œuvres de son groupe, le Photo-Secession. Son but est que la photographie soit reconnue comme un art aussi important que la peinture. Stieglitz est réputé, notamment pour ses clichés de paysages sous la pluie, sous la neige, et de nuit.

▶ *Le trompettiste W.C. Handy est connu pour ses mélodies de blues.*

1906

La flotte britannique se modernise

▶ 10 février 1906 ◀ La marine britannique vient de franchir un grand pas technologique. Le roi Édouard VII inaugure aujourd'hui un magnifique navire de guerre, le *Dreadnought*. C'est le plus rapide et le plus grand des bâtiments de guerre. Il dispose de dix canons de 30, capables de faire feu sur les navires ennemis tout en restant hors d'atteinte de leurs torpilles. Le Premier lord de l'Amirauté avait ordonné la construction de ce navire révolutionnaire, car un rapport l'avait convaincu que la sécurité de la Grande-Bretagne dépendait avant tout de la qualité de sa flotte. Des experts estiment que ce bateau est capable de résister à des ennemis supérieurs en nombre. C'est une nouvelle étape de la course aux armements entre la Grande-Bretagne et l'Allemagne.

▲ *La flotte britannique règne sur les mers.*

Ancêtre du juke-box

Tout nouveau, tout beau, un appareil révolutionne les pistes de danse. Une compagnie américaine vient de lancer, à Chicago, un ingénieux appareil. Il suffit de choisir un air, puis de pousser le bouton correspondant. La musique de votre choix se fait alors entendre. Il n'y a plus qu'à s'élancer sur la piste.

Tremblement de terre à San Francisco

▶ 19 avril 1906 ◀ À 5 h 13 ce matin, San Francisco a été ébranlé jusque dans ses fondations. Cette grande ville de Californie connaît là le plus grave tremblement de terre de son histoire. La ville est en ruine et continue d'être ravagée par de violents incendies provoqués par l'explosion des canalisations de gaz. On déplore au moins 1 000 morts et des milliers de sans-abri. La majorité des habitants a fui. La loi martiale a été proclamée et, dans l'après-midi, 4 pillards ont été abattus.

▼ *La ville de San Francisco, après le tremblement de terre.*

En 1906 aussi...

18 janvier • Armand Fallières devient président de la République française.

10 mars • Catastrophe sans précédent à Courrières (Pas-de-Calais) : 1 200 mineurs de fond sont tués par un coup de grisou.

12 juillet • Réhabilitation du capitaine Dreyfus. Accusé d'espionnage parce qu'il était juif, il avait été injustement condamné, en 1894, à la déportation.

1900 – 1909

Éruption du Vésuve

▶ 7 avril 1906 ◀ Un effroyable torrent de lave déferle sans interruption sur toute la campagne italienne, au pied du Vésuve, entré en éruption. L'armée apporte des vivres en urgence, mais de nombreux villages restent coupés du monde et les routes sont encombrées de gens fuyant la pluie de cendres et de suie. Pour le moment, il est difficile d'évaluer les dégâts. On sait seulement que la ville d'Ottaiano a été rayée de la carte et qu'à Naples 100 personnes sont mortes, écrasées par des toitures ayant cédé sous le poids des cendres.

▲ *Un nuage de cendres s'élève au-dessus du Vésuve.*

▲ *Inauguration du tunnel du Simplon entre la Suisse et l'Italie.*

Le tunnel du Simplon

▶ 1ᵉʳ juin 1906 ◀ Un tunnel vient d'être ouvert entre la Suisse et l'Italie pour permettre le passage du chemin de fer. Les travaux ont duré huit ans. Ses 20 km font de lui le plus long tunnel du monde ; il a été percé sous le massif du Simplon. Les ouvriers ont travaillé dans des conditions épouvantables : températures de l'ordre de 49 °C et inondations souterraines. Il est l'œuvre de l'ingénieur allemand Alfred Brandt qui a conçu un nouveau type de foreuse hydraulique et des méthodes de percement révolutionnaires. Il est mort en 1899, épuisé, et sans avoir vu son tunnel terminé.

Avancée française au Maroc

▶ 31 mars 1906 ◀ La conférence d'Algésiras, en Espagne, se termine. Les accords signés aujourd'hui mettent fin à des mois de crise entre la France et l'Allemagne. Cette dernière voulait limiter les ambitions françaises au Maroc. La France exigeait, au contraire, que l'on y reconnaisse son rôle privilégié. L'Allemagne a accepté cette exigence française mais a obtenu, ainsi que les autres nations, la liberté de commerce avec le Maroc.

La Silver Ghost

▶ 15 mars 1906 ◀ Une nouvelle voiture très luxueuse fait ses débuts. Il s'agit de la Silver Ghost construite par la firme anglaise Rolls-Royce, qui a été créée en 1904. Cette voiture a un moteur de 6 cylindres et est très silencieuse.

« Invention » des corn flakes

William Kellog a fondé la Battle Creek Toasted Corn Flake Company pour commercialiser une nouvelle sorte de céréales inventée par hasard. Dans la cuisine de son frère John, des grains de maïs oubliés dans une poêle ont donné des flocons grillés à point. Ils sont baptisés corn flakes et sont délicieux pour le petit déjeuner.

Des ballons s'envolent

C'est une grande année pour les amateurs de montgolfières. En juillet, sept d'entre elles se sont envolées du jardin des Tuileries, à Paris, pour prendre part à une course de Paris à Whitby, en Angleterre. Cette course est sponsorisée par le quotidien anglais *Daily Mail*. L'Américain Franck Lamm a remporté la victoire.

1907

Émigration record aux États-Unis

▶ **20 février 1907** ◀ Ils partent en masse de chez eux, fuyant la misère ou les persécutions. L'Amérique leur semble être la terre promise. Le Congrès américain vient de voter une loi comme quoi ils pourront être refoulés, sous prétexte que leur arrivée pourrait nuire aux conditions du travail aux États-Unis. La loi autorise également l'exclusion de toute personne venant d'Extrême-Orient. Cette mesure fait suite à la violente agitation qui a eu lieu, l'année dernière, contre les travailleurs japonais.

Quatorze pour cent de la population actuelle américaine est née dans un autre pays mais les immigrants représentent actuellement la moitié de la force de travail. La dernière vague d'arrivants ne débarque pas d'Angleterre, d'Irlande et d'Allemagne comme les fois précédentes, mais vient principalement d'Europe orientale et méridionale. Chaque année, depuis 1880, environ 50 000 Juifs russes ont fui les persécutions, en quête d'une nouvelle vie possible en Amérique. Les dernières attaques antisémites ont entraîné un exode massif des Juifs hors de la Russie tsariste. Cette année, Ellis Island, le passage d'entrée obligé à New York, verra un nombre record d'émigrants – 1 million au total. En une journée, il en est passé 11 747.

▼ *Première vision de New York pour les nouveaux arrivants.*

▲ *Certificat de résidence américain.*

Création des scouts

▶ **29 juillet 1907** ◀ Les scouts sont nés. C'est une organisation de jeunesse calquée sur le modèle des scouts de l'armée anglaise. Elle est due à Robert Baden-Powell, célèbre pour ses exploits durant la guerre des Boers. Son but est de former pour l'avenir de bons citoyens, en leur inculquant le sens de la discipline, de l'altruisme et du devoir accompli.

Vingt jeunes garçons – certains venant de collèges huppés, tandis que d'autres sont issus de quartiers défavorisés de Londres – ont pris part à un camp expérimental sur l'île de Brownsea, sur la côte sud de l'Angleterre. Baden-Powell souhaite faire des scouts un mouvement international.

▼ *Baden-Powell (à gauche) et sa femme (au centre).*

1900 – 1909

▲ *Séance de travail dans une salle de l'école Montessori.*

La première école Montessori

▶ **Mars 1907** ◀ Maria Montessori vient d'ouvrir sa première école à Rome, dans un quartier populaire de la ville. Elle a 37 ans et elle est la première femme italienne à avoir obtenu un doctorat de médecine. Après avoir enseigné avec succès à des enfants handicapés mentaux, elle souhaite appliquer ses méthodes révolutionnaires d'enseignement à des enfants issus de milieux défavorisés. Elle espère enregistrer, là aussi, de bons résultats.

Sa démarche consiste à essayer d'obtenir des enfants le meilleur d'eux-mêmes, par le jeu et le développement de la mémoire, en les laissant libres de progresser chacun à son rythme. Elle veut apprendre à lire et à écrire aux enfants de moins de 5 ans, tout en les habituant à aimer leur travail et à se concentrer longtemps sans se fatiguer.

Kipling reçoit le prix Nobel de littérature

▶ **10 décembre 1907** ◀ Rudyard Kipling vient de recevoir le prix Nobel de littérature. Les enfants du monde entier connaissent bien les aventures de Mowgli, le petit garçon perdu dans la jungle et élevé par une louve. Il est le héros de deux œuvres du romancier, *le Livre de la jungle* et *le Second Livre de la jungle*, parues il y a une dizaine d'années. Né en Inde en 1865, l'auteur a fait ses études en Angleterre,

avant de devenir journaliste globe-trotter. Ses romans ont souvent pour cadre l'Inde où il avait vécu pendant sa jeunesse.
Il a écrit, entre autres, de merveilleuses histoires pour les enfants, comme *le Livre de la jungle*, *Histoires comme ça*, *Capitaine courageux* et *Kim*.

◀ *Rikki-Tikki-Tavi, la mangouste d'un des contes du* Livre de la jungle.

Florence Nightingale reçoit l'ordre du Mérite

▶ **29 novembre 1907** ◀ Florence Nightingale est la première femme à recevoir l'ordre du Mérite. Cette infirmière britannique s'est distinguée au cours de la guerre de Crimée, voilà un peu plus de 50 ans, en réorganisant les hôpitaux de campagne. C'est en imposant de strictes mesures d'hygiène, et en offrant aux soldats une nourriture saine, qu'elle leur sauva la vie. Elle a été la première à demander une formation pour les infirmières et a créé une école en Grande-Bretagne. Grâce à elle, le métier d'infirmière est réellement né.

Ziegfeld Follies

Le public new-yorkais s'enthousiasme pour un nouveau genre de revue musicale donné dans les théâtres de Broadway. Inspiré par les fameuses Folies-Bergère parisiennes, le producteur Florenz Ziegfeld a monté un extravagant spectacle, intitulé *Follies de 1907*, dont la vedette revient à sa femme, Anna Held, une actrice d'origine française.

1907

Pablo Picasso choque

Mars 1907 — Le monde de l'art parisien est habitué aux surprises. Mais la dernière toile du peintre espagnol de 26 ans Pablo Picasso a stupéfait tout le monde. Le tableau, *les Demoiselles d'Avignon*, montre cinq femmes plus ou moins dévêtues, dont le corps et les étoffes sont déformés en de curieuses formes géométriques, et qui rompent avec toutes les règles de l'art, qu'il s'agisse de la composition ou des lois de la perspective.

Ce jeune artiste se renouvelle sans cesse. Pendant quelques années, il a peint en bleu. Puis il est entré dans une période où les tonalités roses dominaient. Mais ce tableau marque une évolution radicale. Certains y voient l'influence du peintre Paul Cézanne, d'autres remarquent des similitudes évidentes entre les visages de certaines de ses demoiselles et des masques de l'exposition africaine qui vient de se dérouler à Paris. Picasso inaugure une nouvelle manière de représenter les objets, l'ensemble étant composé de formes anguleuses figurant le sujet, envisagé sous différentes perspectives.

◀ Les Demoiselles d'Avignon, *de Pablo Picasso.*

La Bakélite

La Bakélite est née. Son créateur, Leo Baekeland, a baptisé cette matière plastique résistante en s'inspirant de son propre nom. Ce chimiste américain d'origine belge a découvert un matériau révolutionnaire qui ne conduit pas l'électricité et qui ne fond pas quand on le chauffe. Lorsqu'elle est liquide, cette résine synthétique peut prendre n'importe quelle forme.

Un zoo modèle

7 mai 1907 — Au zoo de Hambourg, Carl Hagenbeck, dresseur et marchand d'animaux, a transformé la vie des animaux. Envolées les cages minuscules dans lesquelles de pitoyables créatures tournent en rond misérablement ! Dorénavant, grâce à Carl Hagenbeck, les animaux ont droit à de vastes espaces reproduisant leur habitat naturel. Ce sont de larges fosses à ciel ouvert, sans barreaux, où ils évoluent dans la plus grande liberté. Ce pourrait être un modèle pour tous les zoos à venir.

▲ *Repas des morses et des pingouins au zoo de Hagenbeck.*

Des femmes au Parlement finlandais

15 mars 1907 — L'année dernière, pour la première fois en Europe, le droit de vote a été accordé aux femmes en Finlande. La Finlande est ainsi devenue le troisième pays au monde, après la Nouvelle-Zélande et l'Australie, à entrer dans une ère nouvelle. Aujourd'hui, les Finlandaises sont les premières femmes à gagner des sièges dans une assemblée nationale. La majeure partie d'entre elles sont membres du parti social-démocrate, qui détient la majorité des mandats et qui comprend des femmes issues de toutes les couches de la société. Les militants en faveur du vote des femmes attendent de voir quel pays suivra l'exemple.

▲ *Miina Sillanpää, élue au Parlement finlandais.*

▲ *Séance de travail dans une salle de l'école Montessori.*

La première école Montessori

▶ **Mars 1907** ◀ Maria Montessori vient d'ouvrir sa première école à Rome, dans un quartier populaire de la ville. Elle a 37 ans et elle est la première femme italienne à avoir obtenu un doctorat de médecine. Après avoir enseigné avec succès à des enfants handicapés mentaux, elle souhaite appliquer ses méthodes révolutionnaires d'enseignement à des enfants issus de milieux défavorisés. Elle espère enregistrer, là aussi, de bons résultats.

Sa démarche consiste à essayer d'obtenir des enfants le meilleur d'eux-mêmes, par le jeu et le développement de la mémoire, en les laissant libres de progresser chacun à son rythme. Elle veut apprendre à lire et à écrire aux enfants de moins de 5 ans, tout en les habituant à aimer leur travail et à se concentrer longtemps sans se fatiguer.

Kipling reçoit le prix Nobel de littérature

▶ **10 décembre 1907** ◀ Rudyard Kipling vient de recevoir le prix Nobel de littérature. Les enfants du monde entier connaissent bien les aventures de Mowgli, le petit garçon perdu dans la jungle et élevé par une louve. Il est le héros de deux œuvres du romancier, *le Livre de la jungle* et *le Second Livre de la jungle*, parues il y a une dizaine d'années. Né en Inde en 1865, l'auteur a fait ses études en Angleterre, avant de devenir journaliste globe-trotter. Ses romans ont souvent pour cadre l'Inde où il avait vécu pendant sa jeunesse.
Il a écrit, entre autres, de merveilleuses histoires pour les enfants, comme *le Livre de la jungle*, *Histoires comme ça*, *Capitaine courageux* et *Kim*.

◀ *Rikki-Tikki-Tavi, la mangouste d'un des contes du* Livre de la jungle.

Florence Nightingale reçoit l'ordre du Mérite

▶ **29 novembre 1907** ◀ Florence Nightingale est la première femme à recevoir l'ordre du Mérite. Cette infirmière britannique s'est distinguée au cours de la guerre de Crimée, voilà un peu plus de 50 ans, en réorganisant les hôpitaux de campagne. C'est en imposant de strictes mesures d'hygiène, et en offrant aux soldats une nourriture saine, qu'elle leur sauva la vie. Elle a été la première à demander une formation pour les infirmières et a créé une école en Grande-Bretagne. Grâce à elle, le métier d'infirmière est réellement né.

Ziegfeld Follies

Le public new-yorkais s'enthousiasme pour un nouveau genre de revue musicale donné dans les théâtres de Broadway. Inspiré par les fameuses Folies-Bergère parisiennes, le producteur Florenz Ziegfeld a monté un extravagant spectacle, intitulé *Follies de 1907*, dont la vedette revient à sa femme, Anna Held, une actrice d'origine française.

1900 – 1909

1907

Pablo Picasso choque

Mars 1907

Le monde de l'art parisien est habitué aux surprises. Mais la dernière toile du peintre espagnol de 26 ans Pablo Picasso a stupéfait tout le monde. Le tableau, *les Demoiselles d'Avignon*, montre cinq femmes plus ou moins dévêtues, dont le corps et les étoffes sont déformés en de curieuses formes géométriques, et qui rompent avec toutes les règles de l'art, qu'il s'agisse de la composition ou des lois de la perspective.

Ce jeune artiste se renouvelle sans cesse. Pendant quelques années, il a peint en bleu. Puis il est entré dans une période où les tonalités roses dominaient. Mais ce tableau marque une évolution radicale. Certains y voient l'influence du peintre Paul Cézanne, d'autres remarquent des similitudes évidentes entre les visages de certaines de ses demoiselles et des masques de l'exposition africaine qui vient de se dérouler à Paris. Picasso inaugure une nouvelle manière de représenter les objets, l'ensemble étant composé de formes anguleuses figurant le sujet, envisagé sous différentes perspectives.

◀ Les Demoiselles d'Avignon, *de Pablo Picasso.*

La Bakélite

La Bakélite est née. Son créateur, Leo Baekeland, a baptisé cette matière plastique résistante en s'inspirant de son propre nom. Ce chimiste américain d'origine belge a découvert un matériau révolutionnaire qui ne conduit pas l'électricité et qui ne fond pas quand on le chauffe. Lorsqu'elle est liquide, cette résine synthétique peut prendre n'importe quelle forme.

Un zoo modèle

7 mai 1907

Au zoo de Hambourg, Carl Hagenbeck, dresseur et marchand d'animaux, a transformé la vie des animaux. Envolées les cages minuscules dans lesquelles de pitoyables créatures tournent en rond misérablement ! Dorénavant, grâce à Carl Hagenbeck, les animaux ont droit à de vastes espaces reproduisant leur habitat naturel. Ce sont de larges fosses à ciel ouvert, sans barreaux, où ils évoluent dans la plus grande liberté. Ce pourrait être un modèle pour tous les zoos à venir.

▲ *Repas des morses et des pingouins au zoo de Hagenbeck.*

Des femmes au Parlement finlandais

15 mars 1907

L'année dernière, pour la première fois en Europe, le droit de vote a été accordé aux femmes en Finlande. La Finlande est ainsi devenue le troisième pays au monde, après la Nouvelle-Zélande et l'Australie, à entrer dans une ère nouvelle. Aujourd'hui, les Finlandaises sont les premières femmes à gagner des sièges dans une assemblée nationale. La majeure partie d'entre elles sont membres du parti social-démocrate, qui détient la majorité des mandats et qui comprend des femmes issues de toutes les couches de la société. Les militants en faveur du vote des femmes attendent de voir quel pays suivra l'exemple.

▲ *Miina Sillanpää, élue au Parlement finlandais.*

1900 – 1909

BD à la une

Augustus Mutt, flanqué de son compère Jeff, apparaît pour la première fois en novembre 1907 dans les pages de *The Chronicle*, un quotidien de San Francisco. Il s'agira sans doute bientôt du personnage le plus célèbre d'Amérique. Ce n'est pourtant qu'un héros de papier, tout droit sorti de l'imagination et du crayon de Bud Fisher, qui fut journaliste sportif à Chicago, avant de se lancer dans la bande dessinée, en Californie. Le journal est le premier au monde à publier des bandes dessinées tous les jours de la semaine, y compris dans l'édition du week-end. C'est un atout de poids dans la concurrence acharnée que se livrent les quotidiens américains pour gagner des lecteurs.

▲ *Les vignettes en couleurs de la BD mettant en scène les aventures d'Augustus Mutt et de Jeff.*

La peste frappe et tue en Inde

▶ **1907** ◀ Au cours des dix dernières années, la peste a tué 6 millions de personnes en Inde. Les scientifiques qui travaillent pour la seconde commission indienne sur la peste sont désormais certains que la peste bubonique se transmet par les puces du rat. Ils en ont conclu que le seul moyen d'enrayer sa propagation est d'imposer une quarantaine stricte aux navires et de lancer des programmes d'extermination du rat dans le monde entier. Cette maladie infectieuse, épidémique et contagieuse, a tué le quart de la population de l'Europe au Moyen Âge mais elle en a à peu près disparu à la fin du siècle dernier. Ses symptômes sont de caractéristiques bubons (abcès) qui se forment aux glandes de l'aisselle, de l'aine et du cou et qui lui donnent son nom. Maux de tête, fièvre et vomissements les accompagnent. La victime perd conscience et meurt en peu de temps. L'épidémie actuelle a débuté en Chine il y a 50 ans. En 1894, elle a atteint Hong Kong d'où elle s'est répandue, par l'intermédiaire des rats embarqués à fond de cale, en Californie, en Afrique du Sud et en Argentine. L'Inde demeure le pays le plus touché par ce fléau.

▲ *Exposition à Bombay sur les dangers que présentent les rats et les puces.*

Un prince remporte la course Pékin-Paris

▶ **10 août 1907** ◀ Le prince Borghese vient de remporter la course de voitures la plus longue que le monde ait jamais connue. Il a battu cinq autres concurrents. Le Français de Dion et son mécanicien Bouton sont arrivés deuxième. Partis de Pékin il y a deux mois, les concurrents ont rallié Paris en parcourant 12 874 km sur des pistes et des routes accidentées. La course eut du mal à démarrer à cause de la difficulté pour les participants d'obtenir des laissez-passer auprès des autorités chinoises. Apparemment, les Chinois les suspectaient de tramer l'invasion de leur pays. Le prince Borghese faillit bien échouer à la dernière étape lorsqu'un policier belge l'arrêta pour excès de vitesse.

▼ *Voiture bloquée sur une voie ferrée lors de la course Pékin-Paris.*

En 1907 aussi...

21 mars • La Grande-Bretagne ne veut pas d'un tunnel sous la Manche.

10 juin • Le Français Auguste Lumière invente un nouveau procédé de photographie couleur : l'autochrome.

13 novembre • Paul Cornu, un Français, réussit le premier envol d'hélicoptère.

8 décembre • Gustave V devient roi de Suède à 49 ans.

1908

Le premier modèle de Ford T aux États-Unis

▶ 1ᵉʳ octobre 1908 ◀

▲ La Ford T, première voiture avec conduite à gauche.

« L'automobile pour tous. » Le constructeur Henry Ford l'avait promise ; il l'a faite : c'est la Ford T, qui, au prix de 850 dollars, devrait être accessible à beaucoup d'Américains et d'Américaines. Tout a été fait pour réduire son coût. Elle a été conçue par Ford lui-même, selon de nouvelles normes de fabrication, et a été réalisée en série sur une chaîne de montage. Si sa ligne est sobre, elle n'est pas vraiment très belle – au point d'avoir déjà reçu le sobriquet de « tas de ferraille » –, mais elle dispose d'une suspension en trois points et d'une structure en acier léger qui atténue les cahots de la route. Avec son moteur à quatre cylindres et sa puissance de 20 chevaux, elle peut atteindre sans problème les 40 km/h.

Au cours de l'été, Henry Ford en personne a fait un tour dans Detroit au volant du tout premier modèle, et a déclaré s'être beaucoup amusé. Il a poursuivi sa promenade sur les routes de montagne.

Ford demande beaucoup de travail à ses ouvriers et leur impose des cadences très rapides, mais il les paie bien. « Il faut, dit-il, que mes ouvriers puissent acheter mes voitures. » Il pense pouvoir sortir 25 000 unités de ce modèle l'année prochaine.

La Ford T
La Ford T n'est disponible qu'en noir.
•
C'est en 1908 qu'ont lieu les premiers essais de goudronnage des routes.
•
En 1908, encore, Buick a produit 8 487 automobiles, contre 31 en 1904.

Troubles en Turquie

▶ 24 juillet 1908 ◀

▲ Constantinople. Le sultan se rend sur son lieu de prière dans un attelage découvert.

L'Empire ottoman, État turc, est déstabilisé. Le sultan Abdülhamid II – le souverain qui parle de lui-même comme de « l'ombre de Dieu » – a été contraint d'ordonner à tous les districts de l'empire d'organiser des élections au Parlement, pour répondre à l'agitation qui s'est répandue dans tout le pays.

Le mouvement révolutionnaire des Jeunes-Turcs – qui surnomme le sultan « la Vieille Araignée » – exige impérativement l'indépendance religieuse, la liberté de la presse et de l'éducation. Il revendique également le retour à la Constitution de 1876, que le sultan avait écartée autoritairement en février 1878.

Un soulèvement de l'armée a éclaté au début du mois en Macédoine. Les Jeunes-Turcs, en exil à Paris, se sont immédiatement rangés aux côtés de la faction rebelle. Des États européens profiteront de l'affaiblissement de l'Empire ottoman pour occuper une partie de son territoire.

1900 – 1909

Jack Johnson, nouveau roi du ring

Pour la première fois dans l'Histoire, un boxeur noir est sacré champion du monde des poids lourds. Cela se déroulait le 26 décembre dernier à Sydney, en Australie. Le nouveau roi du ring se nomme Jack Johnson et est de nationalité américaine. Il a mis son adversaire Tommy Burns K.-O. ; l'ancien champion en titre a même perdu connaissance durant quelques secondes.

◀ *Jack Johnson a une droite redoutable.*

Le Congo change de mains

▶ **19 août 1908** ◀ Le Congo était la propriété personnelle du roi de Belgique Léopold II. À Bruxelles, le Parlement a voté son annexion à la Belgique. L'État devra verser au roi une coquette somme en échange de cette cession. Le roi a régné en monarque absolu sur le Congo pendant 22 ans. Mais le gouvernement de Bruxelles s'est trouvé dans l'obligation de procéder à ce rachat, à la suite de l'émotion qu'a provoquée dans le monde entier la nouvelle des mauvais traitements infligés à la population.

▼ *Équipement industriel belge arrivant au Congo.*

En 1908 aussi ...

4 juin • Le transfert au Panthéon des cendres de l'écrivain français Émile Zola - mort le 29 septembre 1902 - se fait dans une atmosphère survoltée, car les prises de position de l'écrivain sont contestées par la droite.

5 octobre • L'Autriche-Hongrie annexe la Bosnie-Herzégovine.

10 décembre • Le prix Nobel de physique est attribué au Français Gabriel Lippmann.

Apparition de la Cellophane

La Cellophane est totalement transparente et est issue de la cellulose. Il s'agit d'un tout nouveau matériau créé par Jacques Brandeburger, un chimiste suisse. Il espère qu'une entreprise comme le Comptoir des textiles artificiels pourra fabriquer son produit, idéal pour l'emballage des aliments.

Grèves violentes

▶ **30 juillet 1908** ◀ Quatre morts à Villeneuve-Saint-Georges, à l'est de Paris, après les deux morts de Draveil le mois dernier. La grève des ouvriers du bâtiment, qui se poursuit depuis plusieurs semaines, est très violente. Pour empêcher les ouvriers d'occuper les chantiers, le gouvernement, dont le Premier ministre est Clemenceau, a envoyé l'armée. Les ouvriers ont affronté la police et les soldats, ce qui a eu pour conséquence l'envoi de douze syndicalistes en prison.

1908

Un empereur de Chine

▶ **2 décembre 1908** ◀ Il n'a que 3 ans. Il est pourtant le nouvel empereur de Chine. Il s'appelle Pu Yi et monte sur le trône après les morts mystérieuses de l'empereur et de l'impératrice douairière Ts'eu-hi à l'âge de 73 ans. La vieille impératrice, qui gouvernait comme régente depuis 1875, avait d'abord été concubine de l'empereur Hsien Feng. Elle a soutenu tous les mouvements antieuropéens, dont la révolte des Boxers contre les Occidentaux en 1900.

Pu Yi va vivre dans le palais impérial, derrière les murailles de la Cité interdite de Pékin. Son père assurera la régence jusqu'à la majorité de son fils.

▲ *Pu Yi (à droite) avec son père et son frère.*

La fin des corsets

Fini les corsets trop serrés et les robes qui engoncent. Grâce aux mouvements pour la libération de la femme et au goût du sport qui se développe, la mode évolue : les femmes veulent plus d'aisance dans leurs vêtements. En France, la couturière Madeleine Vionnet prône l'abandon du corset.

Les tailles trop serrées sont abandonnées.

Scandale aux J.O. de Londres

▶ **30 juillet 1908** ◀ En remettant une coupe d'or spéciale à Dorando Pietri, la reine Alexandra a clos la polémique qui s'était déclenchée à l'annonce des résultats du marathon. Pietri, épuisé, avait en effet franchi le premier la ligne d'arrivée, mais il avait été disqualifié, en raison de l'assistance médicale qu'il avait reçue des commissaires de la course durant l'étape finale. Et le deuxième arrivant avait été déclaré vainqueur, ce qui avait provoqué un véritable tollé.

Avec 2 000 participants pour 21 disciplines, les jeux Olympiques de Londres, qui se sont déroulés dans un stade tout neuf, ont remporté un énorme succès. Ils succèdent aux Jeux de Paris et de Saint Louis, ville des États-Unis, dans la lignée du mouvement olympique initié par le baron de Coubertin. Néanmoins, des frictions entre la Grande-Bretagne et les États-Unis se sont fait jour, ces derniers reprochant au pays organisateur d'avoir choisi des jurys exclusivement britanniques.

▲ *La reine Alexandra remet les prix aux vainqueurs des J.O., à Londres.*

Reine d'un jour

C'est la plus belle. Elle a 18 ans, est britannique, et vient de triompher au premier concours international de beauté, à Folkestone (Grande-Bretagne). Elle se nomme Nellie Jarman. Elle a battu des candidates venues de nombreux pays européens.

Albert Ier, roi de Belgique

▶ **23 décembre 1908** ◀ Albert Ier succède à son oncle Léopold II. Le nouveau roi des Belges doit affronter les troubles dus aux problèmes sociaux et à l'hostilité qui règne entre les deux communautés du pays : les Flamands et les Wallons. Il a le soutien de son peuple, qui aime ce roi de 34 ans, calme, courtois et distingué. Sa femme, la reine Élisabeth, est elle aussi très populaire. Il sera surnommé le roi chevalier pour son attitude courageuse face à l'Allemagne pendant la guerre de 1914-1918.

Premier mort en avion

▲ *Le lieutenant Selfridge succombe.*

▶ **17 septembre 1908** ◀ L'avion a fait aujourd'hui sa première victime, aux États-Unis. Le lieutenant Thomas E. Selfridge s'est tué au cours d'une démonstration de vol pour l'armée américaine. Son passager, Orville Wright, pionnier de l'aviation, a été sérieusement blessé. L'immense foule des spectateurs, composée de membres de l'armée et de représentants de la presse, a vu avec horreur l'aile gauche du biplan se disloquer. Le système du gouvernail est parti en lambeaux et l'avion est tombé à pic d'une hauteur de 27 m. En dépit des efforts qui ont été faits, le pilote, souffrant d'une fracture du crâne, n'a pu être sauvé.

Les suffragettes

▲ *Une suffragette s'adresse à la foule.*

▶ **21 juin 1908** ◀ Aujourd'hui, à Londres, plus de 200 000 personnes se sont rassemblées à Hyde Park, afin d'exiger que le droit de vote soit accordé aux femmes. Christabel Pankhurst, qui, avec sa mère, Emmeline, a fondé l'Union féminine sociale et politique, une association consacrée au combat pour le vote féminin, prend la parole. Annie Kenney, qui participa à l'organisation de la première manifestation à Manchester il y a trois ans, prend, elle aussi, la parole au meeting. Elle souligne notamment la présence dans la foule d'un grand nombre d'hommes venus soutenir la cause des femmes.

Depuis deux ans, les militantes de l'Union ont multiplié les actes de provocation. Ainsi, au début de l'année, Emmeline Pankhurst, qui est âgée de 50 ans, a été condamnée à six mois de prison pour avoir gêné les forces de police aux abords du Parlement. Elle a vigoureusement dénoncé les conditions déplorables de sa détention à la prison de Holloway. Dans le même temps, la police avait arrêté 50 autres suffragettes qui tentaient de s'introduire illégalement au Parlement, dissimulées dans un camion qui y livrait des meubles.

Tremblement de terre en Sicile

▶ **28 décembre 1908** ◀ Un tremblement de terre vient de détruire Messine, grand port et deuxième ville de Sicile. C'est le plus violent séisme jamais enregistré en Europe à l'époque moderne. Les sauveteurs recherchent désespérément les éventuels survivants, alors que de nouvelles secousses ébranlent toujours la région. Le cataclysme a engendré un puissant tsunami – un raz-de-marée géant – qui a provoqué de nombreux morts et des destructions de part et d'autre du détroit de Messine. En Calabre, partie la plus méridionale de la botte italienne, la ville de Reggio a aussi été dévastée. À Messine, les pertes sont difficiles à estimer, mais on peut penser que la moitié des 150 000 habitants de la ville ont péri. Un important soutien international a été promis. Les navires britanniques basés à Malte vont sans doute participer au sauvetage et à l'évacuation des victimes.

▶ *Messine, en Sicile, détruite après le terrible tremblement de terre.*

1909

Invention du grille-pain

Une nouvelle invention vient de s'ajouter aux nombreux objets qui améliorent la vie de la femme moderne. La compagnie General Electric vient d'inventer le grille-pain, qui permet de déguster des tartines grillées. Des résistances électriques placées dans la machine les chauffent et leur donnent une appétissante couleur dorée.

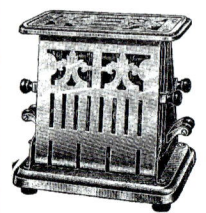

▲ *Le monoplan de Blériot, près du hangar. En médaillon, Louis Blériot.*

Blériot traverse la Manche

▶ **25 juillet 1909** ◀

À 36 ans, le Français Louis Blériot vient de réaliser un exploit sans précédent. Il a franchi la Manche à bord de son monoplan, reliant la France à l'Angleterre en 36 minutes. Parti ce matin de Calais à 4 h 53, il a atterri à Douvres à 5 h 29. Cet aviateur intrépide a dû attendre cinq jours avant de pouvoir décoller. Les conditions météorologiques étaient trop mauvaises. Il s'est tout de même perdu dans les nuages et n'a trouvé le terrain d'atterrissage que grâce à un journaliste du *Matin* qui a agité le drapeau tricolore en entendant le moteur. Il a navigué sans compas, en suivant les navires en route vers Douvres, mais a cassé son hélice en atterrissant. Blériot, le premier à traverser la Manche, a dans le même temps battu deux autres grands aviateurs, Hubert Latham, dont l'avion s'est abîmé en mer il y a six jours, et le comte de Lambert. Il remporte le prix de 1 000 livres sterling offert par le journal le *Daily Mail*. Son succès prouve que les avions sont capables de passer par des endroits qui semblaient jusqu'alors infranchissables.

Meurtre du prince Ito Hirobumi

▶ **26 octobre 1909** ◀

Le prince Ito Hirobumi, Premier ministre du Japon, vient d'être abattu, au cours d'une visite en Mandchourie. Il avait 68 ans. Le meurtrier est un patriote coréen. Le prince a été assassiné à cause de son rôle dans la répression impitoyable qu'il a menée contre les nationalistes coréens. Il y a 25 ans, cet homme d'État avait joué un rôle majeur dans la modernisation du Japon. En dépit de son titre, il était d'origine roturière. Son père était un riche cultivateur qui avait pu acheter un titre nobiliaire.

En 1909 aussi …

Février • Fondation de la N.R.F. : la Nouvelle Revue française, qui rassemble André Gide, Jean Schlumberger, Jacques Copeau et l'éditeur Gaston Gallimard.

16 mars • Les postiers réclament le droit de grève.

27 avril • À Istanbul, le sultan Abdülhamid II est déposé.

23 décembre • Albert Ier monte sur le trône de Belgique.

Une star du muet

« Vous êtes trop grosse et trop petite », lui avait répondu le réalisateur David W. Griffith quand elle s'était présentée pour la première fois devant lui. Mais Mary Pickford n'a pas renoncé. Elle est née à Toronto, au Canada, et a débuté à cinq ans au théâtre. Elle vient de tourner *Her First Biscuits*. Ses doux yeux humides ont fait de Mary une star de seize ans. On la surnomme alors « la petite fiancée de l'Amérique ».

▲ *L'actrice Mary Pickford.*

1900 – 1909

La conquête du pôle Nord

▶ 21 décembre 1909 ◀ Huit mois après qu'il a atteint le pôle Nord, l'explorateur américain Robert E. Peary est officiellement reconnu comme le conquérant du pôle. Il y était arrivé après cinq tentatives infructueuses. Mais Cook, qui l'avait accompagné dans ses expéditions antérieures, prétendait avoir atteint le pôle un an avant lui. La version de Cook a été démentie par les Inuits (les Esquimaux), qui ont dit l'avoir vu faire demi-tour, 32 km avant d'avoir touché le but.

◀ L'explorateur américain Peary et ses compagnons hissent le drapeau américain au pôle Nord.

Nouveau record de vitesse

▶ 8 novembre 1909 ◀ 205 km/h : c'est le nouveau record mondial de vitesse automobile. Il a été obtenu par un Français, le pilote Victor Hémery, au volant d'une Benz fabriquée pour l'occasion à l'usine de Mannheim (Allemagne). Il a accompli cet exploit en Angleterre, à Brooklands. Cette nouvelle performance prouve que, même si les machines à vapeur sont capables d'atteindre de grandes vitesses, les automobiles à essence leur sont bien supérieures lorsqu'il s'agit de records à battre.

▲ Le nouveau prototype Benz.

La première auberge de jeunesse

▶ 8 novembre 1909 ◀ Un instituteur allemand, Richard Schirrmann, a ouvert un dortoir dans son école pour les vacances des jeunes travailleurs. En août dernier, alors qu'il était parti en randonnée avec un groupe de jeunes, ils avaient été contraints par un orage, de dormir à l'école. Son idée d'ouvrir en Allemagne des hébergements bon marché réservés aux jeunes garçons vient de là.

▶ L'auberge de jeunesse de Burg Altena, en Allemagne.

Sur la piste de l'hérédité

C'est une nouvelle science que le botaniste danois Wilhelm Johannsen vient d'inventer. Dans sa dernière publication, il soutient l'existence d'une unité de base de l'hérédité, qu'il nomme gène. Elle serait enfouie dans les cellules de tout système biologique, depuis le haricot jusqu'à l'homme. D'après lui, les gènes seraient responsables des caractères héréditaires de chaque individu.

Mort de Geronimo

▶ 17 février 1909 ◀ Geronimo est mort. Il avait 80 ans. Avec lui disparaît l'un des plus forts symboles de la résistance à l'impérialisme américain. Il fut un chef apache respecté, membre de la tribu des Chiricahua, né en Arizona en juin 1829. Durant l'été 1858, alors qu'il avait fait halte au Mexique, à proximité de la ville que les Indiens nomment Kaskiyed, les Mexicains profitèrent de l'absence des hommes pour massacrer les femmes et les enfants. Il perdit là sa mère, sa femme et ses trois enfants. Dès lors, la guérilla apache – 1862-1872 – se répandit dans le Sud-Ouest américain. Il ne déposa les armes qu'en 1886, lors de sa capture.

De 1910 à 1919

1910

Tout semble stable dans le monde. L'Europe continue d'être la force dominante. Elle exploite d'immenses empires coloniaux et s'enrichit. Les États-Unis pensent à leur croissance et ne s'inquiètent guère des politiques européennes. Mais les données économiques sont en train d'évoluer. Si les progrès techniques et scientifiques se répercutent sur la vie quotidienne, les conflits sociaux se multiplient. Personne ne peut encore imaginer que la décennie va voir le monde s'embraser dans la sanglante Première Guerre mondiale, puis dans la révolution russe, et qu'alors rien ne sera plus jamais comme avant.

La comète de Halley
Elle apparaît dans le ciel tous les soixante-seize ans.
• La comète de Halley figurait sur une tapisserie réalisée entre 1066 et 1082.

Nouvelle anémie

C'est à James Herrick, un professeur de médecine américain, que l'on doit de connaître les causes de la drépanocytose. Sous ce nom rébarbatif se cache une nouvelle sorte d'anémie dont il démontre qu'elle est due à la malformation des globules rouges, qui présentent une curieuse forme de faucille. Il a détecté cette anomalie héréditaire dans le sang d'un patient et publie les passionnants résultats de ses recherches.

La comète arrive !

▶ **20 mai 1910** ◀ « La comète ! » hurlent, pris de panique, les passagers d'un trolleybus de New York en entendant un énorme bruit. Ce n'est qu'une brique qui est tombée sur le toit. Il faut dire que, depuis des jours, les rumeurs les plus alarmistes circulent à propos de l'apparition dans le ciel de la comète de Halley, astre du système solaire constitué de glace, de fragments rocheux et de poussière. Des astrologues prédisent même la fin du monde, par la collision de la comète et de la Terre ! Et, à Chicago, on vend des pilules pour lutter contre les gaz nocifs qu'émettrait la queue de cet astre. La comète illumine le ciel, mais se trouve à 21 millions de kilomètres de la Terre, et les scientifiques estiment qu'elle ne va pas s'approcher plus près. Elle doit son nom à un astronome anglais, Edmond Halley (1656-1742), qui, le premier, a calculé la date exacte de ses apparitions. Elle reviendra en 1986.

▶ *Représentation de la comète de Halley aux États-Unis.*

Le Japon annexe la Corée

▶ **24 août 1910** ◀ Le Japon vient d'annoncer son intention d'annexer la Corée. C'est un pays depuis longtemps convoité par la Chine, le Japon et la Russie. En 1895, les Japonais l'ont envahi et ont assassiné sa reine. Depuis le traité de 1905 de la guerre russo-japonaise, il est sous protectorat japonais. Annexé, il devient colonie japonaise.

1910 – 1919

Le Portugal devient une république

▶ **4 octobre 1910** ◀ Ce soir, le roi Manuel du Portugal s'est réfugié à Gibraltar, chassé de Lisbonne par le soulèvement de son armée. Les révoltés ont pris le contrôle de la capitale, mais des tirs se font encore entendre dans les rues. Ils ont neutralisé les forces royalistes et défilent aux cris de « Vive la république ! ». Durant ces dix dernières années, qui ont vu l'assassinat du père du roi, le Portugal a affronté de graves crises, et les événements actuels sont loin d'être une surprise. Le gouvernement provisoire, présidé par Teófilo Braga, va devoir préparer une Constitution républicaine.

▼ *Le peintre russe Wassily Kandinsky.*

▶ *Portugal. L'artillerie en action, le 4 octobre 1910.*

Paris inondé

▶ **Janvier 1910** ◀ À Paris, on navigue en barque dans les rues d'Auteuil, de Grenelle et du quartier de l'Alma. Le métro est devenu un lac souterrain ; la Seine charrie des troncs d'arbre. Elle est sortie de son lit et a provoqué d'importants dégâts. Le Zouave du pont de l'Alma a de l'eau jusqu'aux genoux. C'est la conséquence des pluies diluviennes qui se sont abattues sur le pays.

Le peintre Kandinsky, père de l'art abstrait

▶ **1910** ◀ Le peintre russe Wassily Kandinsky, âgé de 44 ans, est à la tête d'un mouvement artistique d'avant-garde à Munich (Allemagne). Il exprime ses idées sur l'art dans un ouvrage intitulé *Du spirituel dans l'art*. Il peint des toiles, tel *Improvisation 10*, qui recherchent l'harmonie entre les lignes et les couleurs afin de toucher le spectateur. On le considère comme l'« inventeur » de l'art abstrait. Il explique que, comme la musique, la peinture exprime des émotions et n'a donc pas besoin de faire appel à la représentation exacte de la réalité.

Le jazz est né

Une nouvelle musique, très rythmée, naît à La Nouvelle-Orléans, ville américaine de Louisiane. C'est le jazz, inventé par la communauté noire. Joué par un petit groupe d'instruments, le jazz allie des rythmes forts avec des improvisations d'instruments, surtout de trompette, mais aussi de clarinette et de saxophone.

▶ *Orchestre de jazz à La Nouvelle-Orléans.*

1910

Révolution au Mexique

▶ **20 novembre 1910** ◀ Aujourd'hui, c'est le grand jour pour le peuple mexicain, qui s'est soulevé en vue de renverser son dictateur, le président Porfirio Díaz. Celui-ci dirige le Mexique d'une poigne de fer depuis plus de trente ans, refusant la moindre opposition. Avec pour résultat d'avoir permis l'enrichissement des familles les plus prospères, tandis que les paysans ont vu leur condition devenir totalement désespérée. L'année dernière, Díaz lui-même avait soulevé l'espoir en déclarant à un journaliste américain qu'il pensait son pays prêt pour la démocratie. Le dictateur de 79 ans semblait alors sous-entendre qu'il ne serait pas candidat à l'élection présidentielle de 1910. Néanmoins, quelque temps plus tard, il annonçait le maintien de sa candidature. Francisco Madero, fils de l'une des plus riches familles du pays, décidait, dans ces conditions, de faire campagne contre lui.

En juin, Madero a été arrêté. En septembre, la Chambre des députés a déclaré Díaz réélu. Le mois suivant, Madero s'est évadé de prison et a franchi la frontière américaine. Depuis, réfugié au Texas, il a organisé le financement de la révolution qui vient d'éclater dans son pays.

▲ *Pancho Villa, héros de la révolution mexicaine et fidèle soutien de Madero.*

Les actualités font fureur au cinéma

Après le succès du *Pathé-Journal*, né en France en 1909, les frères Pathé l'exportent aux États-Unis. Ils ont créé l'une des toutes premières compagnies cinématographiques proposant des actualités filmées. Ces news couvrent des sujets aussi divers que des compétitions sportives, des événements politiques, ou des manifestations officielles. Annoncées par un coq, devenu leur image de marque, elles sont projetées en début de séance ou à l'entracte, entre deux films.

▲ *Louis Botha, président de l'Union.*

Afrique du Sud, enfin l'union

▶ **21 mai 1910** ◀ Un jour clé en Afrique du Sud. Par le South Africa Act, la colonie britannique du Cap, le Transvaal, l'État libre d'Orange et le Natal s'unissent pour former l'Union sud-africaine. Les négociations ont été longues et difficiles entre les Boers, de langue néerlandaise, et les colons d'origine britannique, qui se sont tant fait la guerre. Les Anglais, notamment, voulaient donner le droit de vote à une partie de la population noire et métisse, comme c'est déjà le cas au Cap. Ils ont dû céder aux Boers, qui y sont opposés.

En 1910 aussi …

12 février • *La loi sur les retraites ouvrières et paysannes à 65 ans est votée en France.*

11 mars • *Meeting à Paris des suffragettes contre la loi électorale, autour de Marie Bonnevial, d'Hubertine Auclert, de Marcel Sembat.*

6 mai • *Mort du roi Édouard VII d'Angleterre.*

7 septembre • *Marie Curie isole le radium.*

21 novembre • *Mort de l'écrivain russe Léon Tolstoï, à l'âge de 82 ans.*

1910 – 1919

Baden-Powell crée les guides

▶ **31 mai 1910** ◀ Trois ans après la naissance du mouvement scout, Robert Baden-Powell et sa sœur Agnès fondent les guides. Leur but est d'enseigner aux jeunes filles les vertus d'obéissance, de la vie saine, sans oublier l'altruisme ni les bonnes actions.

Le scoutisme se répand dans le monde. Ainsi, à Paris, le pasteur Gallienne s'inspire de la méthode pour l'organisation d'un patronage, la Mission populaire de Grenelle.

▲ *Des guides prêtes pour l'inspection.*

▲ *Le professeur Du Bois est diplômé de Harvard.*

Pour l'égalité des droits aux États-Unis

▶ **1er mai 1910** ◀ C'est une date importante pour les droits des citoyens. Radicaux noirs et réformateurs blancs des États-Unis se sont unis pour créer une association qui se donne pour buts de défendre et de promouvoir les droits des Noirs américains. Ils l'ont baptisée « Association nationale pour le progrès des droits civiques des gens de couleur » (en anglais NAACP, *National Association for the Advancement of Colored People*). L'homme clé du mouvement est William Edward Burghart Du Bois, professeur à l'université d'Atlanta. Il a consacré sa vie à la lutte pour les droits des Noirs dont il a étudié les conditions de vie difficiles dans les États du Sud. Il compte se consacrer à plein temps à la NAACP, qui a son siège à New York.

Le patin à roulettes

Le patin à roulettes, qui fait fureur en Europe occidentale et aux États-Unis, vient d'être reconnu comme discipline sportive. Les figures exécutées sur patins à quatre roues seront désormais jugées selon un barème inspiré de celui du patin à glace.

Mort de Mark Twain

▶ **21 avril 1910** ◀ Le monde vient de perdre l'un de ses écrivains les plus populaires. Mark Twain, le créateur des impérissables héros que sont Tom Sawyer et Huckleberry Finn, n'est plus. De son vrai nom Samuel Langhorne Clemens, il a grandi le long du Mississippi, qui sert de cadre à ses plus grands romans. Celui qui a dû travailler à 11 ans, après la mort de son père, est par la suite devenu pilote de bateau à vapeur sur le grand fleuve. C'est là qu'il a eu l'idée de son pseudonyme, Mark Twain. Ce cri, qui signifie « deux brasses de fond », est celui que lance le sondeur au pilote. Il lui annonce par là que la profondeur est tout juste suffisante pour le passage de son embarcation à faible tirant d'eau. Mais ce n'est qu'après avoir roulé sa bosse en tant que chercheur d'or, puis journaliste, qu'il est devenu le grand écrivain que l'on sait, faisant des *Aventures de Tom Sawyer* et des *Aventures de Huckleberry Finn* des chefs-d'œuvre de la littérature mondiale.

◀ *Huckleberry Finn, personnage populaire dans le monde entier.*

LA COURSE AUX PÔLES

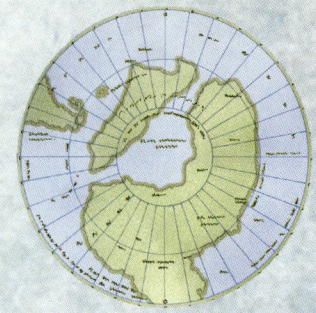

◀ Sur cette ancienne carte, dressée par les premiers explorateurs, le pôle Sud est imaginé dans la mer, et non dans les glaces.

Soudain, à la fin du XIXe et au début du XXe siècle, la passion pour les explorations polaires explose. Européens et Américains se lancent à l'assaut des brouillards et des icebergs de l'océan Arctique comme des glaciers de l'Antarctique.

Ces hommes sont mus par l'intérêt de la science, mais aussi par le désir de gloire, tant nationale que personnelle. Peary a bien l'intention d'être le premier à atteindre le pôle Nord ; Amundsen fait tout pour être le vainqueur du pôle Sud.

Premier au pôle Sud

C'est un Français, Jean-Baptiste Charcot, qui part le premier pour l'Antarctique en 1909-1910, à bord du bateau le *Pourquoi-pas ?* Il en profite pour découvrir deux îles et établir une carte complète des terres australes. Bloqué par les glaces, il doit renoncer à s'enfoncer plus avant vers le sud.

L'Anglais Robert Scott et le Norvégien Roald Amundsen relèvent le défi et conquièrent le pôle. Les traîneaux à moteur et les chevaux de Scott ne résistent pas au froid. Amundsen, lui, choisit un chemin plus court et des chiens de traîneau. Il atteint le pôle le 14 décembre 1911, cinq semaines avant l'expédition de son concurrent.

La mort de Scott

Seuls cinq membres de l'expédition de Scott atteignent le pôle Sud. Ils sont tous disparus. Pris dans le blizzard, ils périssent à 18 km du but. Scott a tenu un journal pendant l'expédition qui a été retrouvé.

▲ Roald Amundsen, en route vers le pôle Nord, apprend que Peary l'a devancé ; il change alors de cap pour vaincre le pôle Sud.

▲ *Le drapeau norvégien flotte sur le pôle Sud. Les Norvégiens emploient des chiens pour mener les traîneaux et se nourrir. Les hommes de Scott finissent, en revanche, par tirer eux-mêmes leurs traîneaux, alourdis par des pierres rapportées pour des expériences scientifiques.*

▲ *Cette ancienne carte situe le pôle Nord au milieu de la banquise.*

◀ *Peary adopte les méthodes des Inuits pour dresser les chiens.*

Expéditions au pôle Nord

La première tentative pour rallier le pôle Nord est faite en 1827 par un officier britannique, Edward Parry. La plus intéressante est celle du Norvégien Fridtjof Nansen, entre 1893 et 1896. Pour affronter les glaces, il conçoit un navire spécial, le *Fram*, qui, plus tard, emmènera Amundsen en Antarctique. Pris dans la banquise, Nansen tente, avec un compagnon, d'atteindre son but à skis et en canoë. Il échoue, mais établit un nouveau record : le pôle n'est plus qu'à 260 km.

Après six expéditions infructueuses en Arctique, Robert Peary plante le drapeau américain au pôle le 6 avril 1909. Il a pris la précaution de déposer à l'avance des provisions tout au long de la route déjà reconnue et franchit les 250 derniers kilomètres en cinq jours. Il est accompagné de Matt Henson et six Inuits (nom que se donnent les Esquimaux).

Les pôles

Les premières explorations de l'Antarctique commencent avec Dumont d'Urville. Il découvre la terre Adélie en 1840.

Charcot reconnaît plus de 1 000 km de terres nouvelles lors de sa première expédition, en 1903. Son deuxième bateau, le *Pourquoi-pas ?*, était équipé pour résister à la banquise.

Bonnet et moufles.

Viande séchée.

◀ *L'équipement des explorateurs est adapté aux conditions polaires. Les vêtements sont en fourrure et la viande est séchée.*

1911

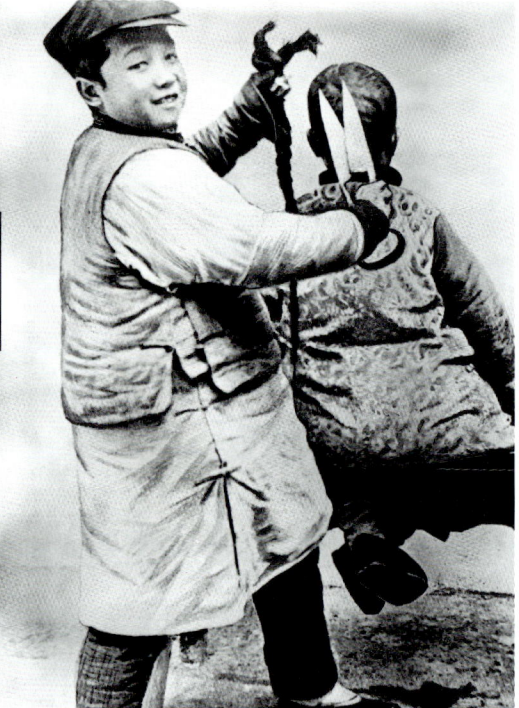

▲ *La révolution incite les Chinois à se couper la natte, qui a été le symbole de la dynastie mandchoue et de ses traditions.*

La république est proclamée en Chine

▶ **29 décembre 1911** ◀

L'empire de Chine vient tout juste de s'effondrer. Un président provisoire de la République chinoise vient d'être nommé dans le sud du pays. Il s'agit du docteur Sun Yat-sen, un chrétien qui a fait ses études de médecine à Hong-Kong et qui se bat depuis trente ans pour la modernisation de son pays. En 1894, il a fondé une société secrète et en a pris la tête. En 1898, il a proclamé les « trois principes du peuple » : nationalisme, démocratie libérale, justice sociale. Il a également créé l'Alliance révolutionnaire, réunissant autour de lui de jeunes intellectuels aussi bien que des représentants des classes moyennes ou de riches marchands. Ceux-ci souffrent des privilèges commerciaux accordés aux étrangers en Chine. Sun Yat-sen, qui vit aux États-Unis, est revenu à la hâte dans son pays natal à l'annonce de la révolution. Il a débarqué à Shanghai le jour de Noël.

La proclamation de la république survient après deux mois de guerre civile acharnée. La révolution a pris naissance en Chine centrale, à l'initiative d'unités de l'armée, soutenues par des groupes révolutionnaires sans lien avec Sun Yat-sen. Pour tenter d'endiguer la rébellion, le prince-régent Chun – l'empereur Pu Yi a tout juste cinq ans – a promis une Constitution démocratique deux mois auparavant. Mais cela arrive bien trop tard. Chun a été forcé de démissionner. Pu Yi abdique le 12 février 1911. La rumeur voudrait qu'il ait quitté précipitamment la Cité interdite, désormais étroitement gardée. Une Assemblée nationale est appelée à élaborer une nouvelle Constitution pour la Chine, mais il est acquis que la monarchie est définitivement abolie. C'est la fin de la dynastie mandchoue qui a régné sur la Chine pendant trois cents ans.

Irving Berlin fait un tabac

Alexander's Ragtime Band est le plus grand succès de l'année aux États-Unis. Et son auteur, Irving Berlin, d'origine russe, qui a débuté à New York comme garçon de café, est sacré roi du ragtime par les journaux américains, enthousiastes. Ses chansons aux airs entraînants n'ont pourtant vraiment rien à voir avec ce type de musique.

À Paris, le triomphe des Ballets russes

Paris fait un triomphe aux Ballets russes pour la première de *Petrouchka*, le ballet du compositeur russe Igor Stravinski. Vaslav Nijinski, le danseur vedette de ces Ballets, fondés en 1909 par Serge de Diaghilev, stupéfie le monde, par l'ampleur de ses bonds, qui font fi des lois de la pesanteur. Dans ce spectacle, les décors, la musique et la danse, contribuent à créer un art nouveau éblouissant.

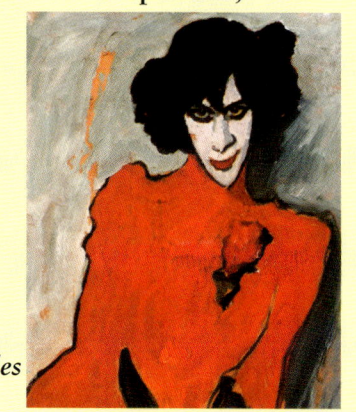

▶ *Portrait de l'un des danseurs des Ballets russes.*

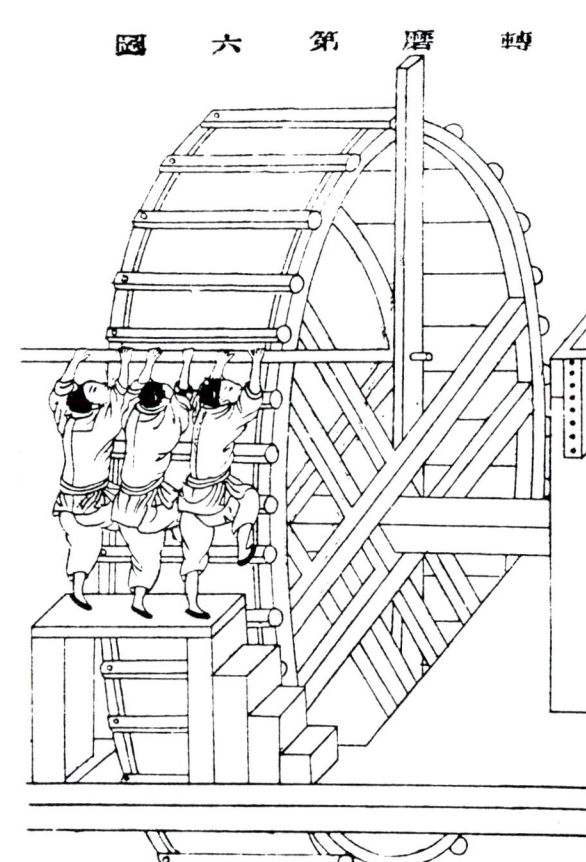

▲ *Roue à eau destinée à l'irrigation des campagnes dans la Chine ancienne.*

En 1911 aussi ...

11 mars
- La France compte 39 601 509 habitants.

25 mai • Au Mexique, le président Porfirio Díaz démissionne.

10 juin • En boxe, le Français Georges Carpentier est sacré champion du monde des mi-moyens.

31 décembre • La physicienne française d'origine polonaise Marie Curie obtient de nouveau le prix Nobel. En chimie, cette fois.

On a volé *la Joconde*

▶ **22 août 1911** ◀ Le musée du Louvre est en émoi. Le tableau le plus célèbre du monde a été dérobé durant la nuit de dimanche à lundi, dans la Grande Galerie, où il était accroché. On s'interroge sur la façon dont le voleur a réussi à mettre en échec les systèmes de sécurité. *La Joconde* est une œuvre exécutée en 1504 par l'artiste Léonard de Vinci, alors que celui-ci résidait à Florence. Le tableau avait été acquis par le roi François Ier, et l'artiste italien était venu s'installer en France. Les experts affirment qu'il va être impossible au voleur de vendre, où que ce soit dans le monde, le fameux chef-d'œuvre représentant Mona Lisa, une femme à l'énigmatique sourire.

▲ La Joconde, *de Léonard de Vinci.*

1910 – 1919

Premier studio de cinéma à Hollywood

▶ **Octobre 1911** ◀ La compagnie Nestor a ouvert le premier studio de cinéma. Elle s'est installée à Hollywood, une petite ville près de Los Angeles. Avec ses nombreux jours d'ensoleillement et sa belle lumière propice aux films, la Californie peut rapidement devenir le lieu de tournage favori des réalisateurs. D'autres compagnies cinématographiques pourraient choisir de venir, s'installer, elles aussi, à Hollywood.

▲ *Tournage d'un film au studio Nestor.*

Le Machu Picchu découvert

Au Pérou, l'explorateur américain Hiram Bingham vient de découvrir une cité inca inconnue, le Machu Picchu, perchée à plus de 2 000 m d'altitude dans la cordillère des Andes. Les bâtiments, enfouis sous la végétation sont pratiquement intacts. Il s'agit d'une des plus grandes découvertes archéologiques de tous les temps.

▼ *L'architecte-explorateur Hiram Bingham.*

Jean Bouin, recordman du monde

▶ **16 novembre 1911** ◀ Aujourd'hui, le stade de Colombes a été le théâtre du remarquable exploit d'un jeune coureur français de 23 ans. Devant un millier de spectateurs, Jean Bouin a en effet établi le record du monde du 10 000 m, distance qu'il a parcourue en 30 min 58 s et 8/10. Il a pourtant dû constamment lutter contre le vent et la pluie.

La folie des puzzles

Le puzzle fait fureur des deux côtés de l'Atlantique. Les premiers remontent au XVIIIe siècle. À cette époque, on pensait que des cartes découpées en morceaux favorisaient l'enseignement de la géographie.

1910

1911

1912

1913

1914

1915

1916

1917

1918

1919

1912

▲ Le Titanic coule à pic avec 1 513 personnes à bord. C'était son premier voyage.

En 1912 aussi …

3 août • Le cargo panaméen SS Cristobal est le premier à franchir le canal de Panamá, qui relie l'océan Pacifique et l'océan Atlantique.

29 juin • Ouverture des jeux Olympiques de Stockholm.

30 juillet • Yoshihito devient le 123ᵉ empereur du Japon.

5 novembre • Woodrow Wilson est élu président des États-Unis.

La tragédie du *Titanic*

▶ **14-15 avril 1912** ◀

1 513 passagers et membres d'équipage disparus : c'est le dramatique bilan du naufrage du plus moderne transatlantique du monde. Cette nuit, vers minuit, le *Titanic* a heurté un iceberg. Il semble que l'avant de la coque ait été éventré. À 2 heures ce matin, le paquebot s'est enfoncé dans l'océan Atlantique, au large de Terre-Neuve.

Le *Titanic* a récemment fait la une des journaux. Les reporters ont décrit dans les moindres détails ses luxueuses installations, qui en font un véritable palace flottant, avec son élégante salle de bal, ses somptueuses cabines, ses jardins intérieurs et sa piscine. Tous ont rappelé qu'il était insubmersible, grâce à une coque à double fond équipée de seize compartiments étanches.

Les enquêteurs auront à déterminer pourquoi le paquebot, qui voguait vers New York, filait si vite – 23 nœuds à l'heure –, pourquoi l'iceberg n'a été repéré qu'au dernier moment, et pourquoi un navire pouvant embarquer 3 500 passagers n'a été équipé de canots de sauvetage que pour 1 178 d'entre eux.

Le signal SOS

Trois traits, trois points, trois traits, sont désormais le signal universel des bateaux en détresse. Il s'agit d'un code sonore - le morse - combinant signaux longs - les traits - et signaux courts - les points. Ils sont le symbole des trois lettres S, O et S, qui signifient en anglais *Save our souls,* « sauvez nos âmes ». Il est déjà utilisé depuis quatre ans par de nombreux opérateurs radios pour signaler leur urgent besoin d'aide.

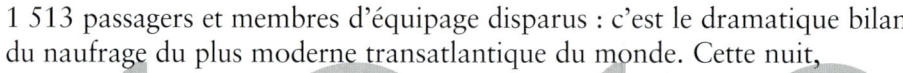

Victoire dans les Balkans

▶ **4 décembre 1912** ◀

Les troupes turques viennent de rendre les armes. Depuis deux mois, l'Empire ottoman subissait les attaques de ses voisins, soutenus par les Russes. La Bulgarie, la Serbie, la Grèce et le Monténégro se sont en effet unis pour chasser les Turcs des Balkans, cette région stratégique du sud-est de l'Europe. Leur victoire met fin à six siècles d'occupation turque dans la région. Depuis quelques années, l'Empire ottoman n'a cessé de faire face à des révoltes et de perdre des territoires.

▼ Les soldats de l'Empire ottoman à Constantinople.

Un Indien aux J.O.

▶ **22 juillet 1912** ◀ Jim Thorpe est la révélation de l'année. Il a fait sensation aux J.O. de Stockholm en remportant la médaille d'or du pentathlon, une discipline constituée de 5 épreuves (cross, équitation, natation, escrime, tir), et en établissant le record du monde du décathlon (10 épreuves de course, saut et lancer). Membre de la tribu des Sacs d'Oklahoma, il est en effet indien et se nomme Wa-Tho-Huck (Sentier lumineux).

La dérive des continents

▶ **Janvier 1912** ◀ D'étonnantes révélations sur l'histoire de la Terre viennent d'être faites par le géophysicien et météorologue allemand Alfred Wegener. Ayant remarqué que l'Afrique et l'Amérique du Sud s'emboîtent l'une dans l'autre si on les rapproche, il a comparé leurs roches et fossiles. Ils présentent des ressemblances troublantes. Ce qui l'a entraîné à une conclusion révolutionnaire. Il y a 250 millions d'années, la Terre n'avait qu'un continent, qui s'est scindé en deux.

Il y a deux cent cinquante millions d'années.

Il y a cent trente-cinq millions d'années.

Il y a soixante-cinq millions d'années.

Les continents actuels.

Les collages de Picasso et de Braque

Pablo Picasso et Georges Braque sont deux jeunes artistes parisiens du groupe des cubistes. Ils peignent des objets comme s'ils étaient vus sous plusieurs angles à la fois. Leurs sujets favoris sont des portraits, des journaux ou des natures mortes, dont ils modifient l'apparence. Ils ont également introduit dans leurs toiles, par collage, des matériaux divers, comme des bouts de tissu, du carton ou des morceaux de papier.

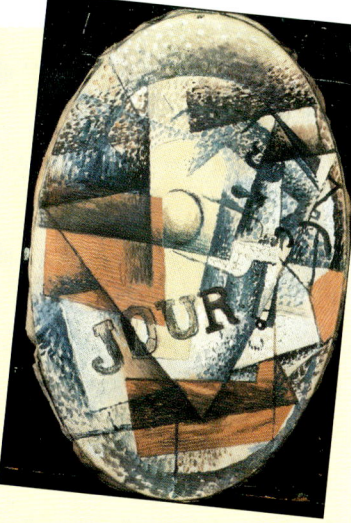
▲ *Collage de Georges Braque.*

La fin de la bande à Bonnot

▶ **27 avril 1912** ◀ Près de Paris, les gendarmes capturent les membres de la bande à Bonnot. Jules Joseph Bonnot, leur chef, est tué. C'est en voiture que ces bandits, pilleurs de banque et meurtriers, opéraient. Ils étaient des partisans violents de l'anarchisme, doctrine politique qui s'oppose à la société et à ses institutions. Par leurs vols, ils estimaient reprendre ce que la société leur avait volé.

Découverte de Néfertiti

▶ **7 décembre 1912** ◀ Elle est âgée de quelque 3 000 ans. Pourtant, sa grande beauté et son expression séduisent toujours ceux qui la contemplent. Il s'agit de Néfertiti, reine d'Égypte et femme du pharaon Aménophis IV Akhenaton, qui vécut vers 1360 av. J.-C. Son buste en calcaire polychrome, qui vient d'être découvert par des archéologues allemands, est d'une étonnante perfection. Il tranche avec la plupart des représentations de hauts personnages, qui se ressemblent toutes. C'est sans doute le premier véritable portrait d'un individu réalisé dans l'Égypte antique.

1913

1911

1912

1913

1914

1915

1916

1917

1918

1919

Le docteur Schweitzer dans la brousse africaine

▶ **16 avril 1913** ◀ À l'emplacement d'un ancien poulailler, un hôpital vient de s'ouvrir, au bord du fleuve Ogooué, à Lambaréné, en Afrique-Équatoriale française (de nos jours, le Gabon). Il est l'œuvre du docteur Albert Schweitzer, qui veut y accueillir et y soigner les milliers de malades qui souffrent de la malaria, de la lèpre et d'autres maladies tropicales. Ce médecin au grand cœur est né et a grandi en Alsace. Il a d'abord fait de solides études pour devenir pasteur et musicien accompli. Puis, à 30 ans, il a entrepris des études de médecine, afin de se consacrer à ceux qui souffrent. Avec ténacité, il a donné des récitals d'orgue et écrit des livres dans le but de collecter assez d'argent pour construire cet hôpital. Avec l'aide de sa femme, Hélène, qui l'assiste dans les soins aux malades, il a élevé ce bâtiment en grande partie de ses propres mains. Les familles viennent s'installer ici pour accompagner leurs malades. Elles vivent sur place, dehors, se chargeant d'apporter leurs provisions et de faire la cuisine.

L'inventeur des chips

Cartier, un chef français, dit avoir inventé les chips, grâce à une nouvelle technique de préparation de la pomme de terre. Il la coupe en tranches fines, qu'il plonge ensuite dans l'huile bouillante. Cette prétention étonnerait bien l'Américain Crum : il semble avoir inventé les chips dès 1853, dans un restaurant de l'État de New York, à la suite d'un mouvement d'humeur des clients. On lui avait demandé de couper ses frites plus fines !

▲ *Des ouvriers assemblent la Ford T.*

Une Ford T montée en 93 minutes

▶ **7 octobre 1913** ◀ Quatre-vingt-treize minutes : c'est le temps de fabrication d'une voiture. Avant que Henry Ford, le constructeur américain, n'inventât la chaîne de montage mobile, il fallait douze heures. Jusqu'alors, le châssis de l'auto stoppait à chaque poste de travail de la chaîne. À l'avenir, il continuera d'avancer. Les ouvriers se plaignent d'un travail fastidieux, mais apprécient leur nouveau salaire, passé de 2 à 5 dollars par jour. Quant au prix de la Ford T, il est passé de 850 dollars en 1908 à 440 cette année.

Une armoire « à faire du froid »

Incroyable mais vrai ! Des appareils capables de fabriquer le froid sont récemment apparus en Europe et aux États-Unis. Ces « réfrigérateurs » sont hors de prix mais, selon leurs premiers utilisateurs, très efficaces. Pourront-ils résoudre un jour, pour tous, le problème de la conservation des aliments pendant l'été ? Cela a toujours été difficile, sauf pour les ménages aisés, qui peuvent se procurer des blocs de glace et les conserver dans des glacières.

1910 – 1919

La plus grande gare du monde

▶ 2 février 1913 ◀ On inaugure aujourd'hui le Grand Central Terminus, la plus grande gare du monde. New York peut être fière de ce monument. Édifié au cœur de Manhattan, il s'étend sur près de 20 hectares et dispose de 48 voies ferrées.

Le grand hall, éclairé par de hautes fenêtres, est une vraie splendeur. Son plafond est comme une voûte céleste d'un bleu intense, cloutée d'étoiles dorées. Il abrite aussi un escalier roulant desservant les différents niveaux. Son horloge monumentale peut devenir un point de rendez-vous.

1913

Poincaré, président de la République

▶ 17 janvier 1913 ◀ Sénateurs et députés se sont réunis en Parlement à Versailles. Ils viennent d'élire Raymond Poincaré président de la République française. Il est partisan d'une politique de fermeté face à l'Allemagne et d'un service militaire porté à trois ans, afin de faire face à l'éventualité d'une guerre.

En 1913 aussi …

17 février • Pour conquérir le suffrage universel, le parti ouvrier belge organise la grève générale.

3 avril • La France adopte le service militaire de trois ans.

23 septembre • Roland Garros est le premier aviateur à franchir la Méditerranée.

12 décembre • On a retrouvé la Joconde, volée au Louvre en 1911.

Hauteur record pour un gratte-ciel

▶ 24 avril 1913 ◀ Le président Wilson inaugure aujourd'hui le gratte-ciel le plus haut du monde. Il s'agit du Woolworth Building, qui se dresse à 241 mètres de hauteur dans le ciel de Manhattan, à New York. Ses 55 étages ont nécessité toute une armada d'ouvriers, qui ont œuvré pendant quatre ans. Sa structure, en acier et béton, est recouverte de carreaux de terre cuite qui lui confèrent une élégante allure de cathédrale gothique. Il a coûté 13,5 millions de dollars.

▶ L'immeuble Woolworth, conçu par Cass Gilbert.

◀ Le jeune compositeur Igor Stravinski.

Un spectacle sifflé

▶ 29 mai 1913 ◀ Pour la première du *Sacre du printemps* au Théâtre des Champs-Élysées, les Ballets russes se sont fait huer. Sifflets et ricanements ont interrompu le ballet, que n'a guère goûté le public parisien. L'œuvre est sans doute trop nouvelle et trop moderne. La musique d'Igor Stravinski, compositeur russe, introduit en effet des dissonances et des rythmes d'une particulière violence, parfois assourdissants.

1914

Vive le confort !

Mary Phelps Jacob, une riche Américaine, est fatiguée d'être étouffée par son corset. Aussi a-t-elle inventé le soutien-gorge : deux mouchoirs taillés en forme de bonnet et attachés par deux rubans roses à nouer derrière le dos. En France, Herminie Cadolle l'a mis au point il y a déjà vingt ans, mais, faute de moyens, n'a pu le rendre populaire. De son côté, Gideon Sundback, un ingénieur suédois installé aux États-Unis, vient de mettre au point une machine à fabriquer plus vite les fermetures à glissière, bien plus pratiques que les boutons.

L'Europe s'embrase

▶ 3 août 1914 ◀ Tôt ce matin, l'Allemagne a envahi la Belgique. À 11 heures, la Grande-Bretagne riposte en déclarant à son tour la guerre à l'Allemagne. C'est l'assassinat le 28 juin à Sarajevo (Bosnie) de l'archiduc François-Ferdinand de Habsbourg, neveu de l'empereur d'Autriche, qui a mis le feu aux poudres. L'Autriche, poussée par l'Allemagne, a envoyé le 28 juillet un ultimatum à la Serbie, accusée d'avoir soutenu l'attentat, et lui déclare la guerre. La Russie, alliée de la Serbie, a mobilisé. L'Allemagne, alliée à l'Autriche, a déclaré la guerre à la Russie.

Cette succession d'événements résulte des tensions qui se sont déclarées en Europe. La France veut prendre sa revanche sur l'Allemagne et récupérer l'Alsace et la Lorraine, provinces perdues en 1871. La Grande-Bretagne craint la concurrence commerciale. L'Autriche et la Russie s'affrontent pour la possession des Balkans. Ces oppositions ont engendré la formation de deux blocs ennemis : l'Entente (France, Grande-Bretagne, Russie) et la Triplice (Allemagne, Autriche-Hongrie et Italie).

▲ *L'archiduc François-Ferdinand, tué à Sarajevo.*

Des armées prêtes pour la bataille

▶ 12 août 1914 ◀ Après dix jours de fébrile activité, les armées françaises, britanniques et allemandes sont prêtes à se battre. C'est la première fois dans l'Histoire que l'on mobilise si vite, grâce notamment au chemin de fer. La France a réquisitionné 4 064 trains pour acheminer ses hommes sur le front de l'est. Le corps expéditionnaire britannique, qui va défendre la Belgique aux côtés des Français, s'est regroupé dans les ports et se prépare à embarquer.

Toutes les grandes nations d'Europe ont de forts contingents de conscrits – de jeunes hommes que la loi oblige à accomplir un service militaire, fréquemment de deux ou trois ans. Le mois dernier, la Russie a ainsi mobilisé 1 million d'hommes, mais, malgré le Transsibérien, elle aura du mal à les acheminer sur le front. L'Allemagne compte déjà 500 000 soldats au front. Seule la Grande-Bretagne, où la conscription n'existe pas, doit faire appel aux volontaires.

Percées allemandes

▶ 31 août 1914 ◀ Sous la direction du général Hindenburg, les troupes allemandes connaissent leurs premiers succès contre la Russie à Tannenberg, en Prusse-Orientale (Pologne actuelle). À l'ouest, où elles occupent la Belgique, elles se sont ruées vers la mer du Nord, afin de contrôler les côtes où débarque l'aide britannique. Forte de ses 340 000 hommes, l'armée belge résiste sur la Sambre, mais l'armée allemande arrive à moins de 100 km de Paris (à Compiègne, le 31 août).

▲ *Les troupes allemandes occupent Bruxelles.*

52

1910 – 1919

Inauguration du canal de Panamá

▶ 15 août 1914 ◀ Aujourd'hui, l'*Ancon* inaugure le canal de Panamá, long de 64 petits kilomètres : il est le premier navire à rallier l'Atlantique au Pacifique sans passer par le cap Horn. Cet étroit chenal creusé dans l'isthme qui relie les deux Amériques, celle du Nord et celle du Sud, fait gagner 11 000 kilomètres aux navires. Il va changer la face du monde.

▲ L'Ancon franchit le canal de Panamá.

▼ Le général Joffre sauve Paris à la bataille de la Marne.

Tarzan, un lord anglais roi de la jungle

Il est né aristocrate anglais mais s'est retrouvé orphelin, perdu dans la jungle africaine, à la suite d'un accident d'avion. Il n'a dû sa survie qu'à une troupe de chimpanzés et à sa mère adoptive, la guenon Chita.
Depuis, son cri retentit dans la jungle. C'est Tarzan, l'homme-singe qui ne se déplace qu'en s'élançant de liane en liane. C'est du moins ainsi que le décrit son créateur, l'écrivain américain Edgar Rice Burroughs.

Plan d'attaque-surprise

▶ 30 septembre 1914 ◀ Le plan Schlieffen prévoyait de battre la France en six semaines, avant que la Russie n'ait fini de mobiliser. C'est pour cela qu'il fallait passer par la Belgique et éviter les forts de l'est de la France.

Vivent les taxis de la Marne !

▶ 10 septembre 1914 ◀ Paris est sauvé ! Grâce au général Joffre qui, aidé du gouverneur militaire de Paris, le général Gallieni, a su rallier des troupes pour la défense de Paris. Comme il n'existe pas de véhicules pour le transport des troupes dans l'armée française, ils ont réquisitionné tout ce qui pouvait servir. En premier, les célèbres taxis, mais aussi les voitures de maître avec les chauffeurs et les omnibus. Tous ces véhicules ont transporté en un temps record les soldats jusque sur le front de la Marne. La bataille dure du 6 au 13 septembre. Les Allemands se replient sur l'Aisne.
À la mi-novembre, le front se stabilise de la mer du Nord à la Suisse. Les armées s'enterrent dans des tranchées.
C'est la guerre de position.

En 1914 aussi...

31 juillet • Assassinat de Jean Jaurès à Paris ; ce leader socialiste a toujours été farouchement opposé à la guerre.

23 août • Le Japon déclare la guerre à l'Allemagne.

27 septembre • La Russie envahit la Hongrie.

14 novembre • En Turquie, le sultan déclare la guerre sainte à l'Entente.

◀ Lors de la bataille de la Marne, les soldats français ont sauvé Paris.

1915

Torpillage du *Lusitania*

▶ **7 mai 1915** ◀ Le paquebot américain *Lusitania* vient d'être envoyé par le fond, vingt minutes après avoir été touché par deux torpilles lancées par un *U-boat*, sous-marin allemand. La scène s'est déroulée au large de l'Irlande, alors que ce transatlantique de la compagnie Cunard reliait New York à Liverpool. Il transportait 1 900 passagers. On dénombre 1 200 victimes civiles, dont 124 Américains. Les autorités allemandes ripostent ainsi au blocus général de leurs ports par les forces de l'Entente, qui les empêchent de se ravitailler à l'étranger. Elles annoncent, par ailleurs, qu'elles couleront tout navire croisant dans les eaux britanniques. Les Américains, qui ne font pas partie des pays en guerre, ont été scandalisés à l'annonce de la nouvelle. Le président, Thomas Woodrow Wilson, a immédiatement protesté. Il accuse les Allemands de ne pas avoir respecté les accords internationaux interdisant formellement l'attaque de navires civils par les sous-marins.

Pour se défendre, les autorités allemandes affirment que le bateau transportait une importante cargaison de munitions destinée à l'Entente.

▼ *Un sous-marin qui a torpillé un navire marchand recueille les survivants.*

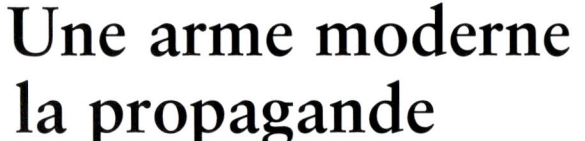

▼ *Les sous-marins sont pourvus de torpilles et de canons.*

L'Italie entre en guerre

▶ **23 mai 1915** ◀ Un nouveau membre vient de rejoindre l'Entente. C'est l'Italie qui déclare la guerre à l'Autriche. Elle est restée neutre jusqu'à présent, fidèle à son alliée autrichienne. Mais celle-ci lui a refusé récemment les territoires qu'elle revendique dans les Balkans. Déjà, le mois dernier, le Premier ministre italien avait approuvé un accord secret avec la France, la Russie et la Grande-Bretagne. En échange, elles lui avaient promis, en cas de victoire, les territoires contestés.

Une arme moderne : la propagande

▶ **1915** ◀ Depuis le début de la guerre, les belligérants multiplient affiches et articles de presse destinés à relever le moral de leurs troupes. Il faut aussi inciter les épargnants à verser leurs économies pour financer la guerre.

◀ *Affiches de propagande française (à gauche), et allemande (ci-contre).*

1910 – 1919

Griffith, maître de la caméra à Hollywood

D.W. Griffith, le réalisateur de *la Naissance d'une nation*, fait preuve d'une grande maestria. Dans ce film où il évoque la fondation du Ku Klux Klan, en 1867, il invente de nouvelles techniques : fondus enchaînés qui font graduellement passer d'une séquence à l'autre, gros plans révélant l'émotion des acteurs, et astuces de montage permettant de montrer des scènes qui se déroulent simultanément.

▲ *Soldats alliés rendus aveugles par les gaz.*

Attaque aux gaz

▶ **22 avril 1915** ◀ Aujourd'hui, pour la première fois dans l'Histoire, des gaz toxiques ont été utilisés pour tuer des hommes. C'est à Ypres, en Belgique, que les Allemands ont attaqué les positions alliées avec un gaz à base de chlore.

Les écrivains meurent aussi

À la guerre, personne n'est épargné. Les écrivains ne font pas exception à cette règle sanglante. On déplore ainsi la mort du poète Charles Péguy, frappé d'une balle en plein front à Villeroy, le 5 septembre 1914. Alain-Fournier, auteur d'un unique et merveilleux roman *le Grand Meaulnes*, a lui aussi été tué, quelques jours plus tard. C'était le 22 septembre près de Verdun. Il avait tout juste 28 ans.

Le retour du Ku Klux Klan

▶ **4 décembre 1915** ◀ Le colonel William Simmons, influencé par le film de Griffith, *la Naissance d'une nation*, vient de ressusciter à Atlanta les vieux démons racistes : le Ku Klux Klan réapparaît. Née après la guerre de Sécession, cette société secrète hostile aux Noirs avait été interdite en 1872. Ses membres veulent provoquer l'effroi en agissant masqués, coiffés de cagoules.

En 1915 aussi …

13 janvier
• La terre tremble en Italie. On dénombre 29 000 victimes.

Février • En Turquie, le génocide arménien est ordonné par le gouvernement turc. Cette extermination de tout un peuple fait 1,5 million de victimes.

10 décembre • Le prix Nobel de littérature récompense *Au-dessus de la mêlée*, une œuvre engagée contre la guerre, du Français Romain Rolland.

▼ *Les Alliés débarquent dans le détroit des Dardanelles.*

Échec des Alliés aux Dardanelles

▶ **20 décembre 1915** ◀ Cette nuit, les Alliés viennent d'abandonner leurs positions dans le détroit des Dardanelles, en Turquie. Depuis avril, date à laquelle ils y avaient débarqué, ils pensaient pouvoir s'emparer du détroit, qui contrôle le passage de la mer Noire à la Méditerranée, de façon à secourir la Russie. Mais ils viennent d'enregistrer un véritable désastre, qui s'est soldé, de part et d'autre, par de nombreux morts.

◀ *Une réunion des membres du Ku Klux Klan.*

LES CIVILS EN GUERRE

▼ *Berlin. Vente de charité pour les enfants de soldats au front.*

La Première Guerre mondiale, que l'on a appelée la Grande Guerre, a été pour chacun une expérience terrible. Conscrits, engagés volontaires, soldats professionnels, civils de « l'arrière » qui ont contribué à l'effort de guerre, tous ont été frappés par les épreuves. Les hommes de toute une génération ont quitté leurs foyers, et des millions d'entre eux ont été tués. Ceux qui en ont réchappé sont souvent revenus blessés, gazés, invalides, et tous ont subi des traumatismes psychologiques inguérissables, aussi cruels pour leur entourage que pour eux-mêmes.

Une vie très difficile

Les régions de Belgique et de France occupées par les Allemands ou proches du front souffrent particulièrement des ravages de la guerre. En Allemagne et en Grande-Bretagne, le rationnement frappe durement les civils. Dans tous les pays, à l'arrière, on s'adapte aux conditions de vie difficiles et on se mobilise. Les familles parrainent des soldats, leur envoient des vêtements, des vivres, ou les accueillent lorsqu'ils sont en permission. On aide l'État en souscrivant aux emprunts pour payer les dépenses nécessaires, qui sont très lourdes.

Partout, les enfants sont touchés par la guerre. Ils font des collectes pour les soldats du front. Beaucoup travaillent dans les usines. Certains adolescents s'engagent très jeunes dans l'armée et se sacrifient pour la patrie.

▼ *Les enfants participent à l'effort de guerre en cultivant des parcelles dont les récoltes fourniront quelque nourriture.*

« Au revoir, papa ! »

La scène se répète dans toutes les gares d'Europe et des États-Unis. De petits enfants embrassent de jeunes pères, partant au front, qu'ils ne reverront peut-être plus. Des millions d'entre eux ne les reconnaîtront pas quand ils reviendront d'une guerre sans fin.

▶ Les adieux d'un soldat américain qui part à la guerre.

Une femme vaut un homme

Les femmes remplacent les hommes partis au front. Pour la première fois, elles remplissent des tâches qui ont toujours été considérées comme trop difficiles ou trop nobles pour elles. Elles se forment, gagnent leur vie, et contribuent à l'effort de guerre. On voit des femmes partout. Elles sont porteuses de bagages, contrôleuses dans les trains, conduisent bus et métros. Elles sont factrices, travaillent dans les champs, dirigent des fermes. Dans les usines d'armement, elles fabriquent obus, canons et explosifs. Au retour des soldats, nombre d'entre elles devront regagner leurs foyers, mais la place de la femme dans la société aura évolué.

▲ Londres. Policières donnant l'alerte de raids aériens.

▶ Ouvrière soudeuse, une tâche jusqu'alors réservée aux hommes.

La Grande Guerre

La Grande Guerre a coûté cher : 8 millions de morts pour 65 millions d'hommes mobilisés.

25 milliards de dollars à la France, 40 milliards de dollars à l'Allemagne.

La France a perdu 1,3 million de soldats. Ils laissent 680 000 veuves et 760 000 orphelins. Un quart de la génération des jeunes gens de 18 à 27 ans a disparu.

1916

1910

1911

1912

1913

1914

1915

1916

1917

1918

1919

◀ *Le capitaine Thomas Edward Lawrence.*

▲ *Dans le désert d'Arabie, les conditions de combat sont difficiles.*

Drôle de bouteille pour Coca-Cola

Cet été, une curieuse bouteille est apparue dans les magasins et les bars des États-Unis et du Canada. Elle a été lancée par la firme Coca-Cola, qui espère ainsi multiplier les ventes de sa boisson qui pétille. Les courbes de la bouteille rappelleraient, semble-t-il, les formes de la noix de cola, qui entre dans la composition, gardée secrète, de la boisson devenue très vite populaire.

▶ *Soldats français dans les tranchées de Verdun.*

Bataille dans le désert

▶ **31 août 1916** ◀

En juin dernier, des tribus d'Arabie et de Jordanie, sous domination ottomane depuis des siècles, ont revendiqué leur indépendance. L'émir Hussein Ibn Ali a pris la tête de la révolte contre l'Empire turc et s'est rendu maître de La Mecque. Ses fils Fayçal, Abdullah et Zeid se sont ensuite emparés de trois villes clés, Ta'if, Djeddah et Médine.

Bien qu'ils aient remporté de grands succès avec leurs méthodes ancestrales, il est clair que les Arabes ont maintenant besoin d'une armée moderne. C'est pourquoi, au cours de ce mois, Hussein a fait appel aux Britanniques. Ils lui ont délégué un jeune officier de 28 ans, le capitaine Thomas Edward Lawrence, qui parle couramment arabe et connaît bien la région. Son but est de rassembler les tribus arabes du désert, afin qu'elles s'unissent et combattent ensemble pour leur indépendance, car les Turcs dominent encore tout le Moyen-Orient.

L'enfer de Verdun

▶ **21 février 1916** ◀

Les Allemands attaquent Verdun. Cette ville va devenir un symbole ; elle ne tombera pas, mais les forts qui l'entourent, Vaux et surtout Douaumont, seront pris et repris. Les Français résistent, sous les ordres successivement des généraux Pétain et Nivelle. Renforts et munitions arrivent par la Voie sacrée, qui relie Bar-le-Duc à Verdun. À l'automne, les Allemands renoncent. Les Français remportent cette bataille très dure. 300 jours, 300 nuits de combat dans le froid, la boue, sous les bombes ; plus de 600 000 morts, tant français qu'allemands. « L'enfer de Verdun » s'achève !

1910 – 1919

La mer en feu

▶ **1er juin 1916** ◀ La première grande bataille navale de la guerre est terminée. À l'heure actuelle, les flottes britannique et allemande quittent les côtes danoises du Jutland, en mer du Nord, et regagnent leurs bases. L'affrontement a commencé hier matin, lorsque l'amiral allemand Scheer a voulu forcer le blocus allié et a fait sortir la flotte de haute mer. L'amiral britannique John Jellicoe a immédiatement tenté de l'encercler. Les pertes sont très lourdes. Chacun revendique la victoire, mais les Britanniques pensent que la flotte allemande n'osera plus sortir. Le blocus continue.

Mort de Raspoutine

▶ **30 décembre 1916** ◀ Le moine russe Grigori Raspoutine est mort assassiné à Saint-Pétersbourg. Moine mystique, il prétendait guérir le tsarévitch (héritier du trône) atteint d'un mal incurable, l'hémophilie. Les nobles russes le haïssaient pour l'influence qu'il avait sur la famille du tsar. Après avoir essayé de l'empoisonner, le prince Ioussoupov l'a achevé à coups de pistolet et a jeté son corps dans la Neva.

En 1916 aussi...

27 janvier • Le service militaire est adopté en Grande-Bretagne.

9 mars • Le dépeçage de l'Empire ottoman est décidé par un accord secret franco-anglais.

1er juillet • Les Alliés lancent une offensive sur la Somme : 65 000 morts.

20 août • Entrée en guerre de la Roumanie aux côtés des Alliés.

15 septembre • Pour la première fois, des chars d'assaut passent à l'attaque.

Sur la Somme

▶ **20 novembre 1916** ◀ Cinq cent mille morts en quelques jours, c'est le triste bilan de la victoire que les Alliés estiment avoir remportée dans la longue bataille de la Somme. Lorsque les soldats français et britanniques sont montés à l'assaut le 1er juillet, les canons allemands les ont fauchés par régiments entiers. Mais les pertes adverses, elles aussi, ont été irréparables. Les chars, la nouvelle arme anglaise, ne sont pas encore assez nombreux pour apporter un appui décisif.

Les dadaïstes défient l'art établi

« Dada » vient de naître à Zurich. À l'initiative de Tristan Tzara, ce mouvement rassemble artistes et écrivains comme Picabia, Duchamp, Man Ray... au cabaret Voltaire. Cet art, né en pleine guerre, refuse toute règle et fait appel à la dérision. Il suffit qu'un objet soit exposé dans une galerie pour qu'il devienne une œuvre d'art. Son nom a été choisi au hasard !

▶ *Man Ray.*

◀ *Soldats de la liberté, Irlande, 1916.*

L'Irlande insurgée

▶ **29 avril 1916** ◀ La rébellion irlandaise est finie. Et l'indépendance de l'Irlande n'est plus qu'un rêve lointain. Elle avait commencé à Dublin, le lundi de Pâques. Les insurgés catholiques avaient mis le feu au palais de justice et pris possession des lieux stratégiques. Le poète Padraic Pearse avait même courageusement proclamé l'indépendance, du haut des marches de la poste, occupée. Mais l'armée britannique a maté la révolte et tiré sur la population civile.

1917

La révolution d'Octobre

▶ **7 novembre 1917** ◀ En ce moment, la Russie subit sa deuxième révolution de l'année. Les bolcheviques, des socialistes révolutionnaires, prennent le pouvoir à Petrograd (ex-Saint-Pétersbourg). On l'appellera « révolution d'Octobre », le calendrier russe ayant treize jours de retard sur celui du reste du monde occidental. La première révolution a eu lieu en mars et a contraint le tsar Nicolas II à démissionner. Ses troupes avaient refusé de tirer sur les manifestants, qui réclamaient la paix et du pain. Un gouvernement provisoire avait alors été formé. Il avait pour objectif d'imposer la démocratie, mais sa faiblesse et son incapacité à mettre fin à la guerre ont donné leur chance aux bolcheviques.

Les bolcheviques sont un groupe de révolutionnaires conduits par Vladimir Lénine et Léon Trotski, qui s'inspirent des idées du philosophe allemand Karl Marx. Ils croient en un État où la propriété privée est abolie. Ils promettent la paix, la terre et du pain. Ils sont très présents dans les soviets (en français, les conseils), créés lors de la révolution de mars. Pour les bolcheviques, ce sont les soviets d'ouvriers et de soldats qui doivent exercer le pouvoir.

▼ *Moscou, Révolution de 1917. L'artillerie bolchevique se prépare au combat.*

▶ *Des soldats bolcheviques gardent la porte du bureau de Lénine.*

Les États-Unis entrent en guerre

▶ **6 avril 1917** ◀ Aujourd'hui, l'Amérique s'engage dans la bataille. Le président Thomas Woodrow Wilson signe la déclaration de guerre contre l'Allemagne, afin de sauver la démocratie dans le monde, aux côtés de la France et de la Grande-Bretagne. Depuis leur création – en 1776 –, les États-Unis ont toujours refusé de se mêler des affaires européennes. Mais les attaques des sous-marins allemands contre les navires américains et la découverte, au début de 1917, d'un plan secret allemand pour persuader le Mexique d'attaquer les États-Unis changent leur politique.

Vous avez dit art ?

Un urinoir. Cette œuvre de l'artiste français Marcel Duchamp a stupéfait le Tout-New York. Il a tout simplement acheté cet urinoir chez un plombier, l'a baptisé *Fontaine* et l'a signé « R. Mutt 1917 ». Duchamp est l'un des fondateurs du dadaïsme, mouvement révolutionnaire dans le monde de l'art.

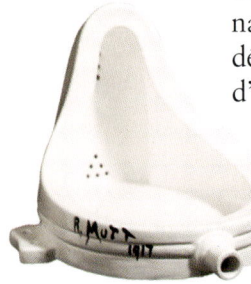

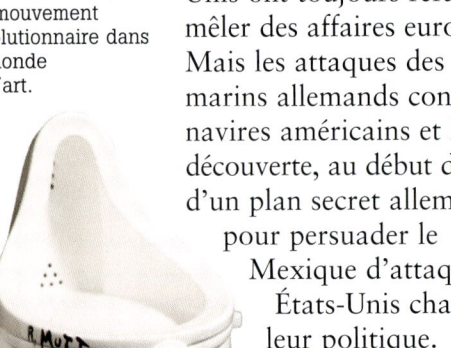

◀ *L'Oncle Sam, symbole des États-Unis, appelle les jeunes Américains à s'engager dans l'armée.*

En 1917 aussi …

avril-juillet • *Mutineries dans l'armée française. Les soldats refusent de se battre. Pétain ramène le calme, améliore leur sort, et fait fusiller les plus durs.*

15 octobre • *Mata Hari, danseuse orientale soupçonnée d'être une espionne allemande, est fusillée à Paris.*

2 novembre • *Lord Balfour, ministre britannique des Affaires étrangères, promet aux juifs un territoire en Palestine.*

Mort de Raspoutine

▶ **30 décembre 1916** ◀ Le moine russe Grigori Raspoutine est mort assassiné à Saint-Pétersbourg. Moine mystique, il prétendait guérir le tsarévitch (héritier du trône) atteint d'un mal incurable, l'hémophilie. Les nobles russes le haïssaient pour l'influence qu'il avait sur la famille du tsar. Après avoir essayé de l'empoisonner, le prince Ioussoupov l'a achevé à coups de pistolet et a jeté son corps dans la Neva.

1910 – 1919

La mer en feu

▶ **1er juin 1916** ◀ La première grande bataille navale de la guerre est terminée. À l'heure actuelle, les flottes britannique et allemande quittent les côtes danoises du Jutland, en mer du Nord, et regagnent leurs bases. L'affrontement a commencé hier matin, lorsque l'amiral allemand Scheer a voulu forcer le blocus allié et a fait sortir la flotte de haute mer. L'amiral britannique John Jellicoe a immédiatement tenté de l'encercler. Les pertes sont très lourdes. Chacun revendique la victoire, mais les Britanniques pensent que la flotte allemande n'osera plus sortir. Le blocus continue.

En 1916 aussi …

27 janvier • Le service militaire est adopté en Grande-Bretagne.

9 mars • Le dépeçage de l'Empire ottoman est décidé par un accord secret franco-anglais.

1er juillet • Les Alliés lancent une offensive sur la Somme : 65 000 morts.

20 août • Entrée en guerre de la Roumanie aux côtés des Alliés.

15 septembre • Pour la première fois, des chars d'assaut passent à l'attaque.

Sur la Somme

▶ **20 novembre 1916** ◀ Cinq cent mille morts en quelques jours, c'est le triste bilan de la victoire que les Alliés estiment avoir remportée dans la longue bataille de la Somme. Lorsque les soldats français et britanniques sont montés à l'assaut le 1er juillet, les canons allemands les ont fauchés par régiments entiers. Mais les pertes adverses, elles aussi, ont été irréparables. Les chars, la nouvelle arme anglaise, ne sont pas encore assez nombreux pour apporter un appui décisif.

Les dadaïstes défient l'art établi

« Dada » vient de naître à Zurich. À l'initiative de Tristan Tzara, ce mouvement rassemble artistes et écrivains comme Picabia, Duchamp, Man Ray… au cabaret Voltaire. Cet art, né en pleine guerre, refuse toute règle et fait appel à la dérision. Il suffit qu'un objet soit exposé dans une galerie pour qu'il devienne une œuvre d'art. Son nom a été choisi au hasard !

▶ *Man Ray.*

◀ *Soldats de la liberté, Irlande, 1916.*

L'Irlande insurgée

▶ **29 avril 1916** ◀ La rébellion irlandaise est finie. Et l'indépendance de l'Irlande n'est plus qu'un rêve lointain. Elle avait commencé à Dublin, le lundi de Pâques. Les insurgés catholiques avaient mis le feu au palais de justice et pris possession des lieux stratégiques. Le poète Padraic Pearse avait même courageusement proclamé l'indépendance, du haut des marches de la poste, occupée. Mais l'armée britannique a maté la révolte et tiré sur la population civile.

1917

La révolution d'Octobre

▶ 7 novembre 1917 ◀ En ce moment, la Russie subit sa deuxième révolution de l'année. Les bolcheviques, des socialistes révolutionnaires, prennent le pouvoir à Petrograd (ex-Saint-Pétersbourg). On l'appellera « révolution d'Octobre », le calendrier russe ayant treize jours de retard sur celui du reste du monde occidental. La première révolution a eu lieu en mars et a contraint le tsar Nicolas II à démissionner. Ses troupes avaient refusé de tirer sur les manifestants, qui réclamaient la paix et du pain. Un gouvernement provisoire avait alors été formé. Il avait pour objectif d'imposer la démocratie, mais sa faiblesse et son incapacité à mettre fin à la guerre ont donné leur chance aux bolcheviques.

Les bolcheviques sont un groupe de révolutionnaires conduits par Vladimir Lénine et Léon Trotski, qui s'inspirent des idées du philosophe allemand Karl Marx. Ils croient en un État où la propriété privée est abolie. Ils promettent la paix, la terre et du pain. Ils sont très présents dans les soviets (en français, les conseils), créés lors de la révolution de mars. Pour les bolcheviques, ce sont les soviets d'ouvriers et de soldats qui doivent exercer le pouvoir.

▼ *Moscou, Révolution de 1917. L'artillerie bolchevique se prépare au combat.*

▶ *Des soldats bolcheviques gardent la porte du bureau de Lénine.*

Vous avez dit art ?

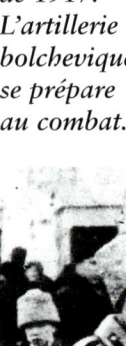

Un urinoir. Cette œuvre de l'artiste français Marcel Duchamp a stupéfait le Tout-New York. Il a tout simplement acheté cet urinoir chez un plombier, l'a baptisé *Fontaine* et l'a signé « R. Mutt 1917 ». Duchamp est l'un des fondateurs du dadaïsme, mouvement révolutionnaire dans le monde de l'art.

Les États-Unis entrent en guerre

▶ 6 avril 1917 ◀ Aujourd'hui, l'Amérique s'engage dans la bataille. Le président Thomas Woodrow Wilson signe la déclaration de guerre contre l'Allemagne, afin de sauver la démocratie dans le monde, aux côtés de la France et de la Grande-Bretagne. Depuis leur création – en 1776 –, les États-Unis ont toujours refusé de se mêler des affaires européennes. Mais les attaques des sous-marins allemands contre les navires américains et la découverte, au début de 1917, d'un plan secret allemand pour persuader le Mexique d'attaquer les États-Unis changent leur politique.

◀ *L'Oncle Sam, symbole des États-Unis, appelle les jeunes Américains à s'engager dans l'armée.*

En 1917 aussi …

avril-juillet • *Mutineries dans l'armée française. Les soldats refusent de se battre. Pétain ramène le calme, améliore leur sort, et fait fusiller les plus durs.*

15 octobre • *Mata Hari, danseuse orientale soupçonnée d'être une espionne allemande, est fusillée à Paris.*

2 novembre • *Lord Balfour, ministre britannique des Affaires étrangères, promet aux juifs un territoire en Palestine.*

1910 – 1919

Mort de Buffalo Bill

William F. Cody, la star du Far West, est mort le 10 janvier à l'âge de 70 ans. Il a tué tant de bisons (*buffaloes*) qu'il leur doit son surnom de Buffalo Bill. Il a, entre autres, ravitaillé en viande de bison les ouvriers qui construisaient la ligne de chemin de fer aux États-Unis. Par la suite, il devient acteur. En 1883, il organise son premier spectacle, où il présente des attaques de diligences, des combats contre les Indiens… Ses représentations ont fait de lui un homme célèbre, aux États-Unis et en Europe.

▲ *Le bombardier Gotha GV.*

Londres meurtri par les bombardements allemands

▶ **13 juin 1917** ◀ Ce matin, un degré vient d'être franchi dans l'escalade de la violence. Les quartiers est de Londres, en Grande-Bretagne, ont reçu un déluge de bombes qui ont tué 100 personnes. Le raid a eu lieu en plein jour. La défense antiaérienne a bien riposté, mais sans toucher un seul avion. Il s'agit de bombardiers Gotha GV, des biplaces rapides équipés de moteurs Mercedes. Ils volent à près de 160 km/h, avec un rayon d'action de 800 km, et peuvent transporter 50 kilos de bombes. Ils ont remplacé les zeppelins, qui ont déjà bombardé Londres mais sont plus vulnérables. En effet, à cause de leur lenteur, ces derniers sont facilement atteints par la D.C.A.

Apparition à Fatima

Un événement curieux se déroule à Fatima, village portugais au nord de Lisbonne. Deux fillettes et un petit garçon affirment avoir vu la Vierge, mère du Christ. Bien que la plus âgée ait tout juste 10 ans, les enfants sont pris très au sérieux. Ils décrivent la scène avec précision, dans un vocabulaire au-dessus de leur âge. Il est difficile de croire qu'ils ont tout inventé.

Tragique bataille dans les Flandres belges

▶ **6 novembre 1917** ◀ Le pont de Passchendaele, au nord-est d'Ypres, en Flandres, vient de tomber aux mains des Britanniques. Le général britannique Douglas Haig a atteint son objectif : déloger les Allemands de ces hauteurs. La bataille, qui devait durer deux jours, s'est prolongée pendant trois terribles mois. Cette troisième bataille autour d'Ypres s'est déroulée dans la boue, les trous d'obus emplis d'eau croupie, sous une pluie torrentielle. Les pertes ont été terribles. Beaucoup d'hommes sont morts noyés dans ce bourbier immonde.

▼ *La pluie et les obus ont transformé les Flandres en bourbier.*

Fin de la retraite en Italie

▶ **12 novembre 1917** ◀ Les Italiens viennent de stopper leur retraite et de stabiliser le front au nord-est de l'Italie. Depuis le 24 octobre, en effet, après l'attaque des Autrichiens et des Allemands à Caporetto, ils n'ont cessé de reculer. Il est vrai que ce sanglant accrochage a fait, du côté italien, des milliers de morts et 275 000 prisonniers. Et à peu près le même nombre de déserteurs. Dorénavant, l'Italie résiste, aidée par les Français et les Britanniques.

1918

La fin des Romanov

▶ **17 juillet 1918** ◀

La nuit dernière, le tsar Nicolas II, la tsarine et leurs cinq enfants ont été exécutés de sang-froid. Le massacre a eu lieu à Iekaterinbourg, dans la cave de la maison où ils étaient retenus prisonniers depuis le mois de mars, sous la garde de bolcheviques. Médecin et domestiques n'ont pas été épargnés. Il n'y aurait aucun survivant.

C'est la fin de la dynastie des Romanov, qui régnait sans partage sur la Russie depuis 1613.

Après la révolution de mars 1917, la famille impériale fut exilée par le gouvernement provisoire à Tobolsk, au cœur de la Sibérie. Puis elle fut transférée en mars 1918 à Iekaterinbourg, au centre de la Russie, en pleine guerre civile. Mais la ville est menacée par les Tchèques, alliés aux Russes blancs, antirévolutionnaires. Afin d'éviter que le tsar et son héritier ne deviennent un instrument entre leurs mains s'ils pénètrent dans Iekaterinbourg, le commissaire local a décidé leur exécution.

▼ *Le tsar Nicolas II, la tsarine Alexandra et leurs enfants, photographiés avant la révolution.*

Paix pour les Russes

▶ **3 mars 1918** ◀

La Russie se retire de la guerre. À Brest-Litovsk (Biélorussie), l'Allemagne, l'Autriche et les représentants du nouveau gouvernement russe signent un traité de paix. En prenant le pouvoir, les bolcheviques l'avaient promis à leurs partisans. Ils y ont été contraints par un ultimatum, et il est vrai qu'ils n'ont plus aucune armée à opposer à l'Allemagne. Ils perdent l'Ukraine, la Finlande et les provinces baltes. Les Alliés voient d'un mauvais œil cet arrêt de la guerre à l'est de l'Europe. Cela signifie qu'ils vont devoir soutenir un effort plus intense sur le front ouest.

▼ *Russes et Allemands signent le traité à Brest-Litovsk.*

La « Grosse Bertha » : l'arme « secrète » de l'Allemagne

▶ **24 juin 1918** ◀

Mille morts. C'est le lourd bilan du bombardement de Paris par les Allemands. À 120 kilomètres de la capitale, un canon géant tire des obus. Ce monstre, établi sur un affût de 33,5 mètres, pèse 200 tonnes et envoie ses projectiles à 18 kilomètres d'altitude, là où la résistance de l'air est moins forte. Bien qu'il soit peu précis, il fait des ravages. Les Parisiens l'ont baptisé « Grosse Bertha ».

▶ *La Grosse Bertha, le canon géant allemand.*

Les femmes votent

▶ 28 décembre 1918 ◀ Droit de vote pour les femmes britanniques. C'est une victoire chèrement acquise par celles qu'on surnomme les suffragettes. Grèves de la faim, églises incendiées, pose de bombes, tout leur fut bon. Mais c'est la reconnaissance du rôle des femmes dans la guerre qui leur vaut ce succès. Une demi-victoire tout de même, puisqu'elles ne votent qu'à partir de 30 ans. Les hommes, eux, votent dès 21 ans.

Clemenceau

▶ 1918 ◀ Clemenceau, Premier ministre français, obtient ce qu'il souhaitait : un commandement unique pour les Alliés. C'est Foch, nommé maréchal, qui l'exercera. Comme Clemenceau, celui-ci souhaite mener contre l'Allemagne une guerre totale, « à outrance », dit-il. Clemenceau fait l'unanimité : sa fermeté dans la conduite de la guerre le fait surnommer « le Tigre ». C'est grâce à cette action que Clemenceau devient le plus populaire des hommes politiques français. Après l'armistice, on l'appellera « le Père-la-Victoire ».

◀ *Clemenceau visite les tranchées.*

▲ *Duel aérien entre avions anglais et allemands.*

Le Baron rouge perd son ultime combat

▶ 21 avril 1918 ◀ Le Baron rouge ne volera plus. Manfred von Richthofen, as de la chasse allemande, a été abattu lors d'un duel aérien au-dessus des champs de bataille de la Somme. Celui qui tenait son surnom de la couleur rouge de son Fokker a, depuis 1916, causé la perte de 78 avions alliés. Les aviateurs français Georges Guynemer, qui abattit 54 avions, et Roland Garros ont aussi été tués. Le premier, dans le ciel de Belgique, et le second à Vouziers.

La contre-offensive a payé

▶ 18 juillet 1918 ◀ Trois jours après la reprise de la contre-offensive allemande dans la Marne, au nord-est de Paris, les Alliés ont lancé une contre-attaque victorieuse, sous le commandement du général Pétain.

L'attaque est dirigée contre le flanc ouest des lignes ennemies, qui se sont avancées au début de l'année sur tout le front. Le 13 juillet, les Allemands ont progressé de nouveau vers l'ouest, et des divisions ont franchi la Marne, menaçant Paris. Pétain veut percer le front allemand, créer une poche, encercler l'ennemi, et poursuivre l'offensive vers l'est. Il dispose de 500 blindés, une force logistique essentielle.

▶ *Les Américains dans la deuxième bataille de la Marne.*

1918

La paix !

▶ **11 novembre 1918** ◀ Le monde entier respire. L'armistice vient d'être signé à Rethondes, en forêt de Compiègne, non loin de Paris. Les armes se sont tues à 11 heures ce matin sur l'ensemble du front. Et les cloches ont sonné à toute volée. Cette guerre, la plus meurtrière de l'histoire européenne, est finie.

Il y a un mois, les Alliés ont mis sur pied une nouvelle série d'offensives. Les succès remportés ont démoralisé les lignes allemandes, qui ont mal résisté et se sont repliées. Le front allemand ne tient plus. Mutineries et émeutes ont, par ailleurs, provoqué l'abdication de l'empereur Guillaume II – le 9 novembre – et la proclamation de la république. Hindenburg et l'état-major voulaient signer un armistice au plus vite et ont envoyé des émissaires à Foch en ce sens. Les Allemands vont maintenant évacuer les territoires qu'ils occupaient et rendre l'Alsace-Lorraine à la France. Elle avait été rattachée à l'Empire allemand en 1871. En revanche, les troupes alliées doivent occuper une partie de l'Allemagne.

▲ *Femme portant un masque antigrippe.*

La grippe tue aussi

Depuis août 1918, la grippe fait rage. C'est la plus meurtrière des épidémies depuis la peste bubonique, au XIVe siècle. Ses dégâts feront plus de 20 millions de morts dans le monde entier. Bien qu'elle soit venue sans doute d'Asie, on l'appelle en France « grippe espagnole ».

La guerre est finie
Les gens s'embrassent dans la rue, à l'annonce de l'armistice. À Paris et à Londres, ils expriment ainsi spontanément leur joie.

Aux États-Unis, la presse annonce l'armistice quatre jours trop tôt. Les Américains l'auront donc fêté deux fois.

▶ *Aux États-Unis, on célèbre l'armistice.*

▼ *11 novembre : défilé de jeunes lycéens sur la place de la Concorde.*

Le bilan de la Grande Guerre

▶ **1918** ◀ Huit millions de morts, 20 millions de blessés, dont certains sont définitivement invalides. Des millions de civils sont morts, victimes de l'Occupation, des bombardements, des pénuries alimentaires et de la grippe espagnole. C'est le lourd bilan que l'on peut tirer de ce que l'on nomme la Grande Guerre. 1,8 million morts pour l'Allemagne, 1,4 million pour la France, 780 000 pour la Grande-Bretagne. En France, on compte 600 000 veuves, 760 000 orphelins et 740 000 mutilés.

Le nord-est de la France et le sud de la Belgique ont été ravagés ; 13 départements sont sinistrés ; 812 000 immeubles sont détruits ; 54 000 km de routes sont à refaire. Le coût matériel et financier est exorbitant. Les nations européennes se sont lourdement endettées auprès des États-Unis.

1910 – 1919

L'Empire austro-hongrois démantelé

▶ 16 novembre 1918 ◀ La république est proclamée en Autriche. L'empereur Charles Ier quitte le pays. L'Empire austro-hongrois a éclaté sous la poussée des peuples qui proclament leur indépendance. C'est le cas des Tchèques le 14 octobre, des Hongrois le 24, des Croates et des Slovènes le 30, des Polonais le 7 novembre. C'est la fin des Habsbourg, qui régnaient sur l'Europe centrale depuis le Moyen Âge. L'Autriche devient un petit État dont les frontières seront fixées lors de négociations internationales.

◀ Rassemblement en face du Reichstag (le Parlement allemand), à Berlin.

En 1918 aussi …

24 janvier
• Le philosophe Henri Bergson entre à l'Académie française.

28 février • Grève générale en Allemagne.

5 mars • Moscou redevient capitale de la Russie, à la place de Petrograd.

12 mars • Paris est bombardé par des avions allemands.

26 mars • Foch est nommé généralissime des forces alliées en France.

La république est proclamée en Allemagne

▶ 9 novembre 1918 ◀ L'aile droite du parti social-démocrate l'a emporté sur les révolutionnaires. La république est proclamée. Philipp Scheidemann, député social-démocrate modéré, l'annonce à une foule immense qui se presse devant le Parlement allemand, le Reichstag. Friedrich Ebert et Philipp Scheidemann forment un gouvernement et demandent l'armistice. L'empereur Guillaume II abdique et s'enfuit aux Pays-Bas. Le prince Max von Bade, dernier chancelier du Reich, est contraint à la démission.

Le succès de *Tarzan*

Immense succès le 27 janvier à la première de *Tarzan, seigneur des singes*. Le Tout-New York a applaudi Elmo Lincoln dans le premier rôle. Certes, le décor a plus à voir avec la Californie qu'avec la jungle africaine, mais personne ne s'en plaint.
Et, créée par le romancier Edgar Rice Burroughs, l'histoire de ce bébé perdu dans la jungle et élevé par des singes n'a pas fini de connaître la gloire.

14 points pour la paix

▶ 8 janvier 1918 ◀ Le président des États-Unis, Wilson, propose un plan pour les pourparlers entre les combattants. Il se présente en 14 points, dont les plus importants concernent les négociations entre les nations, la liberté de commerce et celle des mers, la réduction des armements, la restitution des territoires occupés, le règlement des litiges territoriaux selon le principe des nationalités.
Wilson propose aussi la création d'une Société des nations qui garantirait la paix.

1919

La création des Artistes associés

▶ **17 avril 1919** ◀ C'est un grand jour pour quatre des plus grandes stars de Hollywood. En effet, David W. Griffith, Charlie Chaplin, Mary Pickford et son mari, Douglas Fairbanks, viennent de fonder une nouvelle compagnie cinématographique. Elle s'appelle United Artists (Artistes associés). Grâce à elle, ils comptent distribuer leurs propres films. Ils entendent ainsi s'opposer aux grandes compagnies de Hollywood qui ont monopolisé jusqu'à présent la distribution des films et ont aussi pris l'habitude de payer à leurs stars des cachets fixés à l'avance, sans tenir compte des énormes profits qu'elles tirent ensuite de la projection des films. Les stars qui prennent ce pari risqué sont bien connues. Mary Pickford, actrice favorite des Américains, est aussi l'une des mieux payées. Douglas Fairbanks, héros flamboyant de films d'aventures, est très populaire. David W. Griffith est le réalisateur de *la Naissance d'une nation*. Quant à Charlie Chaplin, créateur de Charlot, il est célèbre dans le monde entier.

Muet hommage

Ce 11 novembre, pour le premier anniversaire de l'armistice, toute vie semble s'être arrêtée. Dans toutes les nations alliées, en effet, les populations ont arrêté le travail pour observer deux minutes de silence en hommage à tous les morts de la guerre. En France, le 11 novembre a été décrété jour national de deuil, et devient jour férié pour tous.

En 1919 aussi…

23 mars • Naissance en Italie du parti fasciste, fondé par Mussolini.

29 mars • Acquittement de Villain, l'assassin de Jaurès. À Paris, le 6 avril, 100 000 manifestants protestent contre ce verdict. Des officiers arrachent leurs décorations.

10 avril • Mort de Zapata. Le leader de la Révolution mexicaine a été assassiné.

▲ *Mary Pickford signe pour les Artistes associés, entourée de Fairbanks (à gauche), Chaplin (au centre), Griffith (le deuxième à droite) et leurs avocats.*

Le traité de Versailles

▶ **21 juin 1919** ◀ La guerre est officiellement terminée. Le traité de Versailles vient d'être signé par les représentants des nations engagées dans le conflit. Il fait 200 pages et a demandé cinq mois de négociations. L'Allemagne, jugée responsable, doit payer 20 milliards de marks-or à titre de réparations, et doit céder de nombreux territoires à la Pologne. Elle perd ses colonies. La Sarre, région d'Allemagne, passe sous le contrôle de la Société des nations pour quinze ans, et ses mines sont cédées à la France, qui récupère l'Alsace-Lorraine.

◀ *Les dirigeants alliés à Versailles.*

1910 – 1919

Gabriele D'Annunzio

Gabriele D'Annunzio vient de prendre possession de la ville de Fiume, le 12 septembre 1919, avec 300 volontaires. Fiume, sur la côte adriatique, fait partie des territoires que l'Italie revendique depuis toujours, mais qu'elle n'a pas obtenus au traité de Saint-Germain entre l'Autriche et les Alliés. D'Annunzio, héros de la Première Guerre mondiale, est un grand poète italien, connu pour son lyrisme et son nationalisme. Il a décidé d'obtenir lui-même ce que le pays n'a pu avoir légalement. Cette action d'éclat lui vaut l'admiration de tous les nationalistes italiens, mais il devra se retirer en 1920, à cause des pressions alliées.

◀ *Le poète D'Annunzio avec ses partisans.*

La flotte allemande se saborde

▶ **21 juin 1919** ◀ Toute la flotte allemande gît, à midi, au fond de l'eau. Quand elle s'est rendue, à la fin de la guerre, environ 70 navires avec leurs équipages furent conduits à la base navale britannique de Scapa Flow, au large de l'Écosse. À l'annonce de la signature du traité de Versailles, les équipages reçurent l'ordre de saborder leurs bateaux au lieu de se rendre. L'amiral allemand, qui commandait la flotte, affirme avoir obéi à un ordre donné au début de la guerre.

▲ *Un navire de guerre allemand coule à Scapa Flow, au large de l'Écosse.*

1ᵉʳ mai violent à Paris

▶ **1ᵉʳ mai 1919** ◀ Un mort et des centaines de blessés, parmi lesquels un député socialiste ayant reçu un coup de sabre, c'est le dramatique bilan des affrontements qui se déroulent à Paris. Les manifestants dressent des barricades et déferlent jusqu'au Palais-Bourbon. D'un côté, le gouvernement avait interdit cette manifestation. De l'autre, la C.G.T. (Confédération générale du travail) avait appelé les ouvriers à exiger la journée de huit heures.

Réaction nucléaire

▶ **1ᵉʳ juin 1919** ◀ Un atome d'azote vient d'être scindé en atomes d'oxygène et d'hydrogène, après avoir été bombardé à coups de particules. C'est une grande première. Elle vient d'être réalisée à l'université de Manchester, en Grande-Bretagne, par Ernest Rutherford, un physicien néo-zélandais, Prix Nobel de chimie en 1908.

▲ *Ernest Rutherford.*

Jusqu'aujourd'hui, les scientifiques étaient nombreux à considérer l'atome comme le plus petit corps existant. Il peut désormais être divisé.

Vol de Terre-Neuve à l'Irlande

▶ **14 juin 1919** ◀ Bières et sandwiches ont soutenu le moral de deux Anglais, le capitaine John Alcock et le lieutenant Arthur Brown, pendant les seize heures et douze minutes qu'a duré leur vol. Dans le brouillard et le grésil, ils ont rallié d'une seule traite Terre-Neuve à l'Irlande. Mais ils ont dû poser en catastrophe leur avion biplace. Cet exploit avait été tenté un mois avant par un Américain, Albert Read. Mais il avait dû faire étape aux Açores pour se ravitailler en carburant.

▼ *Alcock (au centre, avec la maquette de son avion) et Brown (à droite), après le vol.*

De 1920 à 1929

1920

Deux mondes s'entrechoquent en 1920. Celui de la vie facile et des nouvelles modes, et celui des trop pauvres qui ne peuvent participer à cette fête d'après guerre. En Europe et aux États-Unis, on se rue dans les cinémas et les dancings. Le jazz et le charleston font danser tout le monde.

Les femmes revendiquent l'égalité avec les hommes ; les Américains interdisent l'alcool. Ces années profitent d'un véritable boom économique, jusqu'à la crise de 1929, qui changera bien des choses.

La Prohibition
100 000 bars clandestins servent de l'alcool à New York (1929).
1 000 consommateurs sont morts pour avoir bu de l'alcool frelaté (chiffres officiels de 1929).

▲ Réussite assurée pour ce nouvel ustensile.

Du nouveau pour les cheveux !

Le nouveau sèche-cheveux électrique à main vient de sortir. Les risque-tout peuvent aussi essayer la permanente, qui métamorphose les cheveux les plus raides en belles boucles ondulées. Et si vous voulez changer de couleur de cheveux, rien de plus facile, il existe désormais des teintures synthétiques.

▼ La violence de la guerre des gangs a été immortalisée par de nombreux films.

La Prohibition

▶ **16 janvier 1920** ◀

Adieu les saloons ! À partir de ce jour, à 12 h 01, tout Américain qui voudra porter un toast à la santé de la nouvelle décennie ne trouvera rien à boire de plus étourdissant qu'un verre d'eau. Désormais, en effet, comme le veut le 18e amendement de la Constitution américaine, il est strictement interdit de fabriquer, de transporter ou de vendre la moindre boisson alcoolisée.

C'est le début de la Prohibition et un jour de triomphe pour toutes les associations religieuses qui ont fait campagne pendant des années pour l'interdiction de l'alcool. Des États avaient déjà voté des lois en ce sens ; c'est le cas de l'État du Maine dès 1851, suivi par 26 autres États depuis 1917.

De nombreuses personnes craignent que cette interdiction n'entraîne les gens à aller boire dans des bars clandestins. Dans des villes comme Chicago, on sait que les gangsters qui règnent sur la prostitution organisent déjà la fabrication et la vente illégales de boissons alcoolisées. Ce qui va leur rapporter gros. Jim Colosimo, Johnny Torrio et Al Capone, dit Scarface (le Balafré), sont sur le coup. Étant donné que d'énormes profits sont en jeu, les gangsters vont se battre sans merci pour prendre le contrôle du trafic d'alcool et éliminer les gangs rivaux, entraînant les grandes villes d'Amérique dans une spirale de violence.

▲ Des fonctionnaires américains vident des tonneaux de bière.

Des bébés coûte que coûte

▶ **31 juillet 1920** ◀

Contrairement à ce qui s'est passé dans les autres pays d'Europe, la natalité française n'a pas repris après la guerre. Pour enrayer cette chute des naissances qui fait de la France un des pays au plus faible taux de natalité (nombre de naissances pour 1 000 habitants), la Chambre des députés interdit la contraception et en punit la publicité. L'avortement devient un délit et est réprimé par de très lourdes peines de prison.

La première assemblée de la SDN

▶ **11 février 1920** ◀ La première assemblée de la Société des nations (SDN) se tient aujourd'hui à Londres. Elle a été créée pour trancher les différends entre les nations et veiller au maintien de la paix. Des hommes d'État représentant la Grande-Bretagne, la France, le Japon, l'Italie, la Belgique, l'Espagne, le Brésil et la Grèce y participent, mais il n'y a aucune délégation des États-Unis. Ils ont voté contre leur participation à la SDN, car ils ne veulent pas intervenir dans les affaires des autres nations. Les critiques disent que, sans les États-Unis, la SDN ne sera pas assez puissante pour imposer la paix.

▲ *Les membres de la Société des nations en session à Genève, au début de l'année 20.*

La famine en Russie

▶ **Mars 1920** ◀ La famine ravage la Russie. La guerre civile a anéanti l'activité agricole, d'autant plus qu'en pratiquant une politique de réquisition des récoltes les bolcheviques se sont mis à dos une grande partie de la paysannerie. Ne pouvant plus profiter du fruit de leur travail, les paysans ont cessé de semer. On estime qu'il y a au moins 13 millions de personnes qui souffrent de la faim aujourd'hui sur l'ensemble du territoire de l'ancien Empire russe. Déjà, l'année dernière, on a dénombré 22 millions d'affamés, que le pouvoir n'a pu aider.

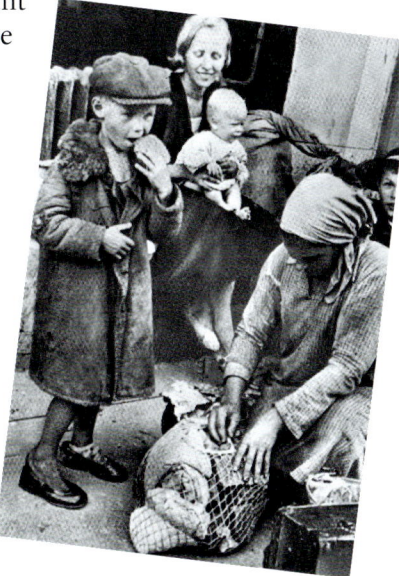

Gains au base-ball

78 000 dollars : c'est la petite fortune que va empocher la star du base-ball américain, Babe Ruth, dont le véritable nom est George Herman Ruth. Pour cette coquette somme, ce joueur de 26 ans, appartenant aux Red Sox de Boston, va rejoindre l'équipe des Yankees de New York. Il a permis à son ancienne équipe de remporter les trophées du base-ball en 1915, 1916 et 1918.

▶ *Babe Ruth est la star incontestée du base-ball.*

Les débuts de la radio

▶ **2 novembre 1920** ◀ Pour la première fois, les résultats d'une élection ont été annoncés par la radio. Il s'agit de l'élection présidentielle, aux États-Unis. C'est Warren Harding qui a gagné. Deux journalistes l'ont annoncé à tout le pays depuis une station basée à Pittsburgh, la KDKA. Il n'y avait qu'un millier d'auditeurs pour les entendre, mais l'intérêt pour la radio ne fait que croître, et le prix de vente des postes est en baisse constante.

▲ *Le siège de la station de radio KDKA.*

Les tests de Rorschach

▶ **Décembre 1920** ◀ Le psychiatre suisse Hermann Rorschach a trouvé une nouvelle façon de faire réagir ses patients. Il leur montre des taches d'encre. Ils doivent lui dire tout ce qui leur passe par la tête en les observant, et tout ce que ces formes leur suggèrent. Il compare leurs réponses à d'autres, qu'il a précédemment analysées. Il affirme qu'elles lui permettent de mieux comprendre divers troubles mentaux.

1920

Les traités de paix

▲ *Les négociateurs des traités veulent réduire les risques de guerre, en attribuant un État à chaque nationalité.*

▶ **4 juin 1920** ◀ La carte de l'Europe a été redessinée. C'est la conséquence des traités signés à la fin de la Grande Guerre. En ce jour, la Hongrie signe avec les Alliés le traité de Trianon, par lequel elle perd la Slovaquie au profit de la Tchécoslovaquie, et la Transylvanie, qui revient à la Roumanie.

L'an passé, l'Autriche a dû renoncer à plus de la moitié de ce qui constituait l'Empire austro-hongrois, démantelé par le traité de Saint-Germain (10 septembre). Deux pays ont alors été créés de toutes pièces, la Tchécoslovaquie et la Yougoslavie, réunissant Serbes, Croates et Slovènes.

La Bulgarie a perdu une partie de ses territoires, au profit du nouveau Royaume serbo-croate et de la Grèce, l'année dernière, lors du traité de Neuilly (27 novembre). La Pologne est devenue un pays indépendant.

Les négociateurs espèrent supprimer toute nouvelle cause de conflit, en satisfaisant les revendications nationales. Mais des tensions subsistent ; de nombreuses minorités demeurent sous la dépendance d'autres nationalités.

Création des robots

Les robots ont été créés pour les besoins de la nouvelle pièce *R.U.R. (Robots universels de Rossum)* du dramaturge tchèque Karel Čapek. Il en fait des ouvriers et leur invente un nom, « robots », à partir du mot tchèque *robota,* qui signifie « travail forcé ». Ses robots conquièrent le monde, après s'être révoltés contre leurs créateurs.

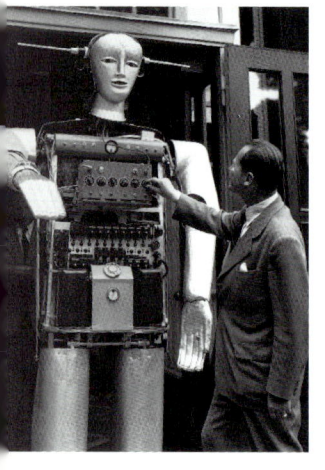

▲ *Le dernier sultan, Mehmed VI, dans un défilé.*

La fin de l'Empire ottoman

▶ **10 août 1920** ◀ C'est aujourd'hui la fin de l'Empire ottoman. Au XVIe siècle, il s'étendait sur une grande partie de l'Europe balkanique, le nord de l'Afrique et l'ensemble du Moyen-Orient. Par le traité de Sèvres, les Turcs signent la perte des quatre cinquièmes du territoire de l'Empire. La Grèce récupère les îles de la mer Égée, la province de Thrace et le port de Smyrne. Des Turcs guidés par Atatürk refusent ce traité et jurent de ne jamais céder les territoires où les Turcs sont majoritaires.

Le premier roman d'Agatha Christie

Hercule Poirot est un détective belge. Il a une tête en forme d'œuf et une grosse moustache soigneusement peignée. Il est le héros de *la mystérieuse affaire de styles (The Mysterious Affair of Styles)*, un roman policier écrit par l'Anglaise Agatha Christie. Il aide son ami, le capitaine Arthur Hastings, à résoudre le meurtre d'une certaine Emily Inglethorp. Les poisons n'ont pas de secret pour Agatha Christie : durant la guerre de 1914-1918, elle a préparé des médicaments au dispensaire d'un hôpital, et connaît donc tout sur leur composition. Son livre vient d'être publié aux États-Unis.

◀ *Agatha Christie, reine du mystère.*

1920 – 1929

Le Cabinet du docteur Caligari

▶ **27 février 1920** ◀ Meurtres et terreur entretiennent un oppressant suspense dans *le Cabinet du docteur Caligari*, un film de l'Allemand Robert Wiene. Tout Berlin en a frissonné. Rien ici ne renvoie au monde réel. Les intérieurs présentent des angles bizarres et les meubles sont déformés. Ce film est une œuvre caractéristique de l'expressionnisme. C'est un mouvement artistique qui met l'accent sur des visions et des émotions exagérées, et même déformées, qui n'ont rien à voir avec la réalité. Les décorateurs ont privilégié les obliques et dénaturé les choses, afin d'accentuer l'effroi et de donner au film son atmosphère trouble qui inquiète et terrorise le spectateur. L'art expressionniste a influencé de nombreux films d'épouvante allemands, mais aussi, quelques années plus tard, hollywoodiens.

▲ *Le matador Joselito avait révolutionné la tauromachie.*

Mort du matador Joselito

L'Espagne est en deuil. Joselito est mort dans les arènes de Talavera de la Reina. C'était le plus grand matador du monde. Il a fini ses jours en toréant. Né en 1895, de son vrai nom José Gomez Ortega, il avait imposé un nouveau style, très audacieux, dans l'arène. Jamais matador avant lui n'avait en effet laissé le taureau l'approcher d'aussi près, pour l'esquiver au dernier moment, avant de lui porter le coup d'épée mortel.

▶ *Le Cabinet du docteur Caligari est un film étrange, « sorti de l'imagination d'un fou ».*

En 1920 aussi …

17 janvier • Paul Deschanel est élu président de la République en France.

16 mai • Jeanne d'Arc est canonisée, à Rome, par le pape Benoît XV.

23 septembre • Alexandre Millerand devient président de la République en France.

16 novembre • Défaite de l'armée blanche de Wrangel en Russie, ce qui met fin à la guerre civile.

Droit de vote pour les femmes

▶ **26 août 1920** ◀ Elles peuvent se réjouir. Celles qui ont tant lutté pour le suffrage des femmes – d'où leur surnom de suffragettes – ont enfin gagné. Le secrétaire d'État américain signe ce jour les directives concernant le 19e amendement de la Constitution qui confère aux femmes le droit de voter.

Les Américaines réclament ce droit depuis soixante-dix ans. Élisabeth Stanton, vétéran de la lutte antiesclavagiste, fut la première à exiger, en 1848, une convention sur les droits de la femme. Aujourd'hui, les militantes du monde entier savourent cette avancée vers l'égalité des droits.

▲ *Les suffragettes célèbrent leur victoire.*

1921

Triomphe de Charlie Chaplin

▶ **6 janvier 1921** ◀ Triomphe pour *le Kid*. C'est le premier long métrage de l'acteur britannique Charlie Chaplin. Il a inventé le personnage de Charlot, petit homme portant chapeau melon, canne et pantalon fatigué. C'est l'un des films les plus coûteux jamais réalisés.

L'affiche prévient qu'il s'agit d'« un film qui prête à rire et peut-être à pleurer ». Et il est vrai qu'il émeut, notamment dans une scène mémorable et touchante, celle où Charlot le vagabond s'endort et rêve du paradis. Tous les personnages, y compris les policiers qui le persécutent, se sont métamorphosés en anges.

Charlot est un innocent dans un monde plein d'embûches. Sa nature confiante semble toujours l'entraîner dans des difficultés sans fin. De son costume, Chaplin a dit : « Je voulais en faire une caricature de l'homme arrivé – la canne, emblème de sa dignité, la moustache, de sa vanité, les bottines, de ses soucis. »

Chaplin est né à Londres en 1889. Plus tard, il fera des tournées aux États-Unis dans un spectacle de music-hall et signera un engagement à Hollywood avec Mac Sennett. C'est sous sa direction qu'il fera ses débuts en tant qu'acteur, en 1913.

◀ *Charlie Chaplin avec Jackie Coogan, dans* le Kid.

N°5 de Chanel

Un grand parfum est né. *N°5* est son nom. C'est le nombre fétiche de sa créatrice, la couturière Coco Chanel. Non contente de lancer un parfum, celle-ci change la vie des femmes. Elle leur offre la liberté de mouvement en jetant les corsets aux orties, en raccourcissant les robes, et en lançant la mode des chaussures à talons plats. Elle a débuté à la fin de la guerre de 1914-1918, en concevant des modèles de vêtements féminins.

▼ *Manifestation en faveur de Sacco et Vanzetti.*

Sacco et Vanzetti condamnés à mort

▶ **14 juillet 1921** ◀ C'est l'indignation générale, aux États-Unis comme dans le monde entier. Un jury de Dedham, dans le Massachusetts, vient de prononcer, cette nuit, une condamnation à mort. Elle concerne Nicola Sacco et Bartolomeo Vanzetti, deux hommes d'origine italienne, et a été prononcée sans qu'aucune preuve ne soit venue étayer l'accusation. L'an dernier, un garde et le caissier d'une usine de chaussures avaient été tués, et la paie des ouvriers, volée. Sacco et Vanzetti faisaient des coupables rêvés aux yeux des conservateurs : ils étaient connus pour leurs idées anarchistes.

L'autonomie de l'Irlande du Sud

▶ **6 décembre 1921** ◀ Un traité signé à Londres fait de l'Irlande un État libre. Mais cette indépendance ne concerne pas toute l'île. Les six comtés de l'Irlande du Nord, qui forment l'Ulster, restent rattachés au Royaume-Uni. Le traité met fin à deux années de guerre entre les autorités britanniques et l'Armée républicaine irlandaise (IRA). Ceux qui ont lutté pour l'unité du pays, tels les membres du Sinn Féin (voir photos ci-dessous), sont déçus. Les députés au Parlement de l'Ulster doivent prêter serment à la Couronne britannique.

◀ *Eamon De Valera.*

▶ *Michael Collins et Arthur Griffith.*

1920 – 1929

Jeux féminins mondiaux

Des Jeux féminins mondiaux viennent de se dérouler à Monte-Carlo, en signe de protestation : les jeux Olympiques sont interdits aux femmes. Le baron Pierre de Coubertin, président du Comité international olympique ne veut pas de femmes dans les stades. Il trouve qu'elles doivent se contenter de la natation et du tennis, épreuves qu'elles peuvent disputer depuis les Jeux de 1900. Il s'appuie sur le fait que, dans l'Antiquité, les Grecques n'avaient même pas le droit de regarder les hommes concourir, sous peine de mort. Aussi est-il déterminé à les interdire de pistes et de compétitions.

▲ *Le départ du 50 m aux Jeux féminins mondiaux, gagné par l'Anglaise Miss Lines.*

Le gratte-ciel de verre

Il est tout de transparence, cet immeuble de bureaux que vient de construire, à Berlin, l'architecte allemand Ludwig Mies van der Rohe. On l'a déjà nommé « le gratte-ciel de cristal ». Il y a deux ans, l'architecte a concouru pour la réalisation de cette tour. Il a remporté le marché avec un projet de bâtiment en forme de prisme utilisant le verre et l'acier.

Mongolie libre ?

▶ **10 juillet 1921** ◀ La Mongolie-Extérieure n'est désormais plus aux mains de la Chine. Les rênes du pouvoir ont été pris par l'Armée rouge. Les Soviétiques sont venus apporter leur aide aux Mongols, quand l'armée blanche, après sa défaite contre les communistes dans la guerre civile de 1918-1920 qui les opposait en Russie, a envahi la Mongolie. L'armée avait pris la capitale, Ourga, et commis de nombreuses atrocités. La Mongolie-Intérieure demeure chinoise.

▲ *Une jeune Mongole portant la coiffe traditionnelle.*

En 1921 aussi ...

Du 7 au 17 mars • En Russie, révolte des marins de la base navale de Cronstadt. Trotski la fait écraser.

12 mars • Le traité de Riga met fin à la guerre russo-polonaise.

10 décembre • Le prix Nobel de physique est attribué à l'Allemand Albert Einstein.

29 décembre • William Mackenzie King devient Premier ministre du Canada.

▲ *La maquette du gratte-ciel de verre.*

L'insuline

▶ **27 juillet 1921** ◀ L'espoir naît pour les malades souffrant de diabète, grâce à deux chercheurs de l'université de Toronto, au Canada, Frederick Banting et Charles Best. Les diabétiques ne produisent pas d'insuline, une hormone qui contrôle la quantité de sucre dans le sang. Si le taux de sucre s'élève trop, ou s'il descend trop bas, cela peut devenir très dangereux. Le malade peut être pris de paralysie, et parfois même perdre la vue. Charles Best et Frederick Banting ont réussi à extraire l'insuline du pancréas des chiens. Et à soigner, grâce à cette insuline, d'autres chiens atteints de diabète. Ils espèrent pouvoir appliquer ce traitement aux humains.

▲ *Charles Best.*

▼ *Frederick Banting.*

Lutte contre la tuberculose

▶ **18 juillet 1921** ◀ Le vaccin contre la tuberculose est né. Il a été mis au point à l'Institut Pasteur par Albert Calmette et Camille Guérin. On le nomme B.C.G., du nom du bacille bilié de Calmette-Guérin, un bacille tuberculeux bovin atténué. Il est le résultat des recherches que les deux savants – le premier est bactériologiste, le second est vétérinaire – ont menées sur la tuberculose bovine. Ils ont vacciné avec succès un nourrisson dont la mère est tuberculeuse. Cette maladie infectieuse très contagieuse, affectant les poumons, est due au bacille de Koch. Elle fait des ravages et est très souvent mortelle. Il faut espérer que la vaccination va se généraliser et que chacun pourra être protégé.

1922

Découverte de la tombe de Toutankhamon

▶ **30 novembre 1922** ◀ Deux archéologues britanniques, Howard Carter et lord Carnavon, viennent de découvrir une tombe royale en Égypte. Elle est vieille de 3 000 ans et renferme des trésors. Le tombeau qu'ils ont ouvert est celui de Toutankhamon, pharaon égyptien qui mourut en 1346 av. J.-C. La tombe est située dans la Vallée des rois, près de Louxor, en Haute-Égypte. Elle est composée de plusieurs salles, qui précèdent la chambre funéraire elle-même. Dans celle-ci gît le corps de Toutankhamon, embaumé et momifié, enfermé dans trois sarcophages. Un masque d'or lui couvre la tête. Il porte le *némès*, coiffure du pharaon à sa mort. Plusieurs pièces de joaillerie étaient placées dans le sarcophage et retenues par les bandelettes qui enserrent la momie.

Les autres chambres renferment, pêle-mêle, des armes, des coffres, des lits, des chaises, des lampes, des statues et même un char. Une coupe d'albâtre présente le jeune pharaon comme une blanche fleur de lotus. L'inscription exprime l'espoir que Toutankhamon pourra passer « des millions d'années assis, le visage effleuré par une brise fraîche, les yeux emplis de bonheur ».

Toutankhamon mourut à 18 ans. Gendre du grand pharaon Akhenaton, qui voulut instituer le culte d'un seul dieu, Aton, il restaura, durant son très court règne, le pouvoir des prêtres d'Amon. Totalement inconnu des historiens, il est en passe de devenir, grâce à cette découverte, le plus célèbre souverain d'Égypte.

▲ *La momie de Toutankhamon repose dans un sarcophage en or.*

La malédiction du pharaon

▶ **Novembre 1922** ◀ Des rumeurs circulent à propos d'une ancienne malédiction que Howard Carter et lord Carnavon auraient ravivée en venant perturber le repos de Toutankhamon. L'Égypte est terre de légendes surnaturelles, et beaucoup de gens croient dur comme fer que les archéologues ont réveillé la puissante malédiction qui s'abat sur ceux qui osent troubler le royaume des morts. De vieilles inscriptions menacent de catastrophes « les vivants qui violent les tombes ». Carter et Carnavon ont cherché ce tombeau dix ans durant et étaient sur le point de renoncer. Maintenant qu'ils l'ont découvert, ils s'apprêtent à le fouiller avec un soin minutieux.

L'Égypte
Les premières momies datent de 2 500 ans av. J.-C.
•
Les organes vitaux des morts étaient déposés dans des récipients appelés vases canopes.
•
Non loin de la pyramide de Khéops a été exhumée une barque solaire. Elle permettait au pharaon d'accompagner le dieu Râ dans sa course solaire. C'est la plus ancienne embarcation du monde.

▶ *L'archéologue Howard Carter surveille les fouilles.*

1920 – 1929

Nosferatu le Vampire

Tous les records de fréquentation ont été battus par un nouveau film d'horreur, réalisé par le cinéaste allemand F. W. Murnau. Il s'agit de *Nosferatu le Vampire*, qui met en scène la terrible histoire d'un vampire, effrayant et pitoyable cadavre vivant condamné à se repaître du sang des humains. Murnau s'est inspiré, sans en avoir le droit, du livre *Dracula* de l'écrivain irlandais Bram Stoker, paru en 1897, et a changé le nom de son vampire en Nosferatu.

◀ *Nosferatu, joué par Max Schreck, doit éviter la lumière du jour, qui lui est fatale.*

▲ *La centrale de l'Ontario utilise de l'eau pour fournir de l'électricité.*

La plus grande centrale hydroélectrique du monde

▶ **Décembre 1922** ◀ Le plus grand barrage du monde a été inauguré. Il s'agit de la centrale hydroélectrique de Queenston-Chippawa, sur la rivière Niagara, dans l'État d'Ontario, au Canada. Elle va produire de l'électricité, grâce à l'énergie fournie par la chute de l'eau qui actionne une turbine pour produire du courant électrique. Le site du Niagara est l'un des plus propices à l'installation de ce type de centrale, grâce à des chutes qui tombent d'une hauteur de 60 m.

La première centrale hydroélectrique vit le jour de l'autre côté de la frontière, aux États-Unis, à Buffalo, dans l'État de New York. Une seconde centrale fut construite sur la rive canadienne des chutes du Niagara. Elle produisit de l'électricité pour la ville voisine, Toronto, dès novembre 1906.

▲ *Les Français signent le traité de Washington.*

Limitation des armements

▶ **6 février 1922** ◀ La course aux armements qui avait débuté à la fin de la guerre de 1914-1918 vient de prendre fin. Des délégations de France, de Grande-Bretagne, d'Italie, du Japon et des États-Unis signent aujourd'hui, à Washington, un accord garantissant que ces pays ne construiront plus ni cuirassés, ni croiseurs, dans les dix années qui viennent. Le traité limite les navires de guerre de chaque pays. Ceux qui dépasseront les quotas accordés devront détruire leurs bateaux.

Accords entre la Russie et l'Allemagne

▶ **16 avril 1922** ◀ Pendant la conférence de Gênes (Italie), l'Allemagne et la Russie soviétique concluent une alliance commerciale et diplomatique. Elles signent un traité à Rapallo qui prévoit que les deux États peuvent coopérer dans les domaines économique et militaire, et qu'ils peuvent s'entendre avant de négocier avec les autres États. Les autres Européens présents, comme le Britannique Lloyd George et le Français Barthou, se sentent exclus et n'arrivent pas à se mettre d'accord sur le montant des réparations que l'Allemagne doit payer.

▲ *Lloyd George et Barthou.*

1922

Nouvelle mode étudiante

Les étudiants anglo-saxons ont adopté un nouveau style de pantalon aux jambes flottantes. Et ils l'ont imposé, au point que l'on ne parle plus désormais que des « sacs d'Oxford ». Consécration suprême, ces « sacs » sont portés par le prince de Galles. Avec cravate voyante, chaussures en daim, casquette ou chapeau mou, la nouvelle tenue fait fureur.

▲ La mode est aux « sacs d'Oxford ».

Naissance de Radiola et de la BBC

Radiola émet pour la première fois en France au mois de novembre. Presque en même temps, la BBC vient de naître en Grande-Bretagne. Radiola appartient à un fabricant d'appareils radio implanté à Levallois, tout près de Paris. Les programmes sont variés, mêlant nouvelles, causeries et musique.

Niels Bohr, prix Nobel de physique

▶ **10 décembre 1922** ◀ Niels Bohr, un scientifique danois, vient de recevoir le prix Nobel de physique pour ses découvertes sur la structure de l'atome. On a toujours pensé que l'atome était la plus petite particule de matière possible et qu'il ne pouvait pas être divisé. Bohr s'est appuyé sur les recherches du physicien néo-zélandais Ernest Rutherford, qui a soutenu que chaque atome est constitué d'un noyau central autour duquel gravitent des électrons, à l'instar des planètes tournant autour du Soleil dans le système solaire. Il affirme que les électrons peuvent passer d'une orbite à l'autre, en libérant une énorme charge d'énergie. Il a développé cette théorie dès 1913, mais le monde scientifique n'était pas prêt alors à la reconnaître.

▼ *Le physicien danois Niels Bohr a fait progresser les connaissances sur la structure de l'atome.*

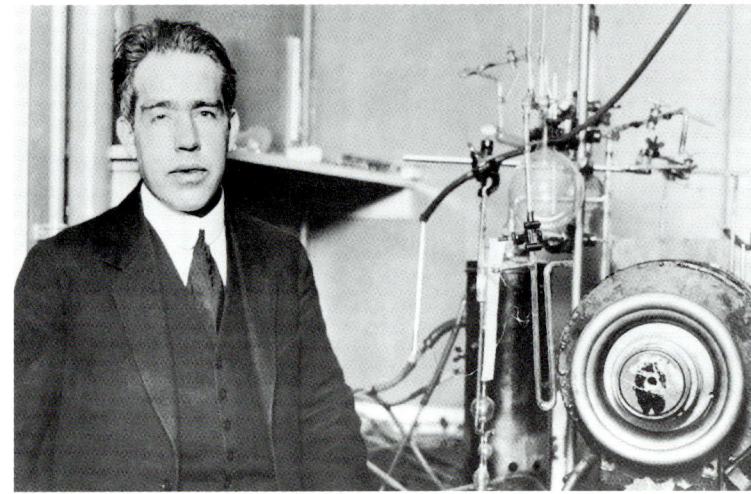

En 1922 aussi...

28 février • *Fin du protectorat anglais sur l'Égypte. Fouad Ier devient roi de cet État indépendant.*

27 mars • *Staline devient secrétaire général du parti communiste en Russie.*

30 décembre • *Russie, Biélorussie, Ukraine et Transcaucasie fondent l'Union des Républiques socialistes soviétiques (URSS).*

La « garçonne »

Ce nouveau type de femme a envahi les rues des grandes villes. On l'appelle la « garçonne ». Elle met du rouge à lèvres, n'hésite pas à fumer une cigarette ou à boire un verre, et s'habille comme ça lui plaît. Elle a raccourci ses robes, montre ses chevilles et ses mollets. Elle a les cheveux coupés au carré, mais les cache sous un chapeau cloche. Les femmes se sont émancipées au cours de la Première Guerre mondiale, car elles ont dû travailler pour remplacer les hommes qui étaient à la guerre. Elles ont prouvé leur valeur. Dorénavant, elles veulent avoir droit à la parole et profiter de la vie dans tous les domaines. La vieille génération a du mal à accepter ce changement.

◀ *La « garçonne » choque l'ancienne génération.*

1920 – 1929

La marche sur Rome

▶ **30 octobre 1922** ◀ Mussolini vient de réussir son pari. Il menaçait de faire un coup de force, si le gouvernement ne mettait pas fin aux activités de l'extrême gauche en Italie. Il a mobilisé ses partisans : 24 000 Chemises noires, hommes débraillés, braillards et déterminés. Ils ont entamé une marche sur Rome. Ils ne sont guère dangereux, et le gouvernement, qui dispose de 26 000 hommes, ne fait rien contre eux. Le roi Victor-Emmanuel III demande à Mussolini de former un gouvernement et le nomme Premier ministre. Benito Mussolini a fondé les Faisceaux italiens de combat – *Fasci italiani di combattimento* – en 1919, pour combattre le socialisme. Il a obtenu le soutien financier d'industriels inquiets de la montée des mouvements de grève. L'année dernière, il s'est proclamé Duce, c'est-à-dire guide tout-puissant des fascistes.

▲ *Mussolini inspecte les troupes fascistes.*

Mort du dernier castrat

▶ **21 avril 1922** ◀ Alessandro Moreschi, le dernier castrat vivant, vient de mourir à 63 ans. Il avait une des plus exceptionnelles voix du monde. Les castrats étaient des chanteurs que l'on castrait avant la puberté, afin de leur conserver la voix cristalline et aiguë de leur jeunesse.

Cette pratique est née en Italie au milieu du XVIe siècle. Elle consistait à déviriliser de jeunes garçons de 6 à 8 ans, remarqués dans les chœurs des églises, tel celui de la chapelle Sixtine, au Vatican où l'on chantait pour le pape. Les premiers castrats ont fait leur entrée à la Sixtine autour de 1565. Mais ils ont aussi tenu de grands rôles, créés pour eux, dans des opéras. C'est le cas de César dans le *Jules César* de Haendel, et d'Orphée dans *Orphée et Eurydice* de Gluck.

Moreschi était né à Montecompatri, près de Rome, en 1858. De 1883 à 1913, il a fait partie du chœur de la chapelle Sixtine. En 1902 et 1903, il a enregistré quelques disques qui illustrent la pureté de ton et la grande échelle de sons que peut utiliser une voix de castrat.

▲ *Alessandro Moreschi, le dernier castrat.*

Mort de l'écrivain Marcel Proust à Paris

▶ **18 novembre 1922** ◀ Marcel Proust est mort aujourd'hui, à Paris. Avec lui disparaît un très grand romancier, auteur d'un chef-d'œuvre en sept parties : *À la recherche du temps perdu*. Dans ce roman, écrit à la première personne, l'auteur étudie minutieusement les facettes des rapports mondains, la société des salons de son temps et la psychologie de ses contemporains. Le premier tome de sa saga, achevé en 1912 et intitulé *Du côté de chez Swann*, a été publié à compte d'auteur, car il avait été refusé par la plupart des éditeurs. Le deuxième tome, *À l'ombre des jeunes filles en fleurs*, a reçu, lui, le prix Goncourt, il y a trois ans.

Johnny Weissmuller bat le record du monde

100 m en moins d'une minute, c'est une grande première au monde. Cet exploit a été réalisé par un nageur de 18 ans, Johnny Weissmuller. 58,6 secondes, c'est le nouveau record établi par ce garçon originaire de Roumanie, mais dont la famille est venue s'installer à Chicago – États-Unis – en 1908.

▶ *Johnny Weissmuller a battu quatre records du monde.*

▲ *Beaucoup d'Américains, abusés par* la Guerre des mondes *à la radio, décident de se défendre contre les envahisseurs martiens.*

LA RADIO

La radio a commencé sous forme de « télégraphie sans fil », ou TSF à la fin des années 1890, grâce à l'Italien Guglielmo Marconi. En 1899, le quotidien *New York Herald* le finance pour qu'il diffuse des commentaires sur les péripéties de l'America's Cup, en la suivant depuis un bateau.

Des innovations techniques permettent de perfectionner les postes de réception. Entre les deux guerres, la TSF conquiert des millions de foyers dans le monde et devient l'une des plus importantes sources d'information.

▼ *L'acteur Orson Welles dirigeant* la Guerre des mondes, *sur CBS, Columbia Broadcasting Systems.*

Une émission cause la panique

31 octobre 1938. Les Martiens débarquent, dans le New Jersey (États-Unis), à la conquête de la planète Terre. Des gens se jettent sur les routes et s'enfuient. Ils viennent d'être avertis de cette invasion par une émission de radio qui transmet les nouvelles de minute en minute.

En fait, la CBS a programmé *la Guerre des mondes*, un roman de H.G. Wells que le comédien Orson Welles fait jouer de manière très réaliste !

La radio

Les découvertes du Français Édouard Branly et de l'Allemand Heinrich Hertz sont à l'origine de l'invention de la télégraphie sans fil par Marconi.

•

La première transmission radio, à partir de la tour Eiffel, a eu lieu en 1921.

•

À tout moment, le nombre de taches solaires affecte le trajet parcouru par les ondes radio autour de la Terre.

La guerre des ondes

Au cours de la Seconde Guerre mondiale, la radio devient une arme de propagande. La BBC, qui émet de Londres, débute ses émissions vers l'étranger par les premières notes de la *Cinquième Symphonie* de Beethoven. Elles correspondent, en morse, aux signaux sonores de la lettre V, symbole de la victoire. En France, les civils écoutent Radio-Londres qui émet de 20 à 22 heures. Les speakers Maurice Schumann ou Pierre Dac, qui sont à Londres avec le général de Gaulle, les informent de l'évolution des combats et transmettent des messages pour la Résistance intérieure. Les civils des pays occupés risquent leur vie en les écoutant. Les nazis eux aussi font de la propagande. Ils essayent de démoraliser les Anglais et les troupes américaines du Pacifique avec de fausses informations, mais ils ne sont pas crus. Ils utilisaient les services d'un traître anglais appelé « lord Haw-Haw » et ceux d'une speakerine surnommée « la rose de Tokyo ».

▶ « *Lord Haw-Haw* » *(en haut, à gauche). Charles de Gaulle (ci-dessus) s'adresse à la France résistante depuis Londres, au micro de la BBC. La « rose de Tokyo » (à droite).*

Tout se vend sur les ondes

La réclame sur les ondes est d'abord un sujet de controverses, mais, à la fin des années 20, de nombreuses stations américaines en font leur principale source de revenus. Elle subventionne les émissions les plus populaires. Lorsqu'une actrice, par exemple, donne ses secrets de maquillage pour le compte d'une société de produits de beauté, des centaines d'auditeurs s'intéressent subitement à ces produits. Les politiciens eux aussi ont rapidement exploité cet accès direct à l'auditeur. Hitler a su utiliser ce moyen de communication.

▶ *Pour les New-Yorkais, la « reine de la radio » est une déesse de la mode.*

1923

République en Turquie

▶ 29 octobre 1923 ◀

Aujourd'hui, Mustafa Kemal proclame la république en Turquie et se nomme lui-même président. Général, il est le leader des nationalistes turcs et commande l'armée, qui, l'année dernière, a chassé les Grecs de Smyrne. Après la défaite de la Turquie dans la Grande Guerre et la perte des territoires à minorité turque de l'Empire ottoman, Mustafa Kemal était déterminé à conserver l'Asie Mineure dans son intégrité, comme fondement d'un nouvel État. Au traité de Lausanne qui mit fin, l'an passé, au conflit gréco-turc, il a réussi, tout en récupérant la Thrace orientale, Constantinople et les détroits, à faire reconnaître les nouvelles frontières de la Turquie. Le traité prévoyait aussi l'échange des populations grecques de Turquie et turques de Grèce. En conséquence, un million de réfugiés de langue grecque vont, entre 1923 et 1925, s'installer en Grèce, tandis que des Turcs, deux fois moins nombreux, vont être placés dans les villages d'Anatolie désertés par les Grecs. Le traité a également aboli la création, récente, des États d'Anatolie et du Kurdistan.

Mustafa Kemal
Pour renforcer sa politique Mustafa Kemal invite ses concitoyens à adopter un nom de famille turc. Il donne l'exemple en prenant celui d'Atatürk, c'est-à-dire « père des Turcs ».

• Atatürk interdit le port du fez. Il abolit la polygamie et impose le mariage civil.

◀ *Mustafa Kemal, le fondateur de la République turque. Il interdit le port du voile pour les femmes.*

Succès du Milky Way

Succès aux États-Unis pour une barre chocolatée qui vient tout juste d'être mise en vente. Sa mise au point a demandé trois ans. Ce chocolat au lait malté a reçu le nom de Milky Way.

Marathons de danse aux États-Unis

Séduits par la promesse de prix importants, femmes et hommes se lancent, aux États-Unis, dans de véritables marathons de danse et rêvent d'arriver en tête. Mais cet espoir peut tourner au cauchemar. Les candidats dansent souvent jusqu'à l'épuisement.

▼ *Danseurs à Washington, après quarante heures de compétition.*

La guerre des ondes

Au cours de la Seconde Guerre mondiale, la radio devient une arme de propagande. La BBC, qui émet de Londres, débute ses émissions vers l'étranger par les premières notes de la *Cinquième Symphonie* de Beethoven. Elles correspondent, en morse, aux signaux sonores de la lettre V, symbole de la victoire. En France, les civils écoutent Radio-Londres qui émet de 20 à 22 heures. Les speakers Maurice Schumann ou Pierre Dac, qui sont à Londres avec le général de Gaulle, les informent de l'évolution des combats et transmettent des messages pour la Résistance intérieure. Les civils des pays occupés risquent leur vie en les écoutant. Les nazis eux aussi font de la propagande. Ils essayent de démoraliser les Anglais et les troupes américaines du Pacifique avec de fausses informations, mais ils ne sont pas crus. Ils utilisaient les services d'un traître anglais appelé « lord Haw-Haw » et ceux d'une speakerine surnommée « la rose de Tokyo ».

▶ « Lord Haw-Haw » (en haut, à gauche). Charles de Gaulle (ci-dessus) s'adresse à la France résistante depuis Londres, au micro de la BBC. La « rose de Tokyo » (à droite).

Tout se vend sur les ondes

La réclame sur les ondes est d'abord un sujet de controverses, mais, à la fin des années 20, de nombreuses stations américaines en font leur principale source de revenus. Elle subventionne les émissions les plus populaires. Lorsqu'une actrice, par exemple, donne ses secrets de maquillage pour le compte d'une société de produits de beauté, des centaines d'auditeurs s'intéressent subitement à ces produits. Les politiciens eux aussi ont rapidement exploité cet accès direct à l'auditeur. Hitler a su utiliser ce moyen de communication.

▶ Pour les New-Yorkais, la « reine de la radio » est une déesse de la mode.

1923

République en Turquie

29 octobre 1923

Aujourd'hui, Mustafa Kemal proclame la république en Turquie et se nomme lui-même président. Général, il est le leader des nationalistes turcs et commande l'armée, qui, l'année dernière, a chassé les Grecs de Smyrne. Après la défaite de la Turquie dans la Grande Guerre et la perte des territoires à minorité turque de l'Empire ottoman, Mustafa Kemal était déterminé à conserver l'Asie Mineure dans son intégrité, comme fondement d'un nouvel État. Au traité de Lausanne qui mit fin, l'an passé, au conflit gréco-turc, il a réussi, tout en récupérant la Thrace orientale, Constantinople et les détroits, à faire reconnaître les nouvelles frontières de la Turquie. Le traité prévoyait aussi l'échange des populations grecques de Turquie et turques de Grèce. En conséquence, un million de réfugiés de langue grecque vont, entre 1923 et 1925, s'installer en Grèce, tandis que des Turcs, deux fois moins nombreux, vont être placés dans les villages d'Anatolie désertés par les Grecs. Le traité a également aboli la création, récente, des États d'Anatolie et du Kurdistan.

Mustafa Kemal
Pour renforcer sa politique Mustafa Kemal invite ses concitoyens à adopter un nom de famille turc. Il donne l'exemple en prenant celui d'Atatürk, c'est-à-dire « père des Turcs ».

• Atatürk interdit le port du fez. Il abolit la polygamie et impose le mariage civil.

◀ *Mustafa Kemal, le fondateur de la République turque. Il interdit le port du voile pour les femmes.*

Succès du Milky Way

Succès aux États-Unis pour une barre chocolatée qui vient tout juste d'être mise en vente. Sa mise au point a demandé trois ans. Ce chocolat au lait malté a reçu le nom de Milky Way.

Marathons de danse aux États-Unis

Séduits par la promesse de prix importants, femmes et hommes se lancent, aux États-Unis, dans de véritables marathons de danse et rêvent d'arriver en tête. Mais cet espoir peut tourner au cauchemar. Les candidats dansent souvent jusqu'à l'épuisement.

▼ *Danseurs à Washington, après quarante heures de compétition.*

1920 – 1929

Impôt sur le sel en Inde

▶ **24 mars 1923** ◀ Le Conseil d'État indien rétablit le très impopulaire impôt sur le sel, pour équilibrer le budget. Cet impôt frappera tout le monde, le sel étant essentiel à la conservation et à la préparation des aliments. M. Sastri, homme politique indien, proteste : les membres du Conseil, dont beaucoup sont des Britanniques, ne connaissent pas les réalités de la vie en Inde, ni les effets que ce nouvel impôt va avoir sur la population déjà très pauvre.

En 1923 aussi ...

26 mai • *Premières 24 Heures du Mans.*

4 avril • *Lord Carnavon, archéologue qui avait découvert la tombe de Toutankhamon, meurt, à la suite d'une piqûre d'insecte. Certains parlent de la « malédiction de Toutankhamon ».*

14 septembre • *Par un pronunciamiento (un putsch), le général Miguel Primo de Rivera prend le pouvoir en Espagne.*

▼ *Le style de Mlle Lenglen s'inspire des Ballets russes.*

Victoire de Suzanne Lenglen

▶ **6 juillet 1923** ◀ Suzanne Lenglen, joueuse de tennis française de 24 ans, vient de gagner, pour la cinquième fois, à Wimbledon, dans le simple dames. Elle domine le tennis féminin français depuis son premier titre de championne, qu'elle a obtenu à l'âge de 15 ans.

Avec sa jupe courte et son très pratique bandeau dans les cheveux, sans compter son service puissant et son revers redoutable, Suzanne Lenglen est une joueuse étonnante. On se rend compte, à la voir, combien le style des joueuses s'est affirmé depuis les timides débuts des tournois féminins.

Tremblement de terre au Japon

▶ **16 septembre 1923** ◀ Le plus catastrophique tremblement de terre jamais enregistré vient de dévaster Tokyo, la plus grande ville du Japon, et Yokohama, le plus grand port du pays. Le bilan provisoire est de 300 000 morts et 2 millions de sans-abri.

Ce gigantesque séisme, causé par un brusque mouvement le long d'une faille – une fissure de l'écorce terrestre –, s'est produit sans aucun signe avant-coureur. Les immeubles qui ne se sont pas effondrés immédiatement ont été rapidement ravagés par des incendies dus aux explosions des tuyaux de gaz et des réservoirs d'essence.

Plus d'un million de survivants ont fui les ruines fumantes pour se réfugier dans les campagnes voisines. Mais, ici, ils ne sont pas non plus en sûreté. Trois fleuves, le Fukoro, le Chiyo et le Takimi, ont rompu leurs digues, provoquant de terribles inondations et laissant de nombreux sans-abri. On redoute des typhons, et les réfugiés, vivant dans des camps surpeuplés et sans hygiène, risquent d'être victimes d'épidémies meurtrières, tels la dysenterie et le choléra.

Il faudra des mois, peut-être des années, pour que la vie des survivants, très choqués, redevienne normale à Tokyo.

◀ *Les habitants de Tokyo enlèvent les décombres, après le séisme.*

Le premier supermarché

Le premier supermarché s'est ouvert à San Francisco. On y vend toutes sortes de produits, moins cher que dans les boutiques spécialisées, car ils sont achetés en grosses quantités. À terme, on risque d'assister à la mort du boucher, du boulanger et du marchand de légumes.

▲ *Au supermarché, les clients se servent eux-mêmes.*

1923

Grave crise financière en Allemagne

▶ **22 juin 1923** ◀ C'est la débâcle monétaire en Allemagne. La hausse des prix est vertigineuse et l'inflation galope. La ménagère échange des saucisses fait-maison contre une nouvelle paire de chaussures, et le médecin soigne les enfants du mécanicien, qui, en échange, répare sa voiture.

La crise économique est la conséquence de l'occupation de la Ruhr par les troupes françaises et belges. En bloquant la production de charbon, elles veulent obliger l'Allemagne à payer les réparations de guerre auxquelles elle a été condamnée. Beaucoup d'Allemands pensent que le pays doit payer trop, et trop vite, pour une guerre dont il n'est pas le seul responsable. Les Britanniques et les Américains souhaiteraient réduire les dettes, mais la France et la Belgique, pays qui furent occupés par l'Allemagne, veulent obtenir complète réparation et ne donnent aucun signe de détente.

▶ *Sans valeur, les billets de banque allemands servent parfois à allumer le feu.*

La succession de Lénine en URSS

▶ **9 mars 1923** ◀ Une nouvelle crise d'hémiplégie vient de terrasser Lénine, le fondateur et le dirigeant de l'Union soviétique. En dépit de précédentes crises, cet homme de 53 ans administrait toujours le pays, avec l'aide de son entourage politique. Mais, depuis cette dernière attaque, qui le laisse paralysé et sujet à des pertes de conscience, il n'est pas pensable qu'il continue à gouverner de son lit.

En son absence, un triumvirat réunissant Grigori Zinoviev, Lev Kamenev et Joseph Staline le remplace. Lénine, pour sa part, aurait préféré que Léon Trotski lui succédât, malgré son idéalisme excessif.

◀ *Lénine s'adresse à la foule, à Moscou.*

Création de la Warner Bros

Les frères Warner, Harry, Albert, Jack (ci-dessous) et Sam, déjà célèbres comme distributeurs, sont devenus producteurs de cinéma. Les Warner Brothers veulent produire des divertissements pas trop chers, proches de la vie des gens du XXe siècle. « J'aime mieux faire une randonnée de 80 km que de m'ennuyer avec un livre », déclare Jack Warner.

1920 – 1929

▲ *Interpol lutte contre le crime.*

Création d'Interpol

▶ **23 septembre 1923** ◀ Les polices de vingt pays se sont réunies à Vienne pour créer l'Organisation internationale de police criminelle, Interpol. Elle souhaite organiser des rencontres dans une capitale différente chaque année, afin d'échanger des informations sur les activités criminelles et les derniers progrès scientifiques pour identifier les criminels. Les voyages aériens se développant, ce genre de coopération est de plus en plus nécessaire. En revanche, les crimes à connotation raciale, religieuse ou politique ne feront pas partie des attributions d'Interpol.

Premier numéro du *Time*

Le premier numéro du magazine *Time* a beaucoup de succès. Fondé par Henry Luce et Briton Hadden, aux États-Unis, l'hebdomadaire compte déjà 12 000 abonnés. Ses directeurs veulent informer les lecteurs des événements internationaux et de l'évolution de la vie politique, parler des arts, du sport, de la mode, offrant ainsi des rubriques variées, des reportages.

Le putsch de Hitler à Munich échoue

▶ **9 novembre 1923** ◀ Les membres du parti national-socialiste allemand des travailleurs, les nazis, ont tenté de prendre le contrôle de la Bavière. Le chef des nazis, Adolf Hitler, d'origine autrichienne, a commencé sa tentative de putsch dans la plus grande brasserie de Munich, un lieu traditionnel de meetings politiques. Hitler s'est précipité dans la brasserie au moment où un autre chef de parti d'extrême droite s'apprêtait à lire une déclaration, devant ses amis politiques, annonçant qu'il souhaitait instituer une dictature en Bavière. Hitler le fait taire, prend la parole, et invite les participants à le rejoindre et à renverser le gouvernement. Il précise qu'il déchirera le traité de Versailles, un « diktat » injuste, dès qu'il sera au pouvoir.

La tentative de Hitler, qui est devenu caporal pendant la guerre, est soutenue par le général Ludendorff. Munich arbore le drapeau à la croix gammée. Le général organise, le lendemain, une manifestation dans la ville pour gagner le soutien de l'armée, mais la police la disperse, tire et tue quelques nazis. Le putsch échoue, faute d'organisation et de soutiens. Ludendorff est assigné à résidence. Hitler est incarcéré dans une forteresse. Mais les nazis se sont fait connaître et ont gagné la sympathie populaire.

▲ *Le magazine américain* Time *s'intéresse aux personnalités et mêle photos, informations et commentaires dans un style vivant.*

▲ *La tentative de putsch de Hitler attire les foules.*

Mort de Sarah Bernhardt

▶ **26 mars 1923** ◀ Sarah Bernhardt est morte, dans son appartement parisien. C'était la première, et certains ajoutent la plus grande, star internationale de la scène théâtrale. Née Henriette Rosine Bernard, aimant s'entourer de mystère, elle n'avait jamais voulu révéler son âge, mais on sait qu'elle avait 78 ans. Son amour pour le théâtre est né lorsque sa mère, dans le but de la dissuader d'entrer au couvent, l'emmena voir une pièce. Le remède fut infaillible, puisqu'elle débuta à 16 ans à la Comédie-Française. Ses interprétations de *l'Aiglon* de Rostand ou du *Phèdre* de Racine sont dans toutes les mémoires.

83

1924

Premiers jeux Olympiques d'hiver

Premiers Jeux d'hiver à Chamonix. Les concurrents viennent de dix-huit pays. Beaucoup de médailles sont revenues aux Scandinaves, qui bénéficient chez eux de conditions idéales à la pratique du ski.

Cinq médailles d'or pour le Finlandais Paavo Nurmi

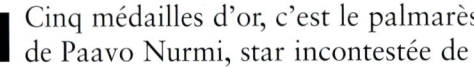
30 juillet 1924

Cinq médailles d'or, c'est le palmarès de Paavo Nurmi, star incontestée de ces VIIes jeux Olympiques, qui se déroulent à Paris sous une chaleur écrasante. Ce « Finlandais volant » a enlevé, en l'espace de deux heures, le 1 500 m et le 5 000 m, tout en établissant de nouveaux records olympiques. Une autre médaille importante est revenue au coureur écossais Eric Liddell. Pasteur presbytérien très strict, il n'a pas voulu participer à sa spécialité, le 100 m, car l'épreuve se déroulait un dimanche. Il a toutefois remporté le 400 m.

Les jeux Olympiques modernes datent d'il y a presque trente ans. Les premiers eurent lieu à Athènes en 1896. Un Français, le baron Pierre de Coubertin, eut l'idée de faire revivre les Jeux que les Grecs anciens organisaient tous les quatre ans, de 776 av. J.-C. à 395 ap. J.-C. Il prit la tête du premier comité international qui organisa les Jeux modernes. Bien qu'il ne soit pas lui-même athlète, il se fait une haute idée du sport. Les concurrents olympiques doivent tous être des amateurs. C'est Coubertin qui instaura le cérémonial de la flamme olympique ; c'est aussi lui qui introduisit le marathon.

Les jeux Olympiques

- L'emblème des JO, composé de cinq anneaux entrelacés, symbolise les cinq continents.
- Dans la Grèce antique, l'intervalle entre deux olympiades, soit quatre ans, servait d'unité de temps.
- Les femmes étaient interdites aux jeux d'Olympie consacrés à Zeus. Elles devaient se contenter de ceux organisés en l'honneur d'Héra.

▲ *Le coureur finlandais Paavo Nurmi bat deux records du monde en deux heures.*

En 1924 aussi...

6 avril • *Élections en Italie. Victoire du parti fasciste, après l'arrestation de nombreux opposants sur ordre de Mussolini.*

17 août • *La France et la Belgique acceptent d'évacuer la Ruhr.*

24 novembre • *Transfert des cendres de Jean Jaurès au Panthéon. C'est une des plus grandes manifestations populaires jamais vues à Paris.*

Instabilité ministérielle en France

11 mai 1924

Le Cartel des gauches, formé de socialistes et de radicaux, remporte les élections à la Chambre des députés. Les précédentes élections, en 1919, avaient porté au pouvoir une majorité de droite où les anciens combattants étaient si nombreux qu'on avait appelé l'Assemblée « la Chambre bleu horizon », à cause de la couleur de l'uniforme des poilus. Malgré la victoire, la France était affaiblie, son économie était désorganisée, sa société, bouleversée par les changements dus à la guerre, et la majorité au pouvoir n'a pas su résoudre ces problèmes. C'est pourquoi les électeurs ont porté la gauche au pouvoir. Mais le pays est bien difficile à gouverner : selon la Constitution de la IIIe République, si les députés refusent leur confiance aux ministres, ceux-ci doivent démissionner. Or il y a plusieurs partis politiques, aucun d'entre eux n'obtient jamais la majorité ; ce sont donc toujours des coalitions qui gouvernent. Comme il suffit qu'un ministre cesse d'être d'accord avec les autres pour que son parti vote contre le gouvernement à l'Assemblée, huit gouvernements successifs doivent démissionner entre 1924 et 1926...

1920 – 1929

▲ *Gershwin exprime le dynamisme de la vie urbaine.*

Gershwin séduit New York

▶ **12 février 1924** ◀ À l'Aleolian Hall de New York, le public applaudit la première d'une œuvre étonnante. Il s'agit de *Rhapsody in Blue*, composé par George Gershwin, un jeune et talentueux pianiste de jazz. Il décrit sa dernière œuvre comme « un essai de musique moderne ». Si son succès ne se dément pas, elle deviendra une œuvre classique.

Formation de l'Arabie Saoudite

▶ **20 octobre 1924** ◀ Deux royaumes se sont fondus en un sous la houlette d'Ibn Saud, l'émir du Nadjd. Occupant la plus grande partie de la péninsule arabique – le centre avec le Nadjd, la côte de la mer Rouge avec le Hedjaz –, ce nouveau royaume d'Ibn Saud sera appelé Arabie Saoudite. Il abrite deux capitales, Riyad et La Mecque.

Mort de Lénine

▶ **28 janvier 1924** ◀ Des milliers de Soviétiques en deuil arrivent à Moscou pour rendre un dernier hommage à Vladimir Ilitch Oulianov, dit Lénine, mort le 21 janvier. Le gouvernement vient d'annoncer que son corps allait être embaumé et exposé en permanence dans un mausolée, sur la place Rouge, en dépit de sa volonté d'être enterré simplement. Les porteurs de son cercueil sont les bolcheviks les plus en vue du moment : Kalinine, Boukharine, Tomski, Kamenev, Molotov et Staline, mais Trotski n'était pas là. Certains affirment que Staline lui aurait donné une fausse date.

Breton publie le *Manifeste du surréalisme*

▶ **Octobre 1924** ◀ Le jeune poète français André Breton vient de publier le *Manifeste du surréalisme,* qui définit le surréalisme, dont il est le chef de file. Il croit que l'art ne peut être limité par la raison et les conventions mais doit faire appel au rêve, à l'inconscient. Des peintres surréalistes, tels Joan Miró ou Salvador Dalí, se laissent guider par leurs rêves et leurs instincts. Ils sont inspirés par la psychanalyse et l'art primitif. Les idées-chocs de Breton ont été approuvées par de nombreux artistes.

▶ *Intérieur hollandais,* par Miró.

▲ *Le record a été établi sur un biplan Douglas.*

Tour du monde aérien

Deux pilotes de l'armée américaine, Lowell Smith et Erick Nelson, viennent de regagner Seattle après avoir bouclé le tour du monde en avion, soit 43 500 kilomètres. Des bases d'étape et de ravitaillement avaient été créées dans de nombreux pays avant même qu'ils ne quittent les États-Unis. La traversée des océans, qu'ils effectuèrent par sauts de puce d'île en île, ne leur posa pas non plus trop de problèmes.

Darwin contesté aux États-Unis

▶ 21 juillet 1925 ◀ Cent dollars d'amende, voilà ce que John Thomas Scopes est condamné à payer par un tribunal du Tennessee. Le délit commis par ce professeur de biologie est d'avoir enseigné à ses élèves la théorie de l'évolution des espèces de Darwin. Une loi d'État interdit tout enseignement qui s'opposerait aux récits de l'Ancien Testament concernant la création du monde. Les fondamentalistes protestants d'Amérique ont utilisé cette loi pour combattre une théorie selon laquelle l'homme est apparenté au singe.

Scopes est poursuivi par un ancien candidat à la Maison-Blanche, William Jennings Bryan, qui affirme la version biblique de la création du monde comme étant la seule valable. Après avoir été questionné par l'avocat de Scopes, Bryan a reconnu que le processus de création a peut-être duré plus de sept jours. Charles Darwin avait repoussé la publication de sa théorie durant vingt ans. Il était effrayé par son impact possible sur les croyances chrétiennes. Cette théorie a été confirmée par l'étude des fossiles. Mais le verdict du juge est en contradiction avec les preuves scientifiques.

▲ *Selon Darwin, les humains sont apparentés aux singes, une idée que certains jugent immorale, car contraire à la Bible.*

▶ *Clarence Darrow, l'avocat de Scopes, et le procureur du Tennessee, William Bryan.*

Mort de Sun Yat-sen en Chine

▶ 12 mars 1925 ◀ Sun Yat-sen, le vénérable chef de la révolution démocratique chinoise, vient de succomber à un cancer, à Pékin. Il avait, en 1911, dirigé la campagne contre le dernier empereur mandchou et fondé le Guomindang, le parti nationaliste chinois. Il est à l'origine de la république en Chine. Il est mort sans avoir réalisé son rêve d'une Chine unie et démocratique, mais ses disciples souhaitent continuer son œuvre. Le général Tchang Kaï-chek, son beau-frère, est en passe de devenir son successeur. Plus militaire que politique, Tchang Kaï-chek revient de Moscou, où il est allé étudier les techniques de l'Armée rouge. Depuis 1923, l'armée du Guomindang reçoit aide et conseils de la Russie soviétique.

◀ *Sun Yat-sen, le « père de la République chinoise ».*

1920 – 1929

▲ Le Bauhaus allie simplicité, fonctionnalité et beauté.

Le Bauhaus

▶ **Mars 1925** ◀ L'école d'architecture et de création du Bauhaus a déménagé de Weimar à Dessau, le nouveau gouvernement conservateur lui ayant retiré toute subvention. Les nationalistes trouvent le Bauhaus trop cosmopolite et affirment que le public est indigné par le fait que ses impôts servent à l'école.

Le Bauhaus a été fondé en 1919 par Walter Gropius. Son but est d'établir une étroite collaboration entre artisans et artistes, afin qu'ils travaillent sur des projets communs en associant leurs savoir-faire au profit du peuple. Le Bauhaus accueille notamment les peintres Wassili Kandinsky et Paul Klee, le décorateur Marcel Breuer et l'architecte Ludwig Mies van der Rohe.

Hitler publie *Mein Kampf*

▶ **18 juillet 1925** ◀ Adolf Hitler annonce son programme politique dans son livre *Mein Kampf* (« Mon combat »). Le leader nazi l'a écrit en prison, après l'échec du putsch de 1923 à Munich.

Hitler veut instituer un IIIe Reich – un empire – allemand qui durera plus de mille ans. Il expose ses théories racistes, prône l'extermination des peuples « inférieurs », d'abord les Juifs et les Slaves. Il compte instituer un nouvel ordre européen, par la guerre, afin d'assurer un espace vital suffisant à l'Allemagne, peuplée d'aryens, la race « supérieure ». La France sera une région agricole qui nourrira l'Allemagne.

Les mots croisés

Les autorités médicales de Chicago viennent d'annoncer que les mots croisés sont un excellent exercice pour le cerveau. Cette idée contredit les conclusions du président des opticiens britanniques, qui affirme que les mots croisés donnent mal à la tête et aux yeux.

▼ *La Rue,* par Georg Grosz, peintre « objectif ».

Le Cuirassé Potemkine

Le réalisateur du *Cuirassé Potemkine* est le cinéaste soviétique Sergueï Eisenstein. C'est l'histoire de la révolte des marins du cuirassé lors de la révolution de 1905. Le navire aux mains des mutins entre dans le port d'Odessa, la foule leur fait un accueil triomphal, mais les soldats ouvrent le feu…

Le nouveau réalisme en peinture

▶ **14 juin 1925** ◀ À Mannheim, les artistes allemands inaugurent l'exposition « Neue Sachlichkeit », ou nouveau réalisme, groupe fondé par Otto Dix et Georg Grosz. Le nouveau réalisme désigne un retour à la sobriété dans la peinture. Les artistes qui font partie de ce mouvement montrent la réalité de la vie dans les grandes villes hantées par les invalides de guerre, les prostituées et leurs souteneurs. C'est un univers sombre : natures mortes empoussiérées, passerelles grisâtres et façades d'immeubles sinistres. Les peintres se veulent témoins de leur temps.

◀ *Otto Dix, artiste majeur de l'école allemande.*

1925

Exposition surréaliste à Paris

▶ 14 novembre 1925 ◀ Une très inhabituelle exposition vient d'ouvrir ses portes à Paris, à la galerie Pierre-Loeb. Elle présente les œuvres de peintres surréalistes, tels Hans Arp, Giorgio De Chirico, Paul Klee, Max Ernst, Juan Miró, André Masson, Pablo Picasso et Man Ray.

Bien que ce soit la première exposition groupée du mouvement, les surréalistes ne se considèrent pas comme un groupe formel ou une école de peinture. La seule loi du surréalisme est qu'il n'y a pas de loi. La vérité surréaliste est dans le pouvoir créateur de l'imagination et de l'inconscient.

Comme les rêves et les créations de l'imagination, leur art est sensible à l'utilisation de matériaux bruts, jusque-là totalement absents de la peinture. Max Ernst utilise la toile grossière, les feuilles, le fil et le bois pour ses tableaux. André Masson invente les « tableaux de sable ». Il envoie des giclées de colle sur une surface posée à plat, peinte ou non, puis la recouvre de sable. Lorsqu'on redresse la toile, le sable glisse et reste accroché là où la colle le retient.

Le porte-parole du mouvement est l'écrivain André Breton. Le café Cyrano, près de chez lui, est l'un des lieux favoris de réunion du groupe où l'on débat sur l'art et les idées nouvelles. Marcel Duchamp, autre grande figure de cette avant-garde artistique française, n'est pas présent à l'exposition – il passe généralement son temps à jouer aux échecs.

▲ *La Forêt* (1923), par le peintre allemand Max Ernst, qui appartient au mouvement dada.

En 1925 aussi...

26 février • Des études suggèrent que la célèbre tour penchée de Pise pourrait bien s'effondrer.

26 avril • En Allemagne, le général Hindenburg devient président.

1er juillet • Les troupes françaises débutent l'évacuation de la Ruhr. Elle devrait durer un mois.

Le prix Nobel pour George Bernard Shaw

▶ 10 décembre 1925 ◀ George Bernard Shaw vient de se voir attribuer le prix Nobel de littérature, prix dont il a refusé de recevoir le montant. Ce célèbre écrivain irlandais, aujourd'hui âgé de 69 ans, fut, jusqu'à 40 ans, l'auteur de nombreuses nouvelles, avant de se mettre à écrire les pièces de théâtre qui lui ont apporté la gloire.

La dernière, *Saint Joan (Sainte Jeanne)*, a connu un tel succès, aussi bien en Grande-Bretagne qu'en Irlande, en Amérique qu'en Europe continentale, qu'elle a fait sa fortune et sa renommée.

George Bernard Shaw est l'homme des grandes causes – socialisme, féminisme –, mais il les transcrit avec tant d'esprit, d'ironie et de charme qu'il arrive à convertir plus de gens qu'il n'en choque. Il montre sa personnalité dans *Pygmalion*, sa pièce la plus populaire, à l'aide du personnage de Henry Higgins, ce professeur de linguistique sarcastique, ironique et élitiste. Le film *My Fair Lady* a été tiré de cette pièce.

1920 – 1929

Succès de Joséphine Baker à Paris

▶ **27 octobre 1925** ◀ Le Tout-Paris se précipite pour aller applaudir Joséphine Baker, vedette de La Revue nègre, une troupe de danse américaine. Ses costumes se réduisent à des fruits ou des plumes qui ne cachent pas grand-chose. L'écrivain Colette dit qu'elle a la grâce d'une panthère – un compliment suggéré par le fait que la danseuse a l'habitude de se promener sur les Champs-Élysées accompagnée de son félin favori. Née il y a dix-neuf ans dans le Missouri, elle a débuté dans un théâtre itinérant alors qu'elle avait à peine 13 ans. Elle compte s'installer à Paris.

La conférence de Locarno

▶ **1er décembre 1925** ◀ Les gouvernements de six pays européens – Allemagne, Belgique, France, Grande-Bretagne, Italie, Pologne – ont ratifié les frontières internationales qui avaient été dessinées après la Grande Guerre. Ils se sont rencontrés en terrain neutre, à Locarno, en Suisse. La nouvelle entente entre la France, représentée par Aristide Briand, et l'Allemagne, par Gustav Stresemann, est d'une importance capitale. Ce dernier a déclaré qu'il s'agissait du meilleur espoir de paix permanente pour l'Europe. Plutôt que de continuer à occuper la Ruhr pour quinze ans, les Alliés se sont mis d'accord pour se retirer. Après Locarno, tout risque de guerre semble écarté.

◀ *La délégation allemande à la conférence de Locarno.*

La sécurité routière en Grande-Bretagne

▶ **29 septembre 1925** ◀ Pour réduire le nombre d'accidents sur la route, de nombreux États se penchent sur la sécurité du trafic routier. Ainsi, en Grande-Bretagne, le ministre des Transports prend aujourd'hui de nouvelles mesures de sécurité, au vu de la multiplication du nombre de voitures sur les routes. D'abord, des lignes blanches indélébiles seront peintes sur les grandes routes, afin de canaliser les flux du trafic dans chaque sens et de signaler le danger. À Londres, des feux tricolores vont intimer aux automobilistes l'ordre de stopper et d'attendre leur tour.

▲ *Joséphine Baker sur scène, vêtue d'un costume étonnant.*

Nouvel appareil photo

Le nouveau Leica est léger et peu encombrant. Il peut prendre 36 clichés sur un même film de 35 millimètres. Déjà qualifié d'« instantané », cet appareil, très souple d'utilisation, est l'invention d'un amateur, Oskar Barnack, spécialiste des microscopes chez le fameux fabricant d'optique Leitz, en Allemagne.

Buster Keaton, l'homme qui ne rit jamais

Dans le film *Go West* (*Ma vache et moi*), Buster Keaton, devenu cow-boy, se lie d'amitié avec une vache, qu'il conduit partout. Cette histoire loufoque donne à l'artiste l'occasion d'inventer une cascade de gags et de scènes burlesques. Mais le comique américain n'abandonne pas pour autant son éternelle expression sérieuse et solennelle. Buster Keaton, qui a joué tout jeune au théâtre avec sa famille, s'est tourné vers le cinéma en 1916, à l'âge de dix-neuf ans.

1920

1921

1922

1923

1924

1925

1926

Winnie l'ourson, un livre pour enfants

▶ **14 octobre 1926** ◀ Alan Alexander Milne vient de publier un nouveau livre pour enfants qui raconte les aventures d'un ours en peluche appelé Winnie, appartenant à Jean-Christophe, un jeune garçon de 6 ans. Winnie l'ourson vit dans la forêt avec ses amis, Bourriquet, Porcinet, Tigrou, Maître Hibou, Gourou et Petit Gourou.

Pour écrire cette histoire, illustrée par E. H. Shepard, l'auteur a longuement observé les activités de son propre fils Jean-Christophe et s'est inspiré de ses jeux. Si l'on en croit le succès de son recueil de vers *When We Were very Young*, qui a déjà été réédité treize fois depuis sa parution en 1924, ce nouveau livre de Milne devrait captiver les jeunes comme les moins jeunes.

▲ *Alan Alexander Milne, l'auteur de* Winnie l'ourson.

▲ *Jean-Christophe, le fils de l'auteur, dans les bras de sa mère.*

▲ *Jean-Christophe rencontre dans la forêt ses amis les animaux.*

1926

1927

1928

1929

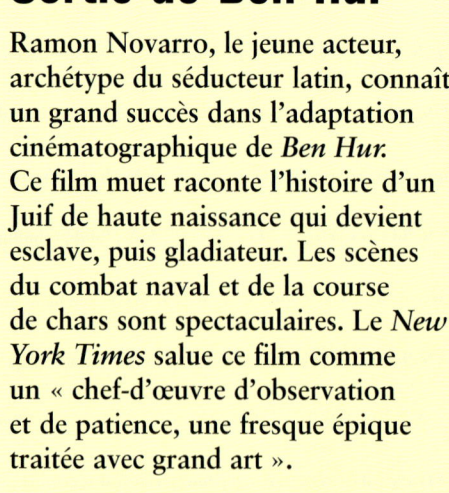

▲ *Winnie l'ourson grimpe sur une chaise pour attraper un pot de miel.*

Sortie de Ben Hur

Ramon Novarro, le jeune acteur, archétype du séducteur latin, connaît un grand succès dans l'adaptation cinématographique de *Ben Hur*. Ce film muet raconte l'histoire d'un Juif de haute naissance qui devient esclave, puis gladiateur. Les scènes du combat naval et de la course de chars sont spectaculaires. Le *New York Times* salue ce film comme un « chef-d'œuvre d'observation et de patience, une fresque épique traitée avec grand art ».

▶ *L'action de* Ben Hur *se situe dans la Rome antique.*

90

1920 – 1929

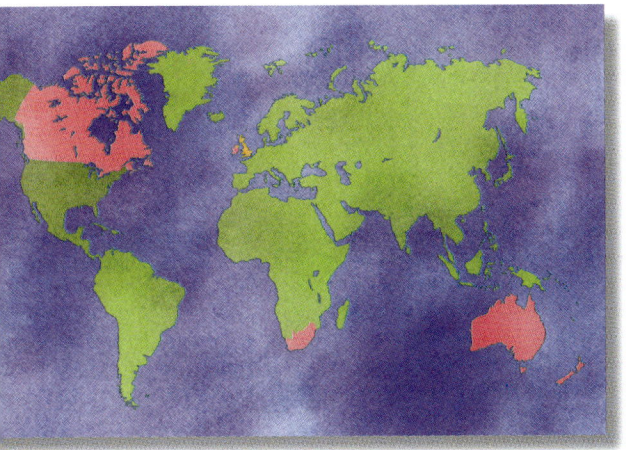

▲ *Le Commonwealth est représenté en rose sur la carte. En font partie le Canada, l'Australie, la Nouvelle-Zélande et l'Afrique du Sud.*

Naissance du Commonwealth

▶ **20 novembre 1926** ◀ Les anciennes colonies de l'Empire britannique – Canada, Australie, Nouvelle-Zélande, Afrique du Sud – deviennent des dominions, États indépendants et souverains, au sein d'une « communauté » de nations, le Commonwealth. À la conférence de Londres est signé un accord de principe : les dominions sont des États autonomes, égaux dans leur statut et qui adhèrent au Commonwealth en reconnaissant qu'ils dépendent de la couronne britannique. L'État libre d'Irlande, inclus dans l'alliance, n'est pas obligé de reconnaître la souveraineté royale.

Ouverture d'un gymnase à New York

Le culturiste Charles Atlas a ouvert un nouveau gymnase où les New-Yorkais peuvent venir développer leur musculature. Atlas, de son vrai nom Angelo Siciliano, a emprunté son nom au géant de la mythologie grecque qui soutient le ciel sur ses épaules.

Des cités mayas découvertes au Mexique

▶ **18 février 1926** ◀ Cinq cités mayas viennent d'être découvertes dans la péninsule du Yucatán, au Mexique. Bien que cette ancienne civilisation amérindienne reste très mystérieuse, on pense que ces maisons en pierre datent de 300 avant J.-C. Elles étaient probablement habitées par les astronomes qui inventèrent les calendriers mayas et organisèrent de grandes fêtes religieuses. L'écriture maya était composée de hiéroglyphes qui demeurent une énigme pour les scientifiques. Peut-être trouveront-ils la réponse dans les forêts du Mexique ?

▲ *Poterie maya, détail.*

▲ *Charles Atlas faisant la démonstration de sa force.*

◀ *L'empereur Hirohito.*

Mort de Gaudí

▶ **10 juin 1926** ◀ Le grand architecte catalan, Antonio Gaudí, est mort à l'hôpital Santa Cruz, trois jours après avoir été renversé par un tramway dans sa chère ville de Barcelone.

Cet architecte de 74 ans travaillait depuis 1884 à la construction d'une gigantesque église, la Sagrada Familia, consacrée à la Sainte Famille. Il savait qu'elle ne serait pas terminée de son vivant. Gaudí cherchait à concilier la nature et la géométrie, de sorte que ses édifices semblent avoir « poussé » naturellement.

▶ *L'église de la Sagrada Familia, à Barcelone.*

Le prince Hirohito empereur du Japon

▶ **25 décembre 1926** ◀ Le prince Hirohito est le nouvel empereur du Japon, même si ses sujets, qui le considèrent comme un dieu, ne l'appellent jamais ainsi. Pour eux, il est *Tenno* ou *Tenno Heika*, c'est-à-dire « Fils du ciel ». Contrairement à ses prédécesseurs, ce jeune empereur de 25 ans connaît bien l'Europe. C'est également un spécialiste de biologie marine.

1926

Une femme traverse la Manche à la nage

▶ 6 août 1926 ◀ Gertrud Ederle, une New-Yorkaise de 19 ans, est la première femme à traverser la Manche à la nage, en un temps record de 14 h 31 min. Elle bat ainsi de deux heures le record établi par l'Argentin Sebastian Tirabocchi.

Il y a deux ans, Miss Ederle avait remporté une médaille de bronze dans le 400 m nage libre aux jeux Olympiques de Paris.

Elle a effectué la traversée de la Manche entre le cap Gris-Nez en France et la côte du Kent en Angleterre, dans des conditions météorologiques très difficiles.

◀ *Les nageuses américaines Gertrud Ederle (à droite) et Lilian Cannon avec leur entraîneur.*

Metropolis, de Fritz Lang

Metropolis, le nouveau film de Fritz Lang, se passe en l'an 2000. Des centaines d'ouvriers travaillent dans les usines d'une ville souterraine, sous la surveillance d'une jeune fille, Maria. Mais celle-ci est remplacée par un horrible robot, inventé par un fou, et également appelé Maria. Ce film totalement futuriste est unique en son genre. Son réalisateur, l'Autrichien Fritz Lang, a suivi des études d'architecture, avant de se lancer dans le cinéma. Son intérêt pour l'architecture transparaît dans les décors spectaculaires de sa ville imaginaire. La catastrophe qu'il décrit annonce les horreurs du nazisme.

▲ *Émeutes à Varsovie pendant le coup d'État.*

Pilsudski prend le pouvoir en Pologne

▶ 12 mai 1926 ◀ Après son coup d'État réussi en Pologne, le maréchal Pilsudski se comporte en dictateur. Nommé ministre de la Guerre et Premier ministre par le président et le cabinet, il règne en maître absolu sur la Pologne.

Pilsudski avait voulu se retirer de la vie politique, il y a trois ans, mais, devant l'instabilité des gouvernements, il changea d'avis et s'empara du pouvoir, le 12 mai, lors d'un coup d'État militaire à Varsovie. Ce patriote d'extrême droite fut emprisonné deux fois par les anciens dirigeants russes de la Pologne. Pilsudski est devenu populaire en s'opposant à la tyrannie de l'occupant russe, avant la Première Guerre mondiale.

1920 – 1929

Survol du pôle Nord

▶ 13 mai 1926 ◀ Deux aviateurs américains, Floyd Bennett et Richard Byrd, annoncent qu'ils ont survolé le pôle Nord. Ils ont décollé de Spitzberg, en Norvège, à bord d'un trimoteur de type Fokker, et ils sont revenus à leur base 15 h 30 min plus tard. Byrd, qui a survolé le Groenland l'année dernière, prépare une expédition au-dessus de l'Antarctique. Deux autres aviateurs, un Italien et un Norvégien, viennent d'atterrir à Nome, en Alaska, après avoir survolé le pôle Nord en dirigeable.

▲ Richard Byrd.

Mort du magicien Houdini

▶ 31 octobre 1926 ◀ Harry Houdini, célèbre prestidigitateur qui réussissait à se libérer de chaînes et de menottes, est mort. Il s'était vanté, devant une classe de Montréal, de pouvoir supporter de violents coups de poing à l'estomac. L'un des étudiants le frappa par deux fois à l'abdomen. Dès son retour aux États-Unis, il fut opéré de l'appendicite, mais décéda des suites d'une péritonite. Né en Hongrie, il s'appelait en réalité Erich Weiss.

▲ Harry Houdini, enchaîné.

En 1926 aussi…

12 janvier • L'Institut Pasteur, à Paris, annonce la découverte d'un sérum contre le tétanos.

21 avril • Naissance de la princesse Élisabeth, future reine d'Angleterre.

23 août • Mort de l'acteur Rudolph Valentino, à l'âge de 31 ans, d'une crise d'appendicite.

10 novembre • Mariage, à Bruxelles, du prince héritier Léopold avec la princesse Astrid de Suède.

◀ Symboles des communautés musulmane (à gauche) et hindoue.

Combats entre hindous et musulmans

▶ 24 avril 1926 ◀ Calcutta est à nouveau le théâtre de violents combats entre les communautés musulmane et hindoue. Ces troubles ont éclaté il y a quelques semaines, des musulmans cherchant à se venger d'atrocités prétendument commises par des hindous. De sanglants combats opposent aujourd'hui des bandes rivales, mettant en danger les membres des deux communautés.

Le « mur d'argent »

▶ 8 mai 1926 ◀ Le Cartel des gauches, au pouvoir de 1924 à 1926, a suscité la peur des possédants. Les capitaux sont partis à l'étranger. Le franc, déjà affaibli par la guerre, s'effondre : c'est le « mur d'argent ». Le nouveau gouvernement, dirigé par l'ancien président de la République Raymond Poincaré, entreprend de revaloriser et de stabiliser la monnaie. Ce sera fait le 25 juin 1928.

Une nouvelle école de danse à New York

Trois ans après son arrivée à New York, la danseuse Martha Graham ouvre, à l'âge de 31 ans, une école de danse sur la 5ᵉ Avenue. Elle souhaite collaborer étroitement avec l'accompagnateur et le compositeur Louis Horst, qui publie le *Dance Observer*, un journal très influent. Cette grande danseuse est également une excellente chorégraphe réputée pour son style à la fois pur et dépouillé.

LES ANNÉES FOLLES

Après 1920, les pays occidentaux connaissent une période de prospérité. L'économie est en pleine expansion. La vie quotidienne se transforme, sous l'influence des progrès techniques.

L'Europe et l'Amérique rapprochent leurs cultures et leurs civilisations, par l'intermédiaire des écrivains, de la radio, de la musique, du phonographe et du cinéma.

Mais la décennie se termine par une crise. Le krach qui frappe la Bourse de New York en 1929 entraîne une récession mondiale, avec la chute du cours des actions et une multitude de faillites de banques et d'entreprises. Le chômage touche des millions de personnes. La dépression commence.

Un saxophone.

Le jazz et le Cotton Club

Le jazz naît à la fin du XIXe siècle à La Nouvelle-Orléans, en Louisiane. Il est inspiré des musiques traditionnelles européennes, africaines et afro-américaines. Le ragtime, au rythme syncopé, apparaît au début du XXe siècle. Les orchestres jouent souvent dans la rue. En 1917, la marine américaine ferme sa base de La Nouvelle-Orléans, et de nombreux musiciens partent pour Saint Louis et Chicago. L'Orchestre original de jazz de Dixieland, de La Nouvelle-Orléans, réalise le premier enregistrement de jazz en 1917, faisant sensation. La radio popularise peu à peu le jazz dans tous les pays. À New York, beaucoup d'amateurs fréquentent le Cotton Club de Harlem, qui ouvre en 1922.

Le Cotton Club peut accueillir 700 personnes. Son décor « primitif » inspire, à l'époque, Duke Ellington pour son style *jungle*. Ce pianiste dirige un groupe et se produit régulièrement, comme d'autres artistes tels que Bill Robinson, Ed « Snakehips » Tucker, Evelyn Welch, ainsi que les orchestres conduits par Cab Calloway, Andrew Preer et Louis Armstrong, ou les chanteurs Lean Horne et Ivie Anderson. Le Cotton Club déménage à Broadway en 1936. Le jazz est devenu une musique à part entière, où dominent les instruments à vent, le piano, la batterie, le rythme et l'improvisation, en solo ou en formation, avec des styles différents.

◄ *Armstrong, dit Satchmo, est un virtuose. Né à La Nouvelle-Orléans vers 1898, il a appris à jouer de la trompette dans une maison de redressement.*

► *Le Cotton Club engage du personnel et de nombreux artistes noirs célèbres, mais il n'admet pas en général la clientèle noire.*

La mode

La mode qui apparaît après la guerre reflète l'optimisme de la jeunesse, impatiente de rattraper le temps perdu pendant le conflit.

Les jeunes femmes transforment leur silhouette. Elles choisissent des robes courtes, à la taille basse, aux tissus souples et variés. Elles sont maquillées et portent des bijoux fantaisie. Elles sont à l'affût de la mode.

Entre 1918 et 1924, le style Chanel s'impose, avec l'ourlet des robes au genou, les habits faciles à porter, les vestes sans col, les couleurs bleu, blanc et noir ; un style destiné aux femmes actives et minces, soucieuses de s'affirmer. La haute couture se développe à Paris, avec Jeanne Lanvin et Paul Poiret. De grandes maisons s'installent autour des Champs-Élysées, rivalisant toutes d'imagination et de créativité.

La mode masculine se démocratise et se simplifie. Les costumes plus amples, l'imperméable, le chapeau de feutre, les chandails rehaussés de dessins et de couleurs, donnent une image de l'élégance adaptée à la modernité et au confort.

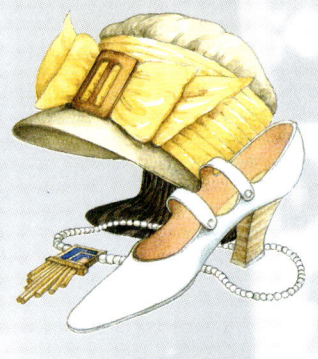

Accessoires chics.

De nouvelles danses

L'Europe adopte toutes sortes de danses nouvelles telles que le one-step et le paso doble.
Le charleston, très rythmé, exprime le désir de vivre et de s'amuser des Années folles. Cette danse, originaire de la ville de Charleston, en Caroline du Sud, gagne tous les États-Unis puis l'Europe autour de 1925.

▶ *Le charleston exige une très grande souplesse des genoux et des chevilles.*

Les années folles

« Paris est une fête » pendant les Années folles : on danse et on écoute du jazz dans les boîtes du quartier Montparnasse. Les grands cafés, comme La Rotonde, sont des centres intellectuels où se croisent et se retrouvent les artistes du monde entier – les Américains Ernest Hemingway et Gertrude Stein, des émigrés russes, les Français Louis Aragon, Jean Cocteau, Blaise Cendrars, etc.

▲ *Le chapeau cloche est très à la mode dans les années 20.*

▶ *Le cinéma popularise les modes et les styles. Cette tenue s'inspire de Rudolph Valentino, dans le Fils du cheik (1921).*

1927

▲ *Charles Lindbergh en tenue d'aviateur.*

▲ *Lindbergh, devant son avion, le Spirit of Saint Louis.*

Lindbergh traverse l'Atlantique

▶ **21 mai 1927** ◀ À 22 h 19, le pilote américain Charles Lindbergh, qui avait décollé de New York, atterrit avec son monoplan monomoteur, le *Spirit of Saint Louis,* au Bourget, près de Paris. Une foule immense est venue le saluer. Il vient d'effectuer la première traversée de l'Atlantique nord sans escale en 33 h 27 min. Muni seulement d'une boussole, il a volé sans carte, et sans visibilité, à cause des réservoirs de carburant installés à l'avant de l'appareil. Le fuselage de son avion est formé de tubes d'acier, et les ailes en bois sont protégées par une toile.

Le capitaine Lindbergh, fils d'un riche membre du Congrès, a appris seul à voler. Officier pilote dans l'armée, il a quitté celle-ci pour entrer au service d'une compagnie assurant le transport aérien du courrier. Sa traversée de l'Atlantique lui rapporte la coquette somme de 25 000 dollars.

Les débuts du violoniste Yehudi Menuhin

Le 6 février, le public parisien est ébloui par un jeune garçon de 10 ans qui exécute avec brio la *Symphonie espagnole,* d'Édouard Lalo, une œuvre pour violon et orchestre extrêmement difficile. Le jeune Yehudi Menuhin, dont les parents sont des Juifs russes, est né à New York, en 1916. Il a donné son premier concert public à l'âge de 7 ans.

Les troupes de Tchang Kaï-chek à Shanghai

▶ **21 mars 1927** ◀ Les troupes nationalistes du Guomindang dirigées par Tchang Kaï-chek viennent d'entrer à Shanghai. Elles se sont emparées de la ville. Les forces nordistes, qui contrôlent encore Pékin, battent en retraite vers le nord face à l'avancée des nationalistes. Il n'a pas été fait de mal aux étrangers, qui sont nombreux dans la ville.

L'alliance entre le parti communiste chinois, dirigé par Mao Zédong, et les nationalistes de Tchang Kaï-chek est rompue, les deux partis se battant pour prendre le contrôle du pays.

1920 – 1929

En 1927 aussi...

12 février • Le dictateur portugais Carmona réprime un soulèvement populaire.

7 avril • Le *Napoléon* d'Abel Gance est projeté sur trois écrans à l'Opéra de Paris.

29 juin • Première éclipse totale du Soleil visible en Grande-Bretagne depuis deux cents ans.

14 septembre • Mort de la danseuse Isadora Duncan, dans un accident de voiture.

Un nouveau type de constructions

▶ **23 juillet 1927** ◀ Un nouveau complexe immobilier comportant 60 appartements vient d'être inauguré aujourd'hui à Weissenhof, en Allemagne. Les logements sont en préfabriqué, ce qui réduit le coût de construction. Bien que destinés à des ouvriers, ils comportent tous des sanitaires et une cuisine équipée. Le Werkbund, qui les construit, réunit depuis 1907 des architectes et des industriels qui ont pour but d'améliorer le cadre de vie. Parmi eux, Le Corbusier.

▲ *Cet ensemble immobilier, esthétique, répond aux besoins de la vie moderne.*

Premier film parlant

Hollywood vient de vivre un grand jour, ce 6 octobre, grâce à la présentation du *Chanteur de jazz*, avec Al Jolson (le troisième en partant de la gauche), le premier film sonore, parlant et musical, réalisé avec les nouveaux disques Vitaphone. Le son est enregistré simultanément à la prise de vues, ce qui exige des acteurs un énorme travail.

Staline contre Trotski

▶ **15 novembre 1927** ◀ Léon Trotski, bras droit de Lénine pendant la révolution bolchevique de 1917, démis de ses fonctions officielles en 1925, a été exclu du parti communiste. Depuis la mort de Lénine, en 1924, Joseph Staline s'est imposé comme le nouveau dirigeant de l'Union soviétique. De nombreux membres du parti ont critiqué les décisions du gouvernement central, mais Staline a rapidement muselé l'opposition. Outre Trotski, plusieurs autres opposants ont été exclus. Certains disent que Staline tente d'assurer l'unité du parti; d'autres pensent que son seul souci est d'étendre son pouvoir.

◀ *Trotski, pêchant, pendant son exil.*

Le sinanthrope de Pékin

▶ **1927** ◀ Le crâne d'un homme a été découvert dans une grotte, près de Pékin. Il a été identifié par le professeur Davidson Black, un Canadien enseignant en Chine, grâce à une dent fossilisée. Selon Black, le sinanthrope de Pékin, ou *Sinanthropus pekinensis*, vivait il y a trois cent cinquante mille ans. Un Français, le père Teilhard de Chardin, travaille sur le chantier des fouilles.

▶ *Le crâne du sinanthrope de Pékin.*

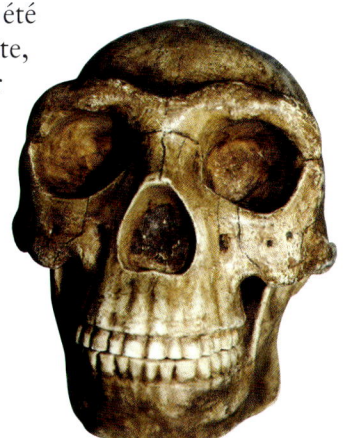

Panneaux de signalisation

La circulation aux États-Unis sera bientôt facilitée par l'utilisation de panneaux routiers identiques dans tout le pays. Actuellement, la signalisation routière varie d'un État à l'autre. Un comité d'experts a recommandé cette uniformisation.

1928

1920

1921
▼ *Les Harlem Globe-trotters transforment le basket-ball.*

1922

1923
Les Harlem Globe-trotters parcourent la terre

1924
Cette année, les célèbres Harlem Globe-trotters ont beaucoup voyagé. Formée à Chicago en 1926, cette équipe est composée de joueurs professionnels noirs. Après de nombreuses tournées dans de petites villes américaines, elle se produit aujourd'hui à l'étranger. Ces joueurs ont fait du basket-ball un véritable divertissement et fascinent le public tant par leur adresse que par leurs facéties.

1925

1926

1927
▼ *Les délégués signent le pacte Briand-Kellogg.*

1928

1929

Alexander Fleming découvre la pénicilline

▶ **30 septembre 1928** ◀ Le milieu médical est en effervescence depuis la découverte par Alexander Fleming, un savant écossais travaillant au Saint Mary's Hospital de Londres, d'une moisissure capable de soigner certaines infections très dangereuses. Ce champignon (ou moisissure), baptisé *Penicillium notatum*, produit une substance, la pénicilline, qui détruit les bactéries. Le professeur Fleming, réputé pour ses travaux sur les vaccins contre la typhoïde, a découvert ce champignon dans un milieu de culture qu'il avait laissé plusieurs jours dans son laboratoire. Celui-ci contenait des bactéries du genre *Staphylococcus*, responsables de nombreuses infections chez l'homme, dont certains abcès et la pneumonie. Il remarqua que ces bactéries avaient complètement disparu autour du champignon, lequel renferme, semble-t-il, une substance chimique qui tue les bactéries. Cette substance ne présente apparemment aucun danger pour l'homme et paraît capable de tuer d'autres bactéries, aussi dangereuses que les *Staphylococcus*. Reste maintenant à extraire la pénicilline et à en étudier les effets.

▶ *Penicillium notatum se développant dans le milieu de culture de Fleming.*

▲ *Fleming, dans son laboratoire.*

La pénicilline
Elle a été découverte par hasard.
•
Fleming observe que la pénicilline garde ses propriétés, même diluée huit cents fois.
•
La pénicilline a ceci d'extraordinaire qu'elle ne détruit pas les cellules humaines.

Le pacte Briand-Kellogg

▶ **27 août 1928** ◀ Un nouveau pas vers la paix a été franchi avec la signature, à Paris, du pacte Briand-Kellogg. Soixante puissances ont accepté de renoncer à la guerre, sauf pour se défendre. Ce pacte porte le nom du ministre des Affaires étrangères français, Aristide Briand, le premier à avoir proposé cet accord entre la France et les États-Unis, et du secrétaire d'État américain, Frank B. Kellogg.

Des médecins en avion

▶ **15 mai 1928** ◀ Un médecin australien visite désormais ses patients en aéroplane. Ce service a été mis en place par John Flynn, un pasteur presbytérien, pour couvrir toute l'Australie centrale. Les patients peuvent contacter le praticien volant à Cloncurry, Queensland, par radio.

1920 – 1929

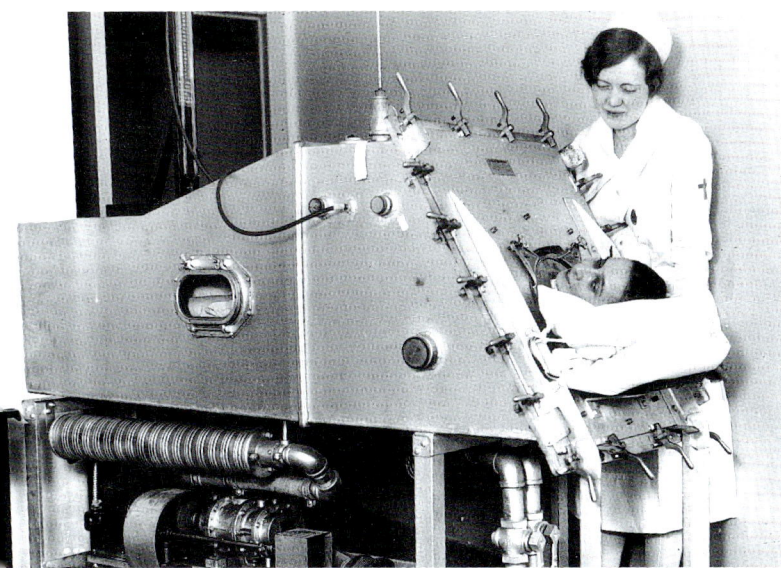

▲ *Patient dans un « poumon d'acier ».*

Le premier « poumon d'acier », espoir pour la médecine

▶ **12 octobre 1928** ◀ Un « poumon d'acier », ou poumon artificiel, est utilisé pour la première fois sur un enfant au Children's Hospital de Boston, Massachusetts. Cet appareil aide le malade à respirer lorsque ses poumons ne fonctionnent pas. Cette machine a été inventée par Philip Drinker, à l'université Harvard, près de Boston. Elle ressemble à un grand réservoir métallique, avec une porte à une extrémité. Le patient est installé à l'intérieur, et la porte est refermée. Seule sa tête dépasse ; un boudin en caoutchouc lui enserre le cou pour que le « poumon » soit tout à fait hermétique. Lorsque la pression à l'intérieur de celui-ci baisse, la poitrine du sujet se dilate et l'air pénètre dans ses poumons. Lorsque la pression augmente, l'air est expulsé des poumons. Le patient peut ainsi être « ventilé » pendant un certain temps.

Le jeune malade traité à Boston souffre de poliomyélite, une maladie infectieuse causée par un virus. Cette maladie, relativement courante aux États-Unis, et particulièrement dangereuse pour les enfants, provoque souvent la paralysie des bras et des jambes, et parfois du système respiratoire.

Les « poumons d'acier » devraient permettre, les médecins l'espèrent, de sauver la vie de nombreux poliomyélitiques.

Plan quinquennal en URSS

▶ **1er octobre 1928** ◀ Le premier plan quinquennal lancé par Staline pour faire de l'URSS une puissance industrielle moderne entre en vigueur. Il fixe des objectifs pour tous les secteurs industriels. Une « révolution » analogue s'organise à la campagne : la collectivisation. Les petites propriétés devront être regroupées dans des fermes collectives contrôlées par l'État, les kolkhozes, ou dans les exploitations d'État, les sovkhozes.

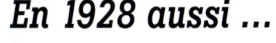

◀ *Un barrage hydroélectrique en Union soviétique.*

En 1928 aussi...

8 juin • *Les forces nationalistes de Tchang Kaï-chek occupent Pékin.*

20 juin • *L'explorateur norvégien Roald Amundsen se tue en avion en participant à une opération de sauvetage dans l'Arctique.*

13 juillet • *La loi Loucheur organise à Paris les HBM, habitations à bon marché réservées aux familles à faibles revenus.*

Schick invente un nouveau rasoir électrique

Les hommes qui se coupent en se rasant sont heureux d'essayer le nouveau rasoir électrique inventé par Joseph Schick, qui devrait mieux fonctionner que les premiers modèles. Les poils entrent dans les trous d'une fine grille métallique et sont coupés par une lame se déplaçant rapidement d'avant en arrière.

▶ *Utilisateur visiblement très content de son nouveau rasoir électrique.*

1928

Mickey à l'écran : un héros qui parle

▶ **18 novembre 1928** ◀ La file d'attente devant le Colony Theater de New York sera longue, ce mois-ci. On y donne en effet le nouveau dessin animé de Walt Disney, *Steamboat Willie*.

C'est le premier dessin animé sonore, qui illustre bien les progrès de la technique cinématographique. La star du film est une souris appelée Mickey. Elle avait d'abord reçu le nom de Mortimer Mouse. Elle a été imaginée par Walt Disney et créée en 1927 par un vieil ami et collaborateur de Disney, Ub Iwerks. Deux courts-métrages muets – *Plane Crazy* et *Gallopin's Gaucho* – précèdent la réalisation de *Steamboat Willie*, mais ne sortiront qu'après, une fois sonorisés. Dans *Steamboat Willie*, c'est Walt Disney lui-même qui prête sa voix à Mickey.

D'autres courts métrages avec Mickey, dont certains en couleurs, sont en projet à Hollywood, au studio Disney.

▲ *Mickey et son amie Minnie.*

Duke Ellington au Cotton Club

▶ **1928** ◀ En ce moment, l'endroit le plus vivant de New York est incontestablement le Cotton Club, situé à Harlem. Le jazz est devenu très populaire, et c'est au Cotton Club que l'on peut écouter le tout dernier orchestre de jazz. Duke Ellington est le compositeur, le pianiste et le chef du groupe. Il est devenu célèbre, notamment grâce à la radio, et prépare des tournées à l'étranger. Son style est unique et il a influencé déjà bien d'autres musiciens et compositeurs.

◀ *Edward Kennedy, dit Duke Ellington, dirige son orchestre tout en jouant du piano.*

L'affaire Anastasia

▶ **6 février 1928** ◀ Une mystérieuse émigrante, une certaine madame Chaikovski, est arrivée à New York aujourd'hui. Elle proclame qu'elle est la princesse Anastasia, fille du dernier tsar de Russie. Or toute la famille a été assassinée en 1918. Pourtant, elle a été formellement identifiée comme étant la princesse par le fils du médecin du tsar. Mais beaucoup restent sceptiques quant à cette possibilité.

▲ *Anastasia est-elle vivante ?*

1920 – 1929

◀ *Les ingénieurs préparent la voiture-fusée pour un essai.*

Voiture-fusée en Allemagne

▶ **23 mai 1928** ◀ Deux cents km/h, c'est la vitesse atteinte aujourd'hui par une voiture-fusée, dans une course qui s'est déroulée à Avus, près de Berlin.

La première voiture-fusée avait fait ses débuts le 15 mars dernier. Il s'agit ici d'une version améliorée, l'Opel-rack 2, conduite par l'ingénieur et industriel Fritz von Opel au cours d'un brillant essai.

Cet engin extraordinairement rapide a été conçu par Opel et l'ingénieur Max Valier. Opel est le petit-fils d'Adam von Opel dont l'entreprise familiale commença à construire des automobiles en 1898. Personne ne pense que la voiture familiale du futur aura besoin d'utiliser la propulsion par fusée. Celle-ci pourrait avoir d'autres applications. Aux États-Unis, Robert Goddard espère qu'elle permettra d'explorer l'espace.

La banquière « escroc »

▶ **5 décembre 1928** ◀ Marthe Hanau vient d'être arrêtée à son domicile parisien du 124, rue de Provence. Cette banquière faisait « bénéficier » ses clients d'informations financières exceptionnelles mais fausses, et assurait à ses souscripteurs des dividendes conséquents. Elle sera inculpée pour escroquerie, infraction à la loi sur les sociétés et action illicite sur les marchés financiers.

◀ *Les femmes disputent maintenant les épreuves d'athlétisme aux jeux Olympiques.*

Émile et les détectives

Énorme succès en Allemagne pour le roman d'Erich Kästner *Émile et les détectives*. C'est la surprise de l'année. Le héros de l'histoire, Émile Tischben, a 10 ans. Orphelin, il se rend à Berlin chez ses grands-parents, où il va vivre désormais. Dévalisé dans le train, il se lance à la poursuite du voleur. Quand il rejoint Berlin, il est aidé dans ses recherches par de jeunes écoliers. Ils mettent la main sur le voleur, qui se trouve être un dangereux escroc. Émile touche une forte récompense et devient célèbre.

▶ *L'une des illustrations d'Émile et les détectives.*

Des femmes aux jeux Olympiques

▶ **12 août 1928** ◀ Les IXes jeux Olympiques viennent de se terminer à Amsterdam, aux Pays-Bas. Quelque 3 000 athlètes y ont participé, représentant 46 nations, contre seulement 13 en 1896. De nombreuses médailles ont été remportées par des athlètes venant de pays en dehors de l'Europe et de l'Amérique du Nord tels que l'Argentine ou le Japon. Pour la première fois, les femmes, qui jusqu'alors ne participaient qu'à certaines disciplines, comme la natation, ont disputé des épreuves d'athlétisme. La médaille d'or du 100 m féminin a été remportée par l'Américaine Élisabeth Robinson.

1920
1921
1922
1923
1924
1925
1926
1927
1928
1929

▼ *Emil Jannings remporte l'Oscar du meilleur acteur.*

Premiers Oscars du cinéma

Le 16 mai a eu lieu, à Hollywood, la première cérémonie d'attribution des Oscars cinématographiques. Les lauréats ont reçu une jolie statuette plaquée or représentant un homme debout sur une bobine de cinéma. La cérémonie de remise des Oscars aura désormais lieu chaque année.

1929

La découverte de l'astronome Hubble

▶ **1929** ◀ L'astronome américain Edwin Hubble vient d'apporter la première preuve en faveur de la théorie du big-bang. Selon celle-ci, l'Univers était à l'origine concentré en un point qui a explosé avec une violence telle (le big-bang) que son expansion continue encore aujourd'hui.

On sait que la Terre tourne autour du Soleil, lequel fait partie d'un vaste système, ou galaxie, la Voie lactée. Il y a cinq ans, Hubble a prouvé l'existence d'autres galaxies dans l'espace. Il démontre aujourd'hui que ces différentes galaxies s'éloignent de la terre – ce qui prouve que l'Univers bouge – et que, plus elles sont éloignées, plus elles se déplacent rapidement. Hubble observe les galaxies avec un télescope très puissant installé à l'observatoire du mont Wilson, aux États-Unis.

▲ *Hubble a découvert l'existence de nombreuses galaxies.*

Hubble
Hubble avançait que l'Univers existait depuis deux milliards d'années. On pense aujourd'hui qu'il existe depuis dix fois plus longtemps.
• Notre galaxie compte environ 100 milliards d'étoiles.

▲ *Un spéculateur ruiné tente de vendre sa voiture pour 100 dollars.*

Le krach de Wall Street

▶ **24 octobre 1929** ◀ L'effondrement du marché financier provoque la panique à Wall Street, la Bourse new-yorkaise. Les investisseurs ont demandé à leurs courtiers de vendre à tout prix, et, au cours de ce « jeudi noir », 12 894 650 actions ont été vendues, donc les cours se sont effondrés. Cette catastrophe frappe aussi bien les grosses fortunes que les petits investisseurs. Onze personnes se sont déjà donné la mort. Ce krach risque d'avoir de graves répercussions à l'échelon international.

Naissance de Tintin

Tintin, un jeune reporter intrépide, fait aujourd'hui son apparition dans le journal belge *le XXᵉ Siècle*. Il est le héros d'une bande dessinée illustrée par Hergé, pseudonyme choisi par l'auteur belge Georges Rémi. Ce jeune reporter rouquin, toujours accompagné d'un chien blanc appelé Milou, fait face avec beaucoup de sang-froid à des situations souvent périlleuses.

▼ *Tintin et son chien, Milou.*

La situation des paysans en URSS

▶ 27 décembre 1929 ◀ En Union soviétique, les agriculteurs doivent céder leurs terres pour rejoindre des fermes collectives censées nourrir les travailleurs. Cette mesure fait partie du plan quinquennal destiné à mettre en place une économie socialiste. De nombreux agriculteurs s'opposent à ces mesures de collectivisation, préférant tuer et manger leur bétail. Les plus riches d'entre eux, les koulaks, sont massacrés ou envoyés dans des camps en Sibérie.

▲ En Union soviétique, les paysans s'opposent à la collectivisation.

1920 – 1929

Mort de Wyatt Earp

▶ 13 janvier 1929 ◀ Wyatt Earp, célèbre aventurier de l'Ouest américain, est mort, à Los Angeles. Dans les années 1870, Earp travaillait pour le shérif de Dodge City, au Kansas. Le 26 octobre 1881, à Tombstone, en Arizona, Wyatt, deux de ses frères et deux amis s'étaient opposés à la famille Clanton dans l'horrible fusillade d'OK Corral. Wyatt, qui se présentait comme un honnête homme, a gagné en fait beaucoup d'argent, grâce au jeu et à la prostitution.

▲ Wyatt Earp (assis au milieu) et ses amis.

Un roman sur la guerre

▶ Décembre 1929 ◀ Le livre d'Erich Maria Remarque, À l'Ouest, rien de nouveau, qui décrit l'horreur des combats dans les tranchées pendant la Grande Guerre, a connu un énorme succès en Allemagne. Il raconte l'histoire de lycéens allemands qui s'enrôlent pour défendre leur pays et sont confrontés au front, à la saleté, aux mesquineries, à la maladie et à la mort.

En 1929 aussi...

11 février • Les accords du Latran sont signés entre le pape et l'État italien. Ils inaugurent de bons rapports entre l'Italie et l'État du Vatican.

1er juillet • Popeye le marin fait son apparition, aux États-Unis, dans une bande dessinée humoristique.

7 octobre • Costes et Bellonte pulvérisent le record du monde du vol en ligne droite sur 9 610 kilomètres, de Paris à Tsitsihar, en Chine, en moins de 48 heures.

Les règlements de comptes d'Al Capone

▶ 14 février 1929 ◀ La police est convaincue que le gangster Al Capone est responsable du massacre de sept membres du gang de « Bugsy » Moran dans une brasserie. Depuis le retrait de son ami Johnny Torrio en 1925, Al Capone a l'entier contrôle du marché du jeu, de la prostitution et de l'alcool à Chicago, et ne souhaite en partager les bénéfices avec personne. Certains gangsters impliqués dans la tuerie portaient l'uniforme de la police.

▲ Al Capone.

FOOTBALL ET BASE-BALL

Le football est l'un des sports les plus populaires du monde. Tous les quatre ans, les meilleures équipes nationales s'affrontent à l'occasion de la Coupe du monde. Beaucoup de pays ont des fédérations de football qui organisent des championnats entre les clubs des différentes villes.
Le base-ball est considéré comme le sport américain par excellence. Les séries mondiales, qui opposent chaque année les vainqueurs de la Ligue américaine et de la Ligue nationale, sont des événements très attendus.

Équipement

Au base-ball, le lanceur envoie une balle recouverte de cuir au batteur, qui porte un casque et joue avec une batte de 1,08 m de long. Le receveur porte un casque, un plastron, des gants, des jambières et des protège-tibias. Placé derrière le batteur, il doit réceptionner la balle avec son gant lorsque le batteur ne l'a pas frappée.

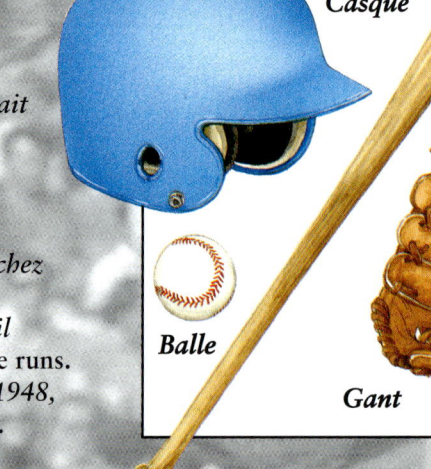

Casque
Batte
Balle
Gant

◀ Babe Ruth, qui était aussi bon receveur que batteur, doit sa réputation à sa performance à ce dernier poste chez les Yankees. Dans sa carrière, il effectua 714 home runs. Ruth mourra en 1948, à l'âge de 52 ans.

Idoles du stade

Babe Ruth et Joe DiMaggio sont les joueurs de base-ball les plus adulés. À eux deux, ils totalisent 34 ans de gloire pour les Yankees de New York. Ruth signe avec les Yankees dès 1920. Lors de sa première saison, il marque 54 *home runs*. Un *home run* est une balle que le batteur frappe hors du terrain et qui lui permet de faire le tour des quatre bases avant qu'elle ne soit renvoyée. En 1927, il marque 60 *home runs*, record qui ne sera battu qu'en 1961. Il arrête de jouer en 1935. DiMaggio rejoint les Yankees l'année suivante et marque 29 *home runs* lors de sa première saison. Les Yankees remportent les séries mondiales de 1936 à 1939. DiMaggio cesse de jouer en 1951. Son mariage avec Marilyn Monroe l'a rendu aussi célèbre que ses prouesses sportives.

▶ DiMaggio réussit l'exploit d'atteindre la première base à chaque fois qu'il envoie la balle, dans 56 matches d'affilée, en 1941.

▶ L'Uruguay a remporté la médaille d'or de football aux jeux Olympiques de 1924 et 1928, et était favori pour la Coupe du monde de 1930.

L'Uruguay gagne la Coupe du monde

Une journée nationale de congé a été déclarée en Uruguay après la victoire de l'équipe nationale par 4 buts à 2 face à l'Argentine. C'était le 30 juillet, lors de la première Coupe du monde de football. Organisée par la Fédération internationale de football (FIFA), seulement quatre clubs européens y ont participé : la Roumanie, la France, la Belgique et la Yougoslavie.

Le roi Pelé

1 090 buts en 1 114 matches pour le club de Santos, voilà le score du joueur de football brésilien Pelé. Il débute à l'âge de 16 ans, en 1957, et marque deux buts l'année suivante lors de la finale de la Coupe du monde, qui oppose le Brésil à la Suède. Avant d'arrêter sa carrière en 1977, il joue pendant deux ans pour le New York Cosmos aux États-Unis. Le dernier match auquel il participe oppose le Santos et le Cosmos au Giants Stadium de New York.

Ils ont gagné la Coupe du monde

1930 Uruguay	(4-2 contre l'Argentine)
1934 Italie	(2-1 contre la Tchécoslovaquie)
1938 Italie	(4-2 contre la Hongrie)
1050 Uruguay	(2-1 contre le Brésil)
1954 RFA	(3-2 contre la Hongrie)
1958 Brésil	(5-2 contre la Suède)
1962 Brésil	(3-1 contre la Tchécoslovaquie)
1966 Angleterre	(4-2 contre la RFA)
1970 Brésil	(4-1 contre l'Italie)
1974 RFA	(2-1 contre les Pays-Bas)
1978 Argentine	(3-1 contre les Pays-Bas)
1982 Italie	(3-1 contre la RFA)
1986 Argentine	(3-2 contre la RFA)
1990 RFA	(1-0 contre l'Argentine)
1994 Brésil	(3-2 contre l'Italie, après prolongation)
1998 France	(3-0 contre le Brésil)

De 1930 à 1939

1930

Le chômage et la pauvreté se généralisent des deux côtés de l'Atlantique dès les années 30. Franklin Roosevelt devient président des États-Unis en 1933 et lance le New Deal, un vaste programme de redressement économique.

En Europe, les affrontements politiques sont violents. En 1933, le parti nazi prend le pouvoir en Allemagne. La France élit en 1936 une coalition de gauche, le Front populaire. Les opposants politiques sont éliminés en U.R.S.S. ; la guerre civile espagnole débute en 1936. À la fin des années 30, la guerre semble inévitable en Europe ; elle éclate en septembre 1939.

▼ *La congélation permet de conserver les aliments.*

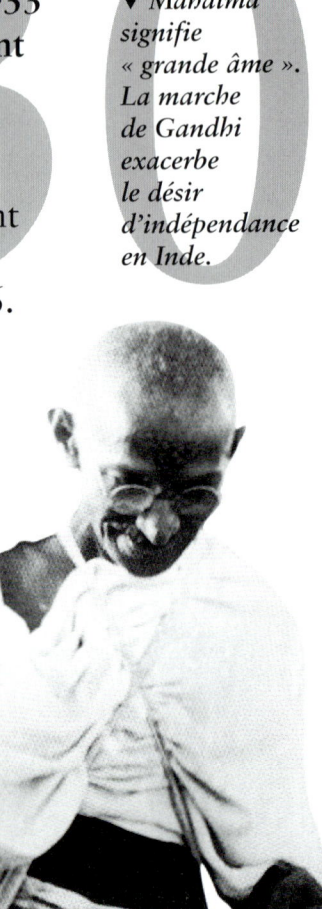

▼ *Mahatma signifie « grande âme ». La marche de Gandhi exacerbe le désir d'indépendance en Inde.*

La marche de Gandhi

▶ **6 avril 1930** ◀ Des centaines d'Indiens menés par le mahatma Gandhi, le militant nationaliste indien, sont arrivés sur la côte indienne après une marche de protestation d'environ 500 km. Ils s'opposent à une loi du gouvernement anglais qui leur interdit de produire leur propre sel. En défi au pouvoir britannique, Mohandas Karamchand Gandhi a ramassé une poignée de sel sur une plage faisant face au golfe de Cambay, dans le nord-ouest de l'Inde. Adepte de la non-violence, celui que l'on appelle le mahatma, la « grande âme », se bat depuis plus de dix ans pour l'indépendance de son pays. Conscient de la gravité de la situation, il demande à ses partisans d'être « prêts au pire, même à mourir, pour lutter contre la taxation du sel », et se prépare lui-même à être jeté en prison.

La congélation

L'homme d'affaires new-yorkais Clarence Birdseye met au point une technique de congélation pour conserver les aliments. Il s'est inspiré des Canadiens du Labrador, qui gardent leur nourriture dans la glace en hiver. Légumes et viandes pris dans la glace sont presque aussi bons que les produits frais.

Pluton, une nouvelle planète

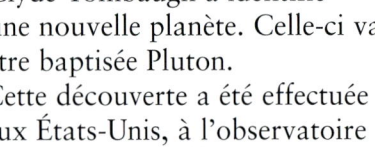

▶ **13 mars 1930** ◀ L'astronome américain Clyde Tombaugh a identifié une nouvelle planète. Celle-ci va être baptisée Pluton. Cette découverte a été effectuée aux États-Unis, à l'observatoire Lowell de Flagstaff, en Arizona. Tombaugh a déniché Pluton le 18 février, en étudiant des photographies du ciel prises la nuit. À son point le plus éloigné du Soleil, la planète est à 7,4 millions de kilomètres de la Terre.

▲ *Photographie de Pluton (à gauche).*

1930 – 1939

Le plus haut building du monde

▶ **Décembre 1930** ◀ On inaugure en fanfare, à New York, le plus haut building du monde, conçu par l'architecte William van Alen. En hommage à la firme automobile Chrysler, qui l'a fait construire, sa flèche en acier a pris la forme d'une calandre de voiture. Il est caractéristique du style Art déco, qui a fait son apparition en Europe dans les années 20.

Un empereur pour l'Éthiopie

▶ **2 novembre 1930** ◀ Le prince ras Tafari est couronné Haïlé Sélassié Ier, empereur d'Éthiopie. Il était régent depuis 1917 et avait aboli l'esclavage en 1924. L'Éthiopie, royaume chrétien, seul État d'Afrique à n'être pas colonisé, suscite la convoitise de l'Italie.

▶ *Haïlé Sélassié.*

▲ *Le Chrysler Building, qui mesure 319 m de haut, est le plus grand édifice du monde.*

La ligne Maginot

▶ **Décembre 1930** ◀ Pour défendre les frontières, André Maginot, ministre de la Guerre, imagine de construire une ceinture de béton. Équipés de puissants canons, bastions et casemates protégeront la France d'une possible invasion allemande.

En 1930 aussi …

12 mai • L'aviateur Jean Mermoz relie Saint-Louis du Sénégal à Natal, au Brésil, en emportant les premiers colis postaux de la ligne.

7 juillet • Le « père » de Sherlock Holmes est mort. L'écrivain anglais Arthur Conan Doyle vient de s'éteindre à l'âge de 71 ans.

Octobre-décembre • En U.R.S.S., les paysans s'insurgent contre la collectivisation des terres.

Montée des nazis

▶ **13 octobre 1930** ◀ « À bas les Juifs ! » hurlent les nazis dans les rues de Berlin en attaquant leurs boutiques. Nazis et communistes s'affrontent violemment au Reichstag, le Parlement. Depuis le 14 septembre, le parti national-socialiste d'Adolf Hitler est le deuxième parti derrière les socialistes, avec un total de 107 sièges au Reichstag.

Malgré leurs méthodes brutales, leurs fraudes et les pressions sur les électeurs, les nazis n'ont pas obtenu la majorité souhaitée. Mais ils sont assez nombreux pour maintenir une agitation permanente.

Succès de *l'Ange bleu* avec Marlene Dietrich

Marlene Dietrich devient une star avec *l'Ange bleu,* film du réalisateur autrichien Josef von Sternberg. Cette jeune Allemande interprète le rôle de Lola-Lola, une chanteuse de cabaret, femme fatale, dont un professeur d'âge mûr tombe amoureux, pour son malheur.

▲ *Marlene Dietrich dans le rôle de Lola-Lola.*

1931

Inauguration de l'Empire State Building

▲ L'Empire State Building.

▶ **1er mai 1931** ◀ Avec ses 102 étages et ses 73 ascenseurs, l'Empire State Building est comme un rayon d'espoir au milieu de la grande crise que traversent les États-Unis. Il mesure 381 m de hauteur et est l'édifice le plus haut du monde. Il a aussi été construit en un temps record : six mois, au lieu des dix-huit annoncés par les architectes. L'ancien gouverneur de la ville, Alfred Smith, a coupé le ruban. Le président Hoover a appuyé sur un interrupteur, et tout l'édifice s'est illuminé. Installé au cœur de New York, le bâtiment ne manque pas de style. Élancé, avec ses lignes verticales et son allure carrée, il mérite de devenir le symbole de la ville. Son sommet en fuseau a été conçu pour servir de mât d'ancrage aux dirigeables.

Un jeu qui fait fureur

Alfred Butts, un architecte au chômage, vient d'inventer un nouveau jeu. Il s'agit de former des mots avec des lettres choisies au hasard ; chaque lettre représente un certain nombre de points. Alfred Butts a baptisé ce nouveau jeu Scrabble, ce qui, en anglais, signifie « jouer des pieds et des mains ».

Les Japonais occupent la Mandchourie

▶ **18 septembre 1931** ◀ Les autorités japonaises accusent les Chinois d'avoir saboté à Moukden, le chemin de fer de Mandchourie, dans le nord-est de la Chine, tout près de la Corée, colonie japonaise. C'est le prétexte que souhaitaient les militaires japonais pour attaquer cette région. Ils veulent s'emparer des mines et accroître leurs possessions. Ils ne tiennent pas compte des protestations de la Société des nations et, l'année suivante, proclament l'indépendance du Mandchoukouo, qui, en fait leur est entièrement soumis.

▶ Prisonniers chinois en Mandchourie.

En 1931 aussi …

19 février • Une foule en délire accueille le cinéaste Charlie Chaplin à Londres.

13 mai • La France a un nouveau président, Paul Doumer.

28 mai • Premier voyage dans la stratosphère ! Il a été réalisé par le professeur Piccard, un savant suisse qui a atterri sur un glacier tyrolien, après avoir volé à plus de 16 000 m d'altitude dans une sphère en aluminium.

L'Espagne devient une république

▶ **14 avril 1931** ◀ Le roi Alphonse XIII et la famille royale espagnole partent pour Paris ; l'Espagne est désormais une république. Le roi a décidé d'abdiquer, devant le succès massif des républicains aux élections municipales.

Depuis 1923, Alphonse XIII avec le général Miguel Primo de Rivera imposaient une sévère dictature. Après la mort de celui-ci, le roi avait été critiqué, notamment pour n'avoir pas su lutter contre la pauvreté. L'ancien souverain et les nouveaux dirigeants espèrent que les récents événements empêcheront l'Espagne de sombrer dans la guerre civile.

▲ *Les républicains fêtent leur victoire en Espagne.*

1930 – 1939

L'hymne national américain

▶ **3 mars 1931** ◀ *La Bannière étoilée* (*The Star-Spangled Banner*), que les Américains chantent depuis la guerre d'Indépendance, devient officiellement, à partir d'aujourd'hui, leur hymne national. Elle a été écrite en 1814 par Francis Scott Key, qui s'est inspiré d'une vieille chanson à boire anglaise.

Une nouvelle loi au Nevada

Aux États-Unis, une nouvelle loi a changé, cette année, la vie de l'État du Nevada. Elle assouplit les lois sur le divorce et légalise les jeux. Cet État, connu pour être faiblement peuplé, espère ainsi attirer les foules et faire flamber ses revenus. Et ça marche : les joueurs ne cessent d'envahir les salles de jeu de Las Vegas.

▲ *Le Nevada, paradis pour les joueurs.*

Union nationale en Grande-Bretagne

▶ **24 août 1931** ◀ La crise mondiale frappe la Grande-Bretagne de plein fouet. Les banques étrangères refusent de reconnaître la livre sterling. Le gouvernement travailliste démissionne. Le Premier ministre James Ramsay MacDonald est obligé de prendre des mesures d'urgence et constitue un gouvernement d'union nationale. Son nouveau cabinet réunit des libéraux, des travaillistes et des conservateurs.

Mort de Thomas Edison

▶ **18 octobre 1931** ◀ Thomas Edison, l'un des plus grands inventeurs de tous les temps, vient de mourir. Autodidacte, il a toujours été fasciné par la science et la chimie. Et, pourtant, ses professeurs le trouvaient « trop brouillon ». Sa première invention a été un « télégraphe » servant à imprimer les cours de la Bourse. Il a inventé le phonographe et la lampe électrique à incandescence. C'est l'un des précurseurs du cinématographe.

▶ *Thomas Edison fait fonctionner un cinématographe. Ce grand savant a fait breveter plus de 1 000 inventions.*

1932

La crise continue

▶ **Décembre 1932** ◀ La crise économique qui secoue l'Occident depuis le krach de Wall Street, en 1929, entre dans sa quatrième année. Les gens ont de moins en moins d'argent et consomment peu, les marchandises ne s'écoulent plus, les usines licencient. 20 % de la population est touchée. Aucun chômeur ne perçoit d'indemnités. Parmi les gens qui sont concernés, beaucoup sont issus de milieux aisés et ne pensaient pas pouvoir se retrouver dans une telle situation. De nombreuses personnes n'ont plus que la soupe populaire pour se nourrir, des bouts de carton pour réparer leurs chaussures, et sont obligées de rapiécer leurs vêtements. Chaque pays tente de trouver une issue à la crise. En Grande-Bretagne, les participants à une marche de la faim présentent une pétition à leur gouvernement. En Allemagne, beaucoup croient trouver une solution dans les idéaux du parti national-socialiste (nazi) d'Adolf Hitler.

▲ *Les Américains font la queue pour acheter du pain.*

La crise économique
Entre 1929 et 1932, 14 millions d'Américains (20 % de la population active) sont au chômage.
•
2,25 millions de Britanniques sont au chômage.
•
Les prix agricoles ont baissé de moitié.
•
44 % des banques américaines ont fait faillite.

Le pont de Sydney

Le plus grand pont en arc du monde vient d'être inauguré en Australie. Le pont du port de Sydney relie le centre-ville aux banlieues nord. Il a fallu neuf ans pour venir à bout des 503 m de long du pont, surnommé « le portemanteau ».

Roosevelt, président

▶ **8 novembre 1932** ◀ Les Américains viennent de remplacer leur président, Herbert Hoover, incapable de mettre fin à la crise. Ils ont élu à sa place le candidat Franklin Delano Roosevelt. Après une campagne menée tambour battant, malgré une paralysie des jambes due à la poliomyélite, F. D. Roosevelt a remporté un succès total. Il a promis de venir rapidement à bout de la crise, grâce à un vaste programme de réformes économiques et sociales, le New Deal (« nouvelle donne »). Il envisage en particulier d'instituer de nouvelles lois sur les salaires, les prix, et les dépenses gouvernementales en matière de construction.

▶ *Roosevelt (à droite) a parcouru plus de 20 000 km en train au cours de sa campagne.*

110

1930 – 1939

Des bébés pour la France

▶ 21 janvier 1932 ◀ Le gouvernement Tardieu vient de faire voter une loi qui prévoit de distribuer des allocations aux familles nombreuses. La natalité française est la plus basse d'Europe : 16,5 ‰ pour un taux de mortalité de 15,7 ‰. Contrairement aux autres pays d'Europe, la France n'a jamais comblé les pertes de la Première Guerre mondiale, sa population stagne et vieillit. Les familles françaises n'ont qu'un ou deux enfants.

▲ António Salazar.

Années noires pour le Portugal

▶ 5 juillet 1932 ◀ Après l'Italie, c'est au tour du Portugal de devenir une dictature d'extrême droite. António Salazar vient d'être nommé à la tête du gouvernement. Il a les pleins-pouvoirs et entend bien imposer sa dictature. Il avait été nommé ministre des Finances en 1926, à la suite d'un putsch militaire. Il envisage d'instituer l'Estado novo (l'« État nouveau »), doté d'une nouvelle Constitution.

Les aviatrices françaises Boucher, Bastié et Hilsz

▶ 21 mai 1932 ◀ Elles sont jeunes, intrépides, et ont un seul amour : leur avion. Hélène Boucher, Maryse Bastié et Maryse Hilsz sont les trois aviatrices françaises les plus populaires. Maryse Hilsz est la spécialiste des grands raids. Après avoir volé de Paris à Saigon en 1930, elle atteint cette année Madagascar. Ces jeunes aviatrices ne sont pas fortunées. Maryse Bastié est mécanicienne ; quant à Maryse Hilsz, elle est modiste. Pour financer leurs vols, elles participent à des concours et des meetings aériens. Maryse Hilsz va même jusqu'à sauter en parachute.

▼ Maryse Hilsz, aviatrice française.

Les mobiles de Calder

Le sculpteur et peintre américain Alexander Calder a fait des études d'ingénieur en mécanique. Cela l'a aidé à créer une nouvelle forme d'art. Il fabrique de drôles de machines, les mobiles. Ce sont de savants assemblages en acier, en cuivre ou en aluminium, le plus souvent peints avec des couleurs vives. Alors qu'ils sont suspendus en l'air, le moindre souffle les fait bouger.

◀ Calder devant l'un de ses « mobiles ».

En 1932 aussi …

4 janvier • Le parti du Congrès est interdit en Inde, Gandhi est arrêté.

10 avril • Le maréchal Hindenburg est réélu en Allemagne. Il bat Hitler à l'élection présidentielle.

6 mai • Assassinat du président français Paul Doumer par un fasciste russe du nom de Gorgulov.

6 novembre • En Autriche, l'ancien ministre de l'Agriculture Engelbert Dollfuss est élu chancelier.

Victoire française en Coupe Davis

▶ 31 juillet 1932 ◀ Les « Quatre Mousquetaires » ont encore frappé ! Brugnon, Lacoste, Cochet et Borotra viennent de remporter la Coupe Davis pour la sixième fois consécutive. La France a battu les États-Unis par trois à deux. La mascotte française est un crocodile, que Lacoste fera broder sur ses célèbres chemises.

DES VILLES TENTACULAIRES

La croissance galopante des villes marque le XXe siècle. Elles explosent littéralement devant l'affluence de ceux qui s'y précipitent avec l'espoir d'y trouver du travail. Dans certains pays d'Europe et aux États-Unis, l'exode rural augmente depuis le XIXe siècle. D'ici à l'an 2000, près de la moitié de la population vivra en milieu urbain. Aujourd'hui, en Europe, en Australie et aux États-Unis, plus des trois quarts de la population vivent déjà dans des villes. Celles-ci se métamorphosent sans cesse. On bâtit, on détruit, on reconstruit, on rénove et on modernise. Dévastées pendant la Seconde Guerre mondiale, de nombreuses villes, comme Tokyo ou Hambourg, ont dû être reconstruites.

◀ *Vue de New York sous le pont de Brooklyn.*

◀ *Ouvrier faisant une pause pendant la construction de l'Empire State Building, à New York.*

Bousculade

Fini la marche à pied ! Grâce au développement des transports – voitures, trains et bus –, les citadins peuvent préférer les banlieues aux centres-villes. Aujourd'hui, les transports publics sont en crise. Ils n'arrivent plus à faire face au nombre croissant des usagers.

◀ *Heure de pointe à Tokyo. Des employés poussent les voyageurs.*

Le développement des villes

Les villes gagnent du terrain. Elles élargissent sans cesse leur territoire, menant la vie dure aux campagnes. Certaines villes industrielles d'Europe et des États-Unis, qui se sont incroyablement développées aux XIXe et XXe siècles, sont désormais dépassées par des villes sud-américaines comme São Paulo ou Mexico. Mexico comptait 5 millions d'habitants en 1960 et 20 millions en 1995, un chiffre qui devrait passer à 31 millions d'ici à l'an 2000.

L'augmentation de la population pousse les villes à se développer. Comme l'espace n'est pas extensible à l'infini, on construit des buildings de plus en plus hauts. C'est le cas de New York ou des principales villes d'Asie du Sud-Est, comme Singapour ou Hong Kong. D'autres villes, qui ont encore la place de s'agrandir, s'étendent en périphérie, comme Paris, Londres ou Los Angeles.

▲ *Réfugiés chinois vivant dans des taudis flottants à Aberdeen, Hong Kong (1962).*

▼ *Femme mendiant dans la rue à Buenos Aires, en Argentine.*

La vie urbaine

La vie est très difficile pour les habitants les plus pauvres dans les grandes agglomérations. Les plus démunis, qui sont souvent ceux qui sont venus en ville pour trouver du travail, vivent, au mieux, dans des logements insalubres, au pire, dans la rue. La violence et l'insécurité augmentent. Il n'est pas rare de voir des sans-abri dormir dans les rues à Paris, Londres ou New York. Dans certains pays, le seuil de pauvreté est tel que de gigantesques bidonvilles se sont créés à la périphérie des grandes villes. Ceux qui y survivent misérablement ont construit des abris avec des matériaux de fortune trouvés dans les décharges publiques. On estime à 5 millions le nombre de familles vivant dans de telles conditions en Amérique latine.

La ville

- Par temps clair, on peut voir jusqu'à 80 km alentour du haut des 381 m de l'Empire State Building, à New York.
- Loger 14 000 personnes sur 60 étages : ce serait possible dans le Woolworth Building, construit à New York en 1913.
- Le nombre de villes de plus de 1 million d'habitants dans le monde est passé de 16 en 1900 à 67 en 1950, à 250 en 1985 et à 400 en 1995.
- Dans les années 80, il y avait plus de téléphones dans la ville de Tokyo que sur tout le continent africain.

Les marchés financiers

Ils sont peu à contrôler l'ensemble de l'économie mondiale et à présider au destin de populations entières : quelques grandes banques et établissements financiers. Toutes les décisions financières sont prises aux Bourses de Paris, de Tokyo, de Londres ou de New York. Chaque métropole a son quartier de la finance, où les banques et les *traders* (les opérateurs de marchés financiers) se sont installés. C'est le cas de Wall Street, à New York. Les villes vivent grâce à la circulation de l'argent. Elles restent réservées à ceux qui ont les moyens d'y habiter ou de venir y dépenser leur argent.

▶ *Les opérateurs intervenant à la Bourse (ici, celle de Londres) influent sur la vie économique.*

Hitler est le nouveau chancelier allemand

▶ *La croix gammée et l'aigle sont les insignes nazis.*

▼ *Les nazis saluent avec le bras droit levé.*

▶ 30 janvier 1933 ◀ Adolf Hitler vient d'être nommé chancelier par le maréchal Hindenburg. Les militants du parti national-socialiste (nazis) défilent en brandissant des flambeaux dans de nombreuses villes pour saluer cette nomination.

À 44 ans, Hitler est chargé de former un nouveau gouvernement. Les députés nazis sont majoritaires au Reichstag (le Parlement). Ils occupent 196 sièges, depuis les élections de novembre 1932. Hitler sait envoûter les foules, grâce à ses talents d'orateur. Sa doctrine politique repose sur le racisme, la haine des socialistes, des communistes, des syndicats, des Juifs, et de tous ceux qu'il estime responsables de la défaite humiliante de 1918. Il développe également la théorie de la supériorité raciale allemande, destinée à mettre l'Europe à genoux. Hitler a promis à son peuple du travail pour les 6 millions de chômeurs. Enfin, il réclame les pleins-pouvoirs afin d'asseoir sa dictature.

Le Reichstag en feu

▶ 27 février 1933 ◀ Cette nuit, le ciel de Berlin est rouge. Le Reichstag (le Parlement) brûle. La police vient d'arrêter le pyromane, un nommé Marinus Van der Lubbe, un jeune Néerlandais. Hitler et le président du Reichstag, Hermann Goering, accusent aussitôt les communistes. Le parti communiste est interdit, les arrestations sont massives. Sous prétexte de protection du peuple et de l'État, la liberté individuelle, la liberté d'expression et la liberté de la presse sont suspendues. L'incendie du Reichstag est un coup monté par les nazis pour supprimer l'opposition.

L'Allemagne quitte la SDN

▶ 14 octobre 1933 ◀ L'Allemagne quitte la Société des nations et la conférence sur le désarmement. Hitler annonce qu'il entreprend le réarmement de son pays, et met progressivement son plan en place. Les partis sont interdits, les opposants politiques et les marginaux sont traqués sans merci, le boycott des commerces juifs est institué. Juifs et communistes sont chassés de la fonction publique. Les nazis enferment les indésirables dans le camp de concentration de Dachau. Les jeunes Allemands sont enrôlés dans les jeunesses hitlériennes.

▲ *Le Reichstag, symbole historique, part en fumée.*

1930 – 1939

◀ À gauche : Kurt Weill.
À droite : Thomas Mann.

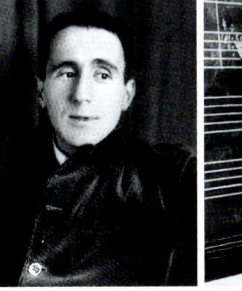

▲ À gauche : Bertolt Brecht.
À droite : Arnold Schönberg.

Les artistes s'enfuient

▶ **15 octobre 1933** ◀ À Berlin, Hitler pose la première pierre de la « maison de l'art allemand ». Cependant, menacés par les nazis, de nombreux artistes et intellectuels fuient l'Allemagne. Les artistes d'avant-garde, surtout s'ils sont juifs ou partisans de la gauche, sont désormais considérés comme « dégénérés » et ne peuvent plus s'exprimer. Beaucoup de livres sont interdits et brûlés.

L'affaire Stavisky

▶ **28 décembre 1933** ◀ Toute la France s'indigne lorsque les journaux révèlent l'affaire Stavisky. Cet escroc profitait de la crédulité des épargnants pour leur vendre de faux bons de crédit soi-disant émis par le Crédit municipal de Bayonne. Personne n'avait eu l'idée de vérifier l'origine de ces bons, car Stavisky, surnommé « le beau Serge », inspirait confiance à tous ; il donnait de somptueuses réceptions, que fréquentaient des députés et des ministres. Un homme qui avait d'aussi brillantes relations ne pouvait pas être soupçonné. En septembre, la police a découvert que les 240 millions de bons étaient des faux. Les autorités ont essayé d'étouffer l'affaire, mais désormais l'opinion soupçonne les hommes politiques d'avoir profité de l'escroquerie.

En 1933 aussi ...

29 mars • Albert Einstein, physicien allemand, fuit l'Allemagne.

2 mai • Les nazis suppriment les syndicats.

20 juin • Le chancelier autrichien Dollfuss interdit les partis communiste et nazi en Autriche.

7 décembre • L'écrivain français André Malraux reçoit le prix Goncourt pour son livre la Condition humaine.

King Kong

Révolutionnaire par ses effets spéciaux, *King Kong* est le film le plus populaire de l'année. On n'avait jamais vu un gorille géant semer la panique dans New York, ni provoquer l'aviation américaine du haut de l'Empire State Building, en brandissant une jolie héroïne !

▲ *Les affiches du film* King Kong.

Roosevelt aide les agriculteurs

▶ **12 mai 1933** ◀ Le président américain Theodore Roosevelt met en application sa politique économique, la « nouvelle donne » (New Deal). Il signe l'Agricultural Adjustment Act (AAA), une politique d'aide nationale aux agriculteurs, victimes de la baisse des prix depuis 1920.

▼ *Les vents de poussière qui ravagent certaines régions des États-Unis aggravent les difficultés des agriculteurs.*

1934

La Longue Marche de Mao Zédong en Chine

▼ *Mao, l'un des fondateurs du parti communiste chinois, en 1921.*

▶ **21 octobre 1934** ◀ Depuis quatre ans, Tchang Kaï-chek, commandant des troupes du Guomindang, essaie d'anéantir les bases communistes créées par Mao Zédong depuis leur rupture. Pour briser l'encerclement, Mao lance ses hommes dans la « Longue Marche ». Elle va durer un an, et ils vont parcourir 12 000 km dans des conditions très dures. Les hommes sont 130 000 au départ, et moins de 30 000 à l'arrivée, mais ils ont rallié des milliers de personnes au fur et à mesure de leur marche. Ils doivent atteindre Zunyi, dans la province du Guizhou.

La Longue Marche
Les communistes chinois ont marché pendant douze mois. Ils ont franchi de formidables obstacles : 24 rivières et 18 chaînes de montagnes, dont cinq couvertes de neige.

Un tiers des marcheurs ont été tués pendant les trois premiers mois de la Longue Marche.

Dollfuss assassiné par les nazis

▶ **25 juillet 1934** ◀ Le chancelier autrichien Engelbert Dollfuss a été sauvagement assassiné par les nazis autrichiens. C'est une véritable tentative de putsch. Ils ont pris des ministres en otage et se sont emparés du bâtiment de la radio. Les forces de l'ordre les ont rapidement maîtrisés. Les membres du commando nazi, au nombre de 150, ont été emprisonnés à Vienne. Le Reich allemand nie sa responsabilité dans cette affaire. Adolf Hitler a officiellement désavoué le parti nazi autrichien. Pendant ce temps, le dictateur italien Benito Mussolini mobilise ses troupes. Il redoute une prochaine invasion de l'Autriche par l'Allemagne.

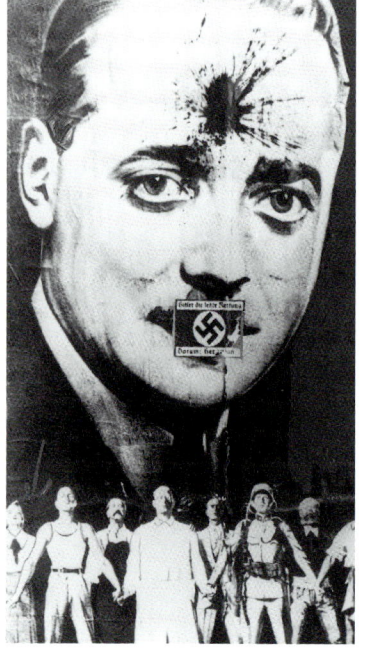

▶ *Affiche parue après le meurtre de Dollfuss par les nazis autrichiens.*

Walt Disney crée Donald

Il rouspète, il n'est pas franchement aimable et il a un sale caractère. C'est un canard. Il s'appelle Donald et il vient de faire son apparition dans le monde du dessin animé. Walt Disney, son créateur, lui donne la parole dans *la Petite Poule sage*. Pas question, cependant, de voler la vedette à Mickey, la souris la plus populaire du globe !

▼ *Donald (en bas, à droite), le nouveau héros créé par Walt Disney.*

1930 – 1939

▲ *Mao Zédong à la tête des participants à la Longue Marche.*

La « nuit des longs couteaux »

▶ **30 juin 1934** ◀ Hitler vient de se débarrasser de l'aile gauche de son parti. Au cours de la nuit dernière, Ernst Röhm, le chef de la Section d'Assaut (SA) a été exécuté avec tout son état major dans un hôtel de Bad Wiesse, en bordure des Alpes. Le massacre dure toute la nuit. Ce règlement de comptes sanglant est connu sous le nom de « nuit des longs couteaux ».

Hitler justifie ses actes au Reichstag. Il parle de complot, de mutinerie et de trahison. En fait, il s'est débarrassé des chemises brunes par calcul politique. En effet, elles ont joué un grand rôle dans l'ascension des nazis. Les SA avaient acquis une grande influence, mais ils se sont peu à peu heurtés à l'aile pro-hitlérienne du Parti national-socialiste. Celle-ci ne pratiquant pas une politique aussi sociale que prévu.

▶ *Le capitaine Röhm, à droite, et le lieutenant Brückner.*

▲ *Un membre de la tribu des Sioux.*

Viva Italia !

▶ **10 juin 1934** ◀ La victoire de l'Italie à l'occasion de la deuxième Coupe du monde de football est également une victoire pour la propagande du dictateur Benito Mussolini. Les joueurs de l'équipe italienne font d'ailleurs le salut fasciste avant de commencer le match. Ils battent la Tchécoslovaquie par 2 buts à 1. Les joueurs d'origine italienne, comme Guaita, Monti et Orsi, qui font partie de clubs argentins, ne sont pas étrangers au score. L'Italie est le premier pays européen à remporter le trophée. L'Uruguay avait gagné la première Coupe du monde en 1930.

▲ *Le trophée de la Coupe du monde.*

Les Indiens aussi ont des droits

▶ **Juin 1934** ◀ Une nouvelle loi américaine autorise les Indiens d'Amérique à posséder les terres de leurs réserves. En 1887, la loi Dawes avait morcelé les réserves indiennes en une multiplicité de petits territoires de 65 hectares environ. Le Congrès américain voulait que les Indiens deviennent cultivateurs, mais la plus grande partie de ces terrains a été revendue à des Américains blancs. La nouvelle loi autorise les tribus à se gouverner de façon autonome. Le bureau fédéral des Affaires indiennes propose de les aider à utiliser efficacement leurs terres.

Le Monopoly est né

Inventé en 1933 par Charles Darrow, le Monopoly, jeu de société, ne cesse de séduire le public américain. Les cases, sur lesquelles chaque joueur avance, représentent les rues d'une grande ville. Chacun peut acheter des rues, y faire construire des immeubles et faire payer les joueurs qui tombent dessus. Les participants s'arrêtent de jouer lorsqu'ils ont tout perdu.

▼ *Le Monopoly, un jeu de société pour tous.*

1934

Mort de Bonnie et Clyde

▲ *Bonnie et Clyde mimant un braquage.*

23 mai 1934 — Le couple de gangsters qui défie les autorités depuis près de deux ans est tombé dans une embuscade tendue par la police, en Louisiane. Bonnie Parker et Clyde Barrow sont morts, criblés de balles. Ils avaient à peine 25 ans.

En 1932, Bonnie quitte son emploi de serveuse à Dallas, au Texas, pour faire équipe avec Clyde, qui sort de prison. Ensemble, ils tuent au moins une douzaine de personnes, dont 6 policiers. La police a mis fin à leurs agissements, après qu'ils ont été dénoncés par une amie de Bonnie.

Pendant 21 mois, ils ont défrayé la chronique américaine en dévalisant les banques, les stations-service et les restaurants du sud-ouest des États-Unis. Ils sont toujours parvenus à échapper aux forces de l'ordre. Même lorsque 200 policiers les ont encerclés dans une aire de pique-nique de l'Iowa ! En avril 1933, ils avaient même défoncé avec leur voiture la porte d'un garage pour s'enfuir. La presse a fait de leurs aventures un feuilleton à sensation. Ce qui n'a pas empêché le célèbre gangster John Dillinger de les qualifier d'amateurs qui « déshonorent la profession ».

Short de tennis à Wimbledon

Les joueuses de tennis étaient cette année autorisées à porter le short à Wimbledon, et ce pour la première fois. Cette nouvelle tenue a, semble-t-il, profité aux Anglais : Fred Perry a remporté la finale du simple hommes en battant l'Australien Crawford, et Dorothy Round a gagné la finale du simple dames, avant de s'imposer aussi dans le tournoi du double mixte.

Lázaro Cárdenas, président du Mexique

2 juillet 1934 — Un ancien soldat de la révolution est nommé président du Mexique. L'heureux élu s'appelle Lázaro Cárdenas. Il représente le premier parti du Mexique, le parti national révolutionnaire (Partido nacional revolucionario, PNR). Il promet d'appliquer le programme du PNR en matière de changements sociaux et de réforme agraire.

La révolution mexicaine a commencé en 1910, lorsque le libéral Francisco Madero s'est soulevé contre le général Porfirio Díaz, qui gouvernait en dictateur depuis plus de 30 ans. Madero est devenu président en 1911 mais n'est pas parvenu à maîtriser la contestation révolutionnaire. Il est renversé en 1913.

En 1917, la nouvelle Constitution proclame la séparation de l'Église et de l'État. Les ressources pétrolières, qui appartiennent à des étrangers, passent aux mains de l'État ; la terre est distribuée. La mise en pratique de ces mesures est lente. Cárdenas doit l'accélérer.

◄ *Lázaro Cárdenas pendant sa campagne électorale au Mexique, parmi ses partisans et ses amis.*

En 1934 aussi …

26 janvier • Pacte germano-polonais de non-agression.

14-15 juin • Première entrevue Mussolini-Hitler à Venise.

1er août • Mort de Hindenburg. Hitler prend les pleins-pouvoirs.

9 septembre • Le roi Alexandre de Yougoslavie est assassiné à Marseille.

18 septembre • L'URSS est admise à la Société des nations.

1930 – 1939

Émeutes sanglantes à Paris

▶ **6 février 1934** ◀ Toutes les organisations de droite et d'extrême droite, parmi lesquelles les Camelots du roi, les Croix-de-Feu, les Jeunesses patriotes et l'Action française, se sont rassemblées place de la Concorde. L'extrême droite s'appuie sur les récents scandales financiers pour tenter de renverser le régime républicain. Les manifestants avancent vers la Chambre des députés et s'affrontent violemment aux barrages des forces de l'ordre. Certains vont jusqu'à tailler les jarrets des chevaux avec des rasoirs. La police riposte, la fusillade éclate. On compte 16 morts et plus de 2 000 blessés.

▲ *Les émeutiers érigent une barricade avec des échelles et un autobus.*

Ouverture du zoo de Vincennes

▶ **Juin 1934** ◀ À Paris, le zoo de Vincennes vient d'ouvrir ses portes au public. 1 500 animaux y vivent dans des espaces spécialement aménagés. L'aquarium, le plateau des lions, le plateau des tigres et le domaine des éléphants sont étonnants. L'immense rocher où vivent les singes est particulièrement impressionnant.

La terreur règne en URSS

▶ **1934** ◀ En URSS, Staline, pour se maintenir au pouvoir, renforce son autorité. Il tue ou emprisonne tous les opposants à son régime. Assassinats, emprisonnements, mais aussi censure, exercée à l'encontre des artistes et des intellectuels : la terreur règne. C'est la dictature du réalisme socialiste. Les artistes et les écrivains doivent désormais glorifier, dans leurs œuvres, le système soviétique, le rôle de Staline et celui du parti communiste. Les artistes qui refusent les normes staliniennes sont impitoyablement pourchassés.

◀ *Affiche russe glorifiant le travail.*

Fred Astaire et Ginger Rogers

Ils ont la souplesse et la grâce, le rythme et la désinvolture. Ils ont apporté leur élégance et leur entrain au film musical. Ils forment un couple séduisant. Fred Astaire et Ginger Rogers présentent le premier film dont ils sont les vedettes. Il s'agit de *la Joyeuse Divorcée (The Gay Divorcee)*, de Mark Sandrich, une histoire d'amour abracadabrante, doublée de formidables numéros de danse. Spécialisés dans les numéros de claquettes éblouissants, les deux acteurs forment un duo de danseurs hors pair. Après avoir débuté vers 1915 avec sa sœur Adèle, Fred Astaire devient rapidement célèbre et arrive à Hollywood en 1932. Ginger Rogers, elle, remporte sa première compétition de danse lorsqu'elle est encore adolescente. Elle vient à Hollywood en 1931. Les deux acteurs ont travaillé pour la première fois ensemble dans *Carioca (Flying Down to Rio)*, un film dans lequel ils n'avaient que des seconds rôles.

▲ *La Joyeuse Divorcée reprend une comédie musicale de Cole Porter.*

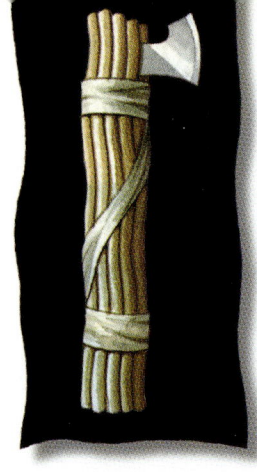

◀ Les faisceaux de la Rome antique sont les emblèmes du fascisme.

LE FASCISME

Les idéologies totalitaires se développent entre la fin de la Première Guerre mondiale et le début de la Seconde. Après le chaos et l'insécurité économique des années de dépression, beaucoup croient trouver une solution en portant des régimes dictatoriaux au pouvoir. Ces nouveaux régimes ont de nombreux traits communs : la concentration des pouvoirs aux mains d'un seul homme, l'existence d'un parti unique, la soumission de l'ensemble de la population à une idéologie totalitaire, la suppression des libertés politiques et individuelles.

Mussolini et Hitler

En 1922, Benito Mussolini impose le régime fasciste à l'Italie et prend la direction du pays. Il modifie le mode de scrutin de façon à contrôler le Parlement, s'octroie les pleins-pouvoirs, et fait du parti fasciste un parti unique. Il emprisonne les opposants, les exile, soumet les journaux à la censure, supprime les libertés publiques.

Adolf Hitler s'inspire de cette ascension et impose la dictature nazie, lorsqu'il prend le pouvoir, en 1933. Les libertés sont abolies, les opposants sont assassinés ou déportés dans des camps de concentration.

Mussolini et Hitler ont des revendications territoriales similaires. Mussolini souhaite contrôler le bassin méditerranéen et les colonies africaines, Hitler cherche à annexer les pays d'Europe centrale et de l'Est à l'Allemagne. En 1936, l'Italie fasciste et l'Allemagne nazie établissent l'axe Rome-Berlin. Mussolini conquiert l'Éthiopie en 1935, les troupes allemandes entrent en Autriche en 1938, puis en Tchécoslovaquie en 1938.

◀ Hitler et Mussolini, à Berlin, en 1936, scellent l'Axe Rome-Berlin.

▼ Mussolini s'adresse à la foule à Trévise, en Italie.

▼ Hitler renforce son pouvoir par des manifestations de masse très organisées.

▼ Le général Franco, dictateur en Espagne.

▲ Les femmes participent à la guerre civile.

Franco

En Espagne, en 1936, le général Franco se soulève contre le gouvernement de Front populaire. Les franquistes, soutenus par l'Allemagne et l'Italie, battent les républicains. Franco devient le seul maître du pays en 1939.

▼ *Rassemblement du parti nazi à Nuremberg, en septembre 1935.*

Jeunesses fascistes

En Italie, personne n'échappe à la propagande fasciste de Mussolini. Les jeunes garçons sont embrigadés, selon leur âge, dans différents corps paramilitaires où ils apprennent à devenir de bons soldats fascistes. Ils sont « fils de la louve » jusqu'à huit ans, « Balilla » jusqu'à douze ans, puis « avant-gardistes » jusqu'à dix-huit ans. Les jeunes filles sont encouragées à ne penser qu'au mariage et à la maternité, afin de peupler les futures colonies italiennes et de subvenir aux besoins de l'armée. L'un des grands axes de la politique fasciste est la bataille des naissances. Les mères de plus de six enfants sont médaillées, les soldats ont ordre de saluer les femmes enceintes, et les hommes paient des impôts spéciaux s'ils ne se marient pas.

En Allemagne, les nazis se préoccupent, eux aussi, de l'éducation physique, intellectuelle et morale de la jeunesse, évidemment dans l'esprit du national-socialisme. Les enfants et les étudiants sont vivement encouragés à entrer dans les organisations de jeunesse, les jeunesses hitlériennes. À travers les activités sportives, les chants patriotiques et les défilés, les jeunes apprennent à devenir les machines de guerre et les travailleurs du IIIe Reich.

Hitler et Mussolini

Mussolini a été renvoyé de l'école pour avoir donné un coup de couteau à un autre élève.

•

La nuit, Mussolini laissait les lumières de son bureau allumées, pour entretenir son image de surhomme.

•

Hitler refusait de porter ses lunettes en public. Ses discours étaient écrits en gros caractères.

◀ *Les fascistes préparent les enfants à combattre pour la grandeur de l'Italie.*

1935

1930

1931

1932

1933

1934

1935

1936

1937

1938

1939

Shirley Temple, la plus jeune star de Hollywood

▶ 27 février 1935 ◀

C'est une révélation ! Shirley Temple, la plus jeune actrice de Hollywood, vient de recevoir un prix spécial du jury des Oscars pour « sa contribution exceptionnelle au cinéma durant l'année 1934 ». Née en 1928, elle commence par jouer, dès l'âge de trois ans, dans des courts métrages comiques comme *Baby Burlesks*. Si elle tourne son premier long métrage en tant que vedette en 1932, elle est véritablement lancée en 1934 par deux films de la Twentieth Century Fox, *Stand up and Cheer*, de Hamilton McFadden, et *Little Miss Marker*, d'Alexander Hall. *Now and Forever*, de Henry Hathaway, et *Bright Eyes*, de David Butler – film dans lequel elle chante *On the Good Ship Lollipop* –, sont ses plus récents succès. C'est l'enfant prodige la plus populaire de Hollywood et la star numéro un du box-office : elle reçoit 15 000 lettres d'admirateurs par jour, et beaucoup de produits sont vendus sous son nom.

▲ *Shirley Temple, l'enfant prodige du cinéma américain, dans un de ses premiers films.*

Le stakhanovisme

▶ 8 septembre 1935 ◀

Alexis Stakhanov, un mineur soviétique de la région de Donetsk, en Ukraine, a obtenu aujourd'hui une récompense pour être parvenu à extraire 175 tonnes de charbon en un temps record. Joseph Staline décide d'instituer une nouvelle méthode de rendement du travail, le stakhanovisme. Les travailleurs soviétiques sont poussés à accroître leur production, à se discipliner, à redoubler d'initiatives et à travailler dur pour le bien du régime. Toutes sortes d'avantages leur sont accordés s'ils parviennent à dépasser les objectifs établis par le plan.

Une nouvelle guitare électrique

La nouvelle guitare électrique ES150 fait son apparition. Elle sort des usines Gibson, un fabricant implanté dans le Michigan. Elle est l'aboutissement de onze ans de recherches sur l'amplification électrique. Elle s'élance sur les traces du succès remporté par les guitares électriques hawaïennes, conçues par Rickenbacker et Beauchamp.

Record de vitesse automobile

Le pilote automobile britannique Malcolm Campbell pulvérise, depuis onze ans, tous les records de vitesse du monde. Le 7 mars, il établissait le record de 484,518 km/h à Daytona Beach, en Floride. Il s'est surpassé, le 3 septembre, au volant de sa Bluebird, conçue spécialement pour lui, en atteignant les 485,750 km/h à Bonneville, dans l'Utah.

◀ *Le pilote automobile Malcolm Campbell.*

▲ *Shirley Temple, vedette de* Bright Eyes.

▼ *Famille juive insultée par des SA.*

Invasion de l'Éthiopie

▶ **3 octobre 1935** ◀ Les troupes italiennes viennent d'envahir l'Éthiopie. Le site d'Adoua a été bombardé par l'aviation. L'empereur Hailé Sélassié demande aux Éthiopiens de défendre leur pays et fait appel à la Société des nations. La guerre a éclaté, à la suite des incidents de frontières du mois de mai, qui ont opposé l'Éthiopie à la Somalie italienne. Si Mussolini fait mine de négocier, il semble préférer la poursuite de la guerre. Ses troupes se massent dans les colonies italiennes – la Somalie et l'Érythrée – depuis le mois de février. Le dictateur italien veut construire un empire aussi vaste que celui de la Rome antique.

▲ *Des Éthiopiens devant un portrait de Mussolini.*

1930 – 1939

En 1935 aussi...

22 mars • *Premières émissions de télévision à Berlin.*

20 octobre • *Fin de la Longue Marche. Les communistes chinois s'arrêtent à Yan'an, dans le nord de la Chine.*

10 décembre • *Irène et Frédéric Joliot-Curie obtiennent le prix Nobel de chimie pour leurs travaux sur la radioactivité artificielle.*

L'Allemagne se réarme

▶ **16 mars 1935** ◀ Le service militaire obligatoire est à nouveau en vigueur en Allemagne. C'est ce que le gouvernement nazi a annoncé, cinq jours après avoir proclamé la création d'une nouvelle force aérienne, la Luftwaffe. L'Allemagne nazie refuse ainsi de respecter le traité de Versailles, qui la limitait militairement. Adolf Hitler souhaite que son armée compte 500 000 hommes, soit cinq fois plus que l'effectif autorisé par le traité. Le retour au service militaire est la réponse, selon les nazis, à l'annonce de réarmement faite récemment par la Grande-Bretagne. Des initiés affirment que l'Allemagne se réarme clandestinement depuis deux ans.

◀ *Un soldat allemand sonne le rassemblement.*

Gallup invente les sondages

George Gallup, un ancien professeur de journalisme américain natif de l'Iowa, va permettre de connaître l'opinion du public sur toutes sortes de sujets. Il travaille depuis 1932 dans une agence de publicité de New York, et vient de mettre au point, à la demande de ses clients, une méthode de sondage prétendument infaillible. Il est sûr de prouver sa qualité lors de la prochaine élection présidentielle. Cette année, il a fondé l'Institut américain d'opinion publique.

Les Juifs hors la loi

▶ **15 septembre 1935** ◀ Adolf Hitler vient d'exposer ses nouvelles lois au congrès du parti nazi de Nuremberg. L'Histoire les appellera les lois de Nuremberg. Elles visent à exclure purement et simplement les Juifs de la vie politique et sociale du pays. Le premier des décrets enlève aux Allemands d'origine juive le droit à la nationalité. Le second interdit les mariages entre Allemands et Juifs, c'est la « loi pour la protection du sang et de l'honneur allemands ». Les nazis refusent l'égalité des races. Selon eux, la race aryenne est une race supérieure qui comprend les Allemands de souche ; la race inférieure est composée de sous-hommes, les Juifs. Pour éviter qu'ils ne se mélangent davantage à la race aryenne, les Juifs sont donc bannis de la société allemande. À cette occasion, le gouvernement supprime leurs allocations et leur droit de vote. De nombreux Juifs parviennent à fuir l'Allemagne.

LA BANDE DESSINÉE

Tintin, Spirou, Astérix, Lucky Luke, Blake et Mortimer : les bandes dessinées nous ont donné les héros les plus attachants de ce siècle.
Par l'abondance de ses sujets et l'audace de certains dessins, par sa façon de refléter le monde ou de faire rêver, la bande dessinée est une forme de culture très appréciée.
Beaucoup d'albums et de feuilletons ont été adaptés pour la radio, la télévision ou le cinéma.

Le savez-vous ?

L'illustrateur Caran d'Ache crée des histoires illustrées à la fin du XIXᵉ siècle.

•

La bande dessinée moderne est préfigurée par Rodolphe Toepffer dès la première moitié du XIXᵉ siècle.

•

Plus de 250 millions d'albums d'Astérix ont été vendus dans le monde.

Premiers héros

Une bande dessinée, c'est une série de dessins qui racontent une histoire. La plus ancienne BD a donc été dessinée sur les parois de la grotte de Lascaux… Les premiers héros français de BD sont le canard Gédéon, la Famille Fenouillard et Bécassine ; ils ne concernent que les enfants. C'est le contraire aux États-Unis, où les quotidiens ont une page de BD destinée aux adultes, qui publie les aventures des *Katzenjammer Kids* (Pim, Pam, Poum), de la petite Annie, de Winnie Winkle (Bicot) ou de Popeye. Arrivent ensuite les super-héros, Dick Tracy le détective, Mandrake le magicien, Flash Gordon, Prince Vaillant et Superman, qui, avec Mickey la souris, envahissent les journaux français. La grande époque de la BD francophone ne commence qu'en 1945 avec l'album des aventures de Tintin et Milou. Dans les magazines *Tintin*, puis *Spirou*, des auteurs donnent naissance à Gaston Lagaffe, Lucky Luke, Astérix et les Schtroumpfs. Les héros de BD deviendront des vedettes de dessins animés : certains, comme Corto Maltese ou Blueberry, seront l'objet d'un véritable culte.

◀ *De jeunes lecteurs new-yorkais lisant des BD avec des lunettes en 3 D.*

De la Famille Fenouillard à Astérix

Christophe, premier auteur français de bandes dessinées, crée *la Famille Fenouillard* en 1889 pour le journal *Le Petit Français illustré*, puis il dessine *le Sapeur Camember* et *le Savant Cosinus*. D'autres héros font leur apparition : Bécassine, une petite Bretonne un peu délurée, en 1905, dans *la Semaine de Suzette* ; les Pieds Nickelés en 1908 ; Bibi Fricotin en 1924. L'année 1929 marque un tournant dans la bande dessinée avec l'apparition de Tintin. Une ère d'extraordinaires héros est née. Ils se nomment Spirou, Lucky Luke, Astérix, Blake et Mortimer, Gaston Lagaffe, Achille Talon, Adèle Blanc-Sec ou Corto Maltese…

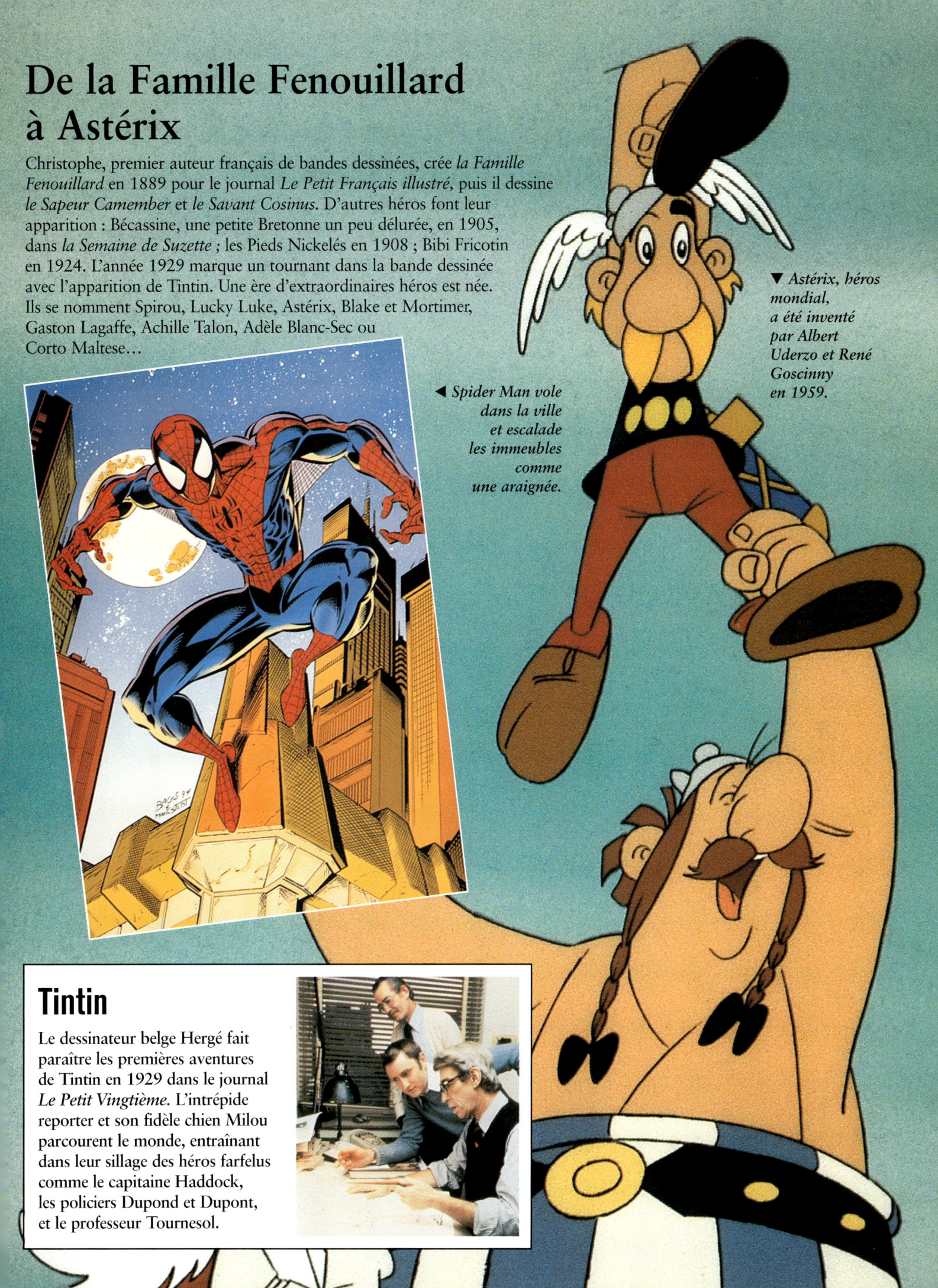

◀ *Spider Man vole dans la ville et escalade les immeubles comme une araignée.*

▼ *Astérix, héros mondial, a été inventé par Albert Uderzo et René Goscinny en 1959.*

Tintin

Le dessinateur belge Hergé fait paraître les premières aventures de Tintin en 1929 dans le journal *Le Petit Vingtième*. L'intrépide reporter et son fidèle chien Milou parcourent le monde, entraînant dans leur sillage des héros farfelus comme le capitaine Haddock, les policiers Dupond et Dupont, et le professeur Tournesol.

1936

▶ Les Brigades internationales, qui luttent aux côtés des républicains espagnols, devant Madrid assiégé.

La guerre d'Espagne

57 grammes de ration alimentaire par personne et par jour : c'est le maigre quotidien de la population pendant le siège de Madrid.

•

Des volontaires du monde entier sont venus combattre aux côtés des républicains espagnols. On les appelle les Brigades internationales.

Une nouvelle mode

Les oreilles percées, voilà la nouvelle mode ! Il faut dire que les boucles d'oreilles à clips se perdent souvent, et celles qui portent des diamants ou des perles rares sont lasses de courir ce risque. Se faire percer les oreilles n'a cependant rien d'original : c'était déjà une pratique courante dans l'Antiquité, chez les femmes comme chez les hommes.

▲ Les villageois espagnols fuient, à l'approche des combats, avant l'arrivée des troupes franquistes.

La révolution en Espagne

▶ **19 juillet 1936** ◀ Une rébellion a éclaté depuis deux jours contre la République espagnole. Le général Franco, qui se trouvait au Maroc espagnol, a débarqué avec ses troupes à Cadix pour déclencher une guerre civile. La droite traditionnelle, l'extrême droite nationaliste et l'armée le soutiennent. L'Italie fasciste et l'Allemagne nazie l'assurent également de leur collaboration. De leur côté, les républicains sont appuyés par la gauche européenne – socialistes et communistes –, ainsi que par l'Union soviétique.

Proclamée en 1931, après la chute du dictateur Primo de Rivera et l'abdication du roi Alphonse XIII, la jeune République espagnole est contestée, à droite par l'Église, l'armée et les grands propriétaires ; à gauche par les ouvriers, les paysans, les Basques et les Catalans, qui critiquent ses mesures. En 1933, un gouvernement nationaliste de centre-droit supprime les nouvelles réformes et écrase l'opposition. La coalition du Frente popular (Front populaire) remporte les élections législatives, le 16 février, et promet des changements radicaux. Les officiers et les conservateurs préparent aussitôt l'insurrection. Les républicains organisent la résistance.

▼ Chômeurs de Jarrow, au nord-est de l'Angleterre, en route vers Londres.

Les chômeurs dans la rue

▶ **5 octobre 1936** ◀ Les manifestations de chômeurs se multiplient dans toute l'Europe. Bien que les années noires de la Grande Dépression soient passées, le chômage reste excessivement élevé, et des millions de gens vivent dans la misère. Jarrow, dans le nord-est de l'Angleterre, illustre bien la situation. Cette ville est sinistrée : depuis la fermeture de ses principaux établissements, les deux tiers des ouvriers sont au chômage. Aujourd'hui, les habitants ont organisé une marche de protestation. Ils vont à Londres, afin de déposer une pétition demandant l'aide du gouvernement. Elle a recueilli 12 000 signatures.

1930 – 1939

◀ *Déclaration officielle de l'abdication d'Édouard VIII en faveur de son frère, le futur George VI.*

Victoire du Front populaire

▶ **3 juin 1936** ◀

L'alliance des partis de gauche français – socialistes, radicaux et communistes – a permis de gagner les élections législatives du 26 avril dernier. C'est la victoire du Front populaire. Le socialiste Léon Blum vient de former un nouveau gouvernement, que les communistes soutiennent mais auquel ils ne participent pas. De nombreuses réformes sociales sont appliquées, parmi lesquelles la semaine de 40 heures et deux semaines de congés payés par an. Après la victoire du Front Populaire, une immense vague de grèves a obligé le patronat à reconnaître le poids de la classe ouvrière. Beaucoup de gens considèrent que ces réformes constituent des acquis qui auraient dû être mis en place depuis longtemps. Blum espère, par ailleurs, réorganiser les banques et les finances.

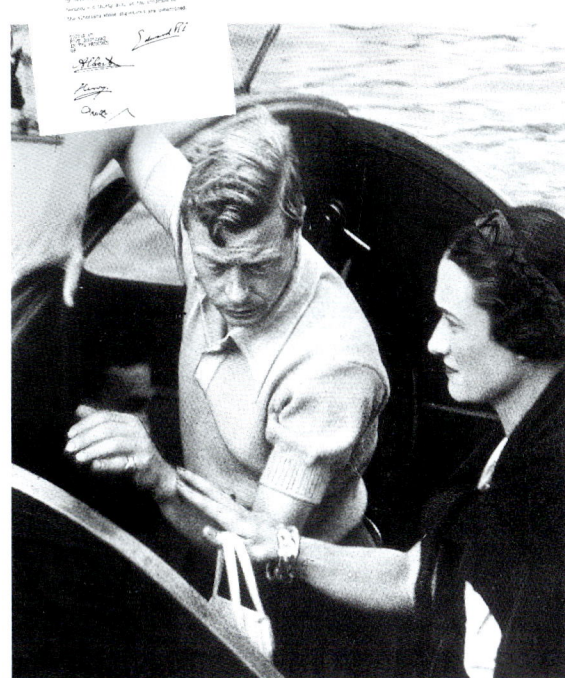

▲ *Édouard et Wallis, la femme qu'il veut épouser après son abdication.*

▲ *Premiers départs en vacances, à l'occasion des congés payés.*

Scandale à la cour d'Angleterre

▶ **11 décembre 1936** ◀

Le roi Édouard VIII, sur le trône depuis le 20 janvier, abdique pour raisons de cœur ! Il souhaite en effet épouser au plus vite la femme qu'il aime, Wallis Simpson. Mais elle est divorcée. Le roi doit choisir : le trône ou l'amour. La romance d'Édouard et de Wallis était restée secrète en Angleterre. Mais, une fois révélée, l'affaire a déclenché un véritable scandale à la cour, très à cheval sur les principes et les devoirs de la monarchie.

La sortie de la « coccinelle »

Adolf Hitler a inauguré une nouvelle usine d'automobiles, le 26 février, à Fallersleben, en Basse-Saxe. Elle fabrique la Volkswagen – la « voiture du peuple » –, qui a été conçue en 1934 par l'ingénieur Ferdinand Porsche. Cette voiture ressemble à une coccinelle et est parfaitement adaptée à la famille traditionnelle.

Son prix est relativement accessible, et sa consommation est raisonnable. Le moteur se trouve à l'arrière, le coffre à bagages, sous le capot. C'est vraiment une voiture originale.

L'étoile du Nord

▶ **28 février 1936** ◀

C'est l'événement des jeux Olympiques d'hiver ! Sonja Henie vient de remporter sa troisième médaille d'or en patinage artistique, dans la catégorie des figures imposées. Cette jeune Norvégienne égale ainsi le record établi par la Suédoise Gillis Grafström en 1928. Elle a remporté sa première médaille d'or à l'âge de 14 ans, en 1927, et a obtenu depuis dix titres mondiaux successifs.

▲ *La Norvégienne Sonja Henie, en route vers son troisième titre olympique de patinage.*

▶ *Adolf Hitler inaugure la nouvelle voiture populaire, la Volkswagen.*

1936

Les fresques de Diego Rivera

▶ **8 décembre 1936** ◀ Le célèbre peintre mexicain Diego Rivera fête aujourd'hui son 50e anniversaire. Il est connu pour ses peintures murales, de gigantesques fresques exécutées sur les murs des bâtiments publics, qui sont généralement inspirées par les idéaux socialistes. Elles ont relancé l'art de la fresque aux États-Unis et en Amérique latine, et décrivent souvent l'histoire et la société mexicaines. L'an dernier, Rivera a effectué un travail titanesque : il a achevé une série de peintures pour l'escalier – monumental – du palais présidentiel de Mexico.

À l'âge de 21 ans, il a obtenu une bourse pour partir en Europe et il y est resté treize ans. Il est alors influencé par les maîtres de la Renaissance, et se lie avec des mouvements artistiques européens révolutionnaires, comme le cubisme. Lorsqu'il retourne à Mexico, en 1921, il se consacre à une nouvelle forme d'art populaire. Ses fresques, allégoriques ou historiques, sont graves, riches de références, mais restent faciles à comprendre.

Premiers cachets de vitamines

▶ **1936** ◀ On peut désormais acheter des vitamines sous forme de cachets ! Les vitamines sont des substances organiques indispensables au bon fonctionnement de notre organisme. Elles doivent être consommées avec modération. Le terme même de « vitamines » a été inventé en 1912, mais leur existence était déjà connue.

▲ *Détail de la fresque de Rivera illustrant la lutte du Mexique pour l'indépendance.*

◀ *Diego Rivera et sa femme, Frieda Kahlo.*

Les Marx Brothers

Une nuit à l'Opéra, le dernier film des Marx Brothers, est sorti le 22 mai à New York. Les talentueux frères Marx, Groucho, Harpo et Chico, stars du comique américain, sèment la panique sur un bateau, ridiculisent une cérémonie officielle, mettent l'univers d'un opéra sens dessus dessous, et sabotent une représentation du *Trouvère* de Verdi.

Ce film fait désormais partie des plus grands classiques du cinéma loufoque. C'est leur dernier chef-d'œuvre depuis *la Soupe au canard.*

Les jeux Olympiques de Berlin

▶ **16 août 1936** ◀ Les théories nazies sur la supériorité de la race aryenne viennent d'être contredites par la victoire d'un Noir américain aux jeux Olympiques de Berlin ! Hitler vient même de quitter précipitamment le stade. En effet, Jesse Owens, un sprinteur noir américain, s'est couvert de gloire en remportant 4 médailles d'or : pour le 100 m, le 200 m, le saut en longueur et le relais 4 x 100 m. Hitler ne supporte pas qu'un athlète noir, qui représente selon lui une race inférieure, remporte la victoire. La foule n'a cependant pas caché son admiration devant les exploits de l'athlète.

Les Jeux rencontrent un réel succès : la capitale du Reich a accueilli 5 000 sportifs représentant 53 pays. De nombreux records ont été battus. Le Néo-Zélandais Jack Lovelock a battu le record du monde du 1 500 m, détenu par l'Américain Glenn Cunningham. La France s'est également distinguée, en boxe avec Despeaux et Michelot, en haltérophilie avec Hostin, en lutte libre avec Poilvé, et en cyclisme avec Charpentier, Lapébie, Chaillot et Georget.

▲ En haut : le relais 4 x 100 m allemand, qui obtient la médaille de bronze.
En bas : Jesse Owens, la star des Jeux.

L'Allemagne défie le traité de Versailles

▲ Les troupes allemandes entrent à Cologne, en Rhénanie.

▶ **7 mars 1936** ◀ Les troupes allemandes viennent d'entrer en Rhénanie, une région allemande qui borde les Pays-Bas, la Belgique, le Luxembourg et la France. Hitler rejette les accords de Locarno (qui stipulent le respect des frontières fixées au lendemain de la Première Guerre mondiale) et la suprême clause militaire du traité de Versailles, selon laquelle cette région devait rester démilitarisée. Les gouvernements français et britannique minimisent l'événement.

En 1936 aussi ...

5 mai • Les troupes italiennes s'emparent de la capitale de l'Éthiopie, Addis-Abeba.

18 juin • Les ligues d'extrême droite françaises sont dissoutes.

26 août • L'Angleterre reconnaît l'indépendance de l'Égypte, mais maintient sa tutelle.

23 octobre • Hitler envoie des renforts à Franco.

Une architecture révolutionnaire

▶ **8 juin 1936** ◀ Voilà un architecte bien peu ordinaire. Frank Lloyd Wright, âgé de 67 ans, vient de révolutionner l'architecture américaine avec deux de ses œuvres, un immeuble de bureaux à Racine, dans le Wisconsin, et une étonnante maison à Bear Run, en Pennsylvanie. Celle-ci, appelée Falling Water, est la très luxueuse résidence secondaire d'Edgar Kaufmann, propriétaire d'un grand magasin de Pittsburgh. L'ensemble s'adapte à la nature ambiante : balcons, terrasses, cascade. Selon Wright, l'architecture doit s'intégrer dans son environnement pour trouver toute sa force.

◀ La « Maison sur la cascade » (Kaufmann House) s'intègre au milieu naturel environnant.

1930 – 1939

1936

1937

▶ À l'aéroport de Lakehurst, dans le New Jersey, le Hindenburg explose au moment de l'atterrissage.

En 1937 aussi …

9 juin • En France, un groupuscule d'extrême droite, la Cagoule, assassine des antifascistes italiens.

21 juin • En France, le chef du gouvernement, Léon Blum, démissionne.

12 novembre • Le prix Nobel de littérature est attribué à l'écrivain français Roger Martin du Gard.

Le dirigeable *Hindenburg* s'écrase

▶ **6 mai 1937** ◀

Le plus grand drame que les transports aériens aient jamais connu vient de se produire aujourd'hui. Le dirigeable allemand *Hindenburg* s'est écrasé à Lakehurst, dans le New Jersey. C'était le plus grand transatlantique aérien du monde. Il mesurait 245 m de long, naviguait à 127 km/h et était porté par 200 000 m³ d'hydrogène. Le *Hindenburg* assurait, depuis un an, des vols réguliers d'une durée de 60 heures, entre Francfort et Lakehurst. Doté d'une bibliothèque, d'un salon et d'un bar, il offrait un réel confort à ses passagers.

L'accident s'est produit lors de l'atterrissage, en plein orage, au moment où l'appareil s'approchait de son mât d'amarrage. L'hydrogène a pris feu avec une rapidité surprenante, le *Hindenburg* a explosé quelques instants après. 34 passagers et membres d'équipage, ainsi qu'un membre du personnel au sol, ont trouvé la mort. Ce drame va ébranler la confiance du public dans les transports aériens.

Massacres en Chine

▶ **13 août 1937** ◀

L'armée japonaise pilonne Shanghai. Des milliers de Chinois ont été tués. Les images de la destruction du port ont bouleversé le monde entier. Shanghai est la dernière victime en date des atrocités commises par les Japonais. Depuis le 8 juillet dernier, la guerre sino-japonaise fait rage : les Japonais ont attaqué plusieurs villes et ports chinois. La Seconde Guerre mondiale commence en Asie. Le Japon s'était emparé de la Mandchourie en 1931. Il est évident qu'il envisage une conquête méthodique du territoire chinois. L'incident de frontières qui a déclenché la guerre est une provocation du gouvernement impérial japonais.

▲ Shanghai après le bombardement japonais.

Grande exposition à Paris

▶ 4 mai 1937 ◀ Le président de la République française Albert Lebrun inaugure aujourd'hui à Paris l'Exposition internationale des arts et techniques de la vie moderne. De nombreux bâtiments ont été construits à cette occasion. Le plus spectaculaire est certainement le palais de Chaillot, édifié sur la place du Trocadéro par les architectes Carlu, Boileau et Azéma. Il frappe par son parti pris académique et monumental. Le peintre espagnol Picasso expose au pavillon espagnol sa célèbre toile *Guernica*, inspirée par les récents événements qui se sont produits en Espagne.

▼ *Inauguration de l'exposition à Paris.*

Bombardement de Guernica

▶ 26 avril 1937 ◀ Guernica, petite localité de la province basque de Biscaye, vient d'être détruite par les bombardements de la légion Condor, une unité de l'aviation nazie au service des franquistes. Après avoir pilonné la ville, les troupes ont massacré 2 000 personnes à la mitrailleuse. Guernica n'est pas une cible militaire d'importance. Le but est de démoraliser la population tout en donnant aux bombardiers nazis l'occasion de s'entraîner. Ce massacre symbolise l'ampleur de la barbarie franquiste.

▼ *Soldats dans Guernica dévastée et déserte.*

Inauguration du Golden Gate

▶ 27 mai 1937 ◀ La ville de San Francisco, aux États-Unis, vient d'inaugurer son nouveau pont. Le Golden Gate Bridge, le plus grand pont suspendu du monde, vient en effet de s'ouvrir à la circulation. Il mesure 1 280 m de long et donne accès à la baie de San Francisco. Sa construction a duré quatre ans et a coûté 35 millions de dollars. Environ 200 000 personnes l'ont pris d'assaut. Un feu d'artifice spectaculaire a clos la cérémonie.

Purges staliniennes

▶ 12 juin 1937 ◀ Les méthodes staliniennes pour éliminer les opposants sont de plus en plus brutales. Les procès de Moscou battent leur plein. Véritables parodies qui se tiennent à huis clos, ils sont orchestrés par Staline et lui permettent d'éliminer les politiques et les intellectuels dont il souhaite se débarrasser. Il procède en particulier à l'épuration des partisans de Léon Trotski, qui conteste le régime avec la plus grande virulence. Ces procès cherchent à impliquer les accusés dans des actes de terrorisme, de sabotage, d'espionnage, d'assassinat et de trahison. L'invraisemblance des charges est considérable. Beaucoup acceptent de faire leur autocritique, c'est-à-dire de s'accuser eux-mêmes, sans doute dans l'espoir de sauver leurs familles.

▶ *Karl Radek, journaliste politique en URSS, a été condamné à dix ans de prison en janvier 1936.*

Margot Fonteyn triomphe à Londres

En janvier dernier, une jeune étoile britannique de 18 ans, Margot Fonteyn, a subjugué le public du Sadler's Wells, théâtre situé au nord de Londres, en interprétant *Giselle*, un célèbre ballet classique. Elle possède la grâce, la sensibilité, le sens de la musique, et impose sa présence à l'occasion d'inoubliables performances. La perfection de son style en fait l'étoile la plus en vue du moment.

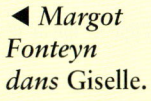

◀ *Margot Fonteyn dans* Giselle.

1930 – 1939

1938

▲ Les nazis aggravent les persécutions et empêchent de plus en plus les juifs de travailler.

▲ Le Premier ministre britannique salue la foule en montrant les accords de Munich.

En 1938 aussi …

4 février • Hitler prend le commandement des forces armées allemandes.

3 juin • Succès du film *Quai des brumes*, de Marcel Carné.

15 novembre • Les enfants juifs sont exclus des écoles allemandes.

19 juin • La Coupe du monde de football commence à Paris.

10 novembre • Le président turc, Mustafa Kemal, meurt.

La Nuit de cristal

▶ **10 novembre 1938** ◀ La communauté juive est mise à feu et à sang. Les assaillants ont dévasté plus de 7 000 magasins juifs, cassé des vitrines, incendié des synagogues, des maisons. Les nazis ont battu et assassiné les juifs qui protestaient. Les rues de Berlin et de plusieurs villes allemandes sont jonchées de verre. La quantité de verre brisé est telle que l'on parle de « Nuit de cristal ».

Le gouvernement allemand a programmé et dirigé cette opération contre la population juive, mais il nie toute responsabilité, en déclarant que des groupes allemands antisémites ont agi de leur propre initiative.

Lorsque Adolf Hitler a pris le pouvoir en 1933, 600 000 juifs environ vivaient en Allemagne. Depuis, près de la moitié d'entre eux ont fui, en raison de la montée de la répression. Après la Nuit de cristal, il n'y a plus aucun doute en ce qui concerne l'avenir de la communauté juive en Allemagne.

Les accords de Munich

▶ **29-30 septembre 1938** ◀ Le chef du gouvernement français Édouard Daladier, le Premier ministre britannique, Arthur Neville Chamberlain, les dictateurs italien et allemand Benito Mussolini et Adolf Hitler, viennent de signer les accords de Munich. Ce pacte à quatre, qui semble sauver la paix de l'Europe, abandonne en fait la Tchécoslovaquie à son destin, et ainsi le dictateur nazi peut continuer son invasion des Sudètes, région du sud-ouest de la Tchécoslovaquie où la population allemande est majoritaire. C'est pour Hitler une victoire retentissante. La France et l'Angleterre ont abandonné la Tchécoslovaquie, et elles autorisent Hitler à avoir recours à la force armée si les Tchécoslovaques rejettent ses conditions.

Invasion des Sudètes

▶ **5 octobre 1938** ◀ Le président tchécoslovaque Edvard Beneš démissionne, après l'invasion des Sudètes par l'armée allemande le 1er octobre. Dans cette région, où la population allemande est majoritaire, Hitler est accueilli en véritable héros par la foule. À celles et ceux qui l'acclament, il déclare : « Je m'adresse pour la première fois à vous comme à mon peuple, et je vous apporte le salut de toute la nation allemande […] Ce salut est en même temps un serment. Ce territoire ne sera plus jamais arraché au Reich. »

L'occupation des Sudètes fait suite aux accords de Munich du 30 septembre, signés par la France, l'Italie, l'Angleterre et l'Allemagne. La Pologne et la Hongrie revendiquent aussi des territoires en Tchécoslovaquie, où vivent des minorités de leurs pays. La voie de la domination nazie sur l'Europe du Sud-Est est ouverte.

1930 – 1939

▲ Les Autrichiens saluent les troupes allemandes à Linz.

L'Allemagne envahit l'Autriche

▶ **13 mars 1938** ◀ Hitler a envahi l'Autriche, deux jours après avoir envoyé un ultimatum au chancelier autrichien Kurt von Schuschnigg. L'Autriche fait désormais partie de l'Allemagne. L'Anschluss (annexion de l'Autriche à l'Allemagne) a été proclamé à Linz. Les sympathisants nazis se pressent dans les rues de la ville et acclament les troupes allemandes, les cloches sonnent en signe de bienvenue, et les drapeaux nazis frappés de la croix gammée flottent aux fenêtres. Des milliers de juifs projettent de partir, à cause de la politique antisémite de Hitler. La communauté internationale ne réagit pas face à cette nouvelle démonstration de force de Hitler.

Benny Goodman : le roi du swing

Le sacre du roi du swing vient d'avoir lieu au Carnegie Hall de New York. Le clarinettiste Benny Goodman a en effet déchaîné les passions de ses admirateurs. Depuis la création de son grand orchestre en 1932, il séduit le public par sa virtuosité et son style. Il s'entoure d'excellents instrumentistes et des meilleurs compositeurs du moment. Il est l'un des premiers musiciens de jazz qui prend l'initiative de lutter contre la ségrégation raciale en jouant avec des vedettes de couleur.

Un « fossile vivant »

▶ **22 décembre 1938** ◀ Un événement attire l'attention de tous les paléontologues (scientifiques qui étudient les fossiles). Un cœlacanthe, ou *Latimeria chalumnae*, vient d'être capturé au large des côtes de l'Afrique du Sud. Cet étrange poisson à colonne dorsale creuse est appelé « fossile vivant ». Il appartient à l'espèce supposée éteinte des cœlacanthes, disparue depuis 70 millions d'années. C'est l'unique survivant connu jusqu'ici. Ce spécimen est plus long et plus lourd que ses ancêtres. Ces derniers sont apparentés aux premières espèces qui sont sorties de l'eau il y a 350 millions d'années, pour vivre sur la terre ferme.

▼ Les troupes nazies arrivent dans les Sudètes, en Tchécoslovaquie.

▼ Nestlé souhaite convertir à son café les amateurs de thé.

Le Nescafé apparaît

▶ **1er avril 1938** ◀ Adieu, moulin à café, cafetière et temps perdu ! Le café instantané est né. Il suffit désormais d'une tasse, d'un peu de Nescafé, d'eau chaude et d'une petite cuiller. Cette merveille de l'alimentation moderne, le Nescafé, vient d'être mise au point par les chercheurs de la compagnie suisse Nestlé. Celle-ci souhaite conquérir le marché européen dès l'année prochaine. Ce remontant devrait convertir les mordus du thé au café. C'est également ce qu'espèrent les producteurs brésiliens. Ils ont accumulé, ces dernières années, des stocks de café gigantesques, et ont été obligés de détruire une partie de leur récolte, afin d'éviter que les prix, déjà très bas, ne s'effondrent encore plus.

1938

▲ Blanche-Neige et les sept nains *remporte un succès mondial.*

Blanche-Neige et les sept nains

▶ **Février 1938** ◀

La dernière création de Walt Disney, *Blanche-Neige et les sept nains* (*Snow White and the Seven Dwarfs*), va bientôt sortir sur les écrans européens. Les spectateurs sont émerveillés par les animaux de la forêt et les personnages des sept nains, dont les noms correspondent à la personnalité de chacun (Grincheux, Dormeur, Atchoum, Joyeux, Timide, Prof et Simplet). Ils sont d'ailleurs en train de devenir de véritables célébrités internationales. Ce dessin animé n'est rien moins que le premier long métrage d'animation sonore et en couleurs ! La critique en parle comme d'un chef-d'œuvre. Il faut dire que l'art de Disney éclate au grand jour. Le film, qui a demandé quatre années de travail et des centaines de milliers de dessins, porte sa marque, même s'il est le fruit d'une création collective.

Adapté du conte des frères Grimm, le film a le souci du détail et du réalisme : le monde qu'il représente est un monde qui obéit à des lois logiques. On parle à son sujet de « réalisme disneyen ». Les événements sont ainsi enchaînés avec soin, les personnages sont animés avec un réel savoir-faire, les décors sont étudiés, les couleurs sont harmonieuses. C'est vraiment la meilleure comédie musicale de Hollywood !

As de la raquette

▶ **2 juillet 1938** ◀

Un jeune joueur de tennis américain, J. Donald Budge, a battu un nouveau record en gagnant la finale du simple messieurs de Wimbledon, contre son homologue allemand Wilfred Austin. Budge a remporté les quatre principaux tournois de tennis du monde – les Internationaux français, britannique, australien et américain – la même année, réalisant l'exploit du grand chelem. C'est la consécration d'une vie pour un sportif ! D'autant que c'est la première fois que cela se produit. Ceux qui suivent la carrière de Budge ne sont toujours pas revenus de sa victoire contre le baron allemand Gottfried von Cramm, lors de la finale de la Coupe Davis de l'an dernier à Wimbledon. L'ancien champion de tennis William Tilden affirme que c'est l'une des plus belles rencontres qu'il ait jamais vues.

▶ *J. Donald Budge, le vainqueur du grand chelem.*

Préparatifs de guerre

▶ **15 juillet 1938** ◀

1 000 personnes ont répondu en un seul jour à l'appel de la Royal Air Force, qui a lancé une campagne de recrutement massif le mois dernier. L'armée de l'air britannique est désormais équipée de 1 000 Spitfire supplémentaires. Cette décision montre à quel point le gouvernement britannique prend au sérieux la menace d'une nouvelle guerre, dans laquelle la défense aérienne jouerait un rôle primordial. Le Spitfire est conçu pour intercepter l'aviation ennemie, comme le Messerschmitt 109, l'avion de combat allemand le plus performant. Parallèlement au développement de la production des Spitfire, la défense passive britannique (Air-Raid Precautions, ARP) s'organise. En Angleterre comme en France, on distribue des masques à gaz et on prépare l'évacuation des enfants des écoles en cas d'attaques aériennes. Des abris antiaériens vont être mis en place.

1930 – 1939

Lancement du *Queen Elizabeth*

▶ **27 septembre 1938** ◀ Le *Queen Elizabeth*, dont le lancement vient de s'effectuer sur la rivière Clyde, en Écosse, est le plus grand paquebot du monde. Il transporte des passagers entre l'Europe et l'Amérique. Les transatlantiques sont de plus en plus imposants. Construit en 1932 aux chantiers de Saint-Nazaire, le *Normandie* ne mesure pas moins de 313 m de long. Il peut contenir 2 000 passagers, ainsi que 1 350 membres d'équipage. Une traversée comme celle de l'Atlantique nord prend environ quatre jours, à la vitesse horaire de 30 nœuds.

▲ Le Queen Elizabeth, le plus grand paquebot du monde.

◀ Le compresseur du système pèse 8 000 tonnes.

Air conditionné à Washington

▶ **26 juillet 1938** ◀ Pour la plus grande joie des membres du Congrès américain, le Capitole est l'heureux bénéficiaire d'un nouveau système d'air conditionné. Un privilège qui est également attribué au Sénat. Le système fonctionne comme un réfrigérateur. Le fréon, un fluide frigorifique, réfrigère 55,65 millions de litres d'eau par jour. Cette eau froide est ensuite distribuée dans un seul circuit à travers les différents bâtiments, rafraîchissant ainsi l'air soufflé par les systèmes de ventilation. Des systèmes identiques sont utilisés dans des usines où le contrôle de l'atmosphère est crucial pour la qualité de certaines denrées, le fil de coton par exemple. L'air conditionné devrait bientôt être disponible pour les bureaux et les maisons.

Les locomotives battent des records de vitesse

C'est la guerre des locomotives à vapeur ! Chacune cherche à battre le record de vitesse. Le dernier vient d'être établi par la Mallard britannique, dont le moteur a été conçu par Nigel Gresley. Elle a roulé à 202 km/h sur plus de 8 km, entre Londres et Newcastle.

Huitième victoire à Wimbledon

▶ **2 juillet 1938** ◀ Helen Wills Moody vient de gagner son huitième tournoi à Wimbledon ! Pour la quatrième fois de sa carrière, elle a remporté le simple dames contre sa compatriote et rivale Helen Jacobs. Helen Wills Moody a 32 ans. Elle a remporté son premier titre à Wimbledon, il y a onze ans. Son assurance lui a valu le surnom de « reine Helen ».

Invention du stylo à bille

Ça ne fait pas de taches d'encre, ça ne se remplit pas et ça ne nécessite pas de buvard… Le journaliste hongrois László Biró a fait breveter une invention extraordinaire : le stylo à bille. Ce stylo révolutionnaire est doté d'une fine cartouche cylindrique qui contient sa réserve d'encre. Cette invention est promise à un bel avenir commercial.

1939

La Pologne envahie par l'Allemagne

▶ **1er septembre 1939** ◀ C'est l'aube. Sans déclaration de guerre ni avertissement d'aucune sorte, les troupes de la Wehrmacht – l'armée allemande – franchissent en masse la frontière polonaise et convergent sur Varsovie. L'aviation nazie bombarde ses objectifs. L'attaque est foudroyante. C'est la guerre-éclair, le Blitzkrieg. Pour justifier son action préméditée contre la Pologne, Hitler prétexte une attaque contre une station de radio allemande de Gleiwitz. Cette opération est en fait l'œuvre d'un commando de SS déguisés en soldats polonais. Elle a été organisée par Heinrich Himmler, le chef des SS – unités d'élite de la Schutzstaffel (« échelon de protection »). L'invasion allemande est ainsi officiellement qualifiée de « contre-attaque ». Hitler réclame la ville de Dantzig et souhaite le retour des territoires autonomes, comme la Prusse, dans le giron du Reich.

Dans le même temps, Staline se prépare à envahir l'est de la Pologne, intervention qui constitue l'un des accords du pacte germano-soviétique. De son côté, Mussolini tente de persuader Hitler d'éviter la guerre. Il demande à être délivré des obligations militaires du traité et déclare la neutralité de l'Italie. Contrairement à ce que pensait Joachim von Ribbentrop, ministre allemand des Affaires étrangères, la France et la Grande-Bretagne mettent l'Allemagne en demeure de retirer ses troupes des territoires polonais, sous menace de proclamation de l'état de guerre. Hitler ne répond pas. La Grande-Bretagne et la France entrent en guerre le 3 septembre, respectivement à 12 heures et à 17 heures.

▲ *La croix gammée flotte sur Dantzig.*

◀ *Les Allemands forcent la frontière polonaise.*

▼ *La ligne Maginot.*

La ligne Maginot

▶ **1939** ◀ Depuis septembre 1939, c'est la « drôle de guerre » : les soldats français attendent l'attaque allemande. Ils se croient bien protégés par la ligne Maginot, une fortification enterrée, construite de 1929 à 1936 sous la direction du ministre de la Guerre, l'ingénieur André Maginot. Sur plus de 140 km de long, tout un monde souterrain s'organise, à des profondeurs de 12 à 30 m. Mais la ligne s'interrompt au niveau des Ardennes. On la croit, à tort, infranchissable, et rien ne protège la frontière entre la France et la Belgique. De plus, elle a coûté très cher. Pour la financer, la France a renoncé à s'équiper en armes modernes (armes automatiques, blindés), alors que l'Allemagne en possède d'énormes quantités.

Le premier hélicoptère

▶ **14 septembre 1939** ◀ Le premier hélicoptère vient de décoller ! C'est l'œuvre de l'ingénieur soviétique Igor Sikorski. Son premier prototype, qu'il avait construit en 1909, n'était pas parvenu à décoller. Il a émigré aux États-Unis, après avoir étudié les inventions de Blériot et de Zeppelin en France et en Allemagne. À l'heure actuelle, Sikorski dirige sa propre entreprise aéronautique.
Sa nouvelle invention va être utilisée par les forces aéronavales américaines.

▲ *Sikorski à bord du VS-300, l'un des premiers hélicoptères, au-dessus de son terrain de Bridgeport, dans le Connecticut.*

1930 – 1939

▲ *Rencontre entre Hitler et Mussolini.*

Le pacte d'Acier

▶ **22 mai 1939** ◀ Mussolini vient de lier son sort à celui de Hitler. Les ministres des Affaires étrangères des deux pays ont signé à Berlin le pacte d'Acier. Cette alliance militaire déclare que les deux nations, « unies par la profonde affinité de leurs idéologies […], sont résolues à agir côte à côte et à unir leurs forces pour obtenir l'espace vital qui leur est nécessaire ». En outre, si l'un des deux signataires est agressé par une autre puissance, l'autre doit lui porter secours.

Autant en emporte le vent

On peut désormais voir l'un des films les plus célèbres de l'histoire du cinéma, *Autant en emporte le vent (Gone With the Wind)*. Le tournage a été mouvementé : les metteurs en scène se sont succédé – c'est finalement Victor Fleming qui signe le film –, le producteur David O. Selznick a mis du temps à trouver son actrice idéale : Vivien Leigh. Cette dernière, qui incarne Scarlett O'Hara et ses amours tumultueuses sur fond de guerre de Sécession, a pour partenaire Clark Gable. Adapté du roman de Margaret Mitchell, le film est en Technicolor et dure 3 h 45.

Le pacte de non-agression

▶ **23 août 1939** ◀ Staline et Hitler, représentés par leurs ministres des Affaires étrangères Ribbentrop et Molotov, signent à Moscou le pacte de non-agression germano-soviétique, conclu pour 10 ans. L'URSS et l'Allemagne ne peuvent s'attaquer l'une à l'autre ; elles se partagent l'Europe, la guerre est inévitable.

▼ *Ribbentrop, Staline et Molotov.*

1939

◄ *Au zoo de New York, l'éléphant Chang prend un bain de DDT qui le débarrasse de ses parasites.*

◄ *Le DDT, un nouvel insecticide.*

Découverte du DDT

▶ 1939 ◄

« Dichloro-diphényl-trichloréthane » n'est pas facile à prononcer. Pourtant, les agriculteurs, les éleveurs et les médecins ne cessent de chanter ses louanges. Découvertes par le biochimiste suisse Paul Müller, les propriétés insecticides de cette nouvelle substance combattent efficacement toutes sortes d'insectes. Excessivement toxique, le DDT vient à bout des puces, des mites, des tiques, des sauterelles et des chenilles. C'est une véritable hécatombe. Beaucoup affirment cependant que le DDT est trop efficace pour être sans effets négatifs. Si une dose de DDT préserve un chou des attaques de chenilles sans éliminer les vers de terre, qu'arrive-t-il au rouge-gorge qui consomme des milliers de vers de terre contaminés ? Et au renard qui dévore le rouge-gorge ? Et à l'homme qui mange le chou ? À l'heure actuelle, les scientifiques ne se posent pas la question de la sauvegarde de l'environnement, ni de savoir si ce produit peut avoir, à long terme, des effets sur la santé humaine. Seule bonne nouvelle : cette substance chimique permettra peut-être de lutter contre la malaria.

Le polyéthylène

Il y a six ans, les chercheurs Reginald Gibson et Eric Fawcett ont découvert un nouveau matériau, léger et transparent, à la suite d'un incident de laboratoire. Il s'agit d'une matière plastique appelée polyéthylène. La firme britannique Imperial Chemical Industries (ICI), a décidé, cette année, de la produire à grande échelle. Le polyéthylène risque de changer nos vies. Pour l'instant, il servira à isoler les câbles sous-marins.

Le *Graf Spee* sabordé par son équipage

▶ 18 décembre 1939 ◄

Le *Graf Spee* a été coulé, la nuit dernière, par son propre équipage. Depuis plusieurs semaines, ce cuirassé régnait en maître sur l'Atlantique sud et avait coulé neuf cargos anglais. Trois croiseurs britanniques, l'*Exeter*, l'*Ajax* et l'*Achilles*, ont engagé les combats, au large de Montevideo, la capitale de l'Uruguay. Sérieusement endommagé, le *Graf Spee* a trouvé refuge dans le port de la ville. Le gouvernement uruguayen a menacé de saisir le bateau. Avec l'autorisation de Hitler, le capitaine a préféré saborder son cuirassé.

▼ *Le* Graf Spee *explose, avant de couler dans le port de Montevideo.*

▼ *Le bas en Nylon.*

1930 – 1939

Premier vol transatlantique

▶ **3 mars 1939** ◀ Le Boeing 314 de la compagnie Pan American vient de réaliser le premier vol au-dessus de l'Atlantique. Aujourd'hui, à Washington, Mme Franklin D. Roosevelt l'a baptisé *Yankee Clipper*, en référence aux voiliers rapides du XIXe siècle. Cet avion est entré dans l'Histoire, voilà une semaine, en atterrissant sans incident à Baltimore, après avoir transporté ses passagers au-dessus de l'Atlantique à la vitesse de 230 km/h. L'intérieur abrite une magnifique cabine de pilotage, ainsi qu'une suite privée et une salle à manger de 14 places.

▲ *Embarquement d'un vol de la Pan Am.*

En 1939 aussi ...

24 janvier
• Un tremblement de terre au Chili fait 30 000 victimes.

28 mars • Entrée des troupes franquistes dans Madrid ; fin de la guerre d'Espagne.

5 septembre
• Déclaration de neutralité des États-Unis.

23 septembre • Mort du psychanalyste autrichien Sigmund Freud, à Londres.

Héroïque défense de la Finlande

▶ **30 novembre 1939** ◀ L'armée finlandaise a réussi à contenir les troupes ennemies russes, tout le long de la frontière, sur une ligne de 240 km. L'URSS souhaite prendre le contrôle des voies d'accès vers Leningrad, et donc s'emparer de la partie finlandaise de l'isthme de Carélie. Staline a ordonné l'invasion, lorsque les Finlandais ont refusé de livrer la Carélie. Contre toute attente, la Finlande, exceptionnellement équipée, oppose une résistance farouche à son agresseur et contient l'offensive, tout le long de la frontière, sur la ligne Mannerheim.

▲ *Exode d'une famille finlandaise.*

Les premiers bas Nylon

Les bas Nylon sont du dernier cri. Certes, leur prix n'est pas très abordable, mais ces bas en soie artificielle sont plus solides, tiennent plus longtemps et sont aussi fins que ceux en soie naturelle. Depuis des siècles, on admirait la capacité du ver à soie à produire des fibres. Le Nylon montre qu'il est possible d'imiter ce savoir-faire. Cette fibre synthétique a été découverte en 1937 par le chimiste américain Wallace Carothers, pour la compagnie Du Pont de Nemours. Elle peut servir à la confection des parachutes.

Attentat contre Hitler

▶ **9 novembre 1939** ◀ Une bombe a détruit la brasserie Bürgerbräukeller, à Munich. Hitler y commémorait, comme chaque année, la tentative de putsch de 1923. Il est certain que la bombe était dirigée contre Hitler. Mais qui est l'auteur de cet attentat ? Les nazis soupçonnent les services secrets britanniques, dont deux agents viennent d'être arrêtés. Ils soupçonnent également un communiste arrêté à la frontière germano-helvétique, en possession d'une photographie de l'intérieur de la brasserie. Mais ne serait-ce pas tout simplement un coup monté par la propagande nazie pour susciter un nouvel élan de sympathie en faveur de Hitler ?

▲ *La brasserie de Munich, en ruine après l'attentat contre Hitler.*

LE CINÉMA

La première représentation publique d'un film a lieu le 22 mars 1895, à l'université de la Sorbonne, à Paris. Elle est organisée par les inventeurs-réalisateurs Auguste et Louis Lumière. Le cinématographe se développe dans le monde entier.

Le cinéma muet règne en maître jusqu'au 6 octobre 1927, date de la première représentation du *Chanteur de jazz (The Jazz Singer)* d'Al Jolson. Ce film parlant fait un triomphe. En 1928, le cinéma muet n'a plus droit de cité aux États-Unis. En France, le premier grand film parlant date de 1930. Il s'agit de *Sous les toits de Paris*, de René Clair. Jean Renoir, Marcel Carné et Jean Vigo tournent à leur tour de somptueux chefs-d'œuvre.

Hollywood

Les grandes compagnies américaines se mettent en place à Hollywood, sur la côte ouest des États-Unis, dans les années 1910. Les principales figures du muet, Mary Pickford, Charlie Chaplin, Douglas Fairbanks, Gloria Swanson, John Gilbert ou Rudolph Valentino, y font leurs débuts. Ils sont souvent cantonnés à un type de personnage bien précis, et leur talent s'exprime à travers leurs mimiques, leurs gestes, leurs attitudes. L'avènement du parlant porte à beaucoup un coup fatal. Les stars sont désormais obligées d'avoir des voix et des accents conformes à leur personnalité. Malgré les cours de diction et la modification de leur timbre de voix, beaucoup ne parviennent pas à s'habituer aux nouvelles techniques. C'est la chute. Certains, comme Buster Keaton et Harold Lloyd, ne dépassent pas l'époque du muet. Assez curieusement, d'autres ne deviennent célèbres que lorsque le public les entend parler. C'est le cas d'Oliver Hardy et de Stan Laurel. La Suédoise Greta Garbo triomphe en imposant son accent dans *Anna Christie (la Reine Christine)*. Quant à Charlie Chaplin, il attend 1940 pour prendre le risque du parlant avec *le Dictateur*.

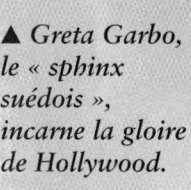

▲ *Greta Garbo, le « sphinx suédois », incarne la gloire de Hollywood.*

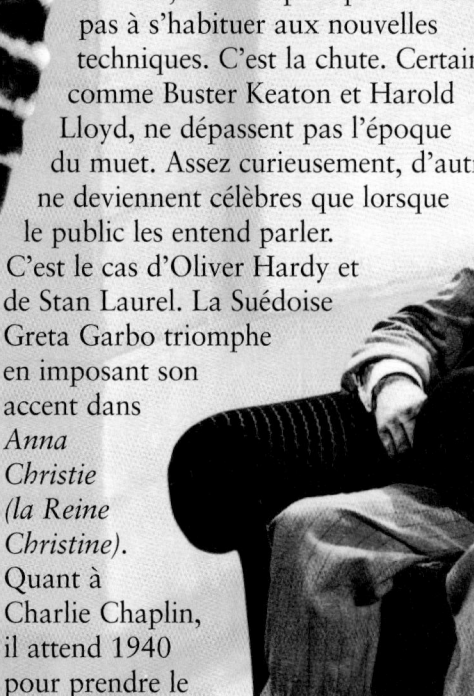

▶ *Laurel et Hardy, grandes vedettes du cinéma comique américain.*

Les plus jeunes actrices de Hollywood

Shirley Temple est née en 1928. Enfant prodige, elle fait ses premiers pas dès l'âge de 3 ans dans des courts métrages comiques, avant d'entamer une carrière d'actrice en 1932 avec le film *The Red Haired Alibi*, de William Christy Cabanne. Elle tourne avec des réalisateurs aussi divers que Fritz Lang, Henry Hathaway, John Ford ou William Dieterle. Dans ses films, elle joue souvent un personnage qui aide les adultes à trouver la bonne voie, grâce à son honnêteté et à son charme comme dans *Heidi*. Une véritable industrie s'est créée autour de son image : poupées Shirley Temple, coloriages, robes, etc. Shirley Temple interrompt sa carrière à l'âge de 21 ans.

Le cas de Judy Garland (1922-1969), de son vrai nom Frances Gumm, est différent. Elle se produit dans un tour de chant dès l'âge de 5 ans, prend son pseudonyme en 1931, et fait un véritable triomphe avec l'excellent film de Victor Fleming, *le Magicien d'Oz* (*The Wizard of Oz*), qui lui vaut un Oscar. Elle en obtient un autre pour *Une étoile est née* (*A Star is Born*), de George Cukor. Entre-temps, elle tourne ses plus célèbres films avec le réalisateur Vincente Minnelli : *le Chant du Missouri* (*Meet Me in Saint Louis*) et *le Pirate* (*The Pirate*). Judy Garland est une actrice de talent dotée d'une voix extraordinaire. Les chansons qu'elle interprète sont un véritable moment d'enchantement.

▲ *Judy Garland obtint un Oscar pour le rôle de Dorothy dans le Magicien d'Oz.*

Le cinéma

- Les Oscars sont décernés à partir de 1929. Il s'agit de statuettes en bronze, dorées à l'or fin.
- Les stars peuvent faire naître des modes : Greta Garbo lance le béret, Marlene Dietrich, le pantalon !
- Le cinéaste Jean Renoir est le fils du peintre Auguste Renoir. Ses films les plus célèbres sont *Boudu sauvé des eaux* (1932), *le Crime de M. Lange* (1935), *la Grande Illusion* (1937) et *la Règle du jeu* (1939).

◄ *Harold Lloyd escalade un gratte-ciel par amour dans* Monte là-dessus *(1923).*

▲ *La jeune actrice américaine Shirley Temple, qui joue ici Heidi, séduit des millions de spectateurs.*

Walt Disney

Les dessins animés de Walt Disney nécessitent des millions de dessins et des années de travail. Les résultats séduisent petits et grands. Il inaugure en 1937 ses longs métrages avec *Blanche-Neige et les sept nains*. Il crée ensuite *Pinocchio* (1940), *Fantasia* (1940) et *Dumbo, l'éléphant volant* (1941). En 1942, *Bambi* raconte l'éducation d'un faon dans la forêt. Le film met en scène exclusivement des animaux aux caractères bien définis, tel Pan-Pan le lapin. Disney est le « père » de nombreux animaux célèbres, comme la souris Mickey, le chien Pluto et le canard Donald.

De 1940 à 1949

1940

La Seconde Guerre mondiale domine la première moitié de la décennie. 55 millions de personnes y trouvent la mort, les civils sont plus touchés que les militaires.

Après la guerre, les nations anéanties se redressent avec lenteur. Après les horreurs d'Auschwitz et de Dresde, après Hiroshima, le monde ne pourra plus jamais être le même. Pourtant, à la fin de la décennie, l'affrontement entre le bloc capitaliste de l'Ouest et le bloc communiste de l'Est commence. C'est le début de la « guerre froide ».

◀ *Charlie Chaplin, dans le rôle du dictateur, danse avec le globe terrestre qu'il veut posséder.*

▼ *Globules rouges.*

Facteur Rhésus

L'immunologiste autrichien Karl Landsteiner a obtenu le prix Nobel de médecine en 1930 pour ses travaux sur les groupes sanguins. Il vient de découvrir le facteur Rhésus. Il permet de comprendre la série d'événements qui peuvent se produire dans le sang de la mère et du fœtus.

Chaplin et *le Dictateur*

▶ **1940** ◀

Pour son premier film parlant, *le Dictateur (The Great Dictator)*, qui sort aux États-Unis, le réalisateur Charlie Chaplin s'offre une fable politique. À travers l'histoire d'un petit barbier juif qui est pris pour le dictateur Hynkel, dont il est le parfait sosie, Chaplin dénonce le Reich et Hitler. Il parodie et ridiculise les gestes, les attitudes et les discours de ce dernier. Ses deux armes, la poésie et l'humour – certaines scènes sont vraiment très comiques –, lui permettent de prendre position avec brio. Le film s'arrête sur un message : les hommes doivent apprendre à s'aimer, et non à se haïr. En des temps aussi troublés, on ne comprend que trop bien ce qu'il veut dire.

Charlie Chaplin

La carrière de Charlie Chaplin commence en 1913-1914. Elle se termine en 1967. Durant cette période, il ne réalise pas moins de 89 films, dont 35 durant la seule année 1914. Il s'éteint en 1977.

• Charlie Chaplin n'a reçu qu'un seul Oscar, pour *les Feux de la rampe (Limelight)*, en 1952.

Invasion de la Belgique

▶ **28 août 1940** ◀

Le roi des Belges, Léopold III, qui avait tenu à conserver la neutralité de son pays, vient de se rendre aux Allemands en début de matinée, contre l'avis de son gouvernement. La campagne de Belgique aura duré dix-huit jours. Le 9 avril, l'armée allemande procédait à l'invasion du Danemark et de la Norvège. Le 10 mai, elle franchissait les frontières du Luxembourg, de la Belgique et de la Hollande. La technique du *Blitzkrieg*, la guerre-éclair, porte ses fruits. Ses forces, qui vont de l'avant avec une étonnante rapidité, surprennent tout le monde.

▲ *Char allemand dans les ruines d'une ville belge.*

▲ *Tableau de Charles Cundell évoquant la retraite alliée à Dunkerque.*

Opération Dynamo à Dunkerque

▶ **4 juin 1940** ◀ Les blindés allemands ont avancé si vite que, dès le 24 mai, ils sont en vue de Dunkerque. Ils ont encerclé et piégé les troupes alliées à Dunkerque.

L'opération Dynamo – l'évacuation des troupes Alliées – a commencé le 27 mai. La Luftwaffe effectue de nombreux bombardements, les pertes en hommes et en matériel sont considérables.

Les Anglais envoient des navires au secours des Alliés mais embarquent les leurs en priorité. 338 000 soldats parviennent à gagner les côtes britanniques, les autres sont fait prisonniers par les Allemands.

Les débuts de la Jeep

Depuis cet automne, l'armée américaine s'est équipée d'une nouvelle voiture. Elle vient en effet d'incorporer la GP, ou plutôt la Jeep, à ses effectifs. Cette voiture, abréviation de *general purpose vehicle* (véhicule tous usages), est conçue par la firme Willys. Ouverte à tous vents, elle est destinée à effectuer des opérations de reconnaissance. C'est un quatre-cylindres dont la vitesse maximale peut atteindre les 105 km/h. La Jeep est extrêmement résistante et peut pratiquement rouler sur tous les terrains.

La France envahie

▶ **23 juin 1940** ◀ L'armée allemande entre à Paris. La convention d'armistice a été signée hier à Rethondes, une petite clairière située en forêt de Compiègne. C'est l'endroit précis où l'armistice de 1918 avait été signé. Le maréchal Pétain avait annoncé, dès le 17 juin, depuis Bordeaux, la capitulation de la France. Les chars allemands avaient traversé la Meuse, près de Sedan, dès le 13 mai. L'avance ennemie avait provoqué l'exode de la population sur les routes. Le 14 juin, les troupes allemandes défilaient à Paris. On estime à environ 2 millions le nombre de soldats français prisonniers en Allemagne.

▶ *Hitler, devant la tour Eiffel, après la chute de Paris.*

Assassinat de Trotski

▶ **21 août 1940** ◀ Léon Trotski vient d'être assassiné, au Mexique, par un agent de Staline, Ramon Mercader. Chef de l'opposition de gauche soviétique, Trotski s'était exilé au Mexique en 1936, afin d'échapper à la répression de Staline.

Le régime de Vichy

▶ **10 juillet 1940** ◀ Selon les conditions de l'armistice, la France est partagée en deux zones. Les deux tiers du territoire, au nord et le long du littoral, sont administrés directement par l'armée allemande d'occupation. Le reste, au sud de la ligne de démarcation, forme la « zone libre ». C'est là que les parlementaires français, réunis à Vichy, donnent les pleins-pouvoirs au maréchal Pétain, qui devient chef de l'État français. Sa devise est Travail, Famille, Patrie.

▶ *Le maréchal Pétain prononce un discours.*

1940 – 1949

1940

Un enfant de 5 ans dalaï-lama du Tibet

▶ **22 février 1940** ◀ Un petit garçon de cinq ans, issu d'un village du nord-est du pays, vient d'être intronisé 14e dalaï-lama ; ce qui fait de lui le souverain politique et spirituel du Tibet.

Les Tibétains, qui vivent dans la contrée la plus haute du monde, sont de fervents bouddhistes. Ils croient que chacun d'entre nous possède une âme immortelle qui prend place dans un autre corps quand nous mourons. La croyance religieuse veut ainsi qu'à la mort du 13e dalaï-lama, en 1933, son âme se soit réincarnée dans un nouveau-né. Les moines, ou lamas, se sont lancés à sa recherche et ont été guidés par un présage : quelques instants avant la cérémonie des funérailles, la tête du 13e dalaï-lama s'est tournée vers le nord-est. Ce signe, associé à d'autres visions, a conduit un groupe de lamas à se rendre au village de Takster, déguisés en marchands ambulants. La légende raconte que, dans la ferme où ils ont été accueillis, un petit garçon de deux ans, Lhamo Thondup, s'est emparé d'un collier ayant appartenu au 13e dalaï-lama et a dit à l'un des lamas : « Tu es un moine de Sera. » Puis, devant un éventail d'objets, il a choisi les anciens biens du défunt en disant : « Ils sont à moi. » Aujourd'hui, le petit garçon porte le nom de Tenzing Gyatso.

▶ *Le dalaï-lama, enfant, vêtu en paysan, au monastère de Kumbum.*

◀ *Le Potala, palais du dalaï-lama à Lhassa, a été construit vers 1645. C'est une véritable ville avec bibliothèques, appartements et sanctuaires.*

En 1940 aussi ...

12 mars • Traité de paix russo-finlandais.

10 juin • Mussolini déclare la guerre à la France et à la Grande-Bretagne.

28 juin • De Gaulle est reconnu chef des Forces françaises libres par le gouvernement britannique.

3 octobre • Vichy décrète un « statut des Juifs ».

24 octobre • Entrevue Pétain-Hitler à Montoire.

Winston Churchill, Premier ministre

▶ **13 mai 1940** ◀ Winston Churchill s'est adressé pour la première fois à la Chambre des communes en tant que Premier ministre. Il y a trois jours, le gouvernement d'Arthur Neville Chamberlain s'est effondré, face aux nombreuses critiques dont il faisait l'objet. Le roi George VI a demandé à Churchill de former un gouvernement de coalition qui rassemble tous les partis. Churchill s'est toujours opposé à Hitler, ainsi qu'à la politique de Chamberlain, trop conciliante vis-à-vis du Reich. Son discours a été particulièrement éloquent : « Je n'ai rien d'autre à vous offrir que du sang, de la peine, de la sueur et des larmes. » Il s'est engagé à poursuivre la guerre « contre une tyrannie monstrueuse et sans rivale ».

▼ *Winston Churchill, nouveau Premier ministre de la Grande-Bretagne.*

La bataille d'Angleterre

▶ **17 septembre 1940** Hitler a lancé l'opération Otarie : l'invasion de la Grande-Bretagne. Comme il ne peut pas débarquer, il veut conquérir l'Angleterre par le ciel. Il organise le bombardement des villes pour faire peur aux civils et pour que les Anglais se rendent. Mais les jeunes pilotes de la RAF résistent aux raids de l'aviation allemande. Les Britanniques possèdent des chasseurs formidables, les Spitfire et les Hurricane. Ils mettent en place des communications sophistiquées, des stations radars performantes et parviennent à déchiffrer le code des transmissions de la Luftwaffe. L'Angleterre est le dernier pays européen qui résiste aux Allemands.

▶ *Enfants devant les ruines de leur école.*

▲ *Mitrailleur allemand à bord d'un Dornier Do-17.*

Le ghetto de Varsovie

▶ **19 novembre 1940** ◀ Les Allemands ont exécuté un Polonais qui a jeté du pain dans le ghetto de Varsovie, quartier dans lequel la population juive de la ville doit vivre. Cet espace, surpeuplé, est coupé du reste de la ville par un haut mur d'enceinte. Les SS ont rassemblé ainsi 400 000 Juifs. Le tiers de la population de Varsovie vit désormais dans un quartier qui représente 2,5% de la superficie totale de la ville. Ils ont interdiction de sortir de l'enceinte, sous peine d'être aussitôt abattus. Ils ne peuvent aller travailler et ne reçoivent des Allemands que des rations de nourriture de 300 calories par jour et par personne. Hans Frank, le gouverneur général de la Pologne du Sud, veut affamer les Juifs jusqu'à la mort.

▲ *Une rue du ghetto de Varsovie.*

Le gouvernement de Pétain

▶ **Juin 1940** ◀ L'article 3 de la convention d'armistice est clair : « Le gouvernement français invitera immédiatement toutes les autorités et tous les services administratifs du territoire occupé à se conformer aux règlements des autorités militaires allemandes et à collaborer avec ces dernières de manière correcte. » Le maréchal Pétain transforme la République en État français, et la devise *Liberté, Égalité, Fraternité* en *Travail, Famille, Patrie*.

Découverte de la grotte de Lascaux

Partis à la recherche de leur chien disparu dans un trou, quatre enfants découvrent le plus beau site préhistorique européen. Il s'agit de la grotte de Lascaux, située au sud de Montignac, en Dordogne. Quatre galeries abritent plusieurs centaines de peintures murales. Ces fresques datent du paléolithique supérieur, 15 000 ans avant notre ère.

▲ *Charles de Gaulle, exilé mais luttant encore.*

L'appel du 18 juin

▶ **18 juin 1940** ◀ Le général de Gaulle, sous-secrétaire d'État à la Défense nationale du gouvernement Paul Reynaud, rejette l'armistice comme un acte inqualifiable. Il s'oppose à la servitude et à la collaboration volontaire du maréchal Pétain. Aujourd'hui, par un message radiodiffusé depuis Londres, il appelle les Français à poursuivre la lutte et donne le signal de la résistance. Il se range ainsi dans l'illégalité.

DU CÔTÉ DES CIVILS

L'Allemagne nazie annexe l'Autriche en mars 1938, puis la Tchécoslovaquie en mars 1939. Le 1er septembre 1939, l'armée allemande envahit la Pologne et provoque l'entrée en guerre de la France et de la Grande-Bretagne. Le 10 mai 1940, elle envahit la Belgique, la Hollande et le Luxembourg. La campagne de France commence. Les Pays-Bas capitulent le 15 mai, la Belgique, le 28 mai. Le 14 juin, Paris est décrétée « ville ouverte ». En 1941, l'Allemagne brise le pacte de non-agression germano-soviétique en attaquant l'URSS. Les États-Unis entrent en guerre en 1941, après le bombardement de Pearl Harbor. L'Allemagne capitule le 8 mai 1945 ; le Japon dépose les armes au mois d'août, après les bombardements atomiques d'Hiroshima et de Nagasaki. Cette guerre aura été l'une des plus meurtrières de l'Histoire.

Villes en ruine

Le bombardement de la petite ville de Guernica par l'aviation nazie, durant la guerre d'Espagne, montre les dégâts que peut provoquer ce type d'offensive. Depuis son commencement, la Seconde Guerre mondiale est menée du ciel, les radars aident à intercepter les bombardiers avant qu'ils ne s'attaquent à leurs cibles. La Luftwaffe a pour missions de détruire les industries de guerre britanniques et de briser la résistance morale de la population. La RAF britannique et l'US Air Force font de même en Allemagne. Pendant la bataille d'Angleterre, la ville de Londres a été pilonnée toutes les nuits. Par la suite, d'autres villes, comme Coventry, sont devenues la cible de bombardements intensifs. 30 000 personnes meurent durant la bataille d'Angleterre.

En France, les bombardements alliés de 1944 détruisent de nombreuses villes. Brest, Nantes, Caen, Le Havre, Amiens, sont totalement en ruine.

À la fin de la guerre, les Alliés bombardent la ville historique allemande de Dresde et font des milliers de morts. Pour mettre fin à la résistance du Japon, les Américains lâchent deux bombes atomiques, sur Hiroshima le 6 août 1945, et sur Nagasaki le 9 août 1945, qui feront d'innombrables victimes.

▲ *Un jeune rescapé, après le raid meurtrier de la Luftwaffe sur Varsovie en septembre 1939. Les Allemands voulaient briser toute résistance en Pologne.*

▼ *Février 1945, Dresde n'est plus qu'un champ de ruines après les bombardements de l'US Air Force et de la RAF.*

▲ *Un quartier de Tokyo, après un raid aérien de l'US Air Force en 1945.*

Évacuation des enfants

Avant que la guerre n'éclate, les gouvernements français et britannique ont préparé l'évacuation des enfants des villes qui, comme Londres, risquaient d'être soumises à des bombardements. La première évacuation a eu lieu le 1er septembre 1939. Près d'un demi-million d'enfants étaient concernés. Les deux autres grandes évacuations se sont produites au début de la guerre-éclair et durant la vague des attaques de roquettes en 1944. Les enfants évacués ont parfois du mal à vivre loin de chez eux. Certains ont été placés chez des parents, mais d'autres ont dû aller dans des familles d'accueil, dans des fermes, par exemple. La situation des enfants juifs est bien plus atroce, car beaucoup vont disparaître et, parmi les survivants, nombreux sont ceux qui ne reverront jamais leur famille.

▲ Les réfugiés fuient l'avance allemande en emportant très peu de choses.

▲ On évacue de jeunes Britanniques vers des zones protégées.

◄ Les écoliers apprennent à mettre le masque à gaz.

► Une étiquette indique l'identité du petit évacué.

Les enfants et la guerre

Il est arrivé que des enfants polonais servent de messagers. Ils parcouraient alors les égouts de leur ville, pour éviter les tireurs allemands.

Au Japon, des milliers d'enfants ont péri, lors de l'explosion de la bombe atomique sur les villes d'Hiroshima et de Nagasaki. Les autres ont été marqués à vie par leurs blessures. Beaucoup sont rapidement morts de leucémie.

▲ Londres. Le métro sert d'abri lors des raids aériens.

Tickets de rationnement pour tous

▲ En Grande-Bretagne, les enfants contribuent à l'effort de guerre en ramassant des mûres.

Tout est rationné : la viande, le lait, le fromage, le beurre, les œufs, le pain, l'huile, le sucre, le savon s'achètent avec des tickets de rationnement, après des heures de queue chaque jour. Tous les pays en guerre sont touchés. Les quantités autorisées sont fonction de l'âge et de l'activité professionnelle de chacun.

▼ Les tickets de rationnement sont obligatoires pour acheter de quoi manger.

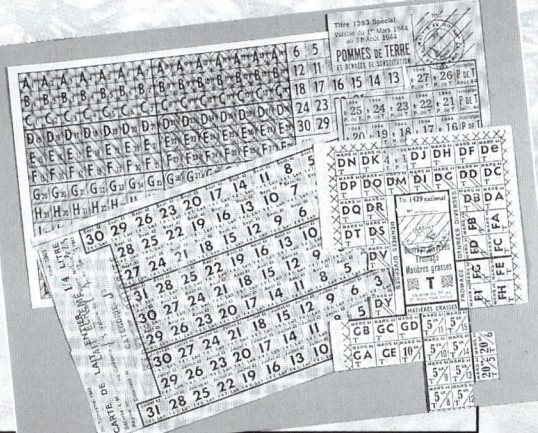

1940

L'ordinateur de Konrad Zuse

1941

C'est l'ancêtre des ordinateurs ! Z3, l'invention de Konrad Zuse, est une machine électronique qui permet aux ingénieurs aéronautiques allemands de calculer les réactions de leurs prototypes en vol. Il lui faut trois secondes pour réussir un calcul en utilisant le système binaire ! Les travaux de Zuse restent secrets en raison de la guerre, mais ils dépassent de loin ceux des autres scientifiques en matière de recherche sur l'intelligence artificielle. Celle-ci repose sur le langage informatique Plankalkül.

1942

1943

1944

1945

1946

1947

1948

1949

1941

Pearl Harbor

▶ 8 décembre 1941 ◀

À 17 h 10, le président des États-Unis, F. D. Roosevelt, déclare la guerre au Japon. Il porte un brassard de deuil, en mémoire des 2043 Américains tués dans l'attaque-surprise que les japonais ont menée contre la flotte américaine du Pacifique basée à Pearl Harbor (Hawaii).

Les pertes américaines sont impressionnantes : 188 avions et 5 croiseurs de combat ont été détruits, et de nombreux bâtiments, gravement endommagés. Seuls les porte-avions ont échappé au désastre.

Le Japon poursuit sa stratégie, qui consiste à s'emparer de tout le Pacifique. Au moment précis où l'amiral Chuichi Nagumo bombarde Pearl Harbor, l'armée japonaise, qui s'était déployée dans le Sud-Est asiatique depuis deux jours, envahit les Philippines, et l'archipel des Mariannes, et débarque en Thaïlande, ainsi que dans les colonies britanniques de Hong Kong et de Malaisie.

Depuis 1937, le Japon essaie de conquérir la Chine et de prendre le contrôle de l'Asie du Sud-Est. Le 28 novembre dernier, Hitler assurait l'empereur du Japon de son soutien en cas d'entrée en guerre des États-Unis. Le conflit est désormais mondial.

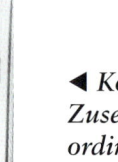

◀ Konrad Zuse et son ordinateur.

▶ Roosevelt déclare la guerre au Japon.

La Collaboration

▶ 1941 ◀

Dès la signature de l'armistice, le maréchal Pétain a engagé la France dans une politique de collaboration avec le régime nazi, ratifiée par sa rencontre avec Hitler à Montoire le 24 octobre 1940. La collaboration est administrative, économique, militaire et intellectuelle. La police participe aux rafles de Juifs ; l'administration désigne des otages ; la milice, police politique fondée par Darnand, traque les résistants. La France paie des indemnités d'occupation à l'armée allemande et livre ses productions.

▼ Scène du film Citizen Kane.

Un grand film d'Orson Welles

Le premier film du réalisateur américain Orson Welles, *Citizen Kane*, est un pur chef-d'œuvre. Metteur en scène de théâtre, animateur d'une célèbre émission de radio, Orson Welles est un véritable homme-orchestre. Il a écrit, réalisé, interprété et produit son film. *Citizen Kane* s'inspire de la vie de William R. Hearst et raconte la grandeur et la solitude du magnat corrompu d'un empire de presse qui vit dans un château, Xanadu, qu'il s'est fait construire.

1940 – 1949

Hitler envahit l'URSS

▶ **19 septembre 1941** ◀ L'armée allemande est entrée dans Kiev, la capitale de l'Ukraine. La ville est truffée de bombes à retardement ; les Soviétiques ont détruit leurs propres réservoirs d'eau ainsi que leurs équipements électriques, plutôt que de les laisser aux troupes adverses.
Le 22 juin, Hitler a dénoncé le pacte de non-agression germano-soviétique. Après la capitulation de la France, il estime pouvoir diriger ses offensives aussi bien à l'ouest qu'à l'est.
L'opération Barbarossa est un succès : l'armée allemande atteint ses objectifs et progresse comme prévu vers Moscou. Hitler souhaite terrasser l'URSS et en raser les principales villes. Il faut qu'il se dépêche, car les pluies d'automne vont bientôt laisser place à l'hiver, à la neige, à un froid inhumain, qui ont été la cause de la défaite de la campagne de Russie menée par Napoléon et sa Grande Armée en 1812. Hitler, pour ces mêmes raisons, veut atteindre Moscou sans plus tarder.

▲ *Un navire américain détruit par le bombardement japonais de Pearl Harbor.*

▼ *Les chars allemands combattent les Soviétiques en Ukraine.*

La Grèce aux mains des nazis

▶ **1er juin 1941** ◀ Le 27 avril dernier, les rues d'Athènes résonnaient sous les chenilles des blindés allemands, obligeant les troupes alliées à se replier en Crète. Cette nuit, douze jours après le débarquement massif des parachutistes allemands sur les lieux, les bateaux de la Royal Navy britannique ont évacué les soldats alliés. L'attaque de la Crète, qui constitue la première invasion aéroportée de l'Histoire, a été conduite avec une minutie d'horlogerie. La Grèce et ses îles sont désormais aux mains du régime nazi.

Des femmes dans l'armée anglaise

▶ **4 décembre 1941** ◀ En Grande-Bretagne, le Premier ministre Winston Churchill a institué la conscription pour les femmes célibataires d'une vingtaine d'années. Elles doivent servir dans l'armée, la police, les pompiers, et peuvent intégrer l'armée de terre, l'armée de l'air ou la marine militaire.
Les plus âgées doivent participer à l'effort de guerre et travailler dans les usines. Dans tous les pays occupés d'Europe, les femmes luttent pour la libération de leur pays. Elles participent aux combats. En France, elles jouent un grand rôle dans la Résistance. Comme les hommes, elles sont arrêtées, torturées, exécutées et déportées par les nazis.

▲ *Les fantassins allemands débarquent en Crète.*

1941

▼ *À Rushmore, aux États-Unis, les têtes en granit de George Washington, Thomas Jefferson, Theodore Roosevelt, Abraham Lincoln (de gauche à droite).*

En 1941 aussi....

24 juillet • La hiérarchie catholique française affirme sa loyauté envers le régime de Pétain.

22 octobre • L'armée allemande exécute en France, à Châteaubriant, 27 otages communistes du camp de Choisel.

11 décembre • Le décret nazi *Nacht und Nebel* (« Nuit et brouillard ») systématise la déportation vers les camps de concentration.

Les têtes sculptées des présidents américains

▶ **1er novembre 1941** ◀ Un saisissant monument patriotique, sculpté dans une falaise de granit, a demandé quinze années de travail. Il a été inauguré aujourd'hui au mont Rushmore, dans les *Black Hills* du Dakota du Sud. Il représente les quatre têtes – hautes de 18 mètres ! – des présidents américains George Washington, Thomas Jefferson, Theodore Roosevelt et Abraham Lincoln. La réalisation a été en elle-même colossale et a demandé l'extraction de 450 000 tonnes de granit, à l'aide d'explosifs, de marteaux piqueurs et de burins. Le sculpteur, Gutzon Borglum, a travaillé à partir de modèles réduits réalisés dans son atelier. Il est mort au printemps dernier et n'a pu, malheureusement, voir son œuvre achevée. Son fils Lincoln a terminé le monument.

Les codes secrets allemands déchiffrés

▶ **30 novembre 1941** ◀ À l'aide d'un radar et de grenades sous-marines, un bombardier de la RAF a coulé aujourd'hui un sous-marin allemand dans la baie de Biscaye. La RAF travaille avec les spécialistes britanniques du décodage. Les forces armées allemandes utilisent un système codé appelé Enigma. Les Britanniques, qui se sont emparés cette année de deux livres codés, sont parvenus à déchiffrer le système. Ils ont localisé le sous-marin en interceptant et en décodant un message. La Grande-Bretagne est en train de gagner la bataille de l'Atlantique.

Étoile jaune obligatoire

▶ **1er septembre 1941** ◀ En Allemagne, en Pologne et dans les États baltes, les nazis obligent tous les Juifs de plus de six ans à porter une étoile jaune, de façon à être immédiatement identifiables. Il s'agit de l'étoile de David, à six branches, découpée sur un fond jaune et portant l'inscription *Jude* (« juif » en allemand) en son milieu. Les « unités spéciales » commencent depuis le mois de juin à rechercher et à massacrer les Juifs, qui sont maintenant reconnaissables grâce à leur étoile jaune.

◀ *Enfant portant l'étoile jaune.*

Pétain

▶ 14 août 1941 ◀ Tous les fonctionnaires français doivent prêter un serment de fidélité au maréchal Pétain. Il est l'objet d'un véritable culte : tous les matins, les enfants des écoles chantent un hymne en son honneur; les livres pour enfants racontent ses « exploits » pendant la Première Guerre mondiale. Mais quelques Français commencent à résister à l'occupant, tandis que la première préoccupation de la majorité d'entre eux est de se procurer du ravitaillement.

Rudolf Hess

▶ 10 mai 1941 ◀ Rudolf Hess, le dauphin de Hitler, s'est envolé pour l'Écosse, à sa seule initiative, dans l'espoir d'y négocier la paix. Il a été aussitôt désavoué par Hitler. Hess a atterri en parachute, non loin de Glasgow. Il affirme que l'Allemagne ne s'attaquera pas à l'Empire britannique si Churchill lui laisse carte blanche en Europe. Cet étrange ambassadeur de la paix a été arrêté et jeté en prison.

Charte de l'Atlantique

▶ 14 août 1941 ◀ Winston Churchill et Franklin D. Roosevelt viennent de signer la charte de l'Atlantique, sur le navire de guerre britannique *Prince of Wales*, au large de Terre-Neuve. Il s'agit d'une déclaration en huit points posant les jalons politiques et économiques de l'après-guerre. Si la défense de la démocratie et de la liberté semble en être la motivation première, certaines clauses concernent plus directement le libre-échange et le désarmement de l'Allemagne. C'est l'origine de l'ONU.

◀ *Roosevelt et Churchill se rencontrent à bord du* Prince of Wales.

La Royal Navy coule le *Bismarck*

▶ 27 mai 1941 ◀ La semaine dernière, l'un des principaux croiseurs de la Royal Navy, le *Hood*, a été coulé en quelques minutes par le plus grand navire de guerre de la flotte allemande, le *Bismarck*. À l'exception de trois d'entre eux, tous les membres d'équipage ont trouvé la mort dans cette offensive. Aujourd'hui, le *Bismarck* a été repéré par la RAF et a été torpillé par le bâtiment de guerre l'*Ark Royal*. À l'instant où le commandant allemand s'apprêtait à saborder son navire, un autre cuirassé britannique, le *Dorsetshire*, l'a envoyé par le fond.

▼ *Le cuirassé* Bismarck *avant l'attaque de la Royal Navy.*

Les dessins de Henry Moore

Le sculpteur britannique Henry Moore est célèbre pour ses œuvres, en bois ou en métal, qui représentent le corps humain comme une forme abstraite. Il est devenu, l'an dernier, l'un des artistes officiels de l'effort de guerre britannique. Il est parvenu à toucher un très large public avec une série de dessins ayant pour sujets les Londoniens endormis dans le métro pendant les attaques aériennes. Moore a su retranscrire avec sensibilité la beauté de ces visages endormis.

1940

1941

1942

1943

1944

1945

1946

1947

1948

1949

La Résistance

Si la Résistance intérieure s'organise dès 1940, trois étapes sont décisives : l'entrée du parti communiste français dans la résistance armée, les événements politiques qui secouent l'État français en 1942, la création des maquis née du refus du STO (Service du travail obligatoire) en 1943.

Les résistants utilisent des noms de code, afin d'éviter de se trahir en cas d'arrestation.

De Gaulle et la Résistance en France

▶ **14 juillet 1942** ◀

Depuis le mois de juin 1940, le général de Gaulle commande les soldats français qui, hors de l'Hexagone, refusent l'armistice signé par le maréchal Pétain. Il s'agit de la France combattante, « présente au combat pour être présente à la victoire ». Aujourd'hui, il s'adresse aux Français et, surtout, aux mouvements de résistance qui s'organisent en France. La Résistance intérieure, qui opère clandestinement et dans des conditions excessivement dangereuses, est formée de plusieurs réseaux très bien organisés. Différents groupes sont spécialisés dans le sabotage, la propagande et l'espionnage. D'autres, comme les FTP (les Francs-tireurs et partisans qui sont communistes), doivent détruire le matériel de guerre des occupants. De nombreux anonymes semi-clandestins distribuent des tracts ou cachent des inconnus traqués. Chaque résistant risque d'être arrêté par la Gestapo, torturé, exécuté ou déporté.

▲ *Un résistant avec une bombe de sa fabrication. Certains réseaux sont spécialistes du sabotage.*

La pénicilline

Le laboratoire pharmaceutique américain Commercial Solvents Corporation, en Indiana, produit d'importantes quantités de pénicilline. Cet antibiotique sera peut-être bientôt disponible pour opérer des miracles. L'an dernier, les scientifiques H. Florey et E. Chain l'ont employé pour soigner un policier atteint de septicémie.

▲ *Chaîne de fabrication de la pénicilline.*

Casablanca

Le dernier film de Michael Curtiz, *Casablanca*, est un véritable mythe. Joué par des acteurs de talent – Humphrey Bogart, Ingrid Bergman, Paul Henreid, Claude Rains, Sydney Greenstreet –, il évoque, de façon très hollywoodienne, l'occupation nazie de la ville marocaine en 1941, à travers une histoire d'amour et de résistance mélodramatique. Malgré la caricature, le film est un réel chef-d'œuvre.

▶ *Casablanca, un film qui colle à l'actualité.*

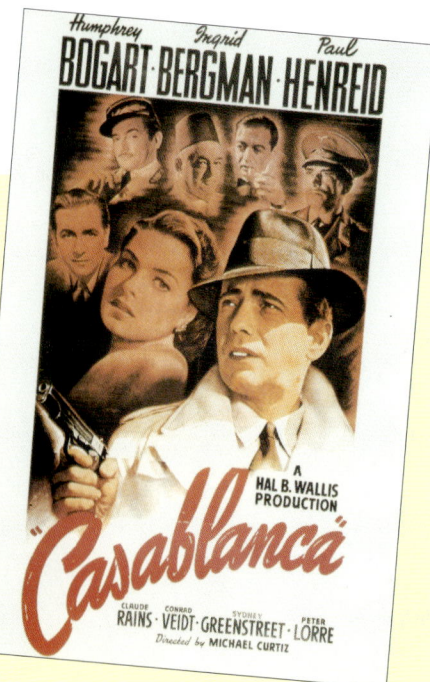

En 1942 aussi…

18 avril • *Tokyo est bombardé par l'armée américaine.*

16 juillet • *À Paris, la police procède à l'arrestation de milliers d'hommes, de femmes et d'enfants juifs. Ils sont dirigés vers le Vélodrome d'hiver, puis vers le camp de concentration de Drancy. C'est la rafle du Vel'd'hiv'.*

11 novembre • *La « zone libre » française est occupée par l'armée allemande.*

1940 – 1949

▲ *Des soldats japonais fêtent la prise d'un canon américain à Batan, aux Philippines.*

Capitulation de Singapour

▶ **15 février 1942** ◀ Les Anglais ont capitulé, ce matin, à Singapour. Soixante mille soldats alliés sont prisonniers. Les Japonais continuent à progresser dans le Pacifique, depuis leur attaque sur Pearl Harbor, le 7 décembre 1941. Après des jours de bombardements, ils ont pris la colonie britannique de Singapour. Forteresse navale stratégique, Singapour est le seul port du Pacifique entre Pearl Harbor et l'Australie. Sa chute est catastrophique pour les Alliés. Il semble que rien ne pourra empêcher maintenant le Japon de conquérir toutes les colonies françaises, américaines, britanniques et néerlandaises en Extrême-Orient.

La bataille des Midway

▶ **7 juin 1942** ◀ Les Alliés viennent de remporter une victoire dans les îles Midway. Atolls de l'océan Pacifique, les îles Midway sont le théâtre de violents combats aéronavals. Lorsque les équipes de décodage américaines ont appris que ces îles étaient une cible pour l'armée japonaise, trois porte-avions ont été dépêchés sur les lieux afin d'intercepter la flotte japonaise. La bataille des Midway a duré trois jours, au terme desquels la flotte japonaise a subi de très lourdes pertes. Elle doit renoncer à son plan d'attaque sur l'Australie et se replier sur les bases des Philippines et du Japon.

▲ *Porte-avions américain touché aux Midway.*

L'Air Force à l'heure du jazz

Le tromboniste et chef d'orchestre américain Glenn Miller a renoncé, au mois de septembre, à son célèbre big band (orchestre), pour s'engager dans l'Air Force. Il y dirigera l'orchestre et aura pour tâche de remonter le moral des troupes. Son grand orchestre de jazz a reçu cette année un Disque d'or pour plus d'un million d'exemplaires de *Chattanooga choo choo*.

Échec des Alliés à Dieppe

▶ **19 août 1942** ◀ Les forces alliées françaises, canadiennes, britanniques et américaines ont tenté de débarquer en France et ont tenu, neuf heures durant, le port de Dieppe, où l'armée allemande a installé sa ligne de défense des côtes françaises de la Manche. Les Alliés ont causé de sérieux dégâts aux installations du port. Les pertes sont importantes des deux côtés, il y a plus de 2 000 prisonniers.

Victoire alliée en Afrique

▶ **4 novembre 1942** ◀ Après des semaines de violents combats, l'Afrikakorps, l'armée allemande de Rommel, et les divisions italiennes sont défaits à El-Alamein, dans le désert égyptien, par la 8ᵉ armée britannique commandée par les généraux Montgomery et Alexander. L'Afrikakorps est désormais anéanti. El-Alamein est l'une des victoires les plus décisives contre les forces de l'axe Rome-Berlin. Dans trois jours, les troupes alliées débarqueront en Afrique du Nord.

▶ *Les Britanniques prennent un char allemand, à El-Alamein, en Égypte.*

Le génocide

60 % des Juifs d'Europe ont été exterminés par les nazis.

76 000 Juifs français, dont 11 000 enfants, sont morts dans les camps nazis.

240 000 Tziganes ont été massacrés par les nazis.

33 771 Juifs d'Ukraine ont été assassinés par les nazis près de Kiev, les 29 et 30 septembre 1941. Et 70 000 autres dans les mois qui ont suivi.

Des Juifs polonais ont été asphyxiés par les nazis avec les gaz des pots d'échappement de camions, à Chelmno, en décembre 1941.

LE GÉNOCIDE

Adolf Hitler et ses adeptes croient en l'existence d'une race pure, la race aryenne, dont font partie les Allemands, destinée à régner sur le monde. En conséquence, les Allemands auraient pour mission d'asservir ou d'exterminer tous les peuples de races qu'ils affirment inférieures, surtout les Juifs, les Slaves et les Tziganes. Les nazis accusent les Juifs d'être responsables de tous les maux qui accablent l'Allemagne. Cette théorie délirante et scientifiquement inacceptable est mise en pratique au cours de la Seconde Guerre mondiale. Dans les pays occupés par l'Allemagne, les nazis raflent systématiquement les Juifs – et les Tziganes –, pour les envoyer vers l'Europe orientale – Allemagne et Pologne surtout – dans des camps d'extermination. Ils feront au moins 6 millions de victimes.

Le *Journal d'Anne Frank*

Son *Journal*, écrit dans un petit cahier rouge et blanc, et publié après la guerre par son père – seul rescapé des quatre membres de la famille –, a fait le tour du monde. L'auteur s'appelle Anne Frank. Petite fille juive de Francfort, en Allemagne, elle avait dû fuir son pays natal pour Amsterdam, avec toute sa famille. Lorsque la ville fut occupée par les Allemands, les Frank échappèrent aux rafles en se cachant avec quatre autres personnes. Ils étaient réfugiés dans une annexe de leur maison, à la porte d'entrée camouflée derrière une armoire pivotante. Des amis les ravitaillaient régulièrement, car ils ne pouvaient pas sortir. Ils furent dénoncés et, en août 1944, firent partie des derniers déportés en partance vers le camp de la mort d'Auschwitz. Anne fut transférée avec sa sœur à Bergen-Belsen, où elle mourut peu de temps avant que les Britanniques ne libèrent le camp. Elle avait quinze ans.

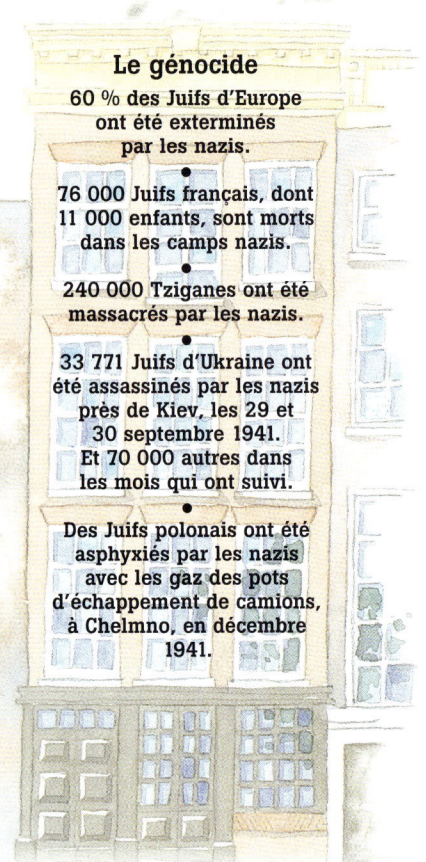

▼ *Anne Frank : le récit de sa vie cachée pendant trois ans, à Amsterdam, sous l'occupation allemande, témoigne de l'horreur au quotidien de la persécution nazie.*

▼ *La cachette des Frank à Amsterdam.*

▶ *En arrière-plan, deux pages extraites du* Journal *d'Anne Frank.*

Parqués et massacrés

Peu de temps après l'invasion de la Pologne, les nazis ordonnent la concentration des Juifs dans les grandes villes. Des ghettos sont institués à Vilnius, Lublin, Lódź. Au printemps 1943, 60 000 Juifs, affamés, emmurés dans le ghetto de Varsovie – uniques survivants des 400 000 personnes parquées là à l'origine –, se soulèvent. Après des jours de combats, rue par rue, maison par maison, ceux qui ne sont pas morts au cours de l'action sont exécutés sur place, et les survivants, déportés. Seule une poignée d'entre eux a survécu.

◄▶ *Les Juifs sont systématiquement séparés des autres personnes, même dans les trams et les écoles.*

La « solution finale »

L'extermination systématique des Juifs débute en 1941. Les nazis l'appellent la « solution finale ». Les Juifs sont raflés, entassés de force dans des wagons à bestiaux, et déportés vers des camps comme Auschwitz, Ravensbrück, Treblinka… Sans eau et sans nourriture, beaucoup meurent en chemin. À l'arrivée, les enfants, les vieillards et les malades sont dirigés vers des chambres où ils sont gazés. Les autres sont mis au travail, jusqu'à ce que mort s'ensuive. Les exactions sont quotidiennes, la sous-alimentation, généralisée. Certains servent de cobayes pour des expérimentations cauchemardesques : on leur inocule le typhus et la gangrène gazeuse, on les soumet à de hautes pressions jusqu'à ce que leurs poumons éclatent… Ils meurent par millions, et leurs cadavres sont brûlés dans des fours crématoires.

▲ *Enfants dans un camp de concentration.*

▼ *Juifs en partance pour un camp de la mort.*

▲ *Patrouilles allemandes dans le ghetto de Varsovie.*

▲ *Le général Stroop (au centre) dans le ghetto de Varsovie.*

Les Juifs se révoltent en Pologne

▶ **19 avril 1943** ◀ Armés de lance-flammes et de dynamite, équipés de chars et de voitures blindées, les Waffen SS (les troupes de combat nazies) ont entrepris de vider le ghetto juif de Varsovie, la capitale de la Pologne. Alors qu'ils progressent dans les ruines du ghetto, les SS du général Stroop ont une surprise : une insurrection juive.

Le ghetto, mis en place par les Allemands, en 1940 a d'abord rassemblé au moins 400 000 habitants. Les conditions de vie y sont effrayantes : en moyenne, sept personnes vivent dans une pièce, et la nourriture manque toujours. Plusieurs milliers de personnes sont mortes de faim et de maladie. La plupart des survivants ont été déportés dans les camps d'extermination. Malgré les horreurs des trois dernières années, le ghetto de Varsovie abrite encore 50 000 Juifs en 1943. Sept cent cinquante d'entre eux décident de résister aux SS. Les insurgés sont dirigés par Mordecai Anielewicz, un jeune Juif de 24 ans. Ils sont armés de 9 fusils, de 59 pistolets et de quelques grenades. Ils luttent rue par rue, maison par maison, et mènent un combat héroïque et acharné dans les galeries des égouts.

La Résistance se développe

▶ **1943** ◀ De plus en plus de jeunes Français rejoignent la Résistance dans les maquis. Ils fuient le Service du travail obligatoire (STO), qui les force à aller travailler en Allemagne. Le gouvernement de Vichy espère qu'en échange de cette mesure les soldats français prisonniers en Allemagne (environ 1 500 000 hommes) pourront être libérés. Avec le STO, l'État français aide l'économie de guerre allemande.

Le Petit Prince

Antoine de Saint-Exupéry publie *le Petit Prince*, livre qu'il a lui-même illustré. Ce conte poétique et philosophique s'adresse aux enfants et aux adultes. Il montre que les petites choses de la vie sont les plus belles. Grand aviateur et résistant, il a dédié son livre à un vieil ami, parce que « tous les adultes ont été des enfants un jour, même si peu s'en souviennent ».

La bataille de Stalingrad

▶ **31 janvier 1943** ◀ Le siège de Stalingrad, en URSS, est levé. Le maréchal von Paulus se rend à un lieutenant soviétique. La plupart de ses hommes sont morts.

La ville de Stalingrad porte ce nom en l'honneur de Staline, qui l'a défendue pendant la guerre civile russe. C'est l'une des raisons pour lesquelles Hitler voulait absolument s'en emparer.

La bataille a commencé en septembre 1942. L'armée allemande a assiégé Stalingrad, mais elle a été elle-même encerclée par les Soviétiques. Pris au piège, sans vivres, les Allemands ont dû se rendre. C'est la première défaite de la Wehrmacht.

▲ *À Stalingrad, les soldats de l'Armée rouge marchent sur les dernières troupes allemandes.*

Une superforteresse volante

▶ **1943** ◀ La première « forteresse volante » de l'armée américaine, le B-17, permettait déjà de bombarder de jour, à condition qu'elle ait un armement suffisant et qu'elle soit accompagnée d'une escorte de chasseurs à grand rayon d'action. La nouvelle « superforteresse » Boeing B-29 est encore plus meurtrière : elle a un rayon d'action de 4 500 km et peut transporter 5 t de bombes. Le B-29 a été conçu spécialement pour bombarder le territoire japonais. Il permettra d'accélérer la victoire des Alliés.

◀ *Le nouveau bombardier américain B-29.*

Un frère et une sœur antinazis exécutés en Allemagne

▶ **22 février 1943** ◀ Hans et Sophie Scholl, un frère et une sœur, viennent d'être condamnés à mort pour résistance, à Munich, en Allemagne. Ils avaient été arrêtés quatre jours plus tôt par la police secrète, la Gestapo. Hans, qui a 24 ans, et Sophie, qui en a 22, sont étudiants. Ils ont créé l'année dernière l'organisation de la Rose blanche, qui appelle les Allemands à lutter contre Hitler et le nazisme. Ils ont été pris alors qu'ils distribuaient des tracts antinazis à l'université. Ils vont être décapités aujourd'hui.

▲ *Hans et Sophie Scholl.*

La chanson pendant la guerre

Frank Sinatra se produit sur la scène du Paramount, à New York. Ce chanteur de charme fait vibrer les cœurs. En France aussi, on chante, malgré l'Occupation. Charles Trenet interprète *Que reste-t-il de nos amours ?*, et Maurice Chevalier *la Symphonie des semelles de bois*. Et, dans la clandestinité, on entonne *le Chant des partisans*, écrit par Joseph Kessel pour les résistants.

1943

Attaques alliées sur tous les fronts

▶ **18 mai 1943** ◀ La Royal Air Force (RAF), l'aviation britannique, a remporté un brillant succès, la nuit dernière, en détruisant les barrages de l'Eder et de la Möhne, qui fournissent l'électricité de la région industrielle de la Ruhr, en Allemagne. Quinze avions Lancaster ont largué des bombes spéciales, rondes, qui rebondissent sur l'eau avant de toucher leurs objectifs. Cette attaque a coûté la vie à 1 500 personnes et provoqué des dégâts que les Allemands mettront des mois à réparer. Depuis le 1er mars, la RAF bombarde aussi systématiquement les lignes de chemin de fer en Allemagne et dans les pays occupés.

Ces succès s'ajoutent aux victoires en Afrique du Nord. Depuis le début de 1943, les unités allemandes, en particulier l'Afrikakorps commandé par le maréchal Rommel, accumulent les défaites. Les forces anglo-américaines et françaises ont obligé les forces de l'axe Rome-Berlin à se rendre, en Tunisie, qui a été libérée le 13 mai. La bataille du désert est gagnée. Désormais, les Alliés peuvent envisager un débarquement en Sicile, qui fera capituler l'Italie.

▼ *Des aviateurs de l'escadrille de la RAF, avant le raid sur la Ruhr, autour du lieutenant-colonel Gibson.*

▶ *Barnes Willis, l'inventeur de la « bombe qui rebondit ».*

L'Italie capitule

▶ **8 septembre 1943** ◀ Les forces alliées ont débarqué en Sicile le 25 juillet, Mussolini a été renversé. L'axe Rome-Berlin n'existe plus : l'Italie signe l'armistice avec les Alliés. Les nazis ont perdu leur principal allié. C'est le maréchal Badoglio qui a négocié en secret la capitulation italienne.

▼ *Des soldats dans les ruines de la ville italienne de Cassino, bombardée par les Alliés.*

Oublier la guerre

La comédie musicale *Oklahoma* triomphe à Broadway, à New York. Les héros en sont des fermiers de l'Oklahoma, un État américain. Le spectacle est truffé de chansons drôles qui font oublier au public les soucis de la guerre. En France, certains artistes s'inspirent, au contraire, de l'actualité. *Le Corbeau*, un film d'Henri Georges Clouzot, se passe dans une petite ville bouleversée par un flot de lettres anonymes. Des lettres comme la Gestapo en reçoit dans la réalité…

Les Japonais torpillent un navire-hôpital

 **14 mai 1943** Un sous-marin japonais torpille sans sommation un navire-hôpital australien, dans le Pacifique sud. Ce drame a provoqué la mort de 300 personnes. Les Japonais n'ont pas attaqué par erreur ce bateau, qui ne pouvait être pris pour un vaisseau de guerre.

Voilà un an, le Japon envisageait d'envahir l'Australie. Des sous-marins de poche nippons avaient même attaqué le port de Sydney. Mais les Japonais sont sur la défensive, depuis leur défaite des Midway, en juin. Cette dernière atrocité pourrait être le signe de leur désespoir croissant.

En 1943 aussi...

9 février • Les forces américaines du Pacifique reprennent Guadalcanal, dans les îles Salomon (Océanie), après six mois de combats.

12 septembre • Un commando SS délivre Mussolini de sa prison et l'emmène dans les Abruzzes, au centre de l'Italie, pour créer un nouvel État fasciste.

28 novembre • Conférence de Téhéran (Iran) entre Churchill, Staline et Roosevelt.

◀ Le port de Sydney, en Australie, après le raid des sous-marins de poche japonais.

Une pin-up pour les GI

Tous les soldats américains (les GI) ont affiché cette pin-up dans leur chambrée. Cette actrice se nomme Betty Grable, la « bombe blonde » de Hollywood. Ses jambes sont assurées pour 250 000 dollars. Elle ne manque pas de charme et représente pour eux la femme idéale. Les GI qui combattent loin de leur pays se remontent le moral en la regardant « punaisée » à leurs murs.

1940 – 1949

Un rein artificiel

Les patients dont les reins fonctionnent mal retrouvent l'espoir, grâce à un médecin danois, Willem Kolff. Il a inventé en effet un appareil pour dialyse, un rein artificiel qui remplace l'organe malade. La dialyse est une opération qui permet de purifier le sang, d'en éliminer les substances toxiques. C'est normalement le travail des reins.

La mort de Jean Moulin

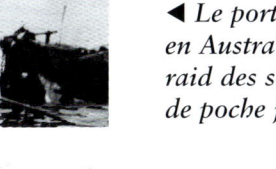 **8 juillet 1943** Jean Moulin est mort pendant son transfert vers un camp de concentration en Allemagne. Il avait été arrêté par la Gestapo le 27 mai, à Caluire, près de Lyon, à la suite d'une trahison. Torturé, il n'a pas parlé. Préfet de Chartres en 1940, il avait été révoqué par le gouvernement de Vichy. Il était parti à Londres rejoindre le général de Gaulle en 1941. En janvier 1942, il fut parachuté en France pour unifier les réseaux de Résistance communistes et non communistes. Il avait réussi à les réunir dans le Conseil national de la Résistance, qu'il avait créé en mai 1943.

◀ Jean Moulin, héros de la Résistance.

1940

1941

1942

1943

1944

1945

1946

1947

1948

1949

▶ *Les forces alliées débarquent sur les plages normandes.*

Roosevelt réélu

En novembre, le président des États-Unis, Franklin D. Roosevelt a été réélu pour quatre ans. C'est son quatrième mandat – un record, aucun autre président n'en ayant détenu plus de deux. Il a une petite majorité, et il est en mauvaise santé, mais, à cause de la guerre, les électeurs ont eu peur du changement.

1944

Le débarquement en Normandie

▶ **6 juin 1944** ◀ À l'aube, les parachutistes alliés ont sauté derrière les lignes allemandes en Normandie. Ils forment l'avant-garde de la formidable flotte qui débarque le long des plages du Cotentin, sur plus de 80 km. L'opération Overlord (son nom de code) est de loin la plus importante attaque navale et aérienne de toute l'Histoire. Sous la direction du général américain Eisenhower, elle engage 150 000 hommes, 5 000 navires et 12 000 avions. Pendant les dernières semaines, les Alliés ont bombardé les défenses et les réseaux de communication allemands en France, tandis que la Résistance a multiplié les sabotages de voies ferrées et de ponts.

Le maréchal von Rundstedt, qui commande les troupes nazies, a été surpris : il doit faire face à des attaques simultanées. Les Américains débarquent près de Carentan et de Vierville, les Anglais et les Canadiens, près d'Arromanches, de Courseulles et de Lion-sur-Mer, les Français, près de Ouistreham. Dès le soir, les Alliés ont pris la côte, sans lourdes pertes, sauf à Omaha Beach.

Marlene Dietrich

L'actrice d'origine allemande Marlene Dietrich fait la tournée des bases militaires américaines. À 43 ans, c'est la plus fascinante des vedettes de cinéma. Elle ensorcelle les soldats et séduit son public. Elle travaille aux États-Unis depuis 1930. Elle a refusé de retourner en Allemagne nazie et a pris la nationalité américaine.

▶ *Les Soviétiques avancent vers Leningrad.*

La fin du siège de Leningrad

▶ **27 janvier 1944** ◀ Le terrible siège de Leningrad est terminé. L'offensive soviétique a obligé les Allemands à se retirer de la voie ferrée Moscou-Leningrad, délivrant la ville. Le siège a duré neuf cents jours. La ville a été bombardée et encerclée dès août 1941. Plus de 650 000 personnes sont mortes de faim et de froid. Le premier hiver a été effroyable. Ensuite, Leningrad a pu être ravitaillé par le nord, depuis le lac Ladoga.

La retraite allemande entraîne l'isolement des Finlandais, qui sont en guerre contre l'URSS depuis 1941. Ils pourraient demander l'armistice.

Londres frappé par un V2

▶ 9 septembre 1944 ◀ Les Allemands ont inventé une nouvelle arme redoutable. Aujourd'hui, Londres a été attaqué par un missile balistique (arme propulsée par une fusée), le V2, qui transporte une ogive de 1 tonne. Avec sa vitesse qui dépasse celle des avions les plus rapides, il ne peut être intercepté. C'est la seconde des armes secrètes de Hitler. Des V1 (Vengeance 1), surnommés « bombes volantes », ont déjà touché Londres le 12 juin. L'année dernière, les Britanniques ont bombardé les sites de construction des V1 et V2. Ils ont réussi à retarder le programme de plusieurs mois.

▲ Un enfant tiré des ruines de sa maison, après un bombardement.

En 1944 aussi...

30 janvier
• À la conférence de Brazzaville (Congo), de Gaulle promet davantage de liberté aux colonies.

10 juin • La division SS das Reich massacre tous les habitants d'Oradour-sur-Glane, en France.

15 août • Les Alliés débarquent en Provence.

3 et 7 septembre • Libération de Liège et de Bruxelles, en Belgique.

La révolte de Varsovie

▶ 1er août 1944 ◀ L'Armée polonaise de l'intérieur soulève Varsovie, la capitale polonaise. Les Polonais pensaient que l'armée soviétique, qui campe tout près, allait venir à leur secours, mais elle n'a pas bougé. Les insurgés combattent au corps à corps. Staline, qui a des visées sur la Pologne, attend que la résistance non communiste soit anéantie avant de faire entrer ses troupes dans Varsovie.

Échec d'un attentat contre Hitler

▶ 20 juillet 1944 ◀ Hitler échappe de peu à un attentat organisé par ses propres officiers. La bombe a explosé en pleine réunion d'état-major au quartier général de Hitler, à Rastenburg, en Prusse-Orientale. Plusieurs officiers ont été tués, mais Hitler a été à peine touché, car il a été protégé par la table. L'engin avait été caché dans une serviette par le colonel von Stauffenberg, un héros de la guerre. Beaucoup d'officiers supérieurs approuvent l'attentat. Cela montre que Hitler doit faire face à une opposition croissante. On entend pourtant peu parler de la résistance allemande, car tous les opposants sont éliminés.

▲ Le général de Gaulle, le chef de la Résistance depuis 1940, dans Paris libéré.

La libération de Paris

▶ 25 août 1944 ◀ La 2e division blindée du général Leclerc est entrée dans Paris hier soir, mettant fin à quatre ans d'occupation. Le général von Choltitz, qui commandait la capitale, n'a pas obéi à l'ordre de Hitler. Celui-ci lui avait ordonner de brûler Paris plutôt que de capituler. Les résistants ont libéré des points stratégiques tels que l'Hôtel de Ville. Paris acclame aujourd'hui le général de Gaulle, qui descend les Champs-Élysées.

LA BOMBE ATOMIQUE

En 1905, Albert Einstein découvre, par la théorie de la relativité, que les atomes – les plus petites particules qui composent la matière, soit toute substance dans l'Univers – peuvent être convertis en énergie. Les physiciens nucléaires font avancer les recherches sur la structure de l'atome et confirment cette théorie dans les années 30. Les neutrons – les particules d'un atome – qui heurtent un atome d'uranium le cassent en deux fragments, le baryum et le krypton. Ce processus de la fission nucléaire dégage beaucoup d'énergie et libère d'autres neutrons, d'où une réaction en chaîne. En 1942, Fermi réalise la première réaction en chaîne contrôlée.

Le projet Manhattan

En 1939, Albert Einstein, à la demande d'autres grands physiciens des États-Unis, envoie une lettre au président Roosevelt. Il explique que, grâce aux récentes découvertes de la physique nucléaire, il est possible de fabriquer une bombe d'une puissance formidable. Roosevelt décide alors de lancer un programme secret d'armement nucléaire. Il faut aller vite : la Seconde Guerre mondiale a commencé en Europe, et les physiciens allemands sont aussi à la recherche de l'arme atomique. L'équipe de spécialistes britanniques du nucléaire rejoint les Américains, après l'entrée en guerre des États-Unis. Les savants réalisent ensemble le programme Manhattan – son nom de code –, dont le site principal se trouve à Oak Ridge, dans le Tennessee, et dont la direction scientifique revient à Julius Robert Oppenheimer.

Le projet aboutit à la construction de trois bombes. La première, « *Little Boy* », est une arme atomique à base d'uranium 235. Elle est larguée par un bombardier américain B-29 sur la ville d'Hiroshima, au Japon, le 6 août 1945. Les deuxième et troisième bombes, à hydrogène, sont plus puissantes. L'une est testée avec succès dans le désert du Nouveau-Mexique, le 16 juillet 1945. « *Fat Man* » est lancée sur Nagasaki, le 9 août 1945. Les deux bombes tuent plus de 100 000 Japonais et font des dizaines de milliers de blessés.

▲ Oppenheimer (à gauche) et le général Groves, après avoir testé la deuxième bombe atomique, dans le désert du Nouveau-Mexique.

La bombe atomique « *Little Boy* », ainsi surnommée d'après le nom de code de Roosevelt, n'avait pas été testée avant d'être lancée sur Hiroshima.
Une bombe atomique dégage un million de fois plus d'énergie qu'une bombe chimique de même poids.
En 1945, seuls les États-Unis possèdent la bombe atomique.

Cobayes humains

États-Unis, 1955. Spectateurs d'un essai nucléaire munis de lunettes noires qui protègent seulement leurs yeux de l'éclair atomique. Les savants qui ont construit les premières bombes ignoraient sans doute que les radiations étaient aussi dangereuses.

Les explosions nucléaires

Les explosions nucléaires tuent de trois façons. D'abord, en raison de la chaleur dégagée. La température extrême occasionne de violents incendies jusqu'à 10 kilomètres alentour. Ensuite, la force de l'explosion provoque un souffle meurtrier. Enfin, les effets des radiations nucléaires sont des plus dramatiques. La radiation directe est liée à l'explosion et touche tout sur le lieu et les environs du sinistre. Mais il y a aussi les retombées, sous forme d'une nappe de poussière fine très radioactive, qui se répand sur des kilomètres, poussée par le vent. Une partie des retombées perd rapidement sa nocivité. Mais une autre reste radioactive pendant des siècles, entraînant chez les êtres humains des maladies mortelles, comme le cancer.

Depuis Hiroshima, le monde vit dans la terreur d'une explosion ou d'un accident atomique. Certains Américains ont construit des abris antiatomiques chez eux pour se protéger. Ces abris souterrains ont des murs en béton, et on peut y survivre une quinzaine de jours.

▲ *Aux États-Unis des enfants testent la fermeture du toit de leur abri antiatomique, à Bronxville, près de New York.*

◀ *Une classe en exercice d'alerte nucléaire. Un bureau ne vous protège pas en cas de guerre atomique.*

Armement et désarmement nucléaires

Les Soviétiques construisent leur première bombe atomique en 1948. Peu à peu, les grandes puissances se lancent dans la course aux armements nucléaires. La Grande-Bretagne effectue son premier essai en 1952. La France fait exploser sa première bombe en 1960, à Reggane, dans le Sahara. La Chine l'obtient en 1964, puis c'est au tour de l'Inde, en 1974. Les essais, qui se multiplient sur terre et en mer, ne tuent pas directement, mais ont des retombées radioactives sur toute la planète.

Jusqu'en 1987, la paix du monde repose sur l'équilibre de la terreur. Chacun des deux Grands peut détruire l'autre et ses alliés, en s'équipant de missiles à tête nucléaire, d'avions et de navires capables de les transporter et de les lancer. Ils entament toutefois des négociations, et parviennent, à partir de 1963, à des accords partiels de non-prolifération. En 1991, le traité START (*Strategic Arms Reduction Talks*) prévoit une réduction de 25 à 30 % des arsenaux nucléaires stratégiques des États-Unis et de l'URSS.

▲ *Manifestation contre les essais nucléaires français dans le Pacifique. Les derniers d'entre eux ont eu lieu en 1995-1996, près de l'île de Mururoa, en Polynésie.*

▶ *Atoll de Bikini, 25 juillet 1946. Premier essai nucléaire des États-Unis dans le Pacifique. La gigantesque colonne d'eau provoquée par l'explosion atteint 1 524 mètres.*

1940

1941

1942

1943

1944

1945

1946

1947

1948

1949

1945

▶ L'équipage de la « superforteresse » B-29 Enola Gay, qui a largué la bombe sur Hiroshima le 6 août.

▶ Les ruines d'Hiroshima après la bombe.

La bombe atomique

Ce n'est pas Nagasaki qui devait être bombardé, mais l'objectif de départ était caché sous les nuages.

Les Américains envisageaient de larguer trois bombes atomiques. Mais, après Nagasaki, la capitulation du Japon était acquise. Le président Truman ne voulut pas faire d'autres victimes.

Fifi Brindacier

Fifi Brindacier, le nouveau livre de la Suédoise Astrid Lindgren, passionne les enfants. L'héroïne, Fifi, est une orpheline de 9 ans qui a les cheveux roux. Elle vit seule avec un poney et un petit singe. Maladroite et pas très soignée, Fifi porte de grandes chaussettes dépareillées, mais elle est dotée d'une force surhumaine : elle est capable de soulever un cheval. Elle fait des blagues et dit des bêtises.

▲ L'édition allemande de Fifi Brindacier.

Capitulation du Japon après Hiroshima et Nagasaki

▶ 14 août 1945 ◀ Le Japon capitule sans condition, après l'attaque foudroyante menée par les Américains, qui ont utilisé une nouvelle arme surpuissante : une bombe atomique a détruit la ville japonaise de Nagasaki, le 9 août. C'était la seconde bombe atomique (1 000 fois plus puissante que la bombe conventionnelle la plus destructrice) que les États-Unis lançaient en une semaine. La première, « Little Boy », a rayé Hiroshima de la carte, le 6 août, tuant 78 000 personnes et en blessant des milliers d'autres. Jusqu'à Nagasaki (36 000 morts et 40 000 blessés), le Japon a refusé de capituler, malgré l'anéantissement presque total de sa flotte. Le président Truman a pris la décision ultime d'employer l'arme nucléaire, afin de hâter la conclusion de la guerre. Il a informé Staline que les États-Unis possédaient une arme à la puissance de destruction inégalée.

L'Armée rouge à Auschwitz

▶ 27 janvier 1945 ◀ Les Soviétiques sont entrés dans le camp de concentration d'Auschwitz, dans le sud de la Pologne. C'est l'un des camps où les nazis ont mis en œuvre la « solution finale », l'extermination des Juifs d'Europe. Comme dans les autres camps qu'ils ont libérés, les soldats de l'Armée rouge ont découvert des scènes d'une horreur insoutenable.
À Auschwitz, les déportés étaient entassés nus dans des chambres à gaz et asphyxiés – le gaz mortel était diffusé par le plafond. Les vêtements des victimes étaient recyclés, et les objets de valeur, partagés entre les SS. Les dents en or des morts étaient arrachées et fondues en lingots. Les corps étaient brûlés dans des fours géants (fours crématoires). On estime que 1 à 3 millions de personnes ont péri à Auschwitz.

▲ Juifs déportés d'Auschwitz, derrière les barbelés.

Conférence de Yalta

▶ **4-12 février 1945** ◀ Les trois grands dirigeants alliés, Winston Churchill, Franklin D. Roosevelt et Joseph Staline, se rencontrent à Yalta, en Crimée (URSS), pour décider de ce qui va se passer après la guerre. L'Allemagne sera occupée par les forces alliées. L'Union soviétique dominera l'Europe de l'Est et prendra des territoires à la Pologne. Churchill se méfie des réelles intentions de Staline dans les pays de l'Est, bien que celui-ci ait promis d'organiser des élections libres. Roosevelt, qui apparaît très affaibli, veut surtout s'assurer l'aide de l'URSS pour vaincre le Japon.

▲ *Churchill, Roosevelt et Staline à Yalta.*

Dresde est détruit

▶ **14 février 1945** ◀ La magnifique ville de Dresde, en Allemagne, est en ruine, victime de l'un des plus terribles raids aériens de la guerre. Les Lancaster britanniques ont bombardé la ville, la nuit dernière. Aujourd'hui, des B-17 américains ont pris le relais. Il y aurait 135 000 morts parmi la population civile. Les Allemands ont opposé très peu de résistance. L'intensité du bombardement et les conditions climatiques ont provoqué des incendies effroyables : tout a brûlé. Certains ont mis en cause la nécessité de ce bombardement, car la défaite de l'Allemagne était désormais certaine.

▲ *La ville de Dresde en ruine.*

En 1945 aussi...

8 mars • En Yougoslavie, Tito forme le nouveau gouvernement avec l'appui de l'URSS.

12 avril • Le président Roosevelt meurt, aux États-Unis.

28 avril • En Italie, Mussolini est exécuté par des résistants.

26 juillet • Winston Churchill est battu aux élections britanniques.

21 octobre • La France élit une Assemblée constituante. Pour la première fois, les femmes votent.

L'armistice en Europe

▶ **8 mai 1945** ◀ La guerre est finie en Europe. Pour les Alliés, c'est le jour de la victoire, si longtemps attendu. Pour les Allemands, c'est la fin pitoyable d'une époque terrible. Aujourd'hui, le maréchal Keitel a signé à Berlin l'acte définitif de la capitulation allemande. Mais il y a en réalité plusieurs jours que la guerre est finie. En Italie, les Allemands ont capitulé le 29 avril. Hitler s'est suicidé à Berlin, le 30 avril, deux jours avant que les Soviétiques ne prennent la ville. À l'ouest, c'est le 4 mai que les forces allemandes se sont rendues au maréchal britannique Montgomery.

▼ *Les soldats de l'Armée rouge hissent le drapeau soviétique sur le Reichstag (le Parlement), à Berlin.*

Be-bop à New York

Les musiciens des clubs de Harlem, le quartier noir de New York, ont inventé une nouvelle forme de jazz, le be-bop. Son nom imite le son de cette musique. Certains affirment que le be-bop, avec son rythme éclaté et ses dissonances, est le début du jazz moderne. Le brillant trompettiste Dizzy Gillespie en est l'une des figures marquantes. Avec les GI le jazz a pénétré en Europe.

▼ *Dizzy Gillespie.*

1940

1941

1942

1943

1944

1945

1946

1947

1948

1949

1946

Festival de cinéma à Cannes

Le premier Festival international du film s'ouvre le 20 septembre, à Cannes, sur la Côte d'Azur. Il est probable qu'il aura lieu chaque année. Il aurait dû commencer dès 1939, mais tout avait été annulé à cause de la guerre. *La Symphonie pastorale,* de Jean Delannoy, reçoit la Palme d'or. Autre œuvre primée : *la Bataille du rail,* de René Clément, qui évoque la résistance des cheminots.

▲ *La Croisette, à Cannes.*

Naissance de la Vespa

▶ **1ᵉʳ septembre 1946** ◀

Vous avez déjà vu une moto. Vous avez déjà vu un vélomoteur. Mais avez-vous déjà vu un scooter ? Vous en verrez bientôt, car la Vespa conquiert l'Italie à toute vitesse et se lance à l'assaut du marché mondial. Le scooter n'est pas une invention nouvelle : il est né dans les années 20, mais sans obtenir de succès. Le nouveau modèle est fabriqué dans des usines italiennes qui fournissaient des équipements militaires et qui se sont reconverties. Cette Vespa – la « guêpe » en italien – fait 125 cm^3, mais il y a fort à parier qu'elle aura vite des concurrentes plus ou moins puissantes. Elle a une conception très originale : les roues sont beaucoup plus petites que celles d'une moto et le moteur est placé très bas, contre la roue arrière. Mais, surtout, le conducteur pose ses pieds sur le plancher, comme s'il était assis sur une chaise. Il est ainsi protégé du vent.

◀ *La première Vespa.*

En 1946 aussi...

20 janvier • Le général de Gaulle démissionne de son poste de chef du gouvernement.

2 juin • L'Italie devient une république.

Septembre
• La guerre d'Indochine commence. Le communiste Hô Chi Minh demande l'indépendance à la France.

13 octobre
• La Constitution de la IVᵉ République est adoptée en France.

Le procès de Nuremberg

▶ **1ᵉʳ octobre 1946** ◀

Les criminels nazis jugés dans la ville allemande de Nuremberg ont entendu aujourd'hui les premiers verdicts. Les procès ont commencé, le 25 novembre dernier, devant le tribunal militaire mis en place par les Alliés. Lors du procès principal, 22 chefs nazis ont été jugés, dont deux ministres de Hitler, Rudolf Hess et Hermann Goering. Les autres dirigeants sont morts (Hitler) ou en fuite. Douze hommes ont été condamnés à mort. Trois ont été acquittés. Tous étaient poursuivis pour crimes contre la paix, crimes de guerre, ou crimes contre l'humanité. Certains ont plaidé non coupables, affirmant qu'ils avaient obéi à des ordres.

▶ *Goering (à gauche) et Hess (son voisin), sur le banc des accusés.*

La France change

▶ **1946** ◀ La France applique le programme du Conseil national de la Résistance et se réforme. Le vote des femmes, la Sécurité sociale, les nationalisations, comme celles des banques ou des usines Renault, ont fondé, dès la fin de 1945, une république soucieuse de justice sociale. La vie politique se renouvelle. Les élections qui se succèdent confirment la domination de trois partis : le Mouvement républicain populaire (MRP, d'inspiration chrétienne), le parti socialiste (SFIO) et le parti communiste.

Le « rideau de fer »

▶ **5 mars 1946** ◀ « Un rideau de fer est tombé sur l'Europe, depuis la Baltique jusqu'à l'Adriatique. » Winston Churchill a fait cette déclaration sinistre dans un discours à l'université de Fulton, dans le Missouri, aux États-Unis. Il estime que les pays occidentaux sont menacés par une puissance hostile, l'Union soviétique. Mais, en cette première année de paix, personne n'a envie de l'écouter.

1940 – 1949

L'explosion du Bikini

Les retraités qui flânent sur les plages de la Méditerranée cet été sont choqués – ou, au contraire, enchantés – par le tout nouveau Bikini. Ce maillot de bain deux-pièces cache en effet bien peu de l'anatomie féminine. Il porte le nom de l'atoll des îles Marshall, dans le Pacifique sud, où les États-Unis réalisent des essais atomiques. Ce petit Bikini provoque lui aussi des explosions, mais moins dangereuses !

Perón, président en Argentine

▶ **4 juin 1946** ◀ L'Argentine fête l'arrivée du général Perón à la tête de l'État. Il est très populaire auprès des classes moyennes et des ouvriers, depuis qu'il a été ministre du Travail du précédent gouvernement militaire. En octobre 1945, quand il avait été écarté du pouvoir, ses partisans avaient déclenché un soulèvement à Buenos Aires, la capitale. Nationaliste et hostile aux États-Unis, Juan Domingo Perón s'inspire des idées fascistes. Il doit l'essentiel de sa popularité à sa femme, la séduisante Eva – Evita, comme le peuple la surnomme –, une ancienne speakerine de radio. L'actuel essor économique du pays joue en faveur du général, qui va pouvoir ainsi financer des réformes sociales.

Les États-Unis aident l'Europe

▶ **1er juillet 1946** ◀ La plus grande partie de l'Europe est en ruine. Les États-Unis, en revanche, sont en plein essor économique. Le niveau de vie y est même plus élevé qu'en 1941. L'Europe a besoin de l'aide américaine. Les États-Unis vont envoyer, cette année, 12 millions de tonnes de céréales outre-Atlantique. Mais la solidarité ne se limite pas à l'action gouvernementale. De nombreuses familles américaines préparent des paquets de vivres, de médicaments et de vêtements pour l'organisation Care, qui se charge de les expédier et de les distribuer dans toute l'Europe.

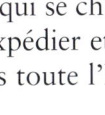

▶ *Juan Domingo Perón.*

1947

1940

1941

1942

La traversée du *Kon-Tiki*

L'âge des fossiles

Le chimiste américain Willard Libby a inventé une méthode pour déterminer l'âge des fossiles. Il les teste au carbone 14. Les plantes et les animaux vivants contiennent en effet une certaine quantité de carbone 14, qui diminue progressivement après leur mort. Les scientifiques savent combien de carbone 14 il y a dans chaque être vivant, et la vitesse à laquelle sa quantité baisse. Ils peuvent ainsi calculer la date de sa mort.

1943

1944

▶ **7 octobre 1947** ◀ Le savant norvégien Thor Heyerdahl et ses cinq compagnons viennent de traverser l'océan Pacifique sur un simple radeau en bois, le *Kon-Tiki*. Les navigateurs sont partis, le 28 avril, de Callao, au Pérou. Ils ont terminé leur périple le 7 août, lorsque le *Kon-Tiki* a heurté un récif de l'archipel de Tuamotu, en Polynésie française. Ils ont accompli un voyage de 6 900 km, sur une embarcation qui ne mesure que 13,7 m de long.

Heyerdahl voulait prouver que des Sud-Américains avaient pu s'installer dans les îles du Pacifique en traversant l'océan il y a des milliers d'années. Il a construit le *Kon-Tiki* avec des rondins de bois de balsa, réunis par de la corde de chanvre. Une rame fixée à l'arrière sert de gouvernail. La voile, rectangulaire, est maintenue par deux mâts. Une petite cabine abrite l'équipage des intempéries.

Heyerdahl a baptisé son radeau *Kon-Tiki* en l'honneur du dieu du Soleil des Incas, le peuple qui occupait le Pérou avant la conquête espagnole du XVIe siècle. Il s'apprête à écrire le récit de ses aventures.

◀ *L'équipage du Kon-Tiki offre au président Truman le drapeau qui a flotté sur le mât du radeau.*

▲ *Les vents et les marées ont guidé le Kon-Tiki vers son but.*

1945

En 1947 aussi...

16 janvier • Vincent Auriol devient président de la République française.

12 mars • Le président américain Truman dit que les États-Unis doivent stopper l'avancée du communisme dans le monde.

5 octobre • Sous la direction de l'URSS, les partis communistes d'Europe de l'Est, français et italien s'unissent dans le Kominform. Le bloc soviétique est né.

1946

1947

1948

1949

Le plan Marshall

▶ **22 août 1947** ◀ Les ministres des Affaires étrangères de l'Europe de l'Ouest viennent d'accepter le plan d'aide américain qui leur permettra de reconstruire leurs pays, ravagés par la guerre. Il est l'œuvre du général George Marshall, le secrétaire d'État et ministre des Affaires étrangères américain, qui l'a exposé le 5 juin dernier. Selon lui, les difficultés dont souffre l'Europe constituent une nouvelle menace pour la paix.

On peut penser que cette aide est en partie destinée à contrer l'influence soviétique en Europe. L'URSS et les pays qu'elle domine en Europe de l'Est ont, ainsi, refusé le plan Marshall. Seize pays ont au contraire sauté sur l'occasion, dont la France, la Grande-Bretagne, l'Italie et les pays scandinaves. En effet, pour beaucoup d'Européens, la vie est aussi difficile que pendant la guerre.

▲ *La pauvre[té] est une mena[ce] pour la paix.*

▶ *George Marshall, le père du plan d'aide américain.*

168

1940 – 1949

Naissance de l'Inde et du Pakistan

▶ **15 août 1947** ◀ L'Inde est indépendante de la Grande-Bretagne depuis minuit. Elle a donné naissance à deux États créés sur des bases religieuses : l'Inde, peuplée en grande majorité d'hindous, et le Pakistan, musulman.

Le dernier vice-roi britannique de l'Inde, lord Mountbatten, avait accepté le projet de partition du pays. Mais beaucoup de musulmans vivent en Inde, et beaucoup d'hindous, au Pakistan. Des conflits violents paraissent inévitables entre les deux communautés.

▼ *Le Bell X-1, premier avion supersonique, peu après son décollage.*

Un avion passe le mur du son

▶ **14 octobre 1947** ◀ Le pilote américain Chuck Yeager est le premier homme à dépasser la vitesse du son. Dans son avion prototype, le *Bell X-1*, il a atteint la vitesse de 1 078 km/h, à une altitude de 12 800 m.

Un avion qui vole à une vitesse inférieure à celle du son envoie des ondes sonores devant lui. Quand il approche de la vitesse du son, ces ondes lui font subir des secousses répétées qui le déstabilisent dangereusement. La forme aérodynamique du *Bell X-1* a été conçue pour réduire ces chocs. Yeager a baptisé son avion *Splendide Glennis*, en l'honneur de sa femme. Il a volé aujourd'hui, malgré deux côtes cassées, résultant d'un accident pendant une fête la nuit dernière.

◀ *Jawaharlal Nehru, le Premier ministre de l'Inde.*

La peinture de Jackson Pollock

L'artiste américain Jackson Pollock n'utilise plus de chevalet : il pose sa toile sur le sol et laisse couler la peinture dessus. Il produit des images abstraites (dans lesquelles on ne reconnaît ni objets quotidiens, ni gens). Pollock pense que sa technique lui permet d'exprimer des sentiments inconscients. « La peinture a une vie propre, dit-il. J'essaie de la montrer. »

▼ *Jackson Pollock dans son atelier.*

Les manuscrits de la mer Morte

▶ **1947** ◀ Une centaine de vieux manuscrits hébreux ont été découverts dans une grotte, près de la mer Morte, en Palestine. Selon les archéologues, ces textes appartenaient aux esséniens. Cette secte religieuse juive occupait le monastère de Qumran, entre 150 av. J.-C. et 68 de notre ère. Certains rouleaux exposent les règles de la communauté essénienne, d'autres sont des livres de l'Ancien Testament.

Une année difficile en France

▶ **1947** ◀ L'année 1947 est difficile en France. Le salaire moyen est tombé à 60 % du niveau d'avant guerre. En mars, le gouvernement Ramadier a créé le salaire minimum vital, en dessous duquel les bas salaires ne peuvent pas descendre. Mais la vie est chère. Beaucoup de produits alimentaires manquent. L'alimentation est toujours rationnée. L'agitation sociale est forte. Des grèves violentes ont éclaté, au printemps, chez les mineurs du Pas-de-Calais, les ouvriers des usines Citroën et Renault, les cheminots.

1940

1941

1942

1943

1944

1945

1946

1947

1948

1949

1948

Création de l'État d'Israël

▶ **14 mai 1948** ◀ Ben Gourion proclame l'État d'Israël. Les Juifs ont fait cette proclamation huit heures avant la fin du mandat (contrôle) britannique sur la Palestine. Le président américain Harry Truman a reconnu le nouveau gouvernement, formé par David Ben Gourion.

Les Juifs s'appuient sur la résolution des Nations unies de novembre 1947 qui partage la Palestine en deux États, l'un arabe, l'autre juif. Mais les Arabes de Palestine rejettent cette solution et sont déterminés à se battre pour conserver leur terre. Aujourd'hui, alors que leurs troupes s'en vont, les Britanniques ont plaidé pour la paix. Mais des armées venues d'Égypte, de Transjordanie, de Syrie et d'Irak s'apprêtent à entrer en Palestine pour soutenir les Arabes. L'armée israélienne, la Haganah, a 30 000 hommes. La guerre semble inévitable. Le plan de l'ONU ne sera jamais respecté. Il n'y aura pas d'État palestinien.

▲ *Des Juifs arrivent à Haïfa, en Israël.*

▼ *Le Premier ministre, Ben Gourion, assiste au départ des derniers Britanniques à Haïfa.*

L'ONU définit les droits de l'homme

▶ **10 décembre 1948** ◀ Réunie à Paris, l'assemblée générale de l'Organisation des Nations unies (ONU) a adopté une liste des droits individuels qui devraient être reconnus partout dans le monde. Cette liste a été préparée par le Français René Cassin. Elle proclame le droit à la vie et à la liberté, l'égalité devant la loi, et le droit à la propriété. Le texte déclare que les gens doivent être autorisés à se réunir pacifiquement, à exprimer librement leurs opinions et à pratiquer leur religion. Il affirme que tout le monde a le droit de travailler, d'adhérer à un syndicat, et que, pour un travail égal, on doit recevoir un salaire égal. Ce texte, la Déclaration universelle des droits de l'homme, a été accepté par les pays qui ont participé au vote. L'Arabie Saoudite, l'URSS, l'Afrique du Sud et les pays de l'Est se sont abstenus.

Un four rapide

Avec le four à micro-ondes, la vie de la cuisine s'accélère ! Les aliments placés dans le four sont bombardés de radiations à la longueur d'onde très courte. Elles pénètrent dans la nourriture et la réchauffent de l'intérieur, beaucoup plus vite que n'importe quel autre four.

◀ *Eleanor Roosevelt a participé à la rédaction de la Déclaration.*

1940 – 1949

▲ *Le nouveau gouvernement sud-africain.*

L'extrême droite en Afrique du Sud

▶ **28 mai 1948** ◀ Le parti national, d'extrême droite, remporte les élections. Seuls les Blancs ont eu le droit de participer au vote. Ce parti prône une politique d'apartheid, selon laquelle les Sud-Africains blancs, asiatiques et noirs doivent vivre de façon séparée. Les « non-Blancs » sont privés de tout droit. Le pasteur D. Malan devient le nouveau Premier ministre. Le parti national est soutenu par les Afrikaners, les descendants des colons néerlandais qui se sont installés dans le pays à partir du XVIIe siècle.

Gandhi assassiné

▶ **30 janvier 1948** ◀ Le leader nationaliste indien, le mahatma Gandhi, a été assassiné à New Delhi, la capitale de l'Inde. Il se rendait à pied, avec ses petites-nièces, à une cérémonie religieuse, quand il a été abattu de trois coups de revolver. L'assassin, Nathuram Godse, est un fanatique religieux hindou. Il a été arrêté immédiatement par un sergent de l'armée de l'air indienne. Gandhi est décédé dans la demi-heure qui a suivi.

Gandhi est le père de l'indépendance de l'Inde, obtenue l'année dernière. Il demandait aux hindous et aux musulmans de mettre fin au conflit religieux, qui a déjà coûté la vie à des milliers de personnes.

◀ *Le monde entier pleure la mort de Gandhi.*

L'invention du Polaroid

L'inventeur américain Edwin Land a créé un appareil photo qui développe et tire lui-même ses clichés dans la minute qui suit la prise de vue. Le Polaroid pèse 2,25 kg, coûte 95 dollars et utilise une pellicule spéciale. Les tirages sortent en noir et blanc. Il faut les enduire d'un vernis pour éviter que leur surface ne s'abîme.

▼ *Edwin Land et son portrait par Polaroid.*

Pont aérien pour Berlin

▶ **26 juin 1948** ◀ Berlin est situé au cœur de la partie est de l'Allemagne, occupée par l'Armée rouge. Les Américains, les Britanniques et les Français contrôlent l'ouest de la ville. Les avions américains et britanniques apportent des vivres et des matières premières aux habitants de Berlin-Ouest ; les Soviétiques, qui occupent la moitié est, empêchent leur ravitaillement par des contrôles. Il y a deux jours, les Soviétiques ont coupé tous les accès qui mènent à Berlin-Ouest. Ils veulent forcer les Occidentaux à quitter la ville. Ceux-ci ont alors répliqué en organisant un pont aérien depuis l'ouest de l'Allemagne.

▶ *Les Alliés disent que les Berlinois de l'Ouest ont besoin de 2 500 tonnes de vivres par jour.*

1948

L'Europe de l'Est

▶ **27 février 1948** ◀ Le « coup de Prague » fait de la Tchécoslovaquie un satellite de l'URSS. Depuis que les Allemands qui l'occupaient ont été vaincus par l'Armée rouge soviétique, le Premier ministre Gottwald est communiste, alors que le président E. Benes est social-démocrate. En 1948, les communistes ont manœuvré pour s'emparer du pouvoir avec l'aide des troupes soviétiques et des milices formées d'ouvriers communistes ; les autres ministres ont laissé faire. Désormais, Staline a les mains libres en Tchécoslovaquie. Depuis 1945, l'Armée rouge a imposé partout des régimes favorables à l'URSS. En Hongrie, le parti des petits propriétaires, vainqueur des élections de 1945, a été peu à peu éliminé. En Roumanie, la monarchie est tombée en 1947. En Pologne, les élections promises par Staline ont été remportées par les communistes, dans des conditions douteuses, en janvier 1947. Désormais, tous ces États sont devenus des « démocraties populaires », où le parti communiste est le seul maître de la vie politique, où l'économie est collectivisée et où les Soviétiques ont tous les droits. Seule la Yougoslavie est parvenue à garder un gouvernement qui, quoique communiste, est indépendant de Moscou.

▲ *Le communiste Klement Gottwald à Prague, en Tchécoslovaquie.*

Truman défie les sondages

▶ **3 novembre 1948** ◀ Surprise aux élections présidentielles américaines : le démocrate Harry Truman est réélu. Les experts et les sondages d'opinion avaient prévu la victoire du candidat républicain, Thomas Dewey. Mais ce matin, Truman est président, et les démocrates ont la majorité au Sénat et à la Chambre des représentants. La presse s'est laissé surprendre par le résultat. La première édition du *Washington Post* titrait ainsi « Dewey sur le chemin de la victoire », tandis que le *Chicago Tribune*, encore plus confiant, annonçait : « Dewey bat Truman ». Truman est président depuis la mort de Roosevelt, le 12 avril 1945.

◀ *Le président Truman ridiculise le* Chicago Tribune, *qui titre : « Dewey bat Truman ».*

Marcel Cerdan, champion du monde

À New York, le boxeur français Marcel Cerdan, surnommé « le boxeur marocain », remporte le titre de champion du monde en battant par K-O l'Américain Tony Zale. Ses amours avec Édith Piaf défraient la chronique, car il est marié et père de famille.

▼ *Marcel Cerdan contre Tony Zale.*

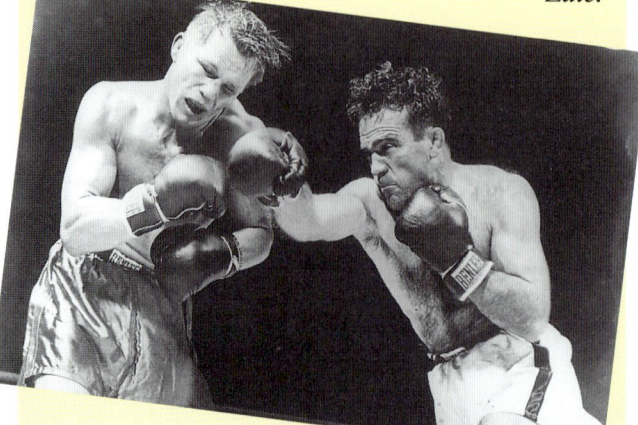

1940 – 1949

1948

L'État-providence

▶ 5 juillet 1948 ◀

À Londres, le gouvernement travailliste (socialiste) vient de créer le Service national de la santé (National Health Service – NHS). Tous les Britanniques vont bénéficier de soins médicaux gratuits, de la naissance à la mort. Les médicaments, les soins dentaires, les lunettes, et même les perruques, seront gratuits.
Le NHS est le principal dispositif du nouvel « État-providence », qui s'engage à aider plus les pauvres, les personnes âgées et les malades. Lorsqu'ils ont gagné les élections en 1945, les travaillistes ont promis une vie meilleure à l'ensemble de la population, après les privations de la guerre. Ils viennent aussi de mettre en place un système d'assurances sociales pour les retraités et les chômeurs.

À la fin de la guerre, la France a adopté les mêmes principes. La Sécurité sociale a été créée en octobre 1945. Le gouvernement veut faire reculer la mortalité en offrant aux citoyens les moyens de se soigner. Les entreprises ont adopté des politiques de prévention de la maladie et de l'invalidité ; les accidents du travail et les maladies professionnelles sont pris en charge.

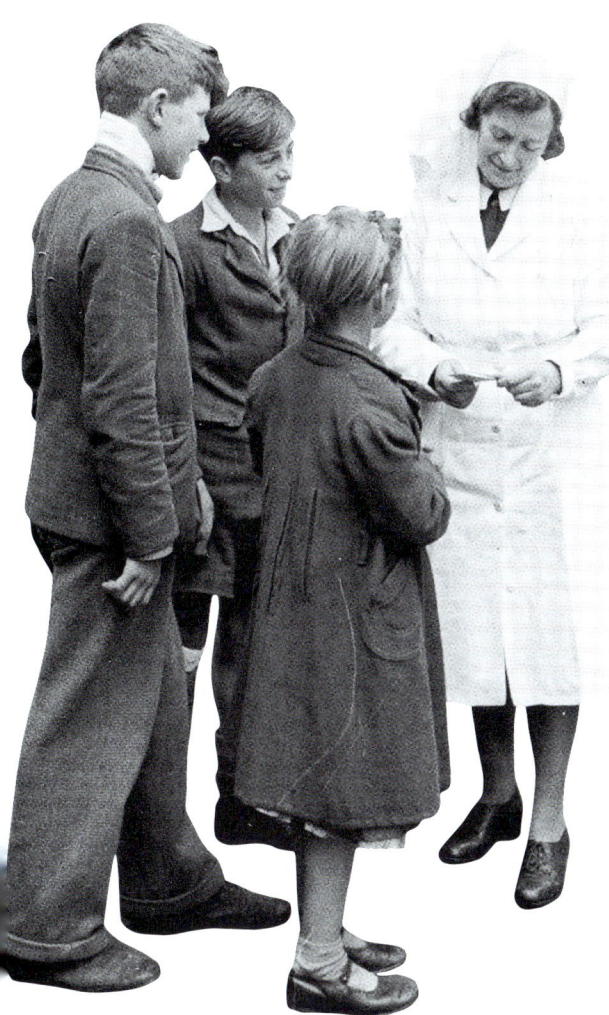

▲ Une infirmière anglaise conseille une famille.

Le 33-tours est né

La compagnie américaine CBS adopte le disque 33 tours. Il offre plus de place pour l'enregistrement, car il a des sillons étroits (microsillons) et tourne à la vitesse de 33 tours à la minute. Il a été inventé par René Snepvangers, un Belge, et Peter Goldenmark, un Américain. Les amateurs de musique devront changer d'électrophone, car les anciens ne tournent pas à la bonne vitesse.

Lyssenko et l'hérédité

▶ Août 1948 ◀

En URSS, le généticien soviétique Vladimir Lyssenko s'attaque aux théories sur l'hérédité de Mendel, au nom du matérialisme scientifique. Il impose les théories de Mitchourine, pour qui le matériel héréditaire des hybrides est fortement influencé par le milieu. Lyssenko affirme que l'homme peut transmettre des « caractères acquis », ce qui permettrait d'envisager une sorte d'« homo sovieticus » parfait. Les savants qui s'opposent à lui sont emprisonnés ou déportés dans des camps en Sibérie. L'affaire prend une tournure mondiale. Ainsi, en France, le physicien Frédéric Joliot-Curie, qui est communiste, est obligé de se taire, alors qu'il sait que cette théorie est absurde.

En 1948 aussi...

3 janvier • En France, l'inflation est si grave que le gouvernement doit dévaluer de 80 %.

24 mars • Les femmes obtiennent le droit de vote en Belgique.

27 mars • En Égypte, la première pierre du grand barrage d'Assouan, sur le Nil, est posée.

Décembre • Le premier McDonald's ouvre à San Bernardino, en Californie.

Une élégante voiture familiale

La Morris Minor est sortie en Grande-Bretagne, au mois d'octobre. Cette voiture familiale est plus large que ses concurrentes et offre un habitacle confortable. Grâce à sa largeur, les passagers ne seront plus secoués dans les virages, car l'écartement de ses roues la rend plus stable. En France, Renault a mis au point la 4 CV ; en Allemagne, Volkswagen produit en série les « coccinelles ».

▼ La Morris Minor.

L'ART DE LA MODE

La mode reflète l'évolution rapide de la civilisation au XXᵉ siècle. Elle offre un kaléidoscope de styles et de couleurs, depuis les robes longues du début du siècle jusqu'aux vêtements simples de la fin des années 50. La mode se diversifie à partir de 1950 et change au fil des années, tout en revenant parfois à des tendances antérieures. Les progrès techniques permettent de fabriquer des vêtements non seulement esthétiques, mais aussi confortables. La technologie a un impact très important, avec le développement des textiles synthétiques comme le Nylon et le Lycra, les fermetures Éclair et les attaches en Velcro. Les nouvelles méthodes de production et les nouveaux colorants ont fait baisser les prix des vêtements, par ailleurs plus faciles à entretenir et à porter.

La mode
- En 1853, Oscar Levi-Strauss taille le premier jean dans une toile de bâche en coton teinte en bleu, venant de Nîmes (toile denim).
- Marlene Dietrich apparaît en pantalon dans le film *Cœurs brûlés* (Morocco).
- Nike fabrique les baskets sur coussins d'air dès 1979.

▶ Jupe au genou et vêtements souples, de style oriental, dans les années 20.

◀ Jupe longue, poitrine étroite, taille fine, un profil typé 1900.

Le créateur Christian Dior fonde le « new-look »

Au printemps 1947, Christian Dior transforme la femme avec sa collection new-look. Il met fin aux lignes droites, aux épaules carrées, aux jupes raccourcies, aux chaussures à semelles compensées, bref à l'austérité des années de guerre, quand il fallait économiser les tissus.

Le grand couturier français dessine des épaules douces, met en valeur le buste, avec une poitrine marquée, en soulignant la taille cintrée. La jupe est longue et ample. Cette silhouette, que renforce le volume des hanches et que prolongent des talons aiguilles, fait le tour du monde. C'est un style romantique, foisonnant, dynamique et optimiste, qui rappelle la mode brillante du siècle précédent. Après les années difficiles et les restrictions, les femmes veulent se mettre en valeur.

▲ La tonalité des tissus des années 50 est vive. Les couleurs et les motifs variés s'associent et s'opposent, pour donner une structure originale.

▲ Un ensemble new-look. Les accessoires, comme le chapeau, les chaussures et les gants, sont essentiels dans ce nouveau style.

Le « deux-pièces » à la mode

En 1909, Annette Kellerman, une nageuse australienne, fait sensation sur une plage de Californie, vêtue d'un maillot de bain une pièce tricoté, comme celui des hommes. Alors qu'elle le porte à Boston, elle est arrêtée pour indécence. Ce maillot dévoile trop les formes féminines et laisse peu de place à l'imagination.

Le 3 juin 1946, à la piscine Molitor de Paris, Louis Réard présente un maillot de bain réduit à deux pièces. Le styliste, spécialiste de l'automobile, lui donne le nom de Bikini d'après celui des îles du Pacifique où des armes nucléaires viennent d'être testées par les Américains : il est sûr que son invention aura du succès.

À la fin du XXe siècle, nombreux sont les estivants qui reviennent à des maillots plus couvrants, pour se protéger des rayons du soleil, qui peuvent être nocifs.

▼ Présentation de maillots au début du siècle.

▲ Après le choc des premiers Bikinis, les deux-pièces des années 50 sont plus sages.

◀ Queue de cheval, jupe cloche et socquettes dans les années 50.

▶ Minijupe et cuissardes dans les années 60.

▶ Tailleur sobre et élégant, épaules marquées, pour la femme cadre des années 80.

La mode innove

La mode change et tente des expériences. Dans les années 60, la jeunesse commence à s'habiller à sa façon, pour se démarquer de la masse tout en affirmant sa personnalité au-delà des contraintes. Les femmes portent le pantalon, mais aussi la minijupe, l'invention de la Londonienne Mary Quant. Les coupes de cheveux géométriques et les grandes bottes en plastique leur donnent une allure futuriste. Les hommes ont des jeans étroits, des vestes sans col et des chaussures pointues.

Au début des années 70, le prêt-à-porter se diversifie, à la recherche des extrêmes. Les stylistes trouvent leur inspiration dans diverses époques et différentes civilisations, proposant parfois une mode unisexe. Les grosses chaussures sont munies d'épaisses semelles compensées. Les jeunes gens, qui renouent avec les favoris, arborent des vestes de satin brillant aux larges revers. Les tissus sont rehaussés de broderies éclatantes. Les pantalons sont étroits, à taille haute, et très larges en bas, et les débardeurs se popularisent. Les cheveux sont longs et flottants.

Les bas Nylon

En 1940, les bas en Nylon apparaissent sur le marché américain. Ils sont munis d'une couture noire qui court tout le long de la jambe. Pendant la guerre, ils sont chers, et les femmes dessinent un trait noir sur leurs jambes nues pour faire illusion.

▼ Mode féminine des années 70 : short étroit, très court et moulant, bottes et collants.

▲ Elton John incarne le style flamboyant des stars du rock des années 70.

1940

1941

1942

1943

1944

1945

1946

1947

1948

1949

1949

République populaire en Chine

▶ À Shanghai, on fête le nouveau pouvoir.

▶ **1er octobre 1949** ◀ À Pékin, Mao Zédong a proclamé la République populaire de Chine. Tchang Kaï-chek s'est enfui à Taiwan, après la victoire des troupes communistes de l'Armée populaire de libération.

La guerre civile entre nationalistes et communistes a commencé dans les années 20. Elle s'est interrompue pendant la guerre. Les deux adversaires ont alors lutté ensemble contre l'occupant japonais. Mais les combats ont repris dès la reddition du Japon, en 1945. Les nationalistes étaient soutenus par les États-Unis, qui veulent combattre le communisme. Leurs troupes étaient bien plus nombreuses que celles des communistes, mais mal commandées. De plus, les communistes ont gagné l'appui des campagnes en aidant les paysans à s'emparer des terres des grands propriétaires. Ils ont pris plusieurs places fortes nationalistes, cette année, dont Shanghai, le 26 mai.

▲ Mao Zédong, chef de la Révolution chinoise.

Le souci de l'apparence

Les Britanniques soignent désormais leur tenue vestimentaire. Le rationnement des tissus, commencé en 1941, pendant la guerre, a pris fin. Pour célébrer l'événement, les boutiques font des soldes. Le gouvernement a prévenu que, si les prix augmentaient trop, il avait le pouvoir de les geler.

George Orwell, une vision du futur

▶ **10 juin 1949** ◀ Le nouveau roman de l'écrivain britannique George Orwell, *1984*, décrit un futur où l'État contrôle toute la vie. Dans ce pays imaginaire, chacun doit vénérer le Grand Frère (Big Brother), le chef du parti politique au pouvoir. On réécrit l'histoire pour l'adapter au présent. Le héros, Winston Smith, tente de résister, mais il est arrêté et torturé par la « police de la pensée ». Orwell veut mettre en garde contre ce qui pourrait se passer si un État fort et centralisé allait jusqu'au bout de sa logique totalitaire.

▼ La foule célèbre la naissance de la République démocratique allemande.

Les deux Allemagnes

▶ **12 octobre 1949** ◀ L'est de l'Allemagne, occupé par les Soviétiques, est devenu un État communiste, la République démocratique allemande (RDA). Otto Grotewohl est le chef du gouvernement. Le 23 mai, les zones d'occupation britanniques, américaines et françaises dans l'ouest de l'Allemagne ont été réunies dans la République fédérale d'Allemagne (RFA), dont la capitale est Bonn. Berlin-Ouest, isolé au milieu de la RDA, reste sous contrôle allié.

▼ Adenauer, chancelier de l'Allemagne de l'Ouest.

1940 – 1949

▲ *La 2 CV a un petit moteur de 375 cm³.*

Naissance de la 2 CV Citroën

Citroën sort une voiture solide et bon marché qui peut rouler partout et qui est décapotable. Elle répond au défi lancé aux ingénieurs de Citroën : concevoir une voiture qui puisse traverser un champ labouré avec un panier plein d'œufs sans en casser aucun. Sa structure montée sur ressorts et sa suspension particulière lui permettent d'affronter les surfaces les plus difficiles. Elle consomme peu : 3 litres aux 100 kilomètres.

L'OTAN

▶ **4 avril 1949** ◀ À Washington, aux États-Unis, douze États (États-Unis, Canada, Italie, France, Grande-Bretagne, Belgique, Pays-Bas et Luxembourg) se sont unis dans une alliance militaire. Ils affirment qu'une attaque armée contre l'un ou plusieurs d'entre eux en Europe ou en Amérique du Nord sera considérée comme une attaque contre eux tous. Cette alliance, l'Organisation du traité de l'Atlantique nord (OTAN), est une réponse au renforcement de la puissance soviétique dans l'est de l'Europe. Les États-Unis ont promis une aide militaire aux pays européens membres de l'OTAN. L'année dernière, la Grande-Bretagne, la France, la Belgique, le Luxembourg et les Pays-Bas avaient signé le traité de Bruxelles, une alliance militaire européenne.

▲ *Le drapeau de l'OTAN flotte à Paris.*

Bombe atomique soviétique

▶ **23 septembre 1949** ◀ Les États-Unis et l'Angleterre annoncent que l'URSS a expérimenté avec succès sa première bombe atomique. Ils savaient que les Soviétiques cherchaient à fabriquer la bombe, mais pensaient qu'ils n'y réussiraient pas avant deux ou trois ans. L'essai a eu lieu dans la République soviétique du Kazakhstan, en Asie centrale. Cela aggrave la tension entre l'URSS et les États-Unis, et va accélérer la course aux armements que se livrent les deux pays pour fabriquer des armes de plus en plus puissantes.

Victoire de Fausto Coppi

▼ *Fausto Coppi, un champion complet.*

▶ **Juillet 1949** ◀ Cet été, l'Italien Fausto Coppi a gagné les deux grandes courses cyclistes d'Europe : le Tour de France et le Tour d'Italie (Giro). Il a battu, dans les deux épreuves, son grand rival et compatriote Gino Bartali, arrivé deuxième. Coppi a pris la place de Bartali dans le cœur des supporters italiens, pour lesquels il est devenu le *campionissimo*, le champion des champions.

Le Tour de France et le Giro sont des courses par étapes. Cette année, dans le Giro, Coppi a écrasé Bartali, à l'issue d'une lutte acharnée dans les Alpes italiennes, le devançant de plus de vingt minutes à l'arrivée de l'étape. Coppi avait déjà gagné le Giro deux fois, mais c'est sa première victoire en Tour de France.

En 1949 aussi...

12 mai • Le blocus de Berlin est terminé. Les Soviétiques ont échoué.

26 juin • Le premier journal télévisé est diffusé en France.

29 juillet • L'avion à réaction met Londres à six heures de New York.

10 août • Le Conseil de l'Europe tient sa première session, à Strasbourg.

15 septembre • Konrad Adenauer devient chancelier de la RFA.

De 1950 à 1959

1950

La guerre froide entre États-Unis et Union soviétique se déroule tout au long de la décennie. Dès le début, il existe une menace de guerre nucléaire mondiale, les deux pays possédant la bombe atomique. Une course aux armements se déclenche des deux côtés. En juin 1950 éclate la guerre de Corée. Les Coréens du Sud sont soutenus par les Américains, qui dépêchent des troupes, tandis que ceux du Nord reçoivent l'appui armé des Chinois. Les Soviétiques créent le pacte de Varsovie, en riposte à la création de l'OTAN par les États-Unis. Les deux grands s'affrontent indirectement sur tous les continents, en Corée – puis au Moyen-Orient –, et rivalisent en Allemagne.

Carte de crédit

Plus besoin d'argent pour payer ! La carte de crédit vient d'être lancée. Créée par les Américains Frank Macnamara et Ralph Schneider, elle permet de boire et de se restaurer en ne réglant la dépense qu'en fin de mois. Cette carte Diner's Club est déjà acceptée dans 28 restaurants dont la liste est inscrite au verso.

Apparition des Peanuts

▶ 2 octobre 1950 ◀

En ce jour, les Peanuts font leur première apparition dans une toute nouvelle bande dessinée. Cette série quotidienne fait naître Charlie Brown, héros créé par le dessinateur Charles Schulz, qui a essuyé six refus avant de pouvoir l'imposer. Dans cette bande de copains, Charlie Brown est le chef. Lucy, une petite fille au caractère volontaire, parfois même peu commode, et son jeune frère Linus, pas très assuré et qui traîne partout avec lui son « doudou » – un vieux chiffon qu'il suce pour se donner du courage – en font partie. Il y a aussi Schroeder, qui passe sa vie à jouer du Beethoven sur son piano-jouet. Mais c'est Snoopy, le chien de Charlie, qui est sans doute le plus malin.

◀ *Le dessinateur Charles Schulz.*

Les *Peanuts* font partie de ces bandes dessinées qui utilisent l'humour pour aborder des sujets sérieux. Cette BD montre combien les enfants peuvent être cruels, mais elle se sert aussi de leurs jeux et de leurs querelles pour critiquer le comportement des adultes. Certes, Charlie Brown est le chef, mais il commet souvent des erreurs et apprend ainsi à quel point la vie de tous les jours est ardue.

◀ *De gauche à droite, Linus, Marcia, Charlie Brown, Peppermint Patty et Snoopy.*

En 1950 aussi...

3 juin • Deux Français conquièrent l'Annapurna. Herzog et Lachenal sont les premiers à atteindre les 8 075 m.

7 juin • Accord franco-allemand pour la création d'un marché agricole commun.

26 octobre • Intervention des troupes chinoises en Corée.

1950 – 1959

▲ Les Chinois bâtissent un pont pour faciliter le transport de leurs troupes.

Victoire de l'Uruguay

▶ **16 juillet 1950** ◀ Le Brésil est en état de choc. Devant 200 000 supporters, dans le stade Maracana à Rio de Janeiro, ses footballeurs ont été impitoyablement vaincus 2 à 1 par l'Uruguay, dans la finale de la Coupe du monde de football. Le Brésil partait pourtant grand favori alors que l'Uruguay venait d'être battu par l'Espagne. Cette victoire marque le retour en force de l'Uruguay, champion des JO de 1924 et 1928, comme de la Coupe du monde de 1930.

Les Chinois envahissent le Tibet

▶ **Octobre 1950** ◀ Le dalaï-lama, chef spirituel du Tibet, n'a pas pu stopper l'invasion des troupes de la République populaire de Chine. Les forces communistes se sont ruées à travers le Tibet, balayant l'opposition tibétaine et se dirigeant vers Lhassa, la capitale. Le gouvernement tibétain appelle l'Inde à son secours, et l'on craint pour la vie du dalaï-lama. Le Tibet est un pays indépendant, situé à l'ouest de la Chine, qui proclame ses droits sur lui depuis des années. En mai, le Tibet s'est vu proposer par Mao Zedong une forme d'autonomie au sein de la Chine. Il est en train de payer le prix de son refus.

Victoire en formule 1

Succès pour Giuseppe Farina. Vétéran italien de course automobile, il remporte, en Alfa Romeo, la première course mondiale de formule 1, qui s'est déroulée à Silverstone, aux États-Unis. Son coéquipier, l'Argentin Juan Manuel Fangio, menait la course mais dut abandonner, ce qui permit à Farina de remporter la première place.

▲ *Giuseppe Farina réussit le temps de 2 h 23 s sur le circuit de Silverstone.*

◀ *Un travailleur noir pousse des poubelles devant une plage réservée aux Blancs, dans le Strand, près du Cap, en Afrique du Sud.*

Apartheid en Afrique du Sud

▶ **1950** ◀ Conformément à la politique de ségrégation raciale – apartheid – du gouvernement d'Afrique du Sud, la minorité blanche doit vivre séparée des autres. Le gouvernement nationaliste a légalisé l'apartheid, qui divise les Sud-Africains en quatre groupes – Blancs, Noirs, métis et Asiatiques –, chaque individu devant porter sur lui un laissez-passer qui atteste son groupe racial. Le gouvernement divise également les villes en zones strictement séparées. Ainsi, Noirs, métis ou Asiatiques ne peuvent vivre dans des quartiers réservés aux Blancs.

La ségrégation raciale existait déjà, mais elle a été renforcée depuis 1948, date à laquelle le parti nationaliste, dirigé par le Premier ministre Daniel François Malan, est arrivé au pouvoir.

1950

La guerre de Corée

▶ 25 juin 1950 ◀ Aujourd'hui, la Corée du Nord a envahi soudainement le Sud. La tension latente entre les États-Unis et l'Union soviétique au cours de ces cinq ans de guerre froide vient d'éclater en conflit armé.

En 1945, lorsque le Japon vaincu fut privé de toutes ses dépendances territoriales, la Corée fut occupée et administrée par l'Union soviétique au nord du 38e parallèle, et par l'armée américaine au sud. Il y a deux ans, l'URSS installait dans le Nord une administration communiste dirigée par Kim Il-sung, alors que les États-Unis renforçaient un régime pro-occidental dans le Sud.

Les forces des Nations unies, placées sous le commandement du général MacArthur, et quelques troupes américaines se précipitèrent au secours des Sud-Coréens. En octobre, alors que MacArthur faisait reculer les communistes jusqu'à la frontière chinoise, la Chine est intervenue. En décembre, l'armée américaine mandatée par l'ONU a dû quitter Pyongyang, la capitale nord-coréenne. Les Nord-Coréens pensent qu'ils vont se retirer définitivement. Le président américain Harry Truman repousserait l'idée d'utiliser la bombe atomique pour arrêter la marche de la guerre.

▲ *Le général Douglas MacArthur en Corée.*

◀ *Parachutistes américains en Corée.*

Insémination artificielle

▶ 1950 ◀ Des scientifiques de l'université du Wisconsin ont annoncé la naissance d'un veau né d'une vache n'ayant pas été saillie par un taureau : ils ont prélevé un œuf fécondé dans l'utérus d'une vache pour le transférer dans celui d'une autre, qui a mis bas tout à fait normalement.

Cette technique offre de nouvelles possibilités pour l'amélioration des troupeaux. L'insémination artificielle, mise au point en Russie et au Danemark au début du siècle, permet à un taureau de concours d'engendrer des milliers de veaux. Maintenant, l'ovule fécondé d'une vache laitière primée peut se développer sans problème dans une autre vache.

▶ *Des survivants de l'un des tremblements de terre en Iran recherchent des victimes dans les décombres des maisons.*

Tremblements de terre en Iran

▶ 29 janvier 1950 ◀ Trois violents tremblements de terre ont secoué le sud de l'Iran, faisant 1 000 morts et 1 500 blessés. Les dégâts sont importants. Vingt villes et villages ont été totalement détruits, et la capitale du Sud, Chiraz, située dans les montagnes de Zagros, est également touchée. De nombreux ports de la côte sud du pays ont été dévastés par des raz de marée.

Saint-Germain-des-Prés

▶ 1950 ◀ À Saint-Germain-des-Prés, Madeleine Renaud et Jean-Louis Barrault découvrent le be-bop, apporté par les troupes américaines. Le quartier est, depuis la guerre, le point de ralliement des artistes et des intellectuels qui avaient l'habitude d'y travailler, car seuls les cafés étaient à peu près bien chauffés.

▲ *Madeleine Renaud et Jean-Louis Barrault en train de danser.*

▼ *De nombreuses vedettes de Hollywood ont manifesté leur opposition à la « chasse aux sorcières » anticommuniste.*

▼ *McCarthy situant des bases communistes.*

McCarthy et la « chasse aux sorcières »

▶ 22 février 1950 ◀ La commission des relations extérieures du Sénat américain a ouvert une enquête sur les affirmations faites par le sénateur du Wisconsin, Joseph R. McCarthy. Ce dernier avait déclaré qu'il détenait une liste de 205 employés du Département d'État qui seraient adhérents du Parti communiste. Il insinue que le secrétaire d'État, Dean Acheson, et le président, Harry Truman, ferment les yeux sur les activités subversives d'agitateurs rouges.

Ceux qui sont soupçonnés sont traduits devant la commission des activités anti-américaines du Sénat. De très nombreux artistes figurent sur des listes rouges, ce qui les empêche de pouvoir travailler.

Décolonisation en Indochine

▶ 26 janvier 1950 ◀ Le Viêt-nam, le Laos et le Cambodge signent un accord par lequel ils deviennent des États associés à la France. Mais, au Viêt-nam, depuis 1946, le communiste Hô Chi Minh fait la guerre à l'armée française pour obtenir une indépendance complète. Les Français ont donc reconnu l'ancien empereur d'Annam, Bao Dai, comme souverain du Viêt-nam, mais aucun Vietnamien ne lui fait confiance, et la guerre continue. En juin, les États-Unis font cause commune avec la France, puisqu'elle aussi est engagée dans une guerre contre le communisme.

▶ *Hô Chi Minh.*

Persécution des catholiques en Hongrie

▶ 30 juin 1950 ◀ Les dirigeants communistes hongrois ont ordonné la fermeture des sections de théologie de toutes les universités. C'est un nouveau pas dans la politique de persécution de l'Église catholique romaine, élément essentiel dans la vie de la plupart des Hongrois. Les prêtres sont arrêtés, et les églises, fermées.

L'an dernier, le cardinal József Mindszenty, primat de Hongrie, a été condamné à la prison à perpétuité, sur des accusations, fabriquées de toutes pièces, de trahison et de spéculation monétaire au marché noir. Le prélat emprisonné est devenu un symbole évident de la résistance politique et religieuse au communisme.

▶ *Le cardinal József Mindszenty.*

▲ *La couronne de saint Étienne fut confiée à l'armée américaine après 1945, pour éviter que les communistes ne s'en emparent.*

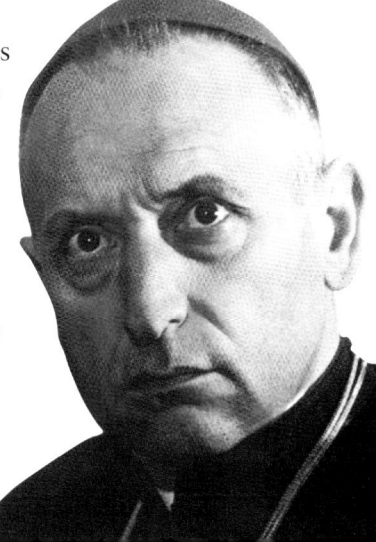

1950 – 1959

L'AUTOMOBILE

L'automobile utilise un moteur à combustion interne, qui fonctionne avec de l'essence. Elle est mise au point en France et en Allemagne entre 1880 et 1900, avec Peugeot, Panhard, De Dion-Bouton, Renault, Daimler et Benz. Mais c'est Ford qui sort la première voiture construite en grande série à partir de 1908 : le Model T. À Detroit, on produit 5 millions de véhicules en 1929. En 1950, les États-Unis dominent la production mondiale. Ils partagent aujourd'hui le marché international avec l'Europe et le Japon.

> **L'automobile**
> En 1892, Rudolf Diesel invente un moteur à allumage par compression.
>
> Les frères Michelin inventent le pneumatique pour automobiles en 1894, à Clermont-Ferrand, et créent leur Guide en 1900.
>
> La première autoroute française a été ouverte en 1946, entre Saint-Cloud et Orgeval.

◀ États-Unis. Le coupé sport Ford Thunderbird apparaît, cinquante ans après le Model T.

Le triomphe de la voiture

L'automobile achève de conquérir l'Europe et les États-Unis entre 1950 et 1960. On construit des routes et des autoroutes, on privilégie le trafic routier : le pétrole est bon marché et semble inépuisable. L'automobile devient le symbole de la réussite sociale et de la prospérité économique. Aux États-Unis, les véhicules sont très spacieux. En Europe, les voitures sont plus petites et plus économiques. La firme allemande Volkswagen produit la « coccinelle » en série à partir de 1945. En France, la 4 CV Renault, mise au point avant la guerre, est commercialisée en 1946. La 2 CV Citroën apparaît en 1948. En 1955, Citroën lance une voiture étonnante, à suspension hydraulique et carrosserie aérodynamique : la DS 19. Elle remplace la Traction-avant.

▶ Dans les drive-in, le spectateur reste dans sa voiture et regarde le film sur un écran géant.

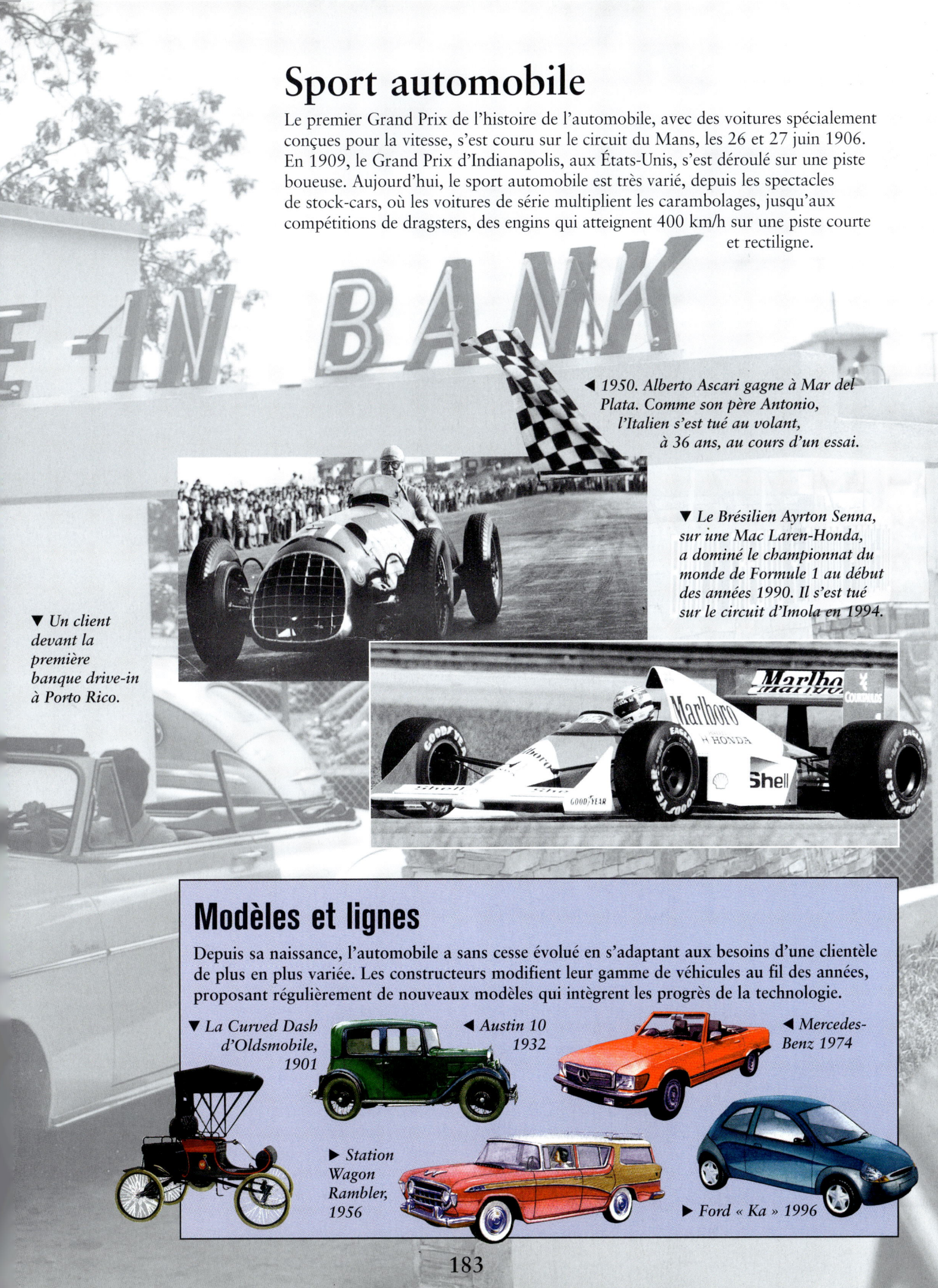

Sport automobile

Le premier Grand Prix de l'histoire de l'automobile, avec des voitures spécialement conçues pour la vitesse, s'est couru sur le circuit du Mans, les 26 et 27 juin 1906. En 1909, le Grand Prix d'Indianapolis, aux États-Unis, s'est déroulé sur une piste boueuse. Aujourd'hui, le sport automobile est très varié, depuis les spectacles de stock-cars, où les voitures de série multiplient les carambolages, jusqu'aux compétitions de dragsters, des engins qui atteignent 400 km/h sur une piste courte et rectiligne.

◀ 1950. Alberto Ascari gagne à Mar del Plata. Comme son père Antonio, l'Italien s'est tué au volant, à 36 ans, au cours d'un essai.

▼ Le Brésilien Ayrton Senna, sur une Mac Laren-Honda, a dominé le championnat du monde de Formule 1 au début des années 1990. Il s'est tué sur le circuit d'Imola en 1994.

▼ Un client devant la première banque drive-in à Porto Rico.

Modèles et lignes

Depuis sa naissance, l'automobile a sans cesse évolué en s'adaptant aux besoins d'une clientèle de plus en plus variée. Les constructeurs modifient leur gamme de véhicules au fil des années, proposant régulièrement de nouveaux modèles qui intègrent les progrès de la technologie.

▼ La Curved Dash d'Oldsmobile, 1901

◀ Austin 10 1932

◀ Mercedes-Benz 1974

▶ Station Wagon Rambler, 1956

▶ Ford « Ka » 1996

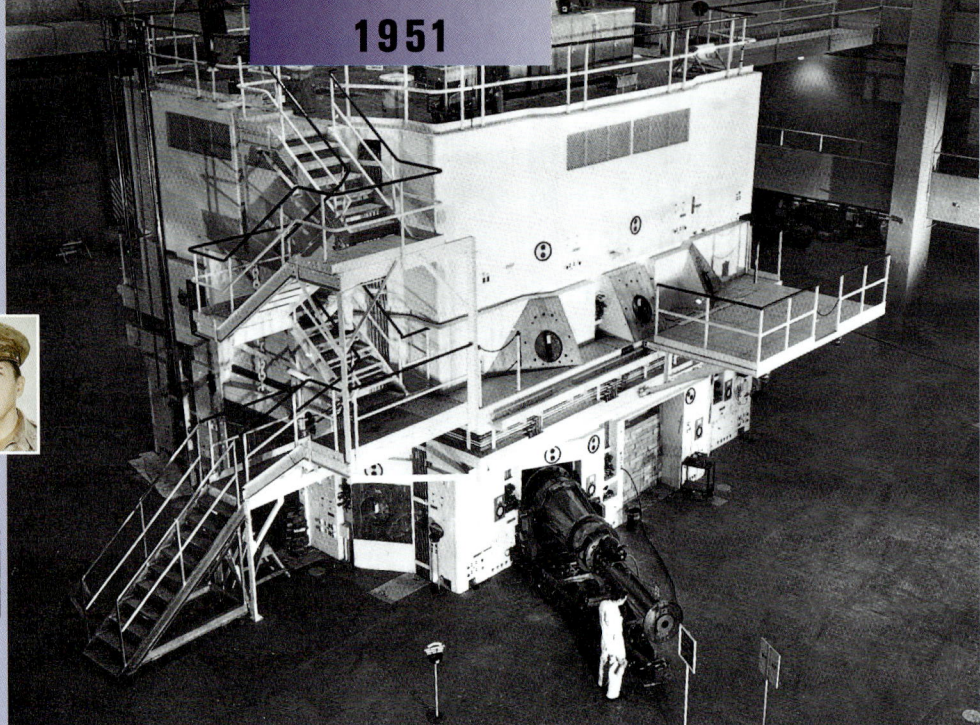

▲ *Réacteur nucléaire au centre d'essais d'Arco Valley, aux États-Unis.*

Électricité nucléaire aux États-Unis

▶ **29 décembre 1951** ◀ La Commission américaine à l'énergie atomique révèle que l'énergie nucléaire, consacrée jusqu'à maintenant à l'équipement militaire, peut avoir des applications pacifiques. Pour la première fois, le réacteur nucléaire expérimental du Laboratoire national de recherche de l'Idaho a produit assez d'électricité pour faire fonctionner toutes sortes d'installations. C'est le premier dans le pays à fabriquer de l'électricité grâce à l'énergie nucléaire. Produisant plus d'énergie qu'il n'en a besoin, le réacteur EBRI fournit la vapeur qui actionne des turbines génératrices d'électricité. Sa production est largement suffisante pour satisfaire une importante consommation en lumière et en électroménager.

En 1951 aussi...

18 avril • La France, l'Italie, l'Allemagne et le Benelux (Belgique, Pays-Bas et Luxembourg) ratifient le traité de Paris, qui fonde la CECA (Communauté européenne du charbon et de l'acier).

27 mai • La Chine prend la direction de la Défense et des Affaires étrangères du Tibet.

Le nucléaire
Albert Einstein a établi de la masse et de l'énergie dans la relation $E = mc^2$.
•
La première centrale nucléaire, ouverte à Obninsk, en Russie, en 1954, était un petit réacteur à eau sous pression.

Truman limoge MacArthur

▶ **11 avril 1951** ◀ Le président Truman a relevé de ses fonctions le général MacArthur, commandant en chef de l'armée américaine en Corée. Le désaccord entre les deux hommes a atteint son apogée lorsque MacArthur a publiquement critiqué la stratégie de Truman en Corée. Le général MacArthur voulait refouler les Coréens du Nord jusqu'à la Chine, pour s'emparer de la Corée du Nord. Il souhaitait même utiliser la bombe atomique. Le président Truman voulait simplement revenir aux frontières de 1945 et empêcher l'extension du communisme. « Nous avons réussi, jusqu'à maintenant, à empêcher la troisième guerre mondiale » a, déclaré le président, affirmant le succès de sa stratégie. Le général M. Ridgway remplace dorénavant MacArthur en Corée.

◀ *Le général Douglas MacArthur.*

1950 – 1959

▲ *Rencontre entre les vedettes de* Show Boat.

Comédie musicale sur le Mississippi

La comédie musicale *Show Boat*, de Hammerstein et Kern, est un magnifique spectacle dont le décor est un bateau sur lequel on chante et on danse. Elle a reçu un accueil enthousiaste. Dans ce film de George Sidney, le rôle de Julie est joué par Ava Gardner, et celui de Joe, par William Warfield.

L'Attrape-cœur de J. D. Salinger

▶ **juillet 1951** ◀ La découverte littéraire de l'année est le premier roman d'un jeune auteur d'une trentaine d'années. *L'Attrape-cœur* de Jerome David Salinger, met en scène un lycéen désœuvré qui dérive dans New York. L'histoire a conquis l'imagination de la jeunesse du monde entier. Le héros, Holden Caufield, âgé de 16 ans, ne sait pas ce qu'il veut, mais il sait qu'il déteste les « nuls » qu'il croise à tous les coins de rue. C'est une étude magistrale d'un jeune homme au seuil de l'âge adulte.

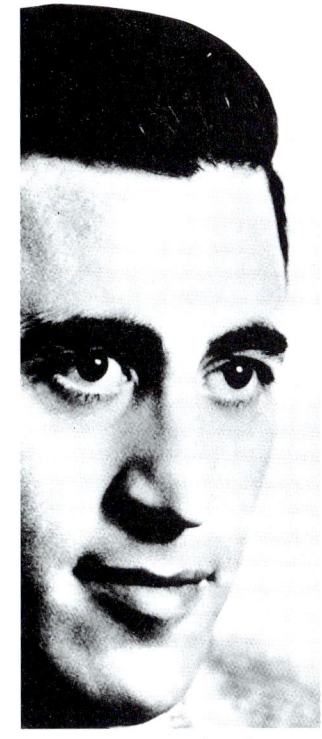

▲ *Jerome David Salinger.*

Espions communistes en Grande-Bretagne

▶ **7 juin 1951** ◀ Les services diplomatiques britanniques sont en émoi depuis la disparition soudaine de Guy Burgess et Donald Maclean, deux hauts fonctionnaires de l'ambassade de Grande-Bretagne à Washington. Cela fait deux semaines qu'ils n'ont plus été vus. D'importantes recherches sont en cours, en Allemagne, en Autriche et en Finlande, le long des frontières avec le bloc soviétique.

Des hypothèses sont émises sur leur appartenance éventuelle à un réseau d'espionnage soviétique. Ils auraient en fait rejoint Moscou. Mais, pour le moment, on n'a aucune nouvelle sérieuse.

▲ *Vue du palais des Expositions, avec les pavillons du Lion et de la Licorne.*

Exposition britannique

▶ **4 mai 1951** ◀ Cet été aura lieu à Londres, sur la berge sud de la Tamise, une « grande exposition britannique ». On s'attend à des couleurs vives et à des démonstrations exaltantes pour faire oublier les longues années de guerre et d'austérité. Parmi les attractions prévues, le dôme des Découvertes présentera des films en trois dimensions, et le Skylon, une gigantesque sculpture en aiguille.

Baudouin, roi de Belgique

▶ **16 juillet 1951** ◀ La crise du régime se termine aujourd'hui en Belgique, avec l'abdication de Léopold III, ce roi qui s'était rendu à l'armée allemande en 1940. Depuis la fin de la guerre, le souverain vivait en exil et refusait d'abdiquer en faveur de son fils. Cette affaire a déchiré la Belgique. Beaucoup n'ont jamais pardonné à Léopold sa reddition si rapide, avec si peu de résistance, et sa collaboration avec les autorités nazies. Son fils Baudouin prend la succession.

1952

La bombe H

▶ **1er novembre 1952** ◀ Les eaux calmes de l'atoll Eniwetok, dans le Pacifique, se sont déchaînées, après l'explosion de la plus puissante bombe nucléaire. Cette nouvelle et effroyable acquisition de l'armée américaine est le premier modèle de bombe thermonucléaire, ou à hydrogène – cousine des bombes atomiques lancées sur Hiroshima et Nagasaki en 1945.

Un éclair lumineux silencieux a accompagné la déflagration. En quelques secondes, l'île principale d'Eniwetok était rasée de la surface du globe. L'explosion équivaut à 10,4 millions de tonnes de TNT – 700 fois la puissance de la bombe d'Hiroshima. Cinq minutes plus tard, un gros nuage de gaz radioactif s'élevait dans l'atmosphère, suivi du nuage en champignon constitué de débris pulvérisés. La bombe a relâché dans la haute atmosphère d'immenses quantités de matériaux radioactifs, qui vont retomber sur la terre pendant des années.

Les scientifiques américains dirigés par Edward Teller ont mis près de trois ans pour concevoir la bombe H. Alors que la puissance de la bombe atomique provient de la fission de l'atome, celle de la bombe à hydrogène est due à la fusion des noyaux de deux isotopes distincts d'hydrogène. Afin d'obtenir le dégagement de chaleur nécessaire pour entamer le processus de fusion, la bombe à hydrogène est elle-même amorcée par une bombe atomique.

Le rock and roll fait exploser les ondes

Un nouveau rythme bat la mesure aux États-Unis : un mélange de folk, de blues et de country joué à un rythme d'enfer. Grâce au disc-jockey Alan Freed, cette musique se répand partout et devient très populaire. On l'appelle rock and roll, car elle donne envie de se balancer *(rock)* et de tourner *(roll)* comme une toupie sur ses rythmes effrénés.

▲ *L'explosion d'une bombe à hydrogène, dans le Pacifique.*

Le Corbusier : un architecte d'avant-garde

▶ **1952** ◀ Le Corbusier, un grand architecte d'avant-garde, d'origine suisse, vient d'achever son fantastique projet, la construction des unités d'habitation à Marseille. Son prototype de « cité verticale » regroupe, dans un seul et même bâtiment, 340 appartements, des magasins, un parc de sculptures et des pistes de course à pied. L'immeuble est autonome, et un réseau de rues intérieures permet d'assurer la circulation des services communautaires.

Cette construction reflète les deux préoccupations principales de son concepteur : la maison est une « machine à habiter » – le logement doit être fonctionnel et pratique –, et l'immeuble doit permettre aux gens de vivre agréablement en communauté.

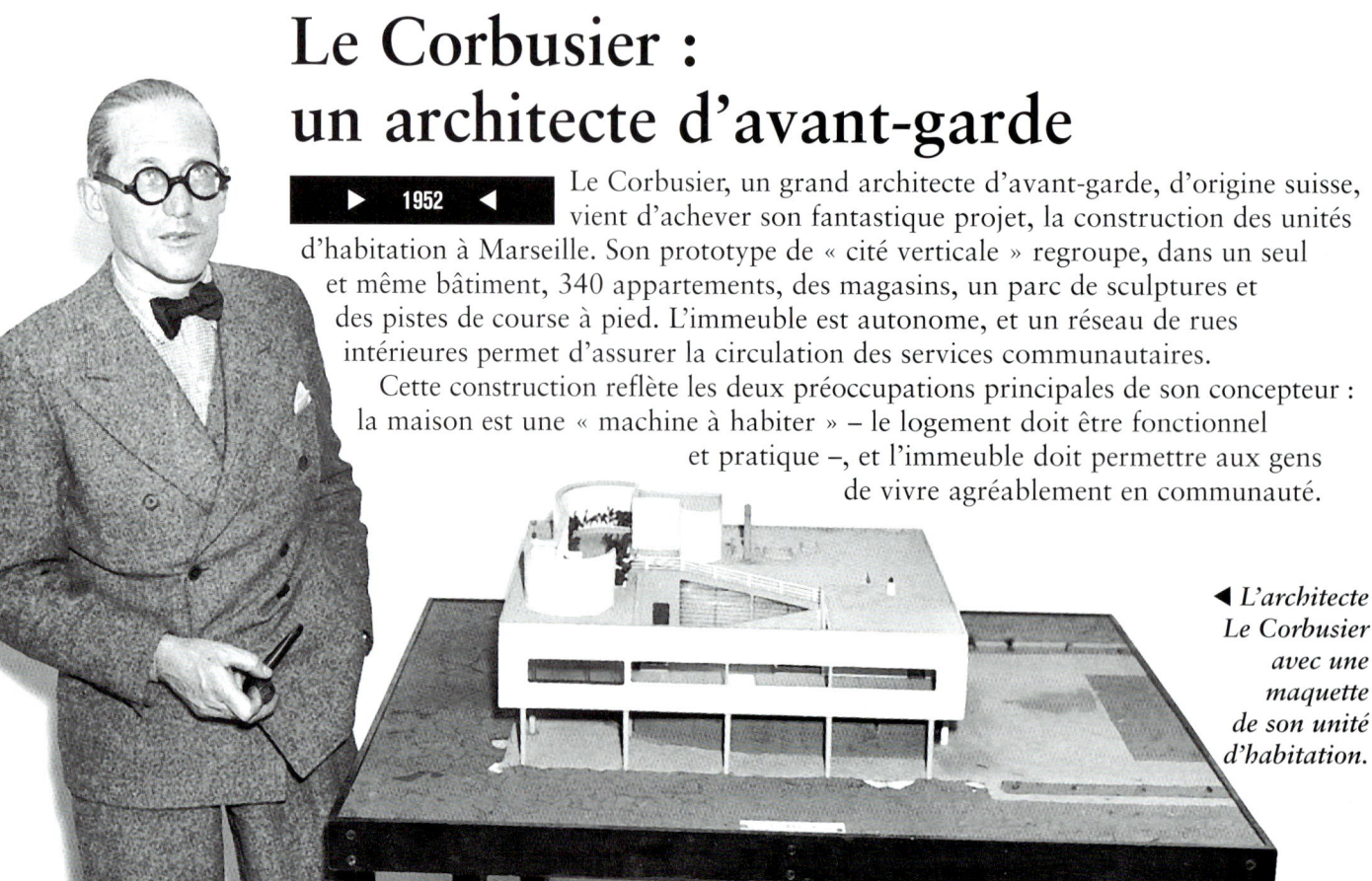

◀ *L'architecte Le Corbusier avec une maquette de son unité d'habitation.*

1950 – 1959

▲ *Rencontre entre les vedettes de* Show Boat.

Comédie musicale sur le Mississippi

La comédie musicale *Show Boat*, de Hammerstein et Kern, est un magnifique spectacle dont le décor est un bateau sur lequel on chante et on danse. Elle a reçu un accueil enthousiaste. Dans ce film de George Sidney, le rôle de Julie est joué par Ava Gardner, et celui de Joe, par William Warfield.

▲ *Vue du palais des Expositions, avec les pavillons du Lion et de la Licorne.*

Exposition britannique

▶ **4 mai 1951** ◀ Cet été aura lieu à Londres, sur la berge sud de la Tamise, une « grande exposition britannique ». On s'attend à des couleurs vives et à des démonstrations exaltantes pour faire oublier les longues années de guerre et d'austérité. Parmi les attractions prévues, le dôme des Découvertes présentera des films en trois dimensions, et le Skylon, une gigantesque sculpture en aiguille.

L'Attrape-cœur de J. D. Salinger

▶ **juillet 1951** ◀ La découverte littéraire de l'année est le premier roman d'un jeune auteur d'une trentaine d'années. *L'Attrape-cœur* de Jerome David Salinger, met en scène un lycéen désœuvré qui dérive dans New York. L'histoire a conquis l'imagination de la jeunesse du monde entier. Le héros, Holden Caufield, âgé de 16 ans, ne sait pas ce qu'il veut, mais il sait qu'il déteste les « nuls » qu'il croise à tous les coins de rue. C'est une étude magistrale d'un jeune homme au seuil de l'âge adulte.

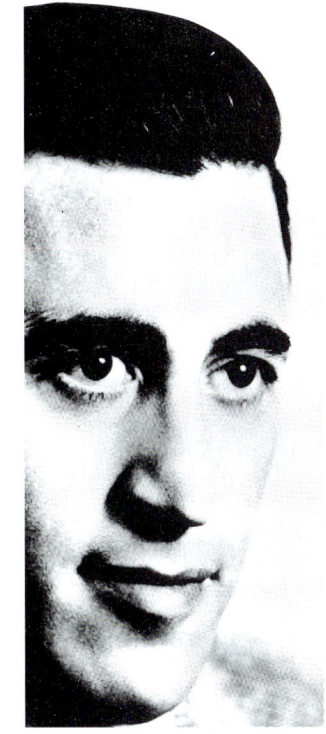

▲ *Jerome David Salinger.*

Espions communistes en Grande-Bretagne

▶ **7 juin 1951** ◀ Les services diplomatiques britanniques sont en émoi depuis la disparition soudaine de Guy Burgess et Donald Maclean, deux hauts fonctionnaires de l'ambassade de Grande-Bretagne à Washington. Cela fait deux semaines qu'ils n'ont plus été vus. D'importantes recherches sont en cours, en Allemagne, en Autriche et en Finlande, le long des frontières avec le bloc soviétique.

Des hypothèses sont émises sur leur appartenance éventuelle à un réseau d'espionnage soviétique. Ils auraient en fait rejoint Moscou. Mais, pour le moment, on n'a aucune nouvelle sérieuse.

Baudouin, roi de Belgique

▶ **16 juillet 1951** ◀ La crise du régime se termine aujourd'hui en Belgique, avec l'abdication de Léopold III, ce roi qui s'était rendu à l'armée allemande en 1940. Depuis la fin de la guerre, le souverain vivait en exil et refusait d'abdiquer en faveur de son fils. Cette affaire a déchiré la Belgique. Beaucoup n'ont jamais pardonné à Léopold sa reddition si rapide, avec si peu de résistance, et sa collaboration avec les autorités nazies. Son fils Baudouin prend la succession.

Le rock and roll fait exploser les ondes

Un nouveau rythme bat la mesure aux États-Unis : un mélange de folk, de blues et de country joué à un rythme d'enfer. Grâce au disc-jockey Alan Freed, cette musique se répand partout et devient très populaire.
On l'appelle rock and roll, car elle donne envie de se balancer *(rock)* et de tourner *(roll)* comme une toupie sur ses rythmes effrénés.

1952

La bombe H

▶ **1er novembre 1952** ◀ Les eaux calmes de l'atoll Eniwetok, dans le Pacifique, se sont déchaînées, après l'explosion de la plus puissante bombe nucléaire. Cette nouvelle et effroyable acquisition de l'armée américaine est le premier modèle de bombe thermonucléaire, ou à hydrogène – cousine des bombes atomiques lancées sur Hiroshima et Nagasaki en 1945.

Un éclair lumineux silencieux a accompagné la déflagration. En quelques secondes, l'île principale d'Eniwetok était rasée de la surface du globe. L'explosion équivaut à 10,4 millions de tonnes de TNT – 700 fois la puissance de la bombe d'Hiroshima. Cinq minutes plus tard, un gros nuage de gaz radioactif s'élevait dans l'atmosphère, suivi du nuage en champignon constitué de débris pulvérisés. La bombe a relâché dans la haute atmosphère d'immenses quantités de matériaux radioactifs, qui vont retomber sur la terre pendant des années.

Les scientifiques américains dirigés par Edward Teller ont mis près de trois ans pour concevoir la bombe H. Alors que la puissance de la bombe atomique provient de la fission de l'atome, celle de la bombe à hydrogène est due à la fusion des noyaux de deux isotopes distincts d'hydrogène. Afin d'obtenir le dégagement de chaleur nécessaire pour entamer le processus de fusion, la bombe à hydrogène est elle-même amorcée par une bombe atomique.

▲ *L'explosion d'une bombe à hydrogène, dans le Pacifique.*

Le Corbusier : un architecte d'avant-garde

▶ **1952** ◀ Le Corbusier, un grand architecte d'avant-garde, d'origine suisse, vient d'achever son fantastique projet, la construction des unités d'habitation à Marseille. Son prototype de « cité verticale » regroupe, dans un seul et même bâtiment, 340 appartements, des magasins, un parc de sculptures et des pistes de course à pied. L'immeuble est autonome, et un réseau de rues intérieures permet d'assurer la circulation des services communautaires.

Cette construction reflète les deux préoccupations principales de son concepteur : la maison est une « machine à habiter » – le logement doit être fonctionnel et pratique –, et l'immeuble doit permettre aux gens de vivre agréablement en communauté.

◀ *L'architecte Le Corbusier avec une maquette de son unité d'habitation.*

1950 – 1959

Farouk abdique en Égypte

26 juillet 1952 — Le roi Farouk d'Égypte vient d'abdiquer. Cette décision intervient trois jours après la prise du pouvoir par le général Néguib et ses « officiers libres », et fait suite à un scandale concernant des négociations secrètes de matériel militaire organisées par ses courtisans. Amer, Farouk déclare : « Bientôt, il ne restera plus que cinq rois : celui d'Angleterre, et ceux de Cœur, de Pique, de Carreau et de Trèfle. »

◀ *L'ex-roi Farouk pose, dans la suite de son hôtel parisien, où le monarque détrôné est en exil.*

En 1952 aussi...

6 février • Le roi George VI est mort. Sa fille aînée devient reine, sous le nom d'Élisabeth II.

24 septembre • Candidat à la vice-présidence des États-Unis, Richard Nixon nie avoir détourné des fonds publics et accepté des cadeaux d'hommes d'affaires.

14 octobre • Première assemblée générale des Nations unies, à New York.

Première opération transsexuelle

15 décembre 1952 — Le secret de Christine Jorgensen, une jolie jeune femme de 20 ans, est percé. Avant de quitter les États-Unis, elle s'appelait George et était un homme. Depuis, elle a subi une série d'opérations et d'injections d'hormones au Danemark. Son opération transsexuelle, la première à être rendue publique, suscite un intérêt énorme auprès de la presse à sensation.

Christine explique qu'elle a toujours voulu être une fille et que, petit garçon, elle préférait jouer à la poupée. Son bref passage à l'armée n'a pas modifié son sentiment. Volontaire pour cette expérience toute nouvelle, elle est enfin devenue, estime-t-elle, la femme qu'elle a toujours souhaité être.

▶ *Christine Jorgensen entre dans l'histoire de la médecine.*

Publication du *Journal d'Anne Frank*

Le *Journal d'Anne Frank*, émouvant témoignage d'une enfance passée à se cacher des nazis, a été publié en juin. Cette jeune fille a passé deux ans dans une cache secrète du bureau de son père, avec sa famille, pendant que les nazis traquaient les Juifs. Elle a finalement été arrêtée, puis déportée. M. Frank, seul survivant de la famille, a publié le *Journal* de sa fille, morte en déportation, pour combattre les théories racistes.

▼ *Gene Kelly, dans la scène qui a donné son titre au film.*

Chantons sous la pluie

Le film de l'année est un chef-d'œuvre de la comédie musicale. Dans *Chantons sous la pluie (Singin' in the Rain)*, une vedette du cinéma muet (interprétée par Jean Hagen) tente de se reconvertir dans le cinéma parlant, mais échoue. Debbie Reynolds joue le rôle d'une adorable choriste, découverte par Gene Kelly, et engagée comme doublure de la star du muet. Le clou du film est la scène qui lui a donné son titre : Gene Kelly, réalisant qu'il est amoureux, se met à chanter et danser sous une soudaine pluie torrentielle.

▲ *Une page du Journal d'Anne Frank.*

1952

Kenya : la guerre des Mau-Mau

▶ **25 novembre 1952** ◀ Les troupes britanniques ont encerclé plusieurs milliers de guerriers kikouyous, alors que la rébellion contre la domination anglaise au Kenya se transforme en un conflit armé. Le soulèvement est mené par une société secrète, les Mau-Mau, suivie par la population autochtone du Kenya, à qui elle a promis d'expulser l'homme blanc. Beaucoup ont fait solennellement le serment de tuer tous les fermiers européens à l'arme à feu ou, si nécessaire, avec des lances.

L'état d'urgence a été proclamé le 20 octobre, après le meurtre de 50 Blancs et opposants noirs, dont le respecté chef Waruhui. Les troupes britanniques sont intervenues pour rétablir l'ordre, les attaques de nuit des Mau-Mau ayant créé un climat de peur dans tout le pays – les colons blancs dorment avec un revolver chargé sous l'oreiller. Mais, malgré l'arrestation cette semaine du dirigeant présumé des Mau-Mau, Jomo Kenyatta, les meurtres continuent.

◀ *Un Kikouyou discute avec un policier kenyan.*

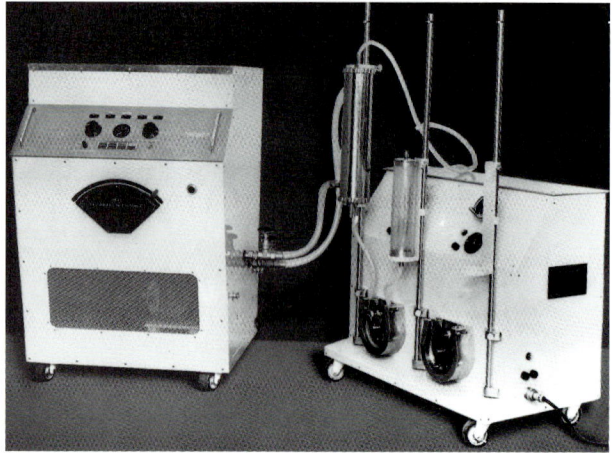

▲ *La « machine cœur-poumons », une sorte de cœur artificiel.*

Inondations en Angleterre

▶ **16 août 1952** ◀ Ce matin, une effroyable inondation a surpris dans leur sommeil les habitants du petit village britannique de Lynmouth, détruisant des rues entières, faisant 36 morts et de nombreux sans-abri. C'est la conséquence des pluies torrentielles tombées dans la région, qui ont entraîné des crues et des glissements de terrain.

L'eau s'est retirée très vite, laissant derrière elle des tonnes de boue et de décombres. Le gouvernement a déclaré Lynmouth zone sinistrée, et la Croix-Rouge a lancé une opération visant à fournir de la nourriture, de l'eau et des abris.

Cœur artificiel

▶ **8 mars 1952** ◀ La chirurgie cardiaque a fait un bond en avant, cette année, lorsqu'un cœur artificiel (mécanique) a permis à Peter During, 41 ans, de rester en vie quatre-vingts minutes, à l'hôpital de Pennsylvanie, aux États-Unis. L'an dernier, le chirurgien américain Heynsham Gibbon inventait la première « machine cœur-poumons », un respirateur artificiel qui remplace le cœur et les poumons en assurant la circulation d'un sang frais et oxygéné dans le corps du patient. Les médecins peuvent arrêter le « vrai » cœur pendant trente minutes ou plus, pour effectuer des opérations compliquées.

« La » Callas triomphe

Le monde de l'opéra a eu le souffle coupé par la brillante interprétation du rôle principal de *Norma*, par Maria Callas. La salle du Royal Opera House de Covent Garden, à Londres, éblouie par « la » Callas, a offert une ovation debout à cette soprano au registre si étendu.

▼ *Avec l'arrivée du brouillard, la circulation se fait au ralenti.*

1950 - 1959

Premiers passagers d'un avion à réaction

▶ **2 mai 1952** ◀ L'âge de l'avion à réaction s'est ouvert avec le premier vol régulier, organisé par une compagnie d'aviation britannique. Le *Comet 1* De Havilland, un quadrimoteur à 36 places, a relié Londres à Johannesburg, en Afrique du Sud, soit 10 750 km. Sa vitesse – proche de 800 km/h – lui permet d'atteindre sa destination en moins de vingt-quatre heures.

▲ *Le personnel de l'aéroport, saluant le Comet 1 De Havilland pour son vol inaugural.*

▲ *Evita, en 1951, avec son mari, Juan, saluant la foule, qui l'adorait et l'admirait.*

Mort d'Evita

▶ **28 juillet 1952** ◀ La Première dame d'Argentine, Eva Perón, est morte d'un cancer à l'âge de 33 ans. Evita, ainsi qu'elle était surnommée, était une héroïne pour les millions de pauvres de son pays, les *descamisados* (« sans-chemise »). Eva Duarte, de son nom de jeune fille, était déjà connue comme actrice de cinéma et de radio, avant d'épouser Juan Perón, vice-président du pays après le coup d'État de juin 1943. Lors de l'emprisonnement de son mari par des opposants, Evita avait soulevé les *descamisados*. Une semaine d'émeutes, de grèves et de manifestations avait convaincu les autorités de le relâcher. Les talents politiques, le style et la grâce d'Evita devinrent des atouts précieux, après l'élection de Perón à la présidence en 1946.

Profondément engagée dans la vie politique argentine, Evita contribua à développer la santé publique, à accélérer l'instauration du droit de vote des femmes et à réformer l'enseignement. Elle comptait se présenter à la vice-présidence de son mari en 1951.

Jeux Olympiques d'Helsinki

▶ **3 août 1952** ◀ Les jeux Olympiques d'Helsinki, en Finlande, auront été marqués par la performance du doublé tchèque Emil Zátopek et Dana Zatopkova, mari et femme dans le civil. Emil avait déjà prouvé ses talents de coureur de fond en accomplissant des prouesses dans le 10 000 m des Jeux de 1948. Cette année, il a dominé les épreuves en récoltant les médailles d'or au 10 000 m et au 5 000 m, puis en remportant son premier marathon devant le Français Alain Mimoun, battu de 92 secondes. Dana a pour sa part établi un nouveau record du lancer du javelot avec 50,46 m.

▼ *Emil Zátopek franchissant la ligne d'arrivée.*

Le smog fait 2 000 morts à Londres

▶ **31 décembre 1952** ◀ Pendant dix jours, cet hiver, les Londoniens ont combattu le pire des brouillards polluants qu'ils aient jamais connu. Une « purée de pois », mélange malsain de particules d'eau (condensation) et de suie, a envahi la capitale. À certains moments, on ne voyait même pas sa propre main, et le public des concerts du Royal Albert Hall n'apercevait même pas l'orchestre. Des masques antibrouillard sont en cours de production, mais 2 000 personnes sont déjà mortes à la suite de problèmes respiratoires.

1953

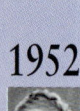

Hillary et Norgay au sommet de l'Everest

▼ *Le Sherpa népalais Tenzing Norgay (à gauche) et le Néo-Zélandais Edmund Hillary.*

▶ 29 mai 1953 ◀ À 11 h 30, ce matin, deux hommes ont foulé le sommet de l'Everest, à 8 848 mètres d'altitude, point culminant de la planète. Le Néo-Zélandais Edmund Percival Hillary et son guide, le Sherpa Tenzing Norgay, se sont poliment serré la main, puis se sont sauté au cou avec enthousiasme. C'était la huitième tentative de Tenzing, et la deuxième de Hillary.

L'expédition, menée par John Hunt, a quitté Katmandou il y a dix semaines avec près de 8 tonnes de matériel. Hillary et Tenzing ont passé la nuit à 8 595 mètres dans une tente installée sous l'arête sud-est. La dernière épreuve s'est présentée sous la forme d'un mur de 12 mètres de haut faisant obstacle à l'accès au sommet. Une petite fissure a permis à Hillary de se hisser centimètre par centimètre sur l'arête, en s'aidant des pointes arrière de ses crampons. Il a pu ensuite aider Tenzing.

Les deux hommes ne sont restés que quinze minutes au sommet – suffisamment pour planter les drapeaux britannique, népalais et des Nations unies. Tenzing a creusé un trou dans la neige pour déposer des offrandes, quelques bonbons et des biscuits, pour remercier les dieux. Hillary a planté une petite croix dans la neige.

▼ *L'ensemble de l'expédition, non loin du sommet de l'Everest.*

▼ *Tenzing, au sommet de l'Everest, avec le drapeau britannique.*

Exécution des époux Rosenberg

▶ 19 juin 1953 ◀ Julius et Ethel Rosenberg ont été exécutés sur la chaise électrique, à New York. Ce sont les premiers Américains condamnés à mort pour espionnage en temps de paix. Tous deux, sympathisants communistes dans leur jeunesse, étaient accusés d'avoir transmis aux Soviétiques des documents secrets sur la bombe atomique. Leurs deux fils, Michael (10 ans) et Robert (7 ans), sont orphelins.

De nombreuses manifestations réclamant le retrait de la peine capitale ont eu lieu dans le monde entier. Leurs défenseurs ont toujours affirmé que le procès était entaché d'irrégularité et que l'implication d'Ethel était incertaine.

▼ *Manifestation, à New York, contre l'exécution.*

L'Everest
À cheval sur la frontière du Népal et du Tibet, l'Everest a hérité son nom de George Everest, un topographe britannique, le premier à avoir enregistré le sommet en 1850.
•
Le nom indigène de l'Everest est Chomolungma, « déesse mère de la Terre » en népalais et en tibétain.
•
George Mallory a échoué trois fois dans ses tentatives pour atteindre le sommet par la face tibétaine, entre 1921 et 1924.
•
Le Népal a autorisé l'entrée des étrangers en 1947, ouvrant la voie à la face sud, plus accessible.

1950 – 1959

▲ *Staline dans son cercueil.*

Mort de Staline

▶ **5 mars 1953** ◀ Joseph Staline vient de succomber à une attaque cérébrale. Né en Géorgie en 1879, Iossif Vissarionovitch Djougachvili, dit Joseph Staline, avait adopté son nom (de *stal*, « acier ») lors de la Révolution russe. En 1922, il était nommé secrétaire général du parti communiste et, sept ans plus tard, après la mort de Lénine, il devenait dictateur de Russie.

Il restera dans l'Histoire comme le créateur de la collectivisation forcée, l'organisateur des purges sanglantes des années 30, et le signataire du pacte germano-soviétique avec Hitler au début de la Seconde Guerre mondiale, puis l'artisan de l'écrasante défaite infligée aux nazis à partir de 1943.

Churchill, Prix Nobel de littérature

▶ **10 décembre 1953** ◀ Le Premier ministre britannique Winston Churchill a obtenu le prix Nobel de littérature. Il a été distingué pour l'ensemble de son travail historique, dont quatre volumes sur la Première Guerre mondiale, et particulièrement pour ses *Mémoires de guerre*, concernant la Seconde Guerre mondiale. Il a également écrit une biographie d'un de ses ancêtres, Malborough.

L'« homme de Piltdown » est un faux

Kenneth Oakley, un géologue du British Museum, a découvert la plus grande escroquerie de l'histoire archéologique. Les tests qu'il a effectués sur le crâne de l'« homme de Piltdown », trouvé dans le Sussex en 1912, ont montré que c'était un faux. En fait du demi-million d'années qui lui était attribué, cette pièce est une mâchoire d'orang-outan associée à un crâne humain datant de cinq cents ans.

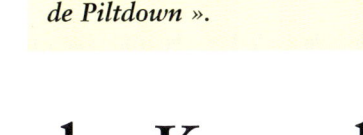

▶ *Moulage du crâne de l'« homme de Piltdown ».*

▼ *Jacky et John coupent le gâteau de mariage.*

Le mariage des Kennedy

▶ **12 septembre 1953** ◀ John Fitzgerald Kennedy et Jacqueline Lee Bouvier viennent de se marier, à Newport, Rhode Island. John, fils de Joseph Kennedy, ancien ambassadeur américain à Londres, est sénateur du Massachusetts. Jacky, fille d'une famille aisée, vient d'abandonner son travail de photographe au *Washington Times Herald*. Kennedy est un jeune et beau politicien issu d'une ambitieuse famille d'Américano-Irlandais. Il a écrit un essai sur la vie politique européenne d'avant guerre, *Pourquoi l'Angleterre a dormi*. En 1943, il était commandant d'un patrouilleur américain détruit par un croiseur japonais dans le Pacifique. L'histoire de sa participation au sauvetage de l'équipage de onze hommes en a fait un des héros de la guerre.

1953

Couronnement d'Élisabeth II

▶ **2 juin 1953** ◀ Des têtes couronnées de toute l'Europe, des chefs d'État, ainsi que de simples citoyens, ont assisté ce jour au couronnement de la princesse Élisabeth à Westminster.

Au cours de la cérémonie – émouvante et pleine de fastes –, la nouvelle reine, accompagnée du duc d'Édimbourg, s'est engagée au service des peuples de Grande-Bretagne et du Commonwealth. La télévision a retransmis la cérémonie du couronnement. C'est la première diffusion mondiale en Eurovision. Le spectacle de la reine dans son carrosse doré, lentement mené dans les rues de Londres par huit chevaux gris, a été inoubliable. Malgré le froid et la pluie, une gigantesque foule s'était amassée sur le trajet, saluant et acclamant le couple royal jusque tard dans la nuit. À minuit, encore, la foule a eu le plaisir d'apercevoir la reine et le duc d'Édimbourg, lors du magnifique feu d'artifice donné au clair de lune sur la Tamise.

▼ *Une scène du nouveau film* The Robe.

▶ *Des millions de spectateurs du monde entier ont assisté au couronnement de la reine Élisabeth II.*

Le CinémaScope est né

La Twentieth Century Fox a livré son premier film en CinémaScope, *The Robe (la Tunique)*, réalisé par Henry Koster. Ce nouveau procédé a été inventé par Henri Chrétien, un physicien français, à la fin des années 20. La caméra est munie de lentilles spéciales, et les images déformées sont rétablies sur un écran très large par un projecteur doté d'un Hypergonar.

Soulèvement ouvrier en Allemagne de l'Est

▶ **17 juin 1953** ◀ Le mécontentement grandit contre le régime communiste d'Allemagne de l'Est. Il a abouti au premier soulèvement dans le bloc soviétique d'après guerre. Les ouvriers se sont mis en grève, manifestant dans les rues de Berlin-Est, pour protester contre l'augmentation des normes de production.

Au bout de deux heures, le régime refusant toujours de leur donner satisfaction, ce sont quelque 100 000 travailleurs qui sont descendus dans la rue, mettant le feu aux bâtiments officiels et exigeant un changement de gouvernement. La révolte s'est étendue à tout le pays et n'a pu être réprimée qu'avec l'arrivée de troupes et de chars soviétiques dans Berlin-Est. Au moins 21 personnes ont été tuées, et des centaines d'autres, blessées. La foule chantait « Ivan, rentre chez toi ! » aux chars russes. Le commandant soviétique de Berlin-Est a déclaré l'état d'urgence et le couvre-feu, du crépuscule à l'aube.

◀ *Le CinémaScope projette une image deux fois et demie plus large que haute.*

En 1953 aussi...

13 août • Des tremblements de terre et raz de marée dans les îles grecques font plus de 1 000 morts.

Mai • Le film de Jacques Tati, les Vacances de M. Hulot, est primé au Festival de Cannes.

17-23 décembre • Au bout du 13ᵉ tour de scrutin, les députés et les sénateurs français élisent René Coty 17ᵉ président de la IVᵉ République.

◀ *Les insurgés manifestent devant la porte de Brandebourg, pendant le soulèvement à Berlin-Est.*

1950 – 1959

Découvertes génétiques

▶ 25 avril 1953 ◀ Le biologiste américain James Dewey Watson et le biochimiste britannique Francis Harry Compton Crick ont travaillé sur la structure de la molécule d'ADN, ou acide désoxyribonucléique, qui compose les chromosomes porteurs des caractéristiques héréditaires.

Depuis quelque temps déjà, les scientifiques savent que l'ADN est composé de quatre éléments. Crick et Watson ont découvert l'ordre d'assemblage de ces éléments. Ils ont pu l'établir à partir de la structure en double hélice révélée par les radiographies aux rayons X de l'ADN, en déduisant le mécanisme de sa duplication et celui de la transmission génétique. Une découverte capitale, ouvrant la voie de la biologie moléculaire.

▲ *James Watson (en haut) et Francis Crick.*

▶ *Représentation de structure en double hélice de l'ADN.*

Grand chelem au tennis

▶ 3 juillet 1953 ◀ Maureen Conolly est la première femme à réaliser le grand chelem au tennis (succès aux Internationaux d'Australie, de France, de Grande-Bretagne et des États-Unis, la même année).

Conolly, qui a commencé le tennis à l'âge de 10 ans, a remporté son premier titre senior en 1951.

▼ *Tito a reconstruit le parti communiste de Yougoslavie en 1937.*

Tito président de la Yougoslavie

▶ 14 janvier 1953 ◀ Josip Broz, connu sous le nom de Tito, a été élu premier président de la Yougoslavie.

Sa politique de non-alignement (ne pas s'allier), tant avec l'Union soviétique qu'avec le bloc occidental, a en grande partie assuré sa popularité et son prestige auprès de son peuple. En juin 1948, lorsque ses relations étaient au pire avec l'Ouest, il a rompu avec Staline, qui revendiquait le contrôle et la direction officieuse du bloc des pays de l'Est.

Tito est le premier et le plus puissant des communistes à rompre avec l'Union soviétique.

Inondations aux Pays-Bas

▶ 3 février 1953 ◀ La tempête en mer du Nord a emporté les digues et dévasté 2 000 km² de terres dans le sud-ouest de la Hollande, faisant plus de 1 000 morts ou disparus. Le gouvernement a déclaré la région de Zélande zone sinistrée.

Comme l'indique son nom hollandais (« terre de la mer »), l'histoire de la Zélande est marquée par une lutte incessante contre la mer. Le gouvernement s'est engagé à lancer le plan Delta, dont les aménagements devraient offrir une solution définitive.

▼ *Les habitants de la Zélande bloqués par l'inondation sont évacués en bateau.*

LA DÉCOLONISATION

Après la Seconde Guerre mondiale, les États européens concernés s'engagent dans la voie de la décolonisation. Les peuples d'Asie et d'Afrique sous domination européenne réclament leur indépendance.

Les Empires britannique, français, belge, néerlandais, portugais et espagnol s'effondrent peu à peu, soit de manière pacifique, comme dans la plupart des pays d'Afrique noire, soit après de terribles guerres, comme au Viêt-nam et en Algérie.

La décolonisation
- **1949.** L'indépendance de l'Indonésie est reconnue par les Pays-Bas, après quatre ans de guerre.
- **1950-1953.** La guerre de Corée oppose les États-Unis, mandatés par l'ONU, et la Corée du Nord, aidée par l'URSS et la Chine.
- **1960-1962.** La plupart des colonies françaises et anglaises d'Afrique noire deviennent indépendantes.

La guerre d'Indochine

L'Indochine française est occupée par le Japon, pendant la Seconde Guerre mondiale. À la libération, le communiste Hô Chi Minh, leader du Viêt-minh (front pour l'indépendance), proclame en septembre 1945 la République du Viêt-nam. En mars 1946, malgré les premiers accords, la France ne se résigne pas à l'indépendance, et bombarde le port d'Haiphong. La guerre s'amorce en novembre. En juillet 1954, après le désastre militaire de Diên Biên Phu (7 mai), la France reconnaît l'indépendance du Viêt-nam. Il est divisé entre le Nord, communiste, et le Sud. La guerre reprend entre les deux États en 1956. À partir de 1960, les États-Unis interviennent contre les communistes. Le cessez-le-feu est signé en 1973 à Paris. En 1975, Saigon est pris par les communistes. Le pays est réunifié.

▼ *La charrette d'un paysan ouvre la voie à un blindé de l'armée américaine, pendant la terrible guerre du Viêt-nam.*

Les pays non alignés

Après 1945, le monde se scinde en deux blocs hostiles : les États-Unis et leurs alliés, les pays occidentaux, contre l'URSS, avec ses pays satellites. Le tiers-monde apparaît, issu de la décolonisation. Tito, Nasser et Nehru fondent en 1961 le mouvement des pays non alignés. Ces États pauvres veulent rester à l'écart des deux blocs, assurer leur indépendance politique et leur croissance économique. Mais ils vont très vite devoir choisir leur camp.

▶ *Le dirigeant nationaliste arabe Gamal Abdel Nasser (au centre, à gauche), en compagnie de responsables indonésiens. Il a gouverné l'Égypte de 1954 à 1970.*

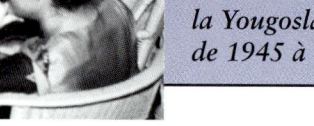

▶ *Tito dirige la Yougoslavie de 1945 à 1980.*

La partition de l'Inde

Le Congrès national indien, fondé en 1885, revendique l'indépendance de l'Inde, cette grande colonie britannique, à partir de 1920. Le mahatma Gandhi donne au mouvement nationaliste une impulsion décisive. Il fait pression sur les autorités britanniques en appliquant la tactique de la désobéissance passive et en prônant la non-violence. En 1945, les Britanniques reconnaissent qu'ils doivent quitter l'Inde, après cent soixante ans de domination.

Face à la perspective de l'indépendance, les conflits religieux entre musulmans et hindous s'intensifient. La Ligue musulmane veut un État séparé. Les hindous défendent une Inde unie, selon le rêve de Gandhi. Malgré les négociations, aucun compromis n'est trouvé. Le 15 août 1947, l'ancienne colonie devient indépendante, mais elle est divisée en deux États. Le Premier ministre de l'Inde est Jawaharlal Nehru, tandis que Muhammad Ali Jinnah dirige le Pakistan, musulman, divisé en deux parties, orientale et occidentale. En 1971, le Pakistan oriental obtient son indépendance et devient l'État du Bangladesh.

▼ *Hindous fuyant le Pakistan en 1947. Après la partition, la guerre du Cachemire fait 2 millions de morts et des millions de réfugiés dans les deux États. Gandhi est assassiné par un hindou fanatique, le 30 janvier 1948.*

▲ *Jinnah, leader de la Ligue musulmane, est d'abord partisan de l'unité hindoue-musulmane, puis se fait l'avocat déterminé de l'État musulman indépendant.*

▶ *Jawaharlal Nehru parle au peuple, à New Delhi, capitale de l'Inde indépendante. À droite, lord Mountbatten, dernier vice-roi britannique.*

1950

1951

1952

1953

1954

Un vaccin contre la poliomyélite

Le docteur Jonas Edward Salk a mis au point un nouveau vaccin contre la poliomyélite, qu'il a commencé à administrer à des enfants. Cette maladie fait des ravages et laisse de nombreuses séquelles, dont la paralysie.

1955

1956

1957

1958

1959

▲ *Le docteur Salk vaccine une petite fille âgée de 8 ans, contre la poliomyélite.*

1954

L'expérience Mendès France

▼ *Le président Pierre Mendès France à son bureau.*

Le sport en 1954
Rugby : la France gagne le Tournoi des Cinq nations.
•
Cyclisme : Louison Bobet gagne son deuxième Tour de France.
•
Football : victoire du Onze de France à Hanovre.

▶ **18 mai 1954** ◀ Après la défaite de l'armée française à Diên Biên Phu, en Indochine, la Chambre des députés confie le pouvoir à un homme de gauche, mais hostile aux communistes, Pierre Mendès France. Il est appuyé par *l'Express*, un nouveau magazine. Son gouvernement fait des réformes économiques et lutte contre l'alcoolisme. Il incite les Français à boire du lait plutôt que du vin. Sa politique coloniale est hardie : les accords de Genève, signés en 1954, mettent fin à la guerre d'Indochine. Il annonce l'autonomie de la Tunisie et du Maroc, mais ne peut empêcher la guerre d'Algérie, qui commence à la Toussaint 1954.

Attentats en Algérie

▶ **1er novembre 1954** ◀ Cette nuit, une vague d'attentats terroristes s'est abattue sur l'Algérie, faisant sept morts et quatorze blessés, ainsi que de nombreux dégâts matériels. Ces violentes attaques seraient le fait du Front de libération nationale (FLN), une organisation dont le but est de débarrasser le pays de la domination française – frein à son développement, selon elle – et de faire de l'Algérie un État souverain et indépendant. Son dirigeant, Ahmed Ben Bella, est un ancien résistant des Forces françaises libres, décoré de la médaille militaire.

Les Algériens, dont beaucoup ont combattu aux côtés de la France libre, ont été très déçus de ne pas obtenir une véritable égalité avec les Français. La seule solution, selon le FLN, est l'indépendance à laquelle il pense parvenir par la guérilla en Algérie. Il espère également être soutenu par les États arabes indépendants, en particulier par l'Égypte de Nasser.

▼ *Soldats français gardant un groupe de combattants pour l'Algérie indépendante.*

Bill Haley et son groupe de rock'n'roll

Bill Haley et ses Comets sont sur le point de faire sauter le hit-parade avec leur tube *Rock Around the Clock*. Cette nouvelle musique aux accents de rhythm and blues endiablés est déjà un succès fou. Les fans s'arrachent déjà ce nouveau disque du groupe, qui a été mis en vente aujourd'hui dans les magasins.

▼ *Bill Haley (au centre) et son groupe.*

▼ *Le baptême du* Nautilus *par Mamie Eisenhower, l'épouse du président américain.*

Toscanini prend sa retraite

▶ **4 avril 1954** ◀ Âgé de 87 ans, le grand chef d'orchestre italien Arturo Toscanini, l'un des plus grands virtuoses de tous les temps, prend sa retraite. Il a donné son concert d'adieux hier soir au Carnegie Hall, avec l'Orchestre symphonique de la NBC. Cet orchestre avait été créé pour lui en 1937, lorsqu'il avait quitté l'Italie de Mussolini.

Toscanini a étudié le violoncelle aux conservatoires de Parme et de Milan. À 19 ans, alors qu'il joue à l'Opéra de Rio de Janeiro, on le sollicite pour prendre au pied levé la direction de l'orchestre dans *Aida*, de Verdi, qu'il exécute de mémoire. C'est ainsi qu'il deviendra un éminent chef d'orchestre en Italie, dirigeant la Scala de Milan de 1898 à 1908, mais également dans le monde entier.

En 1954 aussi…

12 février • *Une étude américaine met en évidence le lien entre certains cancers et la consommation de tabac.*

1er mars • *Deuxième essai de la bombe H par les États-Unis dans l'atoll Bikini, dans le Pacifique.*

2 avril • *Inde : Nehru appelle à l'arrêt de la course aux armes nucléaires.*

▲ *Arturo Toscanini.*

Un sous-marin à propulsion nucléaire

▶ **21 février 1954** ◀ La marine américaine a mis à l'eau le premier sous-marin à propulsion nucléaire sur le Thames, à New London, dans le Connecticut. Le *Nautilus* mesure 97 mètres de long et pèse 3 180 tonnes. Il peut rester immergé durant un mois, fendant les eaux à une vitesse de croisière record de 37 km/h. En chauffant de l'eau, le réacteur nucléaire produit la vapeur qui actionne les turbines du vaisseau. Le *Nautilus* est ainsi le premier sous-marin à pouvoir être immergé de façon prolongée.

Ce bâtiment porte le nom du premier submersible construit en France en 1800 par l'ingénieur Robert Fulton, sur commande de Napoléon. Grâce à sa technologie d'avant-garde, le *Nautilus* est probablement le prototype des futurs sous-marins qui bouleverseront la marine de tous les pays.

1954

▼ *Hô Chi Minh, fondateur et dirigeant du Viêt-minh.*

Défaite de la France en Indochine

▶ **7 mai 1954** ◀ L'armée française a perdu Diên Biên Phu, où elle a subi une écrasante défaite. Depuis près de deux mois, 16 000 soldats français, commandés par le général Navarre, sont assiégés dans le fort de Diên Biên Phu. Ce fort est surplombé de collines tenues par les soldats vietnamiens du général Giap. Très rapidement, les Vietnamiens ont détruit les deux terrains d'aviation, et les Français n'ont plus été ravitaillés que par des parachutages. Il est devenu de plus en plus difficile d'évacuer les blessés.

À Paris, l'annonce de la défaite provoque l'arrivée au pouvoir de Mendès France, qui négocie avec le Viêt-minh. En juillet, les accords de Genève reconnaissent l'indépendance de l'Indochine. Le Viêt-nam est divisé en deux : au nord du 17e parallèle, un État communiste avec Hanoi pour capitale ; au sud, un État capitaliste dont la capitale est Saigon.

◀ *Pendant le siège de Diên Biên Phu, les Français ont parachuté 3 000 soldats supplémentaires.*

Premier vol du Boeing 707

Naissance du transistor de poche

Cette année, la compagnie américaine Regency a conçu le premier radio-transistor. En remplaçant les grosses lampes, on a rendu possible la fabrication de postes petits et transportables.

▶ **15 juillet 1954** ◀ Le premier essai en vol du prototype de Boeing 707 à Seattle a fait entrer les États-Unis dans l'ère du transport des passagers dans des avions à réaction. Les États-Unis sont en retard dans ce domaine, loin derrière la Grande-Bretagne. Depuis le lancement du Comet britannique, en 1952, Boeing a accéléré les recherches. Les constructeurs du Boeing 707 ont l'avantage d'avoir devant eux l'énorme marché américain, qui comprend le transport civil et celui des forces armées. Plus grand que le Comet, le Boeing 707 peut transporter 219 passagers. Ses quatre moteurs sont fixés sous les ailes, orientées vers l'arrière. Cette mesure de sécurité empêche le feu de se propager aux quatre moteurs si l'un d'entre eux est touché.

▼ *Il faudra encore quelques années pour que le Boeing 707 soit mis en service.*

Jasper Johns peint son *Drapeau*

▶ **30 septembre 1954** ◀ Le tableau intitulé *Drapeau* du jeune peintre américain Jasper Johns a provoqué un débat dans les milieux artistiques new-yorkais. Il s'agit de la réplique d'un drapeau américain ordinaire, à ceci près que des traces de pinceau sont apparentes, et ce de façon délibérée. La question que semble poser Jasper Johns est : ceci est-il en soi un objet, ou la représentation d'un objet ?

Premier centre commercial

▶ **1954** ◀ Le centre commercial Northland de Detroit (États-Unis), réalisé par l'entreprise de Victor Gruen, attire des milliers d'acheteurs enthousiastes. Il est salué comme la nouvelle génération de centres commerciaux. Ce lieu fermé, climatisé, propose 200 à 300 magasins sur plusieurs niveaux, avec de la musique, des installations pour enfants, des restaurants, et de nombreux parkings gratuits. On a l'espoir que de tels centres redonneront un peu de vie aux villes américaines quelque peu endormies.

▲ *Vue aérienne du centre commercial Northland, au nord de Detroit.*

▲ *Le Drapeau de Jasper Johns, peinture sur toile et collage.*

▶ *Le photographe, joué par James Stewart, observant ses voisins au téléobjectif.*

Nouveau succès pour Hitchcock

Fenêtre sur cour, le dernier film du maître du suspense, Alfred Hitchcock, attire les foules. Il est annoncé comme le film qui « vous fera connaître une délicieuse terreur ».

Un photographe (James Stewart), immobilisé dans son appartement par une jambe cassée, espionne ses voisins avec sa petite amie (Grace Kelly). La tension et le suspense montent lorsqu'il est témoin du meurtre d'une femme par son mari.

Mariage de Marilyn Monroe et de Joe DiMaggio

▶ **14 janvier 1954** ◀ Deux des plus grandes vedettes américaines, Joe DiMaggio et Marilyn Monroe, ont dit « oui » aujourd'hui. DiMaggio était capitaine de l'équipe de base-ball de New York lors de la Coupe du monde. Et Marilyn Monroe est la plus grande et la plus éclatante des stars de Hollywood. Le public se demande si ce mariage va durer.

◀ *Le baiser de mariage de Joe DiMaggio et Marilyn Monroe.*

L'Allemagne gagne la Coupe du monde de football

▶ **4 juillet 1954** ◀ L'Allemagne a remporté la cinquième Coupe du monde de football, qui se tenait en Suisse, au terme d'une finale palpitante, à Berne. Cette victoire est une surprise, aucune équipe allemande n'ayant participé à une compétition sportive depuis la guerre. Les Allemands ont joué un match enthousiasmant contre la Hongrie. Si les débuts ont été difficiles (les Hongrois menaient 2-0), ils ont finalement arraché la victoire par 3-2, dont deux buts marqués par Rahn, leur puissant ailier.

1955

La folie du jean

La nouvelle mode des blue-jeans fait fureur chez les adolescents. Ces pantalons moulants, à taille basse, populaires aux États-Unis depuis longtemps, sont faits en toile denim (originaire de Nîmes, d'où son nom). On les appelle aussi couramment des Levi's, du nom du premier gros fabricant qui fournissait les cow-boys.

Mort de James Dean à 24 ans

▶ **30 septembre 1955** ◀ James Dean, qui incarnait la nouvelle génération du cinéma américain, s'est tué dans un accident de voiture, en Californie. Il venait de terminer le tournage du film *Géant* et se rendait à Salinas, dans sa Porsche, pour participer à une course. Un policier l'avait arrêté, un peu plus tôt, pour excès de vitesse. Il a percuté une voiture à un croisement. L'autre chauffeur, un étudiant, n'est que légèrement blessé ; le mécanicien accompagnant l'acteur, éjecté de la voiture, est vivant, mais James Dean a eu la nuque brisée. Il n'avait que 24 ans. Avec un seul film, *À l'est d'Eden*, James Dean, jeune vedette rebelle, devenait un héros pour la jeunesse du monde entier. Son deuxième film, *la Fureur de vivre*, qui sort la semaine prochaine, en fera certainement un acteur culte. La nouvelle de sa mort a déjà provoqué des scènes d'hystérie collective chez les adolescents.

▼ *James Dean, dans le film* Géant.

▲ *Lycéennes en jean.*

▶ *La voiture de James Dean après l'accident.*

Le pacte de Varsovie

▶ **14 mai 1955** ◀ L'Union soviétique et ses alliés communistes d'Europe de l'Est ont signé à Varsovie un « traité d'assistance mutuelle », qui devrait prendre le nom de pacte de Varsovie, ville où il a été ratifié. Les pays signataires sont l'Albanie, l'Allemagne de l'Est, la Bulgarie, la Hongrie, la Pologne, la Roumanie, la Tchécoslovaquie et l'Union soviétique. Ils s'engagent à intervenir si l'un d'entre eux est attaqué. Deux ans après la mort de Staline, le bloc de l'Est est toujours solide. L'accord officialise la présence de l'Armée rouge dans toute l'Europe de l'Est. La raison première de ce pacte est une réaction à l'intégration de l'Allemagne de l'Ouest à l'OTAN (Organisation du traité de l'Atlantique nord), malgré les protestations soviétiques.

◀ *Une carte nommant et situant les pays membres du pacte de Varsovie.*

Un million de « coccinelles » !

Les ouvriers de l'usine Volkswagen de Wolfsburg, en Allemagne, ont célébré le succès de la « coccinelle » : 1 million d'exemplaires de cette petite voiture de Ferdinand Porsche, avec moteur à l'arrière, ont été fabriqués depuis son lancement, en 1936. Ce modèle est un véhicule très populaire partout dans le monde.

▼ *L'usine fête le million d'exemplaires.*

En 1955 aussi...

10 février • La police sud-africaine évacue des milliers de personnes du faubourg de Sophiatown, à Johannesburg.

18-24 avril • Conférence de Bandung, en Indonésie : les peuples colonisés demandent leur indépendance.

31 octobre • La princesse Margaret rompt avec un écuyer du roi, le colonel Peter Townsend, divorcé et père de deux enfants.

Tragédie au Mans : 82 morts

▶ **12 juin 1955** ◀ Le plus grave accident de l'histoire de la course automobile a fait 82 morts hier soir. Cela s'est produit sur le célèbre circuit du Mans, premier du genre à avoir été construit. Plusieurs véhicules se sont percutés dans un virage, à une vitesse approchant les 240 km/h, et l'une des voitures a été projetée par-dessus la barrière, sur la foule. Des témoins parlent de corps décapités, de membres arrachés, de cris effroyables. Les organisateurs ont néanmoins refusé d'arrêter la course, une décision très critiquée à l'heure qu'il est. En apprenant l'ampleur de la catastrophe, les vainqueurs ont refusé les prix.

◀ *Des équipes déblaient la route, après le pire accident de l'histoire des courses automobiles, qui a fait 82 morts et une centaine de blessés.*

▼ *Pierre Levegh, pilote français, est mort sur le coup, lorsque sa Mercedes s'est écrasée sur la foule.*

1950 - 1959

« La grande famille de l'homme »

▶ **1er octobre 1955** ◀ Dans le monde entier, de nombreux musées ont déjà réservé l'exposition photographique « La grande famille de l'homme » qui est présentée cet été au musée d'Art moderne de New York. Le fil conducteur de l'exposition est la solidarité, l'unité de l'espèce humaine. Elle a été organisée par Edward J. Steichen, 76 ans, directeur de la photographie du musée, à l'instigation du poète Carl Sandburg, son beau-frère. Pour cette manifestation, Steichen a sélectionné 500 clichés parmi les 2 millions qui lui étaient proposés.

▲ *Clichés rassemblés pour l'exposition.*

Ouverture de Disneyland à Los Angeles

▶ **18 juillet 1955** ◀ Un nouveau parc d'attractions a ouvert ses portes à Anaheim, près de Los Angeles. Disneyland est une création de Walt Disney, producteur de cinéma et père de Mickey Mouse. Les visiteurs déambulent dans une série d'univers imaginaires inspirés des films de Disney. La construction a coûté 17 millions de dollars.

L'URSS reconnaît l'Allemagne de l'Ouest

▶ **13 septembre 1955** ◀ Deux jours après l'arrivée à Moscou du chancelier allemand Konrad Adenauer, l'Union soviétique a officiellement reconnu la République fédérale d'Allemagne comme un État indépendant, admettant ainsi l'existence d'une Allemagne divisée.

Outre la méfiance soviétique, l'une des causes de l'impossibilité de la réunification allemande est l'hostilité d'Adenauer envers le communisme et son refus de reconnaître la République démocratique allemande, sous influence soviétique.

▼ *Les visiteurs de Disneyland sont accueillis par des personnages grandeur nature de Disney.*

1956

Boycott des bus en Alabama

▶ Rosa Parks, assise à l'avant du bus.

▶ **1er mars 1956** ◀ En décembre dernier, Rosa Parks, une femme noire qui ne trouvait pas de place, s'est assise à l'avant du bus, réservé aux Blancs. Son arrestation et son emprisonnement ont provoqué la colère, et le boycott des bus a été organisé. Le meneur de l'opération s'appelle Martin Luther King, un pasteur noir de la ville. L'Alabama est en effervescence avec les manifestations des Noirs contre les lois ségrégationnistes du sud des États-Unis. À Montgomery, la capitale, les Noirs ont arrêté de prendre les bus, ce qui met les sociétés de transport en difficulté financière.

Hier, la Cour fédérale a ordonné la réintégration à l'université d'Alabama d'Autherine Lucy, une étudiante noire. Trois semaines auparavant, alors qu'elle devait commencer les cours, des étudiants blancs s'étaient révoltés, et l'université avait suspendu son inscription – pour sa propre sécurité, selon l'administration. Mais la décision de la cour impose une protection. En 1954, la Cour suprême des États-Unis avait ordonné l'ouverture des écoles publiques aux Noirs, une décision qui n'a jamais été respectée dans les universités des États du Sud.

La ségrégation

Malgré l'arrêté de la Cour suprême des États-Unis déclarant, dès 1954, la ségrégation anticonstitutionnelle (illégale), les autorités blanches d'Alabama n'accepteront pas de Noirs dans les écoles avant 1963.

•

Martin Luther King veut intégrer ses frères de couleur dans tous les rouages de la société américaine. Il a fondé la SCLC (ligue des chrétiens du Sud), qui refuse la violence. Il veut faire connaître ses revendications par des moyens pacifiques.

En 1956 aussi...

2 janvier • Victoire du Front républicain (centre gauche), mené par Guy Mollet, aux élections législatives, en France, sur un programme de paix en Algérie.

29 juin • Marilyn Monroe épouse le dramaturge Arthur Miller.

6 novembre • « Ike » Eisenhower est élu pour un second mandat de président des États-Unis.

Indépendances en Afrique

▶ **20 mars 1956** ◀ Les Français perdent une partie de leur empire colonial. Deux pays du Maghreb obtiennent ainsi l'indépendance : la Tunisie, qui, à partir d'aujourd'hui, est gouvernée par Habib Bourguiba, et le Maroc – français et espagnol – qui est devenu, il y a quelques semaines, le royaume du sultan Mohammed V. Le 1er janvier, le Soudan, sous domination égypto-britannique, obtenait lui aussi son indépendance. Mais, dans un des plus grands territoires français, l'Algérie, en lutte pour l'indépendance, la France intensifie la guerre avec l'envoi de soldats du contingent, c'est-à-dire ceux qui font leur service militaire.

▶ Cette année, le Soudan, le Maroc et la Tunisie sont devenus indépendants.

La crise de Suez

▶ 3 novembre 1956 ◀ Sous la pression de l'Union soviétique et des États-Unis, les Britanniques et les Français ont accepté de retirer leurs troupes de la zone du canal de Suez. La crise de Suez a commencé le 26 juillet, lorsque le dirigeant égyptien Gamal Abdel Nasser a nationalisé le canal, qui appartenait à une colonie franco-anglaise. À la suite de ces événements, les troupes israéliennes envahissent le Sinaï, en Égypte, selon un plan secret établi avec la France et la Grande-Bretagne, qui, à leur tour, envoient une armée dans la zone du canal. Mais l'URSS et les États-Unis interviennent. Ils ne veulent plus de l'influence européenne au Moyen-Orient. L'URSS menace d'utiliser la bombe atomique, et les États-Unis font pression sur la livre et le franc.

▶ Le président Nasser, entouré de la foule en liesse, à Port-Saïd.

Rocky : 43 K-O et aucune défaite

Le boxeur Rocco Francis Marchegiano dit Rocky Marciano, prend sa retraite, à l'âge de 33 ans. Quoique se situant juste au-dessous des 2 mètres et pesant dans les 84 kilos, il a gagné ses 49 combats professionnels, dont 43 par K-O. Il a obtenu le titre de champion du monde des poids lourds en 1952 et l'a défendu six fois avec succès.

Inauguration royale d'une centrale nucléaire

▶ 17 octobre 1956 ◀ La reine Élisabeth II d'Angleterre a inauguré la centrale nucléaire de Calder Hall, sur la côte anglaise, qui fait partie d'un grand complexe comprenant notamment le centre de recherche atomique de Windscale. Le réacteur, refroidi au gaz, a une capacité d'environ 200 mégawatts. C'est une des premières centrales de ce type, conçue pour produire de l'électricité.

▶ La centrale nucléaire de Calder Hall, dans le nord-ouest de la Grande-Bretagne.

De nouvelles lignes de téléphone

On peut maintenant communiquer par téléphone avec l'Amérique aussi facilement qu'avec un ami de la ville voisine. La pose du premier câble de téléphone transocéanique entre Terre-Neuve et l'Écosse, est achevée. Contrairement aux anciens câbles télégraphiques, les nouveaux sont doublés — un pour chaque sens.

L'Autrichien Toni Sailer gagne trois médailles d'or

▶ 6 février 1956 ◀ Les jeux Olympiques d'hiver de Cortina d'Ampezzo, en Italie, sont terminés. Sans conteste, la star de ces Jeux a été Toni Sailer, qui a remporté trois médailles d'or en ski : slalom spécial, slalom géant et descente. Il a dominé de bout en bout le slalom géant, creusant un écart de plus de six secondes avec le médaillé d'argent.

◀ Toni Sailer, nouveau roi autrichien des pistes.

▲ Inauguration des nouvelles lignes de téléphone.

1956

◀ Une statue monumentale de Staline déboulonnée à Budapest. Il sera moins facile de renverser la domination soviétique en Hongrie.

◀ Nikita Khrouchtchev dénonce dans un discours les crimes de Staline.

Khrouchtchev et la déstalinisation

▶ **25 février 1956** ◀ Dans un rapport secret fait aux délégués du XXᵉ congrès du parti communiste, réunis à Moscou, le maître de l'URSS, premier secrétaire du parti communiste, se livre à une violente critique du stalinisme. Il dénonce « le culte de la personnalité » dont Staline était l'objet, la violation des règles démocratiques, et les « crimes staliniens » : arrestations, déportations en Sibérie, exécutions. Il publie des extraits du testament de Lénine, tenu secret jusqu'alors et où l'ancien dirigeant aurait exprimé ses craintes envers la « brutalité » de Staline. Toutes ces révélations semblent incroyables aux délégués communistes étrangers.

L'insurrection de Budapest

▶ **4 novembre 1956** ◀ 200 000 hommes et 2 000 chars soviétiques viennent d'entrer en Hongrie, mettant fin à la libéralisation entamée depuis quelques semaines. Depuis le 23 octobre, des manifestations, organisées par des étudiants, demandaient plus de liberté et des réformes démocratiques ; la police politique avait tiré sur la foule, déclenchant une révolte générale. Encouragés par La Voix de l'Amérique, radio des États-Unis, les Hongrois se montraient de plus en plus hostiles au communisme et à l'URSS. Imre Nagy, ancien Premier ministre communiste, mais favorable aux réformes, a été rappelé au pouvoir le 23 octobre, mais il est trop tard pour rassurer les Soviétiques. Les combats entre Hongrois et militaires russes feront des milliers de morts, sans que l'Occident intervienne. Des dizaines de milliers de Hongrois s'exilent, d'autres sont déportés. Imre Nagy, réfugié dans l'ambassade de Roumanie, sera livré et pendu en 1958.

Elvis Presley bouleverse l'Amérique

Les hit-parades ont été dominés cette année par une nouvelle vedette fracassante, Elvis Presley. Il allie la tradition des chanteurs de blues noirs et de la musique blanche country avec des rythmes durs et rapides. Ses nombreux succès, dont *Heartbreak Hotel*, *Don't Be Cruel* et *Blue Suede Shoes*, ont été vendus à des millions d'exemplaires. Le nombre de téléspectateurs d'une émission à laquelle il participait a franchi le record de 54 millions. Enfant pauvre de Memphis, dans le Tennessee, Elvis est millionnaire à 21 ans. Il provoque une vague de passion hystérique chez ses jeunes fans féminines, mais les adultes sont moins impressionnés. « Vulgaire et sans talent », tel est le verdict d'un critique musical.

▶ Le déhanchement d'Elvis Presley est parfois jugé obscène.

Mariage de Grace Kelly et du prince Rainier

▶ **19 avril 1956** ◀ Un mariage de conte de fées – le prince et la star de cinéma – a été célébré sur la Côte d'Azur. La famille Grimaldi préside aux destinées du minuscule État de Monaco depuis cinq cents ans ; Grace Kelly est, pour sa part, née à Philadelphie, dans une famille riche. Toute la principauté est en fête. À 10 heures, la cérémonie est retransmise en Eurovision : 30 millions de téléspectateurs dans neuf pays suivent, en direct, ce mariage à grand spectacle.

▲ *Rainier III et Grace Kelly, lors de la cérémonie de mariage.*

Pollution de l'air

▶ **5 juillet 1956** ◀ Lorsqu'il entrera en application, dans deux ans, le Clean Air Act (« loi pour l'air propre »), voté à Londres, devrait contribuer à améliorer la qualité de l'air dans les villes britanniques. Les fumées noires ou « sales » sont interdites, et les municipalités peuvent prendre les mesures nécessaires. L'interdiction des feux de charbon devrait mettre fin à la « purée de pois » londonienne (smog), un mélange de fumée, de suie et de brouillard. L'hiver, la capitale reçoit très peu de soleil. Durant l'hiver 1952, où le pic de pollution fut très élevé, on estime à 4 000 au moins le nombre des victimes de maladies du cœur ou des poumons provoquées ou aggravées par la pollution. Depuis 1953, des masques protecteurs sont disponibles, sur ordonnance médicale.

◀ *Des feux spéciaux aident les conducteurs de bus, gênés par le brouillard, aux croisements.*

Les épreuves olympiques d'équitation

▶ **30 septembre 1956** ◀ Commencés en janvier avec les épreuves d'athlétisme, à Melbourne, en Australie, les jeux Olympiques ont duré plus longtemps que de coutume cette année : pour des raisons de distance et de quarantaine, les épreuves d'équitation se sont déroulées à Stockholm, en Suède. La vedette de ces Jeux fut le cavalier allemand Hans Gunter Winckler, qui enleva la médaille d'or du saut d'obstacles en individuel.

▶ *Le champion allemand Hans Gunter Winckler.*

Brigitte Bardot

▶ **8 octobre 1956** ◀ Brigitte Bardot fait scandale. Cette jeune femme de 22 ans, élevée dans une famille bourgeoise, incarne une sauvageonne sensuelle dans *Et Dieu créa la femme*, film tourné par son mari, Roger Vadim. Tous les Français rêvent de sa chevelure blonde, de ses pieds nus et de son déhanchement.

▲ *Brigitte Bardot.*

1950 – 1959

1957

Spoutnik 1, le premier satellite artificiel

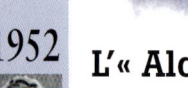

▶ **4 octobre 1957** ◀ L'Union soviétique a lancé son premier satellite artificiel, Spoutnik 1, en orbite autour de la Terre. Il pèse 84 kilos et tourne à plus de 800 kilomètres d'altitude. Chaque rotation autour de la Terre, effectuée à une vitesse de 28 000 km/h, dure quatre-vingt-seize minutes.

L'enthousiasme qu'inspire cet exploit soviétique est partagé dans le monde entier. Des émetteurs placés à bord du satellite envoient un signal radio, que la BBC, en Grande-Bretagne, et la compagnie de diffusion RCA, aux États-Unis, ont capté. Les Américains préparent le lancement d'un petit satellite pesant 1,5 kilo.

▲ *Démonstration du mode d'évolution du satellite soviétique Spoutnik 1 par un guide, à Moscou.*

L'« Alcootest »

La police américaine utilise un « Alcootest » lorsqu'elle soupçonne un automobiliste d'avoir trop bu : elle le fait alors souffler dans un ballon relié à un récipient contenant des cristaux. Ceux-ci changent de couleur selon le taux d'alcool absorbé. Auparavant, l'automobiliste devait prouver qu'il pouvait marcher en ligne droite.

Laïka, une chienne dans l'espace

▶ **3 novembre 1957** ◀ Laïka, une chienne noir et blanc, est en orbite autour de la Terre, à bord du satellite soviétique Spoutnik 2. Elle est le premier être vivant à voyager dans l'espace. Laïka dispose à bord de nourriture, d'eau, et d'une réserve d'oxygène lui permettant de respirer. Il y a également un régénérateur pour éliminer le gaz carbonique et la vapeur qu'elle exhale. Ce vol participe à un programme de recherche sur les réactions d'un animal lors d'un séjour dans l'espace. Des détecteurs et des électrodes placés sur son corps enregistrent les mouvements de Laïka, son poids, sa respiration. Des émetteurs radio envoient ces informations sur Terre. Le voyage de Laïka constitue une expérience préparatoire pour organiser une mission humaine dans l'espace. Mais Laïka n'a aucun moyen de revenir, car le satellite restera en orbite. Elle devrait mourir au bout d'une semaine, quand la réserve d'oxygène sera épuisée.

◀ *L'envoi de Laïka en orbite à bord de Spoutnik 2 apporte la preuve que les êtres vivants peuvent survivre dans l'espace.*

En 1957 aussi...

6 juillet • L'Américaine Althea Gibson est la première Noire à remporter le tournoi de tennis de Wimbledon.

19 septembre • La pièce d'Agatha Christie la Souricière, actuellement à l'affiche à Londres, en est à sa 1998e représentation.

26 septembre • La comédie musicale West Side Story fait un triomphe lors de la première à New York.

Création de la CEE

▶ **25 mars 1957** ◀ Les chefs de gouvernement des Six (France, Allemagne de l'Ouest, Italie, Belgique, Luxembourg et Pays-Bas) viennent de signer le traité de Rome. Ils ont décidé d'établir une zone d'échange commune. Cette Communauté économique européenne (CEE), ou encore Marché commun, implique dans le futur une monnaie commune et la libre circulation des biens et des personnes au sein des États membres. Quelques pays européens n'ont pas participé aux discussions sur la CEE, mais tentent de créer une zone de libre-échange concurrente.

▲ *Le traité de Rome est signé.*

Le premier langage informatique

▶ **Avril 1957** ◀ La récente création du langage de programmation informatique Fortran (*Formula Translator*) va faciliter la réalisation par un ordinateur d'opérations complexes. Jusque-là, ces systèmes étaient binaires – entièrement constitués de combinaisons des chiffres 1 et 0. Fortran utilise des symboles mathématiques. Conçu par John Backus et une équipe américaine d'IBM (International Business Machines), il est destiné aux scientifiques.

La *beat generation*

▶ **Décembre 1957** ◀ L'écrivain américain Jack Kerouac a fait la une des pages littéraires avec la sortie de son roman *Sur la route*. Kerouac appartient à la *beat generation*, un mouvement de jeunes lassés des valeurs américaines et rejetant le confort matériel des années 50, qui se reconnaissent en revanche dans le jazz, la poésie expressive, les drogues douces et les religions parallèles, particulièrement le bouddhisme zen.

Sur la route, rédigé en trois semaines, raconte le voyage de Sal Paradise et de son ami Dean Moriarty à travers l'Amérique.

▲ *L'écrivain américain Jack Kerouac.*

1950 – 1959

Fangio, cinq fois champion du monde

Le coureur automobile argentin Juan Manuel Fangio remporte le Championnat du monde de formule 1 pour la cinquième fois. Sur Maserati 250F, il a gagné les Grands Prix d'Argentine, de Monaco, de France et d'Allemagne. Il termine la saison avec 40 points, 15 de plus que l'Anglais Stirling Moss, qui courait pour Vanwall. Fangio a été champion du monde en 1951, 1954, 1955 et 1956. À 46 ans, il approche de la fin de sa carrière – mais conduit toujours merveilleusement. Sa plus belle course de l'année est celle du Grand Prix d'Allemagne.

▶ *Fangio, le plus grand champion de l'histoire automobile.*

Ségrégation à Little Rock

▶ **25 septembre 1957** ◀ Le président américain Dwight Eisenhower a envoyé plus de 1 000 soldats de l'armée fédérale faire appliquer la loi en Arkansas. La loi interdit en effet la ségrégation, afin qu'enfants noirs et blancs aillent à l'école ensemble. Le gouverneur de l'État d'Arkansas, Orval Faubus, a envoyé la garde nationale de son État pour empêcher les enfants noirs d'intégrer l'école secondaire de Little Rock. Aujourd'hui, neuf d'entre eux, escortés par les troupes fédérales, sont entrés à l'école pour suivre leurs cours aux côtés des Blancs.

▼ *Policiers fédéraux protégeant les enfants des ségrégationnistes.*

L'ÈRE DE LA CONSOMMATION

La société de consommation, née aux États-Unis au début du XXe siècle, se développe en Europe occidentale dans les années 60.
Les consommateurs, dont le niveau de vie ne cesse de s'élever, peuvent acheter plus que les produits de première nécessité et choisir parmi la large gamme de marchandises et de services proposée.
Les fabricants, qui se livrent une rude concurrence, lancent sans cesse de nouveaux produits et baissent leurs prix pour attirer les acheteurs. La publicité, le marketing et les équipes de vente spécialisées jouent un rôle de plus en plus important.

◀ « Le paradis de la ménagère » : c'est ainsi que sont présentées les nouvelles pièces « polyvalentes » (cuisines-salles à manger) au Salon des arts ménagers de New York, en 1952.

▲ Dans les années 50, l'invention d'assiettes et de verres en plastique facilite pique-niques et barbecues.

▼ Habitations caractéristiques des années 50, à Long Island, aux États-Unis.

Des foyers plus modernes

Dans les années 50, la classe moyenne n'a plus les moyens d'entretenir des domestiques à domicile. Mais de nombreux appareils facilitent le travail des ménagères, « libèrent la femme » selon la formule de la marque française Moulinex. Les cuisines sont équipées d'un grille-pain, d'un mixeur, d'une machine à laver, et il n'est plus rare de trouver des fers à repasser électriques et des aspirateurs.
Le chauffage central et l'eau chaude sont désormais courants, et les intérieurs sont aménagés avec des meubles bon marché, colorés et faciles à déplacer.

Les techniques de vente

Dans la seconde moitié du XXe siècle, tout le monde a quelque chose à vendre. Aux États-Unis, les techniques de marketing (toute action qui permet de développer les ventes) se perfectionnent. Les fabricants étudient la taille, la couleur et le prix idéals de chaque produit, ainsi que la manière la plus efficace de le vendre. Ainsi, la publicité télévisée pour un dentifrice promu par une célébrité peut augmenter les ventes. La commercialisation est tout aussi importante que la conception, chaque produit devant paraître unique, donc meilleur que celui du concurrent. Certaines entreprises, comme McDonald's, font fortune en franchisant leurs produits, c'est-à-dire en cédant à des entreprises locales le droit de les vendre dans une zone définie. Dans les supermarchés modernes, la disposition des marchandises influe sur les ventes.

Le porte-à-porte

On sonne à la porte. Un charmant jeune homme entre et salit délibérément votre tapis. Il le nettoie avec un superbe aspirateur qu'il vous propose d'acquérir à crédit. C'est le porte-à-porte.
Une autre technique de vente consiste en des réunions à domicile entre amis ou voisins, où un vendeur propose d'acheter ses produits (encyclopédies, appareils ménagers…).

◀ Dans les années 50, une publicité pour un dentifrice.

La consommation

Le premier Salon des arts ménagers français ouvre ses portes en 1923.

En 1958, 3 % des foyers français ont un réfrigérateur (70 % en 1969).

Le premier hypermarché ouvre en 1963, à Brétigny-sur-Orge. Darty, le premier supermarché de l'électroménager, ouvre en 1966.

En 1995, les ventes de hamburgers McDonald's dans le monde ont représenté environ 30 milliards de dollars.

▶ Le rayon de détergents de ce supermarché est aménagé pour attirer le regard du client.

1958

▲ *Travailleurs brandissant des portraits de Mao.*

Le « Grand Bond en avant »

▶ **Août 1958** ◀ Le dirigeant communiste chinois Mao Zédong lance le « Grand Bond en avant », pour conserver une parfaite égalité au sein du peuple chinois et éviter de reconstituer une bourgeoisie d'État. Toute l'économie est réorganisée. La cellule de base est la commune populaire, qui organise la production : céréales, produits laitiers, viande, mais aussi acier, tissus, machines. La vie privée est aussi « collectivisée » : les familles sont invitées à prendre leurs repas dans les cantines des communes, pour éviter tout individualisme. La désorganisation de l'économie causera une chute de la production et une famine qui fera plusieurs millions de morts.

En 1958 aussi...

1er février • Les États-Unis lancent Explorer, leur premier satellite.

13 mai • Avec les « pieds-noirs » français d'Algérie, les responsables de l'armée française se sont emparés du pouvoir à Alger. Ils redoutent que la métropole n'accorde l'indépendance à l'Algérie.

29 juin • Grâce à Pelé, 17 ans, le Brésil remporte la Coupe du monde de football.

La folie du Hula-Hoop

Les adeptes du rock ne sont plus les seuls à remuer des hanches. Partout, aux États-Unis, enfants et adultes se tortillent pour faire tourner un cercle en plastique autour de la taille. Les premiers Hula-Hoops, inspirés des cerceaux en bambou des enfants australiens, ont été mis sur le marché cet été par deux Californiens, Arthur Melin et Richard Knerr, qui en ont déjà vendu près de 25 millions.

◀ *Mimi Jordan, 10 ans, boit du lait pendant son record du monde de trois heures.*

▼ *600 personnes ont accompli la totalité du parcours.*

Manifestation contre l'armement nucléaire

▶ **7 avril 1958** ◀ Des manifestations contre la bombe atomique ont eu lieu dans plusieurs pays d'Europe. À Berlin-Ouest, 3 000 jeunes ont organisé une marche de protestation. En Grande-Bretagne, 4 000 personnes se sont relayées pour traverser le pays, avant de se regrouper autour de l'usine atomique d'Aldermaston et de finir à 12 000, à Londres. La campagne, entamée le 17 février, presse le gouvernement d'abandonner l'armement nucléaire.

Catastrophe aérienne

▶ **6 février 1958** ◀ Une catastrophe aérienne a plongé le football anglais dans le drame, avec la mort de sept membres de l'équipe du Manchester United. L'avion qui les transportait s'est écrasé au sol, lors du décollage sur une piste verglacée.

La jeune équipe faisait escale à Munich, sur le trajet de retour de Yougoslavie, où les joueurs avaient fait match nul (3-3) contre l'Étoile rouge de Belgrade pour la sélection des demi-finales de la Coupe d'Europe.

▶ *Les sauveteurs passent au crible les débris de l'avion.*

1950 – 1959

Prix Nobel pour un auteur russe

▶ **Octobre 1958** ◀ L'auteur russe Boris Pasternak a reçu le prix Nobel de littérature pour son roman *Docteur Jivago*, une histoire d'amour qui se déroule pendant la Révolution russe.

Les autorités soviétiques refusent de le publier, et l'Union des écrivains russes demande l'expulsion de Pasternak du pays. L'écrivain a donc refusé le prix Nobel, suppliant qu'on l'autorise à rester.

▲ *L'écrivain russe Boris Pasternak.*

Bruxelles et l'Exposition universelle

▶ **17 avril 1958** ◀ Le roi Baudouin de Belgique a inauguré l'Exposition universelle. L'*Atomium*, symbolisant la manifestation, représente un atome de fer agrandi 1 million de fois. Les neuf sphères en acier mesurent chacune près de 18 mètres de haut.

Le pavillon britannique présente des costumes historiques et un « salon des technologies ». Parmi les attractions du pavillon américain, on peut voir des essais de télévision en couleurs. Les Soviétiques montrent une réplique du satellite Spoutnik 2.

Premiers disques en stéréo

L'enregistrement de musique en « stéréophonie » se fait grâce à deux micros placés à des endroits différents. L'enregistrement en stéréo sur magnétophone existe depuis des années, mais la technique sur disque est incomparable. Elle a enthousiasmé tous ceux qui ont pu en apprécier la qualité. Ils jurent depuis qu'ils ne pourront plus s'en passer !

La Ve République

▶ **4 septembre 1958** ◀ Le général de Gaulle présente aux Français la Constitution. Le général s'était retiré de la vie politique. Il a fait sa rentrée, à cause de la tentative de coup d'État militaire en Algérie, le 13 mai. Le président de la République, René Coty, avait alors fait appel à lui, car, depuis son rôle dans la libération de la France, il apparaît comme un homme providentiel. Il a accepté d'être Premier ministre, à condition de pouvoir changer la Constitution. C'est chose faite aujourd'hui. Le 28 septembre, par référendum, les Français approuveront la Constitution de la Ve République, dont de Gaulle sera élu président le 21 décembre.

▲ *Il faut deux enceintes pour écouter les disques en stéréo.*

1959

Fidel Castro renverse Batista

▶ 2 janvier 1959 ◀ Fidel Castro proclame un nouveau gouvernement à Cuba. Pendant plus de deux ans, Castro et ses compagnons ont mené une guérilla contre le dictateur Fulgencio Batista. Hier, Batista a abandonné le pouvoir et fui le pays. Dès que la nouvelle a été confirmée, les Cubains sont descendus dans la rue pour fêter son départ. Le chef des révolutionnaires est Fidel Castro. Celui-ci a déjà fait une tentative contre Batista en 1953, mais il a été arrêté, emprisonné, puis expulsé au Mexique en 1955. Avec quelques compagnons, il prépare son retour et sa révolution. Ils reviennent à Cuba, à bord d'un navire en piteux état, et se cachent dans la Sierra Maestra. Ils ont juré de ne pas se raser la barbe avant d'être parvenus au pouvoir. Au cours de leur marche, un jeune médecin argentin, Ernesto « Che » Guevara, se rend populaire en soignant les paysans. Le combat de Castro et de ses *barbudos* en fait un modèle pour les révolutionnaires du monde entier, mais les États-Unis se méfient de la contagion communiste.

▶ *Castro a été avocat à La Havane, au service des pauvres, avant de diriger la révolution.*

▶ *Batista, qui a dirigé Cuba en dictateur militaire jusqu'à sa chute, s'est exilé en Espagne.*

Scandale à la télé

Les Américains sont sous le choc. Ils découvrent que les héros de leur jeu télévisé favori sont des fraudeurs. Le génial Charles Van Doren, qui avait réponse à toutes les questions du *Vingt et un*, les connaissait en fait avant l'émission. Ce trucage est fréquent. Les sponsors des quiz indiquent souvent au concurrent qu'ils veulent voir gagner.

L'Alaska et Hawaii rejoignent les États-Unis

▶ 21 mars 1959 ◀ Hawaii est devenu le 50ᵉ État des États-Unis, moins de neuf mois après l'admission de l'Alaska, le 49ᵉ État. Il n'y avait pas eu de nouveaux États depuis plus de 45 ans, avec l'intégration de l'Arizona en 1912. Le président Eisenhower a présenté la nouvelle version du drapeau américain, la bannière étoilée. Le drapeau compte désormais 50 étoiles, une pour chaque État.

L'Alaska occupe plus de 1,5 million de km² au nord-ouest de l'Amérique du Nord. Ce territoire réclame depuis plus de 40 ans son admission au sein de l'Union des États. Hawaii, un archipel du Pacifique, a été gouverné jusqu'en 1893 par des rois indigènes. Il a été annexé par les États-Unis en 1898 et a adopté une Constitution en 1950.

▼ *L'Alaska avait été achetée pour 7,2 millions de dollars à la Russie en 1867. Elle célèbre son admission.*

◀ *Van Doren, en direct au* Vingt et un.

212

Le musée Guggenheim

▶ **Décembre 1959** ◀ Le musée Guggenheim ouvre ses portes, à New York, sans son architecte, l'Américain Frank Lloyd Wright, qui est mort à 89 ans, en avril. Le bâtiment, en spirale, se dresse au-dessus de la 5ᵉ Avenue, comme un grand coquillage. À l'intérieur, une rampe circulaire où sont accrochés les tableaux, sur 6 étages, mène en haut de l'édifice, surmonté par une coupole de verre. Cette œuvre est un parfait exemple du « plan ouvert », style dont Wright est le créateur.

◀ *Les expositions longent les murs en spirale du musée Guggenheim.*

Création de la poupée Barbie

Les jeunes Américaines ont une nouvelle amie : Barbie. Cette poupée représente une élégante jeune femme. Ruth Handler a fondé la société des jouets Mattel avec son mari, Elliot. En regardant comment jouait sa fille Barbara, elle a pensé qu'elle aimerait avoir une poupée qui puisse jouer des rôles d'adulte. Barbie a fait son apparition lors de la Foire américaine du jouet, qui a lieu en février à New York.

▶ *La fabuleuse garde-robe de Barbie la transforme en chanteuse ou en mariée.*

Khrouchtchev visite les États-Unis

▶ **27 septembre 1959** ◀ Le dirigeant soviétique Nikita Khrouchtchev est rentré en URSS, après une visite de douze jours aux États-Unis. Il a évoqué avec le président américain la question de Berlin, ville toujours divisée entre les puissances occidentales et l'URSS. Khrouchtchev a visité une ferme de l'Iowa, une usine IBM à San Francisco, et Hollywood. Il n'a pas pu visiter Disneyland, pour des raisons de sécurité.

▼ *Khrouchtchev fait ses adieux aux États-Unis, tandis qu'Eisenhower lit un discours, à l'aéroport.*

La voie maritime du Saint-Laurent

▼ *La reine Élisabeth II, au micro.*

▶ **26 juin 1959** ◀ La voie maritime du Saint-Laurent s'ouvre aujourd'hui. Grâce à de gigantesques travaux, les bateaux pourront circuler sur le grand fleuve canadien entre l'océan Atlantique et les Grands Lacs, le long de la frontière du Canada et des États-Unis. La reine Élisabeth II d'Angleterre, le Premier ministre canadien, John Diefenbaker, et le président américain Eisenhower ont inauguré la voie maritime devant l'écluse de Saint-Lambert, à Montréal.

La voie maritime s'étend sur 3 780 km, de Duluth, au Minnesota, jusqu'à l'ouest du lac Supérieur.

1950 – 1959

1959

Le dalaï-lama fuit le Tibet

▶ **20 avril 1959** ◀ Dans le nord de l'Inde, une foule émue de 7 000 Tibétains en exil a accueilli le dalaï-lama, son chef spirituel. Déguisé en domestique, il a franchi l'Himalaya à dos de yack et atteint l'État d'Assam, hier, sans encombre. Il a fui le Tibet le mois dernier, lorsque la Chine, qui occupe le pays depuis 1951, a lancé un violent assaut contre les rebelles tibétains.

Le dalaï-lama s'est ensuite rendu à New Delhi, pour y rencontrer le Premier ministre indien, Jawaharlal Nehru. Ne souhaitant pas de conflit avec la Chine, il est peu probable que le gouvernement indien accepte une campagne du dirigeant tibétain contre la présence chinoise, tant qu'il vivra en Inde.

▲ *Le Premier ministre indien Jawaharlal Nehru saluant le dalaï-lama.*

Lunik 3 révèle la face cachée de la Lune

▲ *Le vaisseau spatial soviétique.*

▶ **14 octobre 1959** ◀ Pour la première fois, les scientifiques ont pu observer la face de la Lune orientée vers l'espace et invisible de la Terre. Le vaisseau spatial soviétique *Lunik 3* a envoyé des photos révélant 70 % de la face cachée depuis la Lune, dont une grande zone nommée pour la circonstance « mer de Moscou ». Ce programme spatial soviétique est un succès triomphal. Déjà, le 14 septembre, *Lunik 2* avait été délibérément projeté sur la Lune. Avant de s'écraser, il avait communiqué des informations très précieuses sur la radioactivité et les gaz, ainsi que sur les particules de matière dans l'espace, prouvant ainsi que ce n'est pas un vide.

En 1959 aussi...

26 mars • L'écrivain américain d'origine britannique Raymond Chandler, auteur de romans policiers, meurt, à 70 ans.

25 août • Flottant sur un coussin d'air, l'hovercraft traverse la Manche entre Douvres et Calais.

10 novembre • L'assemblée générale des Nations unies condamne l'apartheid en Afrique du Sud.

Un traité pour l'Antarctique

▶ **1ᵉʳ décembre 1959** ◀ L'Antarctique, continent qui comprend notamment le pôle Sud, vient d'être déclaré neutre et réservé à la science. Les douze pays concernés par ce territoire, dont les États-Unis, l'Union soviétique, le Royaume-Uni et la France, se sont engagés par un traité à ne jamais revendiquer la possession exclusive d'une partie de ce continent. L'accord exclut tout essai nucléaire, toute décharge de déchets et toute création de base militaire en Antarctique. Il garantit aux scientifiques de tous les pays le droit d'effectuer des recherches pacifiques. Une fois ce traité officiellement ratifié, il sera définitif et ne pourra être modifié qu'avec l'accord unanime des pays signataires. C'est le premier traité international de ce type.

▶ *Le ministre soviétique des Affaires étrangères, Vassili Kuznetsov, signe pour son pays.*

1950 – 1959

Jean XXIII annonce le concile Vatican II

▶ **25 janvier 1959** ◀ Rome. Jean XXIII annonce sa décision de tenir un concile au Vatican. Cette immense réunion des évêques du monde entier aura pour but la mise à jour *(aggiornamento)* des principes de l'Église catholique, en ce qui concerne la foi et la morale. Le pape pense que les chrétiens ont besoin de points de repère nouveaux dans le monde, où tout change et où tout ce qu'ils croient est remis en question. Jean XXIII, élu l'an dernier, est d'origine paysanne – il est né près de Bergame, en Italie du Nord –, et sa décision brutale inquiète certains catholiques, habitués au raffinement de son prédécesseur, Pie XII. En effet, le nouveau pape a annoncé que le concile sera « œcuménique », c'est-à-dire universel, et qu'il réunira, en plus des catholiques, d'autres responsables chrétiens, orthodoxes et protestants. Compte tenu des difficultés d'organisation, la première séance ne pourra se tenir qu'en 1962.

Triomphe pour *Ben Hur*

Ben Hur a fait plus d'entrées que tout autre film cette année. Charlton Heston joue Ben Hur, un prince juif qui se venge de son ennemi romain, Messala, joué par Stephen Boyd. Le film, réalisé par William Wyler, a coûté 15 millions de dollars. Le clou du spectacle est une course de chars qui dure trente minutes.

▼ *Ben Hur sur son char.*

Grand succès pour la Mini

La nouvelle Mini, lancée cet été par la British Motor Corporation démontre que ce ne sont pas obligatoirement les plus grosses voitures qui sont les mieux. Le concepteur, Alec Issigonis, a créé un véhicule à quatre places étonnamment spacieux dans une toute petite carrosserie. Avec une puissance de 850 cm^3, le petit moteur de la Mini, situé à l'avant, peut entraîner ce poids léger jusqu'à plus de 110 km/h. Les conducteurs impatients de l'essayer ont le choix entre deux modèles – l'Austin Seven et la Morris Mini Minor. L'unique différence est la forme de l'avant.

▶ *La Mini Minor de la British Motor Corporation.*

Johansson, champion du monde de boxe

▲ *L'arbitre arrête le combat au troisième round ; Johansson a mis Patterson K-O.*

▶ **26 juin 1959** ◀ Le boxeur suédois Ingemar Johansson a étonné les supporters du Yankee Stadium ce soir. Avec une facilité déconcertante, il a battu l'Américain Floyd Patterson, champion en titre, qu'il a envoyé sept fois au tapis pendant le troisième round. Johansson a remporté le championnat d'Europe des poids lourds de 1956, et a mis K-O le poids lourd américain Eddie Machen dès le premier round, l'an dernier. Cette victoire fait de lui le premier Suédois à remporter le titre mondial des poids lourds.

La guerre de la morue

▶ **30 avril 1959** ◀ Les hostilités sont ouvertes entre la Grande-Bretagne et l'Islande, au sujet de la pêche à la morue dans les eaux au large des côtes d'Islande. Cette « guerre de la morue », qui dure depuis neuf mois, fait rage : aujourd'hui, une canonnière a fait feu sur un chalutier britannique, l'*Arctic Viking*, le manquant de peu.

Le conflit a débuté l'été dernier, lorsque le gouvernement de Reykjavík a reculé la limite d'interdiction de pêche pour les chalutiers britanniques jusqu'à 19 kilomètres autour de l'île (contre 6,5 km auparavant). Mais les pêcheurs britanniques, soutenus par la Royal Navy, refusent de respecter les nouvelles restrictions et continuent de pêcher dans les eaux désormais interdites.

LES ADOLESCENTS

Dans les années 50, les adolescents ont leurs idées, leurs héros, leur musique et leur manière de s'habiller. Ils consacrent beaucoup de temps et d'argent aux loisirs (vêtements, disques et sorties).

Aux États-Unis, le terme *teenagers* désigne les adolescents entre 13 et 19 ans. Ils forment un monde à part, qui a ses propres valeurs. Un fossé de plus en plus important se creuse entre jeunes et moins jeunes.

Les adolescents
À la sortie du collège, les adolescents se dépêchent de rentrer chez eux pour écouter l'émission *Salut les copains*, apparue en septembre 1959 et diffusée chaque jour sur Europe n° 1. Animée par Daniel Filipacchi, elle s'adresse aux jeunes et leur parle des vedettes et des problèmes qui les intéressent.

La majorité à 18 ans est instaurée en France en 1974.

Le Hula-Hoop

Les jeunes Australiens s'amusaient déjà depuis longtemps à faire tourner autour de leur taille un cerceau en bambou, lorsque le *Hula-Hoop* fit son apparition aux États-Unis. Lancé en 1958 par une entreprise californienne, ce cerceau fait fureur chez les adolescents, se vendant à des centaines de millions d'exemplaires par an.

▼ *La jeune actrice Betty Lou Keim écoutant la musique d'un juke-box dans un café avec ses amis, dans les années 50.*

Des produits pour les adolescents

À la fin des années 50, les enfants du baby-boom arrivent à l'adolescence. Ils ont entre 13 et 19 ans. Journalistes, experts en marketing et publicitaires cherchent à les conquérir, car ils représentent un marché immense. Ils s'intéressent donc aux goûts et aux désirs des adolescents, pour leur proposer de nouveaux produits : revues, maquillage et surtout vêtements et motocyclettes.

Les adolescents s'identifient à des stars du rock et de la pop music, comme Elvis Presley, ou à des acteurs tels que James Dean, dont la vie leur semble refléter la leur, et dont les chansons et les films évoquent leurs problèmes. Ils suivent avec attention l'évolution de leurs idoles, qu'ils vont admirer au cinéma et en concert, achetant disques et magazines par millions. Ils ont leurs propres lieux de rencontre : cafés, boîtes de nuit, music-hall.

Des adolescents rebelles

Aux États-Unis, une partie des adolescents s'identifient à des acteurs qui incarnent la révolte. Un de leurs films culte est l'*Équipée sauvage*, où joue Marlon Brando. C'est le premier film sur les « voyous ». En avance sur la mode, il a lancé celle des blousons cloutés. À partir de ce film, Marlon Brando a construit son image de jeune homme farouche et révolté. La vie de James Dean, qui meurt en 1955, à l'âge de 24 ans, dans un accident de voiture, ressemble à celle du héros qu'il incarne dans *la Fureur de vivre*. Les musiciens s'en prennent eux aussi aux valeurs des adultes. Le mouvement des beatniks, né dans un quartier de New York, Greenwich Village, produit une nouvelle génération de chanteurs engagés, comme Bob Dylan et Joan Baez. Désormais, les jeunes vont critiquer ce à quoi leurs parents étaient attachés.

▶ *Beatniks à Greenwich Village, à New York. Les beatniks sont des adeptes de la* **beat generation,** *mouvement qui, à partir des années 50, rejette les institutions et les discours politiques classiques.*

▶ *James Dean dans sa voiture, en Californie. Les adolescents se retrouvent dans son attitude face à la vie.*

▲ *En arrière-plan, posters et souvenirs de James Dean ornant la chambre de l'une de ses jeunes fans.*

La musique techno

Pour se différencier des autres, les jeunes doivent sans cesse innover. Les musiques « techno », « jungle » et « acid house » se développent ainsi dans les années 80 et 90. Sur des paroles souvent crues, faisant allusion au sexe et à la drogue, elles combinent des rythmes lourds, des sons durs et saturés caractéristiques du rock punk et des sons électroniques.

▶ *Festival techno – The Love Parade – à Berlin, en 1995.*

De 1960 à 1969

1960
Les années 60 représentent l'apogée de la croissance. Les sciences et les techniques font des progrès spectaculaires, tandis qu'interviennent d'importants changements sociaux. La décolonisation s'achève.

En Occident, la musique rock fait son apparition. La mise en vente de la pilule contraceptive est une véritable révolution pour les femmes. En 1962, la crise de Cuba fait trembler pendant une semaine les États-Unis et l'Union soviétique, qui redoutent une guerre nucléaire. Après cette date, on assiste à un apaisement des relations Est-Ouest. L'Union soviétique et les États-Unis commencent leur conquête de l'espace, qui aboutit aux premiers pas de l'homme sur la lune.

John F. Kennedy, président des États-Unis

▶ 9 novembre 1960 ◀

Avec l'une des plus petites majorités de l'histoire politique américaine, John F. Kennedy, le candidat du parti démocrate, vient d'être élu président des États-Unis. Richard Nixon, son rival républicain, a reconnu sa défaite, un peu après 13 heures. Sur les 68 millions de suffrages exprimés, Kennedy a juste 118 000 voix d'avance ; à 43 ans, il est le plus jeune président et le premier président catholique des États-Unis. Sa campagne, basée sur le slogan « Faisons bouger à nouveau l'Amérique », a touché les Américains.

Pour la première fois, la télévision a joué un rôle important dans les élections, les candidats s'y étant affrontés à quatre reprises. Chaque fois, le débat a tourné en faveur de Kennedy, qui « passait mieux » à la télévision.

▼ J.F.K. et Jackie en campagne, à New York.

Mise en vente aux États-Unis d'une pilule contraceptive

Quatre ans après le début des tests médicaux, la pilule contraceptive Enovid-10 a été approuvée par la Food and Drug Administration. Cette pilule empêche l'ovulation en modifiant l'équilibre entre deux hormones, l'œstrogène et la progestérone. Inventée par le Dr Gregory Pincus, elle permet aux femmes de ne pas être enceintes.

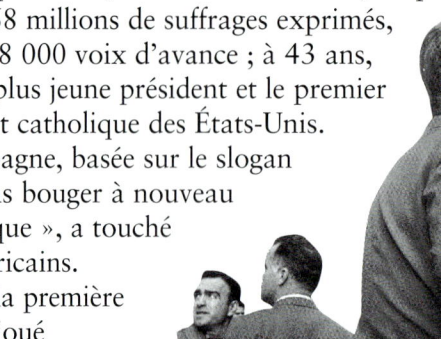

▲ La pilule contraceptive, qui doit être prise tous les jours, ne sera vraiment utilisable que dans quelques années.

Kennedy

- Le père du président Kennedy, Joseph Kennedy, autodidacte millionnaire, fut ambassadeur en Grande-Bretagne de 1936 à 1940.
- Pendant la Seconde Guerre mondiale, Kennedy qui servait dans la marine américaine, fut décoré pour avoir sauvé la vie de plusieurs marins.
- Ses frères Robert et Edward faisaient eux aussi de la politique.

1960-1969

Massacre à Sharpville, en Afrique du Sud

▲ *Manifestation à Sharpville contre les nouvelles lois qui obligent les Noirs à avoir un passeport intérieur.*

▶ **21 mars 1960** ◀ La police a ouvert le feu sur des manifestants dans la ville noire de Sharpville, près de Johannesburg, tuant 69 Africains et en blessant près de 200. Elle a apparemment tiré dans le dos de plusieurs manifestants. Des femmes et des enfants figurent parmi les victimes.

Ce qu'on appelle déjà le « massacre de Sharpville » marque le premier jour d'une campagne contre les nouvelles lois limitant les mouvements des Noirs d'Afrique du Sud.

Psychose, le nouveau film d'Hitchcock

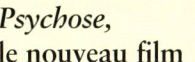

▲ *Janet Leigh.*

Psychose, le nouveau film du maître du suspense, Alfred Hitchcock, vient de sortir sur les écrans. Dans la scène la plus violente de ce film terrifiant, un inconnu frappe à plusieurs reprises Janet Leigh à travers le rideau de la douche ; la caméra montre l'eau teintée de sang qui s'écoule par la bonde. Norman Bates, le propriétaire névrosé du Bates Motel, est joué par Anthony Perkins.

Une femme Premier ministre à Ceylan

▶ **21 juillet 1960** ◀ Mme Sirimavo Bandaranaike devient Premier ministre de l'État de Ceylan (futur Sri Lanka) ; elle est la première femme à assumer cette fonction. Elle est entrée dans la politique l'année dernière, après l'assassinat de son mari, lui-même Premier ministre.

Âgée de 43 ans, elle dirige le parti socialiste de Ceylan qui détient la moitié des 150 sièges au Parlement et souhaite former une coalition avec le parti marxiste, minoritaire.

▲ *Sirimavo Bandaranaike.*

Les Soviétiques abattent un avion américain U2

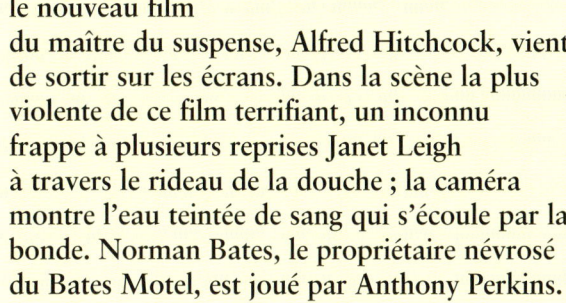

▼ *Jusqu'à il y a peu, l'avion espion américain U2 ne pouvait être intercepté par aucun autre avion.*

▼ *Le pilote américain Powers, condamné pour espionnage.*

▶ **19 août 1960** ◀ La condamnation, à Moscou, d'un espion américain à dix ans de détention porte un coup sévère à la politique étrangère américaine.

Le pilote Francis Gary Powers, abattu le 1er mai au-dessus de Sverdlovsk, alors qu'il effectuait une mission pour les services secrets américains à bord d'un avion U2, risque trois ans de prison et sept ans de travaux forcés. L'U2, qui est équipé d'un matériel photographique et électronique ultra-perfectionné, et peut voler à 21 300 m d'altitude, était supposé être hors de portée des avions et des missiles. Bien que les Américains nient toute activité d'espionnage aérien, le Premier ministre soviétique Nikita Khrouchtchev a annulé la conférence au sommet prévue à Paris avec le président américain Eisenhower. Il a montré des débris de l'appareil et des pellicules prouvant que la CIA avait photographié du ciel les aires d'aviation et les bases militaires soviétiques.

1960

▼ *Explosion de joie au Congo, alors que les forces belges se préparent à quitter l'Afrique.*

En 1960 aussi...

13 février • Première expérience nucléaire française.

2 avril • Mise sur orbite du premier satellite météo américain Tiros I.

11 mai • Lancement du paquebot *France*.

11 octobre • Inejiro Asanuma, le dirigeant du parti socialiste japonais, est assassiné.

14 décembre • Création de l'OCDE, une organisation qui regroupe les pays les plus riches.

Indépendance de plusieurs États africains

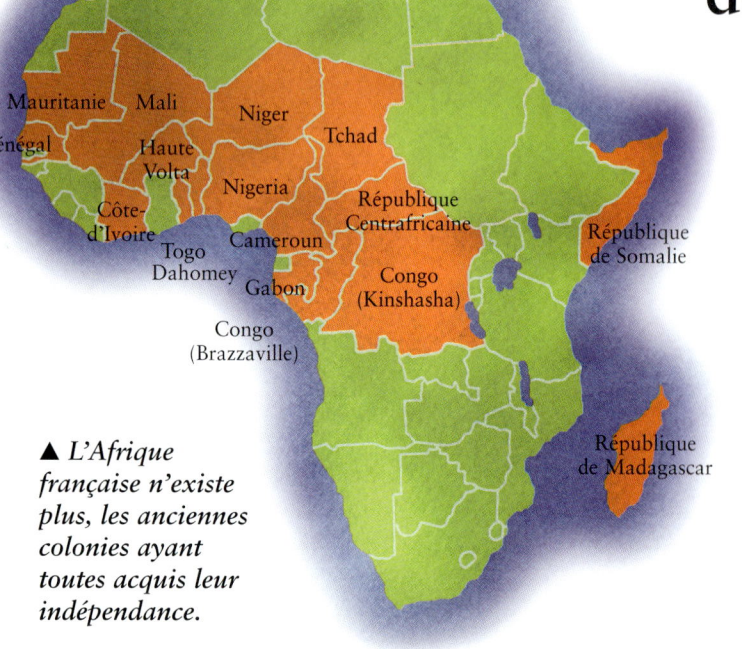

▲ *L'Afrique française n'existe plus, les anciennes colonies ayant toutes acquis leur indépendance.*

▶ **1ᵉʳ octobre 1960** ◀ Le Nigeria vient de rejoindre les rangs de plus en plus nombreux des nations qui n'appartiennent plus aux empires européens. D'ici à quelques années, plusieurs colonies britanniques, dont l'Ouganda, la Zambie et le Kenya, devraient être indépendantes. La France, quant à elle, est en train de renoncer à ses colonies en Afrique occidentale et centrale – Mauritanie, Mali, Sénégal, Côte-d'Ivoire, Haute-Volta, Niger, Tchad, Togo, Cameroun, Gabon et République centrafricaine.

La carte politique de l'Afrique change si vite qu'il est difficile de croire qu'il y a tout juste 40 ans sept pays d'Europe occidentale gouvernaient près de 700 millions de personnes dans les colonies d'outre-mer. Certains craignent la résurgence d'anciennes dissensions dans les pays qui viennent d'accéder à l'indépendance. Bon nombre de ces nouveaux États devront rester en relation avec l'ancien pouvoir impérial pour consolider leur avenir. Si l'on reproche aux Belges d'avoir laissé le Congo dans un état chaotique propice à la guerre civile, les anciennes colonies britanniques sont intégrées dans le Commonwealth, et les anciennes colonies françaises, dans la CFA (Communautés françaises d'Afrique).

Indépendance de Chypre

▶ **16 août 1960** ◀ Hier soir, à minuit, Chypre est devenue une république, après 81 ans de domination britannique. Mgr Makários, l'archevêque de Chypre, est le premier président de la nouvelle République, et le Chypriote turc, le Dr Kutchuk, vice-président. Depuis 1955, les nationalistes grecs chypriotes luttent pour l'Enôsis – l'union avec la Grèce. On espère toutefois que le nouveau gouvernement sera capable d'assurer la paix sur l'île.

1960 – 1969

Médailles d'or pour Wilma Rudolph

▶ **11 septembre 1960** ◀ L'Américaine Wilma Rudolph, originaire du Tennessee, vient de se couvrir de gloire aux jeux Olympiques de Rome, remportant trois médailles d'or (100 m, 200 m et relais 4 × 100 m). Ce triomphe est d'autant plus extraordinaire que, atteinte de la poliomyélite, Wilma n'a pu marcher correctement qu'à l'âge de 8 ans. Les autres héros des Jeux sont l'Éthiopien aux pieds nus Abebe Bikila, qui a remporté le marathon, et le jeune boxeur américain de 18 ans Cassius Clay.

▼ *Wilma Rudolph en pleine action.*

Auguste Piccard atteint 10 916 m sous la mer

Le 23 janvier, l'ingénieur suisse Auguste Piccard et le lieutenant américain Don Walsh ont atteint la profondeur record de 10 916 m dans la fosse Guam, aux Philippines. Avec leur bathyscaphe, *Trieste,* ils ont mis exactement 4 h 48 min pour descendre jusqu'au fond de la mer.

Mort de l'écrivain français Albert Camus

▶ **4 janvier 1960** ◀ L'écrivain français Albert Camus est mort, ce matin, dans un accident de la route. La voiture, qui était conduite par Michel Gallimard, a perdu une roue. Celui-ci s'est tué également. Né en Algérie en 1913, Camus a publié de nombreux romans et essais, dont *l'Étranger, le Mythe de Sisyphe, la Peste, l'Homme révolté* et *le Malentendu.* Prix Nobel de littérature en 1957, cet écrivain et philosophe s'interrogeait sur la condition humaine et le sens de la vie. Sa mort suscite une vive émotion dans le monde entier, où il était admiré par les jeunes et les intellectuels.

▲ *Équipe du Real Madrid.*

Le Real Madrid remporte sa cinquième coupe d'Europe

▶ **18 mai 1960** ◀ Le Real Madrid vient de remporter sa cinquième coupe d'Europe des clubs champions en battant l'Eintracht de Francfort par 7 buts à 3, devant 135 000 spectateurs rassemblés au Hampden Park.

▲ *Le bathyscaphe* Trieste.

Brasília, nouvelle capitale du Brésil

▶ **21 mars 1960** ◀ La capitale du Brésil n'est plus Rio. C'est maintenant Brasília, qui est située à 1 000 km au nord de Rio de Janeiro, dans l'État du Goiás, sur le plateau central du Brésil. Cette nouvelle ville, conçue par les architectes Lúcio Costa et Oscar Niemeyer, est une réussite parfaite. Niemeyer a su donner à l'ensemble une unité plastique. Sa fameuse place des Trois-Pouvoirs, en forme de triangle, rassemble d'un côté la cour de justice, de l'autre le palais du Planalto, et, enfin, le Parlement. L'architecture d'avant-garde de nombreux bâtiments officiels est remarquable.

◀ *La place des Trois-Pouvoirs, à Brasília, dessinée par Niemeyer.*

1960

1961

1961

Le mur de Berlin

▶ 16 août 1961 ◀ La population de Berlin se réveille dans une ville coupée en deux par un mur de 49 km de long et de 1,5 m de haut. Il a été construit durant la nuit. Pendant une semaine, quelques personnes parviendront encore à le franchir. Ce mur a été édifié par les autorités communistes de Berlin-Est pour enrayer le flot d'Allemands de l'Est qui, refusant le communisme, s'enfuient à l'Ouest. Plus de 45 000 personnes se sont réfugiées à Berlin-Ouest avant que les troupes de Berlin-Est ne hérissent ce sinistre mur de fils barbelés.

Les protestations occidentales contre la violation du statut de Berlin, ville libre contrôlée par les quatre vainqueurs de la Seconde Guerre mondiale, sont restées vaines. La force armée répond aux protestations des Berlinois. Tandis que les autorités de la RDA renforcent le mur de Berlin par des tours de guet et des postes armés, les puissances occidentales (France, États-Unis et Grande-Bretagne) s'apprêtent à placer des troupes le long du mur, côté ouest. Bien que Willy Brandt, le chancelier de Berlin-Ouest, ait affirmé aux Berlinois de l'Est qu'ils ne seraient pas emprisonnés à vie, le « rideau de fer » entre l'Est et l'Ouest est devenu une triste réalité.

1962

1963

1964

▲ *Le mur formé de blocs de ciment préfabriqués qui coupe Berlin en deux a été édifié très rapidement.*

▶ *Un soldat de RDA passant à l'Ouest pendant la construction du mur de Berlin.*

1965

Johnny Hallyday

Un chanteur de dix-sept ans bouleverse les variétés françaises. Né Jean Philippe Smet, il se fait appeler Johnny, comme les chanteurs de rock américain, qu'il admire tant. Toute la presse s'accorde pour voir en lui la nouvelle idole des jeunes. D'ailleurs, ses premiers fans copient déjà ses chemises à carreaux, ses jeans et ses santiags.

1966

1967

Mort accidentelle du secrétaire général des Nations unies

▶ 18 septembre 1961 ◀ Dag Hammarskjöld, le secrétaire général des Nations unies, a trouvé la mort, tôt ce matin, dans un accident d'avion. Le DC-6 qui le transportait en Afrique pour rencontrer le chef des rebelles togolais Moïse Tschombé s'est écrasé près de Ndola, dans le nord de la Rhodésie.

Le diplomate suédois, âgé de 56 ans, était secrétaire des Nations unies depuis 1953. Ses interventions dans la crise du canal de Suez en 1956 et dans la crise de Jordanie en 1958 lui ont valu la réputation d'ardent défenseur de la paix. Mais l'envoi de Casques bleus au Congo, l'an dernier, pour empêcher les forces de Tschombé de créer un État indépendant est critiqué par les délégués soviétiques et occidentaux. Doué d'un grand sens diplomatique, Hammarskjöld sera profondément regretté.

▼ *Hammarskjöld, le secrétaire général de l'ONU.*

1968

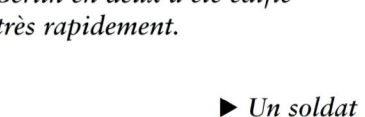

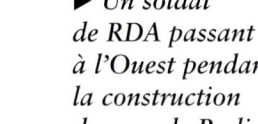

1969

1960 – 1969

Échec américain dans la baie des Cochons

▶ 19 avril 1961 ◀

Le 17 avril, 1 500 exilés cubains – entraînés et équipés par la CIA – débarquaient à Cuba, dans la baie des Cochons, pour évincer Castro.

Ils n'ont pu résister aux chasseurs MIG, ni aux chars de Castro fabriqués par les Russes. Cet échec embarrasse profondément les États-Unis.

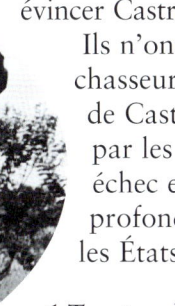

◀ *Troupes de Fidel Castro victorieuses.*

West Side Story au cinéma

West Side Story, la comédie musicale créée à Broadway en 1957 par Stephen Sondheim et Leonard Bernstein, sort sur les écrans. Natalie Wood et Richard Beymer sont les vedettes de ce moderne *Roméo et Juliette* transposé à New York sur fond d'affrontements entre bandes de jeunes rivales. George Chakiris et Rita Moreno sont de parfaits seconds rôles.

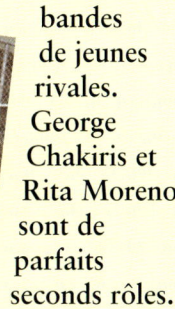

◀ *Danses dans West Side Story.*

L'Afrique du Sud quitte le Commonwealth

▶ 31 mai 1961 ◀

À la suite d'un référendum organisé auprès des électeurs blancs, l'Union de l'Afrique du Sud décide de quitter le Commonwealth et devient une république. En effet, le Commonwealth, dont le chef est la reine d'Angleterre, a condamné la politique d'apartheid. Les dirigeants politiques noirs commencent la lutte contre les Blancs.

Gagarine, le premier homme dans l'espace

▶ 12 avril 1961 ◀

L'URSS a battu l'Amérique dans la conquête de l'espace. Le pilote soviétique Iouri Gagarine a fait aujourd'hui le tour de la Terre à bord d'une fusée Vostok I. Il a décollé à 9 h 07 de la base de Baïkonour, au Kazakhstan. Il a atterri 1 h 48 min plus tard, près de Saratov, en Russie.

Gagarine affirme qu'il a très bien supporté les phases d'accélération et de décélération intenses du décollage et de l'atterrissage.

▲ *Le Premier ministre du Congo, Patrice Lumumba, avant sa mort.*

Guerre civile au Congo

▶ 21 décembre 1961 ◀

La reddition du chef des rebelles katangais Moïse Tschombé, qui lutte pour la sécession du Katanga, marque la fin d'une année agitée au Congo. En janvier, le Premier ministre du Congo, Patrice Lumumba, a trouvé la mort dans des conditions mystérieuses (assassiné sans doute par des Katangais). Alors que l'opinion africaine est plutôt d'accord pour que les forces de l'ONU soutiennent l'armée congolaise, les pays occidentaux et l'Union soviétique déclarent que les Casques bleus n'auraient pas dû intervenir dans le conflit.

▶ *Iouri Gagarine, le premier homme dans l'espace.*

1961

Échec de la « marche de la liberté »

▶ 14 mai 1961 ◀ Dans le sud des États-Unis, des militants antiracistes empruntent les bus, pour vérifier si les lois fédérales sur l'intégration dans les transports publics sont respectées. À Montgomery, en Alabama, des Blancs racistes, aidés par des membres du Ku Klux Klan, ont tenté de brûler un bus et d'en bloquer la sortie, frappant les « marcheurs de la liberté » à coups de matraque.

Robert Kennedy, le ministre de la Justice des États-Unis, a envoyé des officiers de la police fédérale à Montgomery. Le pasteur Martin Luther King appelle à poursuivre la lutte pour l'égalité des droits. Le Dr King avait lancé la campagne de boycott des bus en 1955, en Alabama : on avait alors arrêté 500 manifestants noirs qui protestaient contre la ségrégation raciale dans les bus. Le Dr King, qui sait parler aux foules, affirme que « la résistance passive et l'amour » sont les meilleurs moyens pour lutter contre le racisme.

◀ *Un policier d'une ville du sud des États-Unis ceinture un « marcheur de la liberté ».*

Premier album d'Astérix

Astérix le Gaulois est apparu en 1957 dans le journal *Pilote*. Il est aujourd'hui familier à tous les amateurs de bande dessinée. Ses créateurs, le dessinateur Albert Uderzo et l'écrivain René Goscinny, ont publié le premier ouvrage qui met en scène le combattant de la liberté et ses amis Obélix et Idéfix.

▲ *Les créateurs d'Astérix.*

Création d'Amnesty International

▶ 28 mai 1961 ◀ L'avocat britannique Peter Benenson a décidé d'agir en apprenant la condamnation de deux étudiants portugais à sept ans de prison pour avoir porté un toast à la liberté. Il lance une campagne en faveur des droits de l'homme. Selon Benenson, des milliers de gens sont emprisonnés et torturés, parce qu'ils expriment des idées qui diffèrent de celles de leur gouvernement. Or, selon la Déclaration universelle des droits de l'homme, chacun a droit à la liberté de parole, de croyance, de pensée et d'opinion. L'organisation luttera pour permettre à chacun d'avoir un procès juste et pour obtenir la liberté de tous les gens victimes d'injustices, dans le monde entier.

▶ *Le symbole d'Amnesty, la bougie de l'espoir entourée d'un fil de fer barbelé.*

Les dalmatiens, héros de Walt Disney

Le dernier-né des studios Disney est une magnifique adaptation d'un célèbre conte pour enfants, *les 101 Dalmatiens*.
Les enfants seront passionnés par les aventures de ces adorables chiens qui cherchent à échapper à Cruella, le personnage féminin le plus méchant depuis la sorcière de *Blanche-Neige*.

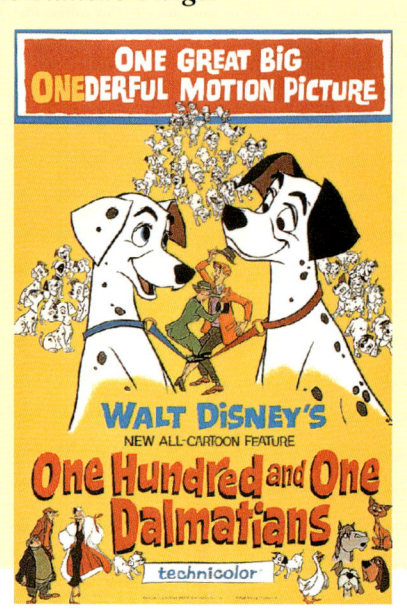

1960 – 1969

Le nazi Eichmann condamné à mort

▶ **15 décembre 1961** ◀ Adolf Eichmann, un ancien colonel allemand SS, est condamné à mort, à Jérusalem. Il était chargé de transporter des millions de Juifs et d'autres « indésirables » vers les camps de la mort, pendant la Seconde Guerre mondiale. Son procès a débuté en avril. Eichmann a été enlevé à Buenos Aires par des agents secrets israéliens, l'année dernière. Les dépositions des témoins et des 90 rescapés des camps ont touché le monde entier. Eichmann a dit qu'il était un modeste exécutant, mais les juges ont estimé qu'il avait joué un rôle clé dans l'extermination des Juifs.

▲ *Adolf Eichmann.*

▲ *Le Vasa repêché.*

Renflouement d'un bateau du XVIIᵉ siècle

▶ **24 avril 1961** ◀ La foule est rassemblée dans le port de Stockholm, attendant avec impatience que le *Vasa* remonte à la surface. Pendant l'été 1628, le bateau a chaviré, devant les habitants de Stockholm venus assister au départ. À l'époque, le *Vasa* était le bâtiment de guerre le plus cher et le plus important que la Suède ait jamais construit. Nul n'a été puni pour ce désastre – où 50 personnes se sont noyées –, car on n'a pas pu déterminer qui était le responsable. Aujourd'hui, les chercheurs vont tenter d'expliquer pourquoi le bateau a sombré.

Découverte du crâne d'Olduvai

▶ **24 février 1961** ◀ Les chercheurs Louis et Mary Leakey analysent les ossements découverts dans la gorge d'Olduvai, en Tanzanie. S'il s'agit d'un hominidé, il prouve que les origines de l'homme remontent à 1,25 million d'année.

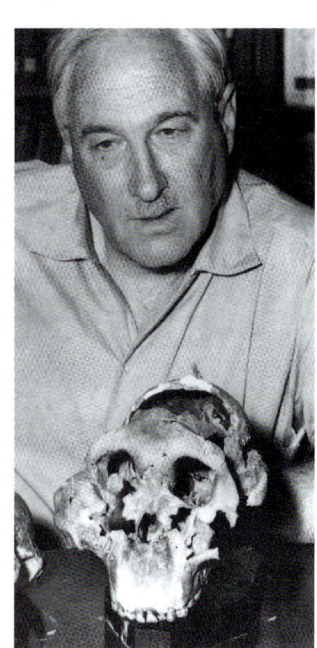

▶ *Louis Leakey et le crâne d'Olduvai.*

En 1961 aussi...

5 mai • *Alan Shepard est le premier astronaute américain. Il effectue un vol de quinze minutes dans l'espace.*

4 juin • *Le président américain Kennedy et le dirigeant soviétique Khrouchtchev se rencontrent à Vienne, pour une entrevue.*

Rudolf Noureïev choisit l'Occident

▶ **16 juin 1961** ◀ Le danseur étoile soviétique Rudolf Noureïev choisit la liberté. Juste avant de monter dans un avion pour Londres à l'aéroport du Bourget, il a échappé à la surveillance de ses « camarades » en faisant un bond gigantesque au-dessus des barrières de la douane. Le gouvernement français lui a accordé l'asile politique. Des représentants de l'Union soviétique ont essayé en vain de le convaincre de rentrer en URSS. Rudolf Noureïev, danseur du ballet Kirov, a un style étonnant qui associe prouesses techniques et virtuosité. C'est un très grand danseur et il est assuré d'obtenir des engagements en Occident.

▶ *Le virtuose de la danse Rudolf Noureïev.*

1962

La thalidomide responsable de graves malformations

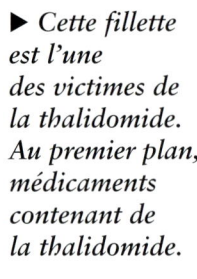

▶ *Cette fillette est l'une des victimes de la thalidomide. Au premier plan, médicaments contenant de la thalidomide.*

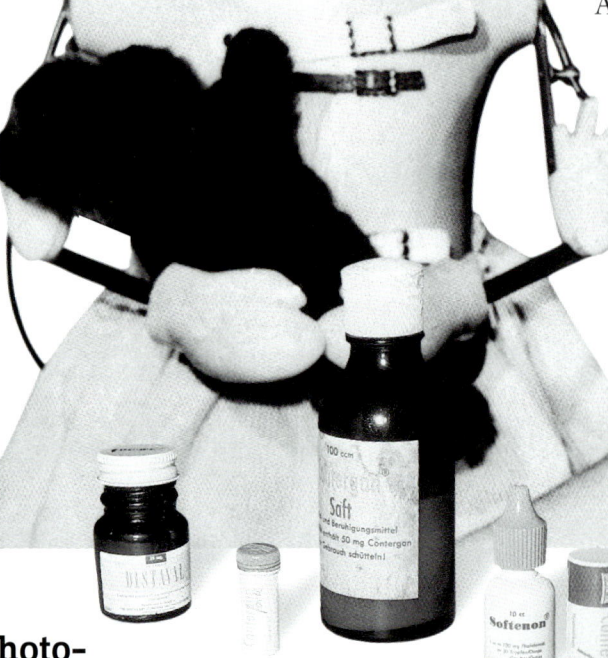

▶ **5 novembre 1962** ◀ Une famille belge et son médecin, accusés d'avoir empoisonné la petite Corinne Van de Put, née sans bras, viennent d'être acquittés. Ils avaient fait ce geste pour épargner de trop grandes souffrances à la petite fille. Au cours de sa grossesse, sa mère avait pris un sédatif contenant de la thalidomide. On sait aujourd'hui que la thalidomide est responsable de malformations des poumons ou des organes internes. De nombreux bébés dont la mère avait absorbé ce produit sont nés avec des malformations de l'oreille et de l'estomac, ou sans bras. 500 bébés sont nés ainsi aux États-Unis et 3 000 en Allemagne. La thalidomide, qui a été mise en vente en 1959, a été prescrite par des médecins dans ces deux pays pour des troubles mineurs : mal de dos, insomnie, fatigue, état dépressif… Elle a bien sûr été immédiatement retirée de la vente, dès que l'on s'est aperçu de son lien direct avec les malformations.

Photographies de Vénus

La sonde américaine Mariner 2 a envoyé ses premières photos de Vénus le 14 décembre. On sait peu de choses de cette planète, du fait de son atmosphère très dense contenant 96 % de CO_2, 3 % d'azote, et des traces de vapeur d'eau, d'argon et de néon. Le gaz carbonique piège la chaleur du soleil et crée une fournaise de 460 °C à la surface de la planète.

En 1962 aussi...

14 janvier • Épidémie de variole en Grande-Bretagne.

24 janvier • Première mondiale du film du réalisateur français François Truffaut *Jules et Jim*.

14 avril • Georges Pompidou est Premier ministre en France.

17 juin • Le Brésil remporte la Coupe du monde de football.

11 octobre • Ouverture du concile Vatican II, à Rome.

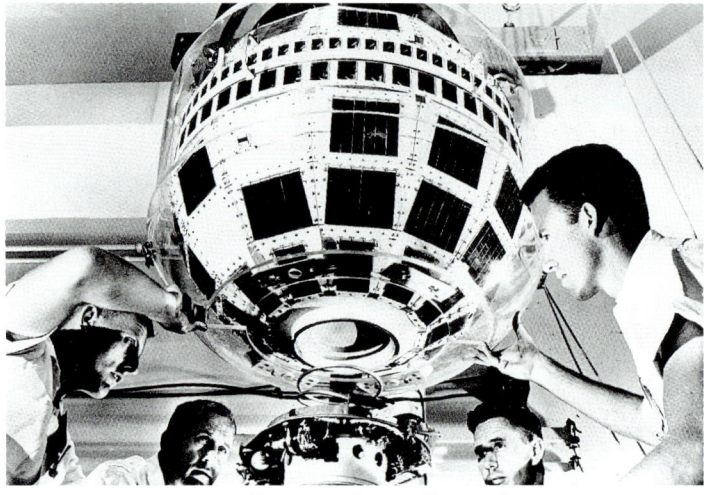

▲ *Techniciens travaillant sur le satellite Telstar.*

Le satellite Telstar

▶ **11 juillet 1962** ◀ La première émission de télévision en Mondiovision a été produite aujourd'hui, grâce au satellite Telstar, lancé hier par l'American Telephone and Telegraph Company. Ce satellite a envoyé des images en noir et blanc depuis Andover, dans l'État du Maine (États-Unis), aux stations de Goonhilly Downs, Cornwall, et de Pleumeur-Boudou en Bretagne (France). La France a envoyé, pour les Américains, des images d'Yves Montand en train de chanter. Ce satellite devrait révolutionner la télévision en permettant de retransmettre des émissions dans le monde entier.

1960 – 1969

▲ *Femmes s'entraînant pendant la guerre sino-indienne.*

Le conflit sino-indien

▶ 21 novembre 1962 ◀ Après la prise de Bomdila, une ville située à la frontière de l'Inde, l'armée chinoise a stoppé son avance. Un cessez-le-feu a été signé, et des discussions s'engagent au sujet du territoire jouxtant la frontière de l'Himalaya, pour mettre un terme à la guerre. L'armée indienne, qui a perdu une grande partie des territoires montagneux du Nord, ne peut que reconnaître sa défaite. Cette zone restera une zone de tensions entre la Chine et l'Inde.

Indépendance de l'Algérie

▶ 3 juillet 1962 ◀ Après plus d'un siècle de domination française et des années de conflits, l'Algérie va devenir indépendante. Plus de 99 % des votants algériens ont dit oui à l'indépendance, lors du référendum organisé il y a deux jours, conformément aux accords d'Évian, signés par Louis Joxe et Benyoussef Ben Kheddah, représentant le gouvernement algérien. Le président français Charles de Gaulle a reconnu solennellement aujourd'hui les résultats du référendum ; demain, l'Algérie deviendra un État souverain indépendant.

◀ *Affiche appelant à la paix.*

▼ *Ben Bella, dirigeant du FLN, participe au scrutin. Il sera élu Président de la République en 1963.*

Suicide de Marilyn Monroe

▶ 5 août 1962 ◀ Le corps de Marilyn Monroe a été découvert, ce matin, dans son appartement de Hollywood. La star de *Certains l'aiment chaud* et d'*Arrêt d'autobus* a été retrouvée nue dans son lit, tenant à la main un tube de somnifères et le téléphone. De son vrai nom Norma Jean Baker ou Mortenson, elle avait eu une enfance difficile et s'était mariée trois fois, la première fois à 16 ans. Son deuxième mariage, avec le célèbre joueur de base-ball Joe DiMaggio, avait duré neuf mois. Son troisième mari était l'écrivain Arthur Miller (Prix Pulitzer), qui a écrit le scénario de son dernier film, *les Désaxés*.

◀ *Marilyn Monroe, la star de Hollywood.*

▶ *Affiche publicitaire d'Andy Warhol pour les boîtes de soupe Campbell.*

Les affiches d'Andy Warhol

Une exposition des œuvres d'Andy Warhol, le représentant du pop' art, s'ouvre à New York, avec, entre autres, ses représentations des boîtes de soupe Campbell, des bouteilles de Coca-Cola et des boîtes de savon Brillo. Né à Pittsburgh, il a étudié le dessin au Carnegie Institute of Technology, puis s'est installé à New York, comme dessinateur publicitaire.

1962

Crise de Cuba

▶ **28 octobre 1962** ◀ Jamais on n'avait frôlé de si près la guerre nucléaire. La crise de Cuba vient de trouver un règlement pacifique. Cette crise couvait depuis mai 1960, date à laquelle Khrouchtchev promit de défendre Cuba contre une éventuelle attaque américaine. Les Soviétiques avaient alors installé des bases de lancement de missiles longue portée, menaçant la côte est des États-Unis.

Le 29 août 1962, des avions espions U2 américains détectent la présence de techniciens soviétiques et la construction de nouvelles bases militaires.

Le 16 octobre, le président Kennedy reçoit des photos des bases de lancement. Il ordonne alors le blocus de Cuba et annonce que les troupes américaines s'empareront des armes offensives et du matériel que les navires soviétiques essaieront de livrer.

Le 24 octobre, les bateaux font demi-tour, mais les bases de lancement restent en activité. Des messages sont échangés entre Kennedy et Khrouchtchev. La tension est à son comble. Finalement, un accord est trouvé : il prévoit le démontage des bases de lancement soviétiques et le rapatriement des missiles en Union soviétique. En échange, Kennedy promet de ne plus jamais tenter d'envahir Cuba. La crise est terminée.

▲ Photo aérienne d'une base de lancement de missiles soviétiques à Cuba.

▶ J.F.K. s'expliquant à la télévision sur le blocus de Cuba.

Premier voyage en aéroglisseur

En ce mois de juillet, 24 passagers viennent de traverser pour la première fois la rivière Dee, entre Rhyl et Wallasey, à bord d'un aéroglisseur britannique. Celui-ci, qui transportait également du courrier, peut circuler aussi bien sur la terre que sur l'eau, grâce au coussin d'air supportant son poids.

Émeute raciste à l'université du Mississippi

▶ **30 septembre 1962** ◀ James Meredith est le premier étudiant noir admis à l'université du Mississippi, dans le sud des États-Unis. Son admission a été entérinée par le University Board of Trustees, conformément à la nouvelle loi interdisant la ségrégation.
Des troupes envoyées par le gouverneur du Mississippi, Ross Barnett, ont empêché Meredith d'entrer dans l'université.
Le président Kennedy a ordonné à la police fédérale d'escorter l'étudiant jusque dans sa classe. Deux personnes ont été tuées, et 28 policiers, blessés, lorsque des Blancs, furieux, encouragés par l'intervention des troupes de Barnett, envahirent l'université pour protester contre l'admission de Meredith.

Le Pan Am Building

▶ **1962** ◀ Le Pan Am Building, construit pour la compagnie américaine de transport aérien Pan American Airways, a été inauguré à New York. Conçu par Emery Roth & Sons, Pietro Belluschi et Walter Gropius, cet édifice de 59 étages domine Park Avenue, entre le New York Central Building et le Grand Central Terminal. Avec la construction de cet immense bâtiment octogonal en béton, l'architecture moderne fait son apparition dans l'une des plus prestigieuses avenues de New York.

▶ *Vue aérienne du Pan Am Building.*

Lancement de la marque Yves Saint Laurent

▶ **15 janvier 1962** ◀ Le protégé de Christian Dior, Yves Saint Laurent, vient d'ouvrir sa propre maison de couture à Paris. Né en Algérie en 1936, Saint Laurent n'a que 21 ans lorsqu'il succède à Christian Dior, célèbre dans le monde entier pour son style novateur baptisé new-look. À son arrivée chez Dior, on reproche à Saint Laurent ses couleurs trop flamboyantes, dues sans doute à ses débuts comme styliste pour des costumes de théâtre. En créant sa propre marque, YSL peut donner libre cours à ses penchants. Abandonnant les jupes courtes, qui lui ont valu tant de critiques, il lance le tailleur – avec pantalon pour femme – et s'intéresse autant aux tenues de ville qu'au sportswear. La marque Saint Laurent est synonyme d'élégance et de sophistication. Les vêtements de la « ligne A », à taille relativement marquée et fabriqués dans des tissus délicats, remportent un grand succès.

▼ *Yves Saint Laurent, entouré de quelques-uns de ses mannequins, lors d'un défilé.*

1960 – 1969

James Bond débute à l'écran

« 007 », le héros créé par l'écrivain anglais Ian Fleming, vient de faire son apparition sur les écrans, dans *James Bond 007 contre Dr No,* avec Sean Connery et Ursula Andress. Fleming a déjà écrit 12 romans policiers racontant les aventures de James Bond. L'adaptation cinématographique de deux d'entre eux, *Bons baisers de Russie* et *Goldfinger,* est déjà en cours.

Le vote en France

▶ **28 octobre 1962** ◀ En avril, le Premier ministre, Michel Debré, hostile à l'indépendance de l'Algérie, a été remplacé par Georges Pompidou, inconnu dans la classe politique. Puis, les centristes se sont déclarés contre le gouvernement, car ils estiment que le Général n'est pas assez favorable à l'Europe. Le 22 août, de Gaulle a échappé à un attentat organisé par des partisans de l'Algérie française ; il décide alors que l'autorité du président, élu jusque-là par des notables, doit venir directement du peuple, donc du suffrage universel. Furieux, les députés votent une motion de censure. Mais de Gaulle dissout l'Assemblée et organise un référendum. Le vote des Français vient de lui donner raison.

AGENTS SECRETS ET ESPIONS

Qu'est-ce qu'un espion ? Un héros à la James Bond ou une jeune fille communiquant en morse avec un pays étranger ? En réalité, il existe toutes sortes d'espions, depuis les agents expérimentés menant une vie « normale » sous une fausse identité jusqu'aux amateurs, recrutés plus ou moins de leur plein gré.

Certains espions travaillent pour de l'argent, d'autres par conviction personnelle, tels certains sympathisants communistes vivant en Occident et divulguant des secrets de la Défense à l'URSS. Ils agissent seuls ou font partie d'un réseau, comme celui de Richard Sorge, un agent allemand travaillant au Japon en 1941.

◀ *De haut en bas : MacLean, Philby, Fuchs, Blunt et Penkovski, célèbres espions en activité pendant la guerre froide.*

Les espions de la guerre froide

De 1945 à 1989, le bloc soviétique s'oppose aux États-Unis et à leurs alliés. Cette période, la guerre froide, ne débouche jamais sur un affrontement direct, mais, dans l'ombre, les agents secrets ne cessent de lutter les uns contre les autres.

Les Russes recrutent ces derniers parmi les sympathisants communistes. Donald MacLean, diplomate britannique à Washington, livre aux Russes des informations confidentielles. « Kim » Philby obtient un grade élevé dans les services secrets britanniques (M16), tout en travaillant pour les Soviétiques. Le physicien allemand Klaus Fuchs, émigré en Angleterre, participe au développement ultrasecret de la bombe atomique et livre des informations techniques à un agent russe. Anthony Blunt, historien d'art anglais, informe les Russes, tout en travaillant pour les services secrets anglais pendant la Seconde Guerre mondiale. Maître de conférences à Cambridge, il recrute des agents pour les services secrets soviétiques. L'Ouest trouve, de la même manière, des sympathisants en Union soviétique. Oleg Penkovski, un colonel des services de renseignements soviétiques (GRU), travaille pour les Britanniques en 1961. Il est arrêté, jugé et exécuté pour haute trahison en 1963.

▼ *Julius et Ethel Rosenberg, des savants atomistes américains, sont exécutés en 1953.*

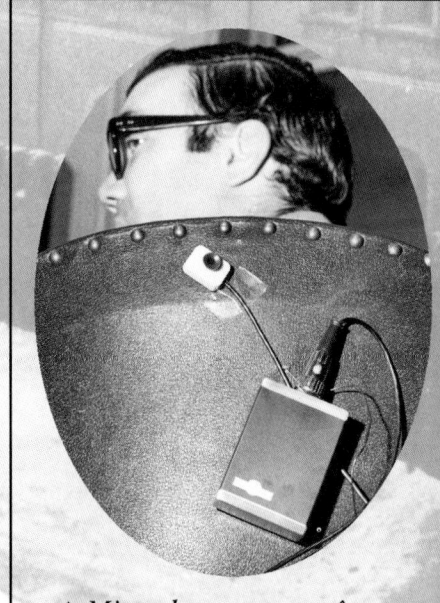

▲ *Microphone pouvant être fixé au dos d'une chaise.*

▼ Elizabeth Schragmüller, espionne en Belgique pendant la Première Guerre mondiale, livre aux Allemands des informations secrètes sur la France.

Les agents secrets et les espions

Les États-Unis, sous l'impulsion du sénateur McCarthy, se livrent à une « chasse aux sorcières » contre les communistes. Les victimes les plus célèbres sont les époux Rosenberg, condamnés pour avoir livré à l'URSS les secrets de la bombe A.

En Russie, durant la guerre froide, une ville « américaine » fut construite pour entraîner les espions en service aux États-Unis.

« Espions » au féminin

L'un des premiers « agents doubles » féminins est Dalila, la femme de Samson, qui révèle aux Philistins le secret de la force de son mari... Quelques femmes figurent parmi les meilleurs agents secrets de l'Histoire, peut-être parce que, à une époque où, institutionnellement, l'homme domine, la femme sait parfaitement user de son charme et de sa force de persuasion pour obtenir ce qu'elle veut.

Bien que très célèbre, Mata Hari n'est pas une espionne très efficace. Comme Dalila, sa force réside dans son charme. Née en Hollande, Margaretha Geertruida Zelle est une danseuse mondialement connue, entretenue par de nombreux amants. Pendant la Première Guerre mondiale, Mata Hari voyage en Europe, fréquentant des dignitaires importants des deux camps. Elle livre à des amis travaillant dans les services secrets allemands des informations secrètes concernant les Alliés. Elle est arrêtée par les Français en 1917 et accusée d'espionnage. Jugée par un tribunal militaire, et condamnée, elle est fusillée.

▲ En arrière-plan, le Kremlin, en 1945, est une véritable forteresse où siège le gouvernement russe.

▶ La séduisante Mata Hari exécutant une danse orientale.

Un matériel sophistiqué

La mission des espions est de transmettre des informations secrètes. Aussi, des techniques de communication ultramodernes sont utilisées. Fini le temps où les espions se promenaient avec de fausses moustaches... Pendant la Seconde Guerre mondiale, des agents de la Résistance contactent Londres avec une radio cachée dans une valise ; trente ans plus tard, les espions disposent de radios de la taille d'une boîte d'allumettes. Pendant la guerre du Viêt-nam, un agent secret est arrêté, car son domestique (agent du camp adverse) avait caché un microphone dans un bouton de sa chemise.

▲ Message secret caché dans un lacet de chaussure.

▶ Appareil photo dissimulé sous un chapeau.

▶ Ce sac de femme est en réalité un appareil photo.

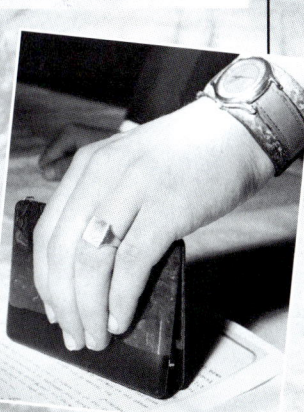

1963

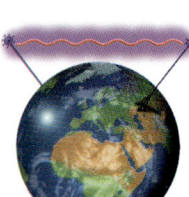

Discours de Martin Luther King

▶ **28 août 1963** ◀ Plus de 250 000 personnes ont défilé dans les rues de Washington et se sont rassemblées sous la statue de Lincoln, après la plus grande marche de l'histoire pour la reconnaissance des droits civiques. Le pasteur noir Martin Luther King s'est adressé à la foule, parmi laquelle Judy Garland, Marlon Brando, Burt Lancaster et Bob Dylan.

« *I have a dream* [je fais un rêve], a-t-il déclaré. Je fais le rêve qu'un jour sur les collines rouges de Géorgie, les fils d'esclaves et les fils des anciens propriétaires d'esclaves pourront s'asseoir ensemble à la table de la fraternité. Je fais le rêve qu'un jour même l'État du Mississippi, un État où on étouffe dans la chaleur accablante de l'oppression, se transformera en une oasis de liberté et de justice. Je fais le rêve qu'un jour mes quatre petits enfants vivront dans un pays où ils seront jugés non pas sur la couleur de leur peau, mais sur leurs propres capacités. »

Mise en service du téléphone rouge

Le téléphone rouge est entré en service le 30 août, entre la Maison-Blanche et le Kremlin, avec la transmission d'un message codé. Ce système de communication directe entre Washington et Moscou doit permettre de régler rapidement tout conflit éclatant soudain entre les deux nations, afin d'éviter une guerre « accidentelle ».

▲ *Le défenseur des droits civiques, le pasteur Martin Luther King, s'adressant à la foule sous la statue de Lincoln, à Washington.*

Traité franco-allemand

▶ **22 janvier 1963** ◀ Après un siècle d'inimitié, la France et la RFA viennent de signer, aujourd'hui, à Reims, un traité de coopération qui marque un tournant pour l'Europe. Le président français Charles de Gaulle et le chancelier allemand Konrad Adenauer ont décidé que les chefs d'État et les ministres des Affaires étrangères, de la Défense, et de l'Éducation des deux pays se rencontreraient plusieurs fois par an pour coordonner leurs politiques. Le but de ce traité est de trouver un terrain d'entente sur tous les problèmes concernant l'OTAN, le Marché commun, le communisme et les pays en voie de développement. Le français sera enseigné dans les écoles allemandes, et vice versa, et des échanges seront organisés entre les établissements français et allemands.

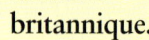

◀ *Les Beatles – John, Paul, Ringo et George.*

« Beatlesmania »

Depuis un mois, les Beatles occupent la première place du hit-parade avec leur chanson *She Loves You*, qui s'est vendue à plus d'un million d'exemplaires, créant ce que l'on appelle la « Beatlesmania ». Des milliers de fans ont envahi le London Palladium, où le groupe se produisait, paralysant la circulation et la voiture du Premier ministre britannique.

1960 – 1969

Le hold-up du train postal

▶ **8 août 1963** ◀ Le plus important hold-up de l'histoire britannique a eu lieu, cette nuit, à bord d'un train postal, après le sabotage d'un signal ferroviaire. Quinze brigands armés et masqués ont sauté dans le train et dérobé 2,6 millions de livres, principalement sous forme de billets de banque usagés destinés à être détruits. Après avoir capturé le mécanicien, descendu du train pour examiner le signal, et blessé grièvement à la tête le conducteur, les bandits se sont enfuis pour se partager le butin.

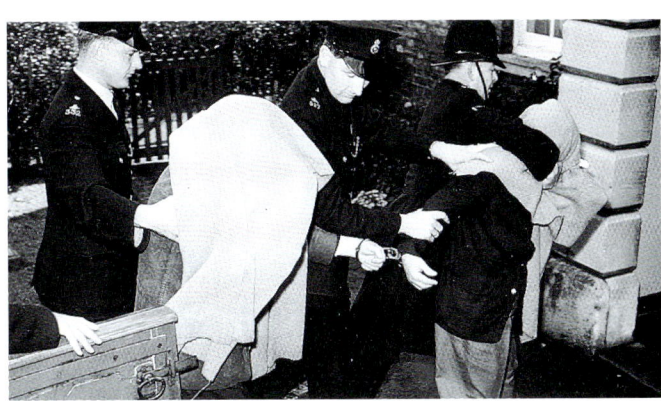

▶ Deux des bandits qui ont participé au « hold-up du siècle », conduits devant le tribunal.

Accord interdisant les essais nucléaires

▶ **5 août 1963** ◀ Les États-Unis, la Grande-Bretagne et l'Union soviétique ont signé, à Moscou, un accord interdisant les essais nucléaires dans l'atmosphère, dans les mers et dans l'espace. La France est la seule puissance atomique qui ait refusé de signer cet accord, estimant qu'il mettrait en danger sa souveraineté nationale.

▼ J. F. Kennedy et sa femme Jackie, traversant Dallas dans leur voiture décapotable, quelques minutes avant l'attentat.

En 1963 aussi...

3 juin • Mort du pape Jean XXIII.

5 juin • John Profumo, le ministre britannique des Armées, est relevé de ses fonctions, à cause de ses relations avec la call-girl Christine Keeler, qui était liée à un réseau d'espionnage.

16 juin • La Soviétique Valentina Terechkova est la première femme cosmonaute.

12 décembre • Le Kenya accède à l'indépendance.

Assassinat de Kennedy

▶ **22 novembre 1963** ◀ John Fitzgerald Kennedy, le 35e président des États-Unis d'Amérique, est assassiné, à Dallas, au Texas, alors qu'il traversait la ville en voiture décapotable. Il était en train de commencer sa campagne électorale, en vue de sa réélection. Un policier a également été tué, et John Connally, le gouverneur du Texas, grièvement blessé.

Devant la foule massée dans la rue, Kennedy, blessé à la tête, s'est écroulé dans les bras de son épouse, Jackie, assise à côté de lui. Transporté d'urgence au Parkland Hospital, Kennedy est décédé, 25 minutes après l'attentat. Soupçonné d'être l'auteur des coups de feu, Lee Harvey Oswald, un ancien marin, a été arrêté.

Abou-Simbel menacé par le barrage d'Assouan

▶ 1964 ◀ Des travaux sont lancés pour sauver les magnifiques temples d'Abou-Simbel, menacés par le réservoir du nouveau barrage d'Assouan. Ce barrage doit régulariser le cours du Nil, permettre d'irriguer des zones agricoles, et fournir de l'électricité. Les temples doivent être déplacés pour ne pas être engloutis. Ces travaux, décidés par l'UNESCO, sont financés par le gouvernement égyptien. Ils sont exécutés par une équipe internationale d'ingénieurs et de scientifiques, qui est financée par des fonds provenant de plus de 50 pays. Ils devraient durer plus de deux ans. L'objectif est de déplacer les quatre statues situées devant le temple principal, puis de découper le haut de la falaise et de démonter les deux temples. Ceux-ci seront remontés et dossés à une falaise artificielle, à 60 m au-dessus du lit du Nil, de sorte qu'ils ne seront pas menacés par les crues du fleuve.

▲ Archéologue mesurant l'une des statues monumentales du temple d'Abou-Simbel.

Abou-Simbel
Les deux temples ont été découpés en 1 050 blocs, le plus lourd pesant 33 tonnes.

Les quatre statues du temple de Ramsès mesurent plus de 20 m de haut. Près d'elles, de plus petites statues – celles de sa femme Néfertari et de ses enfants –, seulement 10 m.

Le coût du déplacement des temples – qui devrait être terminé en 1967 – avait été estimé à 36 millions de dollars.

▲ Temple d'Abou-Simbe construit pour Ramsès II au XIIIe s. av. J.-C.

Création de l'OLP en Palestine

▶ 2 juin 1964 ◀ L'Organisation de libération de la Palestine (OLP) vient d'être créée pour représenter les quelque 4,5 millions de Palestiniens dispersés dans les pays arabes, après la création de l'État d'Israël. Le but de l'OLP est d'unifier les différentes factions palestiniennes organisées en groupes de résistance secrets. Les tendances, au sein de l'OLP, sont diverses, allant de la volonté de négocier avec Israël, pour obtenir la création d'un État palestinien, au désir de détruire Israël et de le remplacer par un État où musulmans, juifs et chrétiens seraient égaux.

Nikita Khrouchtchev est limogé

▶ 14 octobre 1964 ◀ Nikita Khrouchtchev, le chef du gouvernement soviétique, est limogé, à l'âge de 70 ans, par des membres du parti communiste. Alors qu'il était en vacances, il a été rappelé à Moscou par le Politburo, soi-disant pour une réunion. Il a alors été arrêté et accusé, entre autres, d'avoir pris de mauvaises décisions et d'avoir maltraité des dignitaires étrangers. Il est remplacé par Leonid Brejnev à la tête du parti communiste, et Alekseï Kossyguine à la tête du gouvernement.

1960 – 1969

Début de la guerre civile à Chypre

▶ 12 février 1964 ◀ La guerre civile a éclaté à Chypre entre Chypriotes grecs et turcs. De violents combats ont fait vingt morts parmi les Turcs et un mort chez les Grecs. Les troupes britanniques basées à Chypre (la Grande-Bretagne ayant maintenu sa souveraineté sur ses deux bases militaires après l'indépendance de Chypre) n'ont pas obtenu de cessez-le-feu. Les Chypriotes turcs se prépareraient à attaquer le quartier grec. Cette situation est due à l'échec des négociations de Londres, au cours desquelles le Premier ministre turc a réclamé l'intervention de l'ONU pour garantir la liberté des Chypriotes turcs.

▲ Chypriotes turcs quittant leur village après s'être battus contre des Grecs.

Nouveau train à grande vitesse japonais

Une ligne de chemin de fer pour les trains à grande vitesse de 500 km de long a été construite entre Tokyo et Osaka, au Japon. Sur cette « nouvelle ligne de Tokaido », les trains peuvent rouler à plus de 200 km/h, notamment grâce aux traverses en béton précontraint.

Mort de Nehru

▶ 27 mai 1964 ◀ Jawaharlal Nehru, le premier Premier ministre de l'Inde depuis son indépendance, est mort d'une crise cardiaque, à New Delhi, à l'âge de 74 ans. Ce brillant homme politique, qui institua le gouvernement parlementaire indien et mena une politique étrangère « neutraliste », sera profondément regretté.

Nehru sera incinéré selon la coutume indienne, le 29 mai, sur les rives de la Jumna, en présence de nombreux chefs d'État.

◀ *Jawaharlal Nehru.*

▶ *Le Shinkansen, nouveau train à grande vitesse japonais.*

Sidney Poitier remporte l'oscar du meilleur acteur

▶ 13 avril 1964 ◀ Sidney Poitier, l'acteur noir, vient de recevoir l'oscar du meilleur acteur pour son rôle dans *le Lys des champs*, où il aide des religieuses à construire une chapelle dans le désert de l'Arizona. Écrit par James Poe et produit par Ralph Nelson, ce film prône l'harmonie raciale et l'unité des chrétiens. Cela fait du bien de voir un film à petit budget remporter un tel succès.

Mary Quant invente la minijupe

La styliste anglaise Mary Quant révolutionne la mode en inventant la minijupe. Créatrice de la boutique de Chelsea, Bazaar, Mary Quant s'est libérée de l'emprise de la mode parisienne, qu'elle juge rétrograde. Sa minijupe, simple mais osée, arrive largement au-dessus du genou. Cette ancienne étudiante en art va devoir produire en série sa minijupe, pour satisfaire une demande de plus en plus importante.

▶ *Mary Quant, portant sa version de la minijupe.*

▶ *L'acteur Sidney Poitier avec son oscar.*

1964

Premières photographies de la Lune

▶ **31 juillet 1964** ◀ La sonde américaine Ranger 7 – la première sonde non habitée envoyée par la NASA en 1961 – vient de retourner des photos très précises de la Lune. Cette sonde est le premier vaisseau spatial à atteindre la Lune, avant de s'écraser sur son sol, comme prévu. Les photographies, prises par des appareils télécommandés, donnent un certain nombre d'informations sur le sol lunaire, ainsi que sur l'âge, l'histoire et le climat de la Lune.

▲ *Une photographie de la Lune envoyée par Ranger 7.*

En 1964 aussi...

4 janvier • Rencontre historique, à Jérusalem, entre le pape Paul VI et le patriarche de Constantinople, Athênagoras.

16 octobre • Harold Wilson devient Premier ministre et dirige le nouveau gouvernement travailliste britannique. Il n'y en avait pas eu depuis treize ans.

16 octobre • Le pasteur Martin Luther King reçoit le prix Nobel de la paix, à Oslo.

▲ *Nelson Mandela, au début des années 60, avant sa condamnation à la prison à vie.*

Nelson Mandela condamné à la prison à perpétuité

▶ **14 juin 1964** ◀ Nelson Mandela, qui a créé le Congrès national africain (ANC, interdit en 1960), vient d'être condamné à la prison à perpétuité, ainsi que huit autres membres de l'ANC, pour sabotage, trahison, conspiration et complot visant à renverser le gouvernement sud-africain. Mandela est exilé à Robben Island.

Les Rolling Stones aux États-Unis

Les Rolling Stones commencent leur première tournée aux États-Unis, à San Bernardino, en Californie. Le chanteur Mick Jagger, les guitaristes Brian Jones et Keith Richard, le batteur Charlie Watts et le bassiste Bill Wyman remportent un immense succès, comparable à celui des Beatles, depuis la sortie de leur premier disque, *Come on*, et leur première apparition à la télévision, en juin 1963.

▼ *Les Rolling Stones en concert.*

1960 – 1969

Bombardements du Nord Viêt-nam

▶ **7 août 1964** ◀ La résolution sur le golfe du Tonkin, qui donne les pleins pouvoirs au président américain L.B. Johnson dans la guerre du Viêt-nam, a été adoptée par le Congrès, par 88 voix pour et 2 contre. Elle fait suite à l'attaque de destroyers américains par des navires de patrouille nord-vietnamiens. Johnson a ordonné aux aviateurs de guerre américains de riposter en bombardant les bases vietnamiennes, pour détruire les torpilleurs. Cette résolution accroît les pouvoirs du président dans la guerre du Viêt-nam.

▲ *Hélicoptères américains pendant la guerre du Viêt-nam.*

Égalité des droits civiques aux États-Unis

▶ **2 juillet 1964** ◀ Le président L.B. Johnson, déterminé à poursuivre l'œuvre du président Kennedy en faveur des droits civiques, vient de signer une loi interdisant la discrimination raciale dans le travail, les lieux publics, les syndicats et les programmes fédéraux. Johnson a veillé à ce que le Congrès américain ne change aucun point de cette loi.

▲ *Le président Johnson serrant la main du pasteur Martin Luther King.*

Cassius Clay, champion du monde

▶ **25 février 1964** ◀ Avant la fin du 7ᵉ round, le jeune boxeur américain Cassius Clay a été proclamé champion du monde des poids lourds. Il a battu le tenant du titre, Charles Sonny Liston, qui, blessé à l'épaule, a dû déclarer forfait. Cassius Clay a surpris le public par son jeu de jambes ultrarapide et sa technique originale, qui a décontenancé son adversaire, mais a ravi la foule.

Bagarres à Brighton entre Mods et Rockers

▶ **18 mai 1964** ◀ La côte sud de l'Angleterre a été le théâtre de violentes bagarres ce week-end. À Brighton, l'identité de plus de 600 jeunes a été contrôlée, tandis que 76 ont été arrêtés. Les vacanciers ont été terrifiés par les combats à coups de poing, les jets de bouteilles et de pierres et les actes de vandalisme. La tension entre les gangs des Mods, élégamment vêtus, et des Rockers, en blouson de cuir, couvait depuis un moment, mais personne n'avait imaginé qu'elle déboucherait sur une telle violence.

◀ *Mods et Rockers se rassemblant sur la plage de Brighton, avant de se battre.*

1965

L'UNICEF prix Nobel de la paix

▶ 10 décembre 1965 ◀ Le prix Nobel de la paix vient d'être remis à l'UNICEF, le fonds international d'aide à l'enfance de l'ONU. En 1954, un autre organisme de l'ONU, le Haut Commissariat aux réfugiés, avait déjà reçu ce prix. Créé en 1946, lors de la première assemblée générale de l'ONU, l'UNICEF (alors organisme temporaire) devient un organisme permanent en 1953. Son objectif est d'aider les enfants des pays européens dont la vie a été brisée par la Seconde Guerre mondiale, en leur donnant de l'argent, des vêtements, des médicaments, de la nourriture et du lait. Depuis le début des années 50, l'UNICEF concentre ses efforts sur les pays en voie de développement d'Afrique, d'Asie et d'Amérique du Sud. Il aide les gouvernements à créer des programmes d'aide à l'enfance (nutrition, soins…).

▲ *Logo de l'UNICEF.*

Dans les cas d'urgence – famine, guerre… –, il fournit de la nourriture et des médicaments.

Le siège de l'UNICEF est à New York. Les fonds proviennent des contributions volontaires des pays membres des Nations unies, de dons d'associations caritatives ou de particuliers, et de la vente, entre autres, de cartes de vœux. La première de ces cartes fut dessinée et adressée à l'UNICEF par une jeune Tchèque, pour le remercier d'avoir envoyé du lait aux enfants tchèques après la guerre.

▶ *Le prix Nobel de la paix remis à Oslo à Henri Labouisse (à gauche), le directeur de l'UNICEF, par Gunnar Jahn, membre de la commission Nobel du Parlement norvégien.*

Assassinat de Malcolm X

▼ *Malcolm X, le leader noir assassiné.*

▶ 21 février 1965 ◀ Le leader nationaliste noir américain Malcolm X vient d'être assassiné, à New York, lors d'un rassemblement de l'OAAU (Organisation de l'unité afro-américaine). Les auteurs des coups de feu, dont l'un a été arrêté, sont sans doute liés à la secte des Black Muslims (« musulmans noirs »), autrefois dirigée par Malcolm X. Malcolm Little se convertit à la religion des Black Muslims alors qu'il est en prison pour vol. Rejetant, comme d'autres, son nom de famille, considéré comme un nom d'esclave, il se fait appeler Malcolm X. Fondé par Elijah Muhammad, ce mouvement-secte proclame la suprématie des Noirs sur les Blancs, malfaisants. Malcolm X, brillant orateur et journaliste, en est l'un des principaux dirigeants. Mais, il y a un an, après un pèlerinage à La Mecque, il rompt avec Elijah Muhammad et les Black Muslims, et fonde l'OAAU. Cette organisation réclame plus de justice pour les Noirs américains, tout en croyant à l'entente entre les races.

En 1965 aussi…

18 mars • *Le cosmonaute soviétique Alekseï Leonov effectue sa première sortie dans l'espace.*

16 juin • *Ouverture du tunnel du mont Blanc entre la France et l'Italie.*

12 décembre • *Charles de Gaulle est réélu président de la République, lors de la première élection présidentielle au suffrage universel, en France. Il obtient 55,1 % des suffrages.*

1960 – 1969

Panne de courant à New York

▶ **10 novembre 1965** ◀ 30 millions de personnes ont été plongées dans le noir, après une panne d'électricité survenue dans le nord-est des États-Unis et à l'est du Canada. Des milliers de personnes ont été bloquées dans le métro et les ascenseurs de New York, pendant 14 heures. Cela est dû à une défaillance de l'ordinateur répartissant le courant produit par les usines hydroélectriques.

◀ *Seuls les phares des voitures éclairent la ville de New York, plongée dans le noir.*

Indépendance de la Rhodésie du Sud

▶ **11 novembre 1965** ◀ Ian Smith, le Premier ministre de la Rhodésie du Sud, une colonie britannique, vient de proclamer l'indépendance de celle-ci, sans l'accord de la Grande-Bretagne. Smith dirige le Front rhodésien qui lutte pour que les Blancs gardent le pouvoir, comme en Afrique du Sud.

Les dirigeants du Commonwealth pressent la Grande-Bretagne de prendre des sanctions fermes contre ce nouveau régime illégal.

Julie Andrews dans *la Mélodie du bonheur*

La Mélodie du bonheur, qui raconte l'histoire vraie d'une famille autrichienne, remporte cette année un grand succès. Julie Andrews, qui a reçu un oscar pour *Mary Poppins*, joue le rôle de la gouvernante des sept enfants von Trapp, qui s'enfuient dans les Alpes autrichiennes pour fuir les nazis.

▼ *Julie Andrews dans une scène de* la Mélodie du bonheur, *filmée à Salzbourg, en Autriche.*

Dylan choque les amateurs de folk

▶ **25 juillet 1965** ◀ Cette année encore, Joan Baez et Bob Dylan ont été les vedettes du festival de musique folk de Newport, dans l'État de Rhode Island, exprimant à travers leurs chansons les revendications de la jeunesse américaine. Dylan, cependant, a changé de style, basculant dans le « folk rock ». Revêtu d'une tenue flamboyante, il a joué de la guitare électrique avec un orchestre rock, ce qui a choqué les puristes du folk.

▲ *Bob Dylan et Joan Baez, les vedettes du Festival folk de Newport.*

Funérailles de Winston Churchill

▶ **30 janvier 1965** ◀ L'ancien Premier ministre britannique Winston Churchill, mort la semaine dernière à l'âge de 90 ans, a été enterré près de Blenheim Palace, où il est né. 3 000 personnes de 110 pays ont assisté à ses funérailles dans la cathédrale Saint-Paul, à Londres, en présence de la reine. C'est la première fois qu'un monarque assiste aux obsèques de l'un de ses sujets. 350 millions de téléspectateurs ont suivi cette cérémonie en direct.

▲ *Winston Churchill.*

1966

Londres à la pointe de la mode

▶ **11 juin 1966** ◀ La reine Élisabeth vient d'honorer la jeune styliste britannique Mary Quant en la faisant membre de l'ordre de l'Empire britannique. Mary Quant a joué un rôle important dans l'évolution de Londres, qui, en peu d'années, est devenu la Mecque de la culture de la jeunesse internationale. Dans les boutiques de Carnaby Street et de King's Road, les jeunes achètent des disques et des affiches pop, et des vêtements excentriques. Tandis que les jeunes filles adoptent la minijupe et les collants, les garçons se laissent pousser les cheveux. Plusieurs groupes pop, tels les Beatles et les Who, sont les idoles de ces jeunes. « J'ignore ce qui disparaîtra en premier, déclare John Lennon, l'un des Beatles, le rock'n'roll ou la chrétienté. » Les jeunes d'aujourd'hui ont plus d'argent, de pouvoirs et de libertés que n'en avaient leurs parents. Mais, un nouveau fossé se creuse entre les générations.

▲ *Twiggy, la figure dominante du Londres des années 60.*

◀ *Des touristes du monde entier viennent passer le week-end à Londres, dévalisant les boutiques de Carnaby Street et de Chelsea.*

En 1966 aussi...

13 janvier • Le physicien français Louis Leprince-Ringuet entre à l'Académie française.

17 février • Lancement réussi du satellite français Diapason par la fusée *Diamant*.

6 septembre • H. F. Verwoerd, le Premier ministre de l'Afrique du Sud, est assassiné.

28 octobre • La France et la Grande-Bretagne approuvent les plans du tunnel sous la Manche.

Révolution culturelle en Chine

▶ **15 août 1966** ◀ En Chine, Mao Zédong a repris le pouvoir, grâce à la « grande révolution culturelle prolétarienne ». Celle-ci, menée par de jeunes Chinois appelés les gardes rouges, fervents défenseurs du « Petit Livre rouge » de Mao, appelle au rejet de toutes les « vieilles idées et habitudes ». Pour ses victimes, cette révolution n'a rien de culturel. Dans toute la Chine, d'anciens responsables du parti, des intellectuels et des artistes, suspectés d'avoir des idées pro-occidentales ou préréactionnaires, sont dénoncés et obligés de quitter leur travail pour aller travailler dans les champs.

▶ *Manifestation de gardes rouges, appelant à la Révolution culturelle en Chine.*

Tragédie au pays de Galles

▶ **22 octobre 1966** ◀ 144 personnes, dont 116 enfants, ont trouvé la mort, hier, dans le village d'Aberfan, au pays de Galles, à la suite d'un glissement de terrain qui a englouti l'école et plusieurs maisons du village. La colline artificielle surplombant celui-ci, et formée de résidus d'une mine de charbon, regorgeait d'eau, à la suite des violentes pluies de ces derniers jours. Hier matin, elle a commencé à glisser vers le village, et l'école a été engloutie. Les sauveteurs ont travaillé toute la nuit. L'un des instituteurs a été retrouvé vivant ; le corps d'un autre a été retrouvé serrant dans ses bras cinq enfants. Le gouvernement a promis d'ouvrir une enquête. Celle-ci devra déterminer pourquoi personne ne s'est aperçu du danger que représentait cette colline artificielle pour le village et étudier l'état des centaines de collines similaires du pays de Galles.

▲ *Une grande fosse a été creusée, près du village d'Aberfan, au pays de Galles, pour enterrer les nombreuses victimes du glissement de terrain qui a englouti l'école et plusieurs maisons.*

Le président du Ghana renversé

▶ **24 février 1966** ◀ Le président du Ghana, Kwame Nkrumah, en visite officielle en Chine, a appris aujourd'hui qu'il avait été renversé par l'armée. Ce héros africain, chef de file des opposants au régime colonial britannique, devint Premier ministre en 1957, lors de l'indépendance du Ghana. Récemment, les problèmes économiques, la corruption du gouvernement et les abus de pouvoir de Nkrumah ont dressé une grande partie de la population contre lui.

Le trophée de la Coupe du monde réapparaît

Le trophée de la Coupe du monde de football, qui avait été volé au début du mois, vient d'être retrouvé par un chien dénommé Pickles. Le propriétaire de Pickles l'a vu renifler un paquet entouré de papier journal. Il l'a ramassé et a découvert qu'il s'agissait du fameux trophée en or. Un homme soupçonné d'avoir un lien avec ce vol a été arrêté.

Disparition d'une bombe H

▶ **7 avril 1966** ◀ Le Pentagone (ministère de la Défense américain) est soulagé. La bombe H perdue en mer le 17 janvier dernier, après la collision d'un bombardier américain avec un autre avion au large de l'Espagne, a été repêchée, intacte, par des sous-marins de poche, près de Palomares. Le Pentagone avait reconnu, à l'époque, que le B-52 transportait des armes nucléaires, et qu'une bombe H avait disparu.

▼ *Un des bombardiers américains B-52 utilisés pour transporter des armes.*

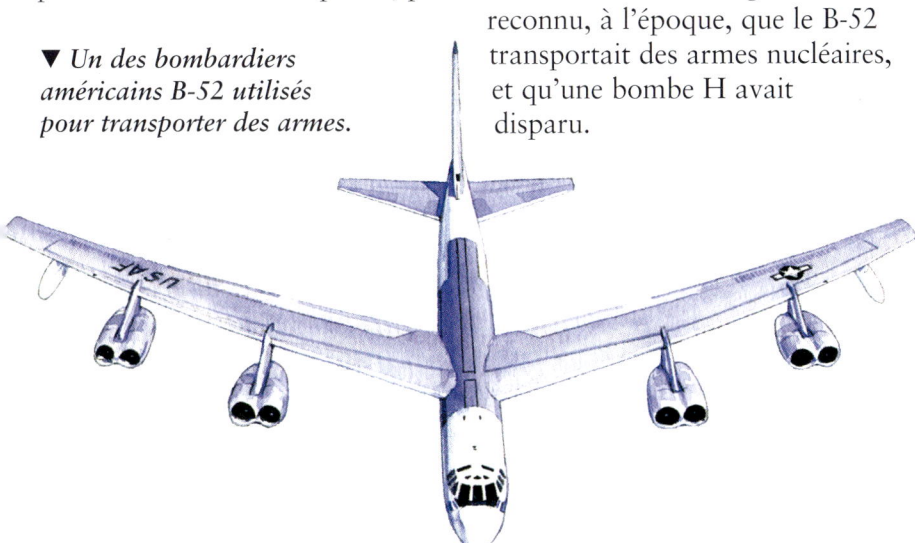

1966

Les Black Panthers proclament le black power

▶ **30 octobre 1966** ◀ Il y a deux ans, le pasteur noir Martin Luther King avait rêvé, dans un discours resté célèbre, qu'aux États-Unis les individus seraient jugés « d'après leur caractère plutôt que d'après la couleur de leur peau ». Au lieu d'attendre que ce rêve se réalise, certains Noirs américains cherchent à perpétuer l'injustice et la pauvreté. À Oakland, en Californie, Hue Newton, Bobby Seale et Eldridge Cleaver ont fondé une nouvelle organisation politique, le parti des Panthères noires, pour l'autodéfense. Celui-ci veut protéger les Noirs contre les exactions de la police raciste ; il souhaite également créer des cliniques et des centres communautaires. Les Panthères noires font partie du black power (« pouvoir noir »), mouvement dont les membres, au lieu d'essayer de se faire accepter par la société blanche, veulent être les maîtres.

◀ *Stokeley Carmichael, le leader noir qui inventa l'expression « black power ».*

▶ *Enfant de Harlem, à New York, apprenant le salut du Black Power.*

L'Angleterre remporte la Coupe du monde

L'Angleterre vient de remporter, pour la première fois, la Coupe du monde de football, battant l'Allemagne par 4 à 2. L'équipe allemande, menée par Franz Beckenbauer, partait favorite. Après 90 minutes de jeu, le score était de 2 à 2. Pendant les prolongations, un but très discuté fut accordé aux Anglais par l'arbitre. Geoff Hurst marqua à la dernière minute son troisième but, qui donna la victoire à l'Angleterre.

◀ *Le capitaine de l'équipe anglaise, Bobby Moore.*

Inondations à Florence

▶ **9 novembre 1966** ◀ Les pluies diluviennes qui se sont abattues sur l'Italie ont fait d'importants dégâts, notamment à Florence. 600 tableaux et plus de 1 000 livres et manuscrits anciens ont été abîmés. Plusieurs chefs-d'œuvre, dont la *Crucifixion* de Cimabue datant du XIIIe siècle, ont été détruits. De nombreux restaurateurs italiens sont déjà au travail, tandis qu'un appel est lancé à la communauté internationale pour restaurer les œuvres d'art endommagées.

▲ *Crue de l'Arno, à Florence, en Italie, projetant une voiture contre un monument.*

1960 – 1969

Mort de Walt Disney

▶ **15 décembre 1966** ◀ Walt Disney, le maître du dessin animé américain, s'est éteint, à Hollywood, à l'âge de 65 ans. Avec son collaborateur Ub Iwerks, Disney réalise ses premiers dessins animés à l'époque des films muets. Dans les années 20, il crée les personnages de Mickey, Donald et Goofy. Il réalisera ensuite de grands classiques, dont *Blanche-Neige*, *Pinocchio* et *Fantasia*.

Un nouveau chancelier en Allemagne de l'Ouest

▶ **1er décembre 1966** ◀ Le nouveau chancelier allemand, Kurt Georg Kiesinger, a prêté serment aujourd'hui. Il succède à Ludwig Erhard, qui est l'auteur du miracle économique allemand, mais qui ne s'entend plus avec son parti, la CDU (chrétiens-démocrates). Kiesinger appartient lui aussi à la CDU, mais il est le premier chancelier à gouverner avec des socialistes. Willy Brandt, le chef du SPD (socialistes modérés) et ancien maire de Berlin-Ouest, devient vice-chancelier et ministre des Affaires étrangères.

Succès de la série télévisée *Star Trek*

Grand succès pour la série télévisée de science-fiction *Star Trek*. William Shatner joue le rôle du capitaine du vaisseau *Enterprise*, dont la mission est d'aller où personne n'est encore allé. L'un des membres de l'équipage, Monsieur Spock, qui vient d'une autre galaxie, est incapable de ressentir la moindre émotion. Il est joué avec talent par Leonard Nimoy.

▶ *Principaux personnages, dans* Star Trek.

▲ *Claus von Amsberg et la princesse Béatrix.*

Mariage de la princesse Béatrix

▶ **10 mars 1966** ◀ La princesse Béatrix des Pays-Bas épouse, à Amsterdam, un diplomate allemand, Claus von Amsberg, qu'elle a rencontré il y a un peu plus d'un an, lors d'un séjour à la montagne. La princesse, qui est âgée de 28 ans et titulaire d'un doctorat en droit, est l'héritière du trône des Pays-Bas. Plusieurs incidents – une bombe fumigène a été lancée sur la voiture des mariés – ont marqué les cérémonies. Le mariage de la princesse avec un Allemand de onze ans son aîné est en effet très mal vu par la population, qui se souvient avec amertume des difficiles années pendant lesquelles les Pays-Bas étaient occupés par les Allemands.

Indira Gandhi, Premier ministre indien

▶ **19 janvier 1966** ◀ Le parti du Congrès vient de nommer Indira Gandhi Premier ministre de l'Inde. Elle succède à Lal Bahadur Shastri, mort brutalement la semaine dernière. Mme Gandhi, qui est veuve et âgée de 48 ans, était déjà ministre dans le précédent gouvernement. Cette femme très expérimentée est la fille de Nehru, le premier Premier ministre de l'Inde ; elle n'a aucun lien de parenté avec le Mahatma Gandhi.

▶ *Mme Indira Gandhi, la première femme Premier ministre de l'Inde.*

1967

Première greffe cardiaque

▶ 3 décembre 1967 ◀

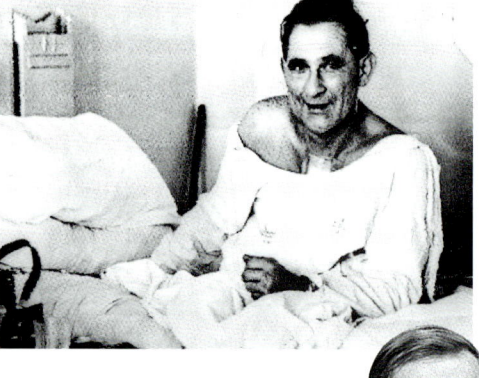
◀ Louis Washkansky, après sa greffe du cœur.

Le professeur Christian Barnard a, pour la première fois de l'histoire de l'humanité, transplanté un cœur sur un être humain, au Groot Schuur Hospital, à Cape Town, en Afrique du Sud. Le patient, Louis Washkansky, âgé de 53 ans, souffrait d'une maladie cardiaque incurable. Il accepta l'opération qui pouvait seule le sauver. Le père de Denise Darwall, une jeune femme morte dans un accident de voiture, autorisa l'utilisation du cœur de sa fille. L'opération, réalisée par le professeur Barnard et une équipe de 30 personnes, dura six heures. Dès qu'il fut en place, le cœur reçut une légère décharge électrique et redémarra. On savait, depuis quelques années, que la greffe d'organes humains était théoriquement possible. Les greffes de rein sont celles qui réussissent le mieux, les patients pouvant être maintenus en bonne santé jusqu'à ce qu'un rein soit disponible. Selon le Pr Barnard, la greffe d'un cœur « n'est pas en soi un problème ». Le danger est que le corps risque de rejeter le nouveau cœur.

Les transplantations
Washkansky, à la suite de complications de santé, est mort dix-huit jours après sa transplantation cardiaque. Son cœur a continué à battre jusqu'au bout.

▶ Le professeur Barnard (à gauche) discutant avec d'éminents spécialistes des maladies cardiaques, Michael de Bakey et Adirn Kantrowitz.

Le dernier album des Beatles

La pochette du dernier album des Beatles, *Sergeant Pepper's Lonely Hearts Club Band*, est l'œuvre de Peter Black, un artiste pop anglais. Elle est tout à fait adaptée au nouveau style psychédélique des chansons des Beatles, qui devraient remporter un grand succès.

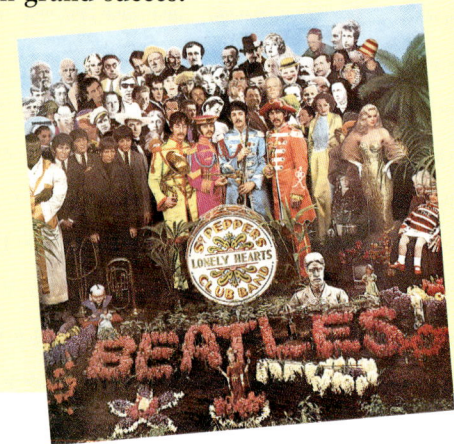

Guerre civile au Biafra

▶ 30 mai 1967 ◀

Le colonel Ojukwu, le chef des Ibos, a déclaré l'indépendance de la région orientale du Nigeria, qui devient la république du Biafra. Cette déclaration fait suite à 18 mois de combats au Nigeria, dont les Ibos, qui y sont minoritaires, sont les principales victimes. Ojukwu est convaincu que les Ibos ne peuvent être en sécurité que dans un État indépendant. Une guerre civile commence entre les Nigérians et le nouvel État du Biafra. Les Nigérians affament les Biafrais. La France tente de leur venir en aide. La Grande-Bretagne et d'autres pays soutiendront les Nigérians.

▶ De jeunes Ibos s'entraînant pour défendre la République indépendante du Biafra.

1960 – 1969

Israël, vainqueur de la guerre des Six Jours

▶ **10 juin 1967** ◀ Après six jours de combats, la guerre opposant Israël à ses voisins arabes s'est achevée, Israël ayant accepté le cessez-le-feu proposé par l'ONU. Israël refuse d'appliquer la résolution 242 de l'ONU qui lui ordonne de quitter les territoires conquis ; c'est-à-dire d'évacuer le Sinaï, la Cisjordanie, Jérusalem-Est, la bande de Gaza et le Golan.

▲ *Moshe Dayan (au centre), le ministre de la Défense israélien, pendant la guerre des Six Jours.*

En 1967 aussi...

27 janvier • Trois astronautes américains meurent brûlés, à l'intérieur d'Apollo, lors d'un exercice préparatoire.

31 juillet • Création à Paris de l'Agence nationale pour l'emploi (ANPE), chargée d'aider les chômeurs à trouver un emploi.

31 juillet • À Paris, l'exposition Toutankhamon a reçu 1,3 million de visiteurs depuis son ouverture en février.

Marée noire en Grande-Bretagne

▶ **31 mars 1967** ◀ Des plongeurs sont en train d'examiner l'épave du *Torrey Canyon*, le superpétrolier qui a coulé, il y a quinze jours, devant les côtes anglaises. Trente mille tonnes de pétrole se sont déversées dans la mer, le pétrolier s'étant cassé en deux pendant les opérations de sauvetage. Des avions l'ont bombardé pour essayer de le couler et de brûler sa cargaison. La nappe de pétrole pollue les côtes de la Cornouaille, de la Bretagne et du Cotentin.

Mort de « Che » Guevara en Bolivie

▶ **9 octobre 1967** ◀ Le héros révolutionnaire d'Amérique latine Ernesto « Che » Guevara a été tué par les troupes boliviennes. Le bras droit de Fidel Castro pendant la Révolution cubaine était originaire d'Argentine. Il disparut de la scène politique cubaine en 1965, pour soutenir les guérilleros en Amérique du Sud.

▲ *Le « Che » (à droite) avec Castro.*

Manifestation contre la guerre du Viêt-nam

▶ **21 octobre 1967** ◀ Des incidents entre manifestants et forces de l'ordre ont marqué la manifestation contre la guerre du Viêt-nam. Cette marche, qui a rassemblé des milliers de personnes, couronne une semaine de protestations contre la politique américaine en Indochine. Depuis la guerre de Sécession au siècle dernier, aucun conflit n'a autant divisé le pays que la guerre du Viêt-nam, dans laquelle seront bientôt engagés plus de 500 000 soldats américains.

▶ *Manifestants pacifistes opposés aux forces de l'ordre.*

LA POP MUSIC

Au début du XXe siècle, l'opéra est très populaire. Avec l'invention du disque, la musique conquiert les marchés du monde entier. En 1902, le célèbre ténor italien Enrico Caruso enregistre ses premiers disques, vendus à des millions d'exemplaires.

Au même moment apparaît, dans le sud des États-Unis, le jazz, mélange de musiques africaine et européenne. Le jazz se diffuse aux États-Unis avec les travailleurs noirs qui sont embauchés dans les villes du nord-est du pays. L'Europe le découvre avec les soldats américains, pendant la Seconde Guerre mondiale. Il donne naissance dans les années 60 à la pop music, qui englobe rock and roll, soul, disco, punk, heavy metal, grunge, techno et rap.

▲ *Le guitariste Chuck Berry commence sa carrière en jouant du blues dans les clubs.*

▼ *Elvis Presley, le « king » du rock and roll.*

▶ *Les Beatles, originaires de Liverpool, forment le premier grand groupe pop.*

Les années rock and roll

Dans les années 50 apparaît le rock and roll, musique dérivée du rhythm and blues. Les barrières raciales entre les musiques noire et blanche commencent à tomber. En 1954, Elvis Presley, un jeune Blanc, enregistre son premier disque. *That's All Right Mama* est l'adaptation d'une chanson noire ; le rock and roll naît de la fusion du rhythm and blues, de la country music et des gospels (chants religieux noirs).

Au milieu des années 50, le guitariste et chanteur noir Chuck Berry compose, entre autres, *Johnny B Good* et *Back in the USA*.

Dans les années 60, de nombreux groupes anglais, dont les Beatles et les Rolling Stones, s'inspirent de sa musique.

Le rôle de la musique dans les années 60

La pop music est aux années 60 ce que le rock and roll fut aux années 50. Cette forme de musique, qui prétend à un rôle social et politique, donne lieu à de grands festivals. Les années 60 voient un regain d'intérêt pour le folk et le blues. D'excellents guitaristes, comme Jimi Hendrix et Eric Clapton, exécutent de longs solos, utilisant de nouveaux gadgets électroniques dans des studios d'enregistrement très sophistiqués. Bob Dylan compose des chansons folks au message délibérément politique, dénonçant le racisme, la guerre du Viêt-nam et la prolifération des armes nucléaires. Il exerce une forte influence sur d'autres artistes, dont les Beatles.

▲ Madonna, dont les exhibitions sur scène et à l'écran comme les chansons provocatrices choquent l'opinion publique.

La pop music

En France, les chanteurs yé-yé les plus populaires sont Johnny Hallyday, Françoise Hardy, Sylvie Vartan, Sheila et Claude François.

•

Danyel Gérard sort le premier disque de rock français, *D'où viens-tu, Billy Boy ?* (texte de Boris Vian).

▶ Les Supremes – Florence Ballard, Diana Ross et Mary Wilson (de gauche à droite).

La soul music

La plupart des grands interprètes noirs américains, comme Aretha Franklin et Marvin Gaye, commencent leur carrière en chantant des gospels. Dans les années 60, ces chants religieux abordent différents sujets, dont les problèmes sociaux. Cette nouvelle musique populaire noire est appelée soul music. Berry Gordy crée à Detroit la firme Motown, maison de disques spécialisée dans la soul music, qui, aujourd'hui encore, vend à des millions d'exemplaires ses enregistrements de Stevie Wonder, de Diana Ross et des Jackson Five.

1968

 1960
 1961
 1962
 1963
 1964
 1965
 1966
 1967
 1968
 1969

Offensive du Têt au Viêt-nam

▶ *La ville de Saigon, où sont entrées les forces du Viêt-cong pendant l'offensive du Têt (nouvel an).*

▶ 24 février 1968 ◀ Voilà trois semaines que les forces communistes du Viêt-nam (le Viêt-cong) ont lancé l'offensive du Têt, attaquant plus de 100 villes et bases militaires dans le sud du Viêt-nam. Cette offensive a rompu le cessez-le feu déclaré pour le Têt, le nouvel an vietnamien. La communauté internationale a été surprise par les images retransmises, qui montrent une armée du tiers-monde infligeant de sévères dommages aux Américains. Le Viêt-cong a prouvé qu'il pouvait atteindre l'armée américaine. Aujourd'hui, les Américains et les Vietnamiens du Sud ripostent et viennent de reprendre Huê. Le général américain Westmoreland demande l'envoi de renforts.

Mai 68

▶ 13 mai 1968 ◀ La France tout entière est paralysée par une grève générale spontanée : employés et ouvriers appuient le mouvement de protestation des étudiants. Celui-ci est parti le 22 mars de la faculté de Nanterre, avec, parmi les meneurs Daniel Cohn-Bendit et Jacques Sauvageot. L'agitation a ensuite gagné le quartier Latin. La protestation contre les brutalités policières est aussi dirigée contre le régime. « Dix ans, ça suffit ! » crient les manifestants. Les ouvriers sont résolus à occuper leurs usines, jusqu'à ce que leurs conditions de travail s'améliorent.

▶ *Des étudiants s'opposant aux forces de l'ordre.*

En 1968 aussi...

10 mai • Début des négociations, à Paris, pour mettre fin à la guerre du Viêt-nam.

1er-2 septembre • Un tremblement de terre fait 11 000 morts en Iran.

20 octobre • Mariage de Jackie Kennedy, la veuve du président Kennedy, avec l'armateur grec Aristote Onassis.

5 novembre • Nixon est élu président des États-Unis.

Assassinat de Bob Kennedy

▶ 6 juin 1968 ◀ Le sénateur américain Robert Kennedy, frère du président John F. Kennedy, et grièvement blessé dans un hôtel de Los Angeles hier matin, est mort. Il venait de remporter les élections primaires de Californie, devenant le candidat démocrate à l'élection présidentielle. Son meurtrier, un Jordanien de 24 ans, a été arrêté. En tirant sur Kennedy, il a crié : « Je l'ai fait pour mon pays. »

▶ *Bob Kennedy avec ses supporters.*

1960 – 1969

1968

Fin du « printemps de Prague »

▶ 20 août 1968 ◀ Les chars soviétiques sont entrés à Prague, pour renverser le gouvernement communiste libéral d'Alexander Dubček. En mars, celui-ci avait adouci la censure de la presse et fait arrêter l'ancien chef de la police secrète. Cette période avait été baptisée le « printemps de Prague ». Mais l'étau soviétique se resserre sur la Tchécoslovaquie ; il semble que l'« hiver » du communisme dur soit revenu. Les Russes craignent que les réformes démocratiques de Dubček n'affaiblissent le communisme dans d'autres pays d'Europe de l'Est. Dubček et cinq membres du gouvernement ont été arrêtés et conduits à Moscou.

◀ Étudiants tchèques faisant face aux chars soviétiques, à Prague.

Retour à l'ordre en France

▶ 30 juin 1968 ◀ Tout semble rentrer dans l'ordre, en France, avec l'éclatante victoire électorale, des gaullistes. Alors que le pays semblait s'enfoncer dans la révolution, l'appel du général de Gaulle, le 30 mai, a poussé ses partisans à se mobiliser. Trois jours avant, le Premier ministre G. Pompidou était parvenu à trouver un accord avec les syndicats. La reprise du travail s'amorce, mais la crise a marqué la société française plus profondément qu'il n'y paraît.

Émeutes après l'assassinat de Martin Luther King

▶ 5 avril 1968 ◀ Partout, aux États-Unis, des Noirs américains descendent dans la rue pour protester contre l'assassinat de Martin Luther King, tué hier à Memphis, dans le Tennessee, par un tireur blanc qui a pris la fuite. Le pasteur noir avait lancé, dans les années 50, un mouvement contre les lois de ségrégation raciale, et prônait la non-violence. Sa mort a provoqué toutefois des émeutes dans 167 villes et sur de nombreux campus.

▶ Émeutes, à la suite de l'annonce de la mort de Martin Luther King.

2001 : l'odyssée de l'espace

Dans son nouveau film, *2001 : l'odyssée de l'espace*, l'Américain Stanley Kubrick offre une vision poétique mais inquiétante du futur. Lors d'une mission dans l'espace, l'ordinateur de bord HAL-9 000 tente de tuer les astronautes. L'un d'eux, David Bowman (Keir Dullea), casse l'ordinateur devenu fou. À la fin, Bowman semble s'évanouir dans l'espace et le temps.

▲ Scène de *2001 : l'odyssée de l'espace*.

Manifestation du Black Power

▶ 16 octobre 1968 ◀ Les athlètes noirs américains Tommy Smith et John Carlos ont profité de leur victoire aux jeux Olympiques de Mexico pour protester contre le racisme aux États-Unis. Alors qu'ils recevaient leurs médailles d'or et de bronze pour le 200 m, tous deux ont levé leur poing ganté de noir au-dessus de leur tête, exécutant ainsi le salut du Black Power, un mouvement noir américain. Ils risquent d'être sanctionnés pour ce geste et d'être renvoyés chez eux.

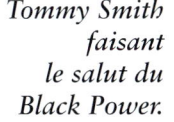

▼ Tommy Smith faisant le salut du Black Power.

1969

Les premiers hommes sur la Lune

▶ **21 juillet 1969** ◀ Des millions d'hommes et de femmes ont allumé très tôt ce matin leur téléviseur, pour suivre les premiers pas de Neil Armstrong et d'Edwin Aldrin sur la Lune. Tandis qu'Apollo 11 se mettait en orbite autour de la Lune, les deux astronautes, équipés d'une caméra, descendaient vers le sol lunaire, à bord du module d'exploration (LEM) *Eagle*. À 3 h 56, Armstrong, puis Aldrin posaient le pied sur la Lune.

Le 16 juillet, la fusée Saturne 5 avait lancé Apollo 11 depuis cap Kennedy, en Floride. Après un voyage de quatre jours, Apollo 11 arriva sur la Lune. Michael Collins resta seul aux commandes de la capsule, tandis qu'Armstrong et Aldrin amorçaient leur descente. Ils restèrent treize heures sur la Lune, prélevant des échantillons de roches et effectuant diverses expériences, avant de rejoindre Collins et d'entamer le long voyage de retour vers la Terre.

▶ *La gravité étant beaucoup plus faible sur la Lune que sur la Terre, les astronautes se déplacent en « bondissant » sur le sol lunaire.*

▶ *Empreinte de pied sur le sol lunaire.*

La Lune
La fusée Saturne 5, qui lança Apollo 11, brûla 2,3 l de carburant pendant les deux premières minutes et demie du voyage, qui dura 4 jours.
•
En souvenir du premier alunissage, les astronautes américains ont laissé sur la lune un drapeau américain et une plaque avec un message signé du président Nixon.
•
À leur retour sur la terre, les astronautes sont restés isolés 17 jours, au cas où ils auraient contracté sur la lune une maladie inconnue.

Mort de Hô Chi Minh

▶ **3 septembre 1969** ◀ Hô Chi Minh, le président du Viêt-nam communiste depuis 1954, est mort d'une crise cardiaque, à l'âge de 79 ans. Pendant presque trente ans, il dirigea la résistance anticolonialiste en Indochine. En 1945, il proclama l'indépendance du Viêt-nam, alors colonie française. La guerre d'Indochine qui suivit aboutit à un accord de paix qui divisa le Viêt-nam en deux, le Viêt-nam du Nord et le Viêt-nam du Sud. Pour les Vietnamiens, Hô Chi Minh était le symbole de la lutte pour la réunification du pays.

◀ *Hô Chi Minh, dont le nom signifie « celui qui éclaire ».*

1960 – 1969

Début du procès de Charles Manson

▶ 24 décembre 1969 ◀ Charles Manson, et quatre membres de sa communauté, ont été accusés ce matin à Los Angeles du meurtre de l'actrice Sharon Tate et de six autres personnes. Manson, âgé de 35 ans, qui se fait appeler « Jésus-Christ », dirige une communauté hippie, La Famille. Lui et d'autres membres de sa secte sont entrés dans la maison de l'actrice à Hollywood et ont assassiné la jeune femme, enceinte de huit mois, ainsi que six autres personnes. Ils ont badigeonné les murs de la maison avec du sang et ont tué deux autres personnes la nuit suivante.

▲ *Charles Manson après son arrestation.*

François Truffaut, Prix Louis Delluc

▶ 9 janvier 1969 ◀ *Baisers volés*, le film du réalisateur français François Truffaut, dont le titre est emprunté à une chanson de Charles Trenet, a reçu le prix Louis Delluc. Ce film est la suite des aventures d'Antoine Doinel, joué par Jean-Pierre Léaud dans *Les quatre cents coups*.

François Truffaut, dont c'est l'un des meilleurs films, a déjà produit *Jules et Jim* (1962) et *Farenheit 451* (1966), qui ont été des grands succès.

Troubles en Irlande

▶ 16 août 1969 ◀ Les troupes britanniques sont arrivées dans les villes d'Irlande du Nord pour maintenir la paix entre catholiques et protestants. Cet été, de nombreux districts catholiques sont devenus « zones interdites » pour la police locale, la Royal Ulster Constabulary, mais les troupes britanniques, jugées impartiales, y sont bien accueillies. Cinq personnes ont été tuées, et des centaines d'autres blessées.

▶ *Soldat Britannique en mission à Belfast.*

Easy Rider, film culte

Un nouveau film, *Easy Rider*, fait fureur aux États-Unis. Deux hippies, joués par Peter Fonda et Dennis Hopper, sillonnent les routes sur leurs motocyclettes. Traversant les États-Unis de Los Angeles à New Orleans, ils rencontrent un avocat déprimé, joué par Jack Nickolson. La bande-son du film comporte des chansons des Byrds et de Jimi Hendrix.

Mme Golda Meir, Premier ministre de l'État d'Israël

▶ 17 mars 1969 ◀ Mme Golda Meir vient d'être nommée Premier ministre de l'État d'Israël. Née en Russie, Golda Meir émigra dans le Milwaukee, États-Unis, avant d'arriver en Palestine en 1921. Elle s'appelait Goldie Myerson. Elle adopta la version hébraïque de son nom lorsqu'elle devint ministre des Affaires étrangères, en 1956. Mme Golda Meir souhaite régler les différends opposant Israël à ses voisins arabes par la voie diplomatique plutôt que par la force.

▶ *Golda Meir, Premier ministre d'Israël.*

1969

Le Festival de Woodstock

▼ *Une fois le festival terminé, des milliers de jeunes quittent Woodstock.*

▶ **17 août 1969** ◀ Les amateurs de rock quittent aujourd'hui Woodstock, dans l'État de New York, convaincus que s'ouvre enfin une nouvelle ère de paix et d'amour. Pendant trois jours, malgré des pluies diluviennes, 400 000 jeunes ont connu le bonheur, près de Woodstock, en écoutant Jimi Hendrix, les Who, Janis Joplin, The Band et Jefferson Airplane. Fumant du haschisch ou de la marijuana, plaisantant et échangeant des signes de paix, ils ont eu l'impression de vivre un grand moment de paix et d'union. Woodstock a été le plus important des nombreux festivals rock organisés cet été. Plus de 100 000 jeunes ont assisté au Festival pop d'Atlanta en juillet, et 80 000, au Festival de jazz de Newport, animé entre autres par Led Zeppelin, BB King et Jethro Tull. La contre-culture hippie, prônant la paix et l'amour, née il y a quatre ans à San Francisco, se répand aujourd'hui dans tous les États-Unis et en Europe. Les hippies ont choisi les fleurs comme symboles de leurs convictions pacifiques, et emploient l'expression *flower power* pour affirmer que l'amour peut l'emporter sur la haine. Tandis que s'amplifie le mouvement de protestation contre la guerre du Viêt-nam, ces valeurs sont adoptées par de nombreux jeunes.

Pétrole en mer du Nord

Les eaux glacées de la mer du Nord cachent peut-être un trésor. Du pétrole brut, de qualité supérieure dans des eaux très profondes. Des compagnies pétrolières étudient ces gisements pour savoir s'ils méritent d'être exploités, le coût des travaux de forage étant élevé.

Arafat, chef de l'OLP

▶ **3 février 1969** ◀ Yasser Arafat est le nouveau chef de l'Organisation de libération de la Palestine (OLP). L'OLP représente les Arabes qui durent quitter la Palestine, lors de la création de l'État d'Israël, en 1948. Plus de 500 000 Palestiniens partirent cette année-là ; 200 000 à 400 000 Palestiniens quittèrent la Palestine pendant la guerre des Six Jours en 1967. La plupart vivent aujourd'hui dans des camps de réfugiés de l'ONU ; le but de l'OLP est de créer un nouvel État palestinien sur un territoire qu'elle veut reprendre à Israël.

Né à Jérusalem, Arafat fit ses études au Caire, puis s'engagea dans l'armée égyptienne et participa aux combats autour de Suez. En 1963, alors qu'il travaillait comme ingénieur au Koweït, il prit la tête du Fatah, la principale organisation militaire de l'OLP.

▶ *Yasser Arafat, le nouveau chef de l'OLP.*

En 1969 aussi...

2 mars • Premier vol de l'avion supersonique franco-britannique Concorde 001.

15 mars • Lancement du *Redoutable*, un sous-marin nucléaire français.

1er avril • Lin Biao a été choisi pour succéder à Mao Zédong à la tête du Parti communiste chinois, lorsque celui-ci se retirera.

21 octobre • Willy Brandt devient chancelier de la RFA.

Kadhafi prend le pouvoir en Libye

▶ **1er septembre 1969** ◀ Des officiers de l'armée, conduits par le colonel Mu'ammar al-Kadhafi, ont proclamé la république en Libye. L'armée a pris le pouvoir alors que le roi Idris, âgé de 70 ans, était en Turquie. Le prince héritier Hassan Rida déclare soutenir le nouveau gouvernement. Kadhafi est né dans une famille de Bédouins vivant dans le désert. Bien qu'il n'ait que 27 ans, voilà plusieurs années qu'il préparait ce coup d'État. Le slogan de ce nouveau régime est « Liberté, Socialisme et Unités ».

◀ *Le colonel Kadhafi est le nouveau dirigeant de la Libye.*

Pompidou président de la République française

▶ **16 juin 1969** ◀ L'ancien Premier ministre du général de Gaulle, Georges Pompidou, vient d'être élu, à 57 ans, président de la République, avec 58,21 % des voix, contre 41,78 % à son concurrent, Alain Poher. Fils d'instituteur, cet agrégé de lettres et auteur d'une *Anthologie de la poésie française* succède à Charles de Gaulle, qui a présenté sa démission le 28 avril dernier.

1960 – 1969

Le Nigeria interdit les secours destinés au Biafra

▶ **16 juin 1969** ◀ Le gouvernement nigérian vient d'interdire à la Croix-Rouge d'envoyer par avion de la nourriture et des médicaments au Biafra, province de l'est du Nigeria, où la guerre fait rage depuis son indépendance. Le Biafra, surpeuplé, subit de lourdes pertes. Des milliers de Biafrais vivent dans des conditions atroces. Le gouvernement nigérian prétend que les rebelles profitent de ces avions pour envoyer des armes au Biafra. Des combats opposent les tribus des Ibos et des Haoussas. En septembre 1966, 30 000 Ibos ont été tués par les Haoussas dans le nord du Nigeria, et 1 million d'Ibos ont fui dans la province orientale, où ils sont majoritaires.

▶ *Enfants biafrais nourris et soignés par la Croix-Rouge, pendant la guerre contre le Nigeria.*

Succès de *1, rue Sésame*

Les petits Américains apprennent à lire et à compter, grâce à *1, rue Sésame (Sesame Street)*. Cette nouvelle émission télévisée, présentée par des adultes, met en scène de charmants animaux en peluche faisant office de professeurs.

◀ *Big Bird, un des « professeurs » de 1, rue Sésame.*

Hommage des Tchèques à Jan Palach

▶ **27 janvier 1969** ◀ Des milliers de jeunes Tchèques ont défilé dans les rues de Prague. Ils ont accroché sur la place de l'Armée-rouge des plaques portant l'inscription « place Jan-Palach », en hommage à l'étudiant qui s'est immolé par le feu, le 16 janvier, pour protester contre l'occupation soviétique. Jan Palach est décédé hier à l'hôpital, à l'âge de 21 ans. Avant de mourir, il a déclaré : « Ma mort a atteint son objectif, mais n'autorise personne à faire la même chose. »

▲ *Obsèques de Jan Palach.*

L'ÂGE DE LA TÉLÉVISION

Le monde est transformé par l'apparition de la télévision, dans la seconde moitié du XXe siècle. Les informations, les sports et les faits divers sont retransmis par satellite dans le monde entier. Les publicitaires se servent de la télévision pour vendre leurs produits, ce qui représente un chiffre d'affaires colossal.

Aujourd'hui, la télévision évolue à toute vitesse. Les téléspectateurs ont le choix entre des dizaines de chaînes. Le matériel de prise de vues et d'enregistrement étant devenu moins encombrant et moins cher, davantage d'émissions peuvent être réalisées. Les écrans sont plus grands, le son et l'image, de meilleure qualité.

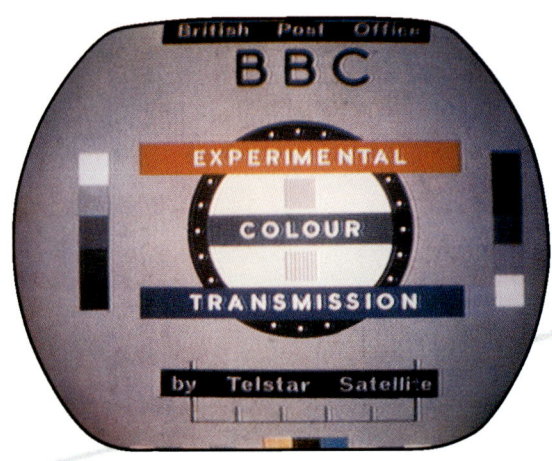

▲ *En 1962, des images en couleurs sont transmises outre-Atlantique par le satellite Telstar. Cette image de la BBC parvient ainsi à New York.*

La télévision trouve sa place dans les foyers

Après la Seconde Guerre mondiale, la télévision devient de plus en plus populaire et commence à remplacer la radio dans les foyers. En 1958, on recense 900 000 téléviseurs pour 45 millions de Français. La France, en 1963, ne compte que deux chaînes publiques. Et c'est en 1965, lors de la première campagne pour l'élection du président de la République française au suffrage universel, que la télévision joue pour la première fois un rôle important auprès des électeurs. En 1990, 98 % des foyers des « pays développés » (Europe et États-Unis) disposent d'au moins un téléviseur.

La télévision propose des programmes de plus en plus variés : jeux, émissions sportives ou de variétés, programmes musicaux, etc. Elle relie la famille au monde extérieur. Elle a parfois un impact considérable sur les téléspectateurs. Dans les années 80, les images d'Africains mourant de faim marquent l'opinion, incitant plusieurs stars du rock et de la pop à recueillir des fonds pour secourir les victimes de la famine.

▼ *Le poste de télévision est souvent placé au centre de la pièce à vivre, au cœur de la famille.*

La télévision
Pierre Sabbagh présente le premier journal télévisé français le 26 juin 1949.

•

La performance de John Fitzgerald Kennedy à la télévision contribue à sa victoire aux élections présidentielles américaines contre Richard Nixon, en 1960.

•

En 1970, la France compte 203 téléviseurs pour 1 000 habitants ; les États-Unis et la Grande-Bretagne en comptent respectivement 405 et 300.

Les émissions pour les enfants

En 1950, alors que pour la première fois les dessins animés font leur apparition à la télévision, les enfants américains passent en moyenne vingt-sept heures par semaine devant le petit écran. L'émission *1, rue Sésame (Sesame Street)*, qui a commencé à être diffusée aux États-Unis en 1969, connaît un énorme succès dans le monde entier ; en 1985, elle est diffusée dans 78 pays différents. En Grande-Bretagne, la BBC lance sa première émission pour les enfants, *For the Children*, en 1946.

En France, dans les années 60, des milliers d'enfants regardent *Bonne nuit les petits*, *le Manège enchanté* et *Kiri le Clown* avant d'aller se coucher. *Ma sorcière bien-aimée*, *Zorro* et *Thierry la Fronde* enchantent les plus grands. Un peu plus tard, *l'Île aux enfants*, avec son gentil monstre orange, Casimir, fascinera pendant de longues années les petits comme les grands.

▼ *Les marionnettes de 1, rue Sésame.*

▼ *John Logie Baird faisant fonctionner une télévision, en 1926.*

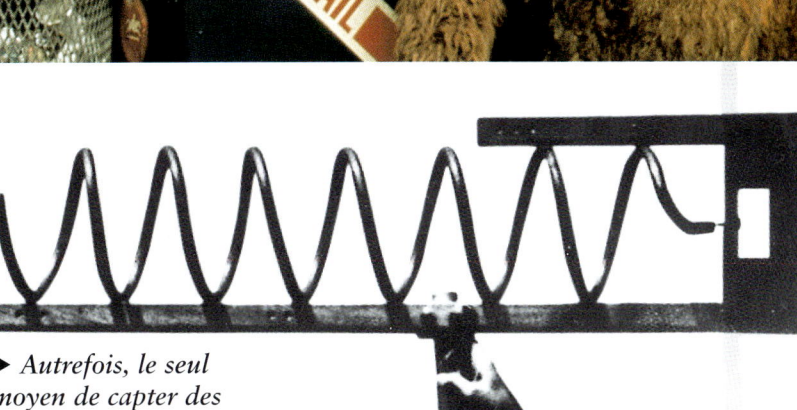

▶ *Autrefois, le seul moyen de capter des émissions télévisées était d'installer une antenne sur le toit. Aujourd'hui, il suffit d'avoir une antenne satellite ou d'être relié au câble. Les antennes ci-contre ont été conçues par des ingénieurs de la Radio Corporation of America.*

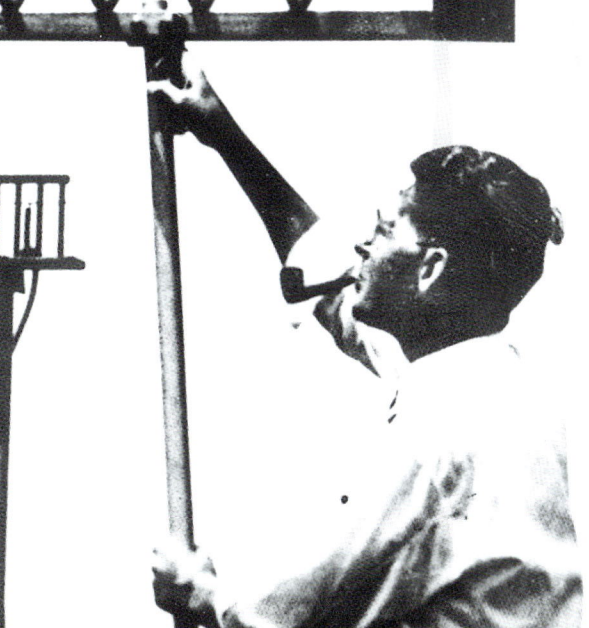

L'inventeur de la télévision

L'Écossais John Logie Baird est le premier à faire fonctionner en public une télévision. Il réussit, le 27 janvier 1926, à transmettre une image entre deux studios. Si la BBC a testé son système en 1929, puis en 1936, elle préfère en adopter un autre. En 1944, Baird invente un procédé de transmission des images en couleurs.

De 1970 à 1979

1970 Dans les années 70, la confiance dans les pays industrialisés s'effondre. La hausse brutale du prix du pétrole, en 1973, désorganise le commerce international et provoque une recrudescence du chômage.

Le progrès ne s'arrête pas pour autant. Les États-Unis et l'URSS acceptent de limiter leur armement nucléaire. Une navette spatiale effectue son premier vol, tandis que naît le premier bébé-éprouvette à partir d'un œuf fécondé en dehors du ventre maternel.

Cyclone au Pakistan

▶ **20 novembre 1970** ◀ Aujourd'hui est une journée de deuil national au Pakistan, après le passage du cyclone qui a fait 150 000 morts au Pakistan oriental la semaine dernière. Le mur d'eau de 9 mètres de haut, accompagné de vents soufflant à 200 km/h, a dévasté les champs, tué de nombreuses bêtes, et détruit des villages entiers.

Des hélicoptères américains et britanniques survolent la région. Mais il sera difficile d'acheminer les secours sur le terrain, de nombreuses routes étant coupées. Des milliers de cadavres flottent sur l'eau ou jonchent le sol, et l'on craint des épidémies. Les survivants sont sous le choc. L'un d'eux a déclaré : « Seul Allah sait pourquoi nous avons été victimes d'une telle catastrophe. »

▲ *En haut, à gauche, un bateau échoué dans un champ. Ci-dessus, un survivant pleurant sa famille.*

IBM invente la disquette

La société américaine IBM vient de révolutionner la micro-informatique en inventant la disquette. Il s'agit d'un petit disque souple en plastique de 20 cm de diamètre, recouvert d'oxyde de fer magnétique. Cette disquette, qu'il suffit d'insérer dans le nouvel ordinateur IBM 3 740, permet d'y entrer des données ou de copier celles stockées dans l'ordinateur.

La guerre du Viêt-nam s'étend au Cambodge

▶ **30 avril 1970** ◀ Le président américain Richard Nixon a annoncé que des soldats américains et sud-vietnamiens ont été envoyés au Cambodge. En effet, c'est par le Cambodge que passe la piste Hô Chi Minh par laquelle les Vietnamiens du Nord envoient du ravitaillement aux maquis du Sud. Cependant, Nixon espère toujours se retirer de la guerre progressivement, en laissant les Sud-Vietnamiens se battre tout seuls.

▶ *Quelques-uns des 10 000 soldats américains, qui devraient progressivement se retirer du Cambodge.*

Les Palestiniens expulsés de Jordanie

▶ 30 septembre 1970 ◀ La paix est revenue au royaume de Jordanie, après les violents combats de ce dernier mois (« septembre noir ») opposant les troupes jordaniennes aux partisans palestiniens. Ces combats ont commencé après que des terroristes palestiniens ont détourné et détruit trois avions occidentaux dans le désert de Jordanie et pris en otages 56 passagers. Les Jordaniens ont battu les Palestiniens et repoussé les Syriens venant soutenir ces derniers. Un accord de cessez-le-feu a été signé il y a trois jours au Caire, la capitale de l'Égypte, entre le roi Hussein de Jordanie et Yasser Arafat, le président de l'Organisation de libération de la Palestine (OLP). Après cette défaite, les Palestiniens lutteront en recourant au terrorisme.

▲ Troupes jordaniennes opposées à des Palestiniens.

Émeutes à Gdansk

▶ 20 décembre 1970 ◀ Après plusieurs semaines de troubles, Wladyslaw Gomulka, le chef du parti communiste polonais, a démissionné en faveur de l'ancien mineur Edward Gierek. Les ouvriers polonais sont de plus en plus hostiles au régime communiste. Ils sont appuyés par l'Église catholique. Les troubles ont démarré à Gdansk, où des manifestations de dockers ont dégénéré en combats dirigés contre le siège local du Parti communiste. Trois cents personnes auraient été tuées.

Love Story

Le dernier film du réalisateur américain Arthur Miller, *Love Story*, d'après le roman d'Erich Segal, fait pleurer dans les salles. Ryan O'Neal joue le rôle d'Oliver, un étudiant amoureux de Jenny (Ali MacGraw), qui meurt d'une leucémie. O'Neal a décroché le rôle, refusé par plusieurs grands acteurs.

▲ Kent State University, dans l'Ohio, aux États-Unis, où quatre étudiants ont trouvé la mort lors d'une manifestation pacifiste.

Tragédie aux États-Unis

▶ 4 mai 1970 ◀ Quatre étudiants ont trouvé la mort aujourd'hui, à la Kent State University, dans l'Ohio, aux États-Unis, lors d'une manifestation contre l'intervention américaine au Cambodge. Après plusieurs jours de désordre, le gouverneur de l'Ohio demanda l'envoi de gardes nationaux sur le campus. À l'heure du déjeuner, ceux-ci essayèrent de disperser une manifestation, lançant des bombes lacrymogènes sur les étudiants, qui ripostèrent par des jets de pierres. De plus en plus nerveux, les gardes nationaux ouvrirent le feu, tuant quatre étudiants, dont deux jeunes filles, et en blessant onze autres. Selon les étudiants, les victimes ne faisaient qu'assister à la manifestation, et l'un d'eux, William Schroeder, appartenait à une organisation militaire formée de volontaires. Deux autres étudiants ont également été tués à la Jackson State University, dans le Mississippi.

▼ Ryan O'Neal et Ali MacGraw dans *Love Story*.

1970

Apollo 13 amerrit dans le Pacifique

▶ **17 avril 1970** ◀ Trois astronautes américains viennent d'amerrir dans le Pacifique, après avoir frôlé la mort pendant leur voyage vers la Lune. Il y a cinq jours, James Lovell, John Swigert et Fred Haise quittaient la Terre, à bord du vaisseau spatial Apollo 13. Après la mise en orbite autour de la Lune de la capsule *Odyssey*, ils devaient descendre vers la Lune à bord du LEM (module d'exploration lunaire) Aquarius. Mais l'explosion soudaine d'un réservoir d'oxygène d'Odyssey les obligea à se réfugier dans le LEM Aquarius, arrimé à la capsule. Ils se mirent alors en orbite autour de la Lune et redescendirent vers la Terre. Juste avant d'entrer dans l'atmosphère terrestre, ils regagnèrent la capsule Odyssey. Après le premier alunissage réussi d'Apollo 11, en juillet 1969, et la marche sur la Lune des astronautes d'Apollo 12, Charles Conrad et Alan Bea, en novembre, la mission Apollo 13, qui a pu cependant rapporter quelques clichés de la Lune, est un demi-échec.

◀ *La capsule Odyssey après son retour sur la Terre.*

Un opéra rock anglais à New York

Tommy, l'opéra rock du groupe anglais les Who, a été représenté en juin au Metropolitan Opera House de New York. Cet opéra raconte l'histoire d'un jeune garçon jouant remarquablement bien au flipper, qui assiste à un meurtre et devient sourd-muet et aveugle. L'album des Who, *Tommy*, remporte un énorme succès aux États-Unis.

▲ *La finale de la Coupe du monde de football.*

Le Brésil remporte la Coupe du monde

▶ **21 juin 1970** ◀ Le Brésil vient de remporter la Coupe du monde de football, battant par 4 à 1 l'Italie, à Mexico, devant 107 000 spectateurs. On a pu admirer l'extraordinaire jeu d'attaque de Pelé, Tostao, Jairzinho et Rivelino, tous en très grande forme. Le Brésil, déjà vainqueur en 1958 et en 1962, conserve donc la Coupe (trophée Jules Rimet).

Obsèques du général de Gaulle

▶ **12 novembre 1970** ◀ L'ancien président de la République française Charles de Gaulle a été enterré à Colombey-les-Deux-Églises. Il dirigea les Forces françaises libres pendant la Seconde Guerre mondiale. Il fut élu président de la République en 1958. Il régla la crise algérienne et fonda la V⁵ République. Fervent patriote, de Gaulle incarnait une France forte au cœur d'une « Europe européenne », par opposition à une Europe dominée par les États-Unis. Les chefs d'État du monde entier ont assisté à la messe célébrée en son honneur à Notre-Dame.

▶ *Le général de Gaulle, figure dominante de l'histoire de la France moderne.*

1970 – 1979

Merckx remporte le Tour de France

▶ **Juillet 1970** ◀ Le coureur cycliste belge Eddie Merckx vient de remporter le Tour de France pour la deuxième année consécutive. Il termine cette longue course divisée en plusieurs étapes avec 17,54 secondes d'avance sur le Français Roger Pingeon. Né en Belgique en 1945, Merckx participa à sa première course cycliste à 14 ans et devint champion du monde amateur à 18 ans. Il remporte également cette année le Tour d'Italie. Sa volonté de vaincre à tout prix lui a valu le surnom de Cannibale.

▲ *Le champion belge Eddie Merckx « volant » vers une nouvelle victoire.*

En 1970 aussi...

1er septembre • Mort de l'écrivain français François Mauriac, auteur de nombreux romans, dont le *Baiser au lépreux*, le *Nœud de vipères* et *Thérèse Desqueyroux*.

18 septembre • Mort du guitariste rock américain Jimi Hendrix, à 27 ans.

15 octobre • Sadate est nommé président de l'Égypte. Il succède au président Nasser, décédé le 28 septembre.

L'Anglais Tony Jacklin remporte l'open de golf américain

L'Anglais Tony Jacklin a remporté en juin l'open de golf américain, sous la chaleur du Minnesota. Menant dès le premier jour, il a terminé avec sept points d'avance sur l'Américain Dave Hill. Jacklin devint célèbre en 1967 : il fut le premier joueur à réaliser un trou en un (c'est-à-dire à mettre la balle dans le trou en un seul coup). En juillet dernier, il fut le premier Anglais, depuis Max Faulkner en 1951, à remporter l'open de golf britannique.

◀ *Le joueur de golf anglais Tony Jacklin, à l'open américain.*

◀ *Germaine Greer, une féministe de la deuxième vague.*

L'égalité pour les femmes

▶ **Décembre 1970** ◀ Germaine Greer, une Australienne travaillant en Angleterre, relance le débat sur le rôle des femmes dans le monde moderne, en publiant *la Femme eunuque*. Cet ouvrage démontre que le mariage traditionnel n'est pour les femmes qu'une forme d'esclavage légalisé. Mme Greer appartient aux féministes de la deuxième vague. Les premières, les suffragettes, se battaient pour les droits politiques des femmes. Aujourd'hui, les féministes, qui appartiennent à divers groupes, tel le MLF (Mouvement de libération de la femme), créé en 1968 en France, mènent campagne pour la liberté sexuelle et l'égalité dans le travail.

▲ *Slogan féministe inscrit sur le socle de la statue de la Liberté à Ellis Island, à New York.*

LA CONQUÊTE SPATIALE

De tout temps, les hommes ont rêvé d'explorer l'Univers. Grâce aux progrès accomplis, l'homme marche sur la Lune en 1969. L'Union soviétique et les États-Unis lancent ensuite des stations spatiales permettant aux astronautes de multiplier les expériences.

Des vaisseaux non habités parcourent des milliers de kilomètres, jusqu'aux confins du système solaire. Les sondes américaines *Viking* (1977) et *Pathfinder* (1997) envoient des informations sur Mars. En 1979, Pioneer 11 est le premier vaisseau spatial à survoler Saturne. Voyager et Pioneer sont programmés pour sortir du système solaire. Ils emportent des messages de la Terre destinés à d'éventuels autres êtres vivants.

▼ *Les astronautes ont fait découvrir une image nouvelle de la Terre.*

La bataille pour l'espace

Dans les années 50 et 60, les États-Unis et l'URSS se livrent un rude combat pour être les premiers dans l'espace. Le 4 octobre 1957, le satellite artificiel Spoutnik 1, construit par les Soviétiques, fait le tour de la Terre. Le 12 avril 1961, le Soviétique Iouri Gagarine effectue, à bord de la fusée Vostok 1 un tour de la Terre en quatre-vingt-neuf minutes.

Le 5 mai, soit moins d'un mois plus tard, l'Américain Alan Shepard, à bord de Liberty Bell 7, est le premier Américain dans l'espace. Le 20 février 1962, John Glenn égale les performances soviétiques, en tournant autour de la Terre, à bord de Friendship 7. Le 21 juillet 1969, les Américains Neil Armstrong et Edwin « Buzz » Aldrin sont les premiers hommes à marcher sur la Lune. Le président américain Richard Nixon décrète qu'il s'agit là du « plus grand moment de l'Histoire depuis la Création ».

L'espace
Le premier lancement d'essai de la fusée européenne Ariane a lieu avec succès le 24 décembre 1979.
• Saliout 1 est la première station spatiale lancée par les Soviétiques, le 19 avril 1971. La première station spatiale américaine *Skylab* est lancée, quant à elle, le 15 mai 1973.
• La chienne Laïka est le premier animal envoyé dans l'espace, le 3 novembre 1957, à bord du satellite soviétique Spoutnik. Elle meurt une semaine plus tard.

▼ *Les gros titres des journaux reflètent l'admiration et la crainte des Américains face aux Soviétiques, qui ont réussi à envoyer un satellite dans l'espace (1957).*

▶ *Iouri Gagarine, le premier homme dans l'espace, vole à 315 kilomètres au-dessus de la Terre, à bord de la fusée Vostok 1, qui pèse 4,7 tonnes.*

Sorties dans l'espace

Le 18 mars 1965, le cosmonaute soviétique Alekseï Leonov sort dans l'espace, relié par une corde au vaisseau spatial Voskhod 2. Tandis que son collègue Pavel Belyaev le surveille de l'intérieur du vaisseau, Leonov teste des instruments, prend des photos et effectue un saut périlleux. Sa sortie – la première dans l'espace – dure dix minutes.

Le 3 juin 1965, l'Américain Edward White sort à son tour dans l'espace. Pendant vingt minutes, il quitte Gemini 4, auquel il est relié par un câble en Nylon. Il parcourt alors 9 600 kilomètres, à la vitesse de 28 000 km/h. Lorsqu'il regagne son vaisseau, l'astronaute déclare que c'est le moment le plus triste de sa vie.

▶ Ed White, qui flotte en apesanteur à 160 kilomètres au-dessus de la Terre, se sert d'un fusil à gaz pour se mouvoir dans l'espace.

▲ Valentina Terechkova.

Des femmes dans l'espace

Le 16 juin 1963, la Soviétique Valentina Terechkova est la première femme dans l'espace. Elle accomplit 48 révolutions autour de la Terre, à bord de Vostok 6, avant d'atterrir au Kazakhstan. Durant ce vol, elle s'entretient avec Nikita Khrouchtchev, le président du Conseil soviétique.

La première Américaine dans l'espace est la physicienne Sally Ride, qui vole à bord de la navette spatiale Challenger le 18 juin 1983.

La première Française dans l'espace, en 1997, est Claudie André-Deshays.

Rendez-vous dans l'espace

Le programme américain Gemini est lancé en 1965-1966, pour apprendre aux astronautes à manœuvrer leurs vaisseaux. Le 15 décembre 1965, Walter Schirra et Thomas Stafford, à bord de Gemini 6, s'approchent à quelques centimètres de Gemini 7, piloté par Frank Borman et James Lovell. Le premier arrimage dans l'espace a lieu entre Gemini 8 et une fusée Agena, le 17 mars 1966.

▼ Gemini 6 s'approchant de Gemini 7.

Greenpeace contre les essais nucléaires

▶ **30 septembre 1971** ◀ Les garde-côtes américains ont empêché des membres de Greenpeace, une organisation écologiste canadienne, de traverser l'archipel des îles Aléoutiennes, au large de l'Alaska. Les huit écologistes, accompagnés par deux journalistes, projetaient de se rendre sur l'île d'Amchitka, où les Américains doivent effectuer des essais nucléaires. Leur bateau de pêche, *Phyllis Cormack*, a été rebaptisé, pour l'occasion, *Greenpeace*. Les membres de Greenpeace veulent mobiliser l'opinion internationale sur les conséquences de ces essais nucléaires. L'île d'Amchitka est une zone sensible, propice aux tremblements de terre. La population redoute qu'une explosion ne déclenche de nouvelles secousses et ne menace l'équilibre écologique de la région.

▲ *Manifestation des membres de Greenpeace à Amchitka.*

Greenpeace

Après la manifestation d'Amchitka, l'association écologiste Greenpeace devient une organisation internationale.

•

Greenpeace contribua à ce que l'Antarctique soit déclaré parc international en 1991.

•

La campagne menée par Greenpeace s'acheva en 1996 avec l'arrêt des essais nucléaires.

La guerre du Bangladesh

▶ **31 mai 1971** ◀ Des millions de Bengladais se sont réfugiés en Inde, et des centaines de milliers sont morts, depuis que le cheikh Mujibur Rahman a proclamé le 26 mars dernier l'indépendance du Bangladesh, l'ancien Pakistan oriental. Des troupes fidèles au président pakistanais Muhammed Yahia Khan veulent que le Bangladesh reste pakistanais. Ils exterminent les rebelles, mais ne font pas de distinction entre les combattants et les civils. L'Inde a permis au Bangladesh de constituer un gouvernement en exil à Calcutta.

▼ *Soldats indiens célébrant la naissance du Bangladesh.*

Jésus-Christ superstar

Chaque soir, des chrétiens manifestent devant le théâtre londonien où se donne la nouvelle comédie musicale d'Andrew Lloyd Webber et de T. Rice, *Jésus-Christ superstar*, qu'ils jugent irrévérencieuse. Cette comédie raconte l'histoire du Christ, sur fond de musique rock, de chansons et de danses. Webber et Rice estiment que la Bible est la plus grande histoire jamais racontée.

▼ *L'auteur T. Rice (à gauche) et le compositeur Andrew Lloyd Webber.*

1970 – 1979

Droit de vote pour les femmes en Suisse

▶ 7 février 1971 ◀ En Suisse, aujourd'hui, les femmes ont obtenu le droit de vote. Le référendum, pour lequel seuls les hommes votaient, a donné 621 403 voix en faveur du vote des femmes et 323 596 contre. Quelques cantons, dont les régions d'Uri, de Schwyz, d'Appenzell, de Saint-Gall et de Thuringe, y sont opposés. Les élections parlementaires d'octobre seront le premier scrutin où les Suissesses s'exprimeront. Comme il y a en Suisse 250 000 femmes de plus que d'hommes, le résultat sera intéressant à analyser.

◀ Suffragettes de la dernière heure menant campagne en Suisse.

Idi Amin Dada prend le pouvoir

▶ 20 février 1971 ◀ Le major Idi Amin Dada, qui a renversé le mois dernier le président ougandais Milton Obote, s'est nommé président et général. Ancien champion de boxe de l'armée, Amin Dada a interdit toute opposition politique ; il a cependant libéré les prisonniers politiques du régime d'Obote et promis des élections libres dans les cinq ans à venir.

▲ Idi Amin Dada.

Un nouveau parc *Disneyworld* :

La ville d'Orlando, en Floride, a un nouveau château – le château de la Belle au bois dormant – et de nouveaux « habitants », dont Mickey Mouse, Goofy et Pluto. La Walt Disney Company y a ouvert ici même son deuxième parc d'attractions. D'ici à la fin de l'année, on attend au moins 10 millions de visiteurs dans ce parc qui a coûté 400 millions de dollars.

En 1971 aussi...

2 janvier
• L'effondrement des barrières provoque la mort de 66 spectateurs assistant à un match de football à Ibrox Park, à Glasgow, en Écosse.

3 mai • Manifestation à Washington, aux États-Unis, pour protester contre la guerre du Viêt-nam.

26 octobre • La Chine populaire est admise à l'ONU (Organisation des Nations unies)

Mort de Jean Vilar

▶ 10 octobre 1971 ◀ L'acteur et metteur en scène français Jean Vilar est mort, à Sète, sa ville natale, à l'âge de 59 ans. Ce passionné de théâtre avait créé en 1943 sa propre compagnie, la Compagnie des 7, et fondé en 1947 le Festival d'Avignon. De 1951 à 1963, il prit en main le Théâtre national populaire (TNP) et le Théâtre de Chaillot. Il révéla de nombreux acteurs, dont le plus célèbre est Gérard Philipe. Celui-ci, star du cinéma français, a accepté les modestes cachets du TNP, pour faire découvrir le théâtre au plus grand nombre.

▲ Mickey Mouse et ses amis défilant dans le nouveau parc Disneyworld d'Orlando, en Floride.

1972

◀ *De gauche à droite : Romano, Zabari et leur entraîneur.*

▲ *Terroriste palestinien dans le village olympique de Munich.*

Tragédie sanglante aux jeux Olympiques d'hiver de Munich

▶ **5 septembre 1972** ◀ Les jeux Olympiques de Munich ont été aujourd'hui le théâtre d'une sanglante tragédie. Vers 5 heures du matin, des terroristes palestiniens appartenant au groupe Septembre noir (organisation clandestine luttant pour la libération de la Palestine) s'introduisent dans les appartements de la délégation israélienne, au village olympique, et tuent l'entraîneur Moshe Weinberg et l'haltérophile Yosef Romano. Neuf athlètes sont pris en otages : les terroristes exigent la libération de 200 Palestiniens prisonniers en Israël. Golda Meir, le Premier ministre israélien, refuse, et Willy Brandt, le chancelier de la RFA, arrive sur les lieux de la tragédie. Les terroristes obtiennent d'être transportés jusqu'au Caire, en Égypte. Le soir même, des hélicoptères les conduisent avec leurs otages vers un aérodrome militaire proche de Munich.

Alors qu'ils s'apprêtent à monter dans un Boeing 727, les lumières de l'aéroport s'éteignent et des tireurs d'élite ouvrent le feu. Les neuf otages ainsi que cinq terroristes et un policier allemand sont tués. Tandis que les survivants de la délégation israélienne s'envolent vers Israël, le comité olympique déclare que les Jeux continuent ; une décision qui est très controversée.

Un Américain champion du monde d'échecs

Bobby Fischer, âgé de 29 ans, est devenu en septembre le premier Américain champion du monde d'échecs. Il a battu le tenant du titre, le Soviétique Boris Spassky, à Reykjavík, en Islande, par 12,5 à 8,5 points. Doué d'un fort tempérament, l'Américain a impressionné tout le monde par la qualité de son jeu.

▲ *Le 69ᵉ coup (1072, tour vers E-1 +) de la partie opposant Spassky à Fischer pour le titre mondial.*

Violents incidents en Irlande du Nord

▶ **30 janvier 1972** ◀ Les troupes britanniques ont dispersé une manifestation en faveur des droits civils, qui avait été interdite, dans le district catholique de Bogside, Londonderry, en Irlande du Nord, tuant treize personnes. Ces violents affrontements, que l'on appelle déjà le « dimanche rouge », vont raviver les tensions entre les forces de sécurité britanniques, arrivées l'été dernier, et les nationalistes. Tandis que le général en chef de l'armée britannique affirme que ses soldats ont ouvert le feu car on leur avait tiré dessus, des témoins déclarent que les manifestants ont seulement lancé des pierres.

◀ *Des soldats britanniques intervenant à Londonderry, en Irlande du Nord, pour disperser une manifestation.*

1970 – 1979

Droit de vote pour les femmes en Suisse

▶ **7 février 1971** ◀ En Suisse, aujourd'hui, les femmes ont obtenu le droit de vote. Le référendum, pour lequel seuls les hommes votaient, a donné 621 403 voix en faveur du vote des femmes et 323 596 contre. Quelques cantons, dont les régions d'Uri, de Schwyz, d'Appenzell, de Saint-Gall et de Thuringe, y sont opposés. Les élections parlementaires d'octobre seront le premier scrutin où les Suissesses s'exprimeront. Comme il y a en Suisse 250 000 femmes de plus que d'hommes, le résultat sera intéressant à analyser.

◀ *Suffragettes de la dernière heure menant campagne en Suisse.*

Idi Amin Dada prend le pouvoir

▶ **20 février 1971** ◀ Le major Idi Amin Dada, qui a renversé le mois dernier le président ougandais Milton Obote, s'est nommé président et général. Ancien champion de boxe de l'armée, Amin Dada a interdit toute opposition politique ; il a cependant libéré les prisonniers politiques du régime d'Obote et promis des élections libres dans les cinq ans à venir.

▲ *Idi Amin Dada.*

Un nouveau parc *Disneyworld* :

La ville d'Orlando, en Floride, a un nouveau château – le château de la Belle au bois dormant – et de nouveaux « habitants », dont Mickey Mouse, Goofy et Pluto. La Walt Disney Company y a ouvert ici même son deuxième parc d'attractions. D'ici à la fin de l'année, on attend au moins 10 millions de visiteurs dans ce parc qui a coûté 400 millions de dollars.

En 1971 aussi...

2 janvier
- L'effondrement des barrières provoque la mort de 66 spectateurs assistant à un match de football à Ibrox Park, à Glasgow, en Écosse.

3 mai • *Manifestation à Washington, aux États-Unis, pour protester contre la guerre du Viêt-nam.*

26 octobre • *La Chine populaire est admise à l'ONU (Organisation des Nations unies)*

Mort de Jean Vilar

▶ **10 octobre 1971** ◀ L'acteur et metteur en scène français Jean Vilar est mort, à Sète, sa ville natale, à l'âge de 59 ans. Ce passionné de théâtre avait créé en 1943 sa propre compagnie, la Compagnie des 7, et fondé en 1947 le Festival d'Avignon. De 1951 à 1963, il prit en main le Théâtre national populaire (TNP) et le Théâtre de Chaillot. Il révéla de nombreux acteurs, dont le plus célèbre est Gérard Philipe. Celui-ci, star du cinéma français, a accepté les modestes cachets du TNP, pour faire découvrir le théâtre au plus grand nombre.

▲ *Mickey Mouse et ses amis défilant dans le nouveau parc Disneyworld d'Orlando, en Floride.*

1972

◀ De gauche à droite : Romano, Zabari et leur entraîneur.

גד צברי
מתאבק
GAD ZABARI
Wrestler

יוסף רומנו
משקולאי
JOSEPH ROMANO
Weightlifter

משה ויינברג
מאמן האבקות
MOSHE WEINBERG
Wrestling Coach

▲ Terroriste palestinien dans le village olympique de Munich.

Tragédie sanglante aux jeux Olympiques d'hiver de Munich

▶ **5 septembre 1972** ◀ Les jeux Olympiques de Munich ont été aujourd'hui le théâtre d'une sanglante tragédie. Vers 5 heures du matin, des terroristes palestiniens appartenant au groupe Septembre noir (organisation clandestine luttant pour la libération de la Palestine) s'introduisent dans les appartements de la délégation israélienne, au village olympique, et tuent l'entraîneur Moshe Weinberg et l'haltérophile Yosef Romano. Neuf athlètes sont pris en otages : les terroristes exigent la libération de 200 Palestiniens prisonniers en Israël. Golda Meir, le Premier ministre israélien, refuse, et Willy Brandt, le chancelier de la RFA, arrive sur les lieux de la tragédie. Les terroristes obtiennent d'être transportés jusqu'au Caire, en Égypte. Le soir même, des hélicoptères les conduisent avec leurs otages vers un aérodrome militaire proche de Munich.

Alors qu'ils s'apprêtent à monter dans un Boeing 727, les lumières de l'aéroport s'éteignent et des tireurs d'élite ouvrent le feu. Les neuf otages ainsi que cinq terroristes et un policier allemand sont tués. Tandis que les survivants de la délégation israélienne s'envolent vers Israël, le comité olympique déclare que les Jeux continuent ; une décision qui est très controversée.

Un Américain champion du monde d'échecs

Bobby Fischer, âgé de 29 ans, est devenu en septembre le premier Américain champion du monde d'échecs. Il a battu le tenant du titre, le Soviétique Boris Spasski, à Reykjavík, en Islande, par 12,5 à 8,5 points. Doué d'un fort tempérament, l'Américain a impressionné tout le monde par la qualité de son jeu.

▲ Le 69ᵉ coup (1072, tour vers E-1 +) de la partie opposant Spassky à Fischer pour le titre mondial.

Violents incidents en Irlande du Nord

▶ **30 janvier 1972** ◀ Les troupes britanniques ont dispersé une manifestation en faveur des droits civils, qui avait été interdite, dans le district catholique de Bogside, Londonderry, en Irlande du Nord, tuant treize personnes. Ces violents affrontements, que l'on appelle déjà le « dimanche rouge », vont raviver les tensions entre les forces de sécurité britanniques, arrivées l'été dernier, et les nationalistes. Tandis que le général en chef de l'armée britannique affirme que ses soldats ont ouvert le feu car on leur avait tiré dessus, des témoins déclarent que les manifestants ont seulement lancé des pierres.

◀ Des soldats britanniques intervenant à Londonderry, en Irlande du Nord, pour disperser une manifestation.

1970 – 1979

▲ Le président américain Nixon et le Premier ministre chinois Chou En-lai.

Mark Spitz remporte sept médailles d'or aux jeux Olympiques

Le nageur américain Mark Spitz s'est distingué aux jeux Olympiques de Munich en remportant, à 22 ans, sept médailles d'or (100 m et 200 m nage libre, 100 m et 200 m papillon, trois épreuves de relais). Ces médailles s'ajoutent aux deux médailles d'or qu'il remporta il y a quatre ans aux jeux Olympiques de Mexico.

▶ L'Américain Mark Spitz, sur le point de remporter sa septième médaille d'or dans le relais 4 x 100 m quatre nages.

Fin de la visite de Nixon en Chine

▶ **28 février 1972** ◀ La visite historique du président américain Richard Nixon en Chine se termine aujourd'hui. À l'invitation du gouvernement communiste chinois, Nixon s'est entretenu avec le président Mao Zédong et le Premier ministre Chou En-lai. Jusqu'à présent, les relations entre la Chine et les États-Unis étaient tendues, du fait de la reconnaissance par les Américains du gouvernement nationaliste chinois de Taïwan. Mais, après ces « discussions sérieuses et franches », les dirigeants américain et chinois ont promis d'œuvrer conjointement pour la paix dans le monde et se sont échangé des cadeaux pour sceller leur rapprochement.

En 1972 aussi...

22 janvier • Le Royaume-Uni, l'Irlande, le Danemark et la Norvège signent à Bruxelles un traité prévoyant leur entrée dans la CEE (Communauté économique européenne).

25 janvier • Première greffe mondiale d'un rein et d'un pancréas, à Londres.

5 mai • Un DC-8 d'Alitalia s'écrase, faisant 115 morts.

Le procès de Bobigny

▶ **Octobre 1972** ◀ Le procès de Bobigny montre que la société française a bien changé. Maître Gisèle Halimi défend une jeune fille qui a demandé à avorter après avoir été victime d'un viol. Selon la loi de 1920, toujours en vigueur, la sage-femme qui a pratiqué l'avortement est passible de la peine de mort. Son acquittement sera une victoire pour les féministes françaises. 1972 est décidément l'année des femmes. Pour la première fois, une jeune fille, Anne Chopinet, est admise à l'école Polytechnique. Au même moment, le Parlement s'apprête à voter une loi sur l'égalité entre les salaires masculins et féminins.

Massacres au Burundi

▶ **6 mai 1972** ◀ Des milliers de personnes ont été massacrées, la semaine dernière, dans la république africaine du Burundi. Ces massacres interviennent après la tentative de rebelles appartenant à la tribu des Hutus, et soutenus par des mercenaires congolais, de renverser le gouvernement tutsi, minoritaire du président Michel Micombero. Selon les survivants, qui se sont réfugiés en Tanzanie, les troupes de Micombero auraient riposté en massacrant des milliers de Hutus. Pendant ce temps, des rebelles hutus sèment la terreur, tuant les Tutsis qu'ils rencontrent.

▼ Soldats appartenant à la tribu des Tutsis, minoritaires au Burundi, surveillant des prisonniers hutus.

1972

Les nouvelles idoles des adolescents

▼ Ci-dessous : les cinq frères Jackson. À droite : les frères Osmond : de gauche à droite, Alan, Wayne, Merrill, Jay et Donny.

▶ 14 octobre 1972 ◀

Aujourd'hui, les jeunes adolescents ont comme idoles des chanteurs à peine plus âgés qu'eux. Ainsi, Michael Jackson, le plus jeune des cinq frères Jackson, âgé de 14 ans, arrive en tête du hit-parade avec *Ben*, la chanson d'un film pour la défense des animaux. L'autre idole des adolescents est David Cassidy, Keith dans le film télévisé *The Partridge Family*. Les frères Osmond, qui appartiennent à l'Église des mormons, sont eux aussi très populaires parmi les jeunes. Après leur grand succès commun *Crazy Horses*, Donny enregistra tout seul *Puppy Love*, et Little Jimmy – 9 ans – triompha avec *Long-Haired Lover from Liverpool*.

▲ Le chanteur et acteur américain David Cassidy, l'idole des jeunes Américains.

Mise en vente du premier magnétoscope

Le groupe hollandais Philips, l'inventeur de la cassette audio, vient de lancer un nouvel appareil. Ce magnétoscope permet d'enregistrer et de projeter des films de télé grâce à une cassette spéciale qui enregistre des signaux vidéo. Une horloge permet de programmer des enregistrements.

La capitale du Nicaragua détruite par un violent tremblement de terre

▶ 24 décembre 1972 ◀

Managua, la capitale du Nicaragua, vient d'être touchée par un violent tremblement de terre. Les secousses, qui atteignaient cette nuit 6,5 sur l'échelle de Richter, ont fait plus de 18 000 morts et 50 000 blessés ; elles continuaient encore ce matin. Le gouvernement a demandé à tous les habitants de quitter la ville, laquelle se vide progressivement.

Parmi les survivants figure le milliardaire américain Howard Hughes, qui se trouvait à l'hôtel Intercontinental au moment du drame et réussit à se réfugier dans le parking de l'hôtel. Le président du Nicaragua, le général Anastasio Somoza – dont le palais a été entièrement détruit –, a déclaré :

« Managua est désormais méconnaissable. Nous devons la reconstruire entièrement. »

▶ Managua, la capitale du Nicaragua, détruite par un tremblement de terre.

1970 – 1979

Accident d'avion dans les Andes

▶ **29 décembre 1972** ◀ On a appris aujourd'hui que les seize survivants de l'avion qui s'est écrasé dans les Andes le 13 octobre ont été obligés de manger les cadavres des morts pour se nourrir. Les rescapés, des membres d'une équipe de rugby uruguayenne, étaient isolés sur un pic montagneux depuis dix semaines. Ayant épuisé leurs vivres au bout de trois semaines, ils ont été persuadés par leur entraîneur que la seule chance de survie était de se nourrir des protéines des cadavres de leurs compagnons. Avant de passer à l'acte, les survivants ont tracé une immense croix dans la neige, pour implorer le pardon divin.

▶ *Après dix semaines de cauchemar, les rescapés de l'accident d'avion acclament l'hélicoptère qui vient les sauver.*

Horreur au Viêt-nam

▶ **9 juin 1972** ◀ La nuit dernière, des avions américains, qui visaient des cibles militaires du Viêt-cong, ont bombardé le village vietnamien de Huynh Cong Ut. Ce matin s'étalent à la une des journaux des photos d'enfants fuyant leur village en flammes. L'un d'eux, une fillette nommée Phan Thi Kim Phuc, a enlevé ses vêtements, brûlés par le napalm. Elle symbolise l'horreur de cette guerre.

▼ *Enfants vietnamiens fuyant leur village bombardé au napalm.*

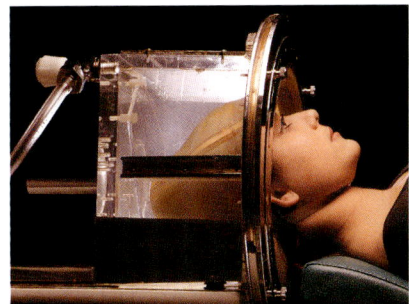

▲ *Appareil de scanographie (scanner).*

Invention du scanner

▶ **Mars 1972** ◀ Un nouvel appareil extraordinaire permet désormais de voir l'intérieur d'un crâne sans l'ouvrir. Inventé par l'ingénieur anglais Godfrey Hounsfield et le physicien d'Afrique du Sud Allan Cormack, le scanographe, ou scanner, utilise un ordinateur pour reconstituer, à partir d'images radiologiques, la coupe transversale du crâne. Il fonctionne en faisant tourner autour de la tête un tube générateur de rayons X, et un détecteur qui mesure la quantité de rayons X absorbée par les tissus.

Les accords SALT-1

▶ **1er juin 1972** ◀ La première visite officielle d'un président américain à Moscou s'achève aujourd'hui avec la signature des accords SALT-1 (Strategic Arms Limitation Talks : accords sur la limitation des armements nucléaires stratégiques). Le président américain Nixon et le secrétaire général soviétique Brejnev se sont engagés à limiter le nombre de missiles balistiques qui ont une portée supérieure à 5 000 km, détenus par chacun des pays, et à ne pas développer d'armes antimissiles.

▶ *Nixon (à droite) et Brejnev (au centre), lors du sommet de Moscou.*

PROTECTION DE L'ENVIRONNEMENT

Depuis les années 70, l'homme prend conscience qu'il doit modifier son comportement vis-à-vis de la Terre. Les marées noires tuent régulièrement des milliers d'oiseaux et de poissons. Les fleuves et les mers sont pollués par les engrais chimiques, les déchets industriels et les égouts.

Un certain nombre d'associations et de gouvernements essaient de sauver la Terre. Les mesures de protection de l'environnement sont primordiales et nous concernent tous.

Croisade contre le nucléaire

L'association Greenpeace est fondée en 1971, au Canada, par des écologistes. Sa première mission est de stopper les essais nucléaires du gouvernement américain sur l'île d'Amchitka, en Alaska. Après ce succès, Greenpeace devient une organisation internationale, financée par ses membres et basée à Amsterdam, en Hollande.

Outre la lutte contre la pollution, Greenpeace tente d'empêcher les essais nucléaires et de sauver les espèces animales et végétales menacées d'extinction. Ses membres prennent souvent des mesures très fermes pour obliger les gouvernements et les industries à protéger l'environnement.

La Terre

On estime à 8 millions le nombre d'espèces animales et végétales existant dans le monde. Seules 1,5 million d'espèces sont répertoriées aujourd'hui.

Les trois quarts des espèces animales et végétales du monde vivent dans les forêts tropicales.

5 929 espèces animales sont en voie de disparition.

En 1972, il n'existait plus que 1 827 tigres en Inde, contre 50 000 en 1905. Grâce aux mesures prises, on en comptait 4 000 en 1986.

▲ Membres de Greenpeace suspendus à un pont au-dessus du Rhin, pour interrompre le trafic fluvial et protester ainsi contre la pollution du fleuve en Europe.

▼ Enfants protestant contre la pollution, en Tchécoslovaquie.

La couche d'ozone

On a découvert un trou dans la couche d'ozone, au-dessus de l'Antarctique : la pollution en est en partie responsable. L'ozone de l'atmosphère terrestre absorbe les rayons ultraviolets du Soleil, qui, en grande quantité, sont nocifs pour les plantes et peuvent provoquer des cancers de la peau chez l'homme.

Les effets de la pollution

L'atmosphère de notre planète est empoisonnée par la pollution. Les « pluies acides », qui abîment les arbres et les plantes, résultent de la production de dioxyde de soufre et d'oxyde d'azote par les gaz d'échappement des automobiles et les émanations des centrales qui fonctionnent au pétrole ou au charbon. En se mélangeant à la vapeur d'eau des nuages, ces gaz produisent des acides sulfurique et nitrique qui polluent la pluie.

L'« effet de serre » est aussi dangereux, à long terme. Certains gaz, parvenus dans l'atmosphère terrestre, empêchent une partie de la chaleur émise par le Soleil de repartir dans l'espace. Plus la quantité de gaz carbonique augmente, plus la quantité de chaleur « piégée » croît. À long terme, les glaciers des pôles Nord et Sud risquent de fondre, et le niveau de la mer, de monter. Notre planète pourrait alors être inondée, et les cycles du climat, modifiés.

▼ Arbres abîmés par les pluies acides.

▲ Les détritus sont une autre forme de pollution. Dans les années 90, des mesures ont été prises pour réduire l'emballage des produits et faciliter leur recyclage.

▲ Les marées noires menacent les espèces aquatiques.

▶ L'ivoire est détruit par l'armée, au Kenya afin d'éviter tout trafic.

Des espèces menacées

Selon les lois de la nature, les espèces animales incapables de s'adapter à leur environnement meurent. Aujourd'hui, certaines espèces sont menacées par l'homme, qui détruit leur habitat. D'autres sont tuées à des fins commerciales, tels les éléphants, dont les défenses en ivoire sont très convoitées (ci-contre). On comptait 2 millions d'éléphants en Afrique en 1970 ; il en reste aujourd'hui 500 000. Le commerce de l'ivoire est interdit dans certains pays d'Afrique.

1973

Coup d'État au Chili

▶ **11 septembre 1973** ◀ La tension est intense au Chili ce soir, après la chute du président Salvador Allende. Le coup d'État du général Augusto Pinochet a commencé tôt ce matin. À son appel, les troupes ont investi les rues de Santiago, la capitale du Chili. Allende s'est barricadé dans le palais présidentiel, qui a subi les bombardements d'avions militaires. La mort du président a été confirmée dans la soirée. Un porte-parole de Pinochet a annoncé son suicide ; les partisans du président affirment qu'il est mort avec les armes à la main, en défendant le palais jusqu'au bout. Le coup d'État met fin au gouvernement socialiste, qui avait été élu démocratiquement. La politique d'Allende, avec des nationalisations, la réforme agraire et la hausse des salaires, avait satisfait les travailleurs, mais elle avait mécontenté les milieux d'affaires. La CIA – les services secrets américains – a aidé à financer les groupes d'opposition qui ont multiplié les actes terroristes. Allende avait perdu le soutien de partis qui lui avaient été favorables. Le Chili est désormais dirigé par une junte militaire de droite.

▼ *Un soldat garde les partisans d'Allende, parqués dans le stade de Santiago du Chili.*

▲ *Le président Allende (avec ses lunettes et son casque) défend le palais, pendant le coup d'État.*

Prix Nobel pour Konrad Lorenz

Konrad Lorenz, le spécialiste autrichien du comportement animal, partage le prix Nobel de médecine avec ses collègues Karl von Frisch et Nikolaas Tinbergen. Lorenz est le fondateur de l'éthologie, la science qui compare les comportements des animaux à ceux des humains. Il est connu pour son étude sur les oies cendrées.

L'Europe des Neuf

▶ **1er janvier 1973** ◀ Le Royaume-Uni de Grande-Bretagne et d'Irlande du Nord, la République d'Irlande, et le Danemark, adhèrent à la Communauté économique européenne, et rejoignent la France, l'Italie, la République fédérale d'Allemagne, la Belgique, les Pays-Bas et le Luxembourg. Les Neuf constituent le plus grand bloc économique du monde. La CEE s'élargit pour la première fois depuis sa création en 1957. Sa population est désormais supérieure à celle des États-Unis. La Grande-Bretagne avait demandé à rejoindre la CEE en 1961, mais le général de Gaulle, président de la République française, s'y était opposé.

▼ *Konrad Lorenz et quelques sujets de recherche.*

En 1973 aussi …

27 janvier • À Paris, les États-Unis et le Viêt-nam signent l'accord de cessez-le-feu mettant fin à l'intervention américaine.

8 avril • Mort du peintre Pablo Picasso.

31 juillet • À Besançon, l'usine Lip (horlogerie) est mise en liquidation. Les salariés s'organisent pour continuer seuls la fabrication et procèdent à des ventes sauvages de montres.

▲ *Des représentants des neuf États de la Communauté économique européenne.*

Le prix du pétrole double

▶ 22 décembre 1973 ◀ À Téhéran, en Iran, les six pays membres de l'OPEP – l'Organisation des pays exportateurs de pétrole – décident de doubler le prix du baril de pétrole brut, qui passe de 5,092 à 11,651 dollars. La première augmentation avait été décidée en octobre, pour gêner les alliés d'Israël. Les pays riches, qui ne produisent pas de pétrole mais l'achètent aux pays producteurs, sont inquiets. La hausse du prix du pétrole va entraîner ainsi plusieurs milliards de dépenses supplémentaires en France. Le prix des carburants nécessaires aux automobiles et le prix des autres produits dérivés du pétrole vont fortement augmenter. Il va falloir faire des économies.

▲ L'Opéra est situé près du port de Sydney.

L'opéra de Sydney

La ville de Sydney, en Australie, possède enfin son Opéra, treize ans après la pose de la première pierre. L'architecte suédois Jörn Utzon a créé une structure étonnante, dominée par de grandes coques en béton. L'Opéra dispose de quatre salles, avec un auditorium pour 1 500 personnes. La reine Élisabeth, chef du Commonwealth, l'a inauguré et a déclaré qu'il était l'une des merveilles du monde moderne.

▼ Le drapeau israélien flotte sur le territoire syrien.

La guerre du Kippour

▶ 24 octobre 1973 ◀ L'Égypte et la Syrie attaquent Israël par surprise, le 6 octobre, le jour du Yom Kippour, la plus grande fête religieuse juive. Les alliés arabes reprennent la rive orientale du canal de Suez et les hauteurs du Golan, dont Israël s'était emparé en 1967. Mais, la semaine dernière, après avoir mené une violente bataille de chars, Israël dépasse les lignes égyptiennes et occupe des territoires sur la rive ouest du canal. L'ONU impose aujourd'hui le cessez-le-feu.

Des Indiens occupent Wounded Knee

▶ 8 mai 1973 ◀ L'extraordinaire révolte des Indiens Sioux de la réserve de Pine Ridge, dans le Dakota du Sud, se termine. Les 120 protestataires acceptent de quitter Wounded Knee, un lieu historique où 200 Sioux avaient été massacrés par les troupes fédérales, en 1890. L'occupation de la ville a commencé en février, pour durer 69 jours. Les Indiens accusent le gouvernement américain de violer les traités et leurs droits civiques. Ils ont mis au défi les autorités de répéter le massacre, et demandent une enquête officielle sur leur situation dramatique.

◀ Des Indiens occupent l'église catholique de Wounded Knee.

▲ La famille royale sur le balcon, après le mariage.

Mariage d'Anne d'Angleterre

▶ 14 novembre 1973 ◀ La Grande-Bretagne, où sévit une crise industrielle et qui est frappée par les restrictions d'essence, célèbre le premier mariage royal depuis dix ans. La cérémonie est suivie par 500 millions de téléspectateurs dans le monde entier. Elle se déroule à l'abbaye de Westminster. La princesse Anne, fille de la reine Élisabeth, se marie avec le capitaine de cavalerie Mark Philips.

1970 – 1979

1974

Démission du président Richard Nixon

▲ Devant la Maison-Blanche, le jour de la démission de R. Nixon, au 2027ᵉ jour de sa présidence.

◀ Nixon, le premier président américain à avoir démissionné.

▶ 9 août 1974 ◀ Le président américain Richard Nixon démissionne aujourd'hui, à la suite du scandale du Watergate qui bouleverse les États-Unis depuis deux ans. En juin 1972, des « cambrioleurs » sont surpris en train de poser du matériel d'écoute dans l'immeuble du Parti démocrate à Washington, le Watergate. L'enquête conclut qu'ils sont liés au comité pour la réélection du président Nixon, qui est républicain. Deux journalistes dénoncent aussi ce scandale dans le *Washington Post*.

Les enquêteurs ont prouvé que de proches collaborateurs du président étaient impliqués et que Nixon était au courant du cambriolage. Nixon, qui a été réélu en novembre 1972, nie sa responsabilité. Mais, voici trois jours, le procureur chargé de l'affaire a obtenu la bande d'un enregistrement audio provenant de la Maison-Blanche. On entend Nixon demander à son équipe de faire obstruction aux enquêtes du FBI sur le cambriolage. Nixon a préféré démissionner plutôt que d'être démis de ses fonctions par le Congrès.

Les Queen, la vidéo et le rock

La *Bohemian Rhapsody* du groupe Queen, une œuvre de 6 minutes qui associe la balade, le hard-rock et la musique heavy metal, bat tous les records de vente au Royaume-Uni. Le groupe a assuré le succès et la promotion du titre en réalisant un court-métrage vidéo.

▼ Le groupe Queen : Brian May, Roger Taylor, Freddie Mercury et John Deacon.

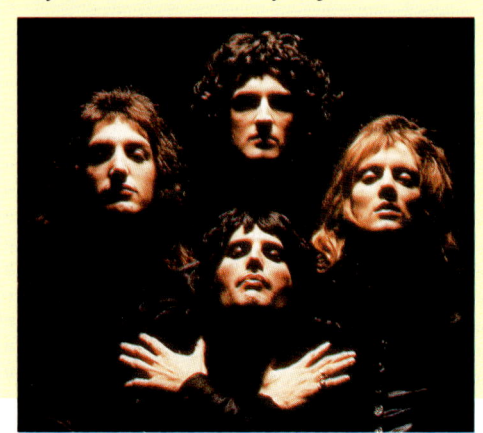

Révolution des Œillets au Portugal

▶ 25 avril 1974 ◀ Les officiers, lassés par les guerres coloniales, mettent fin à la dictature instituée par António Salazar en 1933. Le Mouvement des forces armées du général António Spínola a réussi le coup d'État, qui a fait 3 morts et 40 blessés. Le successeur de Salazar, Marcello Caetano, est renversé. Spínola promet d'établir la démocratie au Portugal et de donner l'indépendance aux colonies. Les Portugais accueillent avec joie la révolution. On voit partout des œillets rouges et blancs, qui symbolisent les espoirs d'un nouvel avenir socialiste.

▼ Les marins soutiennent la révolution des Œillets, à Lisbonne.

Chute de la dictature en Grèce

▶ 24 juillet 1974 ◀ La dictature militaire qui gouverne la Grèce s'effondre, quatre jours après le débarquement des troupes turques dans le nord de Chypre. Celles-ci sont intervenues victorieusement, après qu'un coup d'État a chassé du pouvoir le président Mgr Makários. Celui-ci était parvenu à maintenir la paix dans l'île, malgré l'hostilité qui y règne entre Grecs et Turcs. Mais le gouvernement d'Athènes a poussé les Grecs de l'île à réclamer l'Enósis – réunion avec la Grèce –, car les dictateurs espéraient, en déclenchant une guerre nationale, détourner l'attention des Grecs de la situation intérieure. En effet, depuis 1967, le pouvoir appartient à des colonels, qui ne se maintiennent que grâce à une impitoyable répression. Leur échec à propos de Chypre restaure la démocratie en Grèce. Des négociations sur le statut de Chypre s'ouvrent à Genève.

◀ Des soldats turcs à Chypre.

En 1974 aussi...

22 février • Le Pakistan reconnaît le Bangladesh.

12 septembre • L'empereur d'Éthiopie Hailé Sélassié est renversé par un coup d'État.

29 octobre • Le boxeur Muhammad Ali redevient champion du monde des poids lourds.

26 novembre • M. Tanaka, le Premier ministre du Japon, démissionne, à la suite d'une affaire de corruption.

La tour CN à Toronto

Le Canada va battre un nouveau record. Une formidable tour en béton s'élève peu à peu dans le ciel de Toronto. La tour nationale du Canada atteindra 553 mètres de haut. Elle ne sera pas la réalisation humaine la plus haute, mais sera l'édifice sur pied le plus haut du monde. La tour CN abritera une terrasse d'observation, un restaurant tournant, ainsi qu'un mât d'antenne tout au sommet.

Giscard d'Estaing, président de la République française

▶ 13 novembre 1974 ◀ Le président de la République française, Georges Pompidou, est mort le 2 avril. Une nouvelle élection présidentielle a eu lieu au suffrage universel. Valéry Giscard d'Estaing est élu au second tour, le 19 mai, par 50,8 % des voix exprimées, contre 49,2 % pour François Mitterrand. La France entame alors une série de réformes importantes. Le nouveau président crée un ministère de la Condition féminine. La majorité légale passe de 21 à 18 ans. La même année, la loi Veil autorise l'interruption volontaire de grossesse, dans certaines conditions. Un accord entre les syndicats prévoit d'indemniser les chômeurs pour raisons économiques à 90 % de leur salaire.

Soljenitsyne expulsé d'Union soviétique

▶ 14 février 1974 ◀ L'écrivain russe Aleksandr Soljenitsyne, qui a obtenu le prix Nobel de littérature en 1970, a été arrêté, déchu de la citoyenneté soviétique, et expulsé d'Union soviétique. Son crime est d'avoir publié un nouveau livre, qui raconte la vie des prisonniers déportés dans les camps de travail soviétiques de l'archipel du Goulag. Il est maintenant arrivé à Francfort.

▶ Soljenitsyne et Heinrich Böll.

Découverte d'une armée en terre cuite en Chine

▶ **11 juillet 1975** ◀ Il y a juste un an, des villageois de la région du mont Li, dans le Nord de la Chine, qui creusaient un puits, ont découvert d'étranges sculptures en terre cuite. Les archéologues se sont rendus sur le site et ils ont mis au jour l'extraordinaire armée de terre cuite du premier empereur de Chine. Les statues grandeur nature figurent les soldats de Qin Shi Huangdi. Celui-ci était un tyran très efficace et sans pitié. Il a entrepris le chantier de la Grande Muraille et a décidé de construire dans les environs cette sépulture extraordinaire. Quand il meurt, vers 210 av. J.-C., son armée de terre cuite est achevée. Les chercheurs ont dégagé les 3 000 soldats de la fosse n° 141, qui mesure 210 mètres d'est en ouest, et 60 mètres du nord au sud. Ils sont rangés suivant onze allées parallèles. Chaque visage est différent, comme si toutes les statues représentaient de vrais individus. Il y a aussi des chevaux, des chars, des armes. D'autres fosses attendent les archéologues. L'armée de Qin Shi Huangdi constitue déjà une nouvelle merveille du monde.

▲ *L'infanterie chinoise en terre cuite est en formation de combat.*

Le premier PC

▶ **Mars 1975** ◀ Le premier micro-ordinateur destiné à l'usage familial est disponible, aux États-Unis. On peut l'acheter au prix de 297 dollars. Le MITS Altair 8800 dispose de 256 bits de mémoire. Il se compose de plusieurs éléments. Mais il reste assez compliqué à manipuler. Pour le mettre en marche, il faut appuyer sur une série de 25 boutons, en suivant un ordre précis. Ce nouvel appareil, très original, est donc réservé pour l'instant aux passionnés d'informatique. Toutefois, les constructeurs se sont mis au travail pour créer des produits plus conviviaux.

Mort de Franco

▲ *Franco a durci sa dictature, ces quinze dernières années.*

▶ **20 novembre 1975** ◀ Le généralissime Francisco Franco est mort aujourd'hui. Il a dirigé l'Espagne depuis la fin de la guerre civile, en 1939. Il sera inhumé dans le cimetière militaire officiel où sont enterrés ses compagnons. Le prince Juan Carlos, qui présidera les funérailles du dictateur, montera sur le trône d'Espagne deux jours plus tard, le 22 novembre. Dans son discours devant les Cortes (le Parlement espagnol), le roi dit qu'il favorisera les grands changements. Il a été élevé par Franco pour lui succéder. On l'appelle déjà Juan Carlos le Bref, car on estime qu'il ne pourra rester au pouvoir. Mais il a l'appui de l'armée et la volonté de faire de son pays une véritable démocratie.

En 1975 aussi...

1er janvier • L'ONU proclame 1975 « l'année de la femme ».

4 janvier • Les Khmers rouges, dirigés par Pol Pot, assiègent Phnom Penh, la capitale du Cambodge.

15 mars • Mort du grand armateur grec Aristote Onassis.

1er août • Les accords internationaux d'Helsinki, signés par 35 États, réaffirment les droits de l'homme.

1970 – 1979

Le rendez-vous de l'espace

Deux vaisseaux spatiaux, le Soyouz soviétique et l'Apollo américain se rejoignent et s'arriment au-dessus de l'Europe de l'Ouest. Cette rencontre est historique. Le cosmonaute Alekseï Leonov et l'astronaute Thomas Stafford se serrent la main dans l'espace et se saluent en russe et en anglais. Ils se rendent visite, passant d'un vaisseau à l'autre, travaillent en commun, comparent leurs notes sur leurs expériences et mangent ensemble.

◀ *Rencontre dans l'espace entre spationautes.*

La couche d'ozone et les aérosols

Aux États-Unis, les bombes aérosol à usage familial affichent une mise en garde. Chacun a pris conscience du danger des aérosols depuis l'année dernière. Deux spécialistes ont affirmé que les fluorocarbones qui se répandent dans l'atmosphère en grande quantité détruisent la couche d'ozone. La Terre ne sera plus assez protégée des rayons ultraviolets, et les cancers de la peau risquent d'augmenter.

Guerre civile au Liban

▲ *À Beyrouth, une milice musulmane.*

▶ **16 septembre 1975** ◀ La ville de Beyrouth se transforme en champ de bataille. Le Liban est déchiré et ravagé par la guerre civile. Il y a près de cinq ans, les Palestiniens de l'organisation Septembre noir ont installé au Liban les bases principales de la guérilla contre Israël, qui mène des raids de représailles. La guerre civile a éclaté, car la lutte entre Israël et les Palestiniens a détruit l'équilibre des pouvoirs, déjà fragile, du Liban. Beaucoup de Libanais musulmans soutiennent les actions des Palestiniens contre Israël, mais les chrétiens y sont très opposés. Le Liban compte 14 confessions religieuses. Certaines ont constitué des armées privées, les milices.

Le Viêt-nam réunifié

▶ **29 avril 1975** ◀ Les forces communistes vietnamiennes sont victorieuses. Elles se préparent à entrer dans Saigon, la capitale du Sud-Viêt-nam. La chute de la ville marque la fin réelle de la guerre du Viêt-nam. La paix de 1973 a entraîné le retrait des Américains, mais les combats se sont poursuivis entre le Nord communiste et le Sud.

Depuis des jours, l'ambassade des États-Unis à Saigon est envahie par des milliers de personnes qui veulent fuir avant l'arrivée du nouveau gouvernement communiste.

◀ *Saigon, après les derniers bombardements.*
Ci-dessus : on se bat pour monter à bord d'un avion d'évacuation.

L'année internationale de la femme

▶ **31 décembre 1975** ◀ En Grande-Bretagne, les femmes bénéficient de deux lois qui condamnent la discrimination sexuelle, en matière d'emploi et de salaire, sur les lieux de travail. C'est un triomphe pour les féministes anglaises, qui militent pour la libération de la femme. En Grande-Bretagne, il reste des lieux interdits aux femmes, comme certains pubs et les clubs, réservés aux hommes.

▶ *Trois manifestantes anglaises quittent un pub.*

 1970
 1971
 1972
1973
 1974
 1975
1976
 1977
 1978
 1979

Les Sex Pistols et les punks

En 1976, les jeunes qui se rebellent adoptent le style punk. Les nouveaux groupes de musique comme les Sex Pistols abandonnent les équipements complexes et chers. Ils préfèrent les sons forts, bruts et provocants. Le manager des Sex Pistols, Malcolm MacLaren, dit qu'ils sont des « loubards », mais qu'« ils en sont fiers ».

▼ *Les Sex Pistols sont fiers d'être punks.*

En 1976 aussi...

5 mai • Création du Front de libération nationale corse. Il multiplie les attentats à l'explosif dans l'île.

29 juillet • La ville chinoise de Tangshan est dévastée par un terrible séisme.

25 août • Le Premier ministre français, Jacques Chirac, démissionne.

2 novembre • Jimmy Carter est élu président des États-Unis.

1976

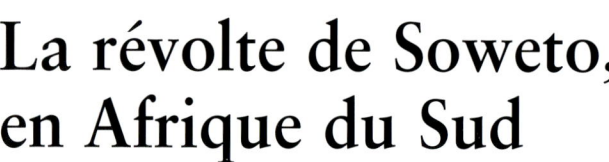

◀ *Les émeutes de Soweto mobilisent le monde contre l'apartheid.*

▼ *La police face aux enfants noirs, en Afrique du Sud.*

La révolte de Soweto, en Afrique du Sud

▶ **18 juin 1976** ◀ Des milliers de Sud-Africains noirs investissent les rues pour protester contre la mesure qu'impose le ministère de l'Éducation du Transvaal : l'afrikaans, la langue des anciens colons hollandais, sera enseigné dans les collèges, à égalité avec l'anglais. Cette mesure exaspère les habitants de Soweto et des autres *townships* – les villes noires de banlieue – autour de Johannesburg. L'afrikaans est le symbole de l'apartheid, fondé sur la ségrégation raciale.

La révolte débute à Soweto, le 16 juin, puis s'étend à tout le pays. La police tue un écolier de 13 ans. Il y a des centaines de morts et plus d'un millier de blessés. La police, chargée de rétablir l'ordre « à tout prix », selon l'expression du Premier ministre Vorster, tire sans sommation. La presse publie les photographies d'écoliers noirs, encore vêtus de leur uniforme, qui ont été abattus par la police.

Raid israélien sur Entebbé

▶ **4 juillet 1976** ◀ Trois avions de transport Hercule débarquent des commandos israéliens sur l'aéroport d'Entebbe, en Ouganda, samedi soir. Ils viennent libérer les 100 otages qui sont détenus par des terroristes propalestiniens. Les commandos israéliens attaquent, profitent de l'effet de surprise total, et s'emparent de l'Airbus. Mais vingt des soldats ougandais qui gardent l'avion, sept pirates de l'air et trois otages sont tués. Les terroristes, qui avaient l'appui du président ougandais Idi Amin Dada, demandaient la libération de prisonniers politiques palestiniens, en Israël, en France et dans trois autres pays.

◀ *Les otages, de retour en Israël, après leur libération.*

Mort de Mao Zédong

▶ 23 octobre 1976 ◀ Mao Zédong, le grand leader de la Chine, est mort, à l'âge vénérable de 82 ans. Dans les minutes qui suivent l'annonce officielle de son décès, des centaines de personnes, bouleversées, se rassemblent sur la place de la Paix-céleste, à Pékin. Les éventuels successeurs de Mao luttent désormais pour le pouvoir. Sa veuve, l'ancienne actrice Chiang Ching, veut continuer la politique de la Révolution culturelle. Les modérés sont inspirés par Deng Xiaoping, et conduits par Hua Guofeng, qui a été le Premier ministre de la République populaire de Chine depuis la mort de Chou En-lai, le second de Mao.

1970 – 1979

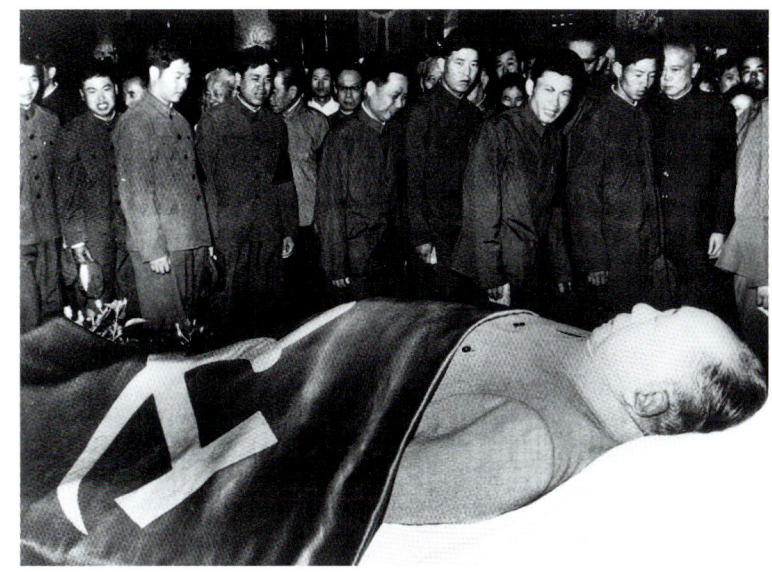

▲ *Les Chinois rendent un dernier hommage à Mao Zédong, décédé après une série de crises cardiaques.*

Enfants en otages à Djibouti

▶ 5 février 1976 ◀ Les enfants français pris en otages à Djibouti ont été libérés. Des membres du Front de libération de la Côte des Somalis, dernière colonie française en Afrique, sont montés dans un car de ramassage scolaire, le 3 février. Ils ont ordonné au chauffeur de se rendre en Somalie, mais le car a été bloqué au poste frontière. La gendarmerie est intervenue le deuxième jour.

10 sur 10 pour Nadia Comaneci

Nadia Comaneci, une gymnaste roumaine de 14 ans, enthousiasme les spectateurs des jeux Olympiques de Montréal, au Canada. Elle remporte trois médailles d'or, une d'argent et une de bronze. Ses 10 sur 10 perturbent l'ordinateur des JO, programmé pour rejeter ces notes maximales.

▶ *Nadia Comaneci, l'héroïne des JO, obtient des 10 sur 10.*

Coup d'État militaire en Argentine

▶ 24 mars 1976 ◀ La présidente Isabel Perón, la veuve de l'ancien président de l'Argentine Juan Perón, a été arrêtée par des chefs militaires, alors qu'elle rentrait à Buenos Aires. Mme Perón avait pris le pouvoir à la mort de son mari, en 1974. La situation économique difficile de l'Argentine explique le coup d'État de l'armée. Une répression sanglante s'abat sur tous les opposants au régime militaire.

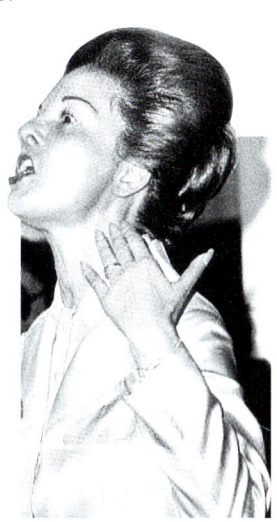

▲ *« Isabel Martínez » Perón, présidente de l'Argentine.*

Catastrophe de Seveso en Italie

▶ 20 juillet 1976 ◀ Un nuage de gaz toxiques s'échappe par accident d'une usine de produits chimiques à Seveso, près de Milan, en Italie. 1 800 hectares ont été touchés, dont 230 sont définitivement impropres à la culture ; 83 000 animaux ont dû être abattus ; 736 personnes ont été évacuées, dont 15 sont très gravement brûlées.

▼ *Une petite victime.*

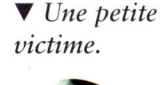

▶ *Il faut se protéger pour inspecter la zone contaminée.*

1970

1971

1972

1973

1974

1975

1976

1977

1978

1979

1977

Drame à Tenerife

30 mars 1977 — L'accident le plus meurtrier de l'histoire de l'aviation a eu lieu, voici trois jours, sur l'aéroport de Tenerife, aux Canaries. Deux jumbo-jets, l'un de la Pan Am et l'autre de KLM, se sont heurtés en pleine piste. Le Boeing américain manœuvrait pour finir son atterrissage, tandis que le Boeing hollandais décollait. Les 248 passagers du jumbo de KLM ont été tués sur le coup. Il y a 70 survivants sur les 326 passagers du jumbo de la Pan Am. Ils ont été hospitalisés. Beaucoup souffrent de brûlures très graves. Les témoins ont vu avec horreur les deux appareils se percuter et exploser en flammes.

Une enquête déterminera les causes de cette catastrophe. L'un des avions aurait dû atterrir à l'aéroport de Las Palmas, et l'autre, en décoller, mais cet aéroport avait été fermé à la suite d'une alerte à la bombe. Les deux Boeing ont été déroutés sur Tenerife, avec ces conséquences tragiques.

▲ *Après l'accident, les soldats dégagent les débris du Boeing 747 de la Pan Am, sur l'aéroport de Tenerife.*

▶ *Un responsable américain vérifie les identités sur les cercueils des victimes, avant leur rapatriement.*

Ouverture du Centre Pompidou

Le Centre culturel Pompidou ouvre le 2 février, dans le quartier Beaubourg, au cœur de Paris. Avec ses tuyaux et conduits extérieurs visibles, aux couleurs brillantes, le bâtiment est une réalisation artistique majeure et étonnante. Les deux architectes du Centre Pompidou sont Renzo Piano et Richard Rogers.

▼ *Le Centre Pompidou, à Paris.*

L'opposition tchèque lance la Charte 77

6 janvier 1977 — Un document révolutionnaire demande le rétablissement des droits de l'homme en Tchécoslovaquie. Il est diffusé dans la presse d'Allemagne occidentale. La « Charte 77 » a le soutien de 240 intellectuels tchèques tels que l'écrivain Václav Havel ou le Dr Jiri Hajek. Ce dernier a été ministre en 1968, pendant le « printemps de Prague ». Le gouvernement d'Alexander Dubček, à la fois communiste et libéral, ouvrait le pays aux libertés. L'intervention soviétique, en août 68, a mis fin à cette expérience. Depuis lors, la police exerce une pression constante. L'opposition au régime communiste s'exprime pour la première fois depuis l'échec du « printemps de Prague ».

Coup d'État au Pakistan

5 juillet 1977 — Zulfikar Ali Bhutto, le Premier ministre du Pakistan, est arrêté par le général Zia ul-Haq, le commandant en chef de l'armée. Le coup d'État du général Zia conclut plusieurs mois d'agitation. Des centaines de personnes sont mortes depuis que le Parti du peuple de M. Bhutto a obtenu la majorité aux élections, en mars dernier, dans des conditions douteuses. En avril, M. Bhutto a imposé la loi martiale dans les villes de Karachi, de Lahore et de Hyderabad. Il a nommé le général Zia à la tête de l'armée. Mais l'opposition a continué à accuser Bhutto d'avoir truqué les élections.

▲ *Zulfikar Ali Bhutto donne une conférence de presse lors d'une visite à Paris.*

1970 – 1979

▲ *Les créatures étranges de* la Guerre des étoiles.

Fantastique et disco

Le réalisateur George Lucas bat des records de recettes avec son film de science-fiction, *la Guerre des étoiles*. *La Fièvre du samedi soir* remporte aussi un immense succès. John Travolta y fait un numéro de danse sensationnel, et la musique des Bee Gees a provoqué une épidémie mondiale de fièvre pour la danse disco.

◀ *John Travolta dans* la Fièvre du samedi soir.

En 1977 aussi...

15 juin • Premières élections démocratiques en Espagne depuis quarante et un ans.

25 juin • M. Jacques Chirac est élu maire de Paris.

26 juin • Djibouti accède à l'indépendance.

31 juillet • Un mort, lors d'une manifestation de protestation sur le site d'une future centrale nucléaire à Creys-Malville, près de Lyon, en France.

Mort d'Elvis

▶ **16 août 1977** ◀ Le roi du rock and roll, Elvis Presley, a été trouvé mort dans la salle de bains de Graceland, son palais de Memphis, dans le Tennessee. Presley, qui avait 42 ans, a régné sur la pop music de la fin des années 50 et du début des années 60. Il a produit plus de 40 albums. En 1968, après huit ans de vie solitaire, il avait repris ses spectacles sur les scènes d'hôtels de Las Vegas. Des millions d'admirateurs pleurent la disparition prématurée du chanteur.

▲ *Elvis Presley chante à Las Vegas.*

Assassinat du Dr Schleyer

▶ **19 octobre 1977** ◀ Le cadavre du Dr Hans Martin Schleyer, directeur de Mercedes-Benz en Allemagne de l'Ouest, et président du patronat allemand, est retrouvé dans le coffre d'une voiture, près de Mulhouse, en Alsace. Le Dr Schleyer a été kidnappé par le groupe Baader-Meinhof, une organisation terroriste allemande, qui réclamait une rançon et la libération de onze de ses membres détenus en prison. Le gouvernement allemand a refusé de céder, mais Schleyer était vivant, hier, quand des commandos allemands anti-terroristes, liés au groupe Baader-Meinhof, ont pris d'assaut un avion de la Lufthansa détourné en Somalie. L'organisation a pris sa revanche sur l'échec en Somalie en assassinant Schleyer.

◀ *Cette photographie de l'homme d'affaires allemand a été adressée par les ravisseurs à un journal français.*

Mort d'un militant noir

▶ **2 décembre 1977** ◀ Steve Biko, le fondateur de l'Association des étudiants sud-africains, qui avait 30 ans, ne serait pas mort des suites de brutalités policières, selon l'enquête officielle. Ses lésions cérébrales sont dues à des blessures diverses à la tête, datant de l'époque où il était en prison. Les policiers qui l'ont interrogé pendant cinq jours ne seront donc pas poursuivis pour sa mort, voici trois mois. La famille et les amis de Steve Biko ont manifesté contre le jugement.

▲ *20 000 personnes accompagnent le cercueil de Biko, en Afrique du Sud.*

LA NOUVELLE GÉNÉRATION

Dans les années 60, de nombreux jeunes s'insurgent contre le mode de vie de leurs parents. En Europe comme aux États-Unis, ils rejettent la tradition familiale, récusent le pouvoir de l'argent et les conflits entre les races et les nations. Ils croient au pouvoir de l'amour et à la vie en communauté.

Certains de ces jeunes en rébellion contre les idées et les convictions de leurs parents veulent transformer la société en un monde meilleur d'amour et de paix. Ce n'est ni la première ni la dernière fois que le conflit des générations s'exprime brutalement...

▼ *En arrière-plan, les vêtements faits main, teintés de couleurs vives, que les hippies portaient volontiers.*

« Peace and love »

Né en Californie au milieu des années 60, le mouvement hippie – de l'argot *hip*, qui désigne un fumeur de marijuana – s'est propagé à l'ensemble des États-Unis et à l'Europe. Les hippies rejettent les conventions, préférant l'amour libre pour tous, et créent des communautés en zones rurales pour se couper de la société.

Ils sont déterminés à changer le monde, qui, tel qu'il est, leur déplaît. Ils s'insurgent contre la participation des États-Unis à la guerre du Viêt-nam et soutiennent des mouvements en faveur des droits civiques. Ils se droguent plutôt avec des drogues douces, étudient les religions et les idées des pays orientaux tels que l'Inde ou le Népal, s'initient au yoga et à d'autres formes de méditation. En déclin vers le milieu des années 70, le mouvement hippie n'en a pas moins marqué les décennies suivantes.

▲ *La troupe de la comédie musicale* Hair, *qui connut un grand succès dès la première représentation, en 1968, incarne le style hippie.*

Paix et harmonie

La chanteuse américaine Joan Baez apparaît pour la première fois en public en 1959, lors du festival folk de Newport, dans l'État de Rhode Island, aux États-Unis. Membre d'un groupe religieux pacifiste protestant (les quakers), elle est une farouche opposante à la guerre et à la discrimination. En 1964, elle refuse de payer l'impôt sur le revenu, pour protester contre les achats d'armes. En 1967, elle est arrêtée et incarcérée pour avoir participé à une manifestation contre la guerre du Viêt-nam.

◄ *Joan Baez, lors d'une manifestation. Sa chanson « Nous vaincrons » (We Shall Overcome) fut souvent reprise au cours de ce genre de réunions protestataires.*

La révolution punk

Au milieu des années 70, le rock punk envahit la scène musicale en Grande-Bretagne, en réaction à la paix et à l'amour prônés par les hippies. D'un tempérament pour le moins direct et belliqueux, les jeunes musiciens de cette tendance sont, de plus, réputés pour ne pas jouer très bien de leurs instruments.

Le groupe anglais des Sex Pistols lance le rock punk avec sa première chanson, « Anarchie au Royaume-Uni » (Anarchy in the UK), en 1976. En mars 1977, il renvoie le guitariste, Glen Matlock, sous prétexte qu'il joue trop bien de la guitare. Celui-ci sera remplacé par Sid Vicious, visiblement plus doué pour la provocation que pour la musique...

La musique punk donne naissance à une nouvelle danse, le « pogo ». Souvent, à la fin des concerts, les jeunes se battent et abîment les sièges. De nombreuses municipalités interdisent, dès lors, les orchestres punk, lesquels se produisent sous de faux noms.

Le mouvement punk ne s'exporte pas très bien aux États-Unis, où il a néanmoins une dimension plus artistique que dans sa version britannique.

▼ Les punks rejettent les conventions. Ils se teignent les cheveux et déchirent leurs vêtements.

▼ Sid Vicious (à gauche) et Johnny Rotten, des Sex Pistols. Le groupe est dissous en 1978, lors d'une tournée aux États-Unis.

Contre-culture

Le premier concert rock hippie eut lieu le 16 octobre 1965, à San Francisco.

•

Sur la pochette du disque God Save the Queen des Sex Pistols, le nez de la reine était affublé d'une épingle à nourrice. Interdit dans de nombreux magasins et par la BBC, ce disque figurait cependant en deuxième position au hit-parade des disques en mai 1977.

•

En France, des groupes comme Starshooters, Trust (Antisocial) et Téléphone (Argent, trop cher et Métro, c'est trop) tenaient le même genre de discours que les Sex Pistols.

1970

1971

1972

1973

1974

1975

1976

1977

1978

1979

1978

Les boat people du Viêt-nam

▶ **17 février 1978** ◀ Des milliers de personnes fuient l'ancien Viêt-nam du Sud et son régime communiste. Beaucoup sont d'origine chinoise et sont persécutées par les autorités vietnamiennes, car la tension monte entre la Chine et le Viêt-nam à propos du Cambodge. La Chine soutient le régime des Khmers rouges du Cambodge, hostile au gouvernement prosoviétique du Viêt-nam. Plus de mille personnes quittent le pays chaque mois par la mer. Ce sont des boat people. Leur volonté de partir est telle qu'ils montent dans n'importe quelle embarcation. En pleine mer, ils risquent de périr dans les tempêtes. Leur souhait est d'être recueillis pour gagner les États-Unis, le Canada, l'Australie et l'Europe. Les associations humanitaires se mobilisent pour les aider.

▲ *Les boat people risquent leur vie pour quitter le Viêt-nam de l'après-guerre.*

En 1978 aussi...

29 janvier • La Suède interdit les bombes aérosols, dangereuses.

25 juin • L'Argentine remporte la Coupe du monde de football.

11 juillet • En Espagne, une explosion dans un camping tue 200 personnes.

30 septembre • Le pape Jean-Paul Ier meurt, après 23 jours de pontificat.

10 décembre • Begin et Sadate partagent le prix Nobel de la paix.

Le premier bébé-éprouvette est né

▶ **26 juillet 1978** ◀ La nuit dernière, vers minuit, la fille de Mme Brown est née dans un hôpital de Manchester, en Angleterre. La maman a subi une césarienne. La petite Louise Brown ressemble à tous les nouveau-nés en bonne santé, mais sa vie a commencé dans une éprouvette. Un œuf de la mère y a été fécondé par le sperme du père. Cette naissance est due aux recherches de Patrick Steptoe et du Dr Robert Edwards.

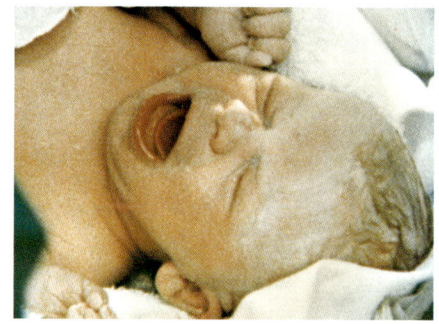

▶ *La petite Louise, un miracle du XXe siècle.*

Begin et Sadate signent les accords de Camp David

▶ *Anouar el-Sadate et Menahem Begin s'étreignent, après la signature des accords de Camp David. Les négociations sont un succès pour la paix.*

▶ **18 septembre 1978** ◀ Le président Carter réussit à réunir le Premier ministre israélien, Menahem Begin, et le président égyptien, Anouar el-Sadate. À Camp David, la maison de campagne des présidents américains, Begin accepte que les Israéliens évacuent progressivement le Sinaï égyptien. Il reconnaît aussi les « droits légitimes des Palestiniens ». Le dirigeant égyptien accepte d'établir des relations normales avec Israël. L'année prochaine, ces accords devraient devenir un traité de paix.

1970 – 1979

▲ *L'Amoco Cádiz dérive dans l'Atlantique, au large de la Bretagne.*

1978

Marée noire sur les côtes de Bretagne

▶ **24 mars 1978** ◀ Une grande partie de la côte bretonne est polluée par une marée noire. Un pétrolier, l'*Amoco Cádiz*, s'est échoué puis s'est brisé en deux, répandant ses 220 000 tonnes de pétrole brut. La nappe d'huile menace la pointe de la Bretagne et les îles Anglo-Normandes. On a installé des barrages flottants et des navires répandent des produits chimiques pour disperser le pétrole. Selon l'enquête, le désastre s'est produit, parce que le capitaine du pétrolier et le capitaine d'un remorqueur ont trop tardé à s'entendre sur le prix du remorquage. La corde du remorqueur s'est cassée, et le pétrolier a dérivé. Les deux capitaines restent détenus par la police.

Suicide collectif en Guyana

▶ **19 novembre 1978** ◀ Les cadavres de près d'un millier de membres d'une secte religieuse américaine ont été trouvés dans leur village de Guyana. Le chef de la secte, appelée Temple du peuple, Jim Jones, a créé cette communauté il y a deux ans. Les rumeurs sur sa cruauté ont conduit le député du Congrès Leo Ryan à se rendre sur place pour enquêter. Ryan et les cinq enquêteurs ont été retrouvés assassinés. Des survivants se sont cachés. Jones s'est sans doute suicidé par balle. Il a convaincu 913 membres de sa secte de boire un poison mortel.

Assassinat d'Aldo Moro

▶ **9 mai 1978** ◀ Le cadavre d'Aldo Moro, le célèbre homme d'État italien, qui a été deux fois Premier ministre dans son pays, est découvert dans le coffre d'une voiture française, au centre de Rome. Aldo Moro avait été kidnappé il y a deux mois par des membres des Brigades rouges, un groupe terroriste italien qui demandait la libération d'autres terroristes détenus en prison. En captivité, Aldo Moro avait écrit des lettres à tous ses amis du gouvernement, mais ceux-ci ont refusé de négocier avec ses ravisseurs, qui l'ont alors tué. Sa famille déplore amèrement ce refus, qui a coûté la vie à Aldo Moro.

▲ *Le service funèbre pour Aldo Moro, victime des terroristes.*

▶ *Trois aérostiers se posent en France.*

Un grand ballon franchit l'océan

Un équipage de trois Américains a atterri, le 17 août, en France. Les aérostiers sont épuisés après leur vol historique au-dessus de l'Atlantique dans un ballon gonflé à l'hélium, le Double Eagle II. Ben Abruzzo, Maxie Anderson et Larry Newman se sont posés dans un champ à 88 kilomètres à l'ouest de Paris. Pendant les six jours du voyage, ils ont lutté contre les pluies et les vents glacés, ils ont mangé des hot dogs et des sardines en boîte. Ils ont dit que c'était « l'expérience la plus formidable qu'ils aient vécue ». Ils seront bientôt reçus par le président Jimmy Carter. Le trio, qui est originaire de l'État du Maine, projette déjà un nouveau vol.

Un pape polonais

Pour la première fois depuis 400 ans, un pape n'est pas italien. L'ancien cardinal de Pologne Karol Wojtyla prend le nom de Jean-Paul II. Au lieu de s'adresser à la foule massée sur la place Saint-Pierre en latin, selon la tradition, le nouveau pape, qui a 58 ans, a parlé italien. Dynamique et intransigeant, il parle aussi anglais, français et allemand.

▲ *Le pape Jean-Paul II, le plus jeune pontife du XXe siècle.*

1979

▲ *Le chah Mohammed Reza Pahlavi et sa femme, Farah, en route vers l'avion qui les conduit à Assouan, en Égypte.*

Exil du chah d'Iran

▶ **16 janvier 1979** ◀ Les rues de Téhéran sont investies par des foules débordant de joie. Le chah, que les Iraniens haïssent, est parti. Il a fait de l'Iran un État riche et puissant, grâce au pétrole. Mais le pays souffre du gaspillage et de la hausse des prix. Les salaires restent bas. La police secrète combat les opposants. Le chah, qui a rapproché l'Iran de l'Occident, se heurte aussi aux chefs religieux. Le mois dernier, des manifestations contre le nouveau gouvernement militaire ont entraîné la paralysie du pays. Le chah a dû appeler un chef de l'opposition, Chahpur Bakhtiar. Celui-ci a accepté le poste de Premier ministre, à condition que le chah quitte le pays.

L'homme le plus puissant de l'Iran nouveau est un chef religieux âgé, l'ayatollah Ruhollah Khomeyni. Il dirige l'opposition depuis son lieu d'exil, en France. Il est attendu à Téhéran dans les prochains jours.

Madame Thatcher Premier ministre

▼ *Margaret Thatcher, surnommée la dame de fer.*

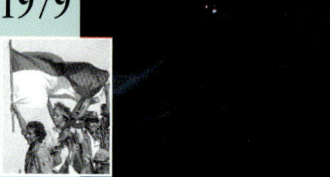

▶ **4 mai 1979** ◀ En Grande-Bretagne, les élections donnent la victoire au Parti conservateur. Le pays va être dirigé pour la première fois par une femme, Mme Margaret Thatcher, chef du Parti conservateur. Le nouveau Premier ministre britannique a 53 ans. Elle appartient à l'aile droite de son parti. Elle veut appliquer une politique libérale : l'intervention de l'État dans l'économie sera moindre. Elle est prête à se battre pour imposer ses idées.

Bokassa est renversé

▶ **20 septembre 1979** ◀ L'empereur Jean Bedel Bokassa, qui régnait en dictateur sur son Empire du Centrafrique, est renversé par son neveu, l'ancien président David Dacko. Bokassa s'est proclamé empereur à vie voici 3 ans. Le terrible dictateur est soupçonné de cannibalisme. Son pays, à l'histoire troublée, redevient une république.

Apparition du rap

Sugar Hill Gang, un groupe du Bronx, un quartier populaire de New York, obtient un grand succès avec *Rapper's Delight*. Le rap, qu'on appelle aussi le hip-hop, a un rythme rapide, saccadé. Il a d'abord été une poésie de la rue, improvisée, avec un fond musical. Le style rap est né chez les adolescents noirs et hispaniques des banlieues de New York. Il fait son apparition peu à peu en Europe.

1970 – 1979

Victoire des sandinistes au Nicaragua

▶ **17 juillet 1979** ◀ Après des mois de guerre civile pendant laquelle les habitants se sont entre-tués, le dictateur du Nicaragua, le général Somoza, a fui son pays. Les partisans du Front national de libération, les sandinistes, sont vainqueurs.

Les nouveaux dirigeants doivent leur nom à Augusto Sandino. Ce leader populaire a été tué, en 1934, sur ordre du chef de la police, Somoza, le père de l'ex-dictateur. Les sandinistes veulent la paix pour tous. Mais ils risquent de se heurter aux milieux d'affaires et au gouvernement américain, qui a longtemps soutenu Somoza.

◀ Les habitants du Nicaragua fêtent la victoire des sandinistes.

En 1979 aussi...

26 mars • Le président égyptien Sadate et le Premier ministre israélien Begin signent le traité de paix qui fait suite à la rencontre de Camp David.

22 juillet • Le Français Bernard Hinault remporte le Tour de France, pour la deuxième fois.

4 novembre • Cinquante Américains sont pris en otages par des étudiants iraniens, à l'ambassade des États-Unis de Téhéran.

Accident dans une centrale nucléaire

▶ **30 mars 1979** ◀ Un accident grave s'est produit, hier, dans la centrale nucléaire de Three Miles Island, en Pennsylvanie, aux États-Unis. La fuite d'un liquide de refroidissement a provoqué la surchauffe du réacteur nucléaire. Les spécialistes estiment que la quantité de radioactivité qui s'est échappée dans les environs est faible. Mais 10 000 personnes ont dû quitter la zone. Il faudra des années pour décontaminer la centrale.

▶ Une vanne défectueuse a provoqué l'alerte nucléaire de Three Miles Island.

Cigarette et cancer

Fumer donne le cancer, une maladie souvent mortelle. C'est la conclusion d'un rapport médical américain. Le rapport, de 1 200 pages, présente en détail les conséquences dangereuses de la dépendance à la nicotine, la substance qui donne son goût au tabac. La cigarette provoque aussi toutes sortes d'autres maladies.

L'URSS envahit l'Afghanistan

▶ **27 décembre 1979** ◀ L'Union soviétique envahit l'Afghanistan. Il y a trois jours, des commandos soviétiques se sont emparés de l'aéroport de Kaboul. Le gouvernement prosoviétique d'Afghanistan a demandé l'aide des Russes. Les Soviétiques ont mis en place un pont aérien pour apporter des armes, des vivres et des troupes. Des convois militaires traversent la frontière soviéto-afghane. Le but de l'invasion est de protéger les intérêts soviétiques. Les Russes font la même erreur que les Américains au Viêt-nam : ils entament une guerre qu'ils ne peuvent pas gagner.

▶ Les convois militaires soviétiques entrent en Afghanistan.

LE TERRORISME

Le terrorisme vise un but politique en commettant des actes de violence qui affaiblissent les gouvernements et terrorisent les populations. Il est employé par des individus qui, ne réussissant pas à obtenir ce qu'ils veulent par des méthodes légales, forment un groupe et sont prêts à commettre les actes les plus odieux pour arriver à leurs fins. Leurs motivations sont diverses : convictions politiques extrémistes, nationalisme, fanatisme religieux, etc.

Les Brigades rouges

Les *Brigate rosse* sont un groupe terroriste italien fondé en 1970 par Renato Curcio qui, pendant une dizaine d'années, a semé la terreur en kidnappant et tuant un certain nombre de juges et d'hommes politiques.

Leur victime la plus célèbre est l'ancien Premier ministre italien Aldo Moro, qui tente de persuader le Parti communiste italien de rejoindre les démocrates-chrétiens. Aldo Moro est enlevé, à Rome, le 16 mars 1978. Les terroristes menacent de le tuer, s'ils n'obtiennent pas la libération de prisonniers communistes. Le gouvernement refuse de négocier. Le cadavre d'Aldo Moro sera retrouvé deux mois plus tard à Rome, dans le coffre d'une voiture. Après ce coup d'éclat tragique, les activités des Brigades rouges diminueront progressivement avant de disparaître, notamment grâce à l'amélioration des méthodes antiterroristes.

▲ *La presse publie les messages des Brigades rouges, ainsi que la photo d'Aldo Moro et ses lettres désespérées à ses amis et collègues.*

▶ *Aldo Moro, photographié par ses ravisseurs en possession d'un journal dont la date prouve qu'il ne s'agit pas d'une vieille photo.*

L'E.T.A. au Pays basque espagnol

Créé en 1959, l'E.T.A. (*Euzkadi ta Azkatasuna* : « Pays basque et liberté ») est l'un des plus anciens groupes terroristes d'Europe. Il se bat pour l'indépendance du Pays basque, dans le nord de l'Espagne. L'aile politique de l'E.T.A. est une organisation non violente appelée Herri Batasuna (« unité populaire »). Depuis 1968, l'E.T.A. est responsable de la mort de plus de 800 personnes. Bien que les revendications des nationalistes basques modérés aient été satisfaites en 1979 par le gouvernement espagnol, l'E.T.A. poursuit ses actions terroristes.

▶ *Funérailles d'un membre de l'E.T.A. au Pays basque.*

L'Organisation de libération de la Palestine

L'OLP est créée en 1964 pour unifier les différents groupes arabes opposés à la présence des Juifs en Palestine. Les plus extrémistes de ces groupes, comme le Fatah, engagent la lutte armée contre Israël. De nombreux pays arabes, qui sont contre les méthodes de l'OLP, en expulsent les membres. Les actes de violence et les tensions à l'intérieur du parti obligent Yasser Arafat (chef de l'OLP depuis 1969) à adopter une attitude plus réaliste pour conclure la paix avec Israël. Mais cette politique est contestée par différents mouvements.

▶ *Libération, à Mogadiscio, d'otages d'un avion détourné par l'OLP.*

▲ *Des réfugiés palestiniens au Liban enrôlés par l'OLP pour former une armée.*

◀ *Portrait-robot d'un membre présumé des Brigades rouges.*

Le terrorisme

7 décembre 1985 : un attentat revendiqué par le groupe Abou Nidal, devant le Printemps et les Galeries Lafayette, à Paris, fait 35 blessés.

• 17 septembre 1986 : une bombe explose devant le magasin Tati, rue de Rennes, à Paris, tuant sept personnes.

L'IRA

En 1919, l'IRA (*Irish Republican Army* – Armée républicaine irlandaise) est officiellement reconnue par le Sinn Féin (parti réclamant une Irlande indépendante). En 1936, elle est déclarée illégale par le gouvernement irlandais. Elle reste active jusqu'en 1969, soutenant les catholiques contre la majorité unioniste protestante.

En 1969, l'IRA se scinde en deux : la branche « officielle » (les *Officials*), qui condamne le terrorisme, et la branche « provisoire » (les *Provisionals*), qui le pratique. Ce dernier groupe organise une série d'attentats contre l'armée britannique. Un cessez-le-feu est signé en 1994, mais l'IRA « provisoire » poursuit ses actions terroristes jusqu'en février 1996. Les gouvernements irlandais et britannique négocient un nouvel accord avec l'IRA en 1998.

◀ *À Canary Wharf, à Londres, immeuble de bureaux soufflé par l'explosion d'un camion piégé par l'IRA.*

▶ *Enterrement d'un des dix jeunes Irlandais morts à l'issue d'une grève de la faim pour avoir essayé d'obtenir le statut de prisonnier politique.*

De 1980 à 1989

1980
La décennie 80 est celle de l'effondrement du « rideau de fer » et de la fin de la guerre froide. En 1985, Mikhaïl Gorbatchev prend la tête de l'Union soviétique, et six ans plus tard l'empire soviétique cesse d'exister.

Le communisme se désintègre en Europe. La démocratie progresse dans le monde. La sécheresse, la famine et la guerre civile accentuent le désespoir dans le tiers-monde. Les inégalités sociales deviennent de plus en plus évidentes en Occident. Les menaces sur l'environnement causent de plus en plus d'inquiétude.

▲ *L'ouvrier des chantiers navals de Gdańsk, Lech Walesa, dirige le nouveau syndicat Solidarité.*

« Solidarité » en Pologne

▶ **17 septembre 1980** ◀

Quelques semaines seulement après avoir obtenu le droit de s'organiser librement en syndicats, les ouvriers polonais viennent de lancer Solidarité (Solidarność), syndicat national indépendant. Son dirigeant prestigieux, Lech Walesa, ouvrier aux chantiers navals, a contribué à la victoire des grévistes. Solidarité, qui est un syndicat non communiste légal, est une preuve de la victoire des ouvriers polonais contre le gouvernement communiste.

Les grèves de l'été en Pologne visaient autant la liberté politique qu'elles contestaient l'augmentation des prix et la pénurie alimentaire. Après avoir consulté l'Union soviétique, le gouvernement polonais a répondu favorablement à de nombreuses revendications, dont l'augmentation des salaires, des pensions et des vacances, la promotion au mérite plutôt que sur la base de l'appartenance au parti, une diminution de la censure, la diffusion d'émissions religieuses et le droit de s'organiser en syndicats indépendants.

Le Rubik-cube

Le cube infernal inventé par le Hongrois Erno Rubik est un casse-tête. C'est un cube dont les six faces de couleurs différentes sont composées de neuf petits carrés imbriqués. Le but du jeu consiste à manipuler le cube, de façon à obtenir neuf petits carrés de couleur identique sur chaque face. Certains y parviennent en quelques minutes, mais la plupart n'y arrivent jamais.

Attentat à Bologne, en Italie

▶ **2 août 1980** ◀

Quatre-vingt-quatre personnes ont été tuées et des centaines, blessées, après l'effroyable attentat à la bombe qui a détruit la gare de chemin de fer de Bologne, dans le nord de l'Italie. L'explosion, qui a laissé un gigantesque cratère, a été provoquée, par une valise bourrée de 50 kg d'explosifs déposée dans une salle d'attente.

Un groupe terroriste d'extrême droite a revendiqué l'attentat. Il semble que ce soit un acte de vengeance en soutien à 8 fascistes poursuivis pour un attentat précédent sur un train, à Bologne, en 1974. Bologne, ville dont la municipalité communiste est très populaire, est une cible de prédilection pour des fascistes.

▼ *La gare de Bologne, en Italie, après l'explosion.*

L'Organisation de libération de la Palestine

L'OLP est créée en 1964 pour unifier les différents groupes arabes opposés à la présence des Juifs en Palestine. Les plus extrémistes de ces groupes, comme le Fatah, engagent la lutte armée contre Israël. De nombreux pays arabes, qui sont contre les méthodes de l'OLP, en expulsent les membres. Les actes de violence et les tensions à l'intérieur du parti obligent Yasser Arafat (chef de l'OLP depuis 1969) à adopter une attitude plus réaliste pour conclure la paix avec Israël. Mais cette politique est contestée par différents mouvements.

▶ *Libération, à Mogadiscio, d'otages d'un avion détourné par l'OLP.*

▲ *Des réfugiés palestiniens au Liban enrôlés par l'OLP pour former une armée.*

◀ *Portrait-robot d'un membre présumé des Brigades rouges.*

Le terrorisme

7 décembre 1985 : un attentat revendiqué par le groupe Abou Nidal, devant le Printemps et les Galeries Lafayette, à Paris, fait 35 blessés.

17 septembre 1986 : une bombe explose devant le magasin Tati, rue de Rennes, à Paris, tuant sept personnes.

L'IRA

En 1919, l'IRA (*Irish Republican Army* – Armée républicaine irlandaise) est officiellement reconnue par le Sinn Féin (parti réclamant une Irlande indépendante). En 1936, elle est déclarée illégale par le gouvernement irlandais. Elle reste active jusqu'en 1969, soutenant les catholiques contre la majorité unioniste protestante.

En 1969, l'IRA se scinde en deux : la branche « officielle » (les *Officials*), qui condamne le terrorisme, et la branche « provisoire » (les *Provisionals*), qui le pratique. Ce dernier groupe organise une série d'attentats contre l'armée britannique. Un cessez-le-feu est signé en 1994, mais l'IRA « provisoire » poursuit ses actions terroristes jusqu'en février 1996. Les gouvernements irlandais et britannique négocient un nouvel accord avec l'IRA en 1998.

◀ *À Canary Wharf, à Londres, immeuble de bureaux soufflé par l'explosion d'un camion piégé par l'IRA.*

▶ *Enterrement d'un des dix jeunes Irlandais morts à l'issue d'une grève de la faim pour avoir essayé d'obtenir le statut de prisonnier politique.*

De 1980 à 1989

1980

La décennie 80 est celle de l'effondrement du « rideau de fer » et de la fin de la guerre froide. En 1985, Mikhaïl Gorbatchev prend la tête de l'Union soviétique, et six ans plus tard l'empire soviétique cesse d'exister.

Le communisme se désintègre en Europe. La démocratie progresse dans le monde. La sécheresse, la famine et la guerre civile accentuent le désespoir dans le tiers-monde. Les inégalités sociales deviennent de plus en plus évidentes en Occident. Les menaces sur l'environnement causent de plus en plus d'inquiétude.

« Solidarité » en Pologne

▲ *L'ouvrier des chantiers navals de Gdańsk, Lech Walesa, dirige le nouveau syndicat Solidarité.*

▶ **17 septembre 1980** ◀ Quelques semaines seulement après avoir obtenu le droit de s'organiser librement en syndicats, les ouvriers polonais viennent de lancer Solidarité (Solidarność), syndicat national indépendant. Son dirigeant prestigieux, Lech Walesa, ouvrier aux chantiers navals, a contribué à la victoire des grévistes. Solidarité, qui est un syndicat non communiste légal, est une preuve de la victoire des ouvriers polonais contre le gouvernement communiste.

Les grèves de l'été en Pologne visaient autant la liberté politique qu'elles contestaient l'augmentation des prix et la pénurie alimentaire. Après avoir consulté l'Union soviétique, le gouvernement polonais a répondu favorablement à de nombreuses revendications, dont l'augmentation des salaires, des pensions et des vacances, la promotion au mérite plutôt que sur la base de l'appartenance au parti, une diminution de la censure, la diffusion d'émissions religieuses et le droit de s'organiser en syndicats indépendants.

Le Rubik-cube

Le cube infernal inventé par le Hongrois Erno Rubik est un casse-tête. C'est un cube dont les six faces de couleurs différentes sont composées de neuf petits carrés imbriqués. Le but du jeu consiste à manipuler le cube, de façon à obtenir neuf petits carrés de couleur identique sur chaque face. Certains y parviennent en quelques minutes, mais la plupart n'y arrivent jamais.

Attentat à Bologne, en Italie

▶ **2 août 1980** ◀ Quatre-vingt-quatre personnes ont été tuées et des centaines, blessées, après l'effroyable attentat à la bombe qui a détruit la gare de chemin de fer de Bologne, dans le nord de l'Italie. L'explosion, qui a laissé un gigantesque cratère, a été provoquée, par une valise bourrée de 50 kg d'explosifs déposée dans une salle d'attente.

Un groupe terroriste d'extrême droite a revendiqué l'attentat. Il semble que ce soit un acte de vengeance en soutien à 8 fascistes poursuivis pour un attentat précédent sur un train, à Bologne, en 1974. Bologne, ville dont la municipalité communiste est très populaire, est une cible de prédilection pour des fascistes.

▼ *La gare de Bologne, en Italie, après l'explosion.*

1980 – 1989

Protéger la nature : une urgence

▶ **Mars 1980** ◀ Pour le malheur des écologistes, le rapport de l'organisation mondiale de protection de l'environnement des Nations unies, concluant trois années de recherches internationales, affirme qu'un million d'espèces végétales et animales risquent de disparaître par la faute des activités humaines, ce qui fragilise les réserves alimentaires et la médecine. La destruction continue des forêts tropicales humides contribue au réchauffement global de la Terre. Si cette tendance se confirme, la destruction deviendra irréversible d'ici à vingt ans. Le rapport demande à chaque pays de mettre en place des programmes de protection de la nature.

▲ *La forêt tropicale du Guatemala, détruite par des méthodes de déboisement par la terre brûlée.*

John Lennon assassiné

▶ **9 décembre 1980** ◀ John Lennon, l'ancien Beatles, a été tué de cinq balles à bout portant, hier soir, devant l'immeuble Dakota où il vivait avec sa femme, Yoko Ono. Son meurtrier, Mark Chapman, avait récemment débarqué d'Hawaii, où il a acheté le pistolet. Il traquait le chanteur depuis plusieurs jours, et a même été pris en photo, quelques heures avant le meurtre, alors qu'il lui demandait un autographe. À l'heure qu'il est, ses motivations restent un mystère.

Mort de Tito

▶ **4 mai 1980** ◀ Le maréchal Tito, père fondateur de la Yougoslavie, vient de mourir, à 87 ans. Tito, de son vrai nom Josip Broz, a dirigé la résistance contre les nazis pendant la Seconde Guerre mondiale et mis en place un régime communiste en 1945. Plus tard, sa politique d'indépendance a entraîné une rupture avec l'Union soviétique et, dans les années 50, il est devenu le chef de file des pays non alignés (indépendants des États-Unis et de l'URSS) au sein des Nations unies. C'est l'autorité de Tito qui maintenait unies les six Républiques de Yougoslavie, qui risquent de s'affronter.

Le Zimbabwe est né

▶ **18 avril 1980** ◀ L'ancienne colonie britannique de Rhodésie est remplacée par la république africaine du Zimbabwe. En 1965, le Premier ministre, Ian Smith, avait proclamé l'indépendance de la Rhodésie, afin de préserver le pouvoir de la minorité blanche. Le refus de la Grande-Bretagne de reconnaître cette indépendance, la résistance armée des groupes noirs africains et le blocus économique international ont poussé Ian Smith à négocier. L'Union nationale africaine du Zimbabwe, de Robert Mugabe, a gagné les élections démocratiques.

▶ *Robert Mugabe, Premier ministre du Zimbabwe indépendant.*

Les nouveaux magazines

À quelques jours de sa première parution, un nouveau magazine britannique est accueilli avec intérêt par les médias internationaux. *The Face*, un journal de plus consacré à l'art, au design, à la musique et à la mode, ne ressemble en rien aux autres magazines de mode. Le développement de l'audiovisuel a fait diminuer les tirages de la presse d'information (quotidiens et hebdomadaires), mais les tirages de la presse spécialisée (journaux techniques, sportifs, mode et beauté) ne cessent d'augmenter.

▶ *La première couverture de* The Face.

1980

La guerre Iran-Irak

▶ 22 septembre 1980 ◀ Aujourd'hui, les forces armées irakiennes ont effectué plusieurs raids sur le territoire iranien. Elles ont détruit la raffinerie de pétrole d'Abadan et avancé de plusieurs kilomètres en divers endroits. Le conflit de frontières s'est transformé en une véritable guerre. L'objectif de l'Irak est le contrôle du Chatt al-Arab qui délimite les deux pays et commande l'accès au golfe Persique. Depuis 1975, il est sous domination commune irako-iranienne.

Le dirigeant irakien Saddam Hussein cherche à tirer profit de l'instabilité de l'Iran. Depuis que le chah d'Iran a été renversé, en janvier dernier, c'est le vieux dirigeant religieux l'ayatollah Khomeyni qui gouverne l'État, devenu intégriste musulman. Il a instauré une nouvelle Constitution basée sur la loi islamique et cherche à faire disparaître toute influence occidentale. Des milliers de gens, dont des cadres de l'armée, ont été exécutés ou ont fui. L'Iran est une république islamique gouvernée par des religieux.

D'autres divergences existent entre ces deux rivaux héréditaires. Et, en particulier, Saddam Hussein, qui se dit laïque, et son gouvernement de tendance sunnite craignent l'influence de la Révolution islamique de Khomeyni sur les chiites (autre famille islamique) d'Irak. Officiellement, les grandes puissances ne prennent pas parti dans ce conflit, mais le golfe Persique est une zone sensible par laquelle transite une grande partie de l'alimentation en pétrole de la planète.

◀ Soldats irakiens faisant le V de la victoire devant une affiche de Khomeyni, criblée de balles.

Le Walkman

La compagnie d'électronique Sony lance le Walkman. C'est une nouvelle génération de lecteur de radiocassettes stéréophonique, portable et résistant aux chocs, suffisamment petit pour une poche, et muni d'un casque. On peut l'écouter en marchant.

◀ Le dernier modèle de lecteur de radiocassettes, le Walkman de Sony.

En 1980 aussi...

11 mars • Marguerite Yourcenar est la première femme admise à l'Académie française.

27 mars • 124 morts dans l'effondrement d'une plate-forme pétrolière en mer du Nord.

30 juin • On estime à 10 millions le nombre de morts par la famine en Afrique de l'Est.

10 octobre • Un violent séisme à El-Asnam en Algérie fait 25 000 morts.

Boycott des jeux Olympiques de Moscou

▶ 3 août 1980 ◀ L'esprit international des jeux Olympiques de Moscou ne sera pas respecté cette année. En effet, 65 pays, dont les États-Unis, l'Allemagne de l'Ouest et le Kenya, ont boycotté les Jeux, pour protester contre l'invasion de l'Afghanistan par l'URSS. 36 records ont été battus. Les champions britanniques ont été particulièrement brillants : le 1500 m pour Sebastian Coe, ou le 800 m pour Steve Ovett. Les athlètes de l'Allemagne de l'Est et de l'Union soviétique ont dominé les Jeux. En natation, les Allemandes de l'Est ont remporté 29 médailles sur 42.

1980 – 1989

Reagan, président des États-Unis

▶ **4 novembre 1980** ◀ Ronald Reagan a battu par une écrasante victoire le président Jimmy Carter aux élections présidentielles américaines. Il a remporté 44 des 50 États, bien que le vote populaire ait été plus serré : 44 millions contre 35. Avant de se lancer dans la carrière politique, Ronald Reagan était un acteur de cinéma connu. Il est républicain conservateur et anticommuniste. Il a montré, lorsqu'il était gouverneur de Californie, ses qualités de dirigeant. Au début de la campagne, on le disait trop vieux, avec ses 69 ans, pour devenir le quarantième président des États-Unis, mais ses manières décontractées, particulièrement à la télévision, ont séduit de nombreux électeurs.

Björn Borg remporte son cinquième Wimbledon

Le joueur de tennis suédois Björn Borg est entré dans le *Livre des records*, le 5 juillet, avec sa cinquième victoire consécutive en simple messieurs du tournoi de Wimbledon. Au cours d'un match marathon d'une durée de quatre heures, il a battu l'Américain John McEnroe en cinq sets.

◂ *Borg reçoit la coupe de Wimbledon pour la cinquième fois. McEnroe, battu de peu, se demande quand le Suédois lâchera prise.*

◂ *Ronald Reagan, avec sa femme, Nancy, sous les acclamations des électeurs républicains, après que Carter a entériné sa défaite aux présidentielles.*

Disparition de la variole

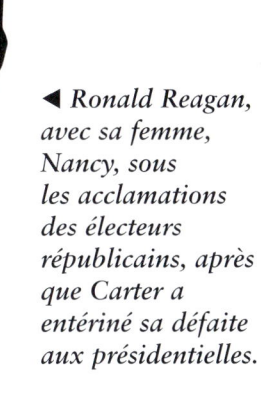

▶ **8 mai 1980** ◀ Selon l'Organisation mondiale de la santé (OMS) la variole a totalement disparu. Le virus n'existant plus sur terre, plus aucun individu n'en étant porteur, personne ne pourra plus l'attraper. C'était une des maladies les plus meurtrières. Ceux qui survivaient à l'infection avaient la peau marquée à vie, et certains restaient aveugles. En 1796, le médecin anglais Edward Jenner découvrit un vaccin mais, sans vaccin, aucun remède ne soignait la maladie. L'OMS mène une campagne contre la variole depuis 1967. En 1977, on pensait que la maladie avait disparu, mais un an plus tard le virus de la variole s'est échappé d'un laboratoire de Birmingham, provoquant plusieurs décès.

Les voitures japonaises en tête

▶ **31 décembre 1980** ◀ Le Japon est devenu le plus gros producteur mondial de voitures. Cette année, il a produit 12,7 millions de véhicules, reléguant les Américains à la deuxième place. De plus, une voiture sur quatre vendue aux États-Unis est japonaise.

L'industrie automobile américaine connaît de graves problèmes. Chrysler a été sauvé de la banqueroute par un prêt garanti par l'État. Ford et General Motors sont lourdement endettés. L'an dernier, la crise du pétrole, qui a provoqué des augmentations importantes du prix du carburant, a incité les acheteurs à se contenter de voitures plus petites. Nissan, Toyota et Honda se sont emparés d'une grande part du marché.

1981

Charles et Diana

▶ 29 juillet 1981 ◀ Ce n'est pas seulement le mariage de l'année, c'est celui de la décennie ! Aujourd'hui, Charles, le prince de Galles, héritier de la couronne, épouse lady Diana Spencer dans la cathédrale St Paul, à Londres. Des foules en liesse massées dans les rues, ainsi qu'un public de 700 millions de téléspectateurs dans le monde entier, ont assisté à la cérémonie. La timide jeune mariée, éclatante de beauté dans sa robe d'une couleur crème originale, est arrivée à la cathédrale dans un carrosse attelé de chevaux. De douze ans plus jeune que Charles, la nouvelle princesse est la fille du huitième comte Spencer, dont une des filles aînées déjà avait été pressentie comme épouse possible du prince. Diana est elle-même d'ascendance royale, par ses illustres ancêtres, les rois Stuarts, Charles II et James II.

▲ Baiser princier des jeunes mariés, à l'issue de la cérémonie.

Charles et Diana
- Charles et Diana se sont rencontrés à la campagne, alors que Charles, ami de la sœur de Diana, participait à une partie de chasse.
- Charles est le premier héritier depuis 1659 à avoir épousé une Anglaise.
- Diana et Charles peuvent faire remonter leur arbre généalogique jusqu'à James Ier.

Mitterrand président de la République française

▶ 10 mai 1981 ◀ Pour la première fois depuis 1958, la France a un président socialiste. François Mitterrand a battu le candidat de la droite, Giscard d'Estaing. C'était la troisième fois que François Mitterrand se présentait devant les électeurs, et cela fait 23 ans que la gauche est absente du gouvernement. Sa victoire tient à sa capacité à avoir forgé l'Union de la gauche avec le Parti communiste. Il a promis la nationalisation des banques, l'augmentation des impôts pour les plus riches, et le plein-emploi. Pour le moment, la majorité à l'Assemblée nationale est de droite, mais il est probable que Mitterrand dissolve l'Assemblée et organise des élections législatives.

▲ François Mitterrand mettant son propre bulletin dans l'urne.

Ronald Reagan échappe à un attentat

▶ 30 mars 1981 ◀ Aujourd'hui, à Washington, l'horreur de l'assassinat du président Kennedy, à Dallas, en 1963, a failli se répéter. Alors qu'il sortait de son hôtel pour prendre sa voiture, Ronald Reagan, président depuis trois mois seulement, s'est fait agresser par John Hinckley Jr, 25 ans, fils d'un magnat du pétrole de Denver. Les médecins ont extrait une balle de la poitrine de Reagan, mais sa vie n'est pas en danger. Trois autres personnes, un assistant du président, un garde du corps et un policier, ont également été blessées par le terroriste, qui a tiré six balles à bout portant avec un petit pistolet 22.

▲ Le terroriste, maîtrisé par les officiers de la sécurité, pendant que Reagan est emmené à l'hôpital.

Émeutes en Grande-Bretagne

▶ **12 juillet 1981** ◀ Un grand désordre règne dans plusieurs villes britanniques. Les émeutes se poursuivent, des bandes de jeunes brûlant, cassant et pillant. L'an dernier, c'est le quartier St Paul de Bristol qui était en ébullition, et cette année des émeutes ont éclaté dans les rues de Brixton, au sud de Londres. Cette semaine, les événements les plus graves se sont déroulés à Toxteth, Liverpool. Ces quartiers sont souvent habités par des Noirs, mais les jeunes blancs sont tout aussi impliqués. Le chômage et les conditions de logement déplorables y sont pour quelque chose.

Le théâtre en Angleterre

Les Anglais adorent aller au théâtre, surtout si la pièce comporte des numéros chantés et dansés. Cette année, le grand succès est une pièce d'Andrew Lloyd Webber, *Cats*, tirée des poèmes de T. S. Eliot. Le public fait la queue pour tenter d'obtenir des places. Ce sera la même chose pour *Miss Saigon*, inspiré de l'opéra Mme *Butterfly*, et surtout, pour les *Miz*, œuvre musicale tirée des *Misérables* de Victor Hugo.

▼ *Les félins séduisants de la pièce* Cats.

Condamnation de la veuve Mao

▶ **25 janvier 1981** ◀ Jiang Qing, la veuve du dirigeant chinois Mao Zédong, a été condamnée à mort pour crime contre l'État. L'ancienne actrice faisait partie de la « bande des Quatre » arrêtée en 1976, alors qu'ils tentaient de s'emparer du pouvoir, à la mort de Mao. Ils sont aussi tenus pour responsables de la Révolution culturelle, qui a laissé de graves séquelles en Chine depuis 1966. Des trois autres accusés, un a été condamné à mort, les autres, à la prison à vie.

▲ *Jiang Qing durant son procès.*

▲ *Sadate (entouré), juste avant son assassinat.*

Assassinat de Sadate en Égypte

▶ **6 octobre 1981** ◀ Anouar el-Sadate, le président de l'Égypte, est mort, tué par ses propres soldats, alors qu'il présidait un défilé militaire au Caire. Les assassins, arrivés en Jeep à la hauteur de l'estrade, ont ouvert le feu tandis que les regards se tournaient vers un avion militaire. Cinq autres personnes ont été tuées.

Sadate avait succédé à Nasser en 1970. Il s'est fait de nombreux ennemis avec les changements radicaux de sa politique extérieure : le traité de paix avec Israël en 1978 a été condamné par la plupart des États arabes. Les meurtriers appartiennent au groupe extrémiste des Frères musulmans, mais certains soupçonnent le gouvernement du colonel Kadhafi, en Libye, d'être impliqué.

En 1981 aussi...

3 février • Gro Harlem Brundtland devient la première femme Premier ministre de Norvège.

23 février • Tentative de coup d'État en Espagne par des officiers de l'armée.

7 juin • Des bombardements israéliens détruisent un site nucléaire en Irak.

23 juin • En France, 4 ministres communistes entrent au gouvernement.

1981

Libération des otages américains en Iran

▶ **21 janvier 1981** ◀ Les otages américains retenus en Iran depuis novembre 1979 sont arrivés aujourd'hui sans encombre à Alger, première étape de leur retour. Il y a 15 mois, des hommes armés représentant le régime intégriste musulman de l'ayatollah Khomeyni ont envahi l'ambassade américaine de Téhéran, maîtrisant les gardes et prenant 100 citoyens américains en otages. La plupart des femmes et tous les otages noirs étaient rapidement libérés ; quelques-uns se sont enfuis plus tard avec des passeports canadiens. Après l'échec de la médiation des Nations unies pour obtenir la libération des autres, les États-Unis ont tenté une intervention aérienne en avril 1980, qui s'est soldée par un drame : la collision de deux avions venant s'approvisionner en carburant dans le désert au sud de Téhéran. Khomeyni a attendu, pour libérer les otages, que Carter, son grand ennemi, ne soit plus au pouvoir. Les 52 otages restant, ont donc dû attendre l'investiture officielle, hier, de Ronald Reagan comme président des États-Unis.

▲ *Accueil chaleureux pour les otages américains retenus pendant 444 jours.*

▲ *Graffiti « Laissez Bobby Sands mourir », dans un quartier loyaliste de Belfast.*

Irlande : Bobby Sands meurt de la grève de la faim

▶ **5 mai 1981** ◀ Alors que le dixième gréviste de la faim de l'IRA vient de mourir à la prison de Maze, ses compagnons ont décidé d'interrompre leur mouvement. À l'annonce de la mort de l'un d'entre eux, Bobby Sands, le 5 mai, des violences avaient éclaté à Belfast. Il avait entamé son jeûne avec d'autres républicains deux mois avant, pour tenter de convaincre les autorités britanniques de les reconnaître comme prisonniers politiques et de les traiter comme tels. Alors qu'il était sur le point de mourir, Bobby Sands avait été élu député au Parlement britannique. Malgré tout, Margaret Thatcher est restée intraitable. Cette attitude a provoqué une indignation internationale.

Dallas et *Dynastie*

En Grande-Bretagne, le succès de la série télévisée *Dallas* explique probablement la sortie de *Dynastie,* une nouvelle série interminable racontant la vie de riches Américains immoraux d'une ville du Sud-Ouest. L'intérêt est un peu renouvelé avec l'arrivée d'Alexis, la mauvaise, jouée par l'actrice anglaise Joan Collins.

▲ *Joan Collins, la mauvaise de* Dynastie.

Mort de Bob Marley

▶ **11 mai 1981** ◀ La star du reggae est morte. Bob Marley a succombé à un cancer, à l'âge 36 ans. Le reggae est apparu dans les bidonvilles de Kingston, en Jamaïque, où est né Bob Marley. C'est grâce à lui, et à son groupe, les Wailers, que cette musique connaît le succès dans le monde entier. Ses chansons sont très morales. Il voulait la fin de la discrimination politique et souhaitait le développement d'un christianisme centré sur l'Afrique.

▶ *Bob Marley, la prestigieuse vedette du reggae.*

État de siège en Pologne

▶ **3 décembre 1981** ◀

« L'homme fort » de la Pologne, le général Jaruzelski, a instauré aujourd'hui l'état de siège. Les frontières sont fermées, et les troupes gouvernementales répriment grèves et manifestations. L'an dernier, le syndicat Solidarité avait obtenu des concessions inédites de la part du gouvernement communiste, mais la situation économique désastreuse de la Pologne, avec des dettes très importantes et une inflation forte, a provoqué de nouveaux remous. Le risque d'une intervention armée de l'Union soviétique persiste. Les Russes comptent sur Jaruzelski, devenu Premier ministre en février, pour rétablir l'ordre. Cette mesure intervient après un voyage de Jaruzelski à Moscou.

▲ *Le train le plus rapide du monde, au départ, à la gare de Lyon.*

Paris-Lyon : 2 h 40 en TGV

Les voyageurs de la SNCF peuvent maintenant effectuer le trajet Paris-Lyon en 2 h 40, soit moitié moins qu'avant. Le train à grande vitesse, électrique, circule sur des voies spéciales, à environ 170 km/h. La ligne sera prolongée sur Avignon et Marseille.

▶ *Des Américains d'origine polonaise manifestent dans les rues de New York, en soutien à la campagne du syndicat Solidarité pour la démocratie et la non-ingérence soviétique en Pologne.*

Premier voyage de Columbia

Le nouveau vaisseau spatial de la NASA, Columbia, vient d'être lancé, en avril. C'est le premier vaisseau réutilisable, lancé dans l'espace à l'aide de fusées de lancement, mais qui atterrit avec son propre moteur comme un avion. Il est capable de transporter des charges de 30 tonnes, dont des satellites à placer en orbite.

◀ *Lancement de la navette Columbia.*

Attentat contre le pape Jean-Paul II

▶ **13 mai 1981** ◀

Ce soir, le pape Jean-Paul II est à l'hôpital, où il se remet de l'attentat dont il a été victime. Il circulait dans sa « papamobile » blanche, bénissant la foule de la place Saint-Pierre, à Rome, lorsqu'un homme a ouvert le feu. Deux spectateurs ont également été blessés, et les policiers du Vatican ont dû protéger le terroriste contre la foule en colère. L'agresseur, un Turc de 23 ans nommé Mehmet Ali Agça, a été appréhendé. Les médecins espèrent que la robuste constitution du pape lui permettra de se rétablir.

▶ *Jean-Paul II vient d'être touché par l'assassin.*

1982

▲ *Le drapeau anglais flotte sur Port Howard, dans l'est des Malouines, après deux mois d'interruption.*

◄ *Les parachutistes britanniques transportant du matériel médical de premier secours aux blessés, à Mont Longdon, dans les îles Malouines.*

La guerre des Malouines

► 14 juin 1982 ◄ Les troupes britanniques ont repris Port Stanley, la capitale des Malouines, après la reddition de la garnison argentine. Cela met fin à 10 semaines de guerre pour le contrôle de ces îles minuscules (que les Britanniques appellent Falkland, et les Argentins, Malvinas) situées à 480 km au large des côtes argentines en Amérique du Sud. Les îles, colonies britanniques depuis 1833, sont revendiquées par l'Argentine. Le gouvernement argentin a envahi le territoire, en avril. Trois jours plus tard, un corps expéditionnaire britannique est parti pour le reconquérir. Avant l'arrivée des troupes britanniques dans les Malouines, des batailles navales et aériennes ont eu lieu. Cette guerre a été un grand succès pour Margaret Thatcher et a provoqué la chute du gouvernement militaire argentin.

Disque compact

Les CD *(compact discs)* lancés par Philips et Sony sont des disques en plastique très légers, d'un diamètre de 120 mm, contre 300 mm pour un 33-tours en vinyle. La musique est enregistrée sur le disque par une série de pits métalliques. Le lecteur de CD fait tourner le disque, et un rayon laser « lit » et convertit ces pits en sons.

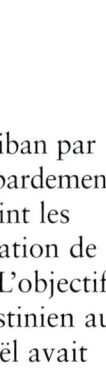

En 1982 aussi…

18 septembre
• Au Liban, les milices chrétiennes profitent de la présence de l'armée israélienne pour massacrer 1 000 Palestiniens dans les camps de réfugiés de Sabra et Chatila.

31 décembre • La loi Roudy autorise le remboursement des actes d'avortement (légalisé en 1974 par la loi Veil) par la Sécurité sociale.

Israël bombarde l'OLP au Liban

► 31 août 1982 ◄ L'invasion du Liban par Israël et le bombardement des positions palestiniennes ont contraint les combattants de l'Organisation de libération de la Palestine (OLP) à quitter Beyrouth. L'objectif de l'OLP est la création d'un État palestinien au Moyen-Orient, ce qu'Israël refuse. Israël avait envahi le Liban le 6 juin, après l'assassinat de son ambassadeur à Londres par un terroriste palestinien. Hier, en quittant Beyrouth dévasté, le dirigeant de l'OLP, Yasser Arafat, s'est juré que la lutte allait continuer.

▶ *La banlieue de Beyrouth, après un bombardement.*

Italie : 3ᵉ Coupe du monde de football

L'Italie vient de remporter la Coupe du monde de football pour la troisième fois, battant la RFA 3 à 1, devant 90 000 supporters à Madrid. Cette victoire met fin à 44 années d'attente pour les supporters italiens. Le premier but de la finale de juillet a été marqué par Paolo Rossi. Dans les demi-finales, l'Italie a battu la Pologne 2 à 0, alors que la RFA a péniblement battu la France aux penalties, après un match nul 3 à 3.

▲ *L'Italien Oraili et l'Ouest-Allemand Foster lors de la finale.*

▲ *L'Antarctique protégé pour la science.*

Protection de l'Antarctique

▶ **7 avril 1982** ◀ Un accord international qui prend effet aujourd'hui protège l'environnement en Antarctique. Pour la première fois depuis le traité de 1959 qui réservait le continent autour du pôle Sud à la science, l'Antarctique est en danger. Bien que la Grande-Bretagne et l'Argentine aient signé ce traité, le conflit des Malouines a été perçu comme une menace pour les bases scientifiques du continent, dont certaines ont été abandonnées.

ET de Spielberg

Steven Spielberg sourit à nouveau devant le succès de son dernier film *ET*, qui bat déjà tous les records. C'est l'histoire d'un extraterrestre attachant aux grands yeux, abandonné sur terre accidentellement par une soucoupe volante, et qu'un petit garçon protège contre les adultes.

Mort de Grace de Monaco dans un accident

▶ **14 septembre 1982** ◀ La princesse Grace de Monaco s'est tuée hier soir : sa voiture a quitté une route de montagne et s'est écrasée dans un ravin 40 mètres plus bas. Sa plus jeune fille, la princesse Stéphanie, passagère, s'en est sortie indemne. Il y a 25 ans, la princesse s'appelait encore Grace Kelly et était une grande vedette de Hollywood. Malgré les premiers rôles dans divers films dont *Fenêtre sur cour* et *Haute société*, elle a abandonné sa carrière en épousant le prince Rainier de Monaco en 1956.

▶ *Grace Kelly sur le bateau qui l'amenait à Monaco pour son mariage.*

Kohl, chancelier d'Allemagne de l'Ouest

▶ **1ᵉʳ octobre 1982** ◀ Aujourd'hui le Parlement de RFA a causé la chute du gouvernement socialiste de Helmut Schmidt. Helmut Kohl, dirigeant des démocrates-chrétiens (CDU) depuis neuf ans, le remplace comme chancelier. Schmidt, à la tête du Parti social-démocrate, dirigeait un gouvernement de coalition. Ce consensus s'est brisé lorsque le Parti démocratique de la liberté a retiré son soutien, car Schmidt refusait de réduire les dépenses sociales. Aujourd'hui, Schmidt a critiqué les lois qui permettent de démettre un chancelier de ses fonctions sans élection. Le chancelier Kohl annonce, quant à lui, qu'il va s'attaquer au chômage.

LES EFFETS SPÉCIAUX

L'un des grands atouts du cinéma est la possibilité d'utiliser des trucages pour faire voir aux spectateurs des choses qui ne se produisent pas en réalité. Les trucages les plus simples procèdent de ce que, contrairement aux apparences, l'image apparaissant à l'écran ne bouge pas, mais est composée d'une série de photographies « fixes » projetées à une cadence très rapide. Pour faire disparaître quelqu'un « par magie », on arrête la caméra, l'acteur descend du plateau, et la caméra est remise en route. Des centaines d'effets plus ou moins complexes peuvent ainsi être obtenus.

▲ *Jurassic Park (1993) a reçu l'oscar des meilleurs effets spéciaux.*

Des artifices spectaculaires

Il existe deux grands types d'effets spéciaux : les premiers consistent à modifier le film ou la bande magnétique, les seconds, à utiliser des accessoires spécialement conçus pour le film, tels des mannequins ou des modèles réduits.

Les effets spéciaux les plus spectaculaires apparaissent dans les films de science-fiction. Le producteur George Lucas est allé jusqu'à créer une société, Industrial Light and Magic, pour concevoir et réaliser les effets spéciaux de son film *la Guerre des étoiles* (1977).

Le roi des effets spéciaux est sans doute Steven Spielberg, le réalisateur de *Rencontres du troisième type*, d'*ET* et de *Jurassic Park*. Le héros d'*ET* (qui signifie extraterrestre) est une adorable créature venue d'une autre planète, abandonnée sur la Terre et qui se lie d'amitié avec des enfants. ET est une marionnette dont les mouvements sont commandés par ordinateur (autrefois, ces marionnettes étaient actionnées manuellement à chaque prise de vues, et les tournages n'en finissaient plus). L'ordinateur a ainsi révolutionné les effets spéciaux, permettant de modifier rapidement et à l'infini n'importe quelle image.

◀ *ET l'extraterrestre regardant s'approcher le vaisseau spatial qui le ramènera chez lui.*

La création d'effets spéciaux

Les studios spécialisés dans les effets spéciaux utilisent souvent des modèles réduits, notamment lorsqu'ils doivent donner l'illusion de gros engins, tels des vaisseaux spatiaux. Les mouvements de la caméra et de l'engin sont commandés par ordinateur, et chaque séquence peut être tournée plusieurs fois, en y ajoutant des détails issus d'autres moments du film. Parfois, on utilise l'engin lui-même et son modèle réduit. Ainsi, dans *Retour vers le futur*, une voiture s'envole et atterrit dans une rue fréquentée. Il s'agit d'un modèle réduit au 1/50, dont les occupants sont des mannequins. Lorsqu'elle atterrit, elle passe derrière un réverbère. La voiture qui réapparaît est une véritable automobile, avec de vrais acteurs.

▲ *Fabrication de modèles réduits pour* l'Empire contre-attaque *(1980), la suite de la Guerre des étoiles. Les montagnes à l'arrière-plan indiquent l'échelle.*

◄ *En arrière-plan : grâce à l'informatique, George Lucas réalise avec la Guerre des étoiles un nouveau genre de films de science-fiction.*

Les effets spéciaux

Le premier trucage a été découvert par hasard en 1896 par Georges Méliès : alors qu'il filmait une foule, sa caméra s'est bloquée ; les gens disparaissaient puis réapparaissaient sur la pellicule.

Dans *Superman*, le héros « vole » sur des fils qui sont « gommés » par ordinateur.

Dans *Forrest Gump*, Tom Hanks apparaît avec des personnalités décédées.

Des films en trois dimensions

Dans les années 50, les producteurs de cinéma cherchent de nouveaux procédés pour faire face à la concurrence de la télévision. C'est ainsi qu'apparaissent les films « en relief », qui nécessitent le port de lunettes spéciales comportant une lentille verte et une lentille rouge. Ces films, généralement de piètre qualité, n'ont guère de succès. Au début, les spectateurs sont très étonnés lorsque des trains ou des ballons leur foncent dessus, mais ces effets s'émoussent vite.

Aujourd'hui, ces films sont devenus plus réalistes, grâce à des effets plus sophistiqués et à des écrans spéciaux renforçant l'illusion du relief.

Roger Rabbit et les stars de Hollywood

Quelques films mêlent des personnages de dessins animés et de vrais acteurs. Le plus connu est *Qui veut la peau de Roger Rabbit ?* (1988). Les mouvements de la caméra et l'éclairage créent l'illusion de personnages animés en relief. L'acteur principal, Bob Hoskins, a en fait joué seul, l'animation ayant été ajoutée après le tournage.

▼ *Bob Hoskins parlant à un personnage animé.*

1980

1981

1982

1983

Manifestations contre le nucléaire

▶ **22 octobre 1983** ◀ Aujourd'hui, en Europe de l'Ouest, deux millions de pacifistes ont manifesté contre les États-Unis. Le commandement de l'Alliance atlantique a annoncé son intention d'installer des fusées Pershing en Allemagne de l'Ouest, en Belgique, aux Pays-Bas et en Italie. En effet, l'URSS a elle-même installé des SS-20 en Pologne, en Allemagne de l'Est, en Tchécoslovaquie et en Hongrie.

Les SS-20 et les Pershing sont des missiles (fusées équipées d'ogives nucléaires) à moyenne portée. Depuis leur base, ils peuvent atteindre une cible située à quelques centaines de kilomètres. Les SS-20 soviétiques menacent donc directement le territoire des pays d'Europe de l'Ouest, alliés des États-Unis ; c'est pourquoi ceux-ci, qui commandent les armées de l'OTAN, ont décidé d'installer à leur tour le même genre de missiles. Les écologistes français s'opposent aussi à l'installation de nouvelles armes nucléaires en Europe, mais Mitterrand a approuvé les États-Unis en disant que « les pacifistes sont à l'Ouest, mais les SS-20 sont à l'Est ». Le président Reagan est furieux que l'on s'oppose aux Pershing ; il annonce que, si cela continue, les États-Unis cesseront de défendre l'Europe contre les Russes, et propose une nouvelle stratégie, l'IDS (Initiative de défense stratégique), ou « guerre des étoiles » : il suffira d'installer des têtes nucléaires dans des satellites géostationnaires au-dessus des États-Unis pour défendre le pays, sans se soucier des Européens.

Les montres Swatch

1983

Le fabricant suisse de montres Asuag-ssih a vu juste avec sa gamme de montres Swatch bon marché et vivement colorées. Ernst Thomke et Nicolas Hayek ont conçu ces montres en plastique, fines mais robustes, pour concurrencer les montres japonaises et de Hong Kong à prix réduits. L'homme d'affaires Max Imgruth a orchestré une stratégie innovante qui présente les montres comme des articles de mode à acheter en même temps que les autres tenues.

1984

1985

▲ Mise en scène symbolique de la mort, lors d'une manifestation en Allemagne de l'Ouest, à l'occasion de la campagne européenne pour la paix.

◀ Le dirigeant de la CDN, Bruce Kent, s'adresse aux manifestants à Hyde Park, à Londres.

1986

Un Boeing 747 coréen abattu au-dessus de l'URSS

1987

▶ **1er septembre 1983** ◀ Cette nuit, un avion de la compagnie aérienne coréenne a été abattu par un avion de combat soviétique. Les 269 passagers ont été tués. L'Union soviétique prétend qu'il s'agissait d'un avion espion. En route pour Séoul au départ de New York, il avait dévié de sa trajectoire habituelle et, juste avant d'être abattu, il survolait la base militaire soviétique de l'île Sakhaline, au large de la Sibérie. 81 victimes sont sud-coréennes, 61 sont américaines. Personne ne comprend les causes de cette attaque.

◀ Un journal mural de Corée publie la liste des victimes de la catastrophe aérienne.

1988

En 1983 aussi...

23 mars • Le président américain Reagan propose la création d'une stratégie de défense nucléaire basée dans l'espace. On parle de « guerre des étoiles ».

5 octobre • Le syndicaliste polonais Lech Walesa reçoit le prix Nobel de la paix.

30 octobre • Un tremblement de terre en Turquie fait 2 000 morts.

1989

1980 – 1989

Émeutes raciales au Sri Lanka

▶ 27 juillet 1983 ◀ Plus de 600 personnes sont mortes dans de nouveaux combats entre Tamouls et Cinghalais. Ces deux communautés s'opposent depuis des siècles. Les Cinghalais, à la peau claire et de religion bouddhiste, sont majoritaires. Les Tamouls, à la peau plus foncée et de religion hindouistes, sont minoritaires.

◀ Rue dévastée au Sri Lanka.

Voile : l'America's Cup

▶ 26 septembre 1983 ◀ Depuis 132 ans, les yachts américains gagnaient toutes les courses de la prestigieuse America's Cup, mais, à partir d'aujourd'hui, la coupe est entre des mains australiennes. *Australia II*, avec le skipper John Bertrand, a remporté une époustouflante victoire devant le yacht américain *Liberty* de Dennis Conner. Le yacht vainqueur, qui appartient à l'homme d'affaires Alan Bond, est remonté de 1 à 3, pour gagner 4 à 3 dans cette course exaltante à sept épreuves.

Le faux journal de Hitler

▶ 14 mai 1983 ◀ Il y a quelques semaines, le magazine allemand *Stern* et le journal britannique *The Sunday Times*, ont publié des extraits des supposés carnets secrets d'Adolf Hitler. Aujourd'hui, alors que Konrad Kujau, l'homme qui les a fabriqués, s'est rendu à la police, ces carnets sensationnels ont été reconnus faux.

▶ Gerd Heidemann, le journaliste qui a « découvert » les carnets secrets de Hitler.

Percée de Madonna,

Une jeune femme de 25 ans, Madonna, s'est imposée dans les hit-parades aux États-Unis avec son tube *Holiday*. Elle travaillait dans une pâtisserie à New York, avant de remporter une bourse pour une formation de danse qui lui a ouvert les portes du succès.

▲ Patrouilles américaines à la Grenade.

Débarquement américain à la Grenade

▶ 25 octobre 1983 ◀ Des troupes américaines, envoyées par le président Reagan, ont envahi l'île de la Grenade, dans l'est des Caraïbes, pour renverser un gouvernement militaire issu d'un coup d'État de gauche. Les 800 marines des troupes d'invasion étaient accompagnés de soldats de la Barbade, de la Jamaïque et d'autres États des Caraïbes. Le Conseil de sécurité des Nations unies a condamné cette invasion d'un État indépendant comme une violation de la loi internationale.

Une Américaine dans l'espace

▶ 24 juin 1983 ◀ Sally Ride, la première femme américaine astronaute, a atterri aujourd'hui avec la navette spatiale Challenger. Elle avait décollé le 16 juin, vingt ans après la cosmonaute soviétique Valentina Terechkova, la première femme dans l'espace, qui s'était envolée à bord de Vostok 6 en 1963.

1984

Le virus du sida est identifié

Le sida

En un an, d'avril 1984 à avril 1985, les cas de sida enregistrés aux États-Unis ont plus que doublé.

Dans les années 90, le virus du sida était appelé HIV *(Human Immunodeficiency Virus)*.

En décembre 1997, le virus avait déjà tué 2,3 millions de personnes.

▶ **23 avril 1984** ◀ Des chercheurs américains et français ont identifié le micro-organisme à l'origine du virus du sida. Les êtres humains sont généralement capables de résister aux infections, grâce à leur système immunitaire. Mais le sida – syndrome d'immunodéficience acquise – s'attaque au système immunitaire, retirant ainsi aux malades toute capacité de résistance à des maladies infectieuses comme la pneumonie ou la tuberculose. Depuis que la maladie a été isolée pour la première fois, en 1981, 3775 cas ont été enregistrés, dont 1642 décès, pour les seuls États-Unis. Des recherches sur des méthodes de dépistage du virus par le sang sont en cours, mais, à l'heure qu'il est, il n'existe aucun remède au sida.

Le virus a été identifié d'abord à l'Institut Pasteur par le professeur Montagnier et son équipe, en France, puis à l'Institut national du cancer, aux États-Unis. Il semble qu'il se transmette par les rapports sexuels et par le sang. En octobre dernier, l'Organisation mondiale de la santé déclarait : « Il n'y a aucun risque de contracter le sida lors de contacts occasionnels et sociaux avec des patients atteints du sida. » Mais certains parlent déjà d'un fléau qui pourrait faire des millions de victimes avant l'an 2000.

◀ *Agrandissement du virus du sida, qui s'attaque aux globules blancs du sang humain chargés de combattre les infections, et les détruit.*

Mort de James F. Fixx

James J. Fixx, auteur du best-seller *Le Guide complet de la course à pied* avait commencé à courir dans l'espoir de déjouer les maladies de cœur fréquentes dans sa famille. Il est mort d'une crise cardiaque, alors même qu'il courait dans le Vermont, aux États-Unis. Il avait 52 ans.

Catastrophe écologique à Bhopal, en Inde

▶ **3 décembre 1984** ◀ Une importante fuite de gaz toxiques dans une usine chimique américaine a tué plus de 2 000 personnes à Bhopal, en Inde. Près de 200 000 autres ont perdu la vue ou souffrent de graves problèmes aux reins ou au foie après l'accident. L'usine fabriquait des pesticides pour la protection des récoltes. Des rapports suggèrent que l'entretien laissait à désirer et qu'il y avait déjà eu des fuites, moins importantes. Le gouvernement indien a fait appel à l'aide internationale.

▶ *L'usine de pesticides d'Union Carbide, à Bhopal, en Inde, une zone aujourd'hui sinistrée.*

En France, Fabius remplace Mauroy

▶ **17 juillet 1984** ◀ La France a un nouveau Premier ministre, Laurent Fabius. Son prédécesseur, P. Mauroy, a donné sa démission, après que le président Mitterrand lui a demandé de retirer un projet de réforme de l'enseignement proposé par M. Savary, ministre de l'Éducation nationale. En effet, les Français avaient manifesté en juin leur désaccord au sujet de cette loi qui menaçait l'école.

1980 – 1989

Barrage d'Itaipú, au Brésil

▶ **Octobre 1984** ◀ La nouvelle centrale hydroélectrique d'Itaipú sur le fleuve Paraná, au Brésil, près de la frontière avec le Paraguay, est entrée en activité. Cette centrale, la plus grande du genre dans le monde, peut produire 12 600 mégawatts d'électricité et alimente directement la ville de São Paulo.

Un barrage de terre et de pierre de 189 mètres de haut bloque le cours du fleuve Paraná et l'eau détournée se précipite dans des turbines pour produire l'électricité. Le barrage d'Itaipú utilise une forme particulière de transmission de l'énergie, le courant direct à haut voltage, la forme la plus rapide de transmission sur de grandes distances.

Succès pour Bruce Springsteen

Born in the USA, de Bruce Springsteen, a été l'album le plus vendu cette année aux États-Unis et en Grande-Bretagne. Les chansons racontant la vie de la classe ouvrière américaine, et les spectacles vibrants de ce chanteur auteur-compositeur né dans le New Jersey, en ont fait une des plus grandes vedettes blanches de rock dans le monde.

▲ *La nouvelle centrale électrique à Itaipú, au Brésil.*

En 1984 aussi...

13 février • Tchernenko devient le dirigeant soviétique, après la mort d'Andropov.

1er avril • Le chanteur américain de soul Marvin Gaye est abattu d'une balle par son père, au cours d'une dispute familiale.

Novembre • Les Canaques, les premiers habitants de la Nouvelle-Calédonie, revendiquent l'indépendance de ce territoire de la France d'outre-mer.

Assassinat d'Indira Gandhi

▶ **31 octobre 1984** ◀ Le Premier ministre indien, Indira Gandhi, a été assassiné par deux hommes de sa garde personnelle. Tous deux adeptes de la religion sikh, ils se vengent ainsi de la prise d'assaut par l'armée indienne en juin dernier du Temple d'or d'Amritsar, le lieu saint le plus sacré des sikhs. Les sikhs, installés dans la région du Pendjab, revendiquent plus d'indépendance. Des militants armés avaient occupé le Temple d'or, que les autorités indiennes ont repris, après quatre jours de violents combats qui ont coûté la vie à 90 soldats et 712 sikhs. Ce soir, le fils d'Indira Gandhi, Rajiv, sera investi Premier ministre.

▶ *Indira Gandhi et son fils Rajiv.*

4 médailles d'or pour Carl Lewis

▶ **8 août 1984** ◀ Avec ses quatre médailles d'or, du jamais vu depuis les Jeux de 1936, le sprinter américain Carl Lewis est la vedette des jeux Olympiques de Los Angeles. La gymnaste roumaine Ecaterina Szabo a également remporté quatre médailles d'or et une d'argent. Ces Jeux sont boycottés par l'URSS et ses satellites, tout comme l'ont été ceux de Moscou en 1980 par les États-Unis et certains pays occidentaux.

1980

1981

1982

1983

1984

1985

1986

1987

1988

1989

1985

Concerts pour les victimes de la famine en Afrique

▶ 13 juillet 1985 ◀ Soixante des plus grandes stars de rock internationales se sont réunies à l'occasion de deux concerts simultanés, l'un en Grande-Bretagne, à Londres, l'autre aux États-Unis, à Philadelphie. Ils ont été organisés par le Band Aid et ont rapporté 40 millions de livres aux victimes de la famine en Afrique. Ces rassemblements gigantesques – plus de 160 000 fans ! – ont été suivis à la télévision par 1,5 milliard de téléspectateurs, qui pouvaient faire des dons par téléphone. Les stars, qui chantaient gratuitement, ont chacune eu droit à dix-sept minutes sur scène. Madonna, Tina Turner, U-2, Dire Straits et Queen étaient de la partie. Bob Geldof et Midge Ure ont créé Band Aid en 1984 avec l'album *Savent-ils que c'est Noël ?*, qui a permis d'envoyer des millions aux victimes de la famine en Éthiopie.

Live Aid
- L'événement Live Aid a été diffusé à la télévision dans 160 pays.
- Des groupes comme The Who, Led Zeppelin, Black Sabbat et Status Quo se sont reformés pour la circonstance.
- Phil Collins a participé aux deux concerts en voyageant en Concorde.

▲ *Bob Geldof pendant le concert.*

Huit oscars pour *Amadeus*

Amadeus, le film du réalisateur tchèque Miloš Forman, adapté de la pièce de Peter Schaffer, montre la rivalité entre deux compositeurs du XVIIIᵉ siècle, Mozart et Salieri. Il a remporté huit oscars, parmi lesquels celui du meilleur film, celui du meilleur réalisateur et celui du meilleur acteur (F. Murray Abraham dans le rôle de Salieri).

En 1985 aussi …

11 mars • À la mort de Konstantin Tchernenko, Mikhaïl Gorbatchev est nommé à la tête du PC (parti communiste) soviétique.

24 mars • Le peintre français d'origine russe Marc Chagall, meurt, à 97 ans.

5 mai • Le président américain Ronald Reagan visite un cimetière militaire allemand où sont enterrés des SS, ce qui provoque l'indignation générale.

Éruption volcanique en Colombie

▶ 13 novembre 1985 ◀ Le volcan colombien Nevado del Ruiz est entré en activité, la nuit dernière. Il a déversé des torrents de pierres, de boue, de cendres et d'eau. Le bilan des victimes est estimé à 25 000 morts. La ville d'Armero, qui abritait 50 000 personnes, est ensevelie sous une couche de boue brûlante.

Le volcan est situé à 130 km de la capitale colombienne, Bogotá, et n'avait connu aucune activité depuis 1845. La cendre et la fumée de l'éruption ont parcouru des centaines de kilomètres. La zone a été déclarée sinistrée sur un périmètre de 180 km.

▼ *Les nominés d'Amadeus avec leurs oscars.*

▶ *Un enfant sauvé de la boue, après l'éruption du Nevado del Ruiz, en Colombie.*

1980 – 1989

Victoire de Bernard Hinault

▶ 30 juin 1985 ◀ Le cycliste français Bernard Hinault vient de remporter le Tour de France pour la cinquième fois, et cela malgré une chute où il a été blessé à la tête. Hinault est arrivé en tête avec 1 min 42 s d'avance sur son concurrent américain Greg LeMond. Le Tour de France est la course de cyclisme la plus importante au monde. Elle a été créée en 1903 et se déroule pendant trois semaines.

▲ *Bernard Hinault.*

Émeutes au stade du Heysel en Belgique

▶ 29 mai 1985 ◀ Les supporters de football britanniques ont provoqué ce soir de violentes émeutes au stade du Heysel, à Bruxelles : il y a 41 morts et plusieurs centaines de blessés parmi les supporters belges et italiens. Les violences ont éclaté juste avant la finale de la Coupe d'Europe entre Liverpool et les Italiens de la Juventus. Le drame n'a pas empêché le déroulement de la rencontre ; la Juventus a gagné 1 à 0. La tragédie est intervenue moins de trois semaines après la mort de 40 supporters dans l'incendie du stade britannique de Bradford.

L'affaire du *Rainbow Warrior*

▶ 22 septembre 1985 ◀ Le gouvernement français vient de reconnaître la responsabilité des services secrets dans l'attentat qui a détruit le bateau de l'organisation écologiste Greenpeace, le *Rainbow Warrior*. Au mois de juillet dernier, celui-ci se trouvait dans le port d'Auckland, en Nouvelle-Zélande, et se préparait à protester contre les essais nucléaires français de Mururoa, dans le Pacifique. Le photographe portugais Fernando Pereira a été tué. L'opinion internationale accuse la France d'être à l'origine du sabotage.

▲ Le Rainbow Warrior *après son explosion.*

Becker gagne Wimbledon

▶ 7 juillet 1985 ◀ Boris Becker, 17 ans, la star du tennis ouest-allemand, vient d'être sacré plus jeune vainqueur du simple messieurs de Wimbledon. Rapide et puissant, il a battu le Sud-Africain Kevin Curren par 3 sets à 1. Chaque année, à Wimbledon, les matches sont tirés au sort, de façon que les meilleurs joueurs ne s'affrontent pas lors des premiers tours de la compétition. Becker ne faisait pas partie des têtes de série. Il est donc le premier joueur vainqueur de Wimbledon à être issu des qualifications, ainsi que le premier champion allemand de ce tournoi.

◀ *Boris Becker, le plus jeune vainqueur de Wimbledon.*

Les « emballages » de Christo

Christo fait sensation à Paris : il vient d'emballer avec plus de 35 000 mètres de toile le Pont-Neuf, qui enjambe la Seine. Il n'en est pas à sa première expérience : en 1983, il a emballé onze îles situées au large des côtes de la Floride dans du tissu rose.

◀ *Le Pont-Neuf revu par Christo.*

1980

1981

1982

1983

1986

Catastrophe nucléaire à Tchernobyl

▶ 6 mai 1986 ◀ Les autorités soviétiques ont livré aujourd'hui des détails concernant l'explosion, le mois dernier, d'une centrale nucléaire, à Tchernobyl, qui a entraîné un accroissement du degré de radioactivité dans l'atmosphère. Les vents ont répandu cette radioactivité sur l'Europe, atteignant la Suède, la Finlande, le nord de la Grande-Bretagne et même la France et l'Italie. L'accident s'est produit le 26 avril, alors que des scientifiques installaient un système de sécurité. Une boule de feu s'est formée, après des explosions qui ont fait sauter le couvercle en béton du réacteur nucléaire.

▶ *Vue aérienne de la centrale nucléaire de Tchernobyl, près de Kiev, après la catastrophe.*

1984

Retour de la comète de Halley

Tous les 76 ans, la boule de glace et de poussières appelée comète de Halley réapparaît au centre du système solaire. Lorsqu'elle est passée à proximité de la Terre, cette année, de nombreux vaisseaux spatiaux ont fait des tests et pris des photos. La comète porte le nom de l'astronome anglais Edmund Halley, qui en a calculé l'orbite en 1705.

1985

1986

1987

Chute de Marcos, président des Philippines

▶ 25 février 1986 ◀ Ferdinand Marcos, président des Philippines depuis vingt ans, a fui le pays aujourd'hui. Corazón Aquino, qui s'est présentée contre lui aux récentes élections, vient d'être investie présidente. Le régime corrompu de Marcos était soutenu par les États-Unis. Mme Aquino est la veuve d'un homme politique assassiné sur ordre de Marcos en 1983.

▶ *Cory Aquino célèbre sa victoire, devant une statue de l'ex-président Marcos.*

En 1986 aussi...

1er janvier • L'Espagne et le Portugal intègrent la Communauté économique européenne.

20 mars • Après la victoire de la droite, Jacques Chirac est nommé Premier ministre. Première cohabitation droite-gauche.

4 décembre • De violentes manifestations étudiantes à Paris font une victime, Malik Oussekine, tué par la police.

▲ *La comète de Halley, en 1986.*

1988

1989

Le drame de Challenger

▶ **28 janvier 1986** ◀ Le vaisseau spatial américain Challenger a explosé aujourd'hui, 1 min 13 s après son lancement, entraînant la mort des sept membres de l'équipage. La navette s'élevait à une vitesse de 3 200 km/h, lorsque la défaillance d'une des fusées de lancement a provoqué un incendie. Les réservoirs de carburant, pleins, ont explosé en un gigantesque bouquet de flammes. Un des membres d'équipage était l'enseignante Christa McAuliffe, choisie par un programme spécial de la NASA pour envoyer des non-spécialistes dans l'espace. Des scientifiques émettent l'hypothèse que le temps, exceptionnellement froid, peut avoir eu une incidence sur la défaillance d'une des fusées de lancement.

▶ *Challenger s'est transformé en une boule de feu orange et blanc.*

Tyson, champion des poids lourds

Le 22 novembre, l'Américain Mike Tyson, 20 ans, a battu le boxeur canadien Trevor Berbick en deux rounds, avec un coup magistral, devenant ainsi le plus jeune champion du monde des poids lourds.

Baby Doc fuit Haïti

▶ **7 février 1986** ◀ La population d'Haïti, dans les Caraïbes, se réjouit à la nouvelle de la fuite en France de son président détesté, Jean-Claude Duvalier. Connu sous le nom de Baby Doc, Duvalier, 34 ans, était encore plus haï que son père, « Papa Doc » à qui il avait succédé comme dictateur, ou « président à vie » d'Haïti. Les Duvalier ont régné sur l'île pendant 28 ans, soutenus par les Tontons Macoutes, une très brutale police secrète.

▶ *Baby Doc se prépare à quitter Haïti.*

▼ *Olof Palme, Premier ministre suédois.*

Le Premier ministre suédois assassiné

▶ **28 février 1986** ◀ Le Premier ministre suédois Olof Palme a été mortellement blessé en pleine rue, hier soir, à Stockholm. Dirigeant du Parti social-démocrate, Palme était Premier ministre depuis 1982, et l'avait déjà été de 1969 à 1976. Il avait critiqué le rôle des États-Unis dans la guerre du Viêt-nam. Avant sa réélection en 1982, l'ONU l'avait envoyé en mission spéciale pour tenter de régler le conflit Iran-Irak.

Élection de Kurt Waldheim

▶ **8 juin 1986** ◀ Kurt Waldheim vient d'être élu président de l'Autriche, malgré sa carrière dans une unité de l'armée allemande qui a commis des atrocités en Yougoslavie. Waldheim, ancien secrétaire général de l'ONU, avoue qu'il n'a pas dit la vérité sur son passé, mais dit qu'on ne peut le rendre responsable de crimes de guerre.

1980 – 1989

1980

1981

1982

1983

1984

1985

1986

1987

1988

1989

1987

Démocratisation et libéralisation en URSS

▶ **29 janvier 1987** ◀ « Le Parti communiste doit être plus ouvert, et les électeurs doivent pouvoir choisir entre plusieurs candidats », a déclaré aujourd'hui le dirigeant soviétique Mikhaïl Gorbatchev. Depuis son élection en mars 1985, son engagement pour le changement et les réformes en Union soviétique n'est un secret pour personne. Les deux axes de sa politique, la perestroïka (« restructuration », en russe) d'une part, et la transparence d'autre part, impliquent une réforme de l'économie et du gouvernement, ainsi que la liberté d'information et de circulation.

La population soviétique est habituée au contrôle étatique strict, mais Gorbatchev a réduit la censure, afin que la presse, les divers médias et les particuliers soient libres de critiquer les membres du gouvernement. En décembre dernier, il y a eu un exemple d'ouverture, lorsque Andreï Sakharov, un défenseur de la démocratie et des droits de l'homme en URSS, a été libéré de son assignation à résidence à Gorki, qui durait depuis sept ans. Partisan du désarmement nucléaire, Gorbatchev a déjà participé à deux réunions au sommet avec le président américain Reagan pour en discuter.

▲ *Mikhaïl Gorbatchev, le réformateur soviétique.*

30 morts dans le métro de Londres

▼ *Un policier dépose des fleurs devant une station de la gare King's Cross.*

▶ **19 novembre 1987** ◀ 30 personnes sont mortes et de nombreuses autres ont été blessées dans l'incendie de la station de métro King's Cross, à Londres, hier soir. Le feu a pris dans un Escalator en bois et s'est propagé très vite à cause de la vétusté du matériel.

La direction des transports est mise en cause, à la suite des réductions des contrôles de sécurité et de l'entretien. La station ne disposait pas de système d'extinction automatique d'incendie, bien qu'il ait été recommandé dans un rapport de sécurité il y a trois ans.

En 1987 aussi...

Mai • À l'approche des jeux Olympiques, les Coréens du Sud manifestent violemment pour demander davantage de démocratie.

22 juin • Fred Astaire, la légende de Hollywood, meurt à 88 ans.

26 juillet • Le cycliste irlandais Stephen Roche remporte le Tour de France.

19 octobre • Krach financier dans toutes les Bourses du monde.

◀ *Un pompier inspecte le hall principal des guichets de la station de métro King's Cross.*

1980 – 1989

Records pour les tableaux de Van Gogh

Cette année déjà, *les Tournesols* du peintre impressionniste hollandais Vincent Van Gogh ont atteint le prix de 225 millions de francs, aux enchères chez Christie's, à Londres, battant tous les records de prix pour un tableau. Mais, plus tard, Christie's, à New York, a vendu *les Iris*, du même artiste, pour la somme de 325 millions de francs. Le premier appartient à la compagnie d'assurances Yasuda, l'acheteur du second ne s'est pas fait connaître.

Succès pour la techno

Avec la baisse des prix des synthétiseurs et des séquenceurs, la musique électronique tient le haut du pavé dans les *raves* et les boîtes de nuit. Les créateurs de la techno préfèrent la technologie du futur aux héros d'hier. Le style « percussif », qui retourne à la vague disco des années 70, est apparu pour la première fois à Detroit.

Naufrage d'un car-ferry

▶ 7 mars 1987 ◀ 200 personnes sont mortes dans les eaux glacées de la Manche, la nuit dernière, dans le naufrage d'un car-ferry. Le *Herald of Free Enterprise* venait de quitter Zeebrugge en Belgique pour rejoindre Douvres, dans le sud de l'Angleterre, lorsque le drame a eu lieu. Des portes du ferry aux deux extrémités permettaient aux véhicules d'entrer d'un côté et de sortir de l'autre sans faire de manœuvre. Une des portes est restée ouverte, et l'eau s'est engouffrée dans la cale des voitures. Beaucoup de personnes sont mortes avant l'arrivée des secours.

▼ Le *Herald of Free Enterprise* après le drame.

La couche d'ozone

▶ 16 septembre 1987 ◀ Un accord international pour la protection de l'atmosphère terrestre a été signé à Montréal, au Canada. 27 pays, dont les États-Unis et la plupart des nations européennes, ont accepté de ne pas augmenter l'utilisation des chlorofluorocarbones (CFC), composés chimiques utilisés pour les bombes aérosol et les réfrigérateurs, et qui attaquent la couche d'ozone. Ils se sont également engagés à diminuer de moitié l'utilisation des CFC d'ici à 1999. La couche d'ozone, autour de la Terre, constitue une protection contre les radiations du soleil, qui peuvent détériorer les récoltes. L'inquiétude est vive face à la diminution de la couche d'ozone dans des régions de l'Antarctique.

▼ Le Cessna de Rust devant l'église Basile-le-Bienheureux sur la place Rouge.

Atterrissage sur la place Rouge

▶ 29 mai 1987 ◀ Un pilote d'Allemagne de l'Ouest de 19 ans a découvert une faille dans le système de défense aérienne le plus performant du monde. Matthias Rust a conduit son avion, un Cessna 172 quatre places, directement au cœur de Moscou, déjouant le radar soviétique en volant juste à hauteur des toits. Il a survolé le Kremlin à très basse altitude, et, après avoir contourné l'église Basile-le-Bienheureux, il s'est posé sur la place Rouge.

1988

▲ *Inspection de la carlingue de l'avion qui a explosé au-dessus de Lockerbie, en Écosse.*

Crash de Lockerbie

▶ **22 décembre 1988** ◀ Une des plus graves catastrophes aériennes depuis les débuts de l'aviation a eu lieu cette nuit, lorsqu'un Boeing 747 américain a explosé au-dessus de la ville écossaise de Lockerbie, à quelques kilomètres au nord de la frontière anglaise. On parle de 270 morts : tous les passagers plus 11 personnes à terre. Parti de Francfort, le vol 103 de la Pan Am volait vers New York, après une brève escale à l'aéroport de Heathrow, à Londres. De nombreux passagers étaient des citoyens américains rentrant chez eux pour les vacances de Noël. Selon des témoins, l'avion s'est soudain embrasé en une boule de feu. Tous, à bord, ont dû mourir instantanément, le pilote n'ayant même pas eu le temps d'envoyer un signal de détresse. L'avion s'est écrasé au sol en fragments incandescents, allumant des dizaines de feux, détruisant plus de 30 maisons, et laissant des cratères de 15 mètres de profondeur. Les corps, dont certains ne sont pas identifiables, et des bouts de carlingue sont éparpillés sur une vaste zone. Bien qu'on n'ait pas encore déterminé les raisons de l'explosion, on privilégie une piste terroriste. Des menaces d'attentats sur la Pan Am circulaient dans les ambassades américaines.

En 1988 aussi...

30 juin • La conférence de Stockholm estime à 5 millions le nombre de porteurs du virus du sida.

3 juillet • Un avion de ligne iranien est abattu par un navire militaire américain, entraînant la mort de 290 personnes.

5 octobre • Les Chiliens rejettent par référendum la dictature militaire de Pinochet.

Trois hommes de l'IRA tués à Gibraltar

▶ **18 mars 1988** ◀ Des troubles ont éclaté lors de l'enterrement à Belfast des trois membres de l'IRA, Sean Savage, Daniel McCann et Maired Farrell, tués à Gibraltar il y a dix jours. Un tireur loyaliste a lancé des grenades et tiré sur la foule en deuil dans le cimetière. Trois personnes ont été tuées, et 50, blessées.

Le déroulement exact des événements qui ont conduit à la mort des trois membres de l'IRA est controversé. Ils étaient surveillés par les forces de sécurité britanniques, probablement le service secret – SAS –, qui pensait qu'ils préparaient un attentat à Gibraltar. Leur voiture a été retrouvée, deux jours après leur mort, avec 64 kg d'explosifs. Selon la version officielle, lorsqu'ils ont interpellé les trois membres de l'IRA, les officiers britanniques se sont sentis menacés et, en situation de légitime défense, ils ont tiré à bout portant.

▼ *Le cortège funèbre des membres de l'IRA.*

▲ *Le Bangladesh après le déluge. Dans de nombreuses régions, on ne peut atteindre les victimes.*

Inondations catastrophiques au Bangladesh

▶ **5 septembre 1988** ◀ Le Bangladesh, un des pays les plus pauvres du monde, est affronté à la plus grande inondation des dernières décennies. Près des deux tiers du pays, dont la capitale Dhaka, sont inondés, et plus de 20 millions de personnes sont sans abri. Les cultures vivrières et fourragères ont été dévastées, ainsi que les routes et les digues. L'aéroport est hors service, et les chemins de fer, construits par des ingénieurs britanniques sur des chaussées surélevées à un mètre au-dessus du niveau présumé des inondations, ont été submergés. On estime qu'il y a 2 000 morts et 43 millions de sinistrés, d'autant que les réserves d'eau potable polluées favorisent la propagation des maladies. Le gouvernement a fait appel à l'aide internationale, mais l'état des voies de communication inondées rend l'acheminement compliqué et urgent.

Ben Johnson perd son titre olympique

Moins d'une semaine après sa victoire en 9,79 secondes au 100 m aux jeux Olympiques de Séoul, le sprinter canadien Ben Johnson a été privé de sa médaille d'or et interdit de représenter son pays. Des contrôles d'urine ont révélé la présence d'anabolisants stéroïdes, une drogue qui augmente les forces.

▲ *Ben Johnson, le champion déshonoré.*

Désarmement nucléaire

▶ **1er juin 1988** ◀ Le traité sur les missiles intermédiaires a enfin été signé aujourd'hui par Ronald Reagan et Mikhaïl Gorbatchev, dirigeants des États-Unis et de l'Union soviétique. C'est le premier accord d'importance pour le désarmement nucléaire et il reflète le souhait de Gorbatchev d'améliorer les relations avec l'Ouest et de réduire les dépenses militaires à l'intérieur. Les États-Unis vont retirer leurs Pershing de moyenne portée et leurs missiles Cruise de leurs bases en Europe de l'Ouest. L'URSS retirera ses missiles équivalents d'Europe de l'Est. Des équipes pour contrôler le bon déroulement des termes de l'accord sont prévues.

▲ *Un manifestant brandit le drapeau palestinien.*

L'Intifada

▶ **4 novembre 1988** ◀ Les Palestiniens de Jérusalem ont publié aujourd'hui leur déclaration d'indépendance. L'annonce a probablement été précipitée par la victoire du parti de droite, le Likoud, aux élections israéliennes, il y a deux jours. Une victoire décrite par l'OLP comme un coup fatal porté à la paix.

L'Intifada est la « guerre des pierres » menée par les gamins palestiniens contre l'armée régulière israélienne. Elle s'accompagne d'une campagne de désobéissance civile et de résistance à la domination israélienne dans les Territoires occupés. Elle a commencé en décembre dernier et se révèle plus efficace que le terrorisme. L'Intifada a mis en évidence la frustration des Palestiniens, qui ne voient pas d'évolution vers une solution diplomatique. Un épisode filmé en secret a montré sur toutes les télévisions du monde la brutalité des soldats israéliens et a soulevé l'indignation.

1980 – 1989

1988

Tremblement de terre en Arménie

▶ **8 décembre 1988** ◀ Le gigantesque tremblement de terre qui a dévasté l'Arménie en plusieurs endroits hier a fait plus de 100 000 morts et au moins dix fois plus de sans-abri. Dans les villes de Leninakan et Spitak, totalement en ruine, les cercueils s'empilent dans le stade. Mal construits, les bâtiments modernes se sont effondrés comme des châteaux de cartes, enterrant vivants leurs occupants. Le temps froid aggrave la situation. L'épicentre du séisme, de 6,9 sur l'échelle de Richter, se situait près de la frontière avec la Turquie. Tandis que les survivants cherchent désespérément leurs proches de leurs mains nues ou avec des outils improvisés, une aide internationale massive est organisée. Mikhaïl Gorbatchev, le président de l'URSS, a annulé sa visite aux États-Unis, pour se rendre en Arménie aujourd'hui. Ce désastre naturel survient après une année de troubles et de violences ethniques dans la région, provoqués par le refus de l'Azerbaïdjan de rendre le Haut-Karabakh, région principalement peuplée d'Arméniens, appartenant à l'Azerbaïdjan depuis 1921.

▲ *Survivants et secouristes marchent dans les ruines de la ville arménienne de Leninakan.*

La vérité sur le saint suaire

Des tests scientifiques, financés par le Vatican, ont jeté le doute sur une des reliques les plus célèbres de la chrétienté. Conservé à la cathédrale de Turin, ce tissu très ancien porte la marque d'un homme. La tradition voulait que ce soit le linceul (suaire) dans lequel fut enterré le Christ, bien qu'on n'en ait aucun témoignage historique antérieur au XIVe siècle. Selon le test, le tissu lui-même ne daterait que de 1260.

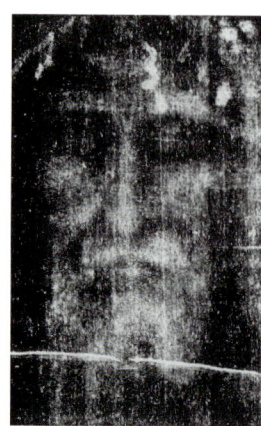

▲ *Le linceul de Turin demeure un mystère, qui n'est plus sacré.*

▲ *Des électeurs félicitent George Bush, futur président des États-Unis.*

George Bush, président des États-Unis

▶ **11 novembre 1988** ◀ Comme prévu, le candidat républicain George Bush, ancien dirigeant de la CIA a aisément remporté l'élection présidentielle américaine. Jusqu'alors, il était vice-président de son prédécesseur, Reagan, qui se retire. Il a obtenu 40 des 50 États et 54 % des voix dans le pays. Bien qu'il ait mené une campagne étonnamment agressive, dérangeant certains rivaux républicains autant que les démocrates, Bush a toujours été assuré de gagner face au candidat démocrate Michael Dukakis, le gouverneur ultralibéral du Massachusetts.

Avec les démocrates majoritaires dans les deux chambres du Congrès, Bush va avoir du mal à tenir ses engagements électoraux, tel celui de ne pas augmenter les impôts. Cela étant, aucun changement notable n'a été prévu par rapport à la politique de l'administration Reagan.

1980 – 1989

Fin de la guerre Iran-Irak

8 août 1988 — Après huit ans d'une guerre qui a fait près d'1 million de morts et un nombre inconnu de blessés, le secrétaire de l'ONU, Javier Pérez de Cuellar, a annoncé un cessez-le-feu entre l'Iran et l'Irak. Il prend effet le 20 août, et des pourparlers de paix se tiendront à Genève sous l'égide des Nations unies. Cette guerre n'a fait ni vainqueur, ni vaincu.

▼ *La foule à Téhéran manifeste sa joie, à l'annonce du cessez-le-feu.*

Le bicentenaire de l'Australie

Les Australiens de toute la planète célèbrent leur 200ᵉ anniversaire. Le 26 janvier 1788, la *Première flotte* britannique jetait l'ancre à Botany Bay, une baie située près de l'actuel Sydney. Les militants aborigènes s'élèvent contre cette commémoration de la colonisation de l'Australie par les Européens.

▲ *Dans le port de Sydney, de grands voiliers miment l'arrivée de la* Première flotte.

Mitterrand réélu

8 mai 1988 — F. Mitterrand commence un second septennat, après avoir battu son rival, le Premier ministre Jacques Chirac. Celui-ci a été désavantagé par les divisions de la droite, par l'affaire des otages français au Liban, ainsi que par les troubles indépendantistes en Nouvelle-Calédonie.

Benazir Bhutto, Premier ministre du Pakistan

17 novembre 1988 — Le Parti du peuple du Pakistan (PPP) a remporté les premières élections démocratiques organisées depuis onze ans. La dirigeante du PPP, Benazir Bhutto, devient la première femme Premier ministre d'un pays musulman. C'est un triomphe pour cette Pakistanaise formée à l'université de Cambridge, et dont le père, Zulfikar Ali Bhutto, ancien Premier ministre, avait été exécuté par le général Zia ul-Haq en 1979. Elle est restée en assignation à résidence ou en exil pendant presque toute la décennie. La mort de Zia, en août dernier, a ouvert la voie à un gouvernement démocratique.

▲ *Benazir Bhutto, la nouvelle dirigeante pakistanaise, en campagne au milieu de la foule des villes.*

Catastrophe de la plate-forme pétrolière Alpha Piper

6 juillet 1988 — Cette nuit, après une série d'explosions, la plate-forme pétrolière Alpha Piper, d'Occidental Petroleum, s'est transformée en une véritable fournaise. Les flammes, dépassant les 100 mètres de hauteur, et la chaleur intense, ressentie à près de 2 kilomètres de distance, entravent les efforts des secours. On redoute la mort de 170 hommes. Beaucoup, endormis au moment de l'explosion, se sont retrouvés coincés dans le bloc d'habitation qui a coulé. D'autres ont pu se sauver en sautant dans la mer brûlante, où ils ont été récupérés par des Zodiacs. Pourtant, il y a huit jours, le contrôle de sécurité jugeait la plate-forme conforme.

▶ *La plate-forme Alpha Piper, encore en flammes, des heures après l'explosion.*

LES ORDINATEURS

À la fin des années 90, les ordinateurs font partie intégrante de la vie quotidienne. Ainsi ce livre a été réalisé à l'aide d'ordinateurs. Les ordinateurs peuvent jouer un rôle éducatif et ludique. Ils permettent de rendre les opérations bancaires plus faciles et même de faire ses courses, ils contrôlent les réseaux de distribution de l'eau et de l'électricité, mais ils servent également à créer les effets spéciaux que l'on voit au cinéma, ou à concevoir certaines musiques. Presque tout ce que nous faisons aujourd'hui nécessite un ordinateur. Et pourtant, les premiers vrais ordinateurs n'ont été conçus qu'au milieu des années 40. Les progrès de l'informatique sont certainement l'une des plus grandes révolutions technologiques du siècle.

Les ordinateurs
Lorsque les ordinateurs sont reliés entre eux, on dit qu'ils sont en réseau.
Aujourd'hui, Internet, premier réseau mondial d'ordinateurs, permet d'échanger des informations et des services sur toute la planète.
Une puce Pentium Pro contient l'équivalent de 5,5 millions de transistors.
Les ordinateurs des années 90 sont 1,5 million de fois plus rapides que ceux des années 50.

◀ Ancêtre des ordinateurs d'aujourd'hui, le calculateur ENIAC en 1943.

Les débuts de l'informatique

L'ère informatique commence en décembre 1943, lorsque le premier ordinateur programmable au monde, une machine appelée Colossus, est mis en service à Bletchley Park – le quartier général du décodage en Grande-Bretagne. Il est composé de 1 500 tubes électroniques qui lui permettent de calculer plus rapidement que ses prédécesseurs mécaniques. Mais Colossus a été vite dépassé par ENIAC (Electronic Numerical Integrator and Computer), construit à l'université de Pennsylvanie en 1945 – trop tard cependant pour pouvoir être utilisé pendant la guerre. L'ENIAC pèse 30 tonnes et occupe à lui seul une vaste pièce ; ses 17 500 tubes électroniques dégagent une chaleur considérable et attirent des nuées de papillons de nuit. Pour exprimer un défaut de fonctionnement des programmes informatiques, le mot « bug », qui en anglais signifie insecte est resté (francisé en « bogue »).

Vers 1980, les ordinateurs sont réservés aux professionnels de l'informatique.

Puces électroniques

La révolution informatique a été rendue possible par les puces électroniques – micro-éléments en silicium contenant un circuit intégré –, élaborées pour la première fois dans les années 60. Les puces sont partout, des cartes bancaires aux jouets, et des moteurs de voiture aux cuisinières.

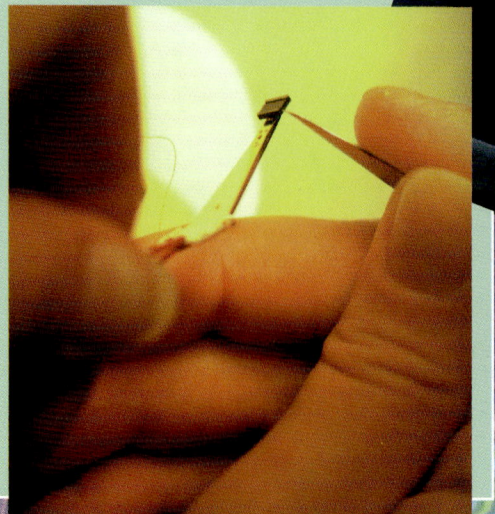

Des ordinateurs pour tous

En 1981, le géant de l'électronique IBM *(International Business Machines Corporation)* lance pour la première fois un ordinateur à usage personnel, le PC *(Personal Computer)*. IBM demande à la firme américaine Intel de fabriquer les puces, et à l'entreprise Microsoft de créer le logiciel MS-DOS du PC (c'est Intel qui a la première regroupé tous les composants d'un ordinateur sur un circuit intégré appelé microprocesseur).

Le PC devient un véritable best-seller. En 1984, au moment où IBM vend plus de 3 millions de PC par an, une autre société américaine, Apple lance un ordinateur rival et radicalement différent, le Macintosh, qui se caractérise par un certain nombre de concepts originaux : une souris, des icônes, etc. Microsoft réagit en créant le logiciel Windows qui utilise les mêmes concepts.

Aujourd'hui l'ordinateur devient de plus en plus puissant tout en étant de plus en plus petit et facile à utiliser. Il se transporte facilement : c'est le portable.

▲ *Le milliardaire Bill Gates, patron de Microsoft, présente le logiciel Windows.*

▲ *John Scully, Steve Jobs et Steve Wozniak, les coinventeurs de l'ordinateur Apple, devant un Apple IIc en 1984.*

◄ *Sur la puce : La planète rouge, un jeu virtuel en 3D, qui se déroule sur Mars.*

Les jeux

Le premier jeu électronique, qui ressemble à du ping-pong sans filet, date de 1972. Il s'agit d'une console conçue par Atari, la Pong, munie de deux manettes de commande et destinée à être branchée sur un téléviseur. Chaque manette commande une raquette qui se déplace verticalement sur l'écran. Cela permet à chaque joueur d'intercepter la balle et de la renvoyer à son adversaire. Les jeux électroniques sont devenus de plus en plus sophistiqués. Les plus populaires restent les simulations de vol et de conduite automobile, les jeux sportifs qui recréent l'atmosphère d'une véritable compétition, les jeux de guerre comme *Mortal Kombat* et *Wolfenstein*, ainsi que les jeux d'aventures comme *Myst*. Ils ont désormais leurs propres vedettes, comme *Lara Croft, Sonic the Hedgehog* et *Super Mario*.

◄ *Gros plan d'une puce au-dessus d'un dessin fait sur ordinateur.*

1989

En 1989 aussi...

15 février
• Les dernières troupes soviétiques quittent l'Afghanistan.

7 mars • La Chine instaure la loi martiale au Tibet.

14 mai • Carlos Menem élu président en Argentine.

3 juin • Mort de l'ayatollah Khomeyni.

14 juillet • Célébration à Paris du bicentenaire de la Révolution française.

▲ Les Berlinois de l'Est et de l'Ouest s'assemblent devant la porte de Brandebourg.

La chute du mur de Berlin

▶ **10 novembre 1989** ◀ Sur les coups de minuit, hier soir, *les checkpoints*, postes de contrôle militaires du mur de Berlin, ont été ouverts par les gardes. Au son des acclamations, des cloches des églises et des klaxons, des milliers de personnes se sont engouffrées à travers ce passage. D'autres ont grimpé sur le mur ou sont passées par-dessus. Certains l'ont attaqué à coups de marteau. Tous étaient heureux de célébrer la fin de la guerre froide, dont le mur était l'un des symboles les plus visibles.

Le mur en béton de 45 km qui traverse le centre de Berlin, la capitale de l'Allemagne d'avant guerre, avait été monté en 1961 pour stopper la migration vers l'Ouest qui, depuis 1949, avait déjà vidé l'est du pays de 2,5 millions de personnes. Depuis sa construction, près de 100 personnes avaient été tuées en tentant de fuir à l'Ouest. Ces dernières semaines, des milliers de réfugiés ont envahi l'Allemagne de l'Ouest, en passant par la Tchécoslovaquie et la Hongrie, où les contrôles aux frontières avaient déjà été levés. Le gouvernement de RDA, réalisant qu'il ne peut plus rien contrôler, a décidé d'ouvrir la frontière, permettant ainsi à tout le monde de passer à l'Ouest. La chute du mur remet à l'ordre du jour la possibilité d'une réunification de l'Allemagne.

Exécution des Ceauşescu

▲ Les Ceauşescu, arrêtés alors qu'ils tentaient de s'enfuir.

▶ **25 décembre 1989** ◀ Le dictateur roumain Nicolae Ceauşescu et sa femme ont été exécutés aujourd'hui, à l'issu d'un procès hâtif. Le vieil empire stalinien d'Europe de l'Est s'est effondré en quelques mois. Depuis juin, la Pologne, la Hongrie et la Tchécoslovaquie ont renversé les communistes et se sont dotées de gouvernements démocratiques. Le mois dernier, l'ancien dictateur bulgare, Todor Živkov, était expulsé, et, au début de ce mois-ci, le gouvernement communiste d'Allemagne de l'Est a démissionné. Le dictateur roumain Ceauşescu est presque le dernier à partir. Depuis son arrivée au pouvoir en 1965, sa politique critique vis-à-vis de l'URSS lui avait assuré un bon accueil auprès de divers gouvernements et politiciens occidentaux. Cependant, Ceauşescu était un dictateur brutal. Sa politique de planification familiale répressive avait accru l'appauvrissement du pays. De plus, il favorisait les membres de sa famille, dont sa femme, Elena.

1980 – 1989

Fatwa islamique contre Rushdie

▶ **15 février 1989** ◀ Au nom de l'Islam, l'ayatollah Khomeyni, chef de la République islamique d'Iran, vient de lancer une *fatwa* (sentence) contre le grand écrivain Salman Rushdie. Il reproche à celui-ci d'avoir manqué de respect envers le prophète Mahomet, dans son dernier livre, *les Versets sataniques*. Tous les musulmans fidèles à Khomeyni ont donc le devoir de tuer Rushdie, dont la vie est désormais en danger.

▲ *Un défenseur de la* fatwa *iranienne, avec un portrait de Khomeyni.*

Massacre de Tian'anmen

▶ **4 juin 1989** ◀ Les dirigeants de la Chine communiste ont réagi rapidement et avec une grande sauvagerie contre les étudiants et les jeunes qui occupaient pacifiquement la place Tian'anmen (« la porte de la paix céleste »), à Pékin, pour revendiquer des réformes démocratiques. L'armée chinoise a envahi et vidé la place par la force, en tirant sans distinction. Des ambulances de fortune tentent de rejoindre les hôpitaux, déjà pleins de mourants et de morts.

Batman, héros du cinéma

Le plus grand film de l'année est inspiré de la bande dessinée *Batman*. Il a déjà fait 200 millions de dollars au box-office aux États-Unis. Certains effets spéciaux sont remarquables ; le personnage le plus extraordinaire n'est pas Michael Keaton avec sa cape de Batman, mais Jack Nicholson en Joker.

▲ *Jack Nicholson en Joker.*

◀ *Un homme seul défie, impassible, les chars sur la place Tian'anmen.*

Intervention américaine au Panamá

▶ **21 décembre 1989** ◀ En réponse à la déclaration de guerre du président du Panamá, Noriega, aux États-Unis et au meurtre d'un soldat américain, les troupes américaines ont envahi le pays aujourd'hui. Leur objectif est la capture de Noriega, leur ancien allié, considéré maintenant comme un criminel. Noriega, arrivé au pouvoir en mai, après des élections truquées de façon flagrante, s'est réfugié dans une ambassade. Les dirigeants de l'opposition ont été tabassés, et des manifestants pour la démocratie, réprimés par les hommes forts de Noriega.

▼ *Un marine américain prend position au Panamá.*

Désastre à Hillsborough

▶ **15 avril 1989** ◀ 96 supporters ont été écrasés dans le stade de Hillsborough, à Sheffield, en Angleterre, où Liverpool jouait contre Nottingham Forest, lors d'une demi-finale de coupe. Un portail ouvert par erreur a permis à des centaines de supporters d'entrer dans un stade déjà plein à craquer. Une barrière en métal qui entourait le stade empêchait toute possibilité de sortir.

Accident de l'*Exxon Valdez*

▶ **24 mars 1989** ◀ 12 millions de gallons de pétrole pur s'échappent du supertanker naufragé l'*Exxon Valdez,* en Alaska. C'est l'une des pires catastrophes écologiques survenues dans les eaux d'Amérique du Nord. Elle menace d'entraîner d'énormes dégâts écologiques. Le bâtiment s'est échoué alors qu'il était commandé par un officier subalterne. Le capitaine somnolait dans sa cabine.

▶ *Le sauvetage du supertanker.*

De 1990 à 1997

1990

Le monde change au début des années 90. En Europe de l'Est, les régimes communistes se sont effondrés, et les pays retrouvent leur liberté. Le système de l'apartheid – ségrégation raciale – disparaît en Afrique du Sud. L'URSS et les États-Unis annoncent que la guerre froide, avec ses tensions dangereuses, est finie.

Mais la guerre touche d'autres parties du globe. La Yougoslavie est ravagée par la guerre civile. Au Moyen-Orient, la guerre du Golfe éclate en 1991. Les terroristes continuent à tuer.

▼ *Mandela et sa femme Winnie font le salut de l'ANC.*

Libération de Nelson Mandela

▶ **11 février 1990** ◀ Nelson Mandela est libre. Après 27 ans de détention, il peut quitter sa prison. La détention de Mandela était le symbole de l'injustice subie depuis des années par la majorité noire opprimée par la minorité blanche. Celle-ci avait instauré l'apartheid, qui maintenait une stricte séparation entre Blancs et Noirs, et n'accordait aucun droit à ces derniers.

Mandela avait adhéré en 1944 au Congrès national africain (ANC), une organisation politique noire interdite en 1960. Il était entré l'année suivante dans la clandestinité, et avait fondé un mouvement de résistance armée appelée Umkoto We Siz We (« la lance de la nation »). Arrêté, Mandela est condamné à cinq ans de prison, puis à la prison à vie. Le président De Klerk a été obligé de mettre fin à l'apartheid, pour rétablir des relations normales avec le reste du monde. En effet, avec la fin de la tension Est-Ouest, l'Afrique du Sud ne bénéficie plus de l'appui des États-Unis, puisque ceux-ci n'ont plus besoin d'allié dans cette partie du monde. Mandela est résolu à ne tirer aucune vengeance de la communauté blanche, mais à faire entrer son pays dans une ère de paix.

Afrique du Sud

Nelson Mandela est avocat. Il a fondé, au début des années 50, le premier cabinet d'avocats noirs d'Afrique du Sud, avec Oliver Tambo, un autre leader de l'ANC.

Mandela a été incarcéré pendant dix-huit ans, de 1964 à 1982, dans la prison de haute sécurité de Robben Island, à 7 km au large de la côte du Cap.

Cinq milliards de terriens

Les ressources de la planète sont limitées, et de plus en plus utilisées. La Terre compte plus de cinq milliards d'habitants. On a constaté, depuis 1985, qu'une femme rwandaise, en Afrique, a en moyenne huit enfants, contre un seul pour une Italienne. Les pays riches puisent beaucoup plus dans les ressources mondiales que les pays moins développés.

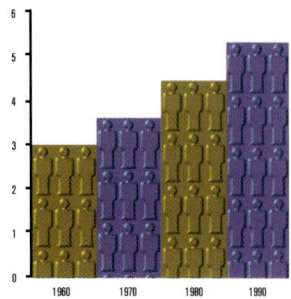

Mme Thatcher démissionne

▶ **22 novembre 1990** ◀ Margaret Thatcher démissionne de ses fonctions après onze ans de pouvoir. Hier, elle n'a pas réussi à obtenir une majorité au sein du Parti conservateur, dont elle était le chef, pour soutenir ses choix politiques. La plupart de ses anciens amis politiques refusent désormais de soutenir ses idées et, surtout, l'énorme augmentation des impôts locaux à Londres. Mme Thatcher s'oppose à l'entrée de la Grande-Bretagne dans la nouvelle Europe, l'Union économique et monétaire, mais beaucoup de parlementaires estiment que son attitude est dangereuse pour l'avenir du Royaume-Uni.

▶ *Mme Margaret Thatcher a été surnommée la « dame de fer ».*

1990 - 1997

Navratilova, championne de Wimbledon

À 33 ans, Martina Navratilova remporte le simple dames au tournoi de tennis de Wimbledon, pour la neuvième fois. Un record. Elle bat Zina Garrison, une Américaine, en deux sets. M. Navratilova, d'origine tchèque, vit aux États-Unis.

▲ *Les partisans du combat pour la libération de la Namibie déploient le drapeau de leur nouveau pays indépendant.*

Indépendance de la Namibie

▶ 21 mars 1990 ◀

La dernière colonie d'Afrique, la Namibie, vient d'accéder à l'indépendance, grâce à l'action de l'ONU. Ancienne colonie allemande, la Namibie avait été donnée à la Grande-Bretagne après la Seconde Guerre mondiale. Elle était administrée depuis par l'Afrique du Sud. En 1964, l'ONU avait déclaré que la Namibie devait devenir indépendante, mais l'Afrique du Sud s'y était toujours opposée, malgré la lutte armée menée par la SWAPO (Organisation du peuple du Sud-Ouest africain) et l'intervention de soldats cubains, communistes, alliés à l'URSS. La fin de la tension Est-Ouest modifie les rapports. L'ONU a pu organiser des élections libres, et, aujourd'hui, le président africain De Klerk a remis le pouvoir au premier président namibien, Sam Nujoma.

Réunification de l'Allemagne

▶ 3 octobre 1990 ◀

À minuit, hier, l'Allemagne de l'Ouest et celle de l'Est ont à nouveau formé une seule Allemagne, 45 ans après la fin de la guerre et la défaite. Les Berlinois ont fêté la nouvelle toute la nuit dans les rues. La réunification s'est faite plus vite que prévu. Il y a moins d'un an, le mur de Berlin, le symbole de la division allemande, se dressait encore au milieu de la ville, sous haute surveillance. La chute du mur, le 10 novembre, avait ouvert la voie aux discussions qui ont débuté en mars.

Lech Walesa, président de la Pologne

▶ 9 décembre 1990 ◀

L'ancien ouvrier des chantiers navals, Lech Walesa, remporte une victoire écrasante à l'élection présidentielle. Il est le premier président de Pologne élu lors d'élections libres et démocratiques depuis 50 ans. Au début des années 80, Walesa avait fondé le syndicat Solidarité et était devenu un héros du combat contre le régime. Il fut emprisonné de la fin 1981 à novembre 1982. En 1989, après sept ans d'interdiction, Solidarité est autorisé.

▶ *Walesa après sa victoire historique.*

En 1990 aussi...

15 avril • L'actrice d'origine suédoise Greta Garbo meurt, à l'âge de 84 ans.

14 mai • Portrait du docteur Gachet, du peintre hollandais Van Gogh, devient le tableau le plus cher au monde. Un homme d'affaires japonais l'a acheté pour 458 millions de francs, dans une salle de ventes de New York.

12 novembre • Le nouvel empereur du Japon, Akihito, monte sur le trône.

1990

L'Irak envahit le Koweït

▶ **8 août 1990** ◀ L'opération « Bouclier du désert » a commencé. Il y a six jours, l'Irak a envahi l'émirat du Koweït. Depuis la fin de la domination britannique, le Koweït et l'Irak formaient deux États différents, mais l'Irak, très peuplé, a toujours revendiqué le Koweït, minuscule, désertique, et très riche en pétrole. L'invasion du Koweït a effrayé la plupart des États, par sa brutalité, mais surtout par la menace qu'elle représente pour les approvisionnements en pétrole. Tous redoutent que l'Irak ne s'en prenne à son autre voisin, l'Arabie Saoudite, premier exportateur mondial de pétrole, plus vaste mais aussi peu peuplée que le Koweït. Il y a deux jours, les Nations unies ont décidé le blocus économique de l'Irak – le pays ne peut plus faire de commerce avec le reste du monde, ni vendre son pétrole, ni acheter des produits. Les États arabes, telles l'Égypte et l'Arabie Saoudite, ont demandé à l'Irak de se retirer du Koweït, mais Saddam Hussein a refusé. Il a massé des troupes à la frontière de l'Arabie Saoudite. Le Conseil de sécurité des Nations unies a décidé d'envoyer en Arabie une force internationale dirigée par les États-Unis.

▲ *Saddam se montre avec les otages occidentaux à la télévision irakienne. Voici Stuart Lockwood, un jeune Britannique.*

▼ *Un cercle dans le blé du Wiltshire. Le résultat de phénomènes météo ou l'œuvre de plaisantins?*

Mystère dans les blés

▶ **30 juillet 1990** ◀ Des farceurs ridiculisent les experts, qui se sont réunis pour enquêter sur les « cercles de blé » dans le Wiltshire, dans le sud de l'Angleterre. Ce sont des motifs circulaires qui sont apparus dans des champs de blé, pendant la nuit. Des experts ont suggéré que ces empreintes seraient dues à de petites tornades ou à des vaisseaux spatiaux venus d'ailleurs. Cette nuit, on a aperçu des éclairs de lumière orange et, le lendemain matin, on a vu de nouveaux cercles. Mais les créateurs des cercles ont laissé derrière eux des traces de leur passage prouvant qu'il s'agit d'une plaisanterie. Une partie de la population a vraiment cru à des extraterrestres.

Les Allemands gagnent leur 3ᵉ Coupe du monde

L'Allemagne remporte la finale de la Coupe du monde de football, pour la troisième fois. Elle bat l'Argentine par 1 but à 0, à Rome. Cette compétition a été décevante, marquée par des tactiques défensives. La Belgique était présente parmi les 24 pays participant aux matches en Italie. La France n'avait pas été sélectionnée.

Gorbatchev reçoit le prix Nobel de la paix

▶ **15 octobre 1990** ◀ Le dirigeant soviétique Mikhaïl Gorbatchev reçoit le prix Nobel de la paix. Ce prix récompense ses efforts pour améliorer les relations internationales. Depuis son arrivée au pouvoir en 1985, les relations entre l'URSS et les pays occidentaux se sont améliorées. De plus, Gorbatchev n'a pas tenté de bloquer la vague de changements en Europe de l'Est. Il a accepté la chute du communisme en Allemagne de l'Est et a approuvé la réunification allemande.

▶ *Mikhaïl Gorbatchev.*

Violente manifestation à Londres

▶ **31 mars 1990** ◀ À Londres, la manifestation organisée pour protester contre les nouveaux impôts locaux se termine en émeute et en pillage. Le défilé devait s'achever au centre de la ville, à Trafalgar Square, par quelques discours. Mais des policiers à cheval sont intervenus. Des manifestants se sont battus avec des bâtons et des projectiles. Ils ont cassé des vitrines de magasins, ils ont incendié des voitures et des bâtiments. Il y a eu de nombreux blessés. 341 personnes ont été arrêtées.

Au Royaume-Uni, les impôts locaux étaient établis, jusqu'à cette année, d'après la valeur de chaque maison, calculée selon sa taille. Mais, avec les nouveaux impôts, chaque adulte doit payer un montant fixé par la commune. Une grande famille vivant dans une petite maison paiera donc beaucoup plus qu'avant. Cette nouvelle mesure de Mme Thatcher est très impopulaire.

▶ *À Londres, les pancartes des manifestants incitent à refuser de payer les nouveaux impôts locaux, la* poll tax.

1990 – 1997

▲ *Un sauteur à l'élastique plonge.*

Le saut à l'élastique

Les amateurs de sensations fortes jouent leur vie au bout d'un fil. Le nouveau sport qui séduit les jeunes est le saut à l'élastique. Les sauteurs s'élancent depuis un pont, ou une tour très haute, au bout d'une corde élastique. Ils plongent dans le vide, mais la corde les retient, en leur évitant de se tuer. Ils se balancent, avec la tête en bas. Les sauteurs cherchent à sentir le danger, pour que leur cœur batte plus vite et plus fort.

Mary Robinson, présidente de l'Irlande

▶ **9 novembre 1990** ◀ Les électeurs de la République d'Irlande créent la surprise. Ils portent Mary Robinson à la présidence. Elle est la première femme élue à cette fonction. Mme Robinson, qui a 46 ans, est avocate. Elle s'est présentée comme candidate indépendante. C'est le premier chef d'État irlandais qui ne soit pas lié au Fianna Fáil – le parti traditionnel qui est au pouvoir depuis 1945. Le président de la République, en Irlande, n'a pas de pouvoir exécutif, il ne gouverne pas. Mais Mme Robinson a fait sa campagne électorale en proposant des idées nouvelles. Quoiqu'elle soit catholique, elle a critiqué certaines idées de l'Église catholique, comme celles sur l'avortement et la contraception. La nouvelle présidente a dit qu'elle serait la représentante de tous les Irlandais, de toutes tendances politiques.

◀ *La présidente de l'Irlande, Mme Robinson, pendant un voyage en France.*

LA FIN DU COMMUNISME

Deux superpuissances dominent le monde après la Seconde Guerre mondiale : les États-Unis, capitalistes, et l'URSS, communiste. Aucun pays ne peut refuser de faire partie d'un des deux blocs. En 1985, Mikhaïl Gorbatchev lance des réformes économiques et politiques en URSS. Quelques années plus tard, l'URSS se désintègre, et les régimes communistes de l'Europe de l'Est disparaissent.

Les deux « Grands »

À partir de 1947, les États-Unis et l'URSS s'affirment nettement comme hostiles et rivaux ; le monde entier redoute une troisième guerre mondiale, mais aucun combat direct n'a lieu. Pourtant, les deux camps se lancent dans une course aux armements qui rend la menace de guerre terrifiante, surtout après 1949 où l'URSS dispose de l'arme atomique. Il y a de nombreux affrontements indirects entre les États-Unis et l'URSS, au Moyen-Orient, en Corée et en Indochine, puis dans différents pays du tiers-monde. Dans tous les points chauds du globe, chaque « Grand » soutient un des adversaires en fournissant des armes et des aides techniques. L'apogée de la guerre froide se situe entre 1947 et 1953, durant la période stalinienne ; elle devient moins intense en 1956, avec Khrouchtchev, puis dans les années 70, quand sont signés les accords Salt I sur le désarmement nucléaire. L'affrontement entre États-Unis et URSS ne cessera qu'en 1989, avec l'effondrement des démocraties populaires.

▲ Les dirigeants des deux superpuissances : le président américain Ronald Reagan, et le président soviétique Mikhaïl Gorbatchev.

Les défenseurs de la liberté politique

▶ Václav Havel, le président de la République tchèque.

Plusieurs hommes politiques d'Europe de l'Est ont commencé leur carrière en s'opposant aux régimes communistes. Avant d'être élu président de la Pologne démocratique, Lech Walesa a dirigé le syndicat Solidarité, qui est devenu le mouvement de réforme démocratique de la Pologne communiste.
En Tchécoslovaquie, le régime communiste au pouvoir depuis 1948 a été renversé en novembre 1989. L'écrivain Václav Havel, cofondateur de la Charte 77, est devenu le premier président de la République tchèque.

▲ Lech Walesa fut un fervent syndicaliste.

La chute du « rideau de fer »

Lorsque, après la Seconde Guerre mondiale, les pays de l'Europe de l'Est passent sous contrôle soviétique, le Premier ministre britannique, Winston Churchill, déclare : « Un rideau de fer est tombé entre l'Europe démocratique et l'Europe communiste. » Cette séparation est symbolisée par le mur de Berlin, construit par les communistes en 1961 pour empêcher les Allemands de l'Est de passer à l'Ouest.

À la fin des années 80, la *glasnost* (« transparence ») instaurée par Gorbatchev encourage les mouvements démocratiques en Europe de l'Est. Le mur de Berlin est détruit le 9 novembre 1989 ; les contrôles aux frontières se relâchent, et les gouvernements communistes de RDA, de Roumanie, de Tchécoslovaquie et de Hongrie tombent. Mais des tensions nationalistes et ethniques refont surface, et la guerre éclate entre les États de l'ancienne Yougoslavie communiste.

◀ En arrière-plan : le marteau et la faucille, anciens symboles de l'URSS.

▶ Soldats hongrois coupant les fils barbelés qui encerclaient la Hongrie communiste.

▶ Ouverture à Moscou, en 1990, d'un restaurant Pizza Hut, fast-food symbolisant l'opulence américaine.

▲ Berlinois de l'Ouest et de l'Est fêtant la chute du mur de Berlin, qui coupait leur ville en deux depuis 1961.

Les dissidents en URSS

En URSS, ceux qui critiquent ouvertement le régime sont considérés comme des traîtres. L'opinion internationale admire le courage de ces dissidents, qui défendent les droits de l'homme. Aleksandr Soljenitsyne, Prix Nobel de littérature en 1970, est expulsé d'URSS à cause de ses récits sur les camps soviétiques. Le physicien Andreï Sakharov proteste contre les essais nucléaires en 1958, et lance un mouvement de défense des droits civiques. Il reçoit le prix Nobel de la paix en 1975.

▲ Le physicien Andreï Sakharov, un pionnier de la dissidence.

◀ Elena Bonner se bat aux côtés de son époux, Sakharov.

▲ Aleksandr Soljenitsyne, écrivain et dissident.

1991

Fin de la guerre du Golfe

▶ 27 février 1991 ◀ La guerre du Golfe est finie. Le conflit se termine par la défaite de l'Irak. Saddam Hussein, le président de l'Irak, a envahi le Koweït en août 1990. Les Nations unies, le 30 novembre, demandent à Saddam Hussein de se retirer du Koweït avant le 15 janvier 1991, pour éviter une guerre. Mais il refuse. Le 16 janvier, les États-Unis et leurs alliés lancent une offensive aérienne, Tempête du désert. Les alliés bombardent des positions et des cibles irakiennes, sans réussir à faire céder Saddam Hussein. Les tanks alliés attaquent alors, le 24 février, en Irak et au Koweït. Les Français y participent. L'armée irakienne recule.

▲ Un soldat égyptien parle avec des prisonniers irakiens qui se sont rendus, après une bataille au Koweït.

▲ Les généraux américains, N. Schwarzkopf (à droite) et C. Powell.

Biosphère II

Huit savants se sont enfermés dans une serre de 1,6 hectare dans le désert de l'Arizona, le 26 septembre. Ils débutent une étude sur l'environnement. L'expérience doit durer deux ans. La serre contient un échantillon des divers milieux de vie de la planète : océan, désert, savane, forêt équatoriale, et marais. Les observations aideront peut-être à construire un jour un milieu artificiel sur une autre planète ou dans un vaisseau spatial.

▲ Les manifestants serrent la main d'un tankiste soviétique.

Fin de l'URSS

▶ 25 décembre 1991 ◀ Mikhaïl Gorbatchev démissionne de ses fonctions de président de l'URSS. L'URSS a cessé d'exister. Gorbatchev a surmonté une tentative de coup d'État organisée le 19 août par des communistes, mais uniquement grâce à l'intervention de Boris Eltsine. Eltsine, le président de la République de Russie, a appelé les citoyens à descendre dans la rue pour résister au coup d'État. Plusieurs Républiques soviétiques ont proclamé ensuite leur indépendance. Le 8 décembre, la Russie, l'Ukraine et la Biélorussie ont annoncé qu'elles allaient créer la Communauté des États indépendants. La CEI a été fondée le 21 décembre, avec la plupart des anciennes Républiques de l'URSS.

Les otages du Liban libérés

▶ 4 décembre 1991 ◀ Terry Anderson, le dernier Américain retenu en otage par les terroristes à Beyrouth, au Liban, est libéré après six ans de captivité. Des négociations secrètes entre les États occidentaux et les groupes terroristes ont permis de libérer des otages depuis 1988. Les Français Marcel Carton et Marcel Fontaine, deux diplomates, Jean-Paul Kauffmann, un journaliste, sont libérés en mai 1988, après plus de trois ans de détention. Mais Michel Seurat, un chercheur kidnappé en 1985, est mort en captivité. Un Irlandais a été libéré en 1990. Le Britannique Terry Waite a été libéré, le 18 novembre.

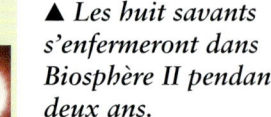

▲ Les huit savants s'enfermeront dans Biosphère II pendant deux ans.

▶ L'ancien otage Terry Waite arrive en Grande-Bretagne. Il salue à sa sortie de l'avion. Il a résisté à 1 763 jours de captivité.

Des Albanais fuient en Italie

▶ **8 août 1991** ◀ Des milliers d'Albanais fuient le chaos politique de leur pays et cherchent refuge en Italie. Des bateaux entiers ont débarqué à Bari, un port de l'Italie du Sud, après une courte traversée de la mer Adriatique. Les Albanais déclarent que dans leur pays les gens meurent de faim, qu'ils sont obligés de survivre avec de maigres rations de pain et d'eau. Les réfugiés ont envahi la ville et les plages. La police italienne les a regroupés pour les refouler. L'exode a commencé voici plusieurs mois. En mars, 25 000 Albanais ont débarqué à Brindisi, un port au sud de Bari. Les élections ont eu lieu en avril en Albanie, mais il y a eu sans doute beaucoup de fraude. Le nouveau gouvernement communiste s'est effondré le 4 juin, après une grève générale de près de trois semaines.

▼ *Les réfugiés albanais entrent à Brindisi, en Italie.*

1990 – 1997

En 1991 aussi...

14 août • La France gagne l'Admiral's Cup.

5 novembre • Robert Maxwell, un riche magnat anglais de la presse, disparaît de son yacht. Il est retrouvé mort dans l'océan Atlantique, au large des Canaries.

22 novembre • Le Français Gérard d'Aboville, parti du Japon, atteint la côte est des États-Unis, après avoir ramé dans un canot pendant 134 jours.

« Hibernatus », l'homme du glacier

▶ **26 septembre 1991** ◀ Le corps d'un homme, âgé de 5 000 ans, est retrouvé dans un glacier des Alpes autrichiennes. Deux Allemands l'ont découvert sous la glace, le 19 septembre, alors qu'ils grimpaient à 3 200 m d'altitude. Quelques jours plus tard, les autorités autrichiennes ont fait descendre le corps à Innsbruck, et les spécialistes de l'Université l'ont étudié. Otzi – comme il a été surnommé – vivait vers 3 350 av. J.-C. Il mesurait 1,50 m. « L'homme du glacier » était allongé dans la glace, avec un arc et une flèche suspendus à son épaule. Il s'est sans doute endormi pendant une tempête de neige, puis il est mort, et son corps a gelé.

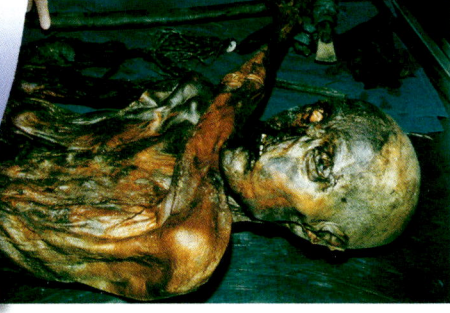

▼ *Le corps momifié d'Otzi, l'homme du glacier.*

Le record de saut en longueur

Le 30 août, à Tokyo, au Japon, l'athlète américain Mike Powell pulvérise l'un des plus anciens records de l'histoire du saut en longueur. Il fait un bond extraordinaire de 8,95 m, repoussant enfin la limite des 8,90 m établie par son compatriote Beamon aux jeux Olympiques de Mexico, en 1968, il y a 23 ans.

▶ *L'Américain Mike Powell dans son bond final.*

La France remporte la Coupe Davis

▶ **1er décembre 1991** ◀ La France remporte la Coupe Davis, 59 ans après sa première victoire de 1932. L'équipe de France, sous la direction de Yannick Noah, a battu en finale celle des États-Unis par 3 à 1, dans le stade Gerland de Lyon. Henri Leconte et Guy Forget ont battu chacun l'Américain Pete Sampras. Ils ont aussi gagné le double.

1992

▼ *Les conséquences tragiques de la guerre : une mère pleure sur la tombe de l'un de ses deux fils, tué au combat.*

▲ *Le Parlement de Sarajevo brûle. Il a été atteint par un obus de l'artillerie serbe, qui pilonne du haut des collines autour de la ville.*

Guerre en Bosnie

▶ 1er mai 1992 ◀ L'ONU vient de voter des sanctions économiques contre la République serbe. Depuis l'an dernier, l'ex-Yougoslavie a éclaté, les Républiques de Bosnie et de Croatie ont proclamé leur indépendance, et l'armée serbe commet les pires atrocités pour rétablir son autorité. La Yougoslavie était un État récent, né en 1918 de la volonté du roi de Serbie de réunir « tous les Slaves du Sud ». Elle est devenue en 1945 un État communiste, gouverné par Tito. Mais elle est formée de peuples différents : les Serbes sont de tradition orthodoxe, les Croates, catholiques, et les Bosniaques, musulmans. La Slovénie est proche de l'Autriche, la Macédoine est revendiquée par la Grèce et la Bulgarie, tandis que les habitants du Kosovo se sentent Albanais. Malgré la réprobation internationale, Slobodan Milosevic, président de la Serbie, se montre prêt à tout pour rétablir l'unité de l'ex-Yougoslavie, et le pouvoir des Serbes.

Disneyland à Paris

Mickey et Donald sont arrivés en Europe. Le parc Disneyland a ouvert le 12 avril, à 30 kilomètres de Paris. Le parc, qui s'étend sur 600 hectares, présente de multiples attractions pour petits et grands, comme les deux parcs Disney des États-Unis. Il comprend aussi six hôtels et un golf.

Partition de la Tchécoslovaquie

▶ 26 août 1992 ◀ Les dirigeants de la Tchécoslovaquie s'accordent pour que le pays soit divisé en deux États, la Slovaquie et la Tchéquie, à partir du 1er janvier 1993. En juin, lors des élections, les Slovaques ont voté pour l'indépendance de leur région et pour maintenir le contrôle de l'État sur l'industrie. Les Tchèques sont favorables à une économie libérale, sans contrôle de l'État.

Sommet de la Terre

▶ 14 juin 1992 ◀ Les délégués de 178 pays ont participé à Rio de Janeiro, au Brésil, à la conférence des Nations unies sur l'environnement et le développement. Ils ont signé une déclaration de 27 principes pour sauvegarder la nature. Les délégués veulent limiter les émissions de gaz à effet de serre.

▶ *Un enfant et un délégué plantent un arbre.*

Guerre et famine en Somalie

▶ **14 septembre 1992** ◀ Les soldats des Nations unies arrivent en Somalie. Les Casques bleus sont chargés d'arrêter les massacres dus à la famine et à la guerre civile. La guerre entre le président Mahdi Mohamed et le chef rebelle Mohamed Aïdid est due à d'anciennes rivalités de clans. Un désordre total règne dans le pays. Des chefs de guerre s'emparent des convois de ravitaillement expédiés par les associations d'aide internationale. Plus des trois quarts des 4,5 millions de Somaliens sont frappés par la famine.

▲ *Un enfant somalien court devant un soldat.*

1990 – 1997

En 1992 aussi...

20 janvier • En France, l'accident d'un Airbus d'Air France fait 87 morts, au mont Sainte-Odile, dans les Vosges.

Février • Jeux Olympiques d'hiver à Albertville, en Savoie. La France remporte 9 médailles.

Juillet-août • Jeux Olympiques d'été à Barcelone, en Espagne. 29 médailles pour la France.

Émeutes à Los Angeles

▶ **3 mai 1992** ◀ Les trois nuits d'émeutes de Los Angeles ont fait 58 morts et des milliers de blessés. La tension raciale entre des Blancs et des Noirs a déclenché ces violences. Le 29 avril, 4 policiers blancs ont été innocentés par un tribunal, malgré un film vidéo prouvant qu'ils avaient battu un automobiliste noir. Des foules scandant « Nous demandons justice » ont investi les rues. Le président Bush a envoyé 4 500 soldats, et l'ordre a été rétabli.

▲ *Actes de violence policière.*

▼ *Bill Clinton et Al Gore.*

Clinton devient président des États-Unis

▶ **3 novembre 1992** ◀ Le candidat du Parti démocrate, William J. Clinton, est élu à la présidence des États-Unis. Il a mené une campagne énergique pour battre ses deux adversaires, le candidat républicain – le président George Bush –, et un candidat indépendant, Ross Perot. Clinton est le premier président démocrate élu depuis 1980. Clinton promet qu'il va changer la vie politique américaine.

Élections en Angola

▶ **30 septembre 1992** ◀ Les premières élections libres ont lieu en Angola. Depuis l'indépendance du pays en 1975, le gouvernement procommuniste du MPLA (Mouvement populaire pour la libération de l'Angola) devait lutter contre la guérilla menée par l'UNITA (Union nationale pour l'indépendance totale de l'Angola) conservatrice, soutenue par l'Afrique du Sud. C'est le MPLA qui remporte l'élection, mais on craint que l'UNITA ne refuse ce résultat.

▶ *Le président Dos Santos, chef du MPLA, vote.*

1993

Israël et l'OLP signent un accord de paix

▶ **13 septembre 1993** ◀ Le Premier ministre israélien Rabin et le leader palestinien Arafat se serrent la main, à Washington. Ce geste historique conclut l'accord de paix signé après de longues négociations. C'est la première étape vers l'autonomie, qui permettra aux Palestiniens de se gouverner eux-mêmes. L'État d'Israël fait un grand pas. Il reconnaît que l'OLP, l'Organisation de libération de la palestine, a le droit et le pouvoir de représenter le peuple palestinien. L'OLP était considérée, il y a peu de temps encore, comme une organisation terroriste. L'OLP fait aussi un grand pas et admet qu'Israël a le droit d'exister. Les Palestiniens auront une autonomie limitée dans les Territoires occupés – la ville de Jéricho et la bande de Gaza. L'accord prévoit que les forces israéliennes se retireront petit à petit et que les Territoires seront administrés par un conseil palestinien.

◀ *Spectacle inattendu. Les drapeaux israélien et palestinien flottent côte à côte.*

◀ *Moment historique entre B. Clinton, Y. Arafat et Y. Rabin.*

Internet

De plus en plus de gens sont « sur le net », le réseau informatique qui permet à chacun de communiquer avec des millions d'autres utilisateurs sur toute la planète. Son histoire commence avec le projet du ministère de la Défense américain, qui voulait relier des chercheurs dans le monde et leur fournir des informations. Le succès de ce projet a encouragé la création d'une multitude d'autres réseaux.

Mort du roi Baudouin Ier

▶ **31 juillet 1993** ◀ La Belgique est en deuil. Le roi des Belges, Baudouin Ier, est mort soudainement dans sa résidence d'été en Espagne. Il a été victime d'une crise cardiaque. Le roi était monté sur le trône en 1951, à l'âge de 20 ans. Il succédait à son père, le roi Léopold III, qui avait abdiqué en sa faveur et lui avait remis tous ses pouvoirs. Baudouin Ier avait épousé en décembre 1960 Fabiola de Mora y de Aragón. Il n'a pas eu d'enfant et donc pas d'héritier direct. Son frère Albert va lui succéder sur le trône.

L'Australie et les aborigènes

▶ **22 décembre 1993** ◀ Les aborigènes d'Australie fêtent la nouvelle loi qu'a votée le Parlement fédéral. Elle reconnaît aux premiers habitants du pays des droits sur les territoires qu'ils possédaient et qui leur ont été pris par les colons européens. La loi a été soutenue par les associations de défense de l'environnement. Mais elle a mécontenté les sociétés qui exploitent les mines. On estime que 10 % du territoire est concerné par cette loi.

▲ *Les aborigènes fêtent la reconnaissance de leurs droits.*

1993

Échec aux communistes

▶ **4 octobre 1993** ◀ Boris Eltsine, président de la Russie, vient de triompher d'une tentative de coup d'État. Quand, le 21 septembre précédent, Eltsine avait ordonné la dissolution du Parlement, trop attaché au communisme, des députés conservateurs avaient refusé de partir et avaient pris possession de la « Maison-Blanche », siège du Parlement, pour rétablir un pouvoir de type soviétique. Mais l'armée est demeurée fidèle à Eltsine, et des commandos ont entouré le bâtiment où étaient les meneurs, Khasboulatov et Routskoï. Ceux-ci viennent de se rendre, après des tirs d'artillerie qui ont fait plusieurs victimes.

▲ *Moscou, le Parlement russe après le siège.*

L'Union européenne

▶ **1er novembre 1993** ◀ Le traité de Maastricht, signé à la fin de 1991 par les dirigeants des pays de la Communauté européenne, prend effet. La Communauté européenne devient l'« Union européenne ». Les Français l'ont accepté par un référendum, avec 51 % de oui contre 49 % de non, le 21 septembre 1992.

▶ *Le drapeau de l'Union européenne avec les douze étoiles des États membres.*

En 1993 aussi...

26 février • À New York, une bombe explose dans le World Trade Center, un grand centre d'affaires. 5 morts.

30 mars • Nouvelle cohabitation gauche-droite en France. Édouard Balladur est Premier ministre.

5 mai • Suicide de l'ancien Premier ministre français M. Bérégovoy, désespéré d'être mêlé à un scandale politique et financier.

Spielberg raconte l'Holocauste

Le cinéaste américain Steven Spielberg obtient un grand succès avec son nouveau film, *la Liste de Schindler,* sur l'Holocauste. Le film est basé sur l'histoire d'un industriel allemand, Oskar Schindler, et de ses ouvriers juifs. L. Neeson (ci-dessous, à gauche) joue Schindler, B. Kingsley est le comptable (à droite).

Les sectes meurtrières

▶ **19 avril 1993** ◀ Le siège de Waco, au Texas, finit par un terrible carnage. Il y a très peu de survivants sur les 120 membres de la secte davidienne. 17 enfants sont morts. Le dirigeant de la secte, David Koresh, se disait le nouveau sauveur du monde. En février, les agents fédéraux ont tenté de prendre d'assaut le ranch, pour l'arrêter et saisir les armes. Le raid a échoué, et le siège a commencé. Aujourd'hui, la police a ouvert le feu, et le bâtiment a explosé en flammes.

▶ *Les rescapés de Waco sont arrêtés.*

LA GÉNÉTIQUE

La génétique est une branche de la biologie qui étudie comment les caractères des êtres vivants se transmettent d'une génération à l'autre, et pourquoi, par exemple, des individus roux ont des chances d'avoir des enfants roux.
La génétique est née il y a un peu plus d'un siècle, lorsque Gregor Mendel, un moine autrichien, a défini les « lois » de l'hérédité, en croisant plusieurs espèces de petits pois. Ces lois, qui passèrent inaperçu de son vivant, sont basées sur l'existence de « particules », ou caractères : les gènes.

◀ *Structure en double hélice d'une molécule d'ADN établie par Crick et Watson.*

▶ *Dolly, la célèbre brebis clonée en 1996 au Roslin Institute, en Écosse.*

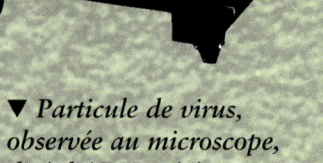

▼ *Particule de virus, observée au microscope, d'où l'ADN a été extrait.*

Dolly, la brebis née par clonage

Un clone est une créature vivante qui a été reproduite, ou copiée, à partir d'un individu, sans acte sexuel. Génétiquement, un clone est exactement identique à son modèle, ou génome. Le clonage se produit dans la nature. Depuis toujours, les jardiniers recourent au bouturage pour multiplier certaines plantes. Des individus identiques se développent lorsque, une fois fécondée, la cellule d'un œuf se divise en deux embryons distincts dont les gènes sont identiques. En imitant ce processus, les scientifiques peuvent produire des animaux clonés en laboratoire. La célèbre brebis écossaise Dolly a été produite en extrayant de l'ADN d'une cellule d'une brebis adulte dont Dolly est la copie conforme. Le succès de cette expérience est capital pour l'avenir de la médecine et de l'agriculture.

L'ADN

Au départ, l'être humain est une cellule chargée d'une énorme quantité d'informations chimiques. Lorsque cette cellule se divise, donnant naissance à des milliers de nouvelles cellules, des copies exactes de ces informations sont transmises. Dans la plupart des cellules, les informations génétiques se trouvent sur plusieurs molécules d'ADN (acide désoxyribonucléique) situées dans le noyau de la cellule. Lorsqu'une cellule est sur le point de se diviser, ses molécules d'ADN deviennent plus épaisses et plus courtes, et peuvent alors être observées au microscope. Une molécule d'ADN a la structure d'une double hélice.

D'ici à l'an 2000, les scientifiques auront sans doute pu établir une liste, ou « carte », des 3 000 millions de « lettres » de l'ADN humain. Une telle carte permettrait d'identifier les gènes responsables de certaines maladies héréditaires, comme la mucoviscidose, la maladie génétique la plus répandue aux États-Unis et en Europe occidentale, identifiée en 1990. Une fois qu'un tel gène est localisé, la thérapie génique devient possible. On peut modifier un « mauvais » gène ou l'empêcher de se diviser.

▶ *Carte d'une molécule d'ADN. En cette fin du XXe siècle, une course est engagée entre les scientifiques pour établir la carte de la totalité du système génétique humain.*

▼ *James Watson découvrit, avec F. Crick, en 1953, la structure en double hélice de l'ADN.*

Génétique

Personne ne sait combien il existe de gènes. L'être humain a sans doute environ 100 000 gènes, en grande partie identiques.

Plus de 98 % des gènes d'un chimpanzé sont identiques à ceux de l'homme.

De nombreuses expériences génétiques sont pratiquées sur une mouche, *Drosophila melanogaster*. Cette minuscule créature pond environ tous les quinze jours, ce qui permet d'observer rapidement les modifications d'une génération à l'autre.

◀ *La capsule de cotonnier de droite a été améliorée génétiquement, contrairement à celle de gauche.*

Manipulations génétiques

Les biochimistes peuvent modifier les gènes d'un organisme vivant et changer ainsi ses caractéristiques. Ces techniques génétiques ont permis d'obtenir, entre autres du raisin sans pépins, des pommes sucrées, et d'énormes pommes de terre. Elles servent également à lutter contre différentes maladies, comme l'hémophilie ou le diabète. Les gènes commandant la production d'insuline peuvent ainsi être introduits dans des bactéries, lesquelles fabriquent de l'insuline qui peut être « récoltée » et utilisée pour soigner les diabétiques.

▶ *Biochimiste étudiant des épis de maïs obtenus grâce à des manipulations génétiques.*

▼ *En arrière-plan, des chaînes de molécules d'ADN grossies 100 000 fois.*

1994

Nelson Mandela, président de l'Afrique du Sud

▶ **10 mai 1994** ◀ Nelson Mandela devient le premier président noir de l'Afrique du Sud. Les Blancs, les Noirs et les métis ont fêté avec joie cet événement. Le chef historique du parti noir, l'ANC, le Congrès national africain, a passé 27 ans de sa vie en prison, pendant la période de l'apartheid (la ségrégation raciale). Dans son discours, il a rendu hommage à F. De Klerk, l'ancien président blanc, qui a renoncé à l'apartheid. De Klerk a libéré Mandela et les autres prisonniers politiques pour que l'Afrique du Sud prenne sa place parmi les grandes nations libres du monde.

Le tunnel sous la Manche

Il suffit désormais d'un voyage de 35 minutes en train pour relier la Grande-Bretagne et la France. Le chantier a débuté vraiment dans les années 80. Deux tunnels, l'un construit à partir de Calais, en France, et l'autre, depuis Folkestone, en Angleterre, se sont rejoints en 1990. Le tunnel a été inauguré en mai par la reine Élisabeth et le président Mitterrand. Le service régulier a débuté fin décembre.

▲ *Nelson Mandela dépose son vote.*

▲ *Le président Mandela avec l'ex-président De Klerk.*

L'IRA annonce un cessez-le-feu

▶ **31 août 1994** ◀ Après 25 ans de violences, l'IRA – l'Armée républicaine irlandaise – annonce qu'elle cesse ses « opérations militaires » en Irlande du Nord. L'IRA se battait pour réclamer l'indépendance. Cette déclaration a été accueillie avec joie. Le gouvernement britannique déclare avec fermeté que le Sinn Féin, le parti politique allié de l'IRA, pourra participer aux négociations sur l'avenir de l'Irlande du Nord, à condition que le cessez-le-feu soit permanent et définitif.

▲ *Les deux Eurostar, à l'inauguration du tunnel.*

Génocide au Rwanda

▶ **4 juillet 1994** ◀ Le Front patriotique rwandais (FPR), dont les partisans appartiennent à l'ethnie des Tutsis, vient de s'emparer de Kigali, la capitale du pays. En avril, le président du Rwanda et celui du Burundi sont morts dans un accident d'avion, dû sans doute à un attentat. Le président appartenant à l'ethnie des Hutus, des milices formées de Hutus se sont déchaînées contre l'autre ethnie du pays, les Tutsis. Un million de personnes ont été tuées ; 2,3 millions de Rwandais se sont réfugiés dans les pays voisins. Il y a un mois, l'ONU a enfin autorisé l'envoi d'une mission humanitaire.

▶ *L'aide humanitaire aux victimes au Rwanda.*

Des soldats américains à Haïti

▶ **19 septembre 1994** ◀ Les États-Unis viennent d'envoyer des soldats à Haïti pour y rétablir le gouvernement légal du président J.-B. Aristide, qui, élu démocratiquement en 1990, avait été évincé par un coup d'État militaire en 1991. Depuis, la violence et la misère n'avaient fait que croître dans l'île, et des milliers d'Haïtiens avaient fui vers les États-Unis. Clinton a agi contre les militaires pour éviter de nouveaux immigrés et pour faire cesser la terreur en Haïti.

▲ *Soldats américains à Haïti. L'invasion est approuvée par l'ONU.*

1990 – 1997

En 1994 aussi...

5 février • Des tirs d'obus de mortier sur le marché de Sarajevo, en Bosnie, tuent 68 personnes.

24 juin • Le Béluga, un Airbus, le plus gros avion du monde, est présenté à Toulouse, en France.

17 juillet • Le Brésil remporte la coupe du monde de football.

31 août • Le champion du monde d'échecs, Kasparov, est battu par un ordinateur.

Ayrton Senna se tue en formule 1

▶ **1er mai 1994** ◀ Ayrton Senna, le coureur automobile brésilien, se tue au Grand Prix d'Imola, à Saint-Marin. Sa voiture, une Williams-Renault, s'est fracassée contre un mur de béton, à 240 km/h. Vainqueur de 41 Grands Prix, Senna était considéré comme le meilleur pilote de course de son temps. La cause du drame reste incertaine.

Tremblement de terre à Los Angeles

▶ **17 janvier 1994** ◀ Le tremblement de terre a tué 30 personnes et a détruit des immeubles. Un pont autoroutier s'est effondré. Des canalisations d'eau et des câbles électriques se sont rompus, provoquant des inondations et des incendies. C'est le séisme le plus violent depuis le début du siècle à Los Angeles.

◀ *Maisons en ruine à Los Angeles.*

Naufrage de l'*Estonia*

▶ **28 septembre 1994** ◀ Neuf cents personnes se noient dans la mer Baltique, dans le naufrage de l'*Estonia*, un ferry. Les portes géantes de la proue ont sans doute cédé sous la pression de la mer déchaînée par la tempête. Le bateau, qui voguait vers la Finlande, a chaviré. Il a sombré en quelques minutes. La température de l'eau de la Baltique est très basse, et il n'y a que 141 rescapés sur un total de 1 000 passagers.

▲ *Une partie de l'*Estonia *a été récupérée.*

1995

▲ La carte d'identité judiciaire d'O.J. Simpson.

◀ La poursuite d'O.J. Simpson, en direct.

O.J. Simpson est libre

▶ 3 octobre 1995 ◀ L'ancien footballeur et acteur américain Orenthal James Simpson est acquitté. Le tribunal juge que le suspect n'est pas coupable des meurtres de son ex-femme, Nicole Brown Simpson, et de son ami Ronald Goldman, l'été dernier. La retransmission télévisée en direct du procès a passionné les Américains, pendant des mois. Il y a eu de nombreux moments dramatiques entre les deux parties, la défense et l'accusation. L'arrestation de Simpson, en juin 1994, a été retransmise en direct à la télévision. La police, après l'avoir accusé des deux meurtres, n'a pas pu le localiser ni le retrouver. Elle l'a déclaré en fuite. Mais la télévision l'a ensuite filmé, au volant de la voiture d'un ami, sur une autoroute de Los Angeles, dans une course-poursuite qui a duré deux heures. Simpson est rentré chez lui, puis s'est rendu à la police.

O.J. Simpson

O.J. Simpson est l'un des meilleurs footballeurs américains professionnels.

Il a joué dans plusieurs films à succès, tel *Capricorn One*, un film de science-fiction, en 1978.

Le procès a fait appel à 100 témoins et a utilisé 1 100 pièces à conviction.

▲ Les obsèques de Rabin ont été retardées, pour que les chefs d'État puissent y assister.

Rabin assassiné en Israël

▶ 4 novembre 1995 ◀ Le Premier ministre israélien, Yitzhak Rabin, est assassiné à coups de revolver. Il regagnait sa voiture, après une manifestation pour la paix entre les Israéliens et les Palestiniens. Il a été tué par un étudiant israélien d'extrême droite qui était contre la paix avec les Arabes. Son assassin, Yigal Amir, a été arrêté. Il a avoué avoir tiré sur Rabin parce que celui-ci voulait « abandonner le pays aux Arabes ». Shimon Peres, le ministre des Affaires étrangères, a été nommé Premier ministre. Il promet de continuer la politique de Rabin.

1990 – 1997

Attentat en Oklahoma

▶ **21 avril 1995** ◀ La terreur a frappé le cœur des États-Unis, voici deux jours. Une bombe a dévasté un grand immeuble administratif à Oklahoma City. La bombe a explosé à 9 h 03 du matin, dans un camion piégé en stationnement devant le bâtiment. Il y aurait soixante-dix-huit morts. Timothy McVeigh, un ancien soldat de l'armée américaine, a été accusé aujourd'hui d'être l'auteur de l'attentat. Son ami Terry Nichols, qui était recherché pour être interrogé, s'est présenté de lui-même à la police de l'État du Kansas.

▲ *Le bâtiment administratif d'Oklahoma City, après l'explosion.*

Séisme à Kobe, au Japon

▶ **17 janvier 1995** ◀ Le port japonais de Kobe, à 450 kilomètres à l'ouest de Tokyo, a été ravagé par un séisme très violent, atteignant 7,2 sur l'échelle de Richter. Le déplacement de la faille de Nojima, au fond de la mer du Japon, a provoqué la secousse. Elle s'est produite à 5 h 46 du matin, et a duré 20 secondes. Les secours luttent pour venir en aide aux victimes. Cinq mille personnes ont péri. Plus de 50 000 bâtiments se sont effondrés. L'autoroute est un amas de ruines.

▼ *L'autoroute de Kobe, après le séisme.*

Terrorisme en Algérie

▶ **27 mars 1995** ◀ Mohamed Abderrahmani, le directeur d'un journal quotidien algérien, est assassiné à Alger. Cet attentat continue la série d'actes terroristes qui ravagent l'Algérie depuis plusieurs années. Certains groupes extrémistes musulmans multiplient les attentats contre des hommes politiques, des journalistes, ou contre la population, afin d'instituer un climat d'insécurité, de violence et de terreur dans tout le pays. Un attentat à la voiture piégée a fait ainsi 42 morts, à Alger, au mois de janvier.

◀ *Des militants de Greenpeace.*

Greenpeace gagne un combat

▶ **20 juin 1995** ◀ Greenpeace, une association écologiste, remporte une victoire avec sa campagne réussie contre la société britannique des pétroles Shell. Shell projetait d'immerger dans l'Atlantique une ancienne plate-forme de forage, Brent Spar, qui n'était plus en service. Mais Shell annonce maintenant qu'il la démantèlera, au lieu de l'immerger.

Mise en vente de Windows 95

Une campagne de publicité lance en août Windows 95, le nouveau système d'exploitation pour ordinateurs de la compagnie américaine Microsoft. À New York, les magasins d'informatique offrent des pizzas gratuites pour attirer les foules, à l'occasion de sa mise en vente.

1995

Jacques Chirac, président de la République

▶ 17 mai 1995 ◀ À l'Élysée, Jacques Chirac (gaulliste) succède à François Mitterrand (socialiste), qui, quoique très malade, est le premier président de la République à achever son second septennat. J. Chirac vient de remporter l'élection présidentielle de 1995, après une campagne brillante, menée contre le candidat socialiste, L. Jospin, et contre son rival de droite, É. Balladur, Premier ministre de 1993 à 1995. J. Chirac a fait campagne sur le thème de la « fracture sociale », des problèmes de société : immigration, inégalités, chômage… Le fort taux d'abstention et le succès relatif de l'extrême droite (15 % des voix pour le Front national) prouvent que les Français sont lassés aussi bien par les difficultés économiques que par les affaires de corruption ou de financement illégal des partis.

▲ *Passation des pouvoirs entre J. Chirac et F. Mitterrand.*

La paix en Yougoslavie

▶ 14 décembre 1995 ◀ Un épisode de la guerre de l'ancienne Yougoslavie se termine. Elle a duré trois ans. Les dirigeants des trois parties en guerre – Serbes, Croates et Bosniaques – signent le traité de paix à Paris. Il confirme les accords conclus à Dayton, aux États-Unis, le mois dernier. Le Croate F. Tudjman, le Bosniaque musulman A. Izetbegovic, et le Serbe S. Milosevic se serrent la main. La guerre a fait 200 000 victimes, mortes ou disparues.

▶ *La poignée de main des trois dirigeants.*

Scandale à la Barings

▶ 2 décembre 1995 ◀ Nick Leeson, un financier anglais de 28 ans, a été condamné à six ans et demi de prison. Les opérations désastreuses qu'il a pu mener sans surveillance ont conduit à la faillite de la Barings, une banque britannique respectée. Leeson (ci-contre), qui travaillait à Singapour, jouait avec l'argent de la banque sur les marchés financiers d'Extrême-Orient. Il a perdu 6,6 milliards de francs.

Babe, nouvelle star

Babe, un cochon au grand cœur, est la vedette la plus inattendue du cinéma. Il sait parler et veut devenir chien de berger. Chris Noonan, le réalisateur de *Babe*, fait jouer des animaux domestiques. Ils sont au centre de l'action. Le cochon garde les moutons pour éviter de finir comme rôti de Noël. Il réussit si bien qu'il remporte avec son maître le concours national des chiens de berger.

1990 – 1997

Interview de Diana à la BBC

▲ *Diana, princesse de Galles, pendant son entretien télévisé.*

▶ **21 novembre 1995** ◀ La princesse Diana, l'ex-femme du prince Charles, l'héritier de la couronne britannique, donne une interview d'une franchise étonnante à la BBC, la télévision anglaise. Elle parle de son mariage malheureux, de son aventure amoureuse avec un officier de cavalerie, et de ses espoirs pour l'avenir. Elle pense qu'elle a peu de chances d'être reine d'Angleterre, mais elle souhaite qu'on la considère comme la « reine des cœurs ».

En 1995 aussi...

5 septembre • Jacques Chirac annonce que la France reprend ses expériences nucléaires dans l'atoll de Mururoa en Polynésie. Elle est condamnée par tous les pays riverains du Pacifique.

7 novembre • Le Premier ministre français, Alain Juppé, modifie la composition du gouvernement et renvoie huit des douze femmes qui en faisaient partie depuis le 17 mai.

Gaz mortel dans le métro de Tokyo

▶ **20 mars 1995** ◀ Les membres d'une secte religieuse japonaise ont répandu un gaz mortel dans une station du métro de Tokyo. Les terroristes ont tué 12 personnes. Cinq mille autres sont gravement malades. La secte de la « Vérité suprême », Aum Shinri-kyo, compte 30 000 disciples. Le chef, Shoko Asahara, a 40 ans. Il pensait que la police allait attaquer son quartier général. Il a ordonné à ses adeptes de fabriquer un gaz mortel, le sarin, que les nazis avaient découvert pendant la Seconde Guerre mondiale. Ils l'ont utilisé contre les voyageurs de la banlieue, pour les terroriser.

▶ *Les sauveteurs, après l'attentat au gaz.*

Atlantis s'amarre à Mir dans l'espace

▶ **7 juillet 1995** ◀ La navette spatiale américaine Atlantis atterrit au Centre spatial Kennedy, en Floride, après une mission réussie de onze jours. La navette a rejoint Mir, la station spatiale russe, qui tourne autour de la Terre. Atlantis a décollé le 27 juin. C'était le 100e vol habité américain. Elle a débarqué les cosmonautes russes A. Soloviev et N. Boudarine dans la station Mir. Elle a récupéré l'astronaute américain N. Thagard pour le ramener sur Terre. Les deux engins se sont arrimés le 29 juin et sont restés ensemble pendant cinq jours. Les hommes ont mené des expériences scientifiques.

▶ *Atlantis et Mir, ensemble dans l'espace.*

1996

Le scandale de la « vache folle »

▶ **22 mars 1996** ◀ Les éleveurs de bovins britanniques sont au bord de la ruine. Le marché de la viande de bœuf s'effondre. On craint que la viande provenant d'animaux atteints de la maladie de la « vache folle » ne transmette aux humains la maladie de Creutzfeldt-Jakob. La Belgique, la France et d'autres pays interdisent l'achat de viande de bœuf britannique. L'encéphalopathie spongiforme bovine, ou ESB., est apparue en 1986. Les experts pensent que le nombre croissant de cas de la maladie de Creutzfeldt-Jakob est lié à l'ESB.

▲ *Les mesures de sécurité n'ont pas réussi à vaincre la peur que provoque la « vache folle ».*

L'ESB
L'ESB provoque des trous spongieux dans le cerveau de l'animal. Elle est sans doute due aux aliments donnés aux bovins, et en particulier aux abats – les parties internes – du mouton.

En Grande-Bretagne, les agriculteurs ont dû abattre le bétail atteint par l'ESB. en 1988. En 1989, le gouvernement a interdit l'emploi des abats de bovins dans la nourriture. Mais les craintes ont persisté, et la consommation de bœuf a diminué.

Folie pour Buzz

Buzz l'Éclair, le héros de *Toy Story* remporte un succès fou dans les magasins de Grande-Bretagne. C'est le jouet le plus demandé pour Noël. *Toy Story* est un dessin animé créé par ordinateur. Buzz le cosmonaute et Woody le cow-boy rivalisent pour obtenir l'affection de leur propriétaire, Andy.

▶ *Les savants français examinent le cerveau d'une vache atteinte de l'ESB.*

Mort de François Mitterrand

▶ **8 janvier 1996** ◀ L'ancien président de la République française François Mitterrand, est mort à son domicile parisien, à l'âge de 79 ans. Il a assuré pendant quatorze ans les fonctions de chef de l'État. Il a d'abord été élu président en mai 1981, contre Valéry Giscard d'Estaing, le président sortant. Il a été élu une seconde fois, sept ans plus tard, en mai 1988, contre Jacques Chirac. Ses obsèques auront lieu à Jarnac, dans sa ville natale, en Charente. Un hommage solennel lui sera rendu à Notre-Dame de Paris, le 12 janvier.

Une bombe aux JO d'Atlanta

▶ **27 juillet 1996** ◀ Une bombe explose dans le parc du Centenaire, à Atlanta, en début de matinée. La ville des États-Unis qui accueille les jeux Olympiques a pourtant mis en place d'importantes forces de sécurité. Une femme est tuée, et plus de 100 personnes, blessées. La police mène l'enquête. Les Jeux, qui ont débuté le 19 juillet, continuent, mais les drapeaux sont en berne, à mi-mât.

▲ *Les sauveteurs donnent les premiers soins aux victimes de l'explosion d'Atlanta.*

Le télescope Hubble

▶ 4 septembre 1996 ◀ Le télescope spatial Hubble a pris des photos étonnantes des galaxies – des groupes d'étoiles –, qui commençaient à se former il y a des millions d'années. Il a été placé en orbite autour de la Terre le 24 avril 1990. Ses objectifs très puissants captent la lumière qui a traversé l'espace pendant des milliards d'années. Il enregistre les images d'événements qui se sont passés voici des milliards d'années. Hubble a déjà réalisé 8 000 observations.

▲ La fantastique photo d'une galaxie, prise par Hubble.

« Magic » Johnson

Le célèbre joueur de basket Earvin « Magic » Johnson revient dans son équipe des Lakers de Los Angeles. Le géant de 2,05 mètres avait quitté le basket en 1991 parce qu'il était atteint du virus du sida.

◀ « Magic » fête une victoire olympique. Il est revenu au sport, parce qu'il sait maintenant qu'il n'y a aucun risque de transmission du sida à son équipe.

En 1996 aussi…

27 mars • Yigal Amir, l'assassin du président israélien Rabin en 1995, est condamné à la prison à vie.

24 septembre • La France, le Royaume-Uni, les États-Unis, la Chine et la Russie signent un traité d'interdiction des essais nucléaires.

25-26 septembre • Les combats entre Palestiniens et Israéliens près de Jéricho et dans la bande de Gaza font 72 morts.

Explosion de l'avion de la TWA

▶ 18 juillet 1996 ◀ Un Boeing 747 explose, après son décollage de l'aéroport de New York, la nuit dernière, au-dessus de l'océan Atlantique. Les 230 personnes à son bord sont tuées. Le vol 800 de la compagnie américaine TWA à destination de Paris décolle à 20 h 19 de l'aéroport Kennedy, mais disparaît soudain des radars de contrôle aérien, à 20 h 32. La cause de l'explosion n'est pas connue. Les recherches commencent aujourd'hui en mer. On espère retrouver la boîte noire de l'avion.

▼ Les débris de l'appareil sont éparpillés dans la mer, après l'explosion.

Des écoliers tués à Dunblane

▶ 14 mars 1996 ◀ Un bandit armé a tué seize enfants et une institutrice dans une école primaire de Dunblane, en Écosse, hier matin. Thomas Hamilton, un ancien animateur de groupes de jeunes de la ville, âgé de 43 ans, est entré dans le gymnase de l'école, à 9 h 30. Il s'est mis à tirer au fusil dans la classe des « cinq-six ans ». Douze autres enfants et une seconde adulte ont été blessés. Hamilton a ensuite retourné l'arme contre lui et s'est tué.

◀ La reine Élisabeth II dépose une couronne devant l'école de Dunblane.

LES JEUX OLYMPIQUES

Tous les quatre ans, les jeux Olympiques, la plus importante de toutes les manifestations sportives, rassemblent les meilleurs athlètes du monde. Des années de préparation physique et mentale sont nécessaires pour que ceux-ci soient au sommet de leur forme.

Fondés à Olympie, en Grèce, il y a presque trois mille ans, les jeux Olympiques sont relancés en 1896 par un Français, le baron Pierre de Coubertin.
Les JO ont comme emblème cinq anneaux entrelacés (bleu, jaune, noir, vert et rouge), qui symbolisent l'union des cinq continents.

▼ *Les athlètes entourent la flamme olympique, lors de la cérémonie d'ouverture des Jeux d'été à Séoul, en 1988.*

▼ *Le Français Jean-Claude Killy remporte les trois épreuves de ski alpin aux jeux Olympiques d'hiver de Grenoble, en 1968.*

Jeux Olympiques d'hiver

Lorsque les jeux Olympiques sont rétablis en 1896, les sports d'hiver n'y occupent pas une place importante. Le patinage artistique est introduit à Londres en 1908, et le hockey sur glace, à Anvers en 1920. Ni le ski ni le bobsleigh ne sont représentés.

La Norvège, la Finlande et la Suède s'opposent à la création de jeux Olympiques d'hiver, craignant qu'ils ne concurrencent les jeux Nordiques. Le CIO (Comité international olympique) organise toutefois les premiers Jeux d'hiver à Chamonix, en France, en 1924.

Les deuxièmes Jeux d'hiver ont lieu en 1928 à Saint-Moritz, en Suisse, avec, comme principales épreuves, le ski nordique, le saut, le patinage artistique, le patinage de vitesse, le bobsleigh et le hockey sur glace. Le skieur norvégien Johan Gröttumsbraaten et le patineur finlandais Clas Thunberg remportent chacun deux médailles d'or.

Depuis 1992, les Jeux d'hiver sont décalés de deux ans par rapport aux Jeux d'été.
Ils ont eu lieu à Lillehammer en 1994, tandis que les Jeux d'été se sont déroulés à Atlanta en 1996.

▲ *La Suissesse Denise Biellmann ravit le public, mais ne se classe que quatrième des Jeux de 1980 en patinage artistique.*

◄ *En 1964, la Soviétique Lidia Skoblikova remporte la médaille d'or dans toutes les épreuves de patinage de vitesse.*

Les cinq plus médaillés

1. L. Skoblikova (URSS, patinage de vitesse) : 6 médailles d'or.
2. E. Heiden (USA, patinage de vitesse), B. Daehlie (Norv., ski nordique) et C. Thunberg (Finl., patinage de vitesse) : 5 médailles d'or chacun.
3. M. Nykänen (Finl., saut à skis) : 4 médailles d'or et 1 d'argent.
4. S. Henje (Norv., patinage artistique) : 3 médailles d'or.
5. K. Witt (RDA, patinage artistique) : 2 médailles d'or.

▶ *Katarina Witt.*

◀ *L'équipe olympique américaine en 1900.*

Jeux Olympiques d'été

En 1896, 211 athlètes représentant 14 pays participent aux premiers jeux Olympiques modernes à Athènes. En 1922, 9 364 athlètes de 169 pays différents sont présents à Barcelone. « Plus vite, plus haut, plus fort », telle est la devise des jeux Olympiques, réservés en principe, aux amateurs. Mais, depuis 1981, quelques professionnels sont admis. En 1980 et 1984, les Jeux, qui doivent se dérouler en dehors de toute considération politique, sont officiellement boycottés (en 1980 par les États-Unis, en 1984 par l'URSS).

◀ *La Canadienne Ann Montinimy en 1992.*

▲ *L'Américain Bob Beamon conserve pendant vingt-trois ans le record du monde du saut en longueur : 8,90 m aux JO de 1968.*

Une étoile est née

Aux Jeux de 1976, à Montréal, la Roumaine Nadia Comaneci remporte, à 14 ans, trois médailles d'or, une d'argent et une de bronze. Elle est la première gymnaste à obtenir la note parfaite de 10, sept fois pendant les Jeux. Remarquée à l'âge de 7 ans par l'entraîneuse roumaine Bela Karolyi, Nadia travaille de manière intensive pendant des années.

▲ *Nadia Comaneci à la poutre.*

Les dix plus médaillés

1. Ray Ewry (USA, athlétisme) : 10 médailles d'or.
2. Larissa Latynina (URSS, gymnastique) : 18 médailles, dont 9 d'or.
3. Paavo Nurmi (Finl., course) : 9 médailles d'or.
4. Mark Spitz (USA, natation) : 7 médailles d'or.
5. Nikolaï Andrianov (URSS, gymnastique) : 15 médailles, dont 7 d'or.
6. Carl Lewis (USA, athlétisme) : 6 médailles d'or et 1 d'argent.
7. Kristin Otto (RDA, natation) : 6 médailles d'or.
8. Jesse Owens (USA, athlétisme) : 4 médailles d'or.
9. Emil Zátopek (Tch., course) : 4 médailles d'or et 1 d'argent.
10. Florence Griffith-Joyner (USA, athlétisme) : 3 médailles d'or et 1 d'argent.

▲ *Jesse Owens.*

▼ *Florence Griffith-Joyner.*

▲ *Carl Lewis.*

▲ *Mark Spitz.*

1997

Mort de Diana à Paris

▶ 6 septembre 1997 ◀

Les obsèques de la princesse de Galles, Diana, se sont déroulées aujourd'hui à l'abbaye de Westminster, à Londres. Une foule considérable s'est pressée pour assister au cortège funèbre, qui a duré deux heures. Le cercueil est parti de Kensington Palace et a traversé la capitale d'ouest en est. Diana est morte à Paris le 31 août, dans un accident de voiture, et son décès a provoqué une vive émotion dans le pays. La limousine Mercedes qui la conduisait a heurté, à très grande vitesse, le mur d'un tunnel situé à proximité des quais de la Seine. Diana, son ami Dodi Al Fayed et le chauffeur de la voiture, Henri Paul, ont été tués sur le coup. Dans les heures qui ont suivi l'annonce de sa mort, la foule s'est progressivement massée aux portes de Kensington Palace. Toute la semaine, les Britanniques ont déposé des fleurs devant sa maison, et sont venus rendre un dernier hommage à celle qui ne s'est jamais assise sur le trône d'Angleterre mais qui est parvenue à être « reine dans le cœur des hommes ».

▲ *La Princesse Diana meurt à Paris le 31 août.*

Les Journées mondiales de la jeunesse à Paris

▶ 18-24 août 1997 ◀

Les XXᵉ Journées mondiales de la jeunesse, organisées par l'Église catholique, se déroulent à Paris. Elles commencent au Champ-de-Mars, où l'archevêque de Paris, Mgr Lustiger, célèbre la messe devant plus de 300 000 jeunes, venus du monde entier, pour discuter et prier ensemble. Le 21, le président de la République, Jacques Chirac, accueille le pape Jean-Paul II. La manifestation atteint son apogée le 24 août à l'hippodrome de Longchamp avec une longue veillée suivie d'une messe à laquelle assistent 1 million de personnes. Une partie de l'opinion française est hostile au pape, en raison surtout de ses prises de position très traditionnelles sur les comportements des couples. Mais la jeunesse lui a fait un accueil délirant, et a écouté son message de justice et d'amour. Des milliers de bénévoles ont travaillé sous une chaleur écrasante pour la réussite de cette rencontre, à laquelle ont collaboré toutes les autorités administratives, quelles qu'aient été leurs opinions religieuses.

▼ *Un accueil triomphal de la jeunesse pour le pape aux JMJ.*

Un sommet pour l'environnement

▶ 1ᵉʳ-11 décembre 1997 ◀

Le président de la République Jacques Chirac participe, à Kyoto, à la Conférence sur le réchauffement de la Terre. Les représentants des 159 pays présents au Japon s'entendent pour faire diminuer de 5,2 % les rejets dans l'atmosphère des gaz qui accroissent « l'effet de serre » d'ici à 2012.

▲ *Manifestation écologiste à Kyoto.*

Tremblements de terre à Assise

▶ 27 septembre 1997 ◀ Une série de tremblements de terre a ébranlé hier le centre de l'Italie, faisant onze morts et plus de 100 blessés. Environ 5 000 personnes sont actuellement sans abri. Ces séismes ont en outre fortement endommagé l'un des plus hauts lieux touristiques de la région de Pérouse, la basilique du XIIIe siècle Saint-François, à Assise. Une partie du plafond s'est effondrée et deux fresques du XIIIe siècle ont été détruites. La tombe de saint François, ainsi que deux fresques du peintre Giotto, sont restées intactes.

▲ Les sauveteurs transportent les pierres de la basilique.

Hommage d'Elton John à Diana

La star de rock britannique Elton John a chanté une version adaptée de son ancien succès, *Candle in the Wind*, aux funérailles de Diana. La chanson, écrite en premier lieu pour l'actrice Marilyn Monroe, a été commercialisée sous le titre *Candle in the Wind '97*. Les bénéfices vont à la Fondation de la princesse. Le 21 octobre, on parlait de 31,8 millions d'exemplaires vendus.

◀ Elton John chante pour la princesse de Galles.

Mort de Mère Teresa

▶ 13 septembre 1997 ◀ Les obsèques de Mère Teresa viennent de se dérouler. La religieuse catholique, née Agnes Gonxha Bajaxhiu, est morte le 5 septembre, à l'âge de 87 ans, d'une crise cardiaque. Celle qui a voué sa vie aux plus déshérités a pris le nom de Sœur Teresa en référence au saint patron des missionnaires, sainte Thérèse de Lisieux. Elle a élu domicile à Calcutta, dans l'est de l'Inde, dès 1948.

▶ Les funérailles de Mère Teresa.

Succès socialistes en Europe

▶ 2 mai-1er juin 1997 ◀ La gauche l'emporte en Europe de l'Ouest. Au Royaume-Uni, les élections à la Chambre des communes ont porté au pouvoir le Parti travailliste conduit par Tony Blair. Cela met un terme à dix-huit années de pouvoir conservateur. En France, où le président Jacques Chirac a dissous l'Assemblée nationale, les électeurs donnent la majorité aux socialistes conduits par Lionel Jospin. Les deux Premiers ministres sont décidés à venir à bout du chômage et des difficultés économiques.

Record de vitesse dans le désert

Le 25 septembre, le pilote de la RAF Andy Green a battu le record de vitesse au sol dans le désert du Nevada. Il a atteint 1 149,272 km/h dans le bolide britannique *Thrust SSC*. Le 15 octobre, il a réalisé un score encore plus performant en atteignant les 1 232,899 km/h. C'est le premier véhicule qui parvient à franchir le mur du son.

La comète Hale-Boop

La comète Hale-Bopp (du nom des astronomes américains Alan Hale et Thomas Bopp) est passée près de la Terre au printemps 1997. Des millions de personnes ont pu découvrir cette comète à l'œil nu. Son retour est prévu en l'an 3200.

▲ Le bolide britannique *Thrust SSC* franchit le mur du son.

1990 – 1997

1997

Hong Kong retourne à la Chine

▶ **1er juillet 1997** ◀

À minuit, la nuit dernière, Hong Kong est redevenu chinois. L'île était devenue une colonie britannique en 1842. L'accord entre les Chinois et les Britanniques conclu en 1984 redonne le contrôle de l'île à la Chine. De magnifiques cérémonies d'adieux ont réuni Chris Patten, le dernier gouverneur de la colonie, le prince Charles d'Angleterre, Tony Blair, le Premier ministre britannique, et le leader chinois Jiang Zemin.

Les Chinois ont promis de ne pas intervenir dans le système économique capitaliste de Hong Kong, fondé sur la propriété privée.

▼ *Chris Patten, le dernier gouverneur de Hong Kong, remet l'Union Jack.*

▲ *Un soldat de l'Armée populaire de libération chinoise entre dans Hong Kong, dans un char.*

Les forêts de Sumatra en feu

▶ **15 octobre 1997** ◀

Le ciel de l'Asie du Sud-Est est assombri par les fumées noires des feux de forêt. Certains ont été déclenchés par des paysans et des marchands de bois qui voulaient déboiser pour dégager des terres. Mais les incendies se propagent et ne sont plus maîtrisés. Le gouvernement de Malaisie a déclaré l'état d'urgence, à cause de la pollution de l'air. Le 24 septembre, 1 000 pompiers sont arrivés à Sumatra. La météo est défavorable. Il fait chaud, et les pluies saisonnières qui devraient aider à éteindre les feux n'arrivent pas.

▶ *Les pompiers se battent contre les feux de forêt, à Sumatra.*

▼ *De gauche à droite, Sporty, Baby, Scary, Posh et Ginger.*

Grand succès pour les Spice Girls

Les Spice Girls, un groupe britannique exclusivement féminin qui joue et chante de la musique pop, s'imposent comme le grand succès de l'année 1997, dans le monde entier. Les cinq jeunes filles ont fait de la publicité pour la firme Pepsi. Elles ont publié un livre, et joué dans un film, *Spiceworld*. Elles ont chacune un style particulier et un surnom original : Posh (Victoria), Baby (Emma), Sporty (Mel C.), Scary (Mel B.) et Ginger (Geri).

1990 – 1997

Vers la paix en Irlande du Nord

▶ 7 octobre 1997 ◀ La recherche de la paix en Irlande du Nord entre dans une nouvelle phase de discussions. Les nationalistes irlandais voudraient que cette région fasse partie d'une Irlande unie. Les unionistes veulent garder leurs liens avec la Grande-Bretagne. Gerry Adams, le leader du parti nationaliste lié à l'IRA, l'Armée républicaine irlandaise, déclare qu'il choisit des méthodes pacifiques.

◀ Le dirigeant du Sinn Féin, Gerry Adams (au centre).

En 1997 aussi...

19 février • Le leader chinois Deng Xiaoping meurt à 92 ans.

16 mai • Mobutu Sese Seko, le dictateur du Zaïre, s'enfuit. Laurent Kabila se prépare à prendre le pouvoir.

1er juin • Les socialistes remportent les élections législatives. Le nouveau Premier ministre est Lionel Jospin. C'est la 3e cohabitation droite/gauche de la Ve République.

Le juge contre les jurés

▶ 10 novembre 1997 ◀ Un juge américain libère Louise Woodward, une jeune fille au pair britannique. Elle risquait la prison à vie, pour le décès du bébé qu'elle gardait. Matthew était mort des suites de lésions cérébrales. Les jurés l'avaient jugée coupable d'homicide par imprudence. Mais le juge Zobel a dit que les 279 jours que Mlle Woodward avait déjà passés en prison, en attendant le procès, suffisaient à sa peine pour homicide involontaire.

▲ Louise Woodward et l'un de ses avocats, au tribunal.

La doyenne du monde

Jeanne Calment est née en 1875. Elle est morte le 4 août, à l'âge de 122 ans. Depuis 1993, elle était la personne la plus âgée du monde. Elle a survécu à sa fille, morte en 1934, et à son petit-fils, mort en 1963. Elle disait que son sens de l'humour l'a aidée à rester en vie.

La planète Mars en photo

▶ 30 septembre 1997 ◀ Les savants ont perdu le contact avec l'engin spatial Pathfinder, qui a atterri sur la planète Mars le 4 juillet. Ils pensent que la batterie n'est plus assez puissante. Mais le programme est considéré comme un grand succès. Pathfinder a travaillé 90 jours, au lieu des 30 jours que les spécialistes avaient prévus. L'engin a envoyé à la Terre 16 000 photos de la « planète rouge », prises par le module d'atterrissage, et 550 ont été prises avec le Sojourner.

▼ Le Sojourner à six roues analyse les roches et prend des photos.

1998

L'ouragan Mitch ravage l'Amérique centrale

▶ **4 novembre** ◀ Le Honduras et le Nicaragua viennent d'être dévastés par l'ouragan Mitch, l'un des plus terribles du siècle. Des pluies diluviennes se sont abattues sur ces deux États d'Amérique centrale ; la boue et les rochers ont recouvert des villages entiers et provoqué des glissements de terrain. On compte 12 000 morts, 13 000 disparus et 2,8 millions de sinistrés. Il faudra plusieurs années pour relever les ruines. En voyage au Guatemala le 15 novembre, le président français Jacques Chirac a assuré les deux États de la solidarité de la France.

▲ *L'ouragan a causé un désastre économique, coupant routes et ponts et détruisant des plantations de bananiers, principale richesse de la région.*

La France remporte la Coupe du monde

▶ **12 juillet** ◀ « On est les champions », hurlent des millions de Français : pour la première fois de son histoire, la France remporte la coupe du monde de football, après avoir battu par 3 à 0 le Brésil, handicapé par la mauvaise forme de Ronaldo. C'est la gloire pour Zidane et Petit, auteurs des buts, pour le gardien de but Barthez et l'entraîneur Aimé Jacquet. Mais la fête a été ternie par la violence de certains supporters : un hooligan anglais a assassiné un passant et un policier est dans le coma après une rixe avec des hooligans allemands.

▲ *Au grand stade de Saint-Denis, Zinedine Zidane marque son deuxième but.*

▼ *Les secouristes fouillent les décombres d'un immeuble de bureaux détruit par l'explosion.*

Attentats meurtriers en Afrique

▶ **7 août** ◀ À 10 heures 30 ce matin, des bombes très puissantes explosent devant l'ambassade des États-Unis à Nairobi, au Kenya, et devant celle de Dar es-Salaam, en Tanzanie. Les auteurs de cet attentat à la voiture piégée sont probablement des extrémistes islamistes, qui ont synchronisé leur action. Douze Américains ont été tués, mais, quoique les États-Unis soient sans aucun doute la cible des terroristes, la plupart des 250 victimes sont africaines ; à Nairobi, plus de 200 personnes ont perdu la vie. Le président Clinton a immédiatement annoncé que tout serait mis en œuvre pour que les coupables soient traduits en justice.

1990–1999

1998

Le président Clinton et l'affaire Lewinsky

▶ **21 septembre** ◀ Le président des États-Unis va-t-il être mis en accusation *(impeachment)* ? Le 7 août, Bill Clinton a reconnu devant un jury de parlementaires avoir menti quant à ses relations avec Monica Lewinsky. Les Américains sont aujourd'hui rivés à leurs téléviseurs pour la diffusion de l'audition ; le monde entier entend Clinton dire que sa relation avec la stagiaire à la Maison-Blanche « n'était pas convenable » et présenter ses excuses à son épouse et à la nation. Au même moment, les tensions en Irak auxquelles les États-Unis répondent par des frappes aériennes détournent l'attention du plublic américain des problèmes personnels du président.

▲ *Pendant son témoignage, le président est resté calme, sauf quand il a manifesté son irritation devant certaines questions.*

En 1998 aussi...

10 avril • L'accord du Vendredi saint fait espérer la fin des violences en Irlande du Nord.

28 mai • Le Pakistan procède à des essais nucléaires en réponse à la reprise des essais indiens.

8 juillet • Plusieurs coureurs cyclistes du Tour de France sont accusés de dopage.

17 octobre • L'ancien dictateur chilien Augusto Pinochet est arrêté à Londres.

John Glenn retourne dans l'espace

▶ **29 octobre** ◀ L'astronaute américain John Glenn est devenu le plus vieil homme à bord d'un engin spatial. Âgé de 77 ans, il fait partie de l'équipage de la navette *Discovery* lancée depuis Cap Canaveral pour une mission de neuf jours. C'est le second voyage dans l'espace de Glenn qui fut, en 1962, le premier Américain en orbite autour de la Terre.

▲ *John Glenn (en haut à gauche) et l'équipage de la navette.*

Le triomphe de *Titanic*

Le film *Titanic*, qui a déjà battu tous les records de fréquentation dans les salles, triomphe à la cérémonie des Oscars d'Hollywood. Il remporte 11 récompenses, autant que *Ben Hur* en 1960. Mais le jury des Oscars n'a pas voulu couronner les vedettes du film, Leonardo Di Caprio et Kate Winslet (ci-dessous).

Maurice Papon condamné

▶ **17 octobre** ◀ Le verdict du procès Papon vient de tomber. La Cour d'assises de Bordeaux condamne Maurice Papon, ancien préfet du général de Gaulle, à dix ans de réclusion pour « complicité de crime contre l'humanité » : le procès a montré qu'il avait activement collaboré à la déportation des juifs alors qu'il travaillait à la préfecture de la Gironde pendant l'Occupation. Maurice Papon, âgé de 88 ans, fait appel de cette condamnation.

Des savants dans l'espace

La construction de *Spacelab*, immense laboratoire spatial international, commence cette année. L'assemblage sera achevé en 2003 grâce à 46 vols de la navette américaine et du lanceur russe Proton. Le lanceur européen Ariane 5 ravitaillera la station.

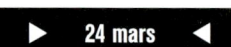

▼ *Distribution de pain aux réfugiés kosovars.*

La guerre au Kosovo

24 mars — L'OTAN lance les premières frappes aériennes contre les Serbes après l'échec des négociations qui se sont tenues ce mois-ci à Rambouillet entre l'OTAN, les Serbes et l'armée de libération du Kosovo (UCK). Les bombardements de l'aviation de l'OTAN, sous commandement américain, s'attaquent à des cibles militaires ou stratégiques, sans toutefois réussir à empêcher que les milices serbes continuent leurs exactions. La crise remonte à 1989, date à laquelle le gouvernement yougoslave de Slobodan Milosevic, dominé par les Serbes, a privé de ses libertés la province autonome du Kosovo, dont 90 % des habitants sont d'origine albanaise, mais que les Serbes considèrent comme le « berceau » de leur patrie. L'armée yougoslave et les milices serbes incendient et détruisent des villages entiers, obligeant leurs habitants à fuir et perpétrant massacres et atrocités. En quelques mois, depuis que le gouvernement serbe de Yougoslavie a lancé ses opérations de « purification ethnique », ce seront près d'un million de Kosovars d'origine albanaise contraints de tout abandonner et de se réfugier dans les pays voisins, ce qui posera de graves problèmes à ces derniers.

◀ *Bâtiment de la télévision serbe incendié par les tirs de l'OTAN à Belgrade.*

En 1999 aussi...

12 février • Le Sénat américain acquitte le président Clinton, mettant fin à l'affaire Lewinsky.

4 mars • Trois millions de chômeurs au Japon, davantage qu'aux États-Unis.

20 avril • Dans une école du Colorado, deux adolescents massacrent 15 de leurs camarades et se donnent la mort.

3 mai • Le préfet de Corse Bonnet est mis en examen pour incendie volontaire.

▼ *L'euro ne sera mis en circulation pour les paiements courants qu'en 2002.*

L'euro, monnaie européenne

1er janvier — Onze des membres de l'Union européenne (UE) ont lancé aujourd'hui leur monnaie unique, l'euro. L'« Euroland » compte 290 millions d'habitants, une population comparable à celle des États-Unis, mais, pour des raisons diverses, le Royaume-Uni, le Danemark, la Suède et la Grèce n'ont pas adopté la monnaie unique. Les anciennes monnaies, comme le franc français et le mark allemand, ne disparaissent pas : elles resteront en usage pour les paiements de chaque jour jusqu'en 2002.

1990 – 1999

1998

Le président Clinton et l'affaire Lewinsky

▶ **21 septembre** ◀ Le président des États-Unis va-t-il être mis en accusation (*impeachment*) ? Le 7 août, Bill Clinton a reconnu devant un jury de parlementaires avoir menti quant à ses relations avec Monica Lewinsky. Les Américains sont aujourd'hui rivés à leurs téléviseurs pour la diffusion de l'audition ; le monde entier entend Clinton dire que sa relation avec la stagiaire à la Maison-Blanche « n'était pas convenable » et présenter ses excuses à son épouse et à la nation. Au même moment, les tensions en Irak auxquelles les États-Unis répondent par des frappes aériennes détournent l'attention du public américain des problèmes personnels du président.

▲ *Pendant son témoignage, le président est resté calme, sauf quand il a manifesté son irritation devant certaines questions.*

En 1998 aussi...

10 avril • L'accord du Vendredi saint fait espérer la fin des violences en Irlande du Nord.

28 mai • Le Pakistan procède à des essais nucléaires en réponse à la reprise des essais indiens.

8 juillet • Plusieurs coureurs cyclistes du Tour de France sont accusés de dopage.

17 octobre • L'ancien dictateur chilien Augusto Pinochet est arrêté à Londres.

John Glenn retourne dans l'espace

▶ **29 octobre** ◀ L'astronaute américain John Glenn est devenu le plus vieil homme à bord d'un engin spatial. Âgé de 77 ans, il fait partie de l'équipage de la navette *Discovery* lancée depuis Cap Canaveral pour une mission de neuf jours. C'est le second voyage dans l'espace de Glenn qui fut, en 1962, le premier Américain en orbite autour de la Terre.

▲ *John Glenn (en haut à gauche) et l'équipage de la navette.*

Maurice Papon condamné

▶ **17 octobre** ◀ Le verdict du procès Papon vient de tomber. La Cour d'assises de Bordeaux condamne Maurice Papon, ancien préfet du général de Gaulle, à dix ans de réclusion pour « complicité de crime contre l'humanité » : le procès a montré qu'il avait activement collaboré à la déportation des juifs alors qu'il travaillait à la préfecture de la Gironde pendant l'Occupation. Maurice Papon, âgé de 88 ans, fait appel de cette condamnation.

Le triomphe de *Titanic*

Le film *Titanic*, qui a déjà battu tous les records de fréquentation dans les salles, triomphe à la cérémonie des Oscars d'Hollywood. Il remporte 11 récompenses, autant que *Ben Hur* en 1960. Mais le jury des Oscars n'a pas voulu couronner les vedettes du film, Leonardo Di Caprio et Kate Winslet (ci-dessous).

Des savants dans l'espace

La construction de *Spacelab*, immense laboratoire spatial international, commence cette année. L'assemblage sera achevé en 2003 grâce à 46 vols de la navette américaine et du lanceur russe Proton. Le lanceur européen Ariane 5 ravitaillera la station.

1999

▼ *Distribution de pain aux réfugiés kosovars.*

La guerre au Kosovo

▶ **24 mars** ◀

L'OTAN lance les premières frappes aériennes contre les Serbes après l'échec des négociations qui se sont tenues ce mois-ci à Rambouillet entre l'OTAN, les Serbes et l'armée de libération du Kosovo (UCK). Les bombardements de l'aviation de l'OTAN, sous commandement américain, s'attaquent à des cibles militaires ou stratégiques, sans toutefois réussir à empêcher que les milices serbes continuent leurs exactions. La crise remonte à 1989, date à laquelle le gouvernement yougoslave de Slobodan Milosevic, dominé par les Serbes, a privé de ses libertés la province autonome du Kosovo, dont 90 % des habitants sont d'origine albanaise, mais que les Serbes considèrent comme le « berceau » de leur patrie. L'armée yougoslave et les milices serbes incendient et détruisent des villages entiers, obligeant leurs habitants à fuir et perpétrant massacres et atrocités. En quelques mois, depuis que le gouvernement serbe de Yougoslavie a lancé ses opérations de « purification ethnique », ce seront près d'un million de Kosovars d'origine albanaise contraints de tout abandonner et de se réfugier dans les pays voisins, ce qui posera de graves problèmes à ces derniers.

◀ *Bâtiment de la télévision serbe incendié par les tirs de l'OTAN à Belgrade.*

En 1999 aussi...

12 février • Le Sénat américain acquitte le président Clinton, mettant fin à l'affaire Lewinsky.

4 mars • Trois millions de chômeurs au Japon, davantage qu'aux États-Unis.

20 avril • Dans une école du Colorado, deux adolescents massacrent 15 de leurs camarades et se donnent la mort.

3 mai • Le préfet de Corse Bonnet est mis en examen pour incendie volontaire.

▼ *L'euro ne sera mis en circulation pour les paiements courants qu'en 2002.*

L'euro, monnaie européenne

▶ **1ᵉʳ janvier** ◀

Onze des membres de l'Union européenne (UE) ont lancé aujourd'hui leur monnaie unique, l'euro. L'« Euroland » compte 290 millions d'habitants, une population comparable à celle des États-Unis, mais, pour des raisons diverses, le Royaume-Uni, le Danemark, la Suède et la Grèce n'ont pas adopté la monnaie unique. Les anciennes monnaies, comme le franc français et le mark allemand, ne disparaissent pas : elles resteront en usage pour les paiements de chaque jour jusqu'en 2002.

1990 – 1999

Funérailles du roi Hussein de Jordanie

▶ **8 février** ◀ Le roi Hussein de Jordanie a été inhumé aujourd'hui en présence de chefs d'État, dont Bill Clinton et Jacques Chirac, et de dignitaires venus du monde entier témoigner de leur respect envers l'un des dirigeants les plus admirés du Proche-Orient. Le « petit roi » de Jordanie, qui avait échappé à plusieurs attentats et sauvé son trône de tous les dangers, a été vaincu par le cancer. Au pouvoir depuis 1952, modéré, il avait toujours agi en faveur du retour de la paix dans cette partie du monde. Son fils Abdullah II, âgé de 37 ans, lui succède.

▲ *Les bédouins de la garde royale portent en terre leur souverain.*

L'an 2000 : les fêtes et le bogue

▶ **1er juillet** ◀ 184 jours avant le deuxième millénaire ! Dans le monde entier, quel que soit le calendrier en vigueur, on s'y prépare. Certains ont prévu de réveillonner plusieurs fois, en jouant sur le décalage horaire, d'autres ont programmé leur bébé pour la nuit du 31 décembre 1999… Les informaticiens, quant à eux, tentent d'éviter le « bogue » qui risque de mettre en panne les ordinateurs et ce qu'ils contrôlent : signaux lumineux, distributeurs, centrales, etc.

▼ *À Sydney, en Australie, l'an 2000 sera avant tout l'année des jeux Olympiques.*

Incendie tragique dans le tunnel de Chamonix

▶ **23 mars** ◀ Un violent incendie a ravagé le tunnel de Chamonix, causant la mort de 41 personnes au moins. Le feu s'est propagé à partir d'un camion qui a bloqué sous le tunnel les autres véhicules ; la chaleur a fait fondre le béton et les structures métalliques, rendant difficile le travail des sauveteurs. Long de 11,6 km, le tunnel sous le Mont-Blanc avait été inauguré en 1965 ; la catastrophe pose la question de la sécurité dans les nombreux tunnels français.

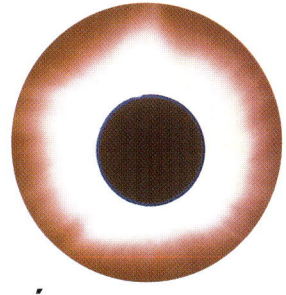

Éclipse totale de Soleil

La dernière éclipse totale du deuxième millénaire a eu lieu le 11 août, au-dessus de l'Europe, du Proche-Orient et du sud de l'Asie. La prochaine éclipse totale de Soleil visible d'Europe aura lieu en 2090.

Michael Jordan se retire

Le 12 janvier, Michael Jordan a annoncé qu'il quittait la compétition. Avec son équipe, les Chicago Bulls, celui qui restera comme le plus grand joueur de basket-ball de tous les temps a remporté entre 1991 et 1998 six championnats ; son salaire de 35 millions de dollars a fait de lui le sportif le mieux payé du monde.

◀ *Michael Jordan est l'un des trois joueurs qui a marqué le plus de points en championnat.*

ÉTAPES DE LA CRÉATION DE L'EUROPE

1951 : fondation de la CECA.
25 mars 1957 : fondation de la CEE à Six (traité de Rome), et de l'Euratom.
1962 : mise en place de la politique agricole commune.
1973 : la CEE admet le Royaume-Uni, l'Irlande et le Danemark.
1979 : mise en place du système monétaire européen, premières élections du Parlement européen au suffrage universel.
1981 : la CEE admet la Grèce.
1986 : la CEE admet l'Espagne et le Portugal.
1987 : Acte unique européen, marché unique entre les Douze à partir du 1er janvier 1993.
1992 : le traité de Maastricht instaure l'Union européenne (UE) à partir du 1er novembre 1993.
1995 : l'UE admet la Finlande, l'Autriche et la Suède.
1998 : premiers pas de l'Euro, monnaie unique européenne.

EUROPE / PAYS MEMBRES

La date d'entrée dans l'Union est donnée pour chaque pays.

Belgique 1958
France 1958
Allemagne 1958
Italie 1958
Luxembourg 1958
Pays-Bas 1958
Danemark 1973
Irlande 1973
Royaume - Uni 1973
Grèce 1981
Portugal 1986
Espagne 1986
Suède 1995
Finlande 1995
Autriche 1995

Sigles CECA : Communauté européenne du charbon et de l'Acier   CEE : Communauté économique européenne   UE : Union européenne

PAYS FRANCOPHONES

(pays où le français est, totalement ou partiellement langue officielle, administrative, ou bien langue d'enseignement)
Haut Conseil de la francophonie : présidé par L. S Senghor (Sénégalais)

Algérie, Andorre, Belgique, Bénin, Burkina, Burundi, Cameroun, Canada (Québec), Centrafrique, Comores, Côte d'Ivoire, Djibouti, États-Unis (Louisiane), Gabon, Guinée, Haïti, Liban, Luxembourg, Madagascar, Mali, Maroc, Maurice, Mauritanie, Monaco, Niger, Rwanda, Sénégal, Seychelles, Suisse, Tchad, Togo, Tunisie, Vanuatu, Zaïre

FRANCE / PRÉSIDENTS DE LA RÉPUBLIQUE

1899-1906, Emile Loubet
1906-1913, Armand Fallières
1913-1920, Raymond Poincaré
1920, Paul Deschanel
1920-1924, Alexandre Millerand
1924-1931, Gaston Doumergue
1931-1932, Paul Doumer
1932-1940, Albert Lebrun
1940-1944, Philippe Pétain
1944-1946, Charles de Gaulle
Janv.- juin, 1946, Félix Gouin
Juin-nov., 1946, Georges Bidault
Déc. 1946-janv. 1947, Léon Blum
1947-1954, Vincent Auriol
1954-1958, René Coty
1958-1969, Charles de Gaulle
1969-1974, Georges Pompidou
1974-1981, Valéry Giscard d'Estaing
1981-1995, François Mitterrand
depuis 1995, Jacques Chirac

FRANCE / PRÉSIDENTS DU CONSEIL

Juin 1899, Charles Dupuy, puis Pierre Waldeck-Rousseau
Juin 1902, Emile Combes
Janvier 1905, Maurice Rouvier
Mars 1906, Maurice Rouvier, puis Ferdinand Sarrien
Octobre 1906, Georges Clemenceau
Juillet 1909, Aristide Briand
Mars 1911, Ernest Monis
Juin 1911, Joseph Caillaux,
Janvier 1912, Raymond Poincaré
Janvier 1913, Aristide Briand
Mars 1913, Aristide Briand, puis Louis Barthou
Décembre 1913, Gaston Doumergue
Juin 1914, Alexandre Ribot, puis René Viviani
Décembre 1915, Aristide Briand
Mars 1917, Alexandre Ribot
Septembre 1917, Paul Painlevé
Novembre 1917, Georges Clemenceau (jusqu'en janvier 1920)
1917-1920, Georges Clemenceau
1920, Alexandre Millerand
1920-1921, Georges Leygues
1921-1922, 1925-1926, 1929, Aristide Briand
1922-1924, 1926-1929, Raymond Poincaré
1924-1925, 1926-1932, Edouard Herriot
1925, Paul Painlevé
1929-1930, 1932, André Tardieu
1930-1931, Théodore Steeg
1931-1932, 1935-1936, 1936, Pierre Laval
1932-1933, 1934, 1938-1940, Edouard Daladier
1933, 1936, Albert Sarraut
1933-1934, 1937-1938, Camille Chautemps
1934, Gaston Doumergue
1934-1935, Pierre Etienne Flandin
1935, Ferdinand Buisson
1936-1937, 1938, Léon Blum
1940, Paul Reynaud
1940, Philippe Pétain
1947, Paul Ramadier
1947-1948, 1948, Robert Schuman
1948, André Marie
1948-1949, 1951, Henri Queuille
1949-1950, Georges Bidault
1950-1951, 1951-1952, René Pleven
1952, 1955-1956, Edgar Faure
1952, Antoine Pinay
1953, René Mayeur
1953-1954, Joseph Laniel
1954-1955, Pierre Mendès France
1956-1957, Guy Mollet
1957, Maurice Bourgès-Maunoury
1957-1958, Félix Gaillard
1958, Pierre Pflimlin
1958, Charles de Gaulle

FRANCE / PREMIERS MINISTRES

1959-1962, Michel Debré
1962-1968, Georges Pompidou
1968-1969, Maurice Couve de Murville
1969-1972, Jacques Chaban-Delmas
1972-1974, Pierre Messmer
1974-1976 Jacques Chirac
1976-1981, Raymond Barre
1981-1984, Pierre Mauroy
1984-1986, Laurent Fabius
1986-1988, Jacques Chirac
1988-1991, Michel Rocard
1991-1992, Edith Cresson
1992-1993, Pierre Bérégovoy
1993-1995, Edouard Balladur
1995-1997, Alain Juppé
Depuis juin 1997, Lionel Jospin

LES PRINCIPALES GUERRES DU XXe SIÈCLE

1904-1905 : guerre russo-japonaise.
1914-1918 : Première Guerre mondiale.
1918-1921 : guerre civile russe.
1922-1923 : guerre civile irlandaise.
1936-1939 : guerre civile espagnole.
1937-1945 : guerre sino-japonaise.
1939-1945 : Seconde Guerre mondiale.
1945-1949 : guerre civile chinoise.
1948-1949 : guerre israélo-arabe.
1950-1953 : guerre de Corée.
1954-1962 : guerre d'Algérie.
1965-1975 : guerre du Viêt-nam.
1967 : guerre des Six-Jours.
1967-1970 : guerre du Biafra.
1968-1998 : guerre civile en Irlande du Nord.
1973 : guerre du Kippour.
1979-1996 : guerre en Afghanistan.
1980-1988 : guerre Iran-Irak.
1991 : guerre du Golfe.
1991-1995 : guerre civile en Yougoslavie.
1991-1997 : guerre en Somalie.
1995-1997 : Guerre civile au Rwanda.
1998 : guerre au Kossovo.

LES MISSIONS SPATIALES DU XXᵉ SIÈCLE

1926 Une fusée au propergol liquide est lancée par Robert Goddard, un physicien américain.
1957 Le premier satellite artificiel soviétique, *Spoutnik 1*, est lancé.
1959 La sonde américaine *Vanguard 2* transmet les premières photographies de la Terre.
1959 La sonde soviétique *Luna 3* transmet les premières photographies de la face cachée de la Lune.
1961 Le Soviétique Iouri Gagarine est le premier homme à effectuer un vol en orbite autour de la Terre à bord du satellite *Vostok 1*.
1963 La Soviétique Valentina Terechkova est la première femme à aller dans l'espace. Elle est restée deux jours en orbite autour de la Terre à bord du satellite *Vostok 6*.
1964 Le premier vol sur Mars est effectué par la sonde américaine *Mariner 4*. Elle transmet à la Terre 22 photographies des cratères de la planète.
1964 Les premiers gros plans de la surface de la Lune sont pris par la sonde américaine *Ranger 7*.
1965 Le cosmonaute Alekseï Leonov réalise la première sortie dans l'espace.
1966 Premier atterrissage sur la Lune de la sonde soviétique *Luna 9*, qui rapporte les premières photos de la surface lunaire.
1968 Premier vol humain autour de la Lune dans la cabine américaine *Apollo 8*, sans alunissage.
1969 Premiers pas sur la Lune des astronautes américains Neil Armstrong et Edwin M. Aldrin.
1970 La sonde soviétique *Venera 7* est la première à atterrir sur Vénus.
1973 La première station spatiale américaine, *Skylab*, est lancée.
1973 La sonde américaine *Mariner 10* prend les premières photos de Mercure.
1975 Premier arrimage en orbite des vaisseaux spatiaux américain et soviétique *Apollo et Soyouz*.
1975 La sonde soviétique *Venera 9* prend les premières photos de la surface de Vénus.
1976 La sonde américaine *Viking 1* confirme qu'il n'y a pas de vie sur Mars.
1977 Les sondes américaines *Voyager 1* et *Voyager 2* rapportent les premières images de Jupiter, Saturne, Uranus et Neptune.
1978 Le premier observatoire international est créé par la Grande-Bretagne, les États-Unis et l'Agence spatiale européenne.
1979 Un satellite et un anneau de la planète Saturne sont découverts par la sonde américaine *Pioneer 11*, au bout de six ans de voyage.
1980 La sonde américaine *Voyager 1* découvre six nouveaux satellites de Saturne après avoir pris des photos en gros plan des anneaux de la planète.
1981 La navette américaine *Columbia* est lancée : c'est le premier vaisseau spatial réutilisable.
1984 Jean-Loup Chrétien est le premier français à effectuer un vol dans l'espace.
1986 L'explosion de la navette spatiale américaine *Challenger* entraîne la mort des sept membres de l'équipage. Le programme spatial est arrêté.
1988 Premier vol de la navette spatiale américaine *Columbia* après l'explosion de *Challenger*.
1989 Six nouveaux satellites de Neptune sont découverts par la sonde américaine *Voyager 2* quand elle atteint la planète.
1990 Le télescope spatial Hubble est lancé, mais son miroir est défectueux.
1990 Les États-Unis et l'Agence spatiale européenne lancent *Ulysse*, le premier satellite qui explore les pôles du soleil.
1994 Le télescope spatial Hubble est réparé.

LES INVENTIONS DU XXᵉ SIÈCLE

1900 Périscope sous-marin
Meccano
Lyophilisation
1901 Appareil auditif
Lame de rasoir
Aspirateur
1902 Motocyclette
1903 Avion à hélices (premier vol)
Insuline
Savon en poudre
1904 Cellule photoélectrique
Centrale géothermique
1906 Juke box
Machine à laver le linge électrique
Émission radiophonique
1907 Bakélite
Télécopieur
Hélicoptère
Chimiothérapie
1908 Cellophane
1909 Grille-pain électrique
1910 Porte-avion
Mixeur
1911 Crème Nivea
1912 Locomotive diesel
1913 Chaîne de montage
Mots croisés
Acier inoxydable
1914 Fermeture Éclair
1915 Air conditionné
Pyrex (verre résistant à la chaleur)
Grenade sous-marine
1916 Tracteur
1917 Détergent
1918 Sonar
Montre électrique
1919 Thé en sachet
1920 Sèche-cheveux
Barre Mars
1921 Détecteur de mensonges
Autoroute
Insuline
1922 Esquimau (glace)
1923 Réfrigérateur
Planétarium
Microphone
Barre Milky Way
Supermarché (le premier à ouvrir aux États-Unis)
1924 Mouchoir jetable
1925 Ski nautique
Scotch
1926 Fusée au propergol liquide
Télévision
1927 Montre à quartz
1928 Pénicilline
Rasoir électrique
Élastoplaste
1929 Yo-Yo
1930 Nourriture congelée
1931 Microscope électronique
Scrabble
1933 Modulation de fréquence
1934 Catadioptre
Monopoly
1935 Parcmètre
1936 Cinéma en couleurs
Magnétophone
1937 Moteur à réaction
1938 Stylo à bille
Photocopieur
Fer à repasser à vapeur
Café instantané
1939 Éclairage fluorescent
Avion à réaction
Plastique
1940 Flipper
Huile solaire
1941 Bombe aérosol
1942 Missile
Réacteur nucléaire
1943 Missile guidé
1944 Fusées V1 et V2
1945 Bombe atomique
Ordinateur (ENIAC)
1946 Bikini
1947 Avion supersonique
Transistor
1948 Bande Velcro
Four à micro-ondes
Polaroid
1949 Télévision par câble
1950 Carte de crédit
1951 Cœur et poumon artificiels
1952 Bombe à hydrogène
1953 Film sur grand écran
1954 Nourriture lyophilisée
Centrale nucléaire
Poste à transistors
Télévision couleur
Casserole avec revêtement antiadhésif
1955 Lego
1956-58 Stimulateur cardiaque
1956 Câble téléphonique transatlantique
Cassette vidéo
Verres de contact
1957 Robot
Satellite
1958 Endoscope
Puce au silicium
1959 Ceinture de sécurité
Aéroglisseur
Circuit intégré
Poupée Barbie
1960 Laser
Prothèse de la hanche
1961 Souris d'ordinateur
1962 Satellite de communication
1963 Fibre carbone
Magnétoscope
Mini-ordinateur
1964 Minijupe
1967 Navigation par satellite
1970 Disquette
1971 Microprocesseur
Scanner
1972 Caméscope
1973 Planche à roulettes
1975 Ordinateur personnel
1976 Couches jetables
Premier vol supersonique avec passagers
1978 Téléphone cellulaire
1980 Baladeur
Rubik Cube
Ordinateurs en réseau
Lampe halogène
Lecteur de code-barres
1981 Airbag
Navette spatiale
Avion furtif
Trivial Pursuit
1982 Champ d'éoliennes
Disque compact
1983 Télescope à infra-rouge
Ordinateur portable
Télévision par satellite
1984 Empreinte génétique
1985 Post-it
Scanner
1986 Chirurgie microscopique
1987 Cassette audio numérique (DAT)
Scalpel laser
1989 Game Boy
1990 Fraise laser (pour les dentistes)
1995 Windows 95
Puce au pentium

Les numéros de page en gras renvoient à l'entrée principale et les numéros en italique aux illustrations.

A

Abdülhamid II 34, *34*, 38
Aboville, Gérard d' 325
Abraham, Murray 304
Abruzzo, Ben 283
Acheson, Dean 181
Acier, pacte d' **137**
Adams, Gerry **345**, *345*
Adenauer, Konrad **176**, *177*, **201**, **232**
Ader, Clément 20
ADN **193**, *193*, *330*, **331**, *331*
adolescents **216-217**
aéroglisseur **228**, *228*
aérosol, bombe 282
Afghanistan **285**, 316
Afrique du Sud **201**, **279**, **318**, 332
  ANC **236**, **318**, **332**
  apartheid **179**, **214**, **318**
  Boers, guerre des 9
  cœlacanthe **133**, *133*
  Commonwealth 223
  national, parti 171
  Sharpville, massacre **219**, *219*
  South Africa Act **42**
  Soweto **276**, *276*
Ağca, Mehmet Ali 295
Aïdid, Mohamed 327
Airplane, Jefferson 252
Akihito 319
Al Fayed, Dodi 342
Alain-Fournier 55
Albanie 325
Albert Ier **36**, 38
Alcock, John **67**, *67*
Aldrin, Edwin 250
Alen, William van 107
Alexandra, reine 36
Alexandre Ier Obrénovitch 19
Algérie **196**, **202**, **227**, **335**
Ali, Muhammad 273
Allemagne
  Algésiras, conférence d' 29
  Anschluss **133**
  Auschwitz **164**, *164*
  Berlin, blocus de **171**, *177*
  Berlin, mur de **222**, *222*, **316**, *316*
  Blitzkrieg **136**
  RDA **176**, **192**
  grève générale 65
  Guerre mondiale (deuxième) **150**, **151**, **153**, **165**, **166**
  Guerre mondiale (première) **52**, **53**, **54**, **58**, **59**, **64**, 66
  inflation 82
  Mein Kampf **87**

Munich, putsch de 83
Nuit de cristal **132**
nuit des longs couteaux **117**
Nuremberg, lois de **123**
Pershing, fusées 300
Rapallo, traité de 75
réarmement **123**
république 65
réunification **319**
RFA **176**, **201**, **243**, **297**
solution finale **155**, 164
traité franco-allemand **232**
zeppelin **10**, *10*
Allende, Salvador **270**, *270*
Alphonse XIII, 109
Amin Dada, Idi **263**, *263*, 276
Amir, Yigal **334**, 339
Amnesty International **224**, *224*
ampoule 25
Amsberg, Claus von **243**, *243*
Amundsen, Roald **44**, *44*, *45*, 99
Anastasia, affaire 100
Anderson, Maxie 283
Anderson, Terry 324
André-Deshays, Claudie 261
Andress, Ursula **229**, *229*
Andrews, Julie **239**, *239*
Angola 327
Anielewicz, Mordecai 156
Anne d'Angleterre **271**, *271*
années folles **94-95**
Anschluss **133**
Antarctique **214**, **297**, *297*
Aquino, Corazón **306**, *306*
Arabie 58
Arabie Saoudite 85
Arafat, Yasser **252**, *252*, **257**, **287**, **296**, **328**
archéologie
  Abou-Simbel **234**, *234*
  carbone 14 168
  Chine (armée en terre cuite) **274**
  Cnossos **9**, *9*
  cœlacanthe **133**, *133*
  Evans, Arthur 9
  Hibernatus **325**, *325*
  Lascaux, grottes de **145**
  Machu Picchu 47
  mayas, cités **91**
  mer Morte, manuscrits de **169**, *169*
  Néfertiti **49**, *49*
  Olduvai, crâne d' **225**, *225*
  Pékin, sinanthrope de **97**, *97*
  Piltdown, homme de **191**, *191*
  Toutankhamon, tombe de **74**
architecture
  Bauhaus **87**

Brasilia **221**, *221*
Chrysler building **107**, *107*
Empire state building **108**, *108*, *112*, 115
Fer à repasser **16**, *16*
Golden Gate **131**
gratte-ciel de cristal 73
habitation, unité d' **186**
Home insurance Building 16
Maison sur la cascade **129**, *129*
Pan Am building **229**, *229*
Sagrada Familia **91**, *91*
Sydney, opéra de **271**, *271*
Sydney, pont de **110**, *110*
tour CN **273**, *273*
Werkbund 97
Woolworth Building **51**, *51*
Argentine **167**, **189**, **277**
Aristide, Jean-Bertrand 333
Arp, Hans 88
armements, course aux **75**, **322**
Armstrong, Louis **94**, *94*
Armstrong, Neil 250
art
  art abstrait 41
  Art nouveau **9**, **15**
  Bauhaus 87
  Calder, mobiles de **111**
  collage **49**, *49*
  dadaïsme, **59**, 60
  Die Brücke (« Le Pont ») 27
  emballage 305
  exposition photographique **201**
  expressionnisme 71
  fauves 25
  Guggenheim, musée **213**, *213*
  Louvre, musée du **47**
  nouveau réalisme 87
  Photo-Secession 27
  Pollock, Jackson, peinture de **169**
  Pompidou, Centre **278**, *278*
  pop' art 227
  réalisme socialiste 119
  Rivera, Diego, fresques de **128**, *128*
  sculpture 60, **150**, *150*
  surréalisme **85**, 88
  vente **310**, 319
Asahara, Shoko 337
Asanuma, Inejiro 220
Ascari Alberto *183*
Assouan, barrage d' **17**, *17*, *234*
Astaire, Fred **119**, 309
Astrid de Suède 93
athlétisme **47**, *325*
Atlas, Charles **91**, *91*
atomique, bombe **162-163**, **177**
  Hiroshima **162**, 163, 164
  Manhattan, projet **162**
  Nagasaki **162**, 164
Auclert, Hubertine, 42

Auriol, Vincent 168
Australie **14**, **16**, **98**, **110**, **313**, **328**
automobile **182-183**
  2 CV Citroën **177**, *177*
  Austin 10 *183*
  Benz *39*
  Buick 34
  course **33**, **81**, **101**
  Curved Dash *183*
  Ford Ka *183*
  Ford T **34**, *34*, **50**, *50*
  Ford Thunderbird *182*
  formule 1 **179**, **207**, **333**
  Japon 291
  Jeep **143**
  Mercedes **13**, *13*, **183**, **279**
  Mini **215**, *215*
  Morris Minor **173**, *173*
  record de vitesse **39**, **122**, **343**
  Silver ghost **29**, *29*
  Station Wagon Rambler *183*
  Volkswagen **127**, *127*, **200**, *200*
Autriche
  Anschluss **133**
  Guerre mondiale (première) **52**
  république 65
Autriche-Hongrie 35
aviation **20-21**, **98**, **103**, **111**, **310**
  accident **267**, **339**, *339*
  Atlantique, traversée de **96**
  avion à réaction **189**
  avion U2 **219**, *219*
  B-29 **157**, *157*
  ballon 283
  Béluga 333
  Boeing 747 coréen 300
  catastrophe **37**, **211**, **278**
  Concorde 252
  course **201**
  Gotha GV 61
  Lockerbie, crash de **310**, *310*
  monde, tour du 85
  pôle Nord, survol du 93
  premier décollage **18**, *18*
  réaction, avion à 177
  Rouge, place **309**, *309*
  son, mur du **169**
  transatlantique, vol **139**
  traversée de la Manche 38
  traversée de la Méditerranée 51
  vol de Terre-Neuve à l'Irlande 67
  vol du Boeing 707 **198**, *198*
  zeppelin **10**, *10*, 61
Azéma 131

B

Bade, Max von 65
Baden-Powell, Robert **30**, *30*, *43*
Badoglio, maréchal 158

Baekeland, Leo 32
Baez, Joan **217**, **239**, *239*, **280**, *280*
Baird, John Logie **255**, *255*
Bakélite **32**
Baker, Joséphine **89**, *89*
Bakey, Michael de *244*
Bakhtiar, Chahpur 284
Balfour, lord 60
Balkans 48
Balladur, Édouard **329**, **336**
Bandaranaike, Sirimavo **219**, *219*
bande dessinée **33**, **124-125**
  Astérix 224
  Little nemo à Slumberland 26
  Peanuts 178
  Popeye 103
  Tarzan 53
  Tintin **102**, *102*
Bandung, conférence de 201
Bangladesh **261**, *273*
Banting, Frederick **73**, *73*
Bardot, Brigitte **205**, *205*
Barnard, professeur **244**, *244*
Barnett, Ross 228
Barrat, Roper 10
Barrault, Jean-Louis **181**, *181*
Barrie, James 22
Barrow, Clyde **118**, *118*
Bartali, Gino 177
Barthou, Louis **75**, *75*
Barton, Edmund 14
Base-ball **19**, **69**, **104-105**
Basket-ball **98**, **339**
Bastié, Maryse 111
bathyscaphe **221**, *221*
Batista, Fulgencio 212
Baudoin (roi de Belgique) **185**, *185*, **211**, **328**
Bea, Alan 258
Beamon, Bob 341
Beatles **232**, *232*, **240**, **244**, *244*, **246**, *246*
Béatrix, princesse **243**, *243*
Beckenbauer, Franz 242
Becker, Boris **305**, *305*
Becquerel, Henri 19
Bee Gees 279
Begin, Menahem **282**, *282*, **285**
Belgique **36**, **328**
  droit de vote des femmes 173
  Exposition universelle **211**
  Guerre mondiale (première) **52**, **55**
  Guerre mondiale (seconde) **142**, **161**
Belyaev, Pavel 261
Ben Bella, Ahmed **196**, **227**
Ben Kheddah, Benyoussef 227
Benenson, Peter 224
Bennett, Floyd 93
Berbick, Trevor 307

INDEX

Bérégovoy, Pierre 329
Bergman, Ingrid 152
Bergson, Henri 65
Berlin, Irving 46
Bernhardt, Sarah **83**, *83*
Berry, Chuck **246**, *246*
Best, Charles **73**, *73*
Beymer, Richard 223
Bhutto, Benazir **313**, *313*
Bhutto, Zulfikar Ali **278**, *278*, 313
Biafra **244**, 253
Biao, Lin 252
Bielmann, Denise *340*
Bikila, Abebe 221
Biko, Steve **279**
Bingham, Hiram **47**, *47*
Birdseye, Clarence 106
Bíró, Lazlo 135
Black Panthers **242**
Black, Davidson 97
Blair, Tony 343, **344**
Blériot, Louis **20**, *20*, **38**, *38*
Bleyl, Fritz 27
Blum, Léon 127, **130**
Blunt, Anthony **230**, *230*
Boers, guerres des **9**, 30
Bogart, Humphrey 152
Bohr, Niels **76**, *76*
Boileau 131
Bokassa, Jean Bedel **284**
bolcheviques 60, 62, **69**
Bolivie 245
Böll, Heinrich **273**
Bonner, Elena **323**
Bonnevial, Marie 42
Bonnot, Jules Joseph **49**
Booth, Hubert Cecil **15**
Borg, Björn **291**, *291*
Borghese, prince 33
Borman, James 261
Borotra, Jean 111
Bosnie 52, **326**, *326*, 333
Bosnie-Herzégovine 35
Botha, Louis *42*
Boucher, Hélène **111**
Boudarine 337
Bouin, Jean **47**
Boukharine 85
Bourguiba, Habib 202
Bouton 33
boxe **35**, 172, **203**, **215**, **237**, **273**, **307**
Boyd, Stephen 215
Braga, Téofilo 41
Brando, Marlon **217**, 232
Brandt, Alfred 29
Brandt, Willy **222**, 243, 252, **264**
Braque, Georges 49
Brazaville, conférence de 161
Brecht, Bertolt 115
Brejnev, Leonid **234**, 267, *267*
Brésil **221**
Breton, André 85
Breuer, Marcel 87
Briand, Aristide 89, **98**
Briand-Kellog, pacte 98
Brown, Arthur 67
Brückner *117*
Brugnon 111

Brundtland, Gro harlem 293
Bryan, William **86**, *86*
Budge, J. Donald **134**, *134*
Buffalo Bill 61
Burgess, Guy 185
Burnham, Daniel H. 16
Burns, Tommy 35
Burroughs, Edgar Rice 53, 65
Burundi 265
Bush, George **312**, *312*, 327
Butts, Alfred 108
Byrd, Richard **93**, *93*
Byrds 251

C

Cadolle, Herminie 52
Caetano, Marcello 272
Calder, Alexandre **111**, *111*
Callas, Maria **188**, *188*
Calloway, Cab 94
Calment, Jeanne **345**, *345*
Calmette, Albert 73
Cambodge **256**, 282
Camp David, accords de **282**
Campbell, Malcolm **122**, *122*
Camus, Albert **221**
Canada 213
Cannon, Lilian 92
Capek, Karel 70
Capone, Al 68, **103**, *103*
Cardenas, Lazaro **118**, *118*
Carlos, Juan 274
Carlu 131
Carmichael, Stokeley 242
Carmona 97
Carnavon, lord 74, 81
Carné, Marcel 132
Carpentier, Georges 47
carte postale **25**
Carter, Howard **74**, *74*
Carter, Jimmy 183, **276**, 291, 294
Cartier 50
Carton, Marcel 324
Caruso, Enrico **22**, *22*, 246
Cassidy, David **266**, *266*
Cassin, René 170
Castro, Fidel **212**, *212*, 223, 245, *245*
Ceausescu, Nicolae et Elena **316**, *316*
CECA 184
CEE, **207**, *207*, 265, 270
Centrafrique **284**
centrale hydroélectrique **75**, *75*, **303**, *303*
Cerdan, Marcel **172**, *172*
Ceylan, voir Sri Lanka
Cézanne, Paul 32
Chagall, Marc 304
Chaillot 129

Chamberlain, Arthur Neville **132**, *132*
Chandler, Raymond 214
Chanel 95
Chanel, Coco **72**
Chaplin, Charlie **66**, *66*, **72**, *72*, 108, **142**, *142*
Chapman, Mark 289
Charcot, Jean-Baptiste **44**, 45
Charles Ier 65
Charles, prince **292**, *292*, 344
Charpentier 129
Che Guevara, Ernesto 212, **245**, *245*
Chevalier, Maurice 157
Chiang Ching 277
Chili 270
Chine
  Boxers, révolte des **9**, 36
  conflit sino-indien 227
  « Grand Bond en avant » **210**
  guerre sino-japonaise 130
  Guomindang **86**, **96**, 116
  Longue Marche **116**, 123
  Mandchourie, **11**, *11*
  Nixon, visite de 265
  république 46
  république populaire **176**
  révolution culturelle 240
  Tian'anmen **317**, *317*
chips 50
Chirac, Jacques 276, 279, **336**, *336*, 337, 338, 342, 343
Choltitz, général von 161
Chopinet, Anne 265
Chou En-laï 265, 277
Chrétien, Henri 192
Christie, Agatha **70**, *70*, 206
Christo 305
Chun 46
Churchill, Winston **144**, *144*, 149, 151, *151*, 165, *165*, 167, *167*, **191**, 239, *239*, 323
Chypre
  guerre civile 235
  indépendance 220
cinéma **140-141**, **298-299**
  2001 : l'Odyssée de l'espace **249**, *249*
  À l'est d'Eden 200
  Amadeus 304
  Arrêt d'autobus 227
  Artistes associés 66
  Autant en emporte le vent 137
  Babe 336
  Baby Burlesks 122
  Baisers volés 251
  Bataille du rail 166
  Batman 317
  Ben Hur **90**, 215
  Cannes, festival de 166
  Casablanca 152
  Certains l'aiment chaud 227

  Chanteur de jazz **97**
  Chantons sous la pluie 187
  cinémaScope **192**, *192*
  Citizen Kane 148
  Cuirasssé Potemkine **24**, 87
  Easy Rider 251
  effets spéciaux **298-299**
  ET 297
  Et Dieu créa la femme 205
  Fenêtre sur cour **199**, 297
  Fièvre du samedi soir 279
  film parlant **97**
  Géant 200
  Go West 89
  Guerre des étoiles, 279
  Her first biscuits 38
  Hollywood **47**, **141**
  James Bond 229
  Jules et Jim 226
  King Kong 115
  l'Ange bleu 107
  l'Équipée sauvage 217
  La Fureur de vivre 200, 217
  La Joyeuse divorcée 119
  la Liste de Schindler 329
  La Mélodie du bonheur 239
  La naissance d'une nation 55
  la Symphonie pastorale 166
  Le cabinet du docteur Caligari 71
  Le Corbeau 158
  Le Dictateur 142
  Le Kid 72
  le Lys des champs 235
  Le voyage dans la Lune 17
  Les Désaxés 227
  Love Story 257
  Mary Poppins 2329
  Metropolis 92
  nickelodeons **14**, *14*
  Nosferatu le Vampire 75
  Oscars **102**, 235, 304
  Psychose 219
  Quai des brumes 132
  Schow Boat 185
  Tarzan, seigneur des singes 65
  The Great Train Robbery **18**, *18*
  Titanic 347
  Une nuit à l'opéra 128
  Vacances de M. Hulot 192
  Warner Bros 82
  West Side Story **223**, *223*
Clapton, Eric 247
Clay, Casius 221, **237**, *237*
Cleaver, Eldridge 242
Clemenceau, Georges 35, **63**, *63*
Clément, René 166
Clinton, William J. **327**, *327*, 328, 332, 347, *347*

Clouzot, Henri 158
Coca-Cola **58**, *58*
Cochet, Henri 111
Coe, Sebastian 290
Cohn-Bendit, Daniel 248
Collins, Joan **294**
Collins, Michael 72
Colosimo, Jim 68
Comaneci, Nadia **277**, *277*, 341
comédie musicale 206
  Jésus-Christ superstar 262
  Oklahoma 158
Commonwealth 91
Congo 35, **223**
Connally, John 233
Connery, Sean **229**, *229*
Connolly, Maureen **193**, *193*
Conrad, Charles 258
consommation **208-209**
continents, dérive des **49**
Coogan, Jackie 72
Cook 39
Copeau, Jacques 38
Coppi, Fausto **177**, *177*
Corée 40
  Corée du Sud 308
  Corée, guerre de 180
corn flakes **29**
Cornu, Paul 33
Costa, Lucio 221
Coty, René 192, 211
Coubertin, Pierre de 36, 73, 84
crédit, carte de **178**
Crick, Francis Harry Compton **193**, *193*, **331**
crise économique **110**
Crum 50
Cuba **212**
  baie des Cochons 223
  crise de **228**
Cunningham, Glenn 129
Curcio, Renato 286
Curie, Marie **19**, *19*, 42, 47
Curie, Pierre **19**, *19*,
Curren, Kevin 305
Curtiz, Michael 152
Cyclisme
  Tour de France **19**, 177, **259**, 285, 305, 309, 347
  Tour d'Italie (Giro) 177, 259
Czolgosz 14

D

D'Annunzio, Gabriele **67**, *67*
Dac, Pierre 79
Daladier, Édouard 132
danse **27**
  ballet **46**, **51**, 131
  charleston **95**, *95*
  cake-walk **8**, *8*
  école 93
  Kirov, ballet 225
  marathon 80
  pogo **281**
Darnand 148

353

Darrow, Clarence 86
Darwin, Charles 86
Davis, Dwight Filley 10
Dayan, Moshe 245
DDT 138, *138*
De Chirico, Giorgio 88
De Gaulle, Charles 79, *79*, 144, **145**, *145*, 152, 159, 161, *161*, 166, *211*, **211**, 227, 229, 232, **249**, 238, 253, **258**, *258*
De Klerk, 318, 319, 332
démocratie populaire 172
De Valera, Eamon 72
Dean, James **200**, *200*, 216, *216*, 217, *217*
Debré, Michel 229
décolonisation **194-195**
Delannoy, Jean 166
Deschanel, Paul 71
Desgrange, Henri 19
Despeaux 129
dessin animé
  Blanche-Neige et les sept nains **134**
  Fantasia 243
  Gallopin' Gaucho 100
  La petite poule sage 116
  Les 101 Dalmatiens **224**, *224*
  Pinocchio 243
  Plane Crazy 100
  Steamboat Willie 100
Dewey, Thomas 172
Diaghilev, Serge de 46
Diana, princesse **292**, *292*, **337**, *337*, **342**, *342*, 343
Diaz, Porfirio 42, 47, 118
Diefenbaker, John 213
Dietrich, Marlene **107**, *107*, **160**, *160*
DiMaggio, Joe **104**, *104*, **199**, *199*, 227
Dion, de 33
Dior, Christian **174**, 229
Dire Straits 304
Disney, Walt **100**, 116, 134, **141**, *141*, 201, 224, **243**
Dix, Otto **87**, *87*
Djibouti 277, 279
Dollfuss, Engelbert 111, 115, **116**
Dolly **330**, *330*
Doren, Van 212
Dos Santos 327
Doumer, Paul 108, 111
Doyen, Eugène Louis 17
Dreyfus, Alfred 28
Drinker, Philip 99
Du Bois, William Edward Burghart **43**, *43*
Dubcek, Alexandre 249
Duchamp, Marcel 59, **60**, 88
Dukakis, Michael 312
Dumont d'Urville 45
Dunant, Henri 13
Duncan, Isadora 97
During, Peter 188
Duvalier, Jean-Claude (Baby Doc) **307**, *307*
Dylan, Bob 217, 232, **239**, *239*, 247

E

arp, Wyatt **103**, *103*
Ebert, Friedrich 65
Ederle, Gertrud **92**, *92*
Edimbourg, duc d' 192
Edison, Thomas 17, **109**, *109*
Edouard VII 17, 28, 42
Edouard VIII **127**, *127*
Égypte 293
  Assouan, barrage d'**17**, *17*, 173, 234
  Farouk, abdication de **187**, *187*
  indépendance 129
  Néfertiti **49**, *49*
  Suez, crise de **203**
  Toutankhamon 74
Eichmann, Adolf **225**, *225*
Einstein, Albert 26, 73, 115, 184
Eisenhower, Dwight 160, 202, 207, 212, *213*, 219
Eisenstein, Sergueï 87
élastique, saut **321**, *321*
Élisabeth II 36, **192**, *192*, **213**, *213*, 240, 271, 332
Ellington, Duke 94, **100**, *100*
Eltsine, Boris 324, 328
Empire ottoman (voir Turquie)
empreinte digitale **15**, *15*
environnement **268-269**, **289**, **324**, **326**, **342**
  ozone **269**, 309
Erhard, Ludwig 243
Ernst, Max 88
Éruption volcanique
  Colombie **304**, *304*
  Italie **29**, *29*
  Martinique 17
espace **260-261**
  Apollo 245, **275**
  Apollo 11 250
  Apollo 13 **258**, *258*
  Atlantis **337**, *337*
  Challenger 301, **306**, *306*
  Columbia **295**, *295*
  Diapason 240
  Discovery 347
  Explorer 210
  extraterrestre 320
  Gemini 6 261
  Gemini 7 261
  Hubble, télescope de **339**
  Laïka **206**, *206*
  Lune **236**, *236*, **250**, *250*
  Lunik 3 **214**, *214*
  Mariner 2 **226**, *226*
  Mir **337**, *337*
  Odyssey **258**, *258*
  Pathfinder **345**
  Ranger 7 **236**
  Sojourner **345**, *345*
  Soyouz 275
  Spacelab 347
  Spoutnik 1 **206**, *206*
  Spoutnik 2 **206**, *206*
  Telstar **226**, *226*
  Tiros I 220
  Vostok 1, 223
Espagne 279, 293
  Front populaire **126**
  Guernica, bombardement de **131**, *131*
  guerre civile **126**, 139
  république 109
espionnage 230-231
États-Unis 190
  Grande-Bretagne 185
ETA 286
États-Unis
  air conditionné 135
  Alaska 212
  attentat **329**, **335**, *335*
  avion U2 **219**, *219*
  centre commercial **199**, *199*
  débarquement à la Grenade 301
  discrimination raciale 237
  Disneyland **201**, *201*
  Disneyworld **263**, *263*
  droit des citoyens 43
  émeutes 327
  émigration 30
  Europe 167
  Guerre mondiale (deuxième) **148**, 159
  Guerre mondiale (première) 54, 60
  Hawaii 212
  hymne 109
  Indiens **117**, **271**, *271*
  MacCarthysme 181
  MacDonald's 173, 209
  Maison-Blanche 15
  manifestation **245**, **257**, 263
  marche de la liberté **224**
  neutralité 139
  Nevada 109
  New Deal 110, **115**
  New York 11, 112, *112*, 239
  nucléaire 184
  panne de courant 239
  plan Marshall 168
  prohibition 68
  racisme 228
  Rushmore, mont **150**, *150*
  ségrégation **202**, 207
  signalisation routière 97
  suffragette **71**, *71*
  Waco, secte de 329
  Wall Street, krack de 102
  Watergate 272
Éthiopie 107, **123**, 129
Europe **329**, 348
  CEE, **207**, *207*, 265, **270**
  conseil 177
Marché commun 232
Evans, Arthur 9
Everest 190

F

abius, Laurent **302**
Fairbanks, Douglas 66, *66*
Fallières, Armand 28
famine 290
Fangio, Juan Manuel 179, **207**, *207*
Farina, Giuseppe **179**, *179*
Farouk **187**, *187*
Farrell, Maired 310
fascisme **120-121**
Fatima, apparition à 61
Faubus, Orval 207
Filipacchi, Daniel 216
Finlande **32**, 139
Fischer, Bobby **264**
Fixx, James **302**, *302*
Fleming, Alexander **98**, *98*
Fleming, Ian 229
FLN 196
Flynn, John 98
Foch, maréchal 63, 64, 65
Fokine, Michel 27
Fonda, Peter 251
Fontaine, Marcel 324
Fonteyn, Margot **131**, *131*
football **104-105**, 263, 317, 333
  Europe, Coupe d' 221
  monde, Coupe du **105**, 117, 132, 179, 199, 226, 241, 242, 258, 282, 297, 320, 347
Ford, Henry 19, 34
Forget, Guy 325
Forman, Milos 304
Fouad Ier 76
France
  1er mai 67
  agitation sociale **169**
  Algérie **196**, 227
  Algésiras, conférence d' 29
  ANPE 245
  appel du 18 juin **145**
  argent, mur d' 93
  aviation 20, 38, 51
  Bobigny, procès de 265
  bombardement 65
  Bonnot, bande à 49
  Cartel des Gauches 84, 93
  catastrophe minière 28
  colonie 220
  Diên Biên Phu 194, 196, 197, *197*
  Disneyland 326
  Eiffel, tour 8
  émeutes 119
  Entente cordiale 23
  Guerre mondiale (première) **52**, 53, 58, 63, 64, 66
  Évian, accords d' 227
  Exposition internationale des arts et techniques de la vie moderne **131**
  exposition Toutankhamon 245
  Exposition universelle 8, 8, 15
  FLNC 276
  Front populaire **127**
  Genève, accords de 196, 197
  grève 35
  Guerre mondiale (deuxième) 134, **143**, **145**, 148, 150, 152, 160, 161
  hypermarché 209
  Indochine, guerre de **194**, 197
  journées mondiales de la jeunesse **342**, *342*
  Mai 68, 248
  marée noire 283
  natalité 68, 111
  Nouveau Salon d'Automne 25
  nucléaire 220
  otages 324
  Paris 8, 9, 46, 316
  Rainbow Warrior, affaire **305**
  Renault, usines 167
  Résistance **152**, 156
  Roudy, loi 296
  suffragette 42
  traité franco-allemand **232**
  travail 11
  V[e] république 166, **211**
  Veil, loi 273
  Vichy, régime de 143, 144
Franco **120**, *120*, 126, 129, **274**, *274*
François-Ferdinand, assassinat **52**, *52*
Freud, Sigmund **10**, *10*, 139
Frank, Anne **154**, *154*
Franklin, Aretha 247
Freed, Allan 186
Frisch, Karl von 270
Fuchs, Klaus **230**, *230*
Fulton, Robert 197

G

able, Clarck 137
Gagarine, Iouri **223**, *223*, **260**, *260*
Gallieni, général 53
Gallienne, pasteur 43
Gallimard, Gaston 38
Gallimard, Michel 221
Gallup **123**, *123*
Gance, Abel 97
Gandhi, Mohandas Karamchand **106**, 111,*106*, **171**, *171*, 195
Gandhi, Indira **243**, *243*, **303**, *303*
Gandhi, Rajiv, 303, *303*
Gapone, Gueorgui 24
Garbo, Greta **140**, 319
Gardner, Ava 185
Garin, Maurice **19**, *19*
Garland, Judy *141*, 232
Garrison, Zina 319
Garros, Roland 51, 63
Gates, Bill *315*
Gaudi, Antonio 91
Gaye, Marvin 247, 303
Geldof, Bob **304**, *304*
Gênes, conférence de 75
génétique **330-331**

INDEX

génocide **154-155**
George VI **187**
George, Lloyd **75**, *75*
Georget **129**
Gerhardt, Charles **18**
Geronimo **39**, *39*
Gershwin, George **85**, *85*
Ghana **241**
Giap, général **197**
Gibbon, Heynsham **188**
Gibson, colonel *158*
Gide, André **38**
Gillepsie, Dizzy **165**, *165*
Gillette, King Camp **12**
Ginnah **195**
Giscard d'Estaing, Valéry **273**, **338**
glace **23**
Glenn, John **347**, *347*
Goddard, Robert **101**
Godse, Nathuram **171**
Goering, Hermann **114**, **166**, *166*
Goldenmark, Peter **173**
golf **259**
Goodman, Benny **133**, *133*
Gorbatchev, Mikhail **304**, **308**, *308*, **311**, **312**, **320**, *320*, **322**, *322*, **323**, **324**
Gordy, Berry **247**
Gore, A. W. **10**
Gore, Al **327**
Goscinny, René **125**, **224**, *224*
Gottwald, Klement **172**, *172*
Gourion, Ben *170*
Grabble, Betty **159**, *159*
Graham, Martha **93**
Grande-Bretagne
　Aberfan **242**, *241*
　automobile **29**
　chômage **126**
　droit de vote **63**
　droit des femmes **275**
　Dunblane **339**, *339*
　éclipse **97**
　émeutes **293**
　Entente cordiale **23**
　État-providence **173**
　exposition britannique **185**
　Guerre mondiale (deuxième) **134**, **145**, **149**, **151**, **161**
　Guerre mondiale (première) **52**, **59**, **61**, **64**
　hold-up **233**
　manifestation **321**, *321*
　marée noire **245**
　marine **28**
　Mods et Rockers **237**, *237*
　morue, guerre de la **215**
　nucléaire **203**
　pollution **205**
　sécurité routière **89**
　smog **189**
　suffragettes **19**, **37**, **63**
　travail **11**
　Union nationale **109**
　variole, épidémie de **226**
Grèce **149**, **273**
Greer, Germaine **259**, *259*
Grenade, île de la **301**, *301*
Griffith, D. W. **55**, *55*
Griffith, Arthur **72**
Griffith, David W. **38**, **66**, *66*
Griffith-Joyner, Florence *341*
Gropius, Walter **87**
Grosse Bertha **62**, *62*
Grotewohl, Otto **176**
Groves, général **162**
Guérin, Camille **73**
Guerre mondiale (deuxième)
　armistice **165**
　Atlantique, charte de l' **151**
　attaques alliées **158**
　Barbarossa, opération **149**
　Belgique, invasion **142**
　Blitzkrieg **142**
　camp de concentration **152**, **155**, **164**
　civils **146-147**
　Collaboration **148**
　débarquement **160**, *160*, **161**
　déclaration de guerre **144**
　Dieppe **153**
　Dresde **165**, *165*
　Dynamo, opération **143**
　El-Alamein **153**, *153*
　Enigma **150**
　étoile jaune **150**, *150*
　évacuation **147**, *147*
　gestapo **152**, **157**, **159**
　ghetto **155**, *155*
　invasion de la France **143**
　Italie, capitulation **158**
　Japon **159**, **164**
　Leningrad, siège de **160**
　Lip, usine **270**
　Londres **161**
　Midway, bataille des **153**
　Nuremberg, procès de **166**
　Otarie, opération **145**
　Paris, libération de **161**, *161*
　Pearl Harbor **148**, *148*
　préparatifs **134**
　rationnement, ticket de **147**
　Résistance **152**
　Singapour, capitulation de **153**
　Stalingrad, bataille de **157**, *157*
　Téhéran, conférence de **159**
　Traité de paix russo-finlandais **144**
　villes **146**, *146*
　Yalta, conférence de **165**
Guerre mondiale (première)
　14 points **65**
　armistice **64**, **66**
　Brest-Litovsk, traité de **62**, *62*
　Caporetto **61**
　civils **56-57**
　Dardanelles, détroit des **55**, *55*
　déclaration **52**, **53**
　Entente **52**, **54**
　États-Unis, entrée en guerre des **60**
　Flandres, bataille des **61**
　guerre de position **53**
　Italie, entrée en guerre de l' **54**
　Jutland, bataille navale du **59**
　Londres **61**
　Lusitania, torpillage du **54**
　Marne, bataille de la **53**, *53*
　Marne, deuxième bataille de la **63**
　mobilisation **52**
　Neuilly, traité de **70**
　propagande **54**
　rationnement **56**
　Saint-Germain, traité de **70**
　Sambre, bataille de la **52**
　Schlieffen, plan **53**
　Sèvres, traité de **70**
　Somme, bataille de la **59**
　Tannenberg **52**
　Trianon, traité de **70**
　Triplice **52**
　Verdun, bataille de **58**, *58*
　Versailles, traité de **66**, **129**
　Ypres, bataille d' **55**
Guillaume II **64**
Guofeng, Hua **277**
Gustave V **33**
Guyana **283**
Guynemer, Georges **63**

H

Haakon VII de norvège **25**, *25*
Hadden, Briton **83**
Hagen, Jean **187**
Hagenbeck, Carl **32**
Haig, Douglas **61**
Hailé Sélassié **107**, *107*, **123**
Hair **280**
Haise, Fred **258**
Haïti **307**, **333**
Hajek, Jiri **278**
Hale-Boop, comète **343**, *343*
Halimi, Gisèle **265**
Halley, Bill **197**, *197*
Halley, comète de **40**, *40*, **306**, *306*
Halley, Edmond **40**, **306**
Hallyday, Johnny **222**, *222*
hamburger **11**, *11*
Hamilton, Thomas **339**
Hammarskjöld, Dag **222**, *222*
Hammerstein **185**
Hanau, Marthe **101**
Handler, Ruth **213**
Handy, W.C. **27**, *27*
Hanks, Tom **299**
Harding, Warren **69**
Hardy, Oliver **140**
Harlem Globe-trotters **98**
Havel, Vaclav **278**, **322**, *322*
Haw-Haw, lord **79**
Hayek, Nicolas **300**
Heckel, Erich **27**
Heidemann, Gerd *301*
Held, Anna **31**
Helsinki, accords d' **274**
Hémery, Victor **39**
Hendrix, Jimi **247**, **251**, **252**, **259**
Henie, Sonja **127**
Henreid, Paul **152**
Henson, Matt **45**
Hergé **102**
Herrick, James **40**
Hess, Rudolf **151**, *151*, **166**, *166*
Heston, Charlton **215**
Heyerdahl, Thor **168**
Hillary, Edmund **190**, *190*
Hilsz, Maryse **111**, *111*
Himmler, Heinrich
Hinault, Bernard **285**, **305**, *305*
Hinckley, John **292**
Hindenburg, dirigeable **130**, *130*
Hindenburg, général **52**, **64**, **88**, **111**, **114**, **118**
hippie **280**, *281*
Hirobumi, Ito **38**
Hirohito **91**, *91*
Hiroshima **186**
Hitchcock, Alfred **199**, **219**
Hitler **83**, **87**, **107**, **116**, **117**, **118**, **120**, *120*, **123**, **127**, *127*, **129**, **132**, **136**, **137**, *137*, **138**, **139**, **143**, **148**, **157**, **161**, **165**, **301**
Hô Chi Minh **181**, *181*, **194**, **197**, **250**, *250*, **256**
Hong-Kong **344**, *344*
Hongrie **181**
　Budapest, insurrection de **204**
　Guerre mondiale (première) **53**, **70**
Hoover, Herbert **108**, **110**
Hopper, Dennis **251**
Hornby, Franck **10**
Horne, Lean **94**
Hoskins, Bob **299**, *299*
Hostin **129**
Houdini, Harry **93**, *93*
Hounsfield, Godfrey **267**
Hsien Feng **36**
Hubble, Edwin **102**
Hugues, Howard **266**
Hurst, Geoff **242**
Hussein, Saddam **290**, **320**, *320*, **324**
Hussein de Jordanie **347**

302, *302*
conflit sino-indien **227**
impôt sur le sel **81**
marche **106**
partition **195**
peste **33**
Indochine
　décolonisation **181**
　guerre de **166**
informatique **207**, **256**, **274**, **314-315**, **335**
inondation
　Bangladesh **311**, *311*
　Florence **242**, *242*
　Grande-Bretagne **188**
　Paris **41**
　Pays-Bas **193**
Internet **328**
Interpol **83**
invention
　aspirateur **15**
　Cellophane **35**
　congélation **106**
　micro-ondes, four à **170**, *170*
　grille-pain **38**, *38*
　Lépine, concours **13**
　magnétoscope **266**, *266*
　polyéthylène **138**
　rasoir **99**
　réfrigérateur **50**
　stylo à bille **135**
Ioussoupov **59**
Irak **293**, **320**, **324**
Iran **284**, **285**, **294**
Iran-Irak, guerre **290**, **313**
Irlande **59**, **72**, **251**, **264**, **294**, **321**, **345**
　IRA **72**, **287**, **310**, *310*, **332**, **345**
　Sinn Fein **72**, **287**, **332**
Islande
　morue, guerre de la **215**
Israël **251**, **275**, **276**, **296**, **328**
　création **170**
　Jérusalem **236**
　Kippour, guerre du **271**
　Six Jours, guerre des **245**, **252**
Issigonis, Alec **215**
Italie
　attentat **288**
　Brigades rouges **283**, **286**
　Chemises noires **77**
　Fiume **67**
　Guerre mondiale (deuxième) **153**, **158**
　Guerre mondiale (première) **54**, **61**
　marche sur Rome **77**
　république
　Seveso, catastrophe de **277**
Izetbegovic **336**

J

Jacklin, Tony **259**, *259*
Jackson Five **247**
Jackson, frères **266**
Jackson, Michael **266**

I

Inde **169**, **243**
　Calcutta **93**
　catastrophe écologique

Jacob, Mary Phelps **52**
Jahn, Gunnar *238*
Jannings, Emil *102*
Japon
 annexion de la Corée **40**
 bombe atomique *162*, **164**
 empereur **91**, *91*
 guerre contre la Russie **22**
 Guerre mondiale (deuxième) *148*, *159*, **164**
 Guerre mondiale (première) *53*
 guerre sino-japonaise **130**
 Hirobumi, Ito **38**
 secte **337**
 Tokyo **112**
Jarman, Nelly **36**, *36*
Jaruzelski, général *295*
Jaurès, Jean *53*, *84*
Jean XXIII **215**, *233*
Jean-Paul Ier *282*
Jean-Paul II **283**, *283*, **295**, *295*, *342*
Jellicoe, John *59*
Jellinek, Émile *13*
Jenner, Edward *291*
jeunesse, auberge de *39*
jeux
 Barbie, poupée **213**, *213*
 Buzz **338**, *338*
 échecs **264**, *333*
 Hula-hoop **210**, *210*, **216**
 informatique **315**, *315*
 Meccano **10**
 Monopoly **117**, *117*
 patin à roulettes *43*
 puzzle *47*
 Rubik-cube **288**, *288*
 scrabble **108**, *108*
 Teddy bear (ours en peluche) **19**, *19*
jeux féminins mondiaux **73**
jeux Olympiques **340-341**
 Amsterdam **101**
 Atlanta **338**
 Berlin **129**
 Chamonix *84*
 Cortina d'Ampezzo **203**
 Helsinki **189**
 Londres *36*
 Los Angeles **303**
 Melbourne *205*
 Mexico **249**
 Montréal **277**
 Moscou **290**
 Munich **264**, *265*
 Paris **11**, *36*, *84*
 Rome **221**
 Saint-Louis *36*
 Séoul **311**
 Stockholm *48*, **49**, *205*
Jiang, Qing **293**, *293*
Jobs, Steve *315*
Joffre, général *53*, *53*
Johansen, Wilhelm *39*
Johensson, Ingemar **215**, *215*
John, Elton *175*, *342*, *343*
Johns, Jasper **199**

Johnson, Ben **311**, *311*
Johnson, Jack **35**, *35*
Johnson, L. B. **237**, *237*
Joliot-Curie, Frédéric *123*, *173*
Joliot-Curie, Irène *123*
Jolson, Al **97**, *97*
Jones, Jim *283*
Joplin, Janis *252*
Jordan, Michael **349**, *349*
Jordan, Mimi *210*
Jordanie *58*, *257*
Jorgensen, Christine **187**, *187*
Joselito **71**, *71*
Jospin, Lionel *336*, *343*, *345*
Joxe, Louis *227*
juif *107*, *114*, *115*, **120**, *121*, *122*, *123*, **132**, *133*, *145*, *147*, *150*, **154-155**, *156*, *164*, *225*
Juppé, Alain *337*

K

Kadhafi **253**, *253*
Kahlo, Frieda *128*
Kalinine *85*
Kamenev, Lev *82*, *85*
Kandinsky, Wassily **41**, *87*
Kantrowitz, Adirn *244*
Kasparov *333*
Kästner, Erich *101*
Keaton, Buster *89*
Keaton, Michael *317*
Keim, Betty Lou *216*
Keitel, maréchal *165*
Keller, Helen **23**, *23*
Kellerman, Annette *175*
Kellog, Frank B. *98*
Kellog, William **29**, *29*
Kelly, Gene *187*
Kelly, Grace **199**, **205**, *205*, **297**, *297*
Kemal, Mustafa **80**, *80*, *132*
Kennedy *228*, *228*, *254*
 assassinat **233**, *233*
 mariage **191**, *191*
 président **218**, *218*
 rencontre avec Khrouchtchev *225*
Kennedy, Jackie **191**, *191*, **218**, *218*, **233**, *233*, *248*
Kennedy, Robert *224*, **248**, *248*
Kenney, Annie *37*
Kent, Bruce *300*
Kenya *188*, *220*, *233*
Kern *185*
Kerouac, Jack **207**, *207*
Kessel, Joseph *157*
Key, Francis Scott *109*
Khan, Muhammed Yahia *262*
Khasboulatov, *328*
Khomeyni, Ruhollah *284*, *290*, *294*, *316*, **317**
Khrouchtchev, Nikita **204**, *204*, **213**, *213*, *219*, *225*, *228*, **234**, *234*, *261*

Kiesinger, Georg *243*
Killy, Jean-Claude *340*
Kim Il-sung *180*
King, Elmo *65*
Kingsley *329*
Kipling, Rudyard **31**
Kirchner, Ernst Ludwig *27*
Klee, Paul *87*, *88*
Knerr, Richard *210*
Kohl, Helmut **297**
Kolff, Willem **159**
Kon-Tiki **168**, *168*
Koresh, David **329**
Kosovo *348*
Kossyguine, Aleksëi *234*
Koweit **320**, *324*
Kremlin *231*
Ku Klux Klan **55**, *55*, *224*
Kubrick, Stanley *249*
Kujau, Konrad *301*
Kutchuk, docteur *220*
Kuznetsov, Vassili *214*

L

Labouisse, Henri *238*
Lacoste, *111*
Laïka **206**, *206*
Lambert, comte de *38*
Lamm, Franck *29*
Lancaster, Burt *232*
Land, Edwin **171**, *171*
Landsteiner, Karl *142*
Lang, Fritz **92**
Lanvin, Jeanne *95*
Lapébie *129*
Latham, Hubert *38*
Latran, accords de *103*
Laurel, Stan *140*
Lawrence, Thomas Edward *58*, *58*
Le Baron Jenney, William *16*
Le Corbusier *97*, **186**, *186*
Leakey, Louis **225**, *225*
Leakey, Mary *225*
Léaud, Jean-Pierre *251*
Lebrun, Albert *131*
Leclerc, général *161*
Leconte, Henri *325*
Leeson, Nick **336**, *336*
Leigh, Janet **219**, *219*
Leigh, Vivien *137*
LeMond, Greg *305*
Lenglen, Suzanne, **81**, *81*
Lénine, Vladimir *60*, **82**, *82*, **85**, *85*, *204*
Lennon, John **289**, *289*
Leonov, Aleksëi *238*, *260*, *275*
Léopold II *35*, *36*
Leopold III *185*
Lépine, Louis *13*
Leprince-Ringuet, Louis *240*
Levegh, Pierre *201*
Lewis, Carl **303**, *303*
Liban *275*, **296**
 Beyrouth, *275*, *275*, *296*
 otage *324*
 Sabra et Chatila, camps de *296*

Libby, Williard *168*
Libye *253*
Liddell, Eric *84*
Lilienthal, Otto **20**, *20*
Lincoln, Elmo *65*
Lindbergh, Charles **96**, *96*
Lindgren, Astrid *164*
Lippman, Gabriel *35*
Liston, Charles Sonny *237*
Littérature
 1984 *176*
 À l'ombre des jeunes filles en fleurs *77*
 À l'ouest, rien de nouveau *103*
 À la recherche du temps perdu *77*
 Au-dessus de la mêlée *55*
 Aventures de Huckleberry Finn *43*
 Aventures de Tom Sawyer *43*
 Bas les armes ! *26*
 Capitaine courageux *31*
 Docteur Jivago *211*
 Dracula *75*
 Du côté de chez Swann *77*
 Du spirituel dans l'art *41*
 Émile et les détectives **101**
 Fifi Brindacier **164**, *164*
 Germinal *17*
 Histoire de ma vie *23*
 Histoire de Pierre le lapin *16*
 Histoires comme ça *31*
 Journal d'Anne Franck **154**, *154*, **187**, *187*
 Kim *31*
 l'Attrape-cœur *185*
 l'Étranger *221*
 l'Homme révolté *221*
 l'Interprétation des rêves **10**
 la Condition humaine *115*
 La mystérieuse affaire de Styles *70*
 la Peste *221*
 le Grand Meaulnes *55*
 le livre de la jungle *31*
 le Malentendu *221*
 le mythe de Sisyphe *221*
 le Petit Prince *156*
 le second Livre de la Jungle *31*
 Lennon, John *289*
 Lénine see above
 Manifeste du surréalisme *85*
 Mémoires de guerre *191*
 Sur la route **207**
 Versets sataniques *317*
 Winnie l'ourson *90*
Lloyd, Harold *141*
Locarno, conférence de *89*, *129*
Lorenz, Konrad **270**, *270*
Loubet, Émile *8*
Loucheur, loi *99*
Louvre, musée du *47*
Lovell, James *258*, *261*
Lovelock, Jack *129*
Lucas, George *279*, *298*

Luce, Henry *83*
Lucy, Autherine *202*
Ludendorff *83*
Lumière, Louis *33*
Lumumba, Patrice **223**, *223*
Lustiger, monseigneur *342*
Luther King, Martin *20*, *224*, **232**, *232*, *236*, *237*, **249**
Lyssenko, Vladimir **173**

M

Maastricht, traité de **329**
MacArthur Douglas *180*, **180**, *184*, **184**
MacCarthy, Joseph R. **181**, *181*
MacDonald, Ramsay *109*
Macédoine *34*
MacGraw, Ali *257*
Machen, Eddie *215*
MacKenzie King, William *73*
MacLean, Donald *185*, **230**, *230*
MacNamara, Frank *178*
Madero, Francisco *42*, *118*
Madonna *247*, **301**, *304*
Magic Johnson **339**, *339*
Maginot, André *107*, *136*
Maginot, ligne *107*, **136**, *136*
Maison-Blanche *15*
Makarios, monseigneur *220*, **273**
Malan, Daniel François *171*, *179*
Malcom X **238**, *238*
Malouines, guerre des **296**, *296*
Malraux, André *115*
Mandchourie **11**, *11*, **108**
Mandela, Nelson **236**, *236*, **318**, *318*, **332**, *332*
Mandela, Winnie *318*
Man Ray **59**, *59*, *88*
Mann, Thomas *115*
Manson, Charles **251**, *251*
Manuel, roi du Portugal *41*
Mao Zédong *96*, *116*, **116**, *176*, *176*, *179*, **210**, *210*, *240*, *265*, **265**, *277*, **277**
Marciano, Rocky **203**, *203*
Marcioni, Italo *23*
Margaret, princesse *201*
Marley, Bob **294**, *294*
Maroc *29*, *202*
Marshall, George **168**, *168*
Martin du Gard, Roger *130*
Martinique *17*
Marx Brothers **128**, *128*
Marx, Karl *60*
Masson, André *88*

Mata Hari 60, **231**, *231*
Matisse, Henri **25**
Mauriac, François **259**
Mauroy, Pierre **302**
Maxwell, Robert **325**
McAuliffe, Christa **306**
McCann **310**
McCay, Winsor **26**
McEnroe, John **291**
McKinley, William **14**, *14*
médecine
  acier, poumon d' **99**, *99*
  alcootest **206**
  anémie **40**
  bébé éprouvette **282**, *282*
  cancer **285**
  cœur artificiel **188**, *188*
  greffe **244**, **265**
  grippe espagnole **64**
  hérédité **39**
  insémination artificielle **180**
  insuline **73**
  Montessori, école **31**
  Nightingale, Florence **31**
  pénicilline **98** , *98*
  pilule contraceptive **218**, *218*
  polyomyélite **196**
  rein artificiel **159**
  Rhésus, facteur **142**
  scanner **267**, *267*
  sida **302**, *302*, **310**
  tétanos **93**
  thalidomide **226**
  transsexuelle, opération **187**
  tuberculose **73**
  variole **291**
  vitamines **128**
Meir, Golda **251**, *251*, **264**
Méliès, Georges **17**, **299**
Melin, Arthur **210**
Mendes France, Pierre **196**, *196*
Menem, Carlos **316**
Menuhin, Yehudi **96**, *96*
Mercader, Ramon **143**
Merckx, Eddie **259**, *259*
Mère Teresa **343**, *343*
Meredith, James **228**, *228*
métropolitain **8**, **9**, **23**, *23*, **308**, *308*, **337**
Mexique
  mayas, cités **91**
  révolution **42**
Michelot **129**
Michton, Morris **19**
Micombero, Michel **265**
Mies van der Rohe, Ludwig **73**, **87**
Milky Way **80**
Miller, Arthur **202**, **227**, **257**
Miller, Glenn **153**
Millerand, Alexandre **71**
Milne, Alan Alexander **90**, *90*
Milosevic, Slobodan **326**, **336**, **348**
Mimoun, Alain **189**
Mindszenty, Jozsef **181**, *181*

Miro, Juan **88**
Mitchell, Margaret **137**
Mitterrand, François, **273**, **292**, *292*, **313**, **332**, **336**, *336*, **338**
mode **174-175**
  années folles **95**
  bas Nylon **138**, **139**, **175**, *175*
  Bikini **167**, *167*, **175**
  corset **36**
  fermeture à glissière **52**, *52*
  garçonne **76**, *76*
  jean **200**, *200*
  Londres **240**
  maillot de bain **175**
  minijupe **235**, *235*
  new-look **174**, *174*
  parfum **72**
  punk **276**, **281**, *281*
  sacs d'Oxford **76**, *76*
  sèche-cheveux **68**
  soutien-gorge **52**
  Yves Saint Laurent **229**, *229*
Mohamed, Mahdi **327**
Mohammed V **202**
Mollet, Guy **202**
Molotov **85**, **137**, *137*
Mongolie **73**
Monroe, Marilyn **104**, **199**, *199*, **202**, **227**, *227*
Montagnier, professeur **302**
Montand, Yves **226**
Montessori, Maria **31**
montgolfière **29**, *29*
Montinimy *341*
Montoire, entrevue de **144**, **148**
Moody, Helen Wills **135**
Moore, Bobby **242**
Moore, Henry **151**, *151*
Moreschi, Alessandro **77**, *77*
Moro, Aldo **283**, *283*, **286**, *286*
Moulin, Jean **159**, *159*
Mountbatten, lord **169**
Mugabe, Robert **289**, *289*
Muhammad, Elijah **238**
Munich, accords de **132**
Murnau, F. W. **75**
musique **246-247**, **266**
  acid house **217**
  be-bop **165**, **181**
  Beatles **232**, *232*, **244**, *244*, **246**
  blues **27**
  castrat **77**
  Cotton club **94**, *94*, **100**
  disque **13**, **173**, **211**
  disque compact **296**, *296*
  festival folk **280**
  folk **239**
  Gibson **122**
  hard-rock **272**
  jazz **85**, **94**, **100**, **133**, **153**, **252**
  juke-box **28**
  jungle **217**
  Live Aid **304**
  opéra **22**, **188**
  opéra rock **258**

pop **246-247**, **252**, **279**, **344**
punk **276**
ragtime **46**
rap **284**
reggae **294**
Rhapsody in blue **85**
rock and roll **186**, **197**, **204**
soul **303**
techno **217**, *217*, **310**
walkman **290**, *290*
Woodstock **252**, *252*
Mussolini, Benito **66**, **77**, *77*, **116**, **118**, **120**, *120*, **123**, **132**, **136**, **137**, *137*, **158**, **159**

N

Nagasaki **186**
Nagumo, Chuichi **148**
Nagy, Imre **204**
Namibie **319**
Nansen, Fridtjof **45**
Nasser, Gamal Abdel **194**, *194*, **203**, *203*, **293**
natation **77**, **92**
Nations unies **187**, **214**, **222**, **245**, **263**, **271**, **274**, **294**, **313**, **320**, **324**, **332**
  Casques bleus **223**, **327**
  droits de l'homme **170**
  forces **180**
naufrage **310**, *310*, **333**, *333*
navire
  Amoco Cadiz **283**, *283*
  Ancon **53**, *53*
  Bismarck **151**, *151*
  Deutschland **11**, *11*
  Dreadnought **28**
  Estonia **333**, *333*
  Exxon Valdez **317**, *317*
  Fram **45**
  France **220**
  GrafSpee **138**, *138*
  Herald of Free Enterprise **310**, **310**
  Kaiser Wilhelm der Grosse **11**
  Lusitania **54**
  Potemkine **25**
  Pourquoi-pas ? **44**, **45**
  Queen Elizabeth **135**, *135*
  Rainbow Warrior **305**, *305*
  SS Cristobal **48**
  Titanic **48**, *48*
  Vasa **225**
Navratilova, Martina **319**, *319*
nazisme **83**, **107**, **110**, **111**, **114**, **115**, **116**, **120-121**, **132**
Neeson **329**
Néfertiti **49**, *49*
Néguib, général **187**
Nehru, Jawaharlal **169**, **194**, **195**, *195*, **197**, **214**, **235**, *235*

Nelson **85**
Nelson, Ralph **235**
Nescafé **133**, *133*
Newman, Larry **283**
Newton, Hue **242**
Nicaragua **285**
Nicholson, Jack **251**, **317**, *317*
Nicolas II **60**, **62**, *62*
Nidal, Abou **287**
Niemeyer, Oscar **221**
Nigeria **220**, **249**
Nightingale, Florence **31**
Nijinski, Vaslav **46**
Nivelle **58**
Nixon, Richard **187**, **218**, **248**, **254**, **256**, **265**, *265*, **267**, *267*, **272**, *272*
Nkrumah, Kwame **241**, *241*
Noah, Yannick **325**
Nobel, Alfred **13**, *13*, **26**
Nobel, prix **13**
  chimie **47**, **67**, **123**
  littérature **31**, **55**, **88**, **130**, **191**, **211**, **221**, **273**
  médecine **22**, **142**, **270**
  paix **26**, **236**, **238**, **282**, **300**, **320**
  physique **19**, **35**, **73**, **76**
non-agression, pacte de (germano-soviétique) **137**
Noonan, Chris **336**
Norgay, Tenzing **190**, *190*
Noriega **317**
Norvège **25**, **293**
Novarro, Roman **90**
Noureïev, Rudolf **225**, *225*
Nouvelle-Calédonie **303**, **304**
nucléaire **279**
  armement **163**
  bombe H **186**, **197**, **241**
  centrale **203**, *203*, **285**
  désarmement **311**
  énergie **184**, *184*
  essai **233**, **337**, **339**
  Greenpeace **262**, *262*, **268**, *268*, **305**, **335**, **335**
  manifestation **210**, **300**
  SALT 1 **267**
  sous-marin **197**, *197*, **252**
  START, traité **163**
  Tchernobyl, **306**, *306*
Nujoma, Sam **319**
Nurmi, Paavo **84**, *84*

O

O'Neal, Ryan **257**
Oakley, Kenneth **191**
OCDE **220**
Ojukwu, colonel **244**
Onassis, Aristote **248**, **274**
Ono, Yoko **289**
Opel, Fritz von **101**

Oppenheimer, Julius Robert **162**, *162*
Orwell, George **176**, *176*
Osmond, frères **266**, *266*
Oswald, Harvey **233**
OTAN **177**, **200**, **232**
Ouganda **220**, **263**, **276**
overcraft **214**
Owell *324*
Owens, Jesse **129**, *129*, *341*

P

Pahlavi, Farah *284*
Pahlavi, Reza **284**
Pakistan **169**, **195**, **313**, **256**, **278**
Palach, Jan **253**, *253*
Palestine **170**
  colonie agricole **13**, *13*
  Intifada **311**
  OLP **234**, **252**, **257**, **287**, **296**, **311**, **328**
Palme, Olof **307**, *307*
Panama **317**
Panama, canal de **53**
Pankhurst, Christabel **37**
Pankhurst, Emmeline **19**, **37**
Papon, Maurice **347**
Parker, Bonnie **118**, *118*
Parks, Rosa **202**, *202*
Parry, Edward **45**
Passy, Frédéric **13**
Pasternak, Boris **211**, *211*
patinage artistique **127**
Patten, Chris **344**, *344*
Patterson, Floyd **215**, *215*
Paul, Henri **342**
Paulus, von **157**
Pavalova, Anna **27**, *27*
Pavlov, Ivan **22**
Pearse, Padraic **59**
Peary, Robert **39**, *39*, **44-45**, *45*,*45*
Péguy, Charles **55**
Peinture
  Drapeau **199**, *199*
  Guernica **131**
  Improvisations 10 **41**
  Iris **310**
  La Forêt **88**
  La Joconde **47**, *47*, **51**
  La Rue **87**
  Les Demoiselles d'Avignon **32**, *32*
  Portrait du docteur Gachet
  Tournesols **310**
Pékin **9**, **36**
Pelé **105**, *105*, **210**
Penkovski, Oleg **230**, *230*
Pereira, Fernando **305**
Peres, Shimon **334**
Perkins, Anthony **219**
Perkins, An **189**, *189*, **277**

Perón, Eva 167, **189**, *189*
Perón, Isabel **277**, *277*
Perón, Juan Domingo **167**, *167*
Perot, Ross 327
Pérou 47
Perez de Cuellar, Javier 313
Pétain 58, 60, 63, 143, *143*, **151**, *151*
pétrole 252, **271**, **383**, 290, 313, *313*, 317
Philby, Kim 230, *230*
Philipe, Gérard 263
Philippines 306
Philips, Mark **271**, *271*
photographie, 9, 27, 33, **89**, **171**
Picabia, Francis 59
Picasso, Pablo **32**, **49**, 88, 131, 270
Piccard 108
Piccard, Auguste 221
Pickford, Mary **38**, *38*, 66, *66*
Pie X 23
Pietri, Dorando 36
Pilsudski, maréchal **92**
Pincus, Gregory 218
Pingeon, Roger 259
Pinochet, Augusto 270, 310, 347
pizza **26**
Planck, Max **11**, *11*
Pluton **106**, *106*
Poe, James 235
Poher, Alain 253
Poilvé 129
Poincaré, Raymond 51, 93
Poiret, Paul 95
Poitier, Sidney **235**, *235*
Pol Pot, 274
pôle
  pôle nord **39**, **44**, **93**
  pôle sud **45**
Pollock, Jackson **169**, *169*
pollution 269
Pologne **92**
  état de siège **295**
  Invasion par l'Allemagne **136**
  Riga, traité de 73
  Solidarité 288, 295, 319, 322
  Varsovie, ghetto de **145**, *145*, **156**, *156*
  Varsovie, révolte de **161**, *161*
Pompidou, Georges 226, 229, 249, **253**, 273
population 318
Porter, Edwin 18
Portugal **41**, **111**
  révolution des Œillets **272**
Potter, Beatrix **16**
Pottier 19
Powell, Mike **325**, *325*
Powers, Francis Gary **219**, *219*
Preer, Andrew, 94
Presley, Elvis **204**, *204*, 216, 246, *246*, **279**, *279*
Primo de Rivera, Miguel
81, 109, 126
Profumo, John 233
prohibition **68**
Proust, Marcel 77
Pu Yi **36**, *36*

Q

Quant, Mary 175, **235**, *235*, 240
quanta, théorie des **11**
Queen **272**, *272*, 304

R

Rabin, Yitzhak **328**, *328*, **334**, *334*, 339
Radek, Karl *131*
radio 69, **78-79**, **198**, *198*, 216
  BBC **76**, 79
  Radio-Londres 79
  radiola 76
Rahman, Mujibur 261
Rainier, prince **205**, *205*, 297
Rains, Claude 152
Ramadier 169
Rapallo, traité de **75**
Raspoutine, Grigori **59**, *59*
RDA (voir Allemagne)
Read, Albert 67
Reagan, ronald **291**, *291*, **292**, *292*, 294, 300, 301, 304, 311, 322
Réard, Louis 175
Reichstag 65, **114**, *114*, 165
relativité **26**
Remarque, Erich Maria 103
Rémi, Georges (voir Hergé)
Renaud, Madeleine **181**, *181*
revue musicale
  follies de 1907 31
  Revue nègre 89
Reynaud, Paul 145
Reynolds, Debbie 187
RFA (voir Allemagne)
Rhodésie du Sud 239
Ribbentrop, Joachim von 136, 137, *137*
Rice 262, *262*
Richtofen, Manfred von (Baron rouge) **63**, *63*
Ride, Sally **261**, **301**
Rivera, Diego **128**, *128*
Roberts, lord 9
Robinson, Bill 94
Robinson, Élisabeth 101
Robinson, Mary **321**, *321*
Roche, Stephen 309
Rogers, Ginger 119
Röhm, Ernst **117**, *117*
Rolland, Romain 55
Rolling Stones **236**, *236*, 246

Romano, Yosef 264, *264*
Romanov **62**
Rommel 158
Röntgen, Wilhelm 13
Roosevelt, Eleanor 170
Roosevelt, Franklin Delano, 106, **110**, *110*, 115, **151**, *151*, **160**, **165**, *165*
Roosevelt, Theodore 14, 15, *15*, 19
Rorschach, Hermann **69**
Rosenberg, Julius et Ethel **190**, *230*
Ross, Diana 247
Rothschild, baron de 13
Rotten, Johnny 281
Roumanie 316
Routskoï 328
Rubik, Erno 288
Rudolph, Wilma **221**, *221*
Rundstedt, maréchal von 160
Rushdie, Salman 317
Russie
  Cronstadt, révolte de 73
  Dimanche rouge **24**
  famine 69
  guerre contre le Japon 22
  Guerre mondiale (première) 53, **62**
  Mandchourie **11**, *11*, 73
  mutinerie **25**
  Octobre, révolution d' **60**
  Rapallo, traité de 75
  Riga, traité de 73
Rust, Matthias **309**
Ruth, Babe **69**, *69*, **104**, *104*
Rutherford, Ernest 67
Rwanda 332

S

Sabbagh, Pierre 254
Sacco, Nicola 72
Sadate, Anouar el- **259**, **282**, *282*, 285, **293**, *293*
Saigon **275**, *275*
Sailer, Toni **203**, *203*
Saint Laurent, Yves **229**, *229*
Saint-Exupéry, Antoine de 156
saint-suaire **312**, *312*
Sakharov, Andrei **308**, **323**, *323*
Salazar, Antonio **111**, 272
Salinger, J.D. **185**, *185*
Salk, Edouard **196**, *196*
Sampras, Pete 325
Sandino, Augusto **285**
Sands, Bobby **294**
Santos-Dumont, Alberto 21
Sauvageot, Jacques 248
Savage, Sean 310
Scheer 59
Scheidemann, Philipp 65

Schick, Joseph **99**
Schirmann, Richard **39**
Schirra, Walter 261
Schleyer, Martin **279**, *279*
Schlumberger, Jean 38
Schmidt, Helmut 297
Schmidt-Rottluff, Karl 27
Schneider, Ralph 178
Scholl, Hans et Sophie **157**, *157*
Schönberg, Arnold 115
Schragmüller, Elisabeth *231*
Schreck, Max 75
Schroeder, William 257
Schulz, Charles **178**, *178*
Schumann, Maurice 79
Schwarzkopf *324*
Schweitzer, Albert **50**
Scopes, John Thomas 86
Scott, Robert **44**
scout **30**
Scully, John *315*
Seale, Bobby 242
Selfridge, Thomas E. 37
Sembat, Marcel 42
Senna, Ayrton **333**, *333*
Serbie **52**
Seurat, Michel 324
Sex Pistols **276**, *276*, 281
Shastri, Lal Bahadur 243
Shaw, George Bernard **88**, *88*
Shepard, Allan 225
Shepard, E. H. 90
Sikorski, Igor **137**
Sillanpää, Miina 32
Simmons, William 55
Simpson, O. J. **334**, *334*
Simpson, Wallis 127
Sinatra, Frank 157
Skoblikova, Lidia *340*
Smith *85*
Smith, Alfred 108
Smith, Ian 289
Smith, Tommy **249**, *249*
Snepvangers, René 173
Société des Nations 65, 66, **69**, *69*, **114**, **118**, 123
Soljenitsyne, Aleksandr **273**, *273*, **323**, *323*
Soloviev 337
Somalie **327**, *327*
Somoza, général 285
SOS, signal **48**
Soudan 202
Spasski, Boris 264
Spice girls **344**, *344*
Spielberg, Steven **297**, *297*, 298, **329**
Spinola, Antonio 272
Spitz, Mark **265**, *265*, *341*
Springsteen, Bruce **303**, *303*
Sri Lanka **219**, **301**, *301*
Stafford, Thomas 261, 275
Stakhanov, Alexis 122
Staline, Joseph 76, 82, 85, **97**, 131, 136, 137, *137*, 139, 157, 164, 165, *165*, 172, **191**, *191*, 200, 204

Stanton, Élisabeth 71
Starshooters 281
Stauffenberg, colonel von 161
Stavisky, affaire **115**
Sternberg, Joseph von 107
Stewart, James **199**, *199*
Stieglitz, Alfred 27
Stoker, Bram 75
Stravinski, Igor 46, **51**, *51*
Streseman, Gustav 89
Stroop, général **156**, *156*
Sudètes, invasion des **132**, *132*
Suez, crise de **203**
Sugar Hill Gang 284
Suisse
  droit de vote pour les femmes 263
  suffragettes 263
Sumatra **344**, *344*
Sun Yat-sen 46, **86**, *86*
Sundback, Gideon 52
Supremes 247
Suttner, Bertha von **26**, *26*
Swatch **300**, *300*
Swigert, John 258
Sydney, George 185
Szabo, Ecaterina 303

T

Tardieu 111
Tarzan **53**
Tati, Jacques 192
Tchang Kaï-chek 86, 96, 99, 116, 176
Tchécoslovaquie 253
  Charte 77 **278**, 322
  partition **326**
  Prague, coup de 172
  Prague, printemps de **249**
Tchernenko, Konstantin 303
Teilhard de Chardin 97
télégraphique, câble **17**
téléphone **203**, *203*, 281
télévision 123, 177, **212**, **226**, 243, **253**, **254-255**, **294**
Teller, Edward 186
Temple, Shirley **122**, *122*, 141
Tennis
  Coupe Davis **10**, **111**, *325*
  grand chelem **193**
  Wimbledon 81, 118, 134, 135, 206, 291, 305, 319
Terechkova, Valentina 233, **261**, *261*, 301
terrorisme **286-287**
Thagard 337
Thatcher, Margaret **284**, *284*, **318**, *318*, 321
The Band 252
The Face, **289**, *289*

génocide **154-155**
George VI **187**
George, Lloyd **75**, *75*
Georget **129**
Gerhardt, Charles **18**
Geronimo **39**, *39*
Gershwin, George **85**, *85*
Ghana **241**
Giap, général **197**
Gibbon, Heynsham **188**
Gibson, colonel *158*
Gide, André **38**
Gillepsie, Dizzy **165**, *165*
Gillette, King Camp **12**
Ginnah **195**
Giscard d'Estaing, Valéry **273**, **338**
glace **23**
Glenn, John **347**, *347*
Goddard, Robert **101**
Godse, Nathuram **171**
Goering, Hermann **114**, **166**, *166*
Goldenmark, Peter **173**
golf **259**
Goodman, Benny **133**, *133*
Gorbatchev, Mikhail **304**, **308**, *308*, **311**, **312**, **320**, *320*, **322**, *322*, **323**, **324**
Gordy, Berry **247**
Gore, A. W. **10**
Gore, Al **327**
Goscinny, René *125*, **224**, *224*
Gottwald, Klement **172**, *172*
Gourion, Ben *170*
Grabble, Betty **159**, *159*
Graham, Martha **93**
Grande-Bretagne
  Aberfan **242**, *241*
  automobile **29**
  chômage **126**
  droit de vote **63**
  droit des femmes **275**
  Dunblane **339**, *339*
  éclipse **97**
  émeutes **293**
  Entente cordiale **23**
  État-providence **173**
  exposition britannique **185**
  Guerre mondiale (deuxième) **134**, **145**, **149**, **151**, **161**
  Guerre mondiale (première) **52**, **59**, **61**, **64**
  hold-up **233**
  manifestation **321**, *321*
  marée noire **245**
  marine **28**
  Mods et Rockers **237**, *237*
  morue, guerre de la **215**
  nucléaire **203**
  pollution **205**
  sécurité routière **89**
  smog **189**
  suffragettes **19**, **37**, **63**
  travail **11**
  Union nationale **109**
  variole, épidémie de **226**
Grèce **149**, **273**
Greer, Germaine **259**, *259*

Grenade, île de la **301**, *301*
Griffith, D. W. **55**, *55*
Griffith, Arthur **72**
Griffith, David W. **38**, **66**, *66*
Griffith-Joyner, Florence *341*
Gropius, Walter **87**
Grosse Bertha **62**, *62*
Grotewohl, Otto **176**
Groves, général **162**
Guérin, Camille **73**
Guerre mondiale (deuxième)
  armistice **165**
  Atlantique, charte de l' **151**
  attaques alliées *158*
  Barbarossa, opération **149**
  Belgique, invasion **142**
  Blitzkrieg **142**
  camp de concentration **152**, **155**, **164**
  civils **146-147**
  Collaboration **148**
  débarquement **160**, *160*, *161*
  déclaration de guerre **144**
  Dieppe **153**
  Dresde **165**, *165*
  Dynamo, opération **143**
  El-Alamein **153**, *153*
  Enigma **150**
  étoile jaune **150**, *150*
  évacuation **147**, *147*
  gestapo **152**, **157**, **159**
  ghetto **155**, *155*
  invasion de la France **143**
  Italie, capitulation **158**
  Japon **159**, **164**
  Leningrad, siège de **160**
  Lip, usine **270**
  Londres **161**
  Midway, bataille des **153**
  Nuremberg, procès de **166**
  Otarie, opération **145**
  Paris, libération de **161**, *161*
  Pearl Harbor **148**, *148*
  préparatifs **134**
  rationnement, ticket de **147**
  Résistance **152**
  Singapour, capitulation de **153**
  Stalingrad, bataille de **157**, *157*
  Téhéran, conférence de **159**
  Traité de paix russo-finlandais **144**
  villes **146**, *146*
  Yalta, conférence de **165**
Guerre mondiale (première)
  14 points **65**
  armistice **64**, **66**
  Brest-Litovsk, traité de **62**, *62*
  Caporetto **61**
  civils **56-57**

Dardanelles, détroit des **55**, *55*
  déclaration **52**, **53**
  Entente **52**, **54**
  États-Unis, entrée en guerre des **60**
  Flandres, bataille des **61**
  guerre de position **53**
  Italie, entrée en guerre de l' **54**
  Jutland, bataille navale du **59**
  Londres **61**
  Lusitania, torpillage du **54**
  Marne, bataille de la **53**, *53*
  Marne, deuxième bataille de la **63**
  mobilisation **52**
  Neuilly, traité de **70**
  propagande **54**
  rationnement **56**
  Saint-Germain, traité de **70**
  Sambre, bataille de la **52**
  Schlieffen, plan **53**
  Sèvres, traité de **70**
  Somme, bataille de la **59**
  Tannenberg **52**
  Trianon, traité de **70**
  Triplice **52**
  Verdun, bataille de **58**, *58*
  Versailles, traité de **66**, **129**
  Ypres, bataille d' **55**
Guillaume II **64**
Guofeng, Hua **277**
Gustave V **33**
Guyana **283**
Guynemer, Georges **63**

H

Haakon VII de norvège **25**, *25*
Hadden, Briton **83**
Hagen, Jean **187**
Hagenbeck, Carl **32**
Haig, Douglas **61**
Hailé Sélassié **107**, *107*, **123**
Hair **280**
Haise, Fred **258**
Haïti **307**, **333**
Hajek, Jiri **278**
Hale-Boop, comète **343**, *343*
Halimi, Gisèle **265**
Halley, Bill **197**, *197*
Halley, comète de **40**, *40*, **306**, *306*
Halley, Edmond **40**, **306**
Hallyday, Johnny **222**, *222*
hamburger **11**, *11*
Hamilton, Thomas **339**
Hammarskjöld, Dag **222**, *222*
Hammerstein **185**
Hanau, Marthe **101**
Handler, Ruth **213**
Handy, W.C. **27**, *27*

Hanks, Tom **299**
Harding, Warren **69**
Hardy, Oliver **140**
Harlem Globe-trotters **98**
Havel, Vaclav **278**, **322**, *322*
Haw-Haw, lord **79**
Hayek, Nicolas **300**
Heckel, Erich **27**
Heidemann, Gerd *301*
Held, Anna **31**
hélicoptère **137**, *137*
Helsinki, accords d' **274**
Hémery, Victor **39**
Hendrix, Jimi **247**, **251**, **252**, **259**
Henie, Sonja **127**
Henreid, Paul **152**
Henson, Matt **45**
Hergé **102**
Herrick, James **40**
Hess, Rudolf **151**, *151*, **166**, *166*
Heston, Charlton **215**
Heyerdahl, Thor **168**
Hillary, Edmund **190**, *190*
Hilsz, Maryse **111**, *111*
Himmler, Heinrich
Hinault, Bernard **285**, **305**, *305*
Hinckley, John **292**
Hindenburg, dirigeable **130**, *130*
Hindenburg, général **52**, **64**, **88**, **111**, **114**, **118**
hippie **280**, **281**
Hirobumi, Ito **38**
Hirohito **91**, *91*
Hiroshima **186**
Hitchcock, Alfred **199**, **219**
Hitler **83**, **87**, **107**, **116**, **117**, **118**, **120**, *120*, **123**, **127**, *127*, **129**, **132**, **136**, **137**, *137*, **138**, **139**, **143**, **148**, **157**, **161**, **165**, **301**
Hô Chi Minh **181**, *181*, **194**, **197**, **250**, *250*, **256**
Hong-Kong **344**, *344*
Hongrie **181**
  Budapest, insurrection de **204**
  Guerre mondiale (première) **53**, **70**
Hoover, Herbert **108**, **110**
Hopper, Dennis **251**
Hornby, Franck **10**
Horne, Lean **94**
Hoskins, Bob **299**, *299*
Hostin **129**
Houdini, Harry **93**, *93*
Hounsfield, Godfrey **267**
Hsien Feng **36**
Hubble, Edwin **102**
Hugues, Howard **266**
Hurst, Geoff **242**
Hussein, Saddam **290**, **320**, *320*, **324**
Hussein de Jordanie **347**

302, *302*
conflit sino-indien **227**
impôt sur le sel **81**
marche **106**
partition **195**
peste **33**
Indochine
  décolonisation **181**
  guerre de **166**
informatique **207**, **256**, **274**, **314-315**, **335**
inondation
  Bangladesh **311**, *311*
  Florence **242**, *242*
  Grande-Bretagne **188**
  Paris **41**
  Pays-Bas **193**
Internet **328**
Interpol **83**
invention
  aspirateur **15**
  Cellophane **35**
  congélation **106**
  micro-ondes, four à **170**, *170*
  grille-pain **38**, *38*
  Lépine, concours **13**
  magnétoscope **266**, *266*
  polyéthylène **138**
  rasoir **99**
  réfrigérateur **50**
  stylo à bille **135**
Ioussoupov **59**
Irak **293**, **320**, **324**
Iran **284**, **285**, **294**
Iran-Irak, guerre **290**, **313**
Irlande **59**, **72**, **251**, **264**, **294**, **321**, **345**
  IRA **72**, **287**, **310**, *310*, **332**, **345**
  Sinn Fein **72**, **287**, **332**
Islande
  morue, guerre de la **215**
Israël **251**, **275**, **276**, **296**, **328**
  création **170**
  Jérusalem **236**
  Kippour, guerre du **271**
  Six Jours, guerre des **245**, **252**
Issigonis, Alec **215**
Italie
  attentat **288**
  Brigades rouges **283**, **286**
  Chemises noires **77**
  Fiume **67**
  Guerre mondiale (deuxième) **153**, **158**
  Guerre mondiale (première) **54**, **61**
  marche sur Rome **77**
  république
  Seveso, catastrophe de **277**
Izetbegovic **336**

I

Inde **169**, **243**
  Calcutta **93**
  catastrophe écologique

J

Jacklin, Tony **259**, *259*
Jackson Five **247**
Jackson, frères **266**
Jackson, Michael **266**

Jacob, Mary Phelps **52**
Jahn, Gunnar *238*
Jannings, Emil *102*
Japon
  annexion de la Corée *40*
  bombe atomique *162*, **164**
  empereur **91**, *91*
  guerre contre la Russie **22**
  Guerre mondiale (deuxième) **148**, *159*, **164**
  Guerre mondiale (première) *53*
  guerre sino-japonaise **130**
  Hirobumi, Ito **38**
  secte **337**
  Tokyo *112*
Jarman, Nelly **36**, *36*
Jaruzelski, général *295*
Jaurès, Jean *53*, *84*
Jean XXIII **215**, *233*
Jean-Paul Ier *282*
Jean-Paul II **283**, *283*, **295**, *295*, **342**
Jellicoe, John *59*
Jellinek, Émile *13*
Jenner, Edward *291*
jeunesse, auberge de *39*
jeux
  Barbie, poupée **213**, *213*
  Buzz **338**, *338*
  échecs **264**, *333*
  Hula-hoop **210**, *210*, **216**
  informatique **315**, *315*
  Meccano *10*
  Monopoly **117**, *117*
  patin à roulettes *43*
  puzzle *47*
  Rubik-cube **288**, *288*
  scrabble **108**, *108*
  Teddy bear (ours en peluche) **19**, *19*
jeux féminins mondiaux *73*
jeux Olympiques *340-341*
  Amsterdam *101*
  Atlanta *338*
  Berlin *129*
  Chamonix *84*
  Cortina d'Ampezzo *203*
  Helsinki **189**
  Londres *36*
  Los Angeles **303**
  Melbourne *205*
  Mexico *249*
  Montréal *277*
  Moscou *290*
  Munich *264*, *265*
  Paris *11*, *36*, *84*
  Rome **221**
  Saint-Louis *36*
  Séoul *311*
  Stockholm *48*, **49**, *205*
Jiang, Qing **293**, *293*
Jobs, Steve *315*
Joffre, général *53*, *53*
Johansen, Wilhelm *39*
Johensson, Ingemar **215**, *215*
John, Elton *175*, *342*, *343*
Johns, Jasper **199**

Johnson, Ben **311**, *311*
Johnson, Jack **35**, *35*
Johnson, L. B. **237**, *237*
Joliot-Curie, Frédéric **123**, *173*
Joliot-Curie, Irène *123*
Jolson, Al **97**, *97*
Jones, Jim *283*
Joplin, Janis *252*
Jordan, Michael **349**, *349*
Jordan, Mimi *210*
Jordanie *58*, *257*
Jorgensen, Christine **187**, *187*
Joselito **71**, *71*
Jospin, Lionel *336*, *343*, *345*
Joxe, Louis *227*
juif *107*, *114*, *115*, **120**, *121*, *122*, *123*, **132**, *133*, *145*, *147*, **150**, *154-155*, *156*, *164*, *225*
Juppé, Alain *337*

K

Kadhafi **253**, *253*
Kahlo, Frieda *128*
Kalinine *85*
Kamenev, Lev *82*, *85*
Kandinsky, Wassily **41**, *87*
Kantrowitz, Adirn *244*
Kasparov *333*
Kästner, Erich *101*
Keaton, Buster *89*
Keaton, Michael *317*
Keim, Betty Lou *216*
Keitel, maréchal *165*
Keller, Helen **23**, *23*
Kellerman, Annette *175*
Kellog, Frank B. *98*
Kellog, William **29**, *29*
Kelly, Gene *187*
Kelly, Grace *199*, **205**, *205*, **297**, *297*
Kemal, Mustafa **80**, *80*, *132*
Kennedy *228*, *228*, *254*
  assassinat **233**, *233*
  mariage **191**, *191*
  président **218**, *218*
  rencontre avec Khrouchtchev *225*
Kennedy, Jackie **191**, *191*, **218**, *218*, **233**, *233*, *248*
Kennedy, Robert *224*, **248**, *248*
Kenney, Annie *37*
Kent, Bruce *300*
Kenya *188*, *220*, *233*
Kern *185*
Kerouac, Jack **207**, *207*
Kessel, Joseph *157*
Key, Francis Scott *109*
Khan, Muhammed Yahia *262*
Khasboulatov, *328*
Khomeyni, Ruhollah *284*, *290*, *294*, *316*, **317**
Khrouchtchev, Nikita **204**, *204*, **213**, *213*, *219*, *225*, *228*, **234**, *234*, *261*

Kiesinger, Georg **243**
Killy, Jean-Claude *340*
Kim Il-sung *180*
King BB *252*
Kingsley *329*
Kipling, Rudyard **31**
Kirchner, Ernst Ludwig *27*
Klee, Paul *87*, *88*
Knerr, Richard *210*
Kohl, Helmut **297**
Kolff, Willem **159**
Kon-Tiki **168**, *168*
Koresh, David **329**
Kosovo *348*
Kossyguine, Alekseï *234*
Koweit **320**, *324*
Kremlin *231*
Ku Klux Klan **55**, *55*, *224*
Kubrick, Stanley *249*
Kujau, Konrad *301*
Kutchuk, docteur *220*
Kuznetsov, Vassili *214*

L

Labouisse, Henri *238*
Lacoste, *111*
Laïka **206**, *206*
Lambert, comte de *38*
Lamm, Franck *29*
Lancaster, Burt *232*
Land, Edwin **171**, *171*
Landsteiner, Karl *142*
Lang, Fritz **92**
Lanvin, Jeanne *95*
Lapébie *129*
Latham, Hubert *38*
Latran, accords de *103*
Laurel, Stan *140*
Lawrence, Thomas Edward *58*, *58*
Le Baron Jenney, William *16*
Le Corbusier *97*, **186**, *186*
Leakey, Louis **225**, *225*
Leakey, Mary *225*
Léaud, Jean-Pierre *251*
Lebrun, Albert *131*
Leclerc, général *161*
Leconte, Henri **325**
Leeson, Nick **336**, *336*
Leigh, Janet **219**, *219*
Leigh, Vivien *137*
LeMond, Greg *305*
Lenglen, Suzanne, **81**, *81*
Lénine, Vladimir *60*, **82**, *82*, *85*, *85*, *204*
Lennon, John **289**, *289*
Leonov, Alekseï *238*, *260*, *275*
Léopold II *35*, *36*
Leopold III *185*
Lépine, Louis *13*
Leprince-Ringuet, Louis *240*
Levegh, Pierre *201*
Lewis, Carl **303**, *303*
Liban *275*, *296*
  Beyrouth, *275*, *275*, *296*
  otage *324*
  Sabra et Chatila, camps de *296*

Libby, Williard *168*
Libye *253*
Liddell, Eric *84*
Lilienthal, Otto **20**, *20*
Lincoln, Elmo *65*
Lindbergh, Charles **96**, *96*
Lindgren, Astrid *164*
Lippman, Gabriel *35*
Liston, Charles Sonny *237*
Littérature
  1984 *176*
  À l'ombre des jeunes filles en fleurs *77*
  À l'ouest, rien de nouveau *103*
  À la recherche du temps perdu *77*
  Au-dessus de la mêlée *55*
  Aventures de Huckleberry Finn *43*
  Aventures de Tom Sawyer *43*
  Bas les armes ! *26*
  Capitaine courageux *31*
  Docteur Jivago *211*
  Dracula *75*
  Du côté de chez Swann *77*
  Du spirituel dans l'art *41*
  Émile et les détectives **101**
  Fifi Brindacier **164**, *164*
  Germinal *17*
  Histoire de ma vie *23*
  Histoire de Pierre le lapin *16*
  Histoires comme ça *31*
  Journal d'Anne Franck **154**, *154*, **187**, *187*
  Kim *31*
  l'Attrape-cœur *185*
  l'Étranger *221*
  l'Homme révolté *221*
  l'Interprétation des rêves *10*
  la Condition humaine *115*
  La mystérieuse affaire de Styles *70*
  la Peste *221*
  le Grand Meaulnes *55*
  le livre de la jungle *31*
  le Malentendu *221*
  le mythe de Sisyphe *221*
  le Petit Prince **156**
  le second Livre de la Jungle *31*
  Manifeste du surréalisme *85*
  Mémoires de guerre *191*
  Sur la route *207*
  Versets sataniques *317*
  Winnie l'ourson *90*
Lloyd, Harold *141*
Locarno, conférence de **89**, *129*
Lorenz, Konrad **270**, *270*
Loubet, Émile *8*
Loucheur, loi *99*
Louvre, musée du *47*
Lovell, James *258*, *261*
Lovelock, Jack *129*
Lucas, George *279*, *298*

Luce, Henry *83*
Lucy, Autherine *202*
Ludendorff *83*
Lumière, Louis *33*
Lumumba, Patrice **223**, *223*
Lustiger, monseigneur *342*
Luther King, Martin *20*, *224*, **232**, *232*, *236*, *237*, **249**
Lyssenko, Vladimir **173**

M

Maastricht, traité de **329**
MacArthur Douglas *180*, *180*, **184**, *184*
MacCarthy, Joseph R. **181**, *181*
MacDonald, Ramsay *109*
Macédoine *34*
MacGraw, Ali *257*
Machen, Eddie *215*
MacKenzie King, William *73*
MacLean, Donald *185*, **230**, *230*
MacNamara, Frank *178*
Madero, Francisco *42*, *118*
Madonna *247*, **301**, *304*
Magic Johnson **339**, *339*
Maginot, André *107*, *136*
Maginot, ligne *107*, *136*, *136*
Maison-Blanche *15*
Makarios, monseigneur *220*, **273**
Malan, Daniel François *171*, *179*
Malcom X **238**, *238*
Malouines, guerre des *296*, *296*
Malraux, André *115*
Mandchourie *11*, *11*, *108*
Mandela, Nelson **236**, *236*, **318**, *318*, **332**, *332*
Mandela, Winnie *318*
Man Ray *59*, *59*, *88*
Mann, Thomas *115*
Manson, Charles **251**, *251*
Manuel, roi du Portugal *41*
Mao Zédong *96*, *116*, *116*, *176*, *176*, *179*, **210**, *210*, *240*, *265*, *265*, *277*, *277*
Marciano, Rocky **203**, *203*
Marcioni, Italo *23*
Margaret, princesse *201*
Marley, Bob **294**, *294*
Maroc *29*, *202*
Marshall, George *168*, *168*
Martin du Gard, Roger *130*
Martinique *17*
Marx Brothers **128**, *128*
Marx, Karl *60*
Masson, André *88*

INDEX

Mata Hari 60, **231**, *231*
Matisse, Henri 25
Mauriac, François 259
Mauroy, Pierre 302
Maxwell, Robert 325
McAuliffe, Christa 306
McCann 310
McCay, Winsor 26
McEnroe, John 291
McKinley, William **14**, *14*
médecine
  acier, poumon d' **99**, *99*
  alcootest **206**
  anémie **40**
  bébé éprouvette **282**, *282*
  cancer **285**
  cœur artificiel **188**, *188*
  greffe **244**, *265*
  grippe espagnole **64**
  hérédité **39**
  insémination artificielle **180**
  insuline **73**
  Montessori, école **31**
  Nightingale, Florence **31**
  pénicilline **98** , *98*
  pilule contraceptive **218**, *218*
  polyomyélite **196**
  rein artificiel **159**
  Rhésus, facteur **142**
  scanner **267**, *267*
  sida **302**, *302*, 310
  tétanos **93**
  thalidomide **226**
  transsexuelle, opération **187**
  tuberculose **73**
  variole **291**
  vitamines **128**
Meir, Golda **251**, *251*, 264
Meliès, Georges **17**, 299
Melin, Arthur 210
Mendes France, Pierre **196**, *196*
Menem, Carlos 316
Menuhin, Yehudi **96**, *96*
Mercader, Ramon 143
Merckx, Eddie **259**, *259*
Mère Teresa **343**, *343*
Meredith, James **228**, *228*
métropolitain **8**, 9, **23**, *23*, **308**, *308*, **337**
Mexique
  mayas, cités **91**
  révolution **42**
Michelot 129
Michton, Morris 19
Micombero, Michel 265
Mies van der Rohe, Ludwig **73**, 87
Milky Way 80
Miller, Arthur 202, **227**, 257
Miller, Glenn **153**
Millerand, Alexandre 71
Milne, Alan Alexander **90**, *90*
Milosevic, Slobodan **326**, 336, 348
Mimoun, Alain 189
Mindszenty, Jozsef **181**, *181*

Miro, Juan 88
Mitchell, Margaret 137
Mitterrand, François, **273**, *292*, *292*, **313**, *332*, **336**, *336*, 338
mode **174-175**
  années folles **95**
  bas Nylon **138**, **139**, **175**, *175*
  Bikini **167**, *167*, 175
  corset **36**
  fermeture à glissière **52**, *52*
  garçonne **76**, *76*
  jean **200**, *200*
  Londres 240
  maillot de bain **175**
  minijupe **235**, *235*
  new-look **174**, *174*
  parfum **72**
  punk **276**, **281**, *281*
  sacs d'Oxford **76**, *76*
  sèche-cheveux **68**
  soutien-gorge **52**
  Yves Saint Laurent **229**, *229*
Mohamed, Mahdi 327
Mohammed V 202
Mollet, Guy 202
Molotov 85, **137**, *137*
Mongolie 73
Monroe, Marilyn 104, **199**, *199*, 202, **227**, *227*
Montagnier, professeur 302
Montand, Yves 226
Montessori, Maria **31**
montgolfière **29**, *29*
Montinimy 341
Montoire, entrevue de 144, 148
Moody, Helen Wills 135
Moore, Bobby 242
Moore, Henry **151**, *151*
Moreschi, Alessandro **77**, *77*
Moro, Aldo **283**, *283*, **286**, *286*
Moulin, Jean **159**, *159*
Mountbatten, lord 169
Mugabe, Robert **289**, *289*
Muhammad, Elijah 238
Munich, accords de **132**
Murnau, F. W. 75
musique **246-247**, **266**
  acid house 217
  be-bop **165**, 181
  Beatles **232**, *232*, **244**, *244*, *246*
  blues 27
  castrat 77
  Cotton club **94**, *94*, 100
  disque **13**, *173*, 211
  disque compact **296**, *296*
  festival folk 280
  folk **239**
  Gibson 122
  hard-rock 272
  jazz 85, **94**, 100, **133**, **153**, 252
  juke-box **28**
  jungle 217
  Live Aid **304**
  opéra **22**, 188
  opéra rock 258

pop **246-247**, 252, 279, **344**
punk **276**
ragtime **46**
rap **284**
reggae **294**
Rhapsody in blue 85
rock and roll **186**, **197**, **204**
soul 303
techno **217**, *217*, 310
walkman **290**, *290*
Woodstock **252**, *252*
Mussolini, Benito 66, **77**, *77*, 116, 118, **120**, *120*, 123, 132, 136, **137**, *137*, 158, 159

N

Nagasaki 186
Nagumo, Chuichi 148
Nagy, Imre 204
Namibie **319**
Nansen, Fridtjof 45
Nasser, Gamal Abdel **194**, *194*, 203, *203*, 293
natation **77**, 92
Nations unies 187, **214**, **222**, **245**, 263, 271, 274, 294, 313, 320, 324, 332
  Casques bleus 223, 327
  droits de l'homme **170**
  forces 180
naufrage **310**, *310*, **333**, *333*
navire
  Amoco Cadiz **283**, *283*
  Ancon **53**, *53*
  Bismarck **151**, *151*
  Deutschland **11**, *11*
  Dreadnought **28**
  Estonia **333**, *333*
  Exxon Valdez **317**, *317*
  Fram 45
  France 220
  GrafSpee **138**, *138*
  Herald of Free Enterprise **310**, 310
  Kaiser Wilhelm der Grosse 11
  Lusitania 54
  Potemkine 25
  Pourquoi-pas ? **44**, 45
  Queen Elizabeth **135**, *135*
  Rainbow Warrior **305**, *305*
  SS Cristobal 48
  Titanic **48**, *48*
  Vasa 225
Navratilova, Martina **319**, *319*
nazisme 83, **107**, 110, 111, **114**, 115, 116, **120-121**, 132
Neeson 329
Néfertiti **49**, *49*
Néguib, général 187
Nehru, Jawaharlal **169**, 194, 195, *195*, 197, 214, *214*, **235**, *235*

Nelson 85
Nelson, Ralph 235
Nescafé **133**, *133*
Newman, Larry 283
Newton, Hue 242
Nicaragua 285
Nicholson, Jack 251, **317**, *317*
Nicolas II 60, 62, *62*
Nidal, Abou 287
Niemeyer, Oscar 221
Nigeria 220, 249
Nightingale, Florence **31**
Nijinski, Vaslav 46
Nivelle 58
Nixon, Richard **187**, **218**, **248**, 254, 256, **265**, *265*, **267**, *267*, **272**, *272*
Nkrumah, Kwame **241**, *241*
Noah, Yannick 325
Nobel, Alfred **13**, *13*, 26
Nobel, prix 13
  chimie **47**, 67, 123
  littérature **31**, 55, 88, 130, **191**, 211, 221, 273
  médecine 22, 142, 270
  paix 26, 236, **238**, 282, 300, 320
  physique 19, 35, 73, 76
non-agression, pacte de (germano-soviétique) **137**
Noonan, Chris 336
Norgay, Tenzing **190**, *190*
Noriega 317
Norvège **25**, 293
Novarro, Roman 90
Nouréiëv, Rudolf **225**, *225*
Nouvelle-Calédonie 303, 304
nucléaire 279
  armement 163
  bombe H **186**, **197**, 241
  centrale **203**, *203*, 285
  désarmement **311**
  énergie **184**,*184*
  essai 233, 337, 339
  Greenpeace **262**, *262*, **268**, *268*, 305, **335**, *335*
  manifestation 210, 300
  SALT 1 267
  sous-marin **197**, *197*, 252
  START, traité 163
  Tchernobyl, **306**, *306*
Nujoma, Sam 319
Nurmi, Paavo **84**, *84*

O

O'Neal, Ryan 257
Oakley, Kenneth 191
OCDE 220
Ojukwu, colonel 244
Onassis, Aristote **248**, 274
Ono, Yoko 289
Opel, Fritz von 101

Oppenheimer, Julius Robert **162**, *162*
Orwell, George **176**, *176*
Osmond, frères **266**, *266*
Oswald, Harvey 233
OTAN 177, 200, 232
Ouganda 220, 263, 276
overcraft 214
Owell *324*
Owens, Jesse **129**, *129*, *341*

P

Pahlavi, Farah *284*
Pahlavi, Reza 284
Pakistan 169, **195**, *313*, **256**, *278*
Palach, Jan **253**, *253*
Palestine 170
  colonie agricole **13**, *13*
  Intifada **311**
  OLP **234**, 252, 257, **287**, *296*, 311, 328
Palme, Olof **307**, *307*
Panama 317
Panama, canal de 53
Pankhurst, Christabel 37
Pankhurst, Emmeline 19, 37
Papon, Maurice 347
Parker, Bonnie **118**, *118*
Parks, Rosa **202**, *202*
Parry, Edward 45
Passy, Frédéric 13
Pasternak, Boris **211**, *211*
patinage artistique **127**
Patten, Chris **344**, *344*
Patterson, Floyd **215**, *215*
Paul, Henri 342
Paulus, von 157
Pavalova, Anna **27**, *27*
Pavlov, Ivan 22
Pearse, Padraic 59
Peary, Robert **39**, *39*, **44-45**, *45*,*45*,
Péguy, Charles 55
Peinture
  Drapeau **199**, *199*
  Guernica 131
  Improvisations 10 41
  Iris 310
  La Forêt 88
  La Joconde **47**, *47*, 51
  La Rue 87
  Les Demoiselles d'Avignon **32**, *32*
  Portrait du docteur Gachet 319
  Tournesols 310
Pékin 9, 36
Pelé **105**, *105*, 210
Penkovski, Oleg **230**, *230*
Pereira, Fernando 305
Peres, Shimon 334
Perkins, Anthony 219
Perkins, An **189**, *189*, 277

Perón, Eva 167, **189**, *189*
Perón, Isabel **277**, *277*
Perón, Juan Domingo **167**, *167*
Perot, Ross 327
Pérou 47
Perez de Cuellar, Javier 313
Pétain 58, 60, 63, 143, *143*, **151**, *151*
pétrole 252, **271**, **383**, 290, 313, *313*, 317
Philby, Kim 230, *230*
Philipe, Gérard 263
Philippines 306
Philips, Mark 271, *271*
photographie, 9, 27, 33, **89**, **171**
Picabia, Francis 59
Picasso, Pablo 32, 49, 88, 131, 270
Piccard 108
Piccard, Auguste 221
Pickford, Mary **38**, *38*, 66, *66*
Pie X 23
Pietri, Dorando 36
Pilsudski, maréchal **92**
Pincus, Gregory 218
Pingeon, Roger 259
Pinochet, Augusto 270, 310, 347
pizza **26**
Planck, Max **11**, *11*
Pluton **106**, *106*
Poe, James 235
Poher, Alain 253
Poilvé 129
Poincaré, Raymond 51, 93
Poiret, Paul 95
Poitier, Sidney **235**, *235*
Pol Pot, 274
pôle
  pôle nord **39**, **44**, **93**
  pôle sud **45**
Pollock, Jackson **169**, *169*
pollution 269
Pologne **92**
  état de siège **295**
  Invasion par l'Allemagne **136**
  Riga, traité de 73
  Solidarité 288, **295**, 319, 322
  Varsovie, ghetto de **145**, *145*, **156**, *156*
  Varsovie, révolte de **161**, *161*
Pompidou, Georges 226, 229, 249, 253, 273
population 318
Porter, Edwin 18
Portugal 41, **111**
  révolution des Œillets **272**
Potter, Beatrix **16**
Pottier 19
Powell, Mike **325**, *325*
Powers, Francis Gary **219**, *219*
Preer, Andrew, 94
Presley, Elvis **204**, *204*, 216, 246, *246*, **279**, *279*
Primo de Rivera, Miguel 81, 109, 126
Profumo, John 233
prohibition **68**
Proust, Marcel 77
Pu Yi **36**, *36*

Q

Quant, Mary 175, **235**, *235*, 240
quanta, théorie des **11**
Queen **272**, *272*, 304

R

Rabin, Yitzhak **328**, *328*, **334**, *334*, 339
Radek, Karl *131*
radio 69, 78-79, **198**, *198*, 216
  BBC **76**, 79
  Radio-Londres 79
  radiola 76
Rahman, Mujibur 261
Rainier, prince **205**, *205*, 297
Rains, Claude 152
Ramadier 169
Rapallo, traité de **75**
Raspoutine, Grigori **59**, *59*
RDA (voir Allemagne)
Read, Albert 67
Reagan, ronald **291**, *291*, **292**, *292*, 294, 300, 301, 304, 311, 322
Réard, Louis 175
Reichstag 65, **114**, *114*, 165
relativité **26**
Remarque, Erich Maria 103
Rémi, Georges (voir Hergé)
Renaud, Madeleine **181**, *181*
revue musicale
  follies de 1907 31
  Revue nègre 89
Reynaud, Paul 145
Reynolds, Debbie 187
RFA (voir Allemagne)
Rhodésie du Sud 239
Ribbentrop, Joachim von 136, 137, *137*
Rice 262, *262*
Richtofen, Manfred von (Baron rouge) **63**, *63*
Ride, Sally **261**, 301
Rivera, Diego **128**, *128*
Roberts, lord 9
Robinson, Bill 94
Robinson, Élisabeth 101
Robinson, Mary **321**, *321*
Roche, Stephen 309
Rogers, Ginger 119
Röhm, Ernst **117**, *117*
Rolland, Romain 55
Rolling Stones **236**, *236*, 246

Romano, Yosef 264, *264*
Romanov **62**
Rommel 158
Röntgen, Wilhelm 13
Roosevelt, Eleanor *170*
Roosevelt, Franklin Delano, 106, **110**, *110*, 115, 151, *151*, **160**, 165, *165*
Roosevelt, Theodore 14, 15, *15*, 19
Rorschach, Hermann 69
Rosenberg, Julius et Ethel **190**, 230
Ross, Diana 247
Rothschild, baron de 13
Rotten, Johnny 281
Roumanie 316
Routskoï 328
Rubik, Erno 288
Rudolph, Wilma **221**, *221*
Rundstedt, maréchal von 160
Rushdie, Salman 317
Russie
  Cronstadt, révolte de 73
  Dimanche rouge 24
  famine 69
  guerre contre le Japon **22**
  Guerre mondiale (première) 53, **62**
  Mandchourie **11**, *11*, 73
  mutinerie **25**
  Octobre, révolution d' **60**
  Rapallo, traité de 75
  Riga, traité de 73
Rust, Matthias 309
Ruth, Babe **69**, *69*, **104**, *104*
Rutherford, Ernest 67
Rwanda 332

S

Sabbagh, Pierre 254
Sacco, Nicola 72
Sadate, Anouar el- 259, **282**, *282*, 285, **293**, *293*
Saigon **275**, *275*
Sailer, Toni **203**, *203*
Saint Laurent, Yves **229**, *229*
Saint-Exupéry, Antoine de 156
saint-suaire **312**, *312*
Sakharov, Andreï 308, **323**, *323*
Salazar, Antonio **111**, 272
Salinger, J.D. **185**, *185*
Salk, Edouard **196**, *196*
Sampras, Pete 325
Sandino, Augusto **285**
Sands, Bobby **294**
Santos-Dumont, Alberto **21**
Sauvageot, Jacques 248
Savage, Sean 310
Scheer 59
Scheidemann, Philipp 65

Schick, Joseph **99**
Schirmann, Richard **39**
Schirra, Walter 261
Schleyer, Martin **279**, *279*
Schlumberger, Jean 38
Schmidt, Helmut 297
Schmidt-Rottluff, Karl 27
Schneider, Ralph 178
Scholl, Hans et Sophie **157**, *157*
Schönberg, Arnold *115*
Schragmüller, Elisabeth *231*
Schreck, Max 75
Schroeder, William 257
Schulz, Charles **178**, *178*
Schumann, Maurice 79
Schwarzkopf *324*
Schweitzer, Albert **50**
Scopes, John Thomas **86**
Scott, Robert **44**
scout 30
Scully, John *315*
Seale, Bobby 242
Selfridge, Thomas E. 37
Sembat, Marcel 42
Senna, Ayrton **333**, *333*
Serbie **52**
Seurat, Michel 324
Sex Pistols **276**, *276*, 281
Shastri, Lal Bahadur 243
Shaw, George Bernard **88**, *88*
Shepard, Allan 225
Shepard, E. H. 90
Sikorski, Igor **137**
Sillanpää, Miina 32
Simmons, William 55
Simpson, O. J. **334**, *334*
Simpson, Wallis 127
Sinatra, Frank 157
Skoblikova, Lidia *340*
Smith *85*
Smith, Alfred 108
Smith, Ian 289
Smith, Tommy **249**, *249*
Snepvangers, René 173
Société des Nations 65, 66, **69**, *69*, **114**, 118, 123
Soljenitsyne, Aleksandr **273**, *273*, **323**, *323*
Soloviev 337
Somalie **327**, *327*
Somoza, général 285
SOS, signal **48**
Soudan **202**
Spasski, Boris 264
Spice girls **344**, *344*
Spielberg, Steven **297**, *297*, 298, **329**
Spinola, Antonio 272
Spitz, Mark **265**, *265*, *341*
Springsteen, Bruce **303**, *303*
Sri Lanka **219**, **301**, *301*
Stafford, Thomas 261, 275
Stakhanov, Alexis 122
Staline, Joseph 76, 82, 85, **97**, 131, 136, 137, *137*, 139, 157, 164, 165, *165*, 172, **191**, *191*, 200, 204
Stanley, Henry 23

Stanton, Élisabeth 71
Starshooters 281
Stauffenberg, colonel von 161
Stavisky, affaire 115
Sternberg, Joseph von 107
Stewart, James **199**, *199*
Stieglitz, Alfred 27
Stoker, Bram 75
Stravinski, Igor 46, **51**, *51*
Streseman, Gustav 89
Stroop, général **156**, *156*
Sudètes, invasion des **132**, *132*
Suez, crise de **203**
Sugar Hill Gang 284
Suisse
  droit de vote pour les femmes 263
  suffragettes 263
Sumatra **344**, *344*
Sun Yat-sen 46, 86, *86*
Sundback, Gideon 52
Supremes 247
Suttner, Bertha von **26**, *26*
Swatch **300**, *300*
Swigert, John 258
Sydney, George 185
Szabo, Ecaterina 303

T

Tardieu 111
Tarzan **53**
Tati, Jacques **192**
Tchang Kaï-chek 86, 96, 99, 116, 176
Tchécoslovaquie 253
  Charte 77 **278**, 322
  partition **326**
  Prague, coup de 172
  Prague, printemps de **249**
Tchernenko, Konstantin 303
Teilhard de Chardin 97
télégraphique, câble **17**
téléphone **203**, *203*, 281
télévision 123, 177, **212**, 226, 243, 253, **254-255**, 294
Teller, Edward 186
Temple, Shirley **122**, *122*, *141*
Tennis
  Coupe Davis **10**, **111**, 325
  grand chelem **193**
  Wimbledon 81, 118, 134, 135, 206, **291**, 305, 319
Terechkova, Valentina 233, **261**, *261*, 301
terrorisme **286-287**
Thagard 337
Thatcher, Margaret **284**, *284*, **318**, *318*, 321
The Band 252
The Face, **289**, *289*

théâtre
  Cats 293
  Festival d'Avignon 263
  La Souricière 206
  Misérables 293
  Miss Saigon 293
  Miz 293
  Mme Butterfly 293
  Peter Pan 22
  Pygmalion 88
  R.U.R 70
  Saint Joan 88
Thomke, Ernst 300
Thorpe, Jim 49
Tibet 184
  dalaï-lama 144, 144, 179, 214, 214, 316
tiers-monde 194
  Bandung, conférence de 201
Tiffany, Louis Comfort 15
Time 83
Tinbergen, Nikolaas 270
Titanic, tragédie du 48
Tito 193, 193, 194, 194, 289
Tolstoï, Léon 42
Tombaugh, Clyde 106
Tomski 85
Torrio, Johnny 68, 103
Toscanini, Arturo 197, 197
Toutankhamon 74, 74
train
  Grand central Terminus 51
  Mallard 135
  Transsibérien 16
  Shinkansen 235, 235
  TGV 295, 295, 332, 332
  train suspendu 15
  Transsibérien 16, 16, 52
  tunnel du Simplon 29, 29
  tunnel sous la manche 33
traité franco-allemand 232
Travolta, John 279
tremblement de terre
  Algérie 290
  Arménie 312, 312
  Chili 139
  Chine 276
  États-unis 28, 333, 333
  Grèce 192
  Inde 27
  Iran 180, 180, 248
  Italie 37, 37, 55, 343, 343
  Japon 81, 335, 335
  Nicaragua 266, 266
  Turquie 300
Trenet, Charles 157, 251
Trotski, Léon 60, 82, 85, 97, 97, 131, 143, 143
Truffaut, François 226, 251
Truman, Harry 164, 168, 170, 172, 172, 180, 181, 184
Trust 281
Tschombé, Moïse 223
Tucker, Ed 94
Tudjman 336
Tull, Jethro 252

Tunisie 202
Turner, Tina 304
Turquie 34, 48, 55, 70
  Guerre mondiale (première) 53, 55
  république 80
Twain, Mark 43
Twiggy 240
Tyson, Mike 307, 307
Tzara, Tristan 59

U

U2 304
Uderzo, Albert 125, 224, 224
UNICEF 238, 238
Union soviétique (voir URSS)
urbanisme 112-113
Ure, Midge 304
URSS 324
  agriculture 103
  avion U2 219, 219
  Boeing 747 coréen 300
  bombe atomique 177
  collectivisation 99
  communisme, fin du 322-323
  déstalinisation 204
  dissidence 323
  fondation 76
  glasnost 323
  Goulag 273
  Guerre mondiale (deuxième) 149, 157, 160
  hérédité, théorie de l' 173
  invasion de l'Afghanistan 285
  kolkhoze 99
  Kominform 168
  Moscou, procès de 131
  perestroïka 308
  plan quinquennal 99
  sovkhoze 99
  stakhanovisme 122
  terreur 119
Utzon, Jörn 271

V

Vache folle 338
Vadim, Roger 205
Valentino, Rudolph 93
Valier, Max 101
Van de Put, Corinne 226
Van der Lubbe, Marinus 114
Van Gogh 310, 319
Vanzetti, Bartolomeo 72
Varsovie, pacte de 200
Vatican II, concile 215, 226
Vénus 227
Verne, Jules 27
Verwoerd, H. F. 240

Vespa 166, 166
Vichy, régime de 143, 144
Vicious, Sid 281, 281
Victor-Emmanuel III 77
Victoria, reine 12, 12
Viêt-nam 237, 250, 256, 267, 270, 275
  boat people 282, 282
  offensive du Têt 248
Vilar, Jean 263
Villa, Pancho 42
Villain 66
Vionnet, Madeleine 36
voile
  Admiral's Cup 325
  America's Cup 301
Voisin, 20
Vorster 276

W

Waite, Terry 324, 324
Waldheim, Kurt 307
Walesa, Lech 288, 288, 300, 319, 319, 322, 322
Walsh, Don 221
Warfield, William 185
Warhol, Andy 227
Washington, Booker T. 15, 15
Washkansky, Louis 244, 244
Watson, James Deway 193, 193, 331
Webber, Andrew Lloyd 262, 262
Wegener, Alfred 49
Weill, Kurt 115
Weinberg, Moshe 264, 264
Weissmuller, Johnny 77, 77
Welch, Evelyn 94
Welles, Orson 78, 78, 148
Westmoreland 248
White, Edward 261, 261
Who 240, 252, 258
Wiene, Robert 71
Willis, Barnes 158
Wilson, Harold 236
Wilson, Woodrow 48, 54, 60, 65
Winckler, Hans Gunter 205, 205
Windsor, château royal de 12
Wonder, Stevie 247
Wood, Natalie 223
Woodward, Louise 345, 345
Wozniak, Steve 315
Wrangel 71
Wright, Frank lloyd 129, 213
Wright, Orville et Wilbur, 18, 18, 20, 27, 37
Wyler, William 215

X

Xiaoping, Deng 277, 345

Y

Yoshihito 48
Yougoslavie 118, 193, 193, 289, 336
Yourcenar, Marguerite 290

Z

Zabari 264
Zaïre 345
Zale, Tony 172
Zambie 220
Zapata 66
Zatopek, Emil 189, 189
Zatopkova, Dana 189
Zemin, Jiang 344
zeppelin 10, 10, 61
Zeppelin, Ferdinand von 10, 20
Zeppelin, Led 252
Zidane, Zinedine 346, 346
Ziegfeld 31
Zimbabwe 289
Zinoviev, Grigori 82
Zola, Émile 17, 35
zoo 32, 119

CRÉDITS PHOTOGRAPHIQUES :

h = haut, b = bas, m = milieu, g = gauche, d = droite

1 hm, bd UPI/Corbis; 8, 9 m Corbis; 11 h Popperfoto; 13 hd, 15 hd, m Corbis, bg Library of Congress/Corbis, bd UPI/Corbis; 17 hd Corbis; 18 b Edison; 19 md Corbis; 21 md Ben Johnson Photography; 23 hd, bd Corbis, bg UPI/Corbis; 24/25 h, 25 hd, hg, m Corbis; 26 h Corbis, m John Frost; 27 bd UPI/Corbis; 30 md Corbis; 31 bg Mary Evans Picture Library; 32 h © Succession Picasso/DACS 1998/Museum of Modern Art, New York, m Radio Times/Hulton Getty Picture Collection, b National Board of Antiquities, Finland; 33 hg (2 pictures) John Frost, hd Corbis; 36 hd, m, bg, bd Corbis, 37 h, b Corbis; 38 b The Kobal Collection; 39 mg Corbis, bg The Bettmann Archive; 40 hg Corbis; 42 b British Pathe PLC; 43 h, mg, md Corbis; 46 m Peter Newark's American Pictures, bd Corbis; 47 m The Kobal Collection, b E.C. Erdis/National Geographic Society; 48 bg, 51 bg, bd et couverture, 53 bg, Corbis ; 53 md Ph. © Archives Larbor ; 54 bd Ph. Bibliothèque nationale de France, Paris ; 55 hd Corbis, md UPI/Corbis; 56/57 photo de fond UPI/Corbis; 56 h, 57 hg, hd Corbis; 58 b Roger Viollet; 60 h, m UPI/Corbis; 61 mg The Bettmann Archive, b Corbis; 62 h, 63 md Corbis, b The Bettmann Archive; 63 m, Ph. © Roger-Viollet; 64 h Corbis ; 64, b, Ph. © Branger/Viollet; 65 md Penguin/Corbis; 67 hg, b UPI/Corbis; 68 b Corbis; 70 bd, 71 b, 72 h et 4ᵉ de couverture , bd, 73 h, mg UPI/Corbis, md Corbis; 75 h Metropolitan Toronto Reference Library; 76 b, 77 h, 79 hg, hd Corbis, m UPI/Corbis, b Underwood & Underwood/Corbis; 80 b, 81 d Corbis; 82 hg Deutsche Bundesbank, bd UPI/Corbis; 83 h Commissioner of Police of the Metropolis, mg AKG London; 84 b, 85 md, bd UPI/Corbis; 86 h, m Corbis; 87 hmd UPI/Corbis, bmd The Bettmann Archive; 88 h Corbis/ADAGP, Paris et DACS, Londres 1998, 89 h Corbis, bg UPI/Corbis; 90 hg, hd, UPI/Corbis, m, bg Corbis, bd The Ronald Grant Archive; 91 md UPI/Corbis, bm Corbis; 93 b UPI/Corbis; 94 photo de fond Penguin/Corbis; 95 md UPI/Corbis, b Underwood & Underwood/Corbis; 97 md Corbis; 98 h St Mary's Hospital Medical School/Science Photo Library; 99 h, bd Underwood & Underwood/Corbis; 100 hd © DISNEY par autorisation spéciale de TWDCF et couverture ; 101 md Popperfoto, mg, b Emil und die drei Zwillinge; 102 hd Science Photo Library; 103 m Corbis; 104/105 photo de fond, 104 b et couverture, 106 h UPI/Corbis; 107 h Stockmarket; 109 h, md UPI/Corbis, b, 110 hd Corbis; 111 hg, hd Hulton Getty Picture Collection; 111 m, Ph.Archives Larbor © DR; 112 h, b Corbis; 113 h UPI/Corbis, m Reuters/Corbis, b Agence France Presse/Corbis; 115 m, b Corbis; 116 h UPI/Corbis, bd Walt Disney Co.; 117 h UPI/Corbis, m Corbis, b, 118 h, 119, h, Ph. © Keystone; 119 hg UPI/Corbis, hd Hulton Getty Picture Collection, bg David King Collection, bd Springer/Corbis; 120/121 photo de fond, 121 b Corbis; 122 h The Bettmann Archive, m The Ronald Grant Archive, b, 123 m, b, 124 b UPI/Corbis; 125 m Marvel Comics; 126 b Hulton Getty Picture Collection/Corbis; 127 hg UPI/Corbis; 127 hd, Ph. © Keystone; 128 bg Springer/Corbis; 129 h, m, 131 hd UPI/Corbis, bd Popperfoto; 131, hg, Ph. © Roger-Viollet; 133 hd UPI/Corbis, b Nestlé UK Ltd; 134 h Walt Disney Co., m UPI/Corbis; 135 h Corbis, m UPI/Corbis, bg, 136 b, Ph. © Harlingue/Viollet; 137 h UPI/Corbis; 138 h (and inset) Corbis, bg Imperial Chemical Industries PLC; 139 h Corbis, 140 g Corbis; 141 h Springer/Corbis; 142/143 h Corbis; 143 bg UPI/Corbis; 143 bd, Ph. © Collection Viollet; 144 h Corbis; 145 hd, hg UPI/Corbis, bg, m Corbis, bd H. Josse/Archives Larbor; 147 hg, hd, bg, bd Corbis, md UPI/Corbis; 147 b, Ph. © M.Didier/Archives Larbor; 148 b Springer/Corbis; 149 bg UPI/Corbis, bd Corbis; 151 hg, Ph. © M.Didier/Archives Larbor/DR; 152 bg, 153 hg UPI/Corbis, hd Corbis; 154/155 photo de fond UPI/Corbis; 157 m Corbis, bd UPI/Corbis; 158, hd Hulton Getty Picture Collection; 159 hd Corbis, m Hulton Getty Picture Collection; 159 b, Ph. ©Keystone; 160 hg UPI/Corbis, b Novosti/Corbis; 161 hg Popperfoto; 162/163 photo de fond, 162 h, 163 h, m UPI/Corbis; 164 bd, Ph. © APN; 166 hg Popperfoto, hd et couverture The World's Motorcycles News Agency; 167 hbd, bd, 168 h, 169 h UPI/Corbis, bg Corbis, bd Jackson Pollock, 1950. Photograph by Hans Namuth © 1991 Hans Namuth Estate. Courtesy, Center for Creative Photography, The University of Arizona; 170 mg, 171 h, 172 h, bg UPI/Corbis, 172 bd, Ph. © Keystone; 173 hg Popperfoto; 176 h UPI/Corbis; 178 h Diners Club International; 179 h, m UPI/Corbis, b Reuters/Corbis; 180 b UPI/Corbis; 181 h, Ph. © Lipnitzki/Viollet; 181 tcr, b Corbis, bmd UPI/Corbis; 182/183 photo de fond, 182 h UPI/Corbis, b UPI/Bettmann; 183 h, b Reuters/Corbis; 185 hg Springer/Corbis, hd UPI/Corbis, m Hulton Getty Picture Collection, b UPI/Corbis; 186 h Corbis; 187 h, m, bg, bd, 188/189 b, 191 m, b UPI/Corbis; 192 m The Kobal Collection; 193 bd, 194 m, 195 b, 196 bg UPI/Corbis; 196 h, Ph. © S.Weiss/Rapho; 197 hg Penguin/Corbis, hd, b UPI/Corbis; 198/199 m Jasper John's/DACS, London/VAGA, New York1998/Ludwig Museum, Cologne/AKG London; 199 h UPI/Corbis, m Corbis, b UPI/Corbis; 200 h, 201 hg, hd, m, b, 202 h UPI/Corbis; 203 bd, 204 b Corbis; 205 m Hulton Getty Picture Collection/Corbis; 205 bd, Ph. © Kipa; 206 h, 207 b, 208/209 photo de fond, 208 b, b UPI/Corbis; 209 b Corbis; 210 m UPI/Corbis, b Corbis; 211 h Corbis, bd Lambert/Archive Photos; 211 bg, Ph. © Archives Photos; 212 bg Corbis; 213 bg, 214 h, b, 215 b, 216/217 photo de fond, 216 b UPI/Corbis; 217 mg Corbis; 219 h Camera Press, mg Corbis, md, b UPI/Corbis; 222 bg, Ph. © G.Dambier/Gamma; 224 h UPI/Corbis, bd Walt Disney Co./The Ronald Grant Archive, bm Amnesty International; 225 hd Camera Press; 226 m UPI/Corbis, bg Corbis; 227 md et 4ᵉ de couverture AKG Photo Londres/The Andy Warhol Foundation for the Visual Arts, mc/ARS, NY et DACS, Londres 1998; 228 mg Corbis, b UPI/Corbis; 229 h, m Corbis, b UPI/Corbis; 230/231 photo de fond UPI/Corbis; 230 from hg down Corbis, Corbis, Corbis, Corbis, Hulton Getty Picture Collection, b Corbis; 231c The Bettmann Archive, b, bd Corbis; 233 hd Popperfoto; 234 b UPI/Corbis; 235 h Corbis, mg UPI/Corbis, md Reuters/Corbis, bd UPI/Corbis; 236 h Lick Observatory California University, m Reuters/Corbis; 237 m UPI/Corbis, bg Corbis; 238 h, m UNICEF; 239 h, m Corbis, bg Springer/Corbis; 240 m Camera Press, b UPI/Corbis; 241 h Corbis, md, b, 242 hg UPI/Corbis, bd, 243 md Corbis, bd, 244 m, bd UPI/Corbis, bg Apple Corps Ltd; 245 m UPI/Corbis; 246/247 photo de fond Springer/Corbis; 247 h, b UPI/Corbis; 248 h Corbis; 249 m Popperfoto, bg Corbis; 251 h, m UPI/Corbis; 252 h UPI/Bettmann, bd, 253 h, bd, 254/255 photo de fond, 254 b, 256 hg, hd, 257 h UPI/Corbis, m Popperfoto; 258 h NASA, m Popperfoto, bg London Features International; 259 m Camera Press, bg UPI/Corbis; 262 bd, bm Hulton Getty Picture Collection; 263 Corbis, m Popperfoto, bd Hulton Getty Picture Collection; 264 hd (all 3) Popperfoto, bg UPI/Corbis, bd Hulton Getty Picture Collection; 265 hd, b UPI/Corbis; 266 h, mg, md UPI/Corbis, bd Hulton Getty Picture Collection; 267 h UPI/Corbis, m Michael Freeman; 268 h Reuters/Corbis; 270/271 b UPI/Corbis; 271 h Corbis; 272 bg London Features International ; 275 bd, 276 m, 277 mg, 278 h, m, bd UPI/Corbis; 279 mg The Ronald Grant Archive, b Michael Ryan/Camera Press; 283 m, b UPI/Corbis; 284 h Popperfoto, bg UPI/Corbis, bd London Features International; 285 m, 286/287 photo de fond, 286 h m UPI/Corbis; bg Agence France Presse/Corbis; 288 h UPI/Corbis; 289 h Dr Morley Read/ Science Photo Library, bg UPI/Corbis, bd The Face Magazine; 290 bd Rex Features, bg Sony UK; 291 h Corbis, bg World Health Organization; 292 m UPI/Corbis; 293 hg, 294 h, m UPI/Corbis; 295 h Corbis, m, 296 hg, hd, bg UPI/Corbis; 297 mg, bd UPI/Corbis; 298 h The Ronald Grant Archive; 299 h The Ronald Grant Archive/Lucas Film; 300 mg, md Camera Press; 301 hg Rex Features, bd UPI/Corbis; 302 h NIBSC/Science Photo Library, bg, 303 h, md, 304 bg UPI/Corbis; 306 h Reuters/Corbis, bg The Bettmann Archive; 307 mg UPI/Corbis, md Rex Features, b, 308 h UPI/Corbis, bg, bd, 310 b Reuters/Corbis; 311 md Frank Spooner Pictures; 312 h, b Corbis, m The Ronald Grant Archive; 313 h The Bettmann Archive, md Frank Spooner Pictures, mg Reuters/Corbis, b, 314 b Corbis; 315 m UPI/Corbis, b Peter Menzel/Science Photo Library; 317 mg The Ronald Grant Archive, bg Reuters/Corbis; 318 h, bd Reuters/Corbis; 320 m Corbis, bg Frank Spooner Pictures; 321 b, 323 bg, bc, bd Reuters/Corbis; 324 hd, bd Reuters/Corbis; 325 bd, 326 bd Reuters/Corbis; 327 bg, bd Reuters/Corbis; 328 b Rex Features; 329 h Reuters/Corbis; 330/331 photo de fond UPI/Corbis; 330 h et 4ᵉ de couverture Corbis, m Popperfoto/Reuter; 331 h Sinclair Stammers/Science Photo Library, mg Frank Spooner Pictures, md UPI/Corbis; 332 m Popperfoto; 333 bg Reuters/Corbis; 336/337 Everett/Corbis; 336 h, Ph. © Gamma; 337 h Camera Press, bd Corbis; 338 h Frank Spooner Pictures, m, bd Corbis, bg Everett/Corbis; 339 h NASA, bg Corbis, bd The Bettmann Archive; 340 h Reuters/Corbis; 342 hg, Corbis, md Popperfoto, b Corbis; 342 bg, Ph. © Gamma, 342, bd Ph. © T.Orban/Sygma; 343 h Popperfoto, m, bd Corbis, b Popperfoto, 344 hg, hd Corbis, md Popperfoto, b David Allen/Corbis; 345 h Popperfoto, mg Frank Spooner Pictures, md Corbis, b, bd NASA.

Toutes les autres photographies de ce livre proviennent de la vidéothèque de Bertelsmann :

Archiv für Kunst und Geschichte, Berlin (12); Associated Press GmbH, Francfort (1); Bauhaus Archiv, Berlin (1); Beltz Verlag, Weinheim (3); Bertelsmann Lexikon Verlag, Gütersloh (35) - NASA (4); Bettmann-Corbis, New York (375) - AFP (8) - Guggenheim Museum (1) - Reuters (52) - Springer (3) - UPI (511); Bildarchiv Preußischer Kulturbesitz, Berlin (2); Botschaft des Staates Israel (1); Cinetext, Francfort (38); Citroën Deutschland AG, Cologne (1); Deutsche Fotothek, Dresde (1); dpa, Francfort (4); Ex Libris, Zurich (1); Giraudon, Paris (1); Greenpeace - Keziere (1); Johnson Space Center, Houston (1); Keystone, Hambourg (5); laenderpress, Mayence (1); Mattel Toys, Dreieich (1); Mauritius, Mittenwald (1); Hans Otto Neubauer, Hambourg (1); Oetinger GmbH, Hambourg (1); Rauch Verlag, Düsseldorf (11); Roger Viollet, Paris (1); Pressebild-Agentur Schirner, Meerbusch (8); Sipa Press, Paris (142); Städt. Galerie im Lenbachhaus, Munich (1); Steiff GmbH, Giengen (12); Süddeutscher Verlag, Bilderdienst, München (20); Transglobe Agency, Hambourg (1).

© Matisse, Stilleben: Succession H. Matisse/VG Bild-Kunst, Bonn 1997.
© Jawlensky, A. Sacharoff; Georges Braque, Stilleben; Marcel Duchamp, Brunnen; Miró, Dutch Interior; George Grosz, The Street: VG Bild-Kunst, Bonn 1997.
© Oskar Schlemmer, Bauhaustreppe: 1997, Oskar Schlemmer, Archiv und Familien Nachlass, Badenweiler.
© Max Pechstein, Plakat Die Brücke: Max Pechstein/Hamburg-Tökendorf.

Illustrations :
Martin Sanders, Nadine Wickenden, Ann Winterbotham, Biz Hull.